I0757624

UNDER TATTERED BANNERS:
A Forgotten Gods Tale

Christian Warren Freed

Copyright © 2022 by Christian Warren Freed

Excerpt from *A Time For Tyrants* 2023 Christian Warren Freed
Cover design by BroseDesignz
Author Photograph by Anicie Freed

Warfighter Books
Holly Springs, North Carolina 27540
https://www.christianwfreed.com

First Edition: August 2022

Library of Congress Cataloging-in-Publication Data
Name: Freed, Christian Warren, 1973- author.
Title: Under Tattered Banners/ Christian Warren Freed
Description: First Edition | Holly Springs, NC: Warfighter Books, 2022. Identifiers: LCCN 2022909740 | ISBN 9781957326061 (trade paperback) | ISBN 9781957326054 (hard cover) | ISBN 9781957326016 (ebook) Subjects: Science Fiction- Space Opera | Science Fiction |Military Science Fiction

Printed in the United States of America

10 9 8 7 6 5 4 3 2 1

"Steven Erickson meets George R.R. Martin!"

"THIS IS IT. If you like fantasy and sci-fi, you must read this series."

Law of the Heretic
Immortality Shattered Book I

'If you're looking for a fun and exciting fantasy adventure, spend a few hours in the Free Lands with the Law of the Heretic.'

Where Have All the Elves Gone?

'Sometimes funny and other times a little dark, Where Have The Elves Gone? brings something fresh and new to fantasy mysteries. Whether you want to curl up with a mystery or read more about elves this book has something for everyone. Spend a few hours solving a mystery with a human and a couple of dwarves - you'll be glad you did.'

The Children of Never

SO, You Want to Write a Book? +
SO, You Wrote a Book. Now What? +

*Forthcoming   + Nonfiction

UNDER TATTERED BANNERS

Christian Warren Freed

PROLOGUE

Final days of the gods, Empyrean Asteroid Belt.

Fear propelled her halfway across the universe in a desperate attempt to survive. A far cry from certain, but a chance she had to take. Her former masters, though in disarray from the total collapse of their civilization, were ruthless. Millenia of hatred drove their actions. Humanity and lesser races were crushed into slavery and hunted to extinction. Violence was their mantra. A philosophy void of morality, eventually leading to their demise. Escaping with her life was but the first step.

She watched the stars flash by through endless days. The long night of impossibility stretched as far as the imagination. A new fear crept into the dark corners of her mind. For the first time, the thought of dying in the void inspired raw terror. Lesser beings had died worse. What more could she, a lone survivor of a burning world, hope to achieve than casting off her shackles and dying a free woman? The prospect enticed her almost as much as it terrified her. The universe might be infinite, but mortality was not.

Nightmares untold stirred. Lost, she had no choice but to entertain their delicious torments. How much time passed was lost? Most of the shuttle's systems were either shut down or in the process of doing so. Time stalked her. Mired between obscurity and delirium, she was startled awake by the awkward chime of the proximity alarm. Raw panic ensued. Certain she had been caught at last, she struggled to retain a modicum of control.

She jerked her head up, shaking off the dim chill of space. A whispered word under her breath and her body warmed. Eyes sharpened as the looming hulk of a freighter filled the viewport. Closer examination showed it was not one of *theirs*. Whose then? The possibility others escaped the madness was there, though she doubted how many could have fled before hunter-killer teams ran them to ground. Lacking food and water, she had no choice but to accept the approaching confrontation.

Gathering her power, she clenched her fists and headed toward the boarding ramp. The shuttle rocked as it set down in a cargo hold. Left with no choice, she summoned the depths of her courage, calming her nerves as best as possible, and activated the hatch. Bright lights flooded the shuttle. She shied away, shielding her sensitive eyes, lest she become blinded. Heavy bootsteps echoed across metallic floor. Shadows crept into the lower edge of her vision.

"You are most fortunate I found you," a gravelly voice greeted.

Throat parched from sustaining on little more than reconstituted water, she raised a hand to protect her eyes. "Who are you? Why have you captured me?"

A pause. "Captured? I am afraid you are quite mistaken. I have come to rescue you, Oracle."

She went rigid. A knife's thrust into her heart. Years of careful planning were wasted. Her voyage across the expanse interrupted by a servant of *him*. Trapped and alone, she decided the need for subterfuge was gone. "I … no longer go by that name."

He cocked his head, blocking the menacing deck lights and allowing Ruma Zzein her first good look. Tall, almost too tall to be human, he was lanky with ill-fitting clothes. Salt and pepper hair blanketed his lower face. A nose that had been broken too many times sat crooked as he stared down at her. She recognized him for what he was, a half-breed. A mistake that never should have lived beyond birth.

"No indeed," he agreed. "Those days are behind us all, I lament. We have been abandoned by all that once was. Cast adrift in an ocean of endless stars. Forever destined to wander paths less taken."

"You seem to know more about me than I care," Ruma replied. "And you still have not given me your name."

Emboldened by his bluster, Ruma stood straighter. She barely reached his stomach. There was little special in his features, save for the depth of understanding trapped in the green flecks of his eyes. A hint of distant recognition she could not quite place.

He answered with the wave of a hand. "I am many things and nothing at all. This universe does not look kindly on men such as me. It is a thankless life I lead, for I was torn from my mother's arms when I was naught but a babe. Raised by powers I will not mention."

He moved away, allowing her the opportunity to continue down the ramp. "My world has been reduced to this ship."

"Are you alone?" she pressed.

"There is one other," he said.

Frustrated, Ruma pulled the hem of her tattered robes up and stepped closer. "Why am I here?"

The twinkle deep in the wells of his eyes brightened. "That is the correct question, Oracle. You have always lived a life of purpose, but you did not know for what. You thought our masters needed you to foretell their futures and predict their fates. How wrong could any of us have been?"

He hung his head. "Shame is an underrated emotion, don't you think?"

"I think you are beginning to waste my time. You speak in riddles and circles, making no mention of why I am here," Ruma countered.

"I speak of change," he said. "Do you know who your parents were?"

She opened and closed her mouth. The bitter retort dying on her lips.

Taking her silence, he continued. "My mother remains a secret. One even I was not privy to. Oh, I am sure she is dead. How could they have let her live, knowing what I was to become?"

Ruma felt drawn in for reasons that chilled her blood. "And your father?"

He tapped a finger against his crooked nose. "My father has many names. Some name him the Third Prince. Others choose to whisper behind his back, calling him what should never be uttered in public."

She clenched her fists and resisted the urge to screw her eyes shut and weep.

"Sorrow."

The name punched her in the gut, robbing Ruma of breath. Sorrow. The Third Prince. One of the three sons of the king and an architect of that civilization's demise. Hundreds of worlds were laid waste by their hands. They were a plague upon the universe. A hate from old times. She needed to flee, lest they discover her and place her back in chains.

"I will not return with you," she said weakly.

He offered a surprised look. "I am not asking you to. My father sent me away before the Fall. I was given explicit instructions. Find the Oracle."

"For what purpose? I am of no use to their kind. *He* will only murder me," she admitted.

"Your fate is woven into the fabric of time, Oracle," he told her with more compassion than she assumed he held. "But your work is just beginning. There is a comet where I shall take you once our task is done. There you will build a grand temple and spend your days in service to the universe."

Temple? Comet? The words barely registered as Ruma struggled with the premature waves of relief threatening to subsume her. "What task must I accomplish?"

"We, Ruma Zzein. We. This game is but beginning. How far into the future it reaches remains to be seen but there are consequences fast approaching us all. My time here is short. A reckoning is coming and I must be prepared, for the day will come when all the violence we have witnessed enacted on life will return to haunt us. Will you take this journey with me? A quest to right old wrongs and restore order?"

She wet her lips. "Who is this other you mentioned?"

"That is someone you should see for yourself," he replied. "Far be it for me to usurp her authority. It is her ship after all."

Ruma stood in shock. She had expected to hear one of the Three named and her life to be forfeit. Instead, the half-breed offered her hope, however slight the glimmer. "I still do not know your name. Tell me and can discuss the future."

He crouched to stare her in the eyes. And he told her his name.

3201 A.G. (After Gods), Inquisition Prison, planet Keltoo.

Of the seven hundred colonized planets in the known universe, several were deemed uninhabitable by the Conclave. Planets rife with hostile environments or native species too invasive for colonists to overcome. These planets became important to the Inquisition as humanity's expansion continued. Ever alert for the first murmurs of heresy, Inquisitors deployed construction crews in secrecy−known only to the highest ranks of the Conclave and Inquisition−to begin work on a great prison system. Heresy was a stain upon the universe. One both Orders sought to stamp out for humanity to continue expansion.

Hidden behind an unstable nebula, Keltoo was all but uninhabitable. High levels of radiation prevented life from existing on the surface. Those few colonies−begun as followers and loved ones of those incarcerated−were forced underground. Lack of natural light and vegetation produced a sickly look, prompting the local Inquisition agents to think of them less than favorably. Desperate to be near loved ones, the underground dwellers remained hidden from all but the most dedicated official.

Alain Nye had little stomach for such places. His upbringing was on a rich world where heresy was as foreign as hardship. Joining the Inquisition was a logical choice, just as his older brothers had done before him. Working for the Inquisitor General proved illuminating far beyond his imagination. He glanced out the shuttle viewport, wincing as blue lightning slashed through the bank of clouds obscuring the ground. Hints of purple skies poked through, providing him with violent images of what might be.

He'd pleaded with Farius Graeme to send another. To spare him the nightmares this experience was bound to inspire. Keltoo, along with several planets under Conclave rule, was never meant to be colonized. Tiny beads of sweat formed under his collar, evidence of his growing discomfort. The shuttle rocked and dipped. Alain gripped his armrests and closed his eyes. The shuttle continued to drop, slicing through the lightning-wreathed clouds. His stomach clenched and twisted. Fears of crashing and being left to die taunted him. Dreams and plans flashed before him, all unfulfilled.

The shuttle jerked up and slowed just as quickly as it dropped. Alain glared at the back of the pilot's head, silently cursing the woman for failing to inform him of their final descent. Her actions were indicative of his standing among the Inquisition. Disliked by most, Alain struggled through the days, knowing he lacked respect from most of the Inquisition. It was an unenviable position that he had yet to turn to his advantage.

"There are biohazard suits in the rear of the compartment. Ensure your mask is sealed," the pilot called, after gently touching down. She had no intention of following him into the prison.

Content with being alone, Alain slipped into the bulky suit and fastened the mask over his head. He placed the heel of his right hand over the filter and breathed, ensuring the seal was intact. He marched down the boarding ramp and crossed the short distance of open terrain to the external decontamination chambers leading into the prison. Black clad Prekhauten Guards watched from behind wide windows, waiting for the all-clear on their monitors.

Heart in his throat, Alain underwent decontamination for the first time, all under the reflective glares on the Prekhauten helmets. He noted they were in full body armor and heavily armed. What sort of prisoners were kept here, so far from the rest of the civilized universe? The possibilities threatened to bring his lunch up. His hands trembled as jets of chemically charged air struck. Everything about this mission reminded Alain that he was not a field man. His position was best served at the Inquisitor General's side, influencing policy and directing the seven hundred worlds into the future.

Memories of his early life did him little justice, interfering when he needed clarity most. Alain was never proud of his origins. They were a detrimental reminder that he would forever be less than his sense of self-worth. It took years of practice to bury his past and focus on tomorrow. Years he was not willing to casually throw away at the first sign of danger.

A stern looking man flanked by two guards greeted him after he was afforded the opportunity to change into a fresh uniform. "Inquisitor, I am General Wael. Welcome to Keltoo."

"Th…thank you, General. I trust you have been informed of my mission?" he asked.

Wael's eyes narrowed. "Enough of it, though I scarcely agree. You are being sent to interview a dangerous being."

"It is my job," Alain replied.

"Better men than you have already failed," Wael pressed. "Have you any idea what you are being asked? The very sound of his voice has driven men to suicide. I would not have another soul on my conscience."

Alain balked at the slight. He was out of his element, true, but he was the aide to the highest-ranking Inquisitor in the universe. Not even a Prekhauten general was allowed to speak to him so. "You know whom I serve. It is with his authority that I come here. Unless you have anything useful to say, I would like to see the prisoner."

Wael bristled at the blatant insult. A career soldier, he was the veteran of a dozen campaigns. A hammer of justice others emulated. The young upstart pretending to stand before him with borrowed strength was an affront to all he had done. Yet Wael was forced to acquiesce. Rank had its privileges but there was only so much that could be done in the face of authority. He snapped his fingers.

A junior lieutenant appeared; hands clasped behind her back. The scar running down the right side of her face was ugly. A ragged hole marred where the eye once sat. "Inquisitor, if you would follow me."

She saluted Wael and stepped off without waiting for Alain's acknowledgement. Cursing under his breath, Alain hurried to catch up. His confidence, already fragile, was reduced and it was all he could do to maintain a professional image.

"Uppity bastard. What game is Vau Prime playing?" Wael asked.

His guards remained at attention. Silent. Blank masks.

She led him through winding corridors and banks of empty cells. Energy bars sealed many of the worst criminals in the universe, those convicted of heresy and worse and deemed a threat to the continuity of civilization, were housed here. All were slated for execution. The Conclave was forgiving on many matters. The Inquisition less so. Alain flinched as human waste was flung at him. The stench assaulted his nostrils.

Disgust twisted his face. "How do you put up with this?"

"You get used to it. These are condemned men. Let them have what fun they may before their bodies are vaporized," she replied.

Alain gave the perpetrator a final snarl and was rewarded with an obscene gesture. "They should have been executed upon capture. This is a monumental waste of funding."

Ignoring him, she marched them down several flights of metal stairs. The air grew heavy, recycled oxygen filtered through failing systems, left many of the lower levels unserviceable. Alain tried, and failed, to keep track of the route. He doubted the lieutenant would be kind enough to see him out once his task was complete.

A thin mist clung to the floor. Ankle high and tinged with phosphorescent green, it reminded him of the gas nebula he travelled through en route. Thicker air rendered him slower. His body failed to respond as it should.

"I am having difficulty breathing. Is this a gas leak?" he decided to break his silence.

"The gravity is more than on Vau Prime. Artificial generators are turned off this far down. We don't want him having thoughts of freedom, now do we?" she replied.

Where would he go? Keltoo was dozens of light years away from the nearest civilized planet. A deliberate end to all hope. Doubts suddenly awakened. The validity of his mission was in question. Why the Inquisitor General would wish to speak with the greatest nightmare the universe had ever known, was a mystery. One he doubted he would ever be privilege to.

"This is it," the lieutenant announced.

Alain jerked to a halt, having failed to notice she had stopped. She waited expectantly. "Not going to talk me out of it?"

"Should I?" she asked.

I almost wish you would. Alain summoned his courage and puffed his chest out. "No. I am to speak with the prisoner alone."

She left without a word, leaving him void of confidence. Alain took several deep breaths before placing his eye over the retinal scans. A green light flashed. A series of doors slid open. His first step was unsteady, for he knew that any hesitation meant his will would melt and he would return to the Inquisitor General in failure. Bright lights flooded the narrow corridor leading deeper into the planet's mantle. They ended at the edge of a wide chamber swathed in darkness. He found it odd they granted the nightmare such luxuries.

Alain Nye halted at the sonic barrier and peered deeper into shadow. A shape stirred. Massive and imposing. Here was the bane of humanity. A scourge best left forgotten. Swallowing his fear, Alain announced, "Amongeratix, I have come under the authority of the Inquisitor General and the Cardinal Seniorus."

Brilliant eyes glowed in the near dark. "Ah, little man. How I've waited for you to come. It does get so terribly lonely this deep in the earth."

Alain's heart hammered as he came to the realization he had just walked into a trap.

ONE

3215 A.G. (After Gods), Warehouse District, Krenz, planet Vau Prime.

Night darkened the city. Current restrictions established by General Kale prevented the beacons lining Redemption Boulevard from being lit. Unnatural darkness settled in, bringing a tide of panic and whispered threats. Stray animals cowered in the shadows, for it was not a night to be caught roaming the streets. Vau Prime was a fragment of its former glory. A broken city struggling to survive a war few understood and even fewer conducted. Entire districts had been cleansed of heresy. Martial law was enacted. Those caught in violation were arrested and sent away, either to clandestine prison camps or conscripted into the Prekhauten Guard. The city remained on edge.

Hours before dawn bore witness to a convoy of ebony assault vehicles speeding through secondary avenues. They moved in silence, guns locked and loaded and hulls filled with combat soldiers. Mobus Kale rode in the turret of the lead vehicle. His face was a grim visage of what was to come. Events from the low continent marred his already hardened face. Haunting visions of flame and nightmare hounded his every step, while whispers of impending demise danced upon the wind.

Mobus, newly promoted to general as the Inquisitor General's insurrection widened, struggled to keep his past where it belonged. Rumors of the end of times reached him. He first heard the Blood Witch's term of "Forever Night" and was romanticized by the potential of burning the universe to the ground and starting over. Infighting between the Conclave and Inquisition showed him the dark heart of humanity's flaws. It spurred his bloodlust and left him convinced the hour of apocalypse was at hand.

He rode in the turret of his favored tank, scarcely watching as the faded gray warehouses drifted past. Hate filled eyes stared off into the predawn. They focused on the already fading horrors of the cult of Rengu fanatics, as they raced into his crossfire. They focused on the debacle on the Prekhauten Guard training compound on Tatarast Island. Insurrectionists snuck ashore in the middle of the night and stole vast stores of ammunition and equipment. Enough to fuel their rebellion for years.

Mobus took the failure personally, a fact reminded by the displeasure of the Inquisitor General. He mistakenly believed Davith Strannan, his former commanding officer, was down to his last and the rebellion would be crushed without need to abandon the southern campaign. Instead, the old tiger proved he still had teeth. There was fight left in the enemy. Were it not for the pressure coming down from the Conclave and Inquisition leadership, Mobus would have broken into a grin. The prospect of engaging the dishonored general of the Prekhauten Guard a final time, spurred his anger.

The unnatural orange-blue glow of city lights bathed the sky an ungodly hue. Mobus ignored it. The convoy through the warehouse district was more than a show of force. It was a retribution force. Punishment for those who failed to see the genius behind all Inquisitor General Nye sought to accomplish. Fools all, Mobus snorted. The time of the gods was returning. Revolution had come to the universe. The flames of anarchy driven by his avenging hand. He would burn the city to the ground for the chance to prove his worth in the eyes of Amongeratix.

Nye had not mentioned the hated of the Three. There was no need. Mobus recognized Nye for being shortsighted. The man was a capable Inquisitor but lacked the stomach to do what was necessary to ensure the successful transition of power. Others waited in the shadows. Men and women eager to slit throats in the dark. Make others disappear, lest their voices continued to be heard in the Forum. Men and women the universe needed.

A senior sergeant waited in the road ahead, forcing Mobus's tank to grind to a halt. The eight-ton vehicle hovered a foot off the ground. Broadfaced and with a decided uninterested look, the sergeant waited for Mobus to climb down to address him. Lines of cuffed prisoners were marched past toward the transports at the rear of the column. Many bore the marks of struggle. A handful of corpses littered a stretch of street.

Mobus set his boots on the ground and removed his helmet. His dark hair was matted to his scalp, tiny beads of sweat clinging to the tips. He noticed the prisoners for the first time and snapped attention back to where it belonged. The sergeant stood before him. His uniform was covered in grime and dark spots that could only be blood. Soot smeared across his face, making him yet more unpresentable.

"Report," Mobus ordered.

The sergeant swallowed, taken aback by the intensity of Mobus's glare. "General, we have secured what appears to be an old insurrectionist base. There is no telling when it was abandoned but there was nothing more than broken equipment and bloodied bandages and blankets."

So, Strannan slips the noose once again. Clever fox. My hunt continues. Mobus gestured to the prisoners with his artificial arm. "And them?"

"Mostly local workers and dock hands for the nearest starport," the sergeant replied. "A few have been separated and taken to the Inquisition assets on hand to see what they know. We are about to begin clearing those two buildings on the right."

"Where is your commanding officer? Why is a sergeant bringing me this intel?" Mobus demanded.

In truth, he preferred the bitter honesty of the noncommissioned officers. They lacked the finesse and intrigue too many officers held when dealing with delicate matters. Mobus knew the rank and file respected the NCO far more than their line officer.

"General, Captain Hessiz is with her command staff. They wished to lead the next breaching teams."

Mobus caught the slightest shift of displeasure in the sergeant's eyes. He considered the move folly. An unnecessary risk. Mobus agreed. He gave a soft nod of agreement. War did odd things to many, not the least of which was a lessening of judgment in mid-level leaders afraid of missing action when armies deployed. Expecting worse in the months to come, Mobus needed to crack down on improper actions and conduct unbecoming before they spread through his forces.

He watched a prisoner stumble and get jerked back to his feet by a young female soldier more than a foot shorter. The ferocity of her actions was spurred by seeing Mobus. She doubted he knew her name but she had stood the line on the low continent when Rengu's minions threatened to overrun them. A proud veteran.

"Sergeant, I be ..."

The explosion rocked the ground. Sparks flew, blinding those using night vision. Balls of shrapnel lanced down alleys and the main street, chased by jets of flame. Several prisoners and Guards fell screaming. Pings of debris striking his tank spurred Mobus into action. He was about to issue new orders to the sergeant, only to see the man was on the ground. A pool of rich blood spilled out from beneath him. Mobus spied a large chunk of metal nearly severing the man's head.

Secondary explosions ripped through another warehouse on the opposite side of the street. Mobus snarled and climbed back into his turret. He pulled his helmet down and activated the comm. "Get me in that building. Prepare to engage anyone standing."

"But General, we might have people inside," his adjutant protested.

Mobus knew the truth. He had just lost an entire command team and an unknown number of Guards to a terrorist act. Hatred seething through his veins, Mobus Kale saw but one thing; revenge. The tank lurched forward. Guns heated. The main barrel was loaded. Active tracking systems engaged, blue and red icons populating the screens to indicated friendly and potential enemy forces. A backward glance showed two lines of infantry forming in the tank's wake. He would be the hammer. They the anvil.

The tank gained speed the closer it got to the wreckage of the warehouse frontage. Melted metal framework sagged on either side of the blast, reminding Mobus of the tears of a clown. Their sad mimicry of life was apropos, all things considered. Tragedy bespoke untold terrors. Vengeance, he vowed, was to be meted out this dawn.

"Hammer it," Mobus snarled, and the tank burst through the debris field.

Without awaiting orders, the adjutant ordered his gunners to open fire. Ion rounds sizzled through the smoke cloud. Puffs of red mist announced vaporized bodies. The main gun fired into the concealed building rear. Mobus watched the scene unfold with morbid fascination developed over decades of military experience, while making a casual glance at the remains of far too many of his Guards who were caught in the initial blast.

Remorseless, he ignored them for the fools they were. Such should not be remembered as it brought disgrace upon their regiments. Letters of reprimand would be filed after. Mobus watched with glee, as icons continued to disappear from his screen. His crew, handpicked, was as merciless as he. A proper reflection.

The first pinpricks of return fire lanced from the shadows. Ineffective against his armor, those that struck left but scorch marks. He braced as the turret swiveled right to engage. Two well placed rounds destroyed the entire corner of the warehouse, causing an entire section to collapse. Infantry swarmed in around the tank and unleashed their full fury. Ion rifles and heavy weapons roared to life. Anything alive was cut down without second thought, until only Mobus's forces remained.

"Cease fire," he called. "Send the infantry forward. Bring any prisoners directly to me."

Again, the tank halted. Mobus popped the hatch and climbed up to watch the operation. A handful of stray rounds crossed the open area between forces. What survivors remained were battered, bloodied, and near their end.

"I need just one," Mobus said.

"Sir?" the adjutant cut in.

Jerking away from the scene unfolding, Mobus realized he had spoken aloud. "Nothing, Captain. Order the rest of the task force to continue mopping up their current positions. We have more than we need."

"Yes, sir." Cold, methodical, his voice was dispassionate.

A thought occurred to Mobus. "Oh, and Captain, I want one hundred prisoners executed in front of the others before they are removed to the processing camps."

Silence answered him.

Inquisition Headquarters, planet Vau Prime.

Pristine halls stretched as far as Gedrick Silk could see. Tile so pure, enough to blind a man, reflected the false overhead lighting. Unused to being in the center of a viper den, the shapeshifter walked with the false confidence his captured uniform inspired. He had been embedded in the heart of enemy territory without word from Strannan for weeks.

Too many times, Gedrick changed his guise, for the enemy was getting closer to discovering his identity. Clever, but outnumbered by thousands, Gedrick was lost in an impossible situation his race was suited for. The last of his kind, so far as he knew, he presented the best opportunity to destroy the usurpers from within. Doing so remained problematic. His conscience weighed heavily, for he was no assassin. Stemming from a peaceful people, Gedrick was forced to adapt to the universe the Conclave shaped through their heretical persecutions. Were times different, he would have slipped away unnoticed and forgotten.

His orders were simple. Eliminate Inquisitor General Alain Nye and end his plan to take over the universe. Gedrick was not averse to fighting. Living among humans for so long, removed any hesitation he was raised with. They were a wicked breed that bore the benefits of rising among the masses, to gain power in the wake of the gods. If only another race had been wise enough, perhaps the universe would not be engulfed in civil war.

Lament was a useless emotion to a man like Gedrick. His one hope of a lasting life was to accomplish his task and find an extraction point out of Inquisition Headquarters. The raid on Tatarast Island forced new security measures complicating his purpose. Nye was, by all accounts, a shrewd man who took few chances. Ensconced in the comforts of his chosen empire, the Inquisitor General saw fit to proceed with armed guards wherever he went. Gedrick thought that spoke ill of the future. Any ruler who feared was determined to end in inglorious demise.

The shapeshifter adjusted his collar and clasped his hands behind his back as he observed other officers do. Uncomfortable, he felt the strain in his shoulders and upper back. The longer he remained in character, the closer he felt to losing his identity. Gedrick surmised Nye must feel the same, for every aspect of his life was manufactured. He briefly wondered what traumatic event transformed a considered meek Inquisitor into a monster bent on universal domination. There was no shortage of suffering in the universe, he lamented.

"Excuse me, Captain, can you direct me to the offices of Heretical Persecution?"

Gedrick stiffened upon being addressed. He turned to find a fresh-faced young woman in an ill-fitting uniform fresh out of supply issue. Human age being difficult for him to judge, he guessed her no more than twenty summers. "You are assigned there?"

She swallowed her fear of addressing a senior officer and gave a clipped nod. "Yes, sir. Newly assigned. I just enlisted."

What lies were you sold? To throw away your future for the greed of one man. "How old are you?"

"Nineteen, sir!" she beamed.

A mere child. Gedrick turned his wince into a weak smile. "You are in the wrong building. Go back to the main entrance and turn left. Third building down."

She snapped a salute, crisp like only a newly trained recruit could accomplish, which he returned and hurried back down the hallway. Gedrick watched her for a moment. The youth were too easily influenced. He doubted she would live to see twenty. Saddened, the shapeshifter continued his trek. There was a man in need of killing.

Gedrick wandered unmolested by others until he reached the central corridor. Hundreds of Inquisitors and Prekhautens filled the avenue. The red robes of Conclave mixed in with them. He was in the center of universal government. The lifeblood of a three thousand year old empire, risen from the ashes of the old gods. Hundreds of trillions of lives with bent knee to the decrees of the Conclave spread across seven hundred worlds. It was, in his limited opinion, a miracle of the first order.

Legends whispered of a time of apocalypse. The ending of all things. Gedrick was not superstitious, though he believed a measure of truth lay buried in each tale to form the basis of modern culture. His own people cultivated tales of horrific beings who ruled the known universe with iron determination. Their violence perpetrated their demise, leaving a vast abyss in their wake, thus allowing humanity to rise. Gedrick did not know the truth, nor was he willing to think on it further. The cold deep of space held secrets no living soul should explore.

Trying his best to blend in, Gedrick presented a false air of confidence. His internal debates brought him to a crisis of faith numerous times since accepting his assignment. Davith Strannan was counting on him to succeed in stealth, where strength of arms failed. Those debates continued as he burrowed deeper into the corridor's traffic. So, it was he failed to notice Alain Nye walking not more than five meters away.

Gedrick's heart quickened. The sidearm on his hip pressed into him. A steady reminder of the severity of the situation. Gedrick knew there would be no escape once he committed. Retribution would be swift. He prayed for a quick demise rather than endless days of torture. Flexing his hands, he slipped in behind his target.

The Inquisitor General was flanked by two lesser ranked Inquisitors and a senior Prekhauten Guard. They conversed in hushed tongues. A full squad of armed guards followed. Getting to Nye in the open was proving more difficult than sneaking into his private quarters. Gedrick cursed his indecision for passing on an earlier opportunity to remove Nye's attendant and taking his identity. This, he decided, was going to be messy.

His right hand slipped around to his thigh and unsnapped his holster. All he needed was one shot to the back of Nye's head. The war would grind to a halt and order would be restored. A natural balance could resume without any more deaths. Well, two at least. Gedrick winced at the thought of being shot as he wondered what it felt like.

He inched closer. A faceless assassin. Why Strannan avoided using the Vaumagians was a mystery, though their allegiance was in question. An organization that could be bought was in position to eliminate the insurrection's entire chain of command. No, Gedrick agreed. Best to take care of business with proven assets. Even one with considerable more talent than the average infiltrator team. Gedrick squinted, as he strained to pick up the conversation.

"Are you certain? I have had no formal word of this," Nye asked. His tone left no question of his surprise.

The Prekhauten Colonel to his right said, "Absolutely. Our networks have picked up a massive ship in the Coellian Sector where Lord Amongeratix was last rumored to be seen. We have every reason to believe it is his ship. He is moving at last."

Nye lengthened his stride. "Impossible, my lord would have informed me of his plans. Send reconnaissance craft to investigate."

An Inquisitor with a pale blue hue to her skin added, "We have, Sir. Every craft, unmanned and piloted, was destroyed before reaching confirmation range. Whoever is on that ship, does not wish to be known."

"Yet you, Colonel, are convinced it is Amongeratix?" Nye questioned. "How can this be when all efforts to make contact or positive identification have been rebuked?"

"Inquisitor General, who else would such a monstrosity belong to? Initial specs taken before our nearest satellite was destroyed, suggest the ship is over three thousand meters long and has thousands of guns," the Colonel defended.

"Guns which could be allied with the enemy," Nye said. His voice was slick, reminding Gedrick of an eel struggling to return to water. "We cannot act on supposition. I want that ship confirmed. It if is

Lord Amongeratix's, as you suggest, we have nothing to be concerned about."

"If it isn't?" the Inquisitor asked.

Nye halted midstride and faced them both. "Then we have greater issues than the rebellion here on Vau Prime."

"Are there any free battle groups in the vicinity, Colonel?" the Inquisitor asked. Her mind raced through scenarios frighteningly fast.

"None. They are all deployed trying to hunt down Admiral Khe'Zhehan's ships. We hold numerical superiority but reports indicate sympathetic ships are starting to gather in support of the old regime."

Nye continued walked. Anger clouded his face. "This must end, and quickly. I want all enemy leaders found and brought before the Conclave to stand public trial for their crimes. There can be no doubt in the general population's minds that we are the true saviors of the universe."

"We have every available force committed. Operations on Mannus Prime have ground to a standstill. Both armies are expending personnel and equipment at impossible rates. We need more men," the Colonel requested.

"There are seven hundred colonized worlds under the Conclave's thumb and countless more that are unaccountable for. How is raising additional troops an issue?" Nye demanded. "I was led to believe we held every advantage needed to win this war."

"Inquisitor General, there was no way to gauge the sheer number of sympathizers with the enemy. The battles in the deserts of An'kuruku showed our vulnerability. The peasantry is rising against us, no matter how hard the hammer falls." The Prekhauten fell silent. He had spoken his mind but was it too much?

The group rounded a corner and halted before a guarded double door. Guards snapped to attention upon seeing Nye. Their blackened ion rifles crossed their chests with fierce pride. Gedrick spied plates in the ceiling concealing additional firepower. Any move here was ended before it began.

"Mannus Prime must not fall," Nye said. "Pull whatever divisions you need to off the line and reinforce what is already in place. The manufactories must be retained for the war effort. Losing that world must not happen."

"Yes, Inquisitor General." The Colonel bowed and excused himself. He brushed by Gedrick, cheeks flushed crimson.

The shapeshifter snapped his holster shut. Killing Nye would have to wait. The intelligence Gedrick learned was too valuable to risk losing his life over. Thoughts of assassination faded, as he turned toward escape. He locked eyes with Nye in passing. It sent chills through him. Whatever humanity the Inquisitor General once had was gone.

The doors hissed open. An orderly in a dark gray uniform saluted. "Sire, Lord Amongeratix commands you to make contact with him at once."

The door shut behind the group, leaving Gedrick lost in his thoughts. Too many pieces were at play. He feared the board lacked room for any more players. War had come to the universe. Wrathful and inspired. Days of peace were ended. He wondered if anyone was to survive the spreading storm.

Her body ached. Every muscle felt as if a hammer had beaten it. Aliz winced as she turned over. The cot she slept on, or tried to, was military issue and not designed for comfort. The lover of the former Cardinal Seniorus wasn't sure if this was on purpose. A quick glance at her wrist chrono showed it was the middle hours of deep night. The time when ghouls prowled nightmares and the dead haunted the streets. No sane person had reason to bear witness to the foul deeds of night, yet she had too much on her mind to sleep.

Aliz often dreamed of Lorenu Phos. They had been together for many years, living a secret life in the center of power in the universe. Politics demanded the Cardinal Seniorus could not sleep with a lesser person of rank. Especially one considered naught but her handmaiden. Aliz remembered their first kiss. Their first tender embrace and the feeling of contentment the next morning, awakening beside her warm body. Long before politics and policy entered. The love they shared became a lie grinding on Aliz's conscience.

None of that mattered now. Lorenu was dead. Killed by men once sworn to defend her. All she once championed was thrown in disarray. War continued spreading across the stars. She knew there was no option of neutrality. This was a battle of faith. Sides must be taken. Families were torn apart by conflicting ideologies. She wished she had tears left for them, but her sympathies had long since dried up. Aliz was hardened by the events of the past two years. A bitter woman by all regards, and in her estimation, far too old for such games.

Recognizing there would be no sleep, she groaned and slipped her feet to the cold floor. Jolts of pain ran up her legs, making her regret again her need to go with the forces to the Prekhauten Guard training facility on Tatarast Island. Strannan insisted she stay behind but Aliz was nothing if not headstrong. Despite mission success, she was left reconsidering her decisions.

It was vengeance that drove her to extreme actions. She had people teach her weapons and how to shoot. How to survive a firefight and treat battlefield injuries. The last vestiges of her former soft life slowly washed away, leaving a hardened and determined woman in their place. Aliz once believed she had not one spiteful bone. Dark times changed that. A product of her environment, she decided to swing by the latrine before checking with the night crew.

Security guards patrolled the exterior and interior of the building. It was the fourth headquarters since she joined Strannan's rebellion. Always the enemy learned their location and persecuted retribution as only the Prekhauten Guard was capable of. Months of constantly looking over her shoulder and wondering if a sniper's round would finally end her pain, filled her waking hours and troubled her dreams. Aliz needed a way out.

Her gaze fell on the empty cot beside her. Not everyone remained dedicated to the cause. The first move Aliz made after Lorenu's assassination, was to find one of the most notorious crime lords in Krenz, Zoraq Darc. They formed a tepid allegiance, each knowing that the moment the union no longer worked for both parties, they would split. The raid on Tatarast Island proved his breaking point. Where she once admired his willingness to look outside of his personal interests, the old scoundrel had returned. He left under cover of night without saying a word.

Frustrated, Aliz ambled through the rows of snoring soldiers and marines. These men and women who had already given so much to the preservation of the Conclave, deserved better. It was a side of the universe she seldom was allowed to glimpse. Perhaps, she mused, if more of the leadership was exposed to the truth, it might not have come to this.

"You carry more weight than you deserve," Strannan told her upon seeing Aliz walk into the makeshift command center. He passed her a metal cup with steam rising from it.

Aliz accepted the tea and drank deeply. The hot liquid soothed many of her fears. "What makes me special?"

He hung his head. Age, wounds, and a fractured conscience colluded to rob him of his former self. "We are all special. Each and every one of these people here and the trillions across the stars. If we fail to remember that for even a moment, we are lost."

"You place great faith in humanity amidst all this," she countered.

"What else have I? Nye and his minions sought to end my life and damned near succeeded, were it not for a twist of fate," Strannan explained.

The sadness in his voice threatened to bring her to tears. She had grown accustomed to sorrow. It was a constant companion to the hatred burning inside. Aliz stared into his eyes, searching for condolence she would not find. Davith Strannan was a lifelong soldier and a proud servant of the Conclave. His days of sympathy were gone.

She finished her tea and handed the cup back. "What keeps you going? We are outnumbered on every count. Wouldn't it be easier to just slip away and find a quiet place to spend the rest of your days?"

"Perhaps, but I am not cut that way." He held up a hand to stay her next comment. "Make no mistake, I am no war monger. The reason I dedicated my life to the Guard was to protect peace and stability, not wage endless conflict across the seven hundred worlds. What sort of man would I be, if I turned my back now, when the universe needs me most?"

She knew the answer. They both did, though neither would speak it aloud. Far too many villains and cowards were already in play. Aliz stifled the yawn building in her chest. Sleep was long in coming, however, for her mind weighed heavy.

"When did Zoraq leave?" she asked.

A cloud passed over Strannan's face before the mask slipped back in place. "Not long ago. I assume it was at dusk, during shift change."

"A coward then," she concluded. The last two years had been a continual let down, yet this hurt the most.

"Don't be so fast to judge. He helped us immensely. Without his networks and access to black market equipment, we would have collapsed long ago," Strannan offered.

She rose, fists clenched. "He left when we needed him the most!"

"He left because he felt he had to. There was no oath or burden of loyalty expected from the man. Zoraq Darc was one of the most wanted men on the planet before the war. That he stepped from the shadows to assist, was unexpected and most appreciated. Even his efforts on the raid of Prekhauten Headquarters. I hold him in no great esteem, but I will not curse his name behind his back," Strannan fell silent, his gaze passing over the bank of portable computer screens and terminals.

"Besides," he continued with an amused look. "He took nothing with him. All the weapons, medicine, and ammunition we confiscated during the raid are accounted for."

Confusion lingered in her eyes. "Then why? What was it all for?"

Strannan shrugged. "Who can say? We are creatures of habit after all. My gut tells me we have not seen the last of him."

"I've seen all of him that I care to." Crossing her arms, she made a show of mock defiance.

"That is immature, especially for one your age," he scolded as a weary father might. "You are tired. Try to get some sleep. I have a feeling we will not be in this location much longer."

"What have you heard?" she asked before he finished speaking.

"Whispers. Snippets of information on the open lines. It appears Kale has been hitting more factories in his hunt for me. Each day, the noose draws tighter."

Reaching out a steadying hand, she slipped back into her chair. "How much longer can we hold out? Honestly, Davith. Will we have to abandon Vau Prime?"

He paused. A small act speaking volumes and her heart plummeted. "I ... do not know. I have done everything I could to build a resistance and keep Nye's hound at bay. We have had many successes, but the sheer weight of opposition drives us into the ground. My hope is to use the vehicles and equipment we stole to make a strong push to break Kale's spine here in the city.

If we hit him hard enough, there is the chance we can slip away. Either to the low continent or off world."

"The low continent? Now?" she blurted. Events there had been broadcast across the planet in real time, all with the propagandized twist of the current political scheme. Images of women and children burning to death, while the armored Prekhauten Guard fought them off, sickened her.

His grin reminded her of the old war hawk. "What better place to hide? Kale has already cleansed the continent and left a skeleton force in place to keep the survivors at bay. He would never think to look there."

"For good reason! They burned everything. Every city, village, and town."

"Not for reasons you suspect," he countered. "I have reports stating a massive cult uprising occurred before Kale was deployed south. They follow one of the old gods. Rengu, I believe. The god of death. How or why this heresy gave birth on Vau Prime is a mystery, but the timing of it bought us over half a year."

Rengu. Cults on Vau Prime. Heresy spreading across the universe unchecked, now the watchdog's gaze is averted. Aliz struggled to understand the implications of it.

"What if we can't find transport?" she asked. One successful midnight raid on a nearby island was one matter. Evacuating tens of thousands of fighters and their equipment, another matter altogether.

"I have means at my disposal. It will not be easy, should it come to that, but I can call upon those who will help us escape." He paused and fixed her with his steel gaze. "The question is, can we afford to abandon all we have done here, and the countless civilians waiting for salvation, when we are needed the most?"

"I don't understand the conflict. How can dying achieve any positivity?" she asked.

He reached out to place a fatherly hand on her knee. "Aliz, we are sworn to defend the populace, not flee when times grow difficult. They need us. Even if it means sacrificing our lives, so that they may live."

Strannan let the words sink in and left her to her thoughts. After pouring a fresh cup of tea, he made his nightly rounds throughout the warehouse. She watched him go, knowing he would stop at every guard point and speak with every Guard still awake. Alize wished he had taken control of the Inquisition instead of Nye. What the universe needed was compassion, not violence. A second yawn struck, but there would be no sleep for her this night. She had much to think on.

TWO

3215 A.G. (After Gods), The Great Library, planet Wexanos.

There was no warmth in the golden light pouring through the bank of windows for Luma Kai. Her mind was troubled. Conflicted with warring emotions, bereft of logic. Lines creased her forehead. Clustered in the corners of her eyes. Random strands of graying hair struck through her once lustrous mane. It was time, she concluded, for a break. Unfortunately for the former Inquisitor of the office of Heretical Persecution, there was none to be had. Open war raged across the universe. Thousands of men and women died daily on forgotten worlds and that was the true sadness.

Luma closed her eyes in private lament and tried to find the beauty in the moment. Wexanos was a dream. One she could ill afford to remain in, given recent circumstances. There was a time, not long ago, when she bridled at the prospect of working with one of the Inquisitions' most famous members. Senior Inquisitor Tolde Breed was a hero among the ranks. His exploits against Amongeratix fueled young women like Luma to join the Inquisition. To do their part.

Tolde first encountered the Three after a prison escape almost thirty years earlier. It was only through a wisp of fate he and the now retired Sergeant Major Matthias survived and brought the villain to justice. The mission was taught in the Prekhauten Academy. A worthy example of how to handle the most extreme situation and find victory at the end. Later, when Tolde encountered the Three working on Crimeat, he again found a way to win. There would be no classes dedicated in honor, however, for his actions there predicated war for the universe.

Luma worked with Tolde for almost a year before Alain Nye made his open bid for power and had the Cardinal Seniorus assassinated. Duty tempted her to remain in the service of the Inquisition, but it was Tolde who whispered her away from the dark ideations spreading through the universe's powers. The break was sharp, forcing her to come to grips with her conscience.

Now, he was dead. She saw the body not long after returning from a mission. Alone and frightened. In the end, he was a broken shell of a man. Luma had accepted it and was content for a time. Until the

Blood Witches arrived with a younger man claiming to have Tolde's soul. Her training demanded she take action and weed out this witchcraft before it took root in others. The impromptu council on Wexanos was already fracturing from increased demands for action. Having a demonspawn among them threatened to unravel all they had sought to preserve.

Yet, when he spoke, it was with Tolde's authority. All the memories and past deeds were easily recounted. Either the man truly was Tolde Breed reborn, or he was a ruse come to slay them in their dreams. Luma had yet to find the balance with which to make a decision. Standing by chafed her. She wanted action. Needed it to calm her mind after the terrible events on An'kuruku. Until that happened, there would be no joy in the fading sunlight of a peaceful day.

Soft footsteps of slippered feet announced a visitor. Luma knew who it was before he spoke.

"Inquisitor, the others are waiting," Chief Librarian Fistel said, his voice uncharacteristically compassionate.

Of course, they are. Never a moment of quiet reflection for any of us. Luma turned, noticing for the first time how pale his yellow robes make him. "Has there been any news of interest in my absence?"

He offered a half bow. Ancient beyond her reckoning, Fistel was Tannus' prime acolyte on Wexanos. "It is not for me to say. I am but a humble librarian."

"One with the training of a Vaumagian Assassin," she threw out to get a response.

Fistel remained bowed but said naught.

Very well. Play your games, old man, but you and I both know you are among the most lethal of us. "Lead on, Chief Librarian. Far be it for me to hold up the council in this hour of need."

Luma knew the way to Tannus' private chambers by heart. The favored of the Three was simplistic in his approach to life, even after several thousand years. He surrounded himself with volumes of books written by every race and species in the universe. It was the true wealth of Wexanos. A world going unnoticed by the Conclave even now. She marveled at that fact. An entire world unaccounted for. If there was one, surely others existed, scattered across the stars waiting for discovery. More likely cowering from prying eyes, she decided.

Fistel halted at the outer doors of Tannus' sanctum. Though master of the libraries, he was seldom invited into the full council. Luma suspected he was also in charge of planetary defenses and the training of the library corps. Earlier, she tried to make a count of the yellow robes moving facelessly about. It was a pointless task, though she surmised they numbered in the thousands.

Crimson flushed up from her throat when the stares of the others fell on her. Friends through conflict, but a handful were unknown to her. Three Blood Witches hovered over the marble floors. Their faces concealed beneath diaphanous robes of shimmering gossamer. They were the harbingers of doom. Watchful angels doling justice where needed. The final stranger was the young man who accompanied Tolde home. A strange boy named Ragan Sandinsol. His youthful innocence was almost gone. Rubbed off by unspeakable horrors on his home world.

"Inquisitor," Tannus addressed her. "We may now begin."

He remained seated, for his twelve-foot frame towered twice over the assembled humans. Luma found him unsettling, despite their continued exposure. He was a giant. Scars covered his hands and neck, though not a one danced across his face. Rationale screamed he should not exist. The gods were forgotten legends. Certainly, they belonged in antiquity.

"My brother continues to make his bid for control," Tannus began. "Word has reached me of his command ship, once thought lost, arisen at last. It is a ship with single purpose. *Behemoth*. The destroyer of worlds."

"No ship is capable of destroying an entire planet," a grim-faced Lieutenant Fies snapped back. He winced and reached down to rub his shin.

"I wish that were so. There was a time when there were far more than seven hundred worlds," Tannus explained. "My brother was ruthless with his execution of our war."

The bald woman who kicked Fies into silence, rubbed a hand over one of the lightning-bolt tattoos on her head. "How do we kill it?"

"If I knew that, Annalilly, I would have done so ages ago. Our best hope is in keeping my brother from reaching the *Behemoth* and starting his war," Tannus said.

"I thought we were already at war," the holographic image of Admiral Falchi said.

"One war, yes. Another is coming. One that will bring civilization to its knees. Amongeratix seeks to remake the universe in his image. Our father could never abide by such greed. Rejection spurred my brother into greater acts of depravity, as the Grand Mistress can attest. With this ship, he with prove unstoppable."

Annalilly folded her arms. Her frown cut deep. "Why don't you have a ship like that and make the field even?"

"I seek to prevent war, not encourage it. There are other weapons, scattered across the stars, for our use. I had hoped to avoid this conflict, but fate was never kind to me."

One of the Blood Witches stirred. "Lord Tannus, you place too much blame on your shoulders. This is not a conflict of your creation, regardless of personal beliefs. Forever Night has been prophesied since the ending of the gods. It is the logical succession of events heralding in a new age."

He tilted his head out of respect. Their relationship stretched back over three thousand years. Ruma Zzein was not always the revered mother of the Blood Witch order. A thin smile creased his lips.

"That does little to justify the grievances in my heart," he replied.

Fies glowered at Annalilly. "If we can't kill it and you have nothing capable of holding it off, how are we supposed to neutralize this…"

"*Behemoth*," Annalilly hissed. "Pay attention, *sir*."

"Keep pissing me off and watch how fast you get promoted," he snarled.

Those who did not know, would never assume they were lovers.

Ruma ignored their bantering. "There is other news. *Behemoth* is but one aspect of Amongeratix's. He secured an army long ago. They lay hidden on a forgotten world for millennia, waiting for their master's call. Skulldaerth he named them."

"Impossible. They were all destroyed at the end of the war. We were both there," Tannus frowned.

"A second army, and potentially more, spirited away, my lord," Ruma supplied. "Sister Alessandra saw them when she recovered the spirit of Tolde Breed and young Ragan."

"It is true. There were thousands of the monstrosities in the monastery," the second Blood Witch added. "It is my belief they are the strength behind the fist of *Behemoth*. Amongeratix will be capable of deploying an invincible force to any world in the universe at will, should he collect them unopposed."

"We can't fight two wars at once," Matthias interrupted. "Our forces are already stretched thin across several worlds. The siege on Mannus Prime already demands more combat divisions than we can afford to spend. Now this? How much more can we stand before the bend becomes a break?"

Tannus felt his patience stretched thin. Unaccustomed to being questioned, he found working with humans continually difficult. "Matthias, you saw what the combined strength of my brother and our … uncle was capable of on An'kuruku."

"Aye," Matthias fired back. "I saw there was a frenzy among his soldiers unlike anything I have seen during my career."

"You also saw how many good civilians were willing to stand up for right and defend their land," the son of the god king lowered his voice. "We may lack trained soldiers and grand space fleets, but the strength of our cause continues to rally thousands. I agree. Mannus Prime must not fall to the enemy. Not if we expect to continue supplying our total war effort."

"Wait, you said uncle? It was our understanding there were no other gods in play," Luma questioned. A glance down showed the tiny hairs on her forearm standing.

Paradise Tear, Tannus' cousin and the key to victory, interjected, "Rengu. The so called god of death. He is beyond vengeful. The fires of war fueled his rage during the great rebellion that nearly ended our people."

"And he's awake?" Fies asked. Dejection lined his already haggard face. Three years of sustained combat with limited resources, and a dwindling number of able bodies, compiled with the catastrophic events on Kharsis, battered his psyche, pushing him to the breaking point.

"Not yet," Tannus' comment eased the mounting tension in the room. "Rengu still sleeps."

Tolde scratched the light brown stubble on his chin. "Surely Amongeratix is searching for him. It makes sense with the number of uprisings spreading."

"He will not find him, Tolde Breed. Rengu is secure," Tannus added.

"How can you be sure?" Matthias asked. Decades of service honed his instincts. Should Amongeratix and Rengu link forces…

"There are three people in the entire universe who know where he is, and we are all sitting in this room," Tannus said. His admission brokered little comfort among the mortals, however. The threat of a tyrant loose among the stars inspired terror in the hollow places of their souls.

Without giving their fears the opportunity to manifest, Tannus continued, "Rengu is my concern. We will handle him should the need arise."

Silence settled over them. Questing eyes looked from one person to the next, each hoping for answers that did not exist. Doubts arose. The validity of their actions suddenly called into question. With mounting pressure on multiple fronts, it felt a matter of time before the walls collapsed and the tide rushed in and drowned them.

"What do we do?"

Ragan's voice broke the still. Youthful, still innocent, he was the beacon they needed. A light to gather all and bring them through the darkness. The smile on Tannus' face was true, for the first time. Paradise Tear rose and placed a soft kiss upon Ragan's cheek. The unspoken gratitude was embarrassing.

"What did I say?" he asked, confused.

"Precisely what needed to be said, lad," Matthias slapped a palm on the table. "We have been through much these past years. Some more than others but our tests remain the same. Somewhere along the way, we lost our course. Tannus is right. There is no way we can stop fighting now. Not when so many need us."

"Well spoken, Matthias," Tannus told him. "We have much to think on. Many actions needing undertaking. I propose we develop contingencies to deal with the imminent threats."

"Wise are the words of Lord Tannus," Ruma Zzein seconded. "Time is needed to prepare a counter offensive. Wisdom, courage, and compassion to deliver unto the voiceless masses. The Blood Witches are at your disposal."

"Thank you, oracle," Tannus said quietly. "You are most welcome in the dire hour."

"My lord, there is a request for my fleet to intercede at Mannus Prime," Falchi took the opportunity to initiate action. "I would secure the planet before Kale sends his fleets."

"A wise move," Tannus said after some thought. "Though I caution against sending your entire fleet. We must be ready to begin the hunt for *Behemoth*."

"I will dispatch resources at once. A ship that large will find it difficult to hide," Falchi decided. "We'll find it and send immediate word, when we do."

His image faded, signaling the end of the meeting.

Luma Kai watched the Blood Witch trio slip away. They were anathema to her training. A source of heresy, the Conclave had long looked the opposite way, when it suited them. She struggled with accepting them as allies. Now that Tolde, the one she knew, was gone, Luma felt more alone than at any point in her young life.

Tolde. She wished there was a way to reconcile her emotions. To accept his rebirth for what it was. A gift to the enemies of malevolence. Yet when she gazed upon the young man, she saw a stranger of similar age. Inexperienced and burdened by the same weight that drove Tolde to his grave. Too many questions remained unanswered and the brief meeting offered no resolve. Luma had much to get off her chest and no one to talk to.

"A word, Luma Kai."

Tossed back into the moment, she found she was alone with Tannus. That old knot reformed in the pit of her stomach. She spent the next hour listening to him explain far more than she imagined or wished to know.

Ruma Zzein waited. Grand Mistress of the Order of Blood Witches, she was the oldest living daughter of humanity's rise. Quiet distraction occupied her thoughts. A distant niggling in the farthest recesses of her mind. It was a thought. Born from the eternal dust among the stars and nurtured by heightened anticipation of events yet to come. Face locked in consternation beneath the veil, Ruma was unable to penetrate the fog of future days. She was, she realized with much lament, blind to the piece of the future she needed to know most. Frustrating.

The door opened and she watched as Luma Kai, face reddened and on the verge of tears, stormed away. Tannus' great shadow fell upon Ruma. His expression suggested he expected this confrontation. *You would have been a grand king, Tannus. If only your kind had not destroyed itself in their lust for power.*

"Oracle," Tannus acknowledged. "It has been a long time since we last took council this way."

"Lord Tannus, it has been longer since I last went by that title. The past is lost to the dim pages of faded memory," she replied. "It is the curse of the living to remember the past."

He nodded slowly as he considered her words. Three thousand years had passed since last he was forced to treat with her cryptic messages. "Indeed. I assume this is a conversation best uttered in private."

"How well you know me," Ruma bowed in return. She followed him into his private chambers. They were a far cry from his palace so long ago.

Tannus sat, knowing the Blood Witch would refuse any offer of comfort. He squinted in the late morning light as he studied his old friend. Much was changed from her days of captivity. A toy for his father's amusement. Regret, washed with guilt, stabbed at Tannus, for there was a time he served as a willing accomplice to her mistreatment. Saving her before the final battle at Occanum was the noblest deed he performed.

"It does my heart good to see you well, Ruma," he began. "Dark times are reborn and I am hard pressed to summon the tools needed to halt them."

"You are not alone."

Her hovering caught his stare. How or why she achieved this talent remained hidden, even from him. Ruma Zzein was the oldest living human in the universe, as close to immortal as possible. Such a feat was not accomplished by the ordinary.

He snorted. "You mean my brother. Sorrow has ever been unpredictable. Many wars have I fought with Amongeratix and few were the times Sorrow intervened. He is lost, more content with discovering immutable truths of the origins of life than accepting his place in the universe. Do not preach to me of his worth. Not now. I beg you."

"He has already set the Paladin on the Forsaken Path," she explained before he finished speaking. "The confluence approaches."

Tannus' eyes opened wide. "The fool! He…"

"He does what he must. I have come to understand Sorrow over the years. He knows the importance of the Paladin and Prophet," Ruma said.

"I understood the Prophet was dead," Tannus suggested. "Killed in the deserts of An'kuruku. Has another been discovered?"

"Perhaps. That moment is clouded. The future is ever in motion. Paladin and Prophet are intertwined. Destined to serve the greater cause at a time not of their choosing. One has fallen. Another will arise. Too many events are in play for the position to remain empty."

Rising, the giant began to pace. "Is Elisa strong enough to master the Forsaken Path?"

"I do not know. Many have tried," Ruma answered.

"All have died. Without the Paladin, Paradise Tear is exposed. We cannot use her powers to stop my people from being destroyed." He paused midstride. "You already knew this. You allowed Elisa to find Sorrow and assume her destiny."

"I offer no apology. There are still matters I can influence before the end," the Blood Witch admitted. "We must all do as we must."

He caught it then. The flicker of sadness buried in her tone. "The Paladin's fate is no longer in our hands. I must accept it. But it is not the reason you wished to speak with me."

"No. There is another matter. One more grave than any I have encountered since I fled your palace all those millennia ago." She froze, hovering in place, while she collected her thoughts. "I fear a schism approaches."

"Among your witches," he concluded. "That is ill news. Have you substantiated evidence? There is little I can do to assist."

"It is a feeling. Discontent rises among the ranks. Much like the rest of the universe, my order is to be faced with its greatest test." Her voice carried a haunted feeling. She was keeping secrets. "My fear is not for my disciples, but for the charge I am guardian of. Should the rebellion succeed…"

"It won't."

"Should it succeed, there is the real possibility of our enemy discovering the one tool they desire most," Ruma finished. "Tannus, he cannot be allowed to walk the stars again."

"Fail safes are in place. Fear not, Ruma Zzein," Tannus said. "The Acumensiis Comet will not fall."

"I hope, for your sake, you are correct," she said after much thought.

Deep space, vicinity Hawker's Gate.

"How much longer are we just going to sit here?"

Captain August did her best to ignore Vicente Blackheart, but his incessant banter and complaining was grinding on her sense of discipline. She considered having the pirate lord tossed in the brig and have done with the situation. Orders prevented that. They were bound to each other until the mission was complete. None of that prevented her from daydreaming of pummeling the man senseless.

Vicente ran his dagger tip beneath his fingernail, again. His boots were propped on the small console in disregard of standard Prekhauten Navy protocol. Weeks in deep space with his newly appointed watchdog left him chafing to return to the lawlessness of his former life. A life that no longer existed. His hope for the future was slender at best. All he had to do was survive to the end and slip away to a life of obscurity.

August arched an eyebrow. "Must you continue doing that?"

He lifted the knife. "What, this? It's not like there's much else for me to do on this tub."

"We've been over this, *pirate*. Your vessel is too familiar to our foes," she hissed, lips pursed.

Blackheart's laugh echoed across the bridge. "You think being on a Prekhauten ship of the line is better than the *Shrike*?"

"At least there is the opportunity of being mistaken for the enemy," she replied. "Besides, sooner or later, you'll cut yourself and I have no desire to see your blood stain my decks."

"Lovely as always, *Captain*," he offered his most charming smile, knowing it was wasted on the disgruntled Guard.

August snorted and turned away. "Tactical, any sign of our prey?"

"None, Captain."

She bit back a curse. It was the same every time. Endless hours of hunting a small frigate out of Kharsis ground on their nerves. Compounding August's angst was the limited intelligence she received before accepting the assignment. Blackheart was the easiest piece of the puzzle. He was out for vengeance for perceived wrongs committed on the planet to himself and his crew. What those were remained elusive in the telling.

Admiral Falchi's orders were simple. Find the vessel carrying Presha Von and stop her from delivering a weapon to the enemy. Finding a lone starship in the deep of space was no easy task. Hundreds of trade routes and travel lanes existed, forcing August to lean on strategy over tactics. Cast from her comfort zone, August reluctantly accepted the criminal wisdom of the pirate lord. At least there was no riddle in Vicente Blackheart.

Blackheart was born into wealth. Instead of accepting his role, he turned his back on the family business and forged a reputation as one of the most notorious pirates in the universe. He was there when a Prekhauten fleet destroyed Drespai. He was involved in the combined campaign on Kharsis before the planet died. Up to his elbows in conspiracy and commitment, Blackheart vowed to see this task through. Knowing this did little to adjust August's ill temper.

"You don't think she knew she was being hunted," Blackheart theorized.

"Do you?" August countered.

He shrugged. "Hard to say. What little I know of the bitch says she is crafty but not wise to the way the greater underbelly of the universe works. She came from royalty or some such on Crimeat. Rumor says she was there when the first battles of the war were waged."

"None of that helps me understand where she would go, if she learned we were after her," August tapped her manicured nails against the console. "Without knowing we were out here, she should have continued straight through to her only haven."

Hawker's Gate was once the largest free meeting station in the universe. Firmly under the Conclave's control. Until war erupted. One of the fiercest naval battles in recent history was fought over the station. Both August and Blackheart were there, veterans on opposing sides. Now they drifted through the debris field surrounding the Gate together.

"She can't go home," he insisted. "I looked into it. Crimeat was thrown into upheaval after the Three finished their battles. Why the Conclave decided on imprisoning Amongeratix instead of executing him, is lost on me. They created their own nightmare."

"That doesn't help," August warned. Fractured as it was, her loyalty remained to the Conclave and the old order. "Wouldn't turmoil conceal her from prying eyes?"

"Not if she was marked. Presha Von is a nasty sort, Captain. She's as cunning as she is attractive and twice as dangerous."

August folded her arms. "Why is this so personal to you, Blackheart?"

He paused, the words dying on his lips. Blackheart winced before saying, "She is with a nasty man responsible for the deaths of too many of my crew. Not to mention my former First Mate. You can have Von. I want Geres Auk."

Falling silent, he left her struggling to piece the answers together.

"Captain, ship falling into real space. Transponder signal marks it as Presha Von's."

Her heart quickened. "Location."

"Three hundred thousand kays and closing slowly. Trajectory suggests it in route to the Gate," her First Mate replied.

"Comms, put all open channels up. I want to hear what she's saying," August ordered.

Garbled chatter filled the bridge's speakers. Most was between incoming supply ships and the Gate's control center. The soft scuff of Blackheart's boots slipping to deck was lost among the chatter.

"Sounds pointless," he commented after minutes passed without results.

August held up a finger. "Amplify and target sensors on the incoming vessel. Weapons, I want torpedoes armed and loaded. Target engines and weapon banks. Helm, prepare an intercept solution. That ship will not reach the Gate."

Several aye captains replied. The hunt was on. Her face was feral. August was the prime huntress in a game that had gone on for far too long. The killing shot was about to strike.

Her First Mate spun around to face. "Captain, target vessel is altering course. They know we're here."

"Full power. Close the gap and launch a spread as soon as we are in range," August barked. The thrill soured to potential failure. Losing Von here presented complications August was ill prepared to accept. Regardless of the lack of intel, she was warned Von had a weapon capable of killing an entire planet.

The *Solstice* buckled as her drives engaged. August decided it was time to abandon the ruse. "Comms, order action stations. I want Marines ready to board the moment that ship is disabled. We're going to war."

"Forget war, we need to stop that ship from dropping back into the space lanes," Blackheart snapped. "Can we hit the engines from here?"

"No, Sir. We are too far out of range."

"Captain Blackheart, so long as you stand on these decks, you will remember that I am shipmaster. Not you," August cast stern reprimand. The pirate shrank away, unwilling to risk being thrown in the brig for enthusiasm. "Is that understood?"

His lower jaw swung from left to right, eyes narrowed. "Yes, Captain. My concern, of course, is for getting that weapon away from Presha Von before she can use it to murder another planet. Forgive my fervor."

August ground her teeth for the fifth time in the last hour. His fervor tested her patience. She knew throwing him into space was the easiest solution but feared the wrath of both Khe-zhehan and Falchi. Being condemned to a garage scow looming in her future, August decided against removing Blackheart from the board.

"Forgiven. We cannot fire upon that ship at this distance," she explained. "Without a full scan, there is no way of knowing how much firepower the enemy has concealed in the debris field around the Gate. Any weapons emissions would only serve to give away our position."

Ah, you have discovered humility. How many times have you envisioned spacing me, I wonder? "I assume we will be able to engage before they flee?"

"I have no intention of letting that ship escape," she ground out. "Engines, best speed to intercept."

"Aye, Captain."

Time slowed. Long range space battles were not things of beauty. August clenched her fists and watched as the stars raced by. The anticipation of the coming fight buoyed her spirits. Redemption was within reach. All she need do was stretch forth a hand to claim it.

Vaade, planet Crimeat.

The man with deep set eyes and his ebony partner with tribal tattoos covering his face were out of place. One hulking, the other wide, they chose to ignore the stares of the locals as they strolled down the city's main avenue. It was a sunny day, yet too many citizens were either at home or not here. The mystery deepened the longer they stayed in the foreign city.

Time presented a feral grin, his tattoos twisting into ugly monsters, to an older man gawking at them. "I hate this world."

Huffing his frustration, his partner rolled his eyes. "We've been through this. Kharsis is dead and we needed to find a nice quiet spot to sit out this damned war. Seems quiet to me."

"Seems like a shit place to ride out the days," Time countered. "Makes me regret not getting that necklace of finger bones 'fore the world ended."

Krimpen Mass resisted the urge to smack his friend on the back of the head. "You complain too much. We got out with our necks, didn't we?"

"Doesn't make it sting less, and if you hit me one more time…"

Smack. Krimpen sidestepped to avoid the angered swing that would have taken his head off.

"I'm going to kill you one day, Krimpen," Time snarled.

"The Gods willing. Now, what I was trying to say before you decided to get all hostile, was we did a good thing by trying to help that pirate princeling…"

"Pirate lord," Time said.

Krimpen squinted against the midday sun. "Huh?"

"He said he was a lord, not a princeling," Time explained. "What is that anyway? Princeling. Sounds like a fancy bird elites eat."

"I should've bought a pet instead of linking up with you," Krimpen Mass groaned.

Time shrugged and continued walking. "So, you were saying why we are here. In this boring city on this boring planet."

"I was?"

"You was. What gives?" Time demanded.

Krimpen fumbled with the latch of his holster. "How would I know why we're here? All I know is I didn't die on Kharsis. Not many can make that claim."

"No, they can't," Time agreed. "I suppose we should find some work. And not for a pirate lord this time. I'm done with this war stuff. A man like me was designed for peace."

"The lap of luxury beckons, eh?"

A nod. "You got that right! Men like us got a reputation to uphold."

"What kind of job you thinking of?" Krimpen asked.

"I thought you was the brains of this outfit," Time replied.

A squad of Prekhauten Guards marched past. Their uniforms were dirty, far beneath their standards, and their weapons slung with power charges locked in. Haggard looks haunted their eyes. These were men and women who had seen too much violence and danced on the beveled edge.

"See them?" Time asked after they passed. "Been through the ringer, I'd say."

"Or worse," Krimpen added. "I did a little digging before we left the ship. Seems this is where the war started. Guard killing Guard. Looks like the fighting's moved on from here."

"Making this the best place to lay low and go unnoticed," Time concluded.

"Precisely. No more stinking pirates, quests, or battles. We're on our own again."

Time straightened. His mood shifted. "Just need to find a job."

"I already got one in mind," Krimpen exclaimed. A sudden breeze tossed his unkempt hair.

"Not gonna like this one, am I?" Time asked.

A hand clasped his shoulder. "When have I ever led you wrong?"

THREE

3215 A.G. (After Gods), the Forsaken Path.

The air was choked with dust and ash. Whatever once lived in this realm was gone, lost to the vagaries of time. Ruins jutted from the detritus. Skeletal remains of a once proud religion from a time before the gods. Sand dunes, charred black, rolled as far as the human eye could see. There was no night. No day. Naught but the cool indifference of perpetual twilight. Or perhaps dawn. Without change, endless leagues of similarity were lost in a haze.

Ah'muf replaced the cap on his canteen. "I do not like this place, farisi. We have entered an ill realm."

He had a point, she accepted. Wherever the Bloody Man sent them was not a place meant for the living. Everywhere she looked was the foul stench of death. *And we're trapped until I find the First Paladin. I'm sorry, Ah'muf. Sorry for everything. I wish now our paths never crossed in that godsforsaken desert. You deserve better than what I can give you.*

"We must trust in our task, Ah'muf. Sorrow sent us here for a reason," she said with as much kindness as she could summon. A pale wind kissed her cheek, sending shivers over her flesh. She felt … haunted.

The desert dweller kicked at a small mound by his sandal. A puff of ashen dust bloomed. "What reason could there be for a place such as this to exist? Only the damned reside herein."

"Maybe, but I have to believe there is a purpose for everything." *Even this.*

Elisa placed her hands on her hips and surveyed the area. No rises. No rivers. Scarce a tree to be found. A glance to the sky showed a similarly bleak outlook. They were stranded with no discernable path forward and no return to the world they left behind. She struggled to recall a more distressing time.

"Farisi, how long are we to stay in this spot? My bones ache from the dust of a million souls. This is an ill land," Ah'muf explained. Narrow eyes darted left, then right, never staying still.

"Indeed, you are correct," a booming voice announced Sorrow's arrival.

The Bloody Man stood in crimson splendor. A miracle of the impossible. He had continuously bled for over a thousand years, after flensing his body of flesh to protest the ignorance of his two brothers. A massive twelve-foot sculpture of madness. Ever the youngest, Sorrow wept for better days.

Ah'muf dropped to his knees and bowed low. "My lord, Sorrow."

Elisa's reaction was different. Old memories returned upon seeing him again. She knew he was the architect of all the wrongs in her life, shaping her direction from early childhood. No memory was stronger, for a pain so grave never fades, as seeing the blood covered giant slaughter everyone in her village. Equally confusing was his apology thereafter.

"Bloody Man," she ground out. "I assumed you had abandoned me again."

He cocked his head and studied her with thoughtful expression. "I do not know why I chose you those many years ago. Like so many of your kind, you lack the patience to wait for matters to unfold, thus limiting your ability to foresee the future unfold. A shame. You hold so much potential."

"I didn't choose this life," Elisa fumed.

"No. Your fate was written long before you were born. Dissecting the past serves no purpose. Here, in this fell realm, we must journey to find the one soul capable of providing you the strength and knowledge to win the war and stop my brother," he explained.

Ah'muf's soft hand on her shoulder stopped the litany of wrath she was ready to unleash. Drawing a deep breath, she blinked slowly. "Sorrow, what is there to be found in a dead realm?"

"Much, if you open your eyes." He knelt and clutched a handful of ash. Sorrow turned his fist and water trickled out.

"Magic!" Ah'muf cried in wonder.

"Magic is in the eye of the beholder. You were correct. This is the ruin of countless civilizations. Older than my own forgotten species," he closed his eyes as visions of what once was returned. "Hundreds of millions of bones collapsed into dust. Such a waste."

"Why are we here, Sorrow?" Elisa felt the pressure of nagging suspicion tug against her conscience. "There is nothing here."

His eyes widened. "Nothing? No. This realm is filled with life, if you choose to see it. There are dangers here you are not prepared to face.

I shall accompany you for a time. At least so far as I deem it takes to formulate a rudimentary understanding of your task."

Her eyes glazed over at his droning. "I fail to see anything in this mess worth fearing, and you still haven't told us where we are supposed to be going."

"The journey is far. How long it will take is unknown, even to me. Navigate this realm successfully and you will discover the embodiment of the First Paladin and the secrets he contains. Secrets needed to end this war and restore order to the universe."

"We know this," she interrupted. "Who is he and why is he so important you stole us from our reality. Tell us how to find him, so we can get back to our friends."

The giant studied her with cocked head. Millenia spent among their kind and he struggled with understanding. Humans were primitive in every regard yet held a fascination for him. So unlike his kind, who bred them for slaves, used them for sport and worse. They represented the best and worst of his legacy. Sorrow, he mused. How apt the name, knowing what he was asking Elisa to do.

"There is a city far to the east. Ruined by time and violence, the skeletal remains mar the landscape for leagues. Goti Tai. This is where you will find the First Paladin," Sorrow explained. "Be warned, do not pause in this ill begotten realm. I warned you there was life here. Ancient creatures stalk the ash fields. Should they catch you, they will eat you, or worse."

Ah'muf struggled to keep his trembling knees from knocking together. "Monsters! We cannot fight this."

"We can avoid them easy enough," Elisa frowned.

Sorrow shook his head. "Regretfully, they know you have invaded their lands. War parties already gather to begin the hunt. Time is now your enemy, Paladin, and I am powerless to assist you."

Slipping the rifle from her shoulder, Elisa checked to ensure the power charge was full. "Can they die?"

"Look around you, all things die. Get to Goti Tai and retrieve the First Paladin before the tribes discover your location," Sorrow explained. "That is the only way to complete your quest and find passage back to the realm of the living."

"You're not coming with us?" Elisa asked, confused by his deliberate subterfuge. Her experience with the Bloody Man left her with numbing sensations she struggled to identify. There was compassion underlying his tone, but the severity of his guise left little room for her to accept his sincerity.

"I shall accompany you to the first menhir but am forbidden to travel further. There are some laws even my kind are not allowed to break."

Frustrations compiling, Elisa snorted and gestured with her head. She knew better than to ask additional questions. "Lead on, Bloody Man. I would get this over with and be done with it."

The ground rocked just then, throwing the humans to the ground. Clouds of dust and ash billowed around them, coating both in pallid grime. An unseen beast cried in the distance. The mournful wail of the last of its kind. Elisa fought down the fear building in her mind. Each heartbeat revealed why this was the Forsaken Path.

Night and day blended into an endless horizon of ash gray. The trio marched with purpose, pausing to relieve themselves, eat, and catch a few hours of sleep when possible. Swarms of insects assaulted them without mercy. Strange creatures shifted beneath the ash, slithering in tempered pursuit. Sorrow plowed ahead without err. He spoke little and spent his time scanning the surrounding area, as if expecting an assault.

Three days into their quest found the weary travelers halted beside a dust filled stream bed. There was no fire for warmth, yet Elisa found sleep easily enough. Curled in her long jacket, the bounty hunter pushed out all worries and fears of the moment. It seldom worked. The Forsaken Path awakened more nightmares than any previous experience in her short life.

She awakened abruptly, shooting up with a hand dropping to her sidearm. Ah'muf's cool tone slowed that hand.

"Farisi, there is no danger yet," he soothed.

Blinking the sleep away, she reluctantly withdrew her hand and rubbed her lower face with a yawn. "What time is it?"

"Does it matter?" he replied.

Elisa cocked her head after catching the sadness in his voice. It evoked a sense of longing she'd carried for the last forty years. "I know, but Sorrow insists this is our purpose."

"The Bloody Man is a pox on us," Ah'muf said. "We are thrice cursed by the gods."

Her grin was regretful. "Indeed, but that doesn't matter. The only way we get back to our reality is by completing out quest. I wish I never pulled you away from An'kuruku, Ah'muf. That was my greatest crime."

"Crime? Nay, farisi. I left with you. I allowed myself to have feelings for an offworlder and it has led me here," he gestured with his chin. "To this lifeless realm, both alike and unlike my desert home."

Her memories of the desert were far different. The combination of her red hair and fair skin left her ripe for burns, heat exhaustion, and worse in the deep deserts of An'kuruku. If not for Mollock Bolle, she would have remained on Crimeat in quiet anonymity.

"You miss the desert," she theorized aloud.

"Not so much, but it is a far cry from the depression surrounding us," he said. "I miss the morning sun kissing my face. The cool night breeze teasing the hairs on my arms. I miss the freedom of not answering to one of the Three."

She did not disagree. The Three were a curse on the entire universe. A galactic joke perpetrated by red robed cardinals in their lofty towers locked in the center of the universe. Legend whispered the gods all but destroyed themselves in a civil war. A handful remained and those were secreted away, their locations known to but a select few. Her encounter with Paradise Tear and the Bone Father opened new fissures in what she thought she knew. None of it made sense, but then neither did watching a blood covered giant slaughter her village in front of her and then kneel to apologize for his actions.

A thought sparked. His actions? Perhaps he apologized for bringing a child into the madness of the gods. Decades later she failed to understand why she was chosen. Never a believer in fate or destiny, Elisa always felt her life had been stolen that day. Absconded by eldritch powers that should not exist. She tore her gaze from Ah'muf and focused on Sorrow's back.

You knew. All those years ago. You knew what I was meant to become. A holy warrior in a cause I knew nothing about. Every event in my life has been dictated by your twisted knowledge of future days. You bastard! I was just a child! You had no right!

"How is it he weeps blood but never spills a single drop?" Ah'muf whispered.

Sorrow's head shifted. "Sound carries further at night, desert dweller. You would do well to remember that after I depart."

Swallowing his apprehension, Ah'muf wrung his hands to prevent his nerves from rising. "This is all wrong. All of it."

"Sweet Ah'muf, that changes nothing. Here we are and here we belong. Find your inner strength. Courage is needed, if we are to navigate the Forsaken Path," Elisa tried to calm him.

Stale wind picked up, carrying the stench of the unfamiliar. Sorrow turned to face the direction they had come. His face was stern, concerned. "We must move now. The menhir is not far. Quickly. Our enemy comes."

Barely giving them time to collect their gear, the Bloody Man hurried the trek on. Darkness rode the eternal twilight. Death stalking them across barren plains of long forgotten empires. Apprehension choked the air. The time of confluence was approaching. Here, at the edge of sanity and buffered by impossibility, the Paladin and her reluctant companion were about to face their strongest challenge.

Seven figures stood in a circle atop the small hill. Squat, each was covered with enough hair, it looked like fur in the unholy light. Each bore a torch in overly muscled arms. Their lower jaws protruded far, lending the appearance of muzzles. Slit irises glared beneath heavy brows. Tails whipped about in anticipation of the future. Long had it been since last they were presented with the challenge. Tribal howls ranged over the hills as a great shadow passed overhead. Shapeless, it was borne on terrible wings and gone in the span of a few heartbeats.

Blue lightning slashed through the sky in its wake. An endless trail of devastation causing further ruin. The seven raised their torches and bellowed ancient cries. The time had come at last. Born for the hunt, they would chase the sky dragon to the edge of forever, hoping to be led to the object of their sole purpose remaining. Only at the end would they find salvation and a chance to fulfill their promise to their now extinct people.

An eighth figure was brought forward at a sharp command. Bound in leather straps and gagged, he was forced to the center of the circle. Locks of gangly hair covered his lowered face. Older than the rest, he was a creature who recognized his fate. One stepped forward to slice his bonds. Death was meant to be met with open arms. The warrior's way. Stone daggers were drawn, each raised to the sky in tribute. The sacrifice added his voice to those of his kin. Raising both hands, he sank to his knees.

Daggers plunged down. Slashing across the throat. Burying in the heart and lungs. Blood sprayed, coating the seven. It was over in moments. The body of their elder lay cold and lifeless. Drops of crimson blood dripped from stone. In reverence, the seven dropped beside the fallen and dipped a single finger in the wound they created. They traced the symbol of their tribe on their cheeks and whispered ancient prayers to gods no longer in play. A sorrowful life, bound to failure, was their legacy.

As one, the last seven of their tribe rose and collected their meager belongings. They ran off in single file. There was a quest to begin. They ran with the wind at their backs, chased by bolts of unnatural lightning. Forgotten so soon, the fallen elder sank into the ash and dirt as he became one with the world of his choosing.

Conclave Manufacturing Facilities, planet Mannus Prime.

The lone shuttle slipped through the ring of industrial haze circling the planet unseen on the fleet's radar. Ships of war hovered in debris fields of their slaughtered compatriots. The initial engagements over Mannus Prime were brutal. Thousands died in the opening salvos. Former friends twisted by opposing ideologies. The universe continued to splinter, tearing civilization asunder with reckless glee. For the survivors, it was the death of all things.

"We are entering the upper atmosphere," the pilot announced.

Three passengers strapped into their chairs and waited for the inevitable turbulence of entry. Two bowed their heads to whisper prayers forgotten in all but one language and not heard in the universe for millennia. The third, pushed a lock of hair from her face and stared out the window. No stranger to war, Kaline took in her first sights of besieged Mannus Prime. Cold memories assailed her, for it was a rich world of green continents and vast blue oceans. How like home.

"Will the enemy not spot our signature?" she asked the pilot.

"They shouldn't. We are equipped with the latest Prekhauten technology and coded to align with forces loyal to the Inquisitor General," he replied.

The answer provided less comfort than intended. Kaline trusted neither side. Loyalties ran too deep on many levels, despite the chasm widening across the seven hundred worlds. The universe was changing. Reverting to a time before human rule. A time of the gods. Mannus Prime was but the latest of her charges. Ripe for conversion. Seriousness hardened her face into a stone visage. Kaline knew better than to take her latest task for granted. Her failures on An'kuruku fresh in her mind, this was her one opportunity to atone. Her master was unforgiving.

Kaline leaned forward, hand curled on the back of the pilot's chair. "Ensure we are not interrupted until we reach the ground. Your fate will frighten children for generations, should you fail in this, Captain."

His silence filled the cabin.

The shuttle rocked and jerked as it sped into the atmosphere. Enough, Kaline feared they would be torn apart and burnt to cinder, drifting like ash across the continents. Thoughts of flames disturbed her, for she had learned of the cleansing purge of Vau Prime's low continent. Hundreds of thousands of faithful reduced to memory and then nothing as their kin fell around them. Her heart cried out against the travesty.

Being sent to Mannus Prime offered the chance for revenge. She found it a useful tool when converting new followers to the eternal joys of Rengu. Kaline drew her cloak tight and closed her eyes until the shaking subsided. The revolution was close. A fire that would claim billions of souls in tribute. She was the harbinger of doom. Riding the whirlwind of devastation across the stars. Hands balled into tiny fists, she tilted her head back as cabin pressure changed.

The shuttle tracked the coast of the largest continent. No anti-aircraft defenses awaited. No coastal emplacements to repel marine assaults. Kaline absorbed this new world with youthful vigor she seldom felt. Life had not been kind to her, despite her efforts to broaden the cause. She stared with amazement at the rich trees spearing high into the sky. Flocks of white and green birds soared over the treetops. Reptilian heads popped up in response. Calculating eyes tracking their flight.

Kaline grew giddy. So long had it been since she last witnessed sights worth seeing. Mannus Prime was ripe. Filled with impossible lifeforms so many across the universe never saw or comprehended. It was then she decided her true role. She was a pilgrim. A wanderer across the stars bringing a new future by offering to return all to what once was. The idea calmed her. Pilgrim. She was … truth.

Touching down, the pilot began his post flight operations. Kaline unbuckled and stretched; experience trained her not to trust her body those initial moments when gravity resumed control. She shifted her jaw back and forth as her ears popped. A cursory glance showed her colleagues doing similar exercises. Acolytes, they were ordered to serve her needs by spreading the message of Rengu.

"Mistress Kaline, we have secured a landing zone and there are no sentient lifeforms showing on the scanners. We are alone," the pilot announced.

"An inauspicious beginning, wouldn't you say?" she replied. "How far to the nearest village?"

He paused to check the holographic maps. "Less than ten clicks, due west. There is a settlement of approximately thirty structures."

She nodded, already thinking through her introductions. "What of the land to the east. I assume we are secure from attack?"

"As much as can be, though nowhere near enough to make me comfortable," he said.

"You were a soldier," Kaline suggested.

His shoulders lifted. "Thirteen years in the Prekhauten Marines. I fought in seven major engagements."

"No doubt earning accolades at every turn," she added.

"No real soldier does it for medals."

Her grin softened the defiance growing in him. "What is your name? I refuse to keep calling you captain."

He told her and she did not believe him.

"Everyone got everything? We won't be returning to the shuttle for a few days, if all goes well," he asked the group.

They shouldered packs, secured weapons, and filed down the back ramp. There was a world to be conquered. Kaline exhaled a pensive breath. Her stomach churned with nerves. The pneumatic hiss of the shuttle closing behind them announced the start of a glorious adventure.

Far from the major cities and farther from the manufactories that supplied a healthy portion of Prekhauten combat gear, was the land chosen by both sides to fight their war. Vast webs of trenches and tunnels stretched across open expanses. Command posts were dug into hills. Wire, anti-personnel mines, and worse separated the armies by a hundred meters. The land was pockmarked from concentrated artillery barrages. Between the lines, no living thing grew. Once rich plains of cadmium green had become a mud churned wasteland. Broken tree trunks stuck up like time-worn teeth. The stink of bodies decaying beneath hundreds of pounds of mud and grime permeated all. It was death. Pure and simple.

"Commander, looks like the enemy is getting ready to assault again. There's too much movement on their front lines."

The audible sigh rising from the back of the command bunker said it all. Commander Torgast slipped his mud crusted boots off the three-legged table. Tall, he stood almost a full head over his staff and a fair portion of his soldiers. A week's worth of beard peppered his chin, covering the hallow draw of his cheeks. He was a man who had seen the worst humanity offered.

"Whose turn is it?" he asked.

The orderly checked the duty rotation. "Seventh company."

Torgast stared out across the field to where his foe prepared. Foe. He snorted. How many of those Guards facing him were once friend? Boon companions as they rose through the ranks in service to the Conclave. How many were now dead? Slain for reasons he failed to understand, in a war neither side wanted. Crossed ideologies at their worst, he surmised.

Torgast licked the corner of his lips. "Very well. Get 'em up and ready. You know the drill. No one exposes themselves until the artillery is done. Heavy weapons and mortars to open fire at will the moment the first rank crawls out of the mud. It's going to be a long day."

"Yes, sir."

Satisfied he had done what he could, Torgast wrapped his officer's cloak around his shoulders and headed off to make his rounds among the army. His first stop was the aid station. The first artillery rounds were announced by subsonic booms. Outgoing and incoming, the cannon crews dueled without ever seeing each other or their targets, relying on forward observers entrenched on the front. Should those observers get killed, the artillery became blind. Useless.

Torgast had been in command of Mannus Prime for almost two years. Most of it involved attempts at preventing the planet from betraying the founding principles of the Conclave. A handful of pitched battles broke out soon after open war was declared. In the time following, Torgast and his opponent settled into their trenches for the long campaign. It was an archaic form of warfare but one suited to this planet.

He no longer ducked as plasma fueled rounds rocketed overhead. Ignored the pounding of impact up and down the line. War did terrible things to one's soul. Torgast was a mediocre leader at best before the war. Here, locked in one long battle that felt it had no end, he was forced to become better. Nine months of trench warfare, tens of thousands of casualties on both sides, and the unflinching desire to survive, honed his army into men and women who would follow him to the ends of the universe. Torgast only wanted to go home.

Scores of Guards murmured good morning in passing. Saluting was prohibited in combat. Snipers claimed far too many officers and senior NCOs, forcing a change to military protocol. No one seemed to mind. Extended time at the sharp end turned them into more than units of collected personality. They became family.

A stiff breeze blew the acrid smoke residue from the firing batteries across the camps. Battle flags and banners high above the field announced who stood the line with pride. Many of those banners were tattered from stray rounds and pieces of shrapnel. Torgast refused to allow them to be retired. They were the symbols of each unit. A constant reminder that they were not dead yet and hope still bloomed in each beating heart. Who was he to refuse such?

There had been a time when he would not leave the command bunker until the engagement ended. Time and experience changed his perceptions, forcing him to adjust as the battle evolved. In over nine months of battle, neither army successfully made it far enough to secure the other's front trench. Most of the time, units were decimated to the point of combat ineffectiveness and pulled from the line. Torgast had no reason to believe this day would be any different.

He was wrong.

Torgast glared from the pair of Inquisitors and back to Cardinal Virom. Not only had they interrupted what amounted to breakfast on the front, but their arrival went unreported by every sentry position leading back to Eger City. Those responsible would be dealt with, but after this unscheduled meeting. Stomach growling, he leaned back in his chair and folded his arms.

"Commander, we must have an answer," the taller Inquisitor pressed.

Torgast knew little about the man. "You'll forgive me but I am in the middle of fighting a battle."

The female Inquisitor snorted. "It seems to me you were in the middle of breakfast."

Ah yes, you, I know. Bela Cass. Cold hearted bitch. How many of your own kind have you condemned to death, or worse? "A man has needs. What do you want, Inquisitor?"

"Don't play games. You know precisely what we have come for," Bela hissed.

"Stop the fighting and return to the fold," he recited the same line he had been forced to listen to for the last year, if not longer. It was a tired game they played. Torgast might never know what made him adhere to General Strannan and his principles. He doubted it would matter when the dust settled. Loyalties went deep.

Cardinal Virom leaned forward, wringing his hands. "Commander, this senseless slaughter is pointless. We are all on the same side. The only true enemy is heresy."

"Cardinal, while I respect your station, this is a military matter," Torgast's face turned to stone. "The Conclave is in enough disarray. I need to win this war and get back to the business of keeping this sector of space safe."

"Your forces are the reason there is violence!" Bela Cass shouted.

Torgast stifled a groan. He admired her passion, misplaced as it was. Aside from that, there was no defining aspect of the woman worth noticing. Short of stature and plain faced, Bela Cass was pent up fury. He was surprised her eyes had not turned red during what he imagined was her exile on Mannus Prime.

"Inquisitor, this is a military matter. Your counsel is received. I apologize for your having come this way for no reason," Torgast fired back.

"Careful, Torgast. You border heresy. I have every right to place you in custody."

He spied her clenched fists, noticing the way the flesh was bled white. "I have a hundred and twenty-seven thousand soldiers who might disagree with that. We're finished here. Leave by your will or I will have my guards escort you back to Eger City."

Lips pursed, Bela Cass decided against snapping at him. She gestured toward the exit. The second Inquisitor followed, leaving Cardinal Virom behind. They left without another sound, though Torgast understood the potential repercussions from this failed engagement. Blowing out his frustrations, he turned to the Conclave's representative.

"You should tread carefully with her, Torgast," Virom cautioned. "She's dangerous."

"Aye, a bloody snake in the weeds. I know her sort, Virom. She's an idealist and that's what makes her dangerous. Take out her fangs and she'll go whimpering into obscurity." He tossed his battered and stained cap on the table and ran a hand through his salt and pepper hair. "I know why they came. It's the same story every time. But what could be so important as to get you out of your lap of luxury?"

Virom scoffed, knowing Torgast was better appraised of the actual situation concerning the entire planet. Mannus Prime was mired in steady decline, as the war demanded more and more. Food shortages loomed and the medical staff was woefully undermanned. Soldiers on both sides of the line suffered for it.

"I have received word from our friends," Virom lowered his voice and glanced to the tent flap.

Torgast's eyes widened. He slipped to the flap and poked a head through to ensure they were alone. A pair of guards stood five meters away. Of the Inquisitors, there was no sign. Satisfied, he went back to face his friend.

"How? I understood the communications were jammed," he said. They had not received any messages from the loyalist faction since the siege began.

Virom's face brightened, unable to contain his glee. "You have your secrets, I have mine."

"You make a man want to drink," Torgast fumed.

"At this hour? My liver can't take it," the Cardinal waved him off. "Relief is coming."

"How soon?"

"I don't know. The line was cut before we could get that far. A fleet is being assembled with ground troops pulled from across the universe. It should be enough to break the siege and allow your personnel enough downtime to refit and prepare for the next offensive."

Torgast started to pace. His nerves coiled, threatening to snap and undo him. Rudimentary plans formed. His mind raced through possibilities. Casualty statistics. Logistics. Food. Water. Time. A professional soldier, Torgast saw an endless succession of sleepless nights and thinning hair before any help arrived. A predator trapped in a cage, he was ready to break free and reclaim what destiny offered.

"You dare raise my hopes, Virom," he said. "Without any actionable intelligence, I can't start planning a breakout. Damnation, I need to speak with the commanding officer well in advance to…"

Virom held up a staying hand, hoping to calm his friend before the man spun out of control. "Patience, Torgast. We have only just begun to unravel this mess. There is still time." He paused to sit, folding the muddied crimson robes over his knees. "How goes the battle here?"

Torgast tossed a hand toward the trenches where companies of men and women were engaged in a bloody contest, not for liberty of ideals but for sheer survival. He knew there was no soldier on the line, on either side, still clinging to antiquated principles or delusions of grandeur. Walking away alive was reward enough.

"Nothing changes on this damned world. Every week, I throw forces at him and every other week he does the same. We are bleeding our most precious resource at an unsustainable pace," he replied.

Virom jumped at the sudden roar of multiple cannons firing.

Torgast chuckled. "That means the battle is ending, for now. Care to tour the line with me?"

"I doubt my robes will inspire much among the troops, Torgast. Too many view my office as the reason this war started," Virom admitted. "Perhaps it best I slip quietly away without drawing undue notice on myself."

"Virom, we may be at war but many, if not most, of my people are firm believers in what the Conclave stands for. That faith might be misplaced and even forgotten since the first shots were fired last year, but never underestimate the power of faith in a fighter."

"Would that were true for all of us," Virom bowed his head. "Another time, Torgast. You have casualties to see to. Moral and welfare. I won't keep you."

He hurried to the exit before his friend of many years could change his mind, pausing to look over his shoulder a final time, "I will do what I can to placate our Inquisitor friends but I fear they will strike soon. Our comms might be jammed, but theirs most certainly are open. Alain Nye is a vindictive man. His vengeance will be swift. Until the next time, my friend."

And he was gone, leaving Torgast trapped in a crossfire of intricate unreconcilable emotions. *Not all wars are visible. Here I stand, a vast army at my fingertips, yet I fail to control my own mind. How much longer must I endure where so many others have already broken? We weren't created to fight like this. This world will be the death of me.*

Commander Torgast snatched his cap before heading to inspect what he knew was going to be a thoroughly mauled and demoralized company of what was once among his best infantry. The day was just beginning.

One soldier remained behind. Knees drawn to his chin. Arms wrapped around them. Red streaked eyes wept uncontrollably as he stared at the mounds of bodies stretching out between the trench lines. Men and women he ate with, showered with, joked with. Now they were gone. food for crows. Others staggered by, stumbling back to the trench in disbelief.

Pushed to the point of breaking, the soldier let them go. He failed to understand the greed corrupting those in power and vowed to take his measure of revenge on those responsible. Mannus Prime had seen bloodshed, but it had never withstood the fury surging through his veins this day.

FOUR

3215 A.G. (After gods), the Great Library, planet Wexanos.

"Sergeant Major, a word."

Matthias paused midstride, taking a moment to recall the speaker before turning. The last glow of fading daylight painted their faces crimson and blue.

"Sergeant Major no longer, I'm afraid. I was retired after An'kuruku," Matthias admitted. "You are Ishis Gul, correct?"

The tall, rapier thin man with a hooked nose, half bowed. "I am flattered you remember, given the circumstances of our last meeting."

"You saved lives. What can I do for you?"

Matthias kept his tongue. The man, for whatever reasons he chose to help on the desert world, was a smuggler and potential security risk.

"I have learned of your pending assault on Mannus Prime," the smuggler began.

Matthias stiffened. "That is classified information, Gul. You should not know this."

Ishis waved at the luxury surrounding them. "Even in such a secure location, the walls have ears. Lord Tannus would do well to remember that. No, friend, I am not suggesting there are spies in the midst, lurking behind bookcases and the like. No. I come to you with an offer of help."

"No doubt for a price," Matthias jabbed.

"I am a humble man who has needs. I'm sure you can understand. A modest fee to ensure your campaign meets proper success," Ishis replied. The words were practiced, flowing off his silvered tongue like so many lies delivered to rulers and petty warlords the universe over, with the intent of building a quiet coffer with which to retire and forget the pains of the present situation.

"Uh huh. What are you offering?"

"There are hidden forces available to come to your aid. Through them you hold the potential to secure Mannus Prime and obtain your objectives with minimal loss of life on your part," the smuggler offered.

Matthias's eyes narrowed as comprehension crept into his mind. "Mercenaries. We haven't stooped to that level, Gul. We have enough soldiers to take and secure the planet."

"And after that?"

"Come again?" Matthias asked.

Ishis Gul smiled, pencil lips pressed together. A predatory gaze, with the knowledge his prey was in striking distance. "What happens after you take the world? Your meager forces will be depleted and open for retaliation. The universe is vast and not every force lies between the strict lines of Prekhauten Guards. Vau Prime can play its games, using our lives as the balance, but it does not control every aspect of life."

He paused, more for dramatic effect than natural means. "Fighters exist in the shadow. Most are former soldiers. Some thirst for violence, while the majority seek an end to warfare. The opportunities of peace are strong motivators, Matthias. All it takes is a bridge to reach out and connect."

The possibilities were fraught with inherent peril. Bringing unreliable forces into play threatened to undermine the already unstable foundations their operation was built upon and expose them to Nye's war machine. Matthias doubted even Tannus had the strength to fend off that number of wolves. Yet, dismissing Ishis Gul out of hand was a tactical mistake few experienced commanders would make. The only conclusion was he was not qualified to make the decision alone.

"What group do you have in mind?" he asked with hesitation.

Rubbing his hands together, Ishis Gul answered, "The Shadow Hammers."

It took a moment to sift through his memories. Matthias vaguely recalled past exploits of the band. They were not known for mercy. "You're insane. They are the most bloodthirsty lot in the universe. Involving them opens too many doors, Gul."

"Who better to stem the tide of your enemy, than a mighty hammer that will not bend?" The smuggler licked his lips. "What other options do you have? The hour grows late. Time is nearly expired. I bring to you the offer of salvation from a demise most terrible."

Shaking his head, Matthias struggled with duty and common sense. Inviting the Shadow Hammers into the fight ensured the slaughter of hundreds of former comrades and ripened the arena for future engagements, possibly on both sides. That responsibility was once well above his pay grade. Forced retirement changed much. Ultimately, there was little real choice.

"Come with me," he decided. "We need to tell the others."

Ishis bowed again. The tail of his robes scraping over the pristine floor. "As you wish."

Matthias turned, rolling his eyes. *Nothing is as I wish, Gul, and you are the latest in a string of alarming surprises.* He led them back to the only person on Wexanos capable of seeing the bigger picture.

"Are you certain this is the correct move?" Tannus asked, staring down his visitors.

Matthias glanced to Ishis, allowing the smuggler the opportunity to present his case. "Ah, my lord, I do not presume to harness great wisdom, not in your lofty company."

"Platitudes are meaningless to me, smuggler," Tannus warned. "Mercenaries? I know of this band. Ruthless by all accounts. You jeopardize unveiling my refuge to the universe and my brother."

Ishis bowed low, dropping his gaze to the floor. "Lord, would that were true! I was held captive en route here. Blindfolded and secured against my will by Matthias to mitigate the risk to your precious libraries. Indeed, I do not know the name of your world."

Tannus looked to Matthias for assurance but the human could only shrug. "The Shadow Hammers are infamous among human circles. How is it you have their contact information, when so many others, the pirate lord Blackheart included, do not?"

"As has been pointed out several times, I am a smuggler," Ishis's voice tightened, though from embarrassment or frustration, remained unknown.

"He may prove a valuable asset, Matthias," Tannus suggested. "Winning this war requires less than desirable assets."

Lacking the resources inherent to the Inquisitor General and his renegade forces, Tannus recognized necessity. Old tactics used against Amongeratix through their many wars over the years showed him the truth of human reserves. Two opposing forces comprised of similar soldiery could only be broken by an outside contingent.

"Very well, smuggler. I accept your request. Take Matthias and find these mercenaries. Offer them what you can and deploy to Mannus Prime with all dispatch. We may yet win this campaign." *If only they knew how important it was*. Tannus lacked the heart to tell the others what dark twist of fate awaited should the planet fall.

The threat of duplicity in the smuggler was high, though his experience showed him that mortals were often unpredictable, especially through emotional manipulation. Faith in Matthias presented higher chances of success. Funding was no obstacle, for Tannus had accumulated one of the largest treasures in the universe.

"Ishis Gul, you have my leave to depart at once. Speak with the Chief Librarian about a credit line enough to entice these mercenaries to our cause. Matthias will join you shortly," Tannus ordered. The authority in his tone kept the smuggler in line. At least until he was far from Wexanos.

Waiting for the desert dweller to finish bowing and excuse himself, Tannus drank from a crystal glass. "Honeyed mead. An acquired taste I discovered twenty-seven hundred years ago on a primitive world filled with vicious clans of fur clad warriors. Their civilization is long gone, faded into the dust of ages. A shame. I have been unable to find a distiller capable of recreating the same recipe."

"Do you trust him?" Matthias asked, declining a glass of the golden liquor. His only experience with mead had not ended well.

"Enough to deliver you to these mercenaries and enlist their aid. He has a dishonest heart, but a clean one. Confused he is. The man struggles to maintain his façade, while plying between factions he fails to understand."

Tannus set the empty glass down and strode to the bank of windows overlooking sweeping rivers rimmed by purple trees. "He will prove his use, though it might not come in the form he chooses. Take care to keep our secrets, Matthias. Should Amongeratix learn of Wexanos, he will deploy the full fury of his armies. We are not strong enough yet to face him head to head."

"I'll keep a watch on him," the former Guardsman accepted. "Has Tolde departed yet?"

Tannus glanced skyward. "He faces demons of another sort."

Pacing to avoid succumbing to her mind's creations, Luma Kai focused on the tread of her boots plunging into the lush carpet. Black over red, the sight presented two sides of a coin. As an Inquisitor of the Office of Heretical Persecution, Luma was trained to view cases of heresy and adjudicate without prejudice. By all standards of sanity, Tolde Breed had become the very thing he once swore to oppose. An anomaly that should not exist. Should not stride the fabric of time and should not be seated across from her now.

Struggling with the basic concept of reincarnation, in conjunction with the sorcery of the Blood Witches, Luma failed to reconcile how a man who died on Wexanos, could awaken in another body light years away and find his way back to them. The sheer impossibility of it threatened to subsume her notion of common sense and unravel all she thought she knew. *I watched you die!*

The pain she felt from his passing and the countless days of standing vigil while he faded away from wounds sustained in battle, was for naught. Grief was robbed from her but at what cost? Reality was altered and she lacked the knowledge of how to proceed in that absence. An ache in her calves, Luma spun on her former partner.

"Damn you, Tolde! You're dead. I saw you die. This isn't right," she shouted. Fists clenched, she screwed her eyes shut to avoid looking at him. "How many times do you get to die? How many times do you get to abuse our emotions like this? I'm not as strong as you, Tolde. I … I can't do this."

For his part, Tolde Breed sat in silence. Allowing her to vent years' worth of frustration was the only gift he had.

"When you died, a part of each of us died with you. You were our rock. The common denominator we needed to establish a sense of order in this new universe. Gods and the Three. None of this should be happening. Our brethren slaughtered each other on a hundred worlds, while our former leaders assert dominance with an iron fist. Any hope I once had of surviving this pointless war was lost the day you returned."

She threw her head back and screamed to the ceiling. "How? How did you return, and in a different body? Your actions are familiar, yet your face, your mannerisms, and your presence are wholly changed. I need answers, Tolde. Give me something to make sense of this before I lose what remains of my mind. Please."

Tolde whet his lips. Clenching the arms of the antique wooden chair he occupied, the Inquisitor wished he had what she was searching for. "I remember being shot. My life force fading on a solitary bed far from the rest of you. Time and space folded in my mind and I felt myself pulled away, to a distant shore, where a task awaited."

He paused as hazed memories of his quest to the fabled mountain of Braewynd played out. "How or why are unknown, but I had renewed purpose. Every action on that alien world propelled me closer to … reunion. It was not until after my quest was complete that I was awarded with the memories of my former life by Sister Alessandra."

Luma snorted. "Blood Witch! Their ilk has interfered with human lives for far too long."

"Without them, I would be dead," Tolde cautioned. "Don't be so hasty to evince your wrath on them without greater understanding. The Grand Mistress is a key player in the drama unfolding. We need them as allies, if we are going to stop Amongeratix and end Nye's quest for power."

"We're going to need more than that, Tolde," Luma interrupted. "There are forces at play you have no idea of. Our enemy killed an entire planet. Every sentient being, tree and shrub down to the last blade of grass faded to dust. Amongeratix has a weapon of unimaginable power and Tannus admits there is nothing we have capable of contending with it. We are going to lose this war."

Trapped among visions of unmitigated disaster and the inability to fully understand what happened during his time in another body, Tolde failed to imagine what sort of weapon could destroy all life at will. He had heard whispers from some of the Prekhauten Guards who were there. Stolen phrases and imagined monster looming in the shadows, but until Luma's confession, there had been no concrete evidence.

"Where is this weapon now?" he asked.

Luma tossed her hands in the air. "We don't know. Blackheart claims it was stolen away during the final battle. He has been assigned a Guard escort to hunt down the villain and retrieve the weapon before it can be used again, but they could be anywhere in the universe by now."

"This is a wicked game we are forced to play," he said, his voice a bare whisper.

"You've been there from the beginning, haven't you?" Luma asked. Her rage was calmed enough she was able to sit without the urge to leap up. "Do you ever feel like you've been manipulated?"

He paused, never having considered the possibility. The former Inquisitor General deployed him, along with a contingent of Guards led by Matthias, to hunt down the escaped Amongeratix long ago. While successful at the cost of many lives, Tolde again found himself mired in the realm of the Three years later when Amongeratix was freed from his prison on Crimeat. His life was intricately intwined with the Three now, all but one. Sorrow remained an unknown. A concealed figure on the board.

"It does appear that way," he said after much thought. "I have been fighting against the Three for so long, it becomes one blurred succession of events. Tannus and Amongeratix have all but dominated my life for decades. If I have been manipulated, it is by a power higher than any we know to exist."

"I don't suppose it matters much. Nothing we can do to change the past."

The finality of her words echoed long in his mind. Tolde studied his partner. She had changed much since they first started working together. Once he viewed her as a raw mold to shape in his own fashion. A force for good in a universe where too many undeserving rose to lofty positions, while keeping better sons and daughters under their heel. Ultimately, Luma Kai had become a victim. Perhaps as much from his blind innocence, as the whirlwind of decay threatening to consume them all.

"What's it like, Tolde? Being in another body?" she asked.

He offered a wry grin. The best he could manage given the sudden revelations. "I'll let you know when I figure it out."

Vaade, planet Crimeat.

"I look ridiculous," Time growled, holding his arms in front of him.

Krimpen Mass stared at the bright yellow and amethyst jacket his friend wore. It was the same he was issued, though he had the good sense to say thank you and accept the position as private security for Lord Ossu, newly elected leader of the Plateau City of Reven. Initial misgivings were waylaid when Ossu explained they would remain in Vaade for the duration of their employ, thus avoiding the near inhospitable mountain terrain. That did little to assuage their pride upon being issued their uniforms.

Krimpen chewed a slice of green apple thoughtfully. "The color suits you. Gives you a pleasant appearance."

Red faced, Time jabbed a thick finger at his friend. "Keep that up and I'll show you just how pleasant I can be. I look like a clown. The colors are all wrong. And these puffed pants! Who, in their right mind, finds this effective?"

"No one said the boss is in his right mind. I heard whispers from some of the staff. The war started here and it was through the previous boss things went weird. Fella named Scura aligned with the wrong guy and paid for it," Krimpen explained. "Matter of fact, if it weren't for him, we wouldn't have a job!"

"Mighty nice of him dying like that and leaving no heirs," Time grumbled.

"Oh, there's an heir, only she don't want anything to do with politics and rulership. No sir. Smart woman that. I heard she collected her belongings, what remained that is, and booked it for the nearest spaceport. No telling where she is now." He gestured skyward. "Out there wandering among the stars. Too bad. Ain't no safe place left in this universe."

Time glanced down. "Why don't you have puffy pants?"

"Huh? Me? Oh, that. Well, you see, Time, my lad, I ain't a public figure. Boss wants to keep one of us out of sight, just in case something bad were to happen," Krimpen beamed, exposing brown stained teeth.

"Convenient, that," Time said.

"Just so. Now, what do you say we go about spending some of the boss's hard-earned coin and get some chow? My stomach is about to rebel," he suggested.

They started walking. Krimpen watched the passersby with interest. His purse was already filled with a score of careless pedestrians wandering too close to eager hands. Indeed, he was starting to like their decision to visit Crimeat.

"You know, I'm thinking of growing a beard," he ventured.

He never saw Time raise a clawed hand and reach for the back of his neck.

Hurtling through space burned the small shuttle. Refugees from their larger cruiser, the two occupants were all that remained. A Prekhauten frigate intercepted them en route to Crimeat and captured them. Only two managed to escape. Two out of fifteen hundred. There was no way of telling how many of the former crew were killed or wounded during boarding operations, nor did either occupant think much on it. Survival belonged to those who desired it most.

The shuttle touched down on Vaade's northern spaceport. Disguised to prevent any official recognition, the passengers slinked down the ramp, small bags in hand, and hurried to the transportation stand. Armed soldiers patrolled the area, alert for signs of foul play. It was a far cry from the days before the war. Where peace and tranquility once reigned, now there was only suspicion. The ruling lords of Lethendweil, ashamed for failing to stop the spread of civil war from taking to the stars, were determined to do all in their power to prevent further mishaps. They failed to realize it was already too late.

"I never thought to see this place again," Geres Auk complained.

Hulking over the diminutive Presha Von, his massive frame was heavy with muscle and more body hair than she was used to in her companions. An almost Neanderthal face glared at everyone. Deceptive, for he was lethal in what he was meant for. His time as Baron Scura's enforcer left him with peculiar ideations of how the universe ran. Since fleeing his home several years ago, Geres Auk had proven his worth in the field many times.

Presha Von took a deep breath, enjoying the familiarity of the scents. She was home at last. But she was not safe. Her hunters would soon discover she had fled the cruiser and track her course to Crimeat. It was but a matter of time before they came searching. Presha needed to disappear and there was one group still at large who could help.

"Even you should be able to appreciate the comforts of home, Geres," she chided. Her voice dripped honey. Seductive. Demure.

"Home? What use is that? My home was destroyed by raiders when I was still a boy. Baron Scura took me in and gave me a job." He paused to brush away the willowed remains of a bugeon flower as it danced over the bridge of his nose. "There is no home for me here, Lady Von. No home for me anywhere. You shouldn't feel safe either. There's no time for reminiscing of ancient pasts. It won't take those Prekhauten's long to realize where we went."

"Leave that to me," she said. "I must make contact with the dark council. They will provide our escape."

He snorted. "If they still exist. Who knows if they have been purged since we've been away."

She paused. It was a valid point. One born of years of toil tempered through a stream of disappointments. Until now, she had not anticipated the council being wiped out in the aftermath of Scura's failed bid for power. Prekhauten Guards patrolled the walkways and concourses. Local soldiery operated out of established positions sprinkled throughout the spaceport, and she counted no fewer than seven Inquisitors searching passengers and conducting customs inspections. Vaade had changed, and none for the better.

Presha Von had come home to a militarized state where suspicion remained high. Flashing lights on the comms boards announced captures of dissidents alongside images of men and women wanted in conjunction with efforts to destabilize the government. She started to think coming home was a mistake. Was the council already rounded up? Executed for high crimes against the state, their bodies left swaying in the wind. Reminders to all. She shuddered as the image of a rope being placed around her neck flashed by.

"Have I made a mistake, Geres?" she whispered.

Geres continued walking. His stride forced others to step aside. The anointed bodyguard ignored her question, though the admission startled him. He was unused to following those who lacked confidence, even if they had already proven themselves in the field. "I figure we don't have much time before those bastards in space come down to the spaceport. We'll have Guards swarming us in no time. Did your people get the message?"

Doubts swirled in her fragile mind, threatening to tear away her carefully constructed ideations. "I don't know. The Captain assured me the transmission was delivered to a ground facility here but was unable to determine if the enemy intercepted. We were attacked before he received confirmation."

"Meaning we are in a bad way if not," Geres concluded.

Face trapped in perpetual scowl, he wondered why he hadn't walked away when he had the chance. Why he had to stick his nose where it did not belong. Life might be better elsewhere, away from the manipulations of secret councils, obscure cults risen from the ashes, and a power play by one of the Three. Geres scoffed. There was no fun in watching the universe burn.

"We must get off the street," he suggested.

Presha agreed and led him away from the main concourse and into a shadowed area bereft of guards or security. There, she leaned against the grime-stained wall and closed her eyes. The way ahead was clouded. Her mind's eye dazed. Nothing had gone right for her since accepting the administrator role on Hawker's Gate. Her dreams of living among the stars were dashed when Prekhauten soldiers and renegade Inquisitors, foolishly aligned with the old powers, made a frenzied attempt at reclaiming the space station in the name of a crumbling entity long absent from the common folk.

Madness. All had turned to insanity as the war crept across the blanket of space. So mad, she decided that she was forced to flee to her home world in search of a new path forward. Her foes pursued with ruthless aggression, for they knew what she bore. An item of unimaginable power capable of murdering an entire world. The weight threatened to crush her soul. Each night, visions of the ruination of Kharsis tormented her. How many millions of lives were lost, turned to ash and dust by her hand? Humanity, Presha knew, was a wicked creature best returned to the primordial pool.

"The transportation facility isn't far. We should be able to make it that far at least," Geres said. The short hairs on his neck tickled his exposed flesh. A warning. "Look, see there? More Guards are arriving. Our time is up, Lady."

"Take the case and leave all else," Presha stared at the three troop transports on the far side of the concourse dislodging soldiers in full battle gear. "Steal a vehicle if you have to."

"Where are we headed?" he asked. His strides ate the distance between them and freedom with ease, forcing her to trot to keep up.

"There is a safehouse in the city. We should be secure there long enough for the council to find us," she panted as she ran.

Geres Auk knew the plan was weak, bordering on suicidal, but he held his tongue. He was a man who knew the value of silence. He picked up the pace, the sound of military bootsteps echoing at his back.

"Not a bad day, all things considered," Krimpen Mass declared, as he pushed away an empty plate of what had been stuffed pastries and some odd kind of slimy fruit the waiter insisted was properly cooked.

"We haven't done anything," Time said.

"Precisely my point. Look, my friend, we are free at last. Away from that nonsense on poor Kharsis. The pirate boy and his Guard friends are probably dust by now. Not many made it to the transports, from what I saw," he replied. A tear welled, threatening to spill.

Time raised his half empty glass of bitter ale. "To good friends no longer with us."

"We'll be along soon," Krimpen finished.

They clinked glasses, much to the shock of the establishment's other patrons. Both men looked around with murderous intent, daring anyone to voice their concerns. Only a handful of brave souls met their stares, and those withered in moments. All, that is, save for a small boy of ten summers who gawked openly at the offworlders dressed in funny clothes.

"I don't think these people are civilized, Time," he said after heads turned away in shame.

Time offered the boy a half shrug. "You don't say. What are we doing here? We don't need the money. The Prekhautens paid handsomely."

"True, but pirate boy left us in the lurch," Krimpen waggled a finger at his friend. "I had grand designs before that mess. We were going places, Time."

Time wanted to point out they would both be dead, if not for Vicente Blackheart and his schemes, but the moment passed when he spied a giant of a man walking beside a smaller woman.

"Are you listening? Time?" Krimpen fumed after realizing he was being ignored.

Time pointed across the street where the odd duo were about to round the corner. "They look familiar to you?"

Krimpen Mass turned, hand sliding to his concealed blaster under his jacket. "Who?"

"Them two? The big boy with the woman."

Squinting in the sunlight, Krimpen felt a cold sensation run through him. "Aye, that's that big bastard that nearly killed us. Well, well. Looks like we can settle old scores after all."

"As much as I'd like to crack that man's skull, are you sure this is the right place?" Time cautioned.

Fixing his friend with a one-eyed glare, Krimpen asked, "What? Are you afraid, all of a sudden? They killed everyone we ever knew. Sure, some of them were rotten good-for-nothings, but they didn't deserve to die like that. We have him here, now. Let's break his neck and have done with it all."

"No man calls me a coward and gets away with it, Krimpen. You know I ain't afraid to break a few bones, but this don't feel right. Alls I'm saying is, we need to be smart about how we go about getting our revenge."

Caught trying to figure out how many times his friend said about, Krimpen missed their potential targets slipping around the corner, and out of sight. Autumn was approaching and a brisk wind ran down the streets. Pedestrians hurried about their way, eager to escape the unexpected chill pushing down from the north. The wind caressed his face, threatening to render Krimpen lost in the odd chasm between memory and the future.

"You ain't listening," Time threw a half-eaten pastry at his friend. "Krimpen, this is a dangerous place. I'm all for getting him here and now, but my bones are screaming warning."

"The woman," Krimpen said.

Time nodded. "She's dangerous. Got an air of evil surrounding her."

"So what? We've faced evil before. You think she's got a hint of magic?" Krimpen asked, as fresh doubt awakened.

"I'm not willing to find out the hard way."

"Yeah, I think you're right. Ah well. We got them now. I suppose revenge can wait another day or so. Besides, you stick out in a crowd, my friend. Can't have that, if we're trying to act all stealthy. Come on, let's get back to the estate and get you into some decent clothes."

Time's fist landed right between his eyes.

Prekhauten Frigate *Solstice*, far orbit of planet Crimeat.

Lines of prisoners were marched down the corridor, hands on their heads. Guards and Marines funneled them from lower decks and compartments. Barked commands ensured the civilian crew, fanatics to the last, were cowed enough to prevent any from acting foolishly. Bodies already lined the breach points. Several crewers carried the body bags with red eyes for they bore the chosen of Rengu, forever denied the glory of his return.

Captain August stood with hands clasped behind her back, watching the procession with a critical glare. Beside her, Vicente Blackheart fidgeted with unease. Two of his crew had been killed during the assault. They were the only friendly casualties and he was responsible, insisting his people had a part in capturing the killers of

Kharsis. Enthusiastic, they failed to account for the enemy's fervor. *Never be the first through the door. A lesson I should have learned decades ago.*

"Still no sign of Von or Auk," August frowned.

Her displeasure swallowed what small measure of patience she had remaining. Catching the ship before it reached Crimeat was a small miracle by itself. The *Solstice* had suffered damage in the pursuit, losing power in one engine and threatening to cripple the Prekhauten ship in deep space. Necessity forced August's hand. Capturing Von was all that mattered.

"Reluctant as I am to admit it, she might have escaped during boarding operations," she managed.

Blackheart grunted. Questioning the passengers offered little information, for they were dedicated to their twisted ideations of what god meant. Most were consumed with Rengu. The pirate lord watched them with suspicion, for many appeared … devolved. Blackheart could only guess, but their humanity felt less. *What power is capable of twisting the human mind and ruining the spirit to the point it becomes far less than what it was meant to be?*

"These people," he said. "Look at them. They are almost ape-like."

August studied her prisoners for the first time. Emaciated, starving, and deprived of life supporting nutrients, they shuffled as ghosts trapped in a realm straddling life and death. "Some great evil is at work here."

"Why doesn't that surprise me? Captain August, this cult of Rengu is a stain upon the universe. These people should be eliminated before we dock," Blackheart declared.

"They are prisoners of war and will be treated accordingly," she replied.

"They are a hazard and a threat to us all. You risk losing this ship and everyone on it, based on an antiquated notion of propriety," he fumed. "Their brand of filth has already spread to scores of worlds. Will you let this one suffer, as well? Worse, are you willing to expose your crew to their taint?

"I know evil, Captain. I've lived it every day for years," Blackheart pushed when he saw her hesitancy. "These people are evil."

"I refuse to believe that … otherwise, what are we fighting for?"

"To keep Kharsis from happening again."

She shifted her lower jaw several times. Desperate times called for strength above all else. The courage to do right, over easy. Soldiers and marines were dying on a hundred battlefronts. Masses of humanity no longer existed thanks to the spreading plague of the cult of Rengu. August understood she stood at the edge of civility and barbarism. Ship of the line captains were expected to make quick and efficient decisions. Her internal deliberations threatened to stymy her quest.

"Sergeant, I want these prisoners confined to the cargo hold. Jettison all life pods and have engineering shut down all but the essential ship systems. Have food and water brought in immediately. I want this vessel to become a prison, until we can find a place to rehabilitate them," she ordered.

Blackheart stiffened at the sound of her true authority. He did not think she had it in her. This new power resonated deeply. He now had another aspect to reckon on his personal quest. The game heightened, sucking him deeper.

"Captain Blackheart, we have prey to stalk on the surface."

"Yes, Captain August, I believe we do."

Prekhauten and pirate, the duo hurried back to the *Solstice's* bridge. Their hunt was about to take on a new direction.

FIVE

3215 A.G. (After gods), Krenz, planet Vau Prime.

Tinus Har stared out his office window to the now extinguished light columns lining Redemption Boulevard. The massive lights were ordered off under martial law, leaving the center of the universe in darkness long forgotten. His heavy sigh reflected the weight in his heart, for his beloved city was plunging deeper into chaos. Rumors of the low continent purge had reached Krenz and the Conclave was impotent to prevent the spread to every block and city center. Tinus knew all it would take to spark widespread panic was a gust of wind.

Stifled beneath his new robes of office, the current Cardinal Seniorus felt every bit the imposter he was. The memory of Lorenu Phos haunted these chambers. A life robbed in exchange for the lure of power. He, like so many others in the Conclave and Prekhauten Guard, owed allegiance to Alain Nye. Day by day, the cardinals were forced to endure humiliation by their Inquisition handlers. Tinus Har had ascended the steps of the Conclave to serve as the puppet leader.

Air cars sped by, their red lights providing little to the expansive darkness smothering Krenz. In contrast, the bright lights of the multiple domes of Inquisition headquarters presented the lie of safety. Salvation. Tinus fumed. He was mired in bureaucracy, kept busy with aimless tasks lesser clergy should be performing. His life had become a lie.

A low chime disturbed him. Tinus waved without looking and was rewarded moments later with the reflections of a handful of the Forum filtering into his office. A nest of vipers in themselves, they represented both salvation and damnation. Several jockeyed for position to take his place after his fall. And fall he would. The universe was fickle that way. No great believer in fate, Tinus recognized the potential for disaster. He was a pale simulacrum of greater rulers.

"Sit," he commanded and waited for the rustling of their robes to calm before turning to face them. He stared into their eyes, seeing the truth laid bare in their expressions. "There's no point in delaying the inevitable. I find my time greatly reduced these days, as you are no doubt aware."

"Better you than us, Tinus," Cardinal Shri mocked. Her violet eyes glowered at him, whispering silent curses.

Cardinal Thent echoed her sentiments. "Yes, Tinus, you coveted Lorenu's position for far too long. My mother always said be careful what you wish for."

"Your mother is naught but dust on Uon, Thent. Do not push my perceived generosity for accepting this meeting," Tinus frowned.

"Why are we here? Chaos descends upon us and you seek to keep us locked away with pointless gatherings," Cardinal Arbalas accused. Her demeanor left a sour feeling in his stomach.

"Enough. All of you!" Tinus struggled to keep his tone under control, lest the Inquisitors standing guard in the far hallway overhear and investigate. "You know why we are here. The time has come."

Murmurs rippled through the cardinals. More than one glanced back to the doors, expecting Nye's minders to storm in and arrest them in the name of heresy. Tinus studied each, pleased his ruse worked as they betrayed their private thoughts. *You may be vipers, but so am I. Beware my friends. The game grows fraught with peril. Step wrong and you will fall forever.*

"Martial law and this insane desire to hunt down Davith Strannan is unraveling everything this body has sought to achieve since any of us were elected to our positions in the Conclave," Tinus began. "The only thing his purge has accomplished is cowering the populace into submission, while his commando units burn and assault at will. Let us not forget the razing of the low continent. How many souls were robbed of their immortality under this monster Mobus Kale's whim?"

"They were already condemned through their worship of Rengu," Thent dismissed his concern. "Kale did us a favor by preventing the spread of the disease."

"They were living beings, not animals meant for slaughter," Arbalas chided. "You should show more compassion. What would you do should Nye turn his predations to Uon?"

"Uon has given him no reason to suspect they are against him," Thent's voice dropped. "We are a peaceful world. Nye's vision is fixed on worlds with known insurrectionists. The low continent proved disloyal and were administered to according to his new laws."

"They were citizens of the Conclave and deserved better than incineration by the drove," Arbalas said. "Are we to become bloodthirsty killers without compassion? Slaughterers of our own kind, until only a handful remain?"

Tinus watched the conflict rage between them. That dissent undid the pollution of Alain Nye's lies by setting his deceitful cardinals against each other. Keep the pack distracted long enough and they would return to the fundamental understanding that they were a necessity in the universe. A restoration of divinity too many worlds now lacked. Only through that would he be able to undo many of the wrongs he helped create.

"The point is what would happen should Kale slip his leash? Who left to preside over, when entire worlds are naught but wastelands bereft of life?" Shri interrupted. "Like Kharsis."

Her statement cast the chamber in silence. Until now, the members of the Forum, the Conclave's ruling one hundred cardinals, were loath to mention the now dead world. Shame consumed them. Each morning was the casual reminder of unerasable failure. The cosmic screams of billions echoing through eternity in mockery of all the Conclave represented.

Thent threw his hands in the air. The artificial lights made his liver spots glow. "What can we do against such power? He has the ability to murder entire worlds. We are sorely outmatched and underprepared for the levels of violence Nye has unleashed."

"Does that matter to the trillions of citizens in our care?" Tinus countered. "We are at war, Cardinals. Not a war of our choosing but one we accepted from inception. Each of us in this room conspired to put Nye on the throne. He has taken that trust, murdered our peers, and began a purge across the universe in our holy name. We have failed the gods and we have failed our people."

"What are you suggesting?" Arbalas asked, her words drawled out with suspicion.

Her eyes wore a wicked gleam emphasized by the reflection of light. Tinus Har stiffened. Was this it? *Am I at last betrayed?* Calculating how long it would take the guards outside his door to react, if indeed they remained loyal to the Conclave and the office of the Cardinal Seniorus, Tinus knew death sped faster. He slipped the hand under his desk deeper into the folds of his robe, questing for the composite feel of his hidden blaster.

Swallowing his rising fear, he replied, "Is there any question what needs to be done?"

He swept his gaze around the room, desperate to gauge the intent of his chosen cardinals. Proven usurpers, they were equally capable of being Nye's accomplices. The moment was rife with peril. Tinus stood upon the precipice of greatness or condemnation. Ever at his core, he desired to be a true man of the people. His initial conception of what that meant prompted him to join Nye's insurrection. Years passed and the body count rose at considerable pace, culminating with the utter devastation of planet Kharsis. One act proving the turning point in his decision-making process. Tinus knew there might not be another opportunity to sunder their alliance and reclaim his soul.

Shocked, Cardinal Thent rocked back in his seat. His flesh turned ashen. "You cannot be serious!"

His fright was met by muted stares from those around him. Conversation halted, words unsaid hanging on the air like a cold winter night. The ask threatened to tear the already fragile coalition apart before it had the chance to earn redemption.

"Is there a choice? A real choice?" Arbalas asked.

"We play a dangerous game, fellows," Tinus suggested. "What say you, Shri? Do you stand with us?"

Licking her lips, the violet eyed cardinal contemplated her words. When she spoke, it was measured, oratory. "How can you expect an honest answer so immediately? We are a deliberate body. The actions of we few are not representative of the entire body. If we act now, the Inquisitor General will sniff us out and end our coup before it begins. I prefer my neck on my shoulders, Tinus. Should we choose to pursue your course of action, I fear you place the entirety of the Conclave in irreversible jeopardy."

"You choose what?" Thent demanded. "Answer the man's question."

"I choose … survival, my friends. Many of us have already been claimed by the purge. No doubt Nye has little qualm with adding our necks to his trophy wall. I do not suggest we act now, only that the possibility exists," he answered. Shri's use of Nye's proper title did not go unnoticed, marking her a potential traitor.

Rivals among rivals. Tinus felt the first strains of defeat, arousing the secondary protocol he dreaded. Killing the others and claiming an assassination attempt. Every way he foresaw the outcome, Nye won.

"Perhaps your way is best, for now," he concluded. "Do not speak of this with anyone, including the other cardinals. We few must reach agreement before matters proceed. I give you one standard week."

Arbalas grunted, folding her hands in the sleeves of her robes. "Fair enough, though I question the sanity of prolonging this beyond necessity. The longer we delay, the greater the odds of Nye discovering our agenda."

"Agreed," Thent added. "We stand upon a ledge because of you, Tinus."

"You mean Nye. His actions have pushed the Conclave to the breaking point. We are not strong enough to stand on our own." *Thanks in large part to our roles in this little game. What fools we were to fall for his scams. Will the universe ever forgive us?*

Nothing left to say, the cardinals filed out, leaving Tinus Har secluded in obscure thoughts. It was not until the doors hissed closed that he removed his hand from the blaster. Deflated from the expected resistance, his thoughts turned to the one entity capable of enacting his plans. The only question was whether the Vaumagian Assassin Guild was pledged to Alain Nye or not.

Inquisition Headquarters.

General Mobus Kale marched down the center of the main hall with impunity, daring anyone to halt him. His Prekhauten uniform was immaculate, pressed and starched to present a professional appearance. Rows of ribbons representing various medals and campaigns covered most of his left breast. The crisp gray of his cloth contrasted with the darker blacks of the Inquisition. Those who recognized him hurried to step aside, pausing to stare at him in passing. Those who did not invited disaster to fall upon them should his mood shift.

There was no time for pleasant hostility. He was here on purpose, delivering messages to the office of the Inquisitor General in person. It was a luxury he seldom afforded. The echo of his bootsteps, polished to bright sheen, was angry. A proud warrior prone to violent tendencies, Mobus became one with his position, yet the ghosts of his greatest failure haunted him late at night. Heavy bags clung beneath his red lined eyes. His shoulders sagged from exhaustion. Mobus knew he pushed too hard, but it was the only way he felt he was going to win the war for Vau Prime. Destiny held little regard for weak men.

A quartet of Inquisitors, resplendent in their combat uniforms, filed from a side hall to block his progress. Mobus clenched his fists, the metal contrasting obscenely with his remaining flesh. Each Inquisitor bore an electrified baton capable of rendering his body immobile. Considering his metallic arm, Mobus halted.

"I have no time for this," he grated, balancing pride with caution.

"Sir, we have orders not to allow any … interruptions to the Inquisitor General today."

An interruption, am I? How the sands shift. You should have considered what you inspired when you chose me to be your right hand, Nye. "Step aside. My business will not wait."

To their credit, the squad braced. "General, you have been instructed to remain here until he wishes to speak with you."

"Wishes to speak with me? Your precious leader would be nothing without my assistance. Am I now a dog to adhere to his master's wishes?" Mobus fumed. "Stand aside now, before you spike my anger."

"We have our orders. If you do not cooperate, we are authorized more extreme measures," the lead Inquisitor said. His voice trembled with the understanding of what was about to occur.

Mobus straightened to his full height and glowered at them. Though they were following orders and he expected the same from his men, the Inquisitor risked sparking internal conflicts he was willing to entertain. Already disillusioned with how matters were developing between the Inquisition and the Prekhauten Guard, Mobus was willing to push to achieve his goals.

"I have zero issue with striking you down within your own halls. Is the Inquisitor General willing to lose the support of my Guard over a disagreement of priority?" he projected his best authoritative tone to cow them into submission.

Exchanging glances, the Inquisitors eased aside. Mobus smirked down on them for their lack of conviction. Any Guard doing the same would be punished without mercy. He stormed past, only half expecting an assault from behind. The door hissed open, and he continued on unmolested.

Familiar with the offices, Mobus stalked through the antechamber, brushed aside a sputtering Burl Icks as he tried to stop him, and entered Nye's inner sanctum. The lights were lowered, bathing the room in semi-darkness. He paused to allow his eyes time to adjust before moving to the far end of a small hallway. Statues and plaques depicting previous Inquisitor Generals and their greatest achievements lined the walls. All monuments to the past. Mobus halted at the final door. It was a room he had yet to enter, and for reasons he might never comprehend, felt apprehensive about.

Where the Inquisition found space to craft secret chambers deep within their command building was unknown, though he was certain none of this existed the last time he visited. Mobus was the curious sort, but only when it allowed for personal advancement. There was danger lurking behind the door and it gave him pause. Lowered voices echoed through the thin door. He cocked his head and listened.

"… consolidating power on a hundred worlds. Our efforts are hampered by the persistence of the loyalists to the old regime, my lord."

Lord? Who pulls your strings, Alain Nye? What terrible master do you serve? And how delicious it is to find you little more than a puppet.

"That is unacceptable. You promised me a world ripe for my return, Nye. Am I wrong to have misgivings of you?"

The voice was deep, thundering through the small space. Hackles rose across Mobus' flesh. This was a voice of true power. One he could willingly follow without question.

"M…my lord," Nye stammered, "You must understand, there is a vacuum across the stars, left by the reducing of the Conclave's authority. Vau Prime will be ready for your return as promised. My agents continue to undermine the former regime, thus paving the way for you."

The unnatural pause made Mobus' eyes narrow.

"See that it is so, Inquisitor General. I go now to seek my command carrier and bring my reign to the universe. It will begin on Vau Prime."

The transmission ended, announced by Nye's frustrated growl. Mobus, sensing the moment to assert his strength, forced his way into the chamber. Alain Nye jerked, caught off guard. His face dropped, flushing crimson.

"How much did you hear?" he asked in hushed tones.

Mobus folded his arms and leaned against the door frame. "Enough. Who is coming, Alain?"

"That … is my business for now," Alain replied. "My motivation for this power bid is my own. It shall be revealed in time. Know that there are forces at play, even your wrath cannot contend with. Careful how you tread, Kale. Matters are only beginning."

The general broke into a grin. Stained teeth shining in the gloom. "Threatening me, Nye? And I had come to do the same to you."

They stared in silence. Each lost in their private schemes. Mobus' desire for power, and the subsequent elimination of his hated rival, drove his actions. Foul deeds arose through the night, terrorizing millions in their zeal. He was vengeance made flesh. A terrible angel come to claim them all. If only Nye stepped aside to allow him the opportunity to fulfill his purpose.

"Very well. Keep your secrets," Mobus said after the tension grew unbearable. "I imagine I will meet this secret benefactor in due time."

"Why are you here, Mobus? Shouldn't you be out purging Krenz of General Strannan?" Nye scoffed. His quest to rid the universe of the former Prekhauten Guard commanding officer had grown stale. A paltry reminder of failed greatness.

"I need authority to have a man released from an Inquisition prison facility."

Alain bit back his initial retort. "You disturb my privacy for this?"

"It is necessary," Mobus reinforced.

"Doubtless this man will turn the tides and bring you victory in a matter of days."

"Do not mock me, Nye."

Alain dismissed him with a wave. "This is not a game, Mobus. I propped you up, supported your becoming the Guard commander. You serve at my discretion, or are you so foolish as to believe every member of your precious Guard is loyal to you? Remember your place, Mobus. I may serve another master, but I am not tolerant to subordinates."

"One day we shall settle this, but I need you to release this man."

Bristling with fury, Mobus chose to ignore the barb. There was a time and place for everything and Alain Nye would learn the truth of what darkness resided in his soul in due time.

"Who is this man?" Alain asked after spying the coldness buried deep in Mobus' eyes.

"Utan Husk."

He balked as his past returned to haunt him. "Husk! Murderer. Have you any idea how many of his own people he killed before we placed him in that cell to rot? He cannot be trusted. The man is a cancer upon humanity."

"Precisely the reason I need him," Mobus added. "Grant me this one request."

Alain shook his head, flashes of Husk's previous treason slipping through his guard. "He cannot be trusted. Letting him loose upon the universe is an agony I will not be responsible for."

"I can handle him. He is but one man," Mobus said. "Perhaps he can succeed where I … failed."

The admission stung, for Mobus had spent the better part of two years dedicated to hunting Davith Strannan. Pride had its uses, the one-armed general concluded, but so, too, did humility.

Sensing the conversation turning back to his favor, Alain pressed. "How can you guarantee you will keep him under your heel?"

"Every man has a breaking point. Threaten him enough and he'll perform the way I want," Mobus replied. He failed to keep the confused look from twisting his face.

"And when he doesn't?"

"A round to the back of his head will solve both our problems."

No truer words have been spoken in this chamber, Mobus Kale. Beware the beast you unleash, General. It may return to destroy your bald ambitions. "Just so. Very well. I shall have the written order drawn up shortly. You may have your man, Mobus, but do not seek to trust him."

Mobus turned to leave.

"Perhaps he will succeed where you have failed," Alain called to his back.

The door hissed shut.

*

A steady stream of uniformed personnel filed out of the Inquisition Headquarters, to be replaced by incoming streams of similar personnel. The shift change occurred twice daily with thousands of menials returning to perform odd tasks few in the field witnessed. The dregs of labor fueling the hierarchy ruling seven hundred worlds. Thankless performances bereft of acknowledgement. Without them, however, the universe would grind to a halt and cease to function.

Gedrick Silk tucked his chin into the top of his black jacket, scowling at the rough scrub of the wool fabric, and fell into line. Unable to ditch his stolen Inquisitor uniform for more practical attire, he shuffled along without making eye contact. The exit was still a hundred meters away and armed guards were on heightened security for reasons he failed to ascertain. Disappointed by the sudden turn of events, Gedrick's only priority was finding a way, whether in person or through messengers, to deliver his news to Strannan and the resistance. Nothing else mattered, least of all his survival.

The shapeshifter languished under the bright lights, for he was prevented from shifting into another persona. The prospect of being discovered was too real. His one saving grace was the Inquisition wore no name identifications. The rank on his chest was another matter. Odds were, he would be noticed and stopped. Commotion rose from behind. He kept walking, knowing any movement out of the ordinary for a ranking Inquisitor drew immediate suspicion.

Gedrick felt the crowds parting behind and stepped aside moments before a squad of Prekhauten Guards in full battle armor, weapons at the ready, swept by. Visors concealed their intent, but the shapeshifter knew they were hunting. Their weapons were charged, suggesting to his experience they were authorized to use force if necessary. Adrenaline quickened his step. The possibility they were after him arose and it chilled him. For all his traits and unique quality, Gedrick Silk was not a fighter.

"Wonder what they're doing."

"Who knows. Rumor has it that one armed Guard threatened the Inquisitor General."

Gedrick perked at the suppositions of the crowd. Paranoia often led to wild speculation. Rumors would swarm the building in no time, affording him a moment of protection. He walked as fast as the pace of the crowd allowed.

"Looks like those bastards are ready to gun us all down."

"I just want to get home and forget today. We had thirteen false alarms over General Strannan. My mind can't handle much more stress."

"You need a vacation."

"Doesn't look like she's going to get one. None of us are. I heard it from a friend in operations that something big is in the works. Looks like we might finally get the chance to end the war."

"War. Bah! I haven't seen a bit of it and neither have you. In fact, I doubt there's really one. More like propaganda to keep the people in line."

"But the low continent."

"What about it?"

"Newsvids say the entire continent was burned to the ground."

"When have the newsvids ever been right? The Conclave has lied to us for generations. If there is a war, and I'm not saying there is, we could do a lot better than those robed freaks."

Gedrick's heart hung heavy. The disillusionment of humanity ran deep, stretching back through decades of misplaced ideology. As one of the last of his kind, he was in a unique position to understand the reckoning they were heading for. Should Amongeratix regain his command ship and his private armies, the universe would burn for a thousand years. The need to find Strannan grew stronger, more urgent. Gedrick and those around him filed out past the Guards, thankful their attention was turned elsewhere.

The first breath of fresh air calmed his nerves without doing much to prevent a haunting image burned in his mind as hundreds of people filed onto awaiting trains to take them to the edge of damnation. Humanity seemed the willing participants of its own demise.

"A few more trips and that should do it," Davith Strannan said as he strode up behind Aliz and Captain Julian. "The evacuation will be done before dawn."

Aliz watched as three cargo haulers slipped from their moorings to disappear in predawn traffic. The warehouse district was no longer tenable. Mobus Kale and his marauders were eliminating entire blocks each night, reducing the number of places to hide a large force. Unwilling to risk becoming trapped, Strannan opted to split his forces into smaller commands and facilitate a true guerilla war across Krenz.

"Are you sure you want to occupy the low continent?" Aliz asked without turning. The artificial orange glow of millions of lights hazed the horizon. She failed to remember the last time she saw an honest night sky.

"It seems the strongest tactical decision. Kale's already ruined it, perhaps for good. There's no reason for him to redeploy forces down there," Strannan explained. "We should be safe enough for a while."

Clinging to doubts lodged from past experience, Aliz wondered at what he hoped to accomplish. All they worked toward over the past year was for naught. The raid on Tatarast Island, while successful, did little to advance their agenda. Kale stepped up his assaults, pushing the resistance to the breaking point. She knew, as did the others in her company, that recovery was impossible, if it devolved that far. Immediate executions awaited, if they were fortunate. Endless years languishing in an Inquisition prison otherwise. She felt trapped. Suddenly Zoraq Darc's defection made sense.

How easy would it be for me to slip away? Quit this foolish quest for revenge and create a new life? The potential teased her, prompting the realization that no one in the Inquisition or the Conclave knew her name. Lorenu went to great lengths to keep their relationship secret. Had she known the day would come when one of her trusted compatriots would betray her and done what she had to ensure Aliz stayed alive?

"This is an unwinnable war, Davith," she replied. "I fear we have lost the initiative, and in doing so, abandoned our people to a fate undreamed of."

"Nonsense. True, we have endured losses, but our numbers swell despite the odds. We now have enough weapons, equipment and ammunition to keep fighting for years. Kale and his cronies will not expect wide dispersal, nor will he anticipate me largely abandoning the capital city. Given time, we should be able to execute a new campaign across the planet."

"You overestimate our chances of survival," she said coldly.

"I underestimate the value of my name. There are still many in uniform and those recently out of it, who adhere to the old ways. The founding principles the Guard once stood for. Hundreds have joined us. More will come."

His words lacked the comfort in which they were meant. Numbers. Aliz ignored the bravado, choosing to focus on the abstract he avoided. Media coverage off world was limited, with the civil war ignored in favor of pacifying stories. Aliz reckoned the war had to have stretched across scores of worlds by now and continued growing. Battle lines were drawn, siphoning men and material away from Vau Prime. How long before the prime world was abandoned and forgotten as broken fragments struggled to maintain what little area of space they controlled?

She offered a sad smile. "I wish I had your faith, General, but the past two years have all but destroyed my trust in mankind. Whatever dark power spawned this conflict has left a rotten spore deep in our souls. The war won't stop until one side is left in utter ruin."

He placed a fatherly hand on her shoulder, amused that they were of similar age. "And I vow to continue resisting until my last breath. We cannot abandon our principles now, Aliz. They are all we cling to when the night grows too dark."

Strannan wanted to say more. To let her know Lorenu would be proud of all she had accomplished these past few years. Ultimately, he decided it was not his place. No one needed to be reminded of the pain of loss.

"I know," she whispered before the sadness became too strong.

Captain Julian, having chosen to remain silent, glanced at his commanding officer. "Sir, where do you want me?"

"I need you to command the cell in the housing districts north of Conclave. You will coordinate with my post by nontraditional means. No transmissions," Strannan informed the young officer.

"Our objectives, sir?" Julian asked.

"Disruption of enemy propaganda efforts. Eliminate high value targets as they present themselves," he replied. "I knew your father, Julian. He was a good man. A good friend. Learning of his passing left a hole in my heart. I could use him now."

"My father was fond of you, General. It was his pleasure to have trained you," Julian said. Painful memories of his father's last days as disease claimed him, seeing the once proud soldier unable to lift his head without assistance, brought a tear to his eye. He fought for the memory of his father, and all those who served alongside him.

"I am going with Julian," Aliz interrupted. She spoke with defiance, daring either man to deny her the right.

"Are you certain, Aliz? He will be marching into the very mouth of our foe," Strannan explained. "This one cell is perhaps the most exposed, the most ready to suffer grievous losses. I would see you somewhere safe instead."

"The choice is mine, Davith. It is all I can do to honor the memory of Lorenu as well. She deserved a better fate," Aliz postured.

The sound of small arms fire echoed through the city streets far to the west.

"Aye. That she did. Lorenu was a good woman and a better leader," Strannan agreed.

"She was a poor leader, Davith, for she failed to see the sparks before they fanned into open flame."

His tone grew harsh. "Nonsense. None of us predicted Alain Nye would betray us or that he was the progenitor of this war. Lorenu Phos did all within her power to keep this rebellion from spreading. She is the reason I continue to fight. So should it be for you."

Rebuked, Aliz clenched her fists in defiance. "General Strannan, I am not some child to be lectured to. I knew Lorenu more than you or anyone other than her family. Think you it does not pain me to see the failure, the ruin her name has become? In one fell swoop, Alain Nye has destroyed her achievements and placed blame for so many problems in the universe. My heart weeps each night because I know there is nothing I can do to reverse this."

"But there is," Julian interrupted softly. His kindly gaze stole a piece of her venom. "You can continue to fight. I confess to not knowing the Cardinal Seniorus, but I am versed in all she has done for us. The lies of the Inquisitor General must be stopped before all dignity and human decency is left smote upon empty battlefields."

"Captain Julian, you are a wise soul for one so young," Aliz broke into a smile. "Thank you for reminding me of what truly matters."

She turned back to Strannan. "Very well, Davith. I concede your point. We will fight Nye and bring his hired killer to heel. Krenz will once again be made safe."

Chuckling under his breath, Strannan replied, "Just staying alive will suffice, my dear. But the hour grows late and the noose tightens. Captain, take command of your teams. Until we meet again."

They clasped forearms in the old tradition. Aliz found it a deed rooted in finality. Did both men know a secret truth they were unwilling to share? A dark future growing less distant as the universe continued plunging out of control. It was then cold realization slapped her across the face. Neither man expected to live through this stage of the insurgency. She had resigned herself to a sinking ship.

"I know what you are thinking. Your eyes betray your thoughts, Aliz," Strannan told her as Julian walked off. "Perhaps we shall die. We all must at some point. Do not let that truth dissuade you from the direction in which we move. We are desperate, yes, but those are the moments when the extraordinary rise and take control of their destiny. Even should we fail, the universe will know the strength of our conviction."

"Inspiring a new generation to rebel against Nye's tyranny," Aliz concluded. "I have underestimated you, Davith."

"Perhaps, though it's not you who worries me. Aliz, it has been my sincerest pleasure getting to know you. Would that times were different …" he let the thought fall away. There were times when words did no justice.

"Goodbye, General. The pleasure was mine."

Heart pounding, Aliz hurried into the semi gloom of the warehouse before Strannan found the tears building in her eyes. Though they were of similar age, she found herself thinking of him as a fatherly figure, prone to dispensing sage advice when needed and stern discipline at other times. He was the rock she anchored herself on during the darkest moments of her life.

"Is everything all right with you two?" Julian asked. He grunted under the weight of the field pack and reached for his rifle.

"Yes," she admitted. "Is all in order?"

"It is. There's room in the lead air car, if you like," Julian offered.

Offering her most motherly glare, Aliz reached for a weapon. "Thank you, Captain, but I am perfectly capable of walking. Though I will accept your offer for my pack."

Grinning, Julian said, "As you wish."

A jerk with his head and a young soldier stepped out of ranks to take her kit to the air car. A nervous pall clung to the men and women in Julian's new command. Many knew they would not survive. Others were in denial. Aliz admired them all and resigned to serve the same fate.

"Move out," Julian ordered.

Aliz gave the warehouse a final look before heading out into the dying night. Once again, the war was changed by a single stroke of brilliance. Or so she liked to think.

SIX

3215 A.G. (After gods), Front lines, planet Mannus Prime.

Night fell over the front lines, bathing the trenches in blessed darkness, marred only by the accented moans from hospital tents and the occasional sobs of Guards pushed to the breaking point. Endless days turned to months of seeing comrades slaughtered by those once considered allies broke many, on both sides. This was the worst mankind had lurking in the wells of its soul. A simple hatred spanning back to the time of the gods, where violence was currency. Most never expected to see protracted warfare on such scale, for the schism was swift and allowed little time to draw sides. Some turned to archaic texts of worship to escape the fatalism of the moment. Others turned to drinking.

Jelin Quint was no stranger to fighting. Born the third son of a lowly banker, he was left without inheritance and forced to join the Prekhauten Guard at a young age or be left to languish on the backwater world of his birth. Veteran of a score of campaigns, he had never seen combat this intense. Losing most of his company during the last ill-fated assault pushed him to the bottle, where he remained. Other guards surrounded him in the makeshift bar. Commander Torgast initially banned alcohol, thinking the campaign would be finished in days. A year and a half later, the ordnance was forgotten, though still on record. Quint did not care. None of them did anymore.

He took a long pull from the bottle, grimacing as the homemade alcohol burned down to the pit of his stomach. All supplies of proper alcohol were long since gone. Savvy soldiers confiscated the empty bottles, built stills in abandoned bunkers dug into the trenches, and brewed a form of swill capable of bringing down a herd of bellurns. Nothing a true tavern would consider serving, Quint drank it for what it was meant to do.

"'Nother day getting slogged on the lines. I'm tired of the godsdamned artillery. Tired of this swill and tired of the whole mess!"

Quint narrowed his eyes, failing to push the negative thoughts away. His experience with soldiers like that was always bad. They usurped authority and stole morale. Military units needed their esprit de corps to perform effectively on the battlefield. Bellyachers robbed that, damning a campaign before it began.

"More so, I'm tired of being told to go on the line. What did we do to deserve this? Nothing, I tell ya. We're being thrown out like yesterday's lunch."

"You call that shit lunch?" a second encouraged him.

"Eh? What? Lunch? It's past supper, you daft bastard. Now, where was I?"

"You were about to shut the fuck up, trooper," Quint snapped and slammed his bottle on the field table.

"Says who?"

Jelin Quint was on his feet and closing the gap between them in the blink of an eye. Larger, wider, and covered in tattoos, the other Guard was a beast of a man. He lacked Quint's natural aggression, however. It was over before the braggart knew what hit him. Quint's fist slammed into the side of his head, felling him with one terrible blow. Blood and spittle burst from the Guard's nose and mouth as he collapsed. Satisfied the dissent was ended, Quint returned to his bottle. The stares of a dozen dirt smeared Guards followed him.

"There he is. That's the guy who knocked out Sergeant Borus."

Mind fogged by drunkenness, Jelin Quint barely registered the words before gloved hands gripped his upper arms, jerking his hands behind his back and clasping them in shackles. He tried picking his head up from the vomit smeared tabletop he had passed out on but lacked enough leverage. Instead, his face splashed in a cooling pool of his own vomit.

"On your feet, trooper. You're under arrest."

A bubble of mucus formed in one nostril. "Arrest? For what?"

"Assault of a superior officer. Conduct unbecoming of a Guard. Drunk and disorderly conduct. We can keep going, if you like," the provost barked.

Two men jerked Quint to his unsteady feet and half dragged him out of the bunker and into the sunlight. Vision swimming, he groaned as the light burned into his brain. Mud and piss splashed his boots and lower trousers. Unconcerned for his wellbeing, the provosts paraded him through the trenches. Veterans and recruits fresh from Mannus Prime's western cities stared in disbelief at the cruelty exhibited. No man on the line deserved such treatment. Not in the midst of battle.

"Let him go!"

"Damned provosts. Ain't never around when you need 'em!"

"Let him go!"

Flushed with anger, the lead provost drew his shock baton and jabbed it into the nearest Guard's stomach. The trooper fell in convulsions. "Back off! Next trooper gets in our way shares his fate!"

A senior lieutenant, having assumed command from his late captain, slipped from his sleeping cot, long coat covered in mud, and glowered at his men. "What's the meaning of this? You're loud enough the enemy will know where we are." He spotted the source of the commotion. "What do you want?"

"Lieutenant, we have orders to arrest this man for assaulting a noncommissioned officer last night. Broke his damned jaw," the provost answered.

"Is he one of yours, sir?" the second asked.

Striding closer for a better look, the lieutenant shook his head. "Never seen him before, though he's a damned disgrace. Smells like vomit and shit. Clear a hole! Anyone keeps these men from doing their duty gets thirty days of recon duty."

The masses parted. None were willing to spend the next few weeks sticking their necks out to get intel on enemy lines for no reason. The provosts took advantage and hurried down the trench.

"Damned drunks are going to be the ruin of this army," the lieutenant muttered.

"What am I doing in here?" Quint demanded.

The day was gone, faded into the latest of a string of unmemorable moments. His back ached and his arms were sore. A quick inspection showed him deep red rings around his wrists. Head pounding, Quint took in his surroundings. Iron bars framed the small space. A small cot and an empty chamber pot were the only other items aside from him. Two rows of similar cells lined the large tent but stood empty.

"A damned jail," he groaned. "Put your foot in it this time, didn't you? Foolish bastard."

Quint leaned back against the bars, careful not to hit his head, and drew a deep breath. The stench gagged him. His uniform was filthy, soiled several ways. Fresh cuts and tears peppered his legs. Disgusted with himself, Quint forced the breath out and closed his eyes.

"What did I do this time?"

Boots thumped down the mud-stained floorboards. "Name and unit, trooper?"

"Quint, Jelin. Corporal in the second company, eighty-fifth assault infantry. What are the charges?" he asked.

"That'll be explained to you when you stand before the commander. On your feet, trooper. You need to get cleaned up. Resist and it's the stockade for you for the duration of this campaign."

Quint snorted, the idea of missing the rest of the battle somehow comforting. He took in his captors, guessing neither had spent a moment on the line here or any other world. Only a rear echelon Guard would treat a veteran so. Rather than protest, Quint gathered what composure remained to him, dignity having long since abandoned him, and followed the provost to the adjourning showers. The cold water burned in ways he failed to expect but provided welcome respite from the self-induced grime coating him. An orderly arrived in the middle of the shower to remove his soiled uniform and boots, replacing them with fresh prison fatigues. Quint spied the giant "P" on the back of the blouse.

"Not the royalty you're accustomed to, is it?" the provost asked. "You deserve it, and more. Broke the sergeant's jaw and took him off the line for weeks until he heals. The man might not be able to talk again from what I heard."

What man?

Groaning at the gaps in his short-term memory, Quint finished showering. The uniform fit poorly but at least it was clean. He forgot the last time his unit was issued new fatigues. Aromas from the nearest mess tents drifted to him and his stomach churned. Not wanting to vomit again, Quint exhaled and stuck to breathing out his mouth as he was marched past the hundreds of staring troopers in line for chow.

Cannons went off from firebases well behind the lines. Personal experience told Quint they were kilometers away and having a good war. How could they not? Only the forward observers saw the effects of their bombardments. The cost in human life and the ruin it left on those still alive. Quint respected the artillerymen for what they did, just not how they did it.

They passed through the combat troops and into an area of bunkers and command tents. Antennas poked the sky like a forest of saplings. This was the army's nerve center. A few well-placed rounds and they lost the ability to coordinate movements and fight the war with any standard of effectiveness. Why the enemy had not done this yet was a mystery to Quint. What better way to kill the beast than by cutting off the head?

He caught the eye of a dark brown uniformed soldier in passing. The other Guard was camouflaged, his face and hands covered in black face paint. His rifle was not standard issue and he wore no identifying accoutrements declaring unit or allegiance. Curiously, the man had only a small ammunition pack on his back, foregoing the usual Guard infantry kit. Several others, all similarly dressed and equipped, filed behind their leader. Stone faced and determined. Quint wondered where they were heading and decided it was best not to know.

"Wait here," the provost barked, jarring him out of his thoughts.

Quint looked up to see the sprawling command tent before him. *Looks like I don't have to sit around to learn my fate. Only wish I knew what it was I was being accused of. Ah, shit. What a way to start the day.*

"Commander Torgast will see you now. No funny business. March in all professional like and halt two paces from his desk. Salute like you mean it. Might be the difference between the rope or chains. Stand at attention until he directs you otherwise. You are still a noncommissioned officer in the Guard and are expected to act like it. Understand?" the provost leered.

Quint glared back but kept his tongue, instead choosing to inspect the non-regulation moustache curling down over the provost's upper lip, enough the man could chew on the ends when bored. Why certain individuals thought all military prisoners abandoned their discipline and turned rogue was beyond him. *At least in my case, I still don't recall what I am accused of. This isn't going to be fun.*

"Well, enough," he growled.

The provost flinched, hand slipping for the baton swinging from his hip.

Sneering back, Quint slipped through the fabric doors. Noncombatants ever felt the need to prove themselves in front of veterans. The only problem was no veteran worth his salt was going to bow down to it. Quint halted before the makeshift table, catching a glance of the three additional officers and senior NCOs standing off to the right. Ignoring them, he locked eyes on Torgast and threw the crispest salute of his career.

"Sir, Corporal Jelin Quint reporting as ordered." His tone was sharp, the words uttered with total confidence, despite his situation.

Leaning back in his chair, hands folded over his stomach, Torgast studied the man before him dispassionately. Every detail whispered Quint was a fighter. A no nonsense man with sharp discipline and the tactical knowledge to prove effective on the battlefield. Just the sort of man he needed in his army. Torgast removed the chewed toothpick from his mouth and returned the salute.

"At ease, Corporal."

Quint's arm dropped and he locked his hands behind his back, feet spread shoulder width apart. A vein on the side of his forehead thumped with each heartbeat, betraying his only emotion.

Damned impressive. "Why are you here, Corporal? I have better things to occupy my time than deal with drunk and disorderly conduct. Or are you under the impression this is giving me a welcome break?"

"No, sir," Quint answered.

"You didn't answer my question."

He blinked rapidly, desperate to recall even a sliver of the previous night. "Sir, I am told I put a man in the infirmary."

The officers to the side shuffled nervously.

"Told, were you?" Torgast struggled not to laugh. "I have it on good authority you broke a sergeant's jaw and was discovered passed out in a pool of your own vomit. Not terribly professional of you and far from indicative of how I run my army."

Quint stiffened as he waited for the hammer to fall.

"Fortunately for you, there were several witnesses, all claiming this sergeant was urging desertion and insurrection," Torgast continued. "If you ask my opinion, I think you went too easy on him. Men like that are cancerous. Best removed before the tumor grows. Today is your lucky day, Sergeant. All charges are dropped."

"Corporal, sir," Quint said.

Torgast leaned forward to reclaim his toothpick. "Are we adding disobeying a direct order to your list of infractions?"

Bastard. You got me by the balls now, don't you? "Not at all, sir. Thank you, sir."

"Don't thank me yet. You are hereby reassigned to my personal detail. Report to the adjutant immediately after this for your assignment. And for the gods' sake, get out of that damned prisoner uniform. You represent me now, Jelin Quint."

Quint saluted, did an about face, and marched out before full realization it him.

Fuck.

"Are you sure that was wise?"

Torgast took advantage of being unseen to roll his eyes. The longer he remained in command of the campaign on Mannus Prime, the more subordinates felt the need to openly question his decisions. It grew tiresome. Unfortunately, shooting them was out of the question. He needed every available body to throw at his foes.

"Yes, Cardinal. Jelin Quint may have anger issues but he is precisely what I need."

A pause before the comms reopened. "He could be a liability. Men like that are unpredictable. Dangerous even."

Torgast smiled despite himself. "Cardinal, we are an army at war. Danger is part of the job title. I'll be fine. If anything, the poor bastard has no idea what is coming to him."

"What of the man he accosted? Having that type of dissent in the ranks can unravel all you are trying to accomplish."

Trying to accomplish? Hells, I just want to survive. "He is being reassigned to mess detail. You are correct and as much as I'd like to ship him away, I can't afford to lose the manpower. Losses from the past attack were enough to break two combat battalions. If I don't get support soon, this planet will fold."

"Faith, Torgast. You must hold to faith," Virom reminded in his best fatherly tone.

"So, you remind me," Torgast said. "Have you made any progress with our Inquisitor friends?"

"No. They seem content with biding their time before accusing you of treason and executing you in front of the army. Not a very pleasant sort," the Cardinal answered.

"I should have had them shot the moment we went to war," Torgast cursed.

"What would that accomplish?"

"Nothing, but it would remove these chains from around my neck."

Virom said, "We are ever plagued by the chains of our past. Even now, while you fight under tattered banners, old truths cling to us. Weighing us down through burdens uncounted. This war may prove the damnation of us all."

"Always a pleasure speaking with you, Cardinal," Torgast said dryly. "Lovely as this has been, I have a mission briefing to give."

"You're still going through with it?" Virom asked.

"There is no choice. I can't count on imaginary reinforcements. They will either succeed or I lose another ten troopers," Torgast said.

"May the gods bless you, Torgast."

The line went dead, leaving Commander Torgast lost in a swirl of emotions.

They slipped through the night, lethal shadows with singular focus. Palms sweat in leather gloves. Weapons gripped loosely, they bore no armor. No identification, and no items capable of giving their presence away. Each wore a uniform made of material concealing body heat signatures, neutralizing enemy thermal imaging. Grim faced, they were death manifest. Night vision built into their mesh facemasks brightened the gloom to a musky green, pinpointing enemy pickets and gun emplacements directly ahead.

Once slipping through their outer lines, the squad formed a wedge and hurried across the no man's land separating both armies. Night combat was rare on Mannus Prime. Each commander found their fill in bloodshed and failure during the daylight. Night was the only time soldiers found to forget the horrors of the moment and pretend there was a shade of normalcy left in their lives. A farce, but a welcome one, nonetheless.

As such, the enemy pickets were caught unawares. Blades flashed. Throats were slit and the bodies quietly slumped to the bottom of their foxholes. A cursory look at her sensors told the squad sergeant all her people were still with her. Satisfied with their initial progress, she led them to the first trench. A massive bunker anchored the end of the line. Dozens of machine gun barrels poked through the concrete den of lethality. Knowing the squad lacked the firepower to deal with the threat, the sergeant ordered her people to converge in a single file behind her. They slipped to the exposed area on the side and prayed the enemy had not deployed a minefield.

Sweating, the squad was past the trench and into the enemy army encampment. Standard Prekhauten protocols were the same for both armies, allowing her to pinpoint their target in short order. The night was half finished, the world trapped in deep darkness. Perfect for her work. The squad continued at the same pace through rows of tents filled with sleeping soldiers. Those few on guard duty or those who failed to find sleep, ignored her. Heat pounding, her squad reached the inner defenses protecting her target.

Security was much tighter here. Armed guards patrolled at random intervals while static guards were positioned at every entrance. Those on duty at the main gate had dogs. Cursing, the sergeant had not planned on dogs. Several hand signals later, the squad broke apart into two-man teams. She stared at the chrono counting down on her facemask. Her heart pounded, for this was the most dangerous task she had been called upon to perform in her short career. There had been finality in Torgast's voice as he relayed his orders. Did he know they would not be coming back? She suspected so but followed orders. Anything to help end this pointless war and keep her friends from dying.

The countdown hit zero. She raised her rifle and sighted on the nearest guard. Muffled shots disturbed the night calm. Guards and dogs fell in lifeless heaps. A whispered prayer and the sergeant charged through the main gate. Her mask switched off night vision the moment her boot stepped into the light. There was no pause. No consideration of how easy their infiltration was. She took their skill for granted and should not have. Too late to stop, she opened fire on every living target within the command tent. When it was finished, a score of bodies draped chairbacks, map tables, and the floor. Still, not one of her squad was missing. Lost in the realization her mission was a success and her failure in formulating a complete escape plan, she lowered her rifle and ordered the squad to form on her.

One of her soldiers snatched the rank from the collar of their dead target and nodded. Satisfied the enemy general was dead, the sergeant headed for the door. Night was rushing away, as if eager to escape the torments conducted in her name. Guards rushed out of the tent. Bright lights bathed the cordon, halting the squad in place as the last man existed the command tent. Blinded, they staggered into one another while throwing off their night vision.

Blinking her tears away, the sergeant squinted into the lights. Scores of shadowy figures surrounded her. When her vision cleared, she saw they were trapped and the man in front of her was the one she thought she had killed. The hum of charging rifles buzzed, electrifying the very air. Tiny hairs on the back of her neck rose. Outgunned and thrust into the worst imaginable situation, she lowered her weapon.

The enemy fired as one.

"This land smells of death."

Kaline continued walking. The jungle was unkind, thick and impenetrable at times. Countless insect bites peppered her exposed, sweat drenched flesh. The promise of enlightenment wavered. Her resolve weakened under the harsh realities of the sun. Snakes slithered along vines, under leaves. Spiders the size of her palm raced in front of her. Deep in the foliage whispered predatory cats and other creatures she wished to avoid. The very air was closed in. She felt small. Insignificant.

"We keep moving. The village is not far," she affirmed.

Her disciples exchanged worried looks.

"Mistress, this is not a game. Night is falling and the jungle is unkind to unwary travelers," the former Marine said.

Kaline halted in midstride. "All the more reason to push forward."

"We risk being trapped here. You would damn us all." His face twisted with concern. Experience echoed in his gaze.

"When was the last time you led troops into a jungle?" she asked.

He swallowed, thoughts swirling. Kaline was a dangerous woman, unlike any he'd encountered during his time in service. A true fanatic, she represented the very worst in the human soul. *So why then do I follow? Not for glory or the promise of a burned future. What then? Am I lost?* "Seventeen years ago."

She eased a step closer and laid a hand on his forearm. "We cannot allow old fears to cripple our work. I have need of both of you, if I am to successfully spread the word of Rengu to this planet. Will you stay by my side and deliver enlightenment to those worthy souls?"

Resolve weakened. "I … I do not know what lies ahead, Mistress, but this land is thirsty for human blood. I smell it in the air. Musky, humid. We risk becoming lost before reaching our target."

The briefest hint of sadness lingered in her eyes. Kaline nodded slowly. Her breath was heavy, laden with understanding. "I believe you, but I also need you. Stay by me. Protect me from the horrors that plague you, while I deliver the message of our lord. I beg you."

Slumped shoulders were his first sign of resignation. Why, he might never know, but the power of her voice, that singular conviction pouring from the center of her heart, offered him a split second of promise he lacked.

"Aye," he whispered. "I will accompany you."

Her smile genuine, Kaline removed her hand and resumed her trek. "Come, gentlemen, we have a long way to go and the jungle is unkind to trespassers."

They continued as darkness and temperature dropped.

Kaline led them to a small overhang behind a bamboo stand. A stream babbled nearby, though she figured the water was unsafe to drink. They had a small fire going as the last ribbons of light fled the jungle. No one spoke, for the creatures of the night held their own conversation.

Unable to stand the forced silence, Kaline stirred the fire. "You know, it has occurred to me that I know neither of your names. An unfortunate circumstance, given our reliance on one another to remain alive."

The Marine snorted his amusement. "Captain works fine. I was a Marine on the *Monttle*. That sleeping princess is Mott."

"Did the two of you serve together?" she asked. Her gaze lingered on the rise and fall of Mott's chest.

"No, and I'm glad I didn't. Word is, he escaped a prison colony a few years back and is wanted by the Inquisition for unsavory crimes," the Captain explained.

"Rengu accepts us all," Kaline explained after some thought. "It is not my position to choose who answers the call. We are all inspired by individual choice. The ability to decipher our unique path through life is what makes us the right choice to rule the universe."

"How so? I've encountered more than a few species during my time. None of them seem to want the job. The gods left this universe to us," he said.

"Perhaps, but that does not suggest divine inheritance. Our past is checkered. You do not think the Conclave was the initial dominant power after the gods fell?"

"Who else would it be?"

Flames reflected in her deep blue eyes. "There are tales of organizations, tribes of primitive humans who sought dominance. Many were eliminated outright, their genetic code lost to eternity. It was humanity who rose through the ashes, true humans such as you and I, who deciphered the code. We alone are capable of reasoning. It is that skill that enables imagination and drives innovation. The wheels of industry were built upon the bones of the gods. The first members of the Conclave were vicious, brutal tyrants with the desire to control all.

"They needed a military arm and a division of special volunteers to stamp out anyone speaking against their message. Thus was born the power structure you know today. How many millions died during those first wars is lost to us, though I've no doubt those pious bastards on Vau Prime have pristine records in their vaults."

The howl of a troop of primates high in the canopy disturbed her thoughts.

"Isn't piety the reason we are here? You serve one of the old gods, even if he is no longer in the universe," he countered.

"Isn't he?"

"What do you mean?"

Kaline's grin reminded him of a serpent. "Gods get their strength, their eternal power from believers. Without faith, they wither and die. Abandoned to the dark stain of space. True, there was a war between the gods and most were destroyed. Killed by their kin. Those who lived, fled to the uncharted regions of the universe, where I believe they remain today."

"You are suggesting they are waiting for us?" the Captain asked. He found it difficult to meet the passion in her gaze.

"Or biding their time for our fall to regain their rightful thrones," Kaline suggested. "Who knows the mind of a god."

"If that is true, how is it none have been discovered during three thousand years? Surely they have been encountered in the past."

"Can you contend with the will of a god? I cannot. There are many secrets in this vast universe. Some we will learn. Others we were never meant to know. My heart is filled with both joy and terror at the thought of confronting the unknown."

He leaned back against the cool stone. "So why do it?"

"Do what?"

"Serve a god you have never met and one you don't want to?" he asked.

"Faith."

The word left him chilled.

The Captain awoke to screams. The old soldier reached for his rifle as his vision adjusted. Kaline was scrambling behind him, eyes wild with raw terror. Instincts kicking in, he swung his rifle to address the immediate threat. His stomach rebelled when he spied the giant snake swallowing a slime covered Mott. Blood painted the man's face. An outstretched arm reached for him, desperate to be saved. It was too late. He raised his rifle and put a round between the man's eyes before emptying the power charge on the snake. The impossible creature died with a hiss and was still.

"You saved him," Kaline said through forced tears.

"I failed him, and you. We should have never come here, Kaline."

Unconcerned, she continued staring at what remained of both snake and man. The jungle fell silent and in the absence of all sound, He was left with little but the thump of his own heart.

"His sacrifice was inevitable. It was the will of Rengu," she whispered.

Rising, Kaline gathered her robes close and went to inspect the remains. A sickening aroma filled the air as flesh began dissolving. The acids and venoms of the snake leaked free, consuming the corpse slowly. Fascinated, she watched as an army of insects emerged from the night to feast. The jungle took care of its own.

He contemplated shooting her, if only to end his misery. "Bull. He died because this jungle is filled with predators. How can you defend that against some god no one has seen in over three millennia?"

"My dear, Captain. I had thought it would be obvious," she chided. "Faith."

"You keep using that word," he growled.

"Indeed, for it is the shield upon which we may grow, basking in the confidence that ours is the cause of righteousness and we shall not be denied," Kaline returned to her spot by the fire. "Without faith, we are little more than animals."

"I find it difficult to place faith in something I can't see."

"Therein lies the great cosmic joke. To achieve our full potential, we must rely on that which cannot be seen," Kaline replied. "We should get some rest. Dawn is still a ways off and it will prove taxing convincing the villagers to join our cause."

Kaline pulled her hood over her head, locks of crimson hair falling around her neck, and leaned back against the stone, confident he would protect her.

He stared at her until he heard the soft grunts of her snores. *Sleep? How in the hells am I supposed to do that?*

Far to the south, two Inquisitors plotted their next move. It was a precarious time, one neither felt shifted to their favor, despite the most recent news. Rumors traveled back from the front, detailing a brazen mission aimed at ending the campaign. Choosing to keep Cardinal Virom from their counsel, the Inquisitors spoke in hushed whispers from deep within a hidden chamber in the main government building.

"Torgast oversteps his authority. He must be removed."

Dowan Mun studied his companion with deep regard. Fiery by every standard, she was filled with venom. How or why Bela Cass found herself on Mannus Prime was unknown to him, though he suspected her being outspoken had much to do with it. The Inquisition had changed over the past three years. Unique voices were extinguished, forced to bow to the will of the Inquisitor General. What was once a hunt for heretics, devolved into a hunt for loyalists to the old regime.

"This is a dangerous junction. We lack authority to remove him," he replied with measured tone. More than once, the idea of slipping a blade in her back crossed his mind.

Bela turned on him with hate filled eyes. "Torgast is a snake. If he had succeeded in his assassination attempt it would have prompted a total surrender. We would have lost this world and both you and I would feel the sting of Nye's enforcers."

"What do you propose? Arrest him in front of his soldiers?" Dowan asked.

They were crossing the line from Inquisitor to murderer, and despite orders from Krenz, Dowan felt no rush to end his assignment. Leaving Mannus Prime now only served to enhance his career and get him shipped to another battlefield. He was tired and needed a break from the endless cycle of violence gripping the universe.

Bela fumed, her tiny hands clenched. "If needs be. He is a soldier, a servant of the Conclave. All true sons and daughters owe their allegiance to Nye and the new order. His actions are heretical and demand punishment."

"We are the only Inquisitors on this planet. Though an entire army of Guards loyal to Nye sit not far from us, we are alone in enemy territory. Giving away our hand now will see us hanging from the church spire," he cautioned.

"What are you saying, Dowan Mun?"

He stiffened. Her tone hardened. Suspicion caused severe actions. As much as it amused him to think of killing her, Dowan knew Bela Cass harbored no hesitation if it came to ending his life.

"I am saying we must exercise patience, if we are to trap the bear in his den," he said. "Torgast will expose himself soon enough. Opportunity to remove him and force this army to its knees will arise only then."

"For your sake, I pray you are right."

She stormed off, leaving him mired in dark and twisted thoughts.

SEVEN

3215 A.G. (After gods), the Forsaken Path.

The air choked with ash. Falling like a light rain, it covered the landscape for as far as the eye could see, turning the horizon a hellish inferno of violent colors reflected off the shimmer of twilight. The travelers spied rocky outcroppings just ahead, though admitted time and distance meant little in this distorted realm. Wails tormented the quasi-darkness. On edge, Elisa and Ah'muf huddled in the Bloody Man's shadow. It was an illusion of comfort, if nothing else.

They had already covered leagues, struggling to match his great strides. The youngest of the Three marched with purpose, for this was a realm he well knew. And feared. Sorrow bore no weapons. His eyes narrowed to prevent ash from obscuring his vision, he watched for the first signs of trouble.

"What could trouble the son of the king of the gods?" Ah'muf whispered.

Elisa did not want to know. She had seen too much she once thought impossible. Whether it was the devastation of her village as a child or the violence of battle between the Three on Crimeat, the bounty hunter shuddered at the thought of her bloody protector knowing fear.

"Some questions are best unanswered, desert dweller," Sorrow called over his shoulder. "There are fouler creatures in the false night than I."

Disturbed by Sorrow's heightened sense of hearing, Elisa decided to choose her words carefully for the duration of their time together. The dying branch of a scrub tree brushed against her leg. "Sorrow, this is no time for games. If the Forsaken Path is as dangerous as you claim, we have every right to know what awaits."

"You have me," he replied. "For now."

"What do you mean for now?" she demanded, their earlier conversations forgotten amongst the unveiling of new horrors.

The Bloody Man kept walking. His crimson footprints were obscene in the ash. "I cannot follow you through the first portal. I tried to pass through once and was nearly killed for my effort. It is not an event I wish to do twice."

An eerie call echoed across the plains. A cross between roar and howl, it chilled the humans. Boulders the size of small houses cascaded down the mountainside to their right. Artificial thunder pounded the ground and air. Elisa struggled not to scream. *Madness. This realm in madness made real. We will not survive this.*

She ran her tongue across the roof of her mouth as realization struck. "You are leaving us alone. Here? In this land of dread."

"You are the Paladin," he said with a shrug. "What more can I do for you than you for me?"

"You are a god!" Ah'muf exclaimed. "How can one such as you know fear?"

Sorrow's shoulders drooped for a stride only before resuming his march. "We all bear secrets. Perhaps one day, should we meet again, I will tell you ancient truths that will tear your notion of the universe apart. First you must find the First Paladin and retrieve the item."

"What item?" Elisa asked, her mind lingering on his previous comment. "You remain elusive with your answers, Sorrow."

Frustration boiled. She had grown used to his stigmatic approach to conversation. The Bloody Man spoke in broken riddles and a combination of confusion and wisdom. She deemed him either insane from centuries of isolation or cunning beyond measure.

"Our kind is not much different. We are both children of misunderstanding. The First Paladin guards the *Grimfurvor*. It is a weapon capable of killing my brother. One of the few left remaining from our final days," Sorrow said. "I hid it while my kind slaughtered each other at Occanum."

"Why have you not used this weapon before? Why wait until the universe tears itself apart?" she asked.

Suspicions overrode her frustration, leaving Elisa mired in new doubt. The Three were true enemies of humanity. How she found herself tied to his weave was beyond her ability to comprehend. She wondered how life might have turned out had he not slaughtered everyone she ever knew and loved. Hindsight being moot, Elisa continued in his footsteps.

Sorrow paused. His face twisted in quiet debate. "Elisa, I do not know why it was that I chose you to bear this burden, but it was not out of charity. Any weapon that can kill my brother will also be my undoing in the wrong hands. Find the weapon and take it to my brother Tannus."

Crossing her arms, she asked, "What is to keep me from killing you before, or after?"

"An act of faith on my part," he said. "Perhaps it is best for your species that we are all removed from reality. I often wonder what death will be like. I certainly deserve it."

"You're not getting off that easy," she answered swiftly. "Judgment will come to you in due course, but we must stop your brother first. How will I know this *Grimfurvor*? Is it a rifle, a sword? What?"

"That is a question more difficult to answer. *Grimfurvor* is a weapon of unparalleled majesty, crafted by witches and warlocks using the primordial energy created when time began. It does not bear singular shape, rather molds to fit the holder. *Grimfurvor* was a spear when last I looked upon it."

Ah'muf made a sign of blessing and kissed the edge of his index finger before spitting. "We are doomed."

"All in due course, desert dweller. This task is not suited for you. That much is clear to me. I will take you back to your realm," Sorrow offered.

"He stays with me," Elisa shook her head. "I … I might have need of him."

Sorrow blinked twice. "You are the Paladin. This task is appointed for you alone. He is a mere hindrance to success."

"He stays with me."

The Bloody Man swept his gaze from the fire consuming her visage, to the meekness of barely disguised terror of his. The dichotomy interested him, for he often felt pulled in opposite directions without resolution. Hers was an empty life designed for specific purpose only he knew. He cried the day he was confronted with killing her family. A single tear that continued to ripple across space and time as empires crumbled; a species stood on the brink of extinction should his brother succeed. Sorrow had not cried since. Such was the power of portent.

"Very well, though I do not offer promise of protection from all that dwell within this realm," Sorrow said. Thought bereft of emotion, his words delivered the subtle promise of hope. "We must hurry. The portal is not far and time is desperately short. Come. We must not stop again. Our hunters press ever closer."

He took off without waiting to see if they followed.

"Farisi, are you certain? I do not wish to be a burden," Ah'muf asked. The trepidation in his voice rattled her resolve.

"Yes, Ah'muf. I do not wish to do this without you," she laid a calming hand on his shoulder. *Besides, I need you. You may not realize it, but I do, and I am terrified to admit it.* "Come on, he's not waiting for us."

They hurried on, pushed to the edge of exhaustion. Their packs dug into shoulders, cutting off blood flow and wearing down the longer they marched. Elisa felt her hands swell as a result. Her weapon grew heavy but she refused to sling it and leave them defenseless with an unknown foe pursuing them. Sweat beaded her brow, though there was little warmth to be found in this realm.

A storm rippled across the sky. Dark clouds smelling of brimstone roiled in an endless clash. Brilliant flares of lighting slashed the darkness, charging the air. Elisa quickened her pace. The mountains were close. Her thoughts raced over a myriad of concerns, most of which centering on Ah'muf's lack of fighting skills. Far from an honest man, he was best suited for subversive work, picking pockets and talking from the corners of his mouth. She owed him her life. Good for a quick stab of his dagger when the opponent was distracted, Ah'muf managed to find a special place in her heart. That alone excited her with fear.

Elisa's reasons for keeping him by her side were purely selfish. She could complete Sorrow's task alone, but the prospect of his companionship to keep her from barreling into a pocket of imagination that did not belong in her mind calmed her. Aside from what she determined was growing affection, Ah'muf reminded her how fragile life could be.

"There! The portal lies just ahead," Sorrow called over his shoulder.

He pointed toward the mountains, now looming high overhead, to where a pale light shimmered into the dusk sky. A rainbow of drowned colors flickered with the wind. Greens and blues collided with purples and umbers. Emboldened by nearing the completion of his part of their quest, Sorrow broke into a grin. He readied to explain more when slight vibrations in the ash and sand drew his attention.

The Bloody Man knelt and placed his palm on the ground. Vibrations roared in his mind, transforming into raw hatred. His eyes widened. They were out of time. "Go! To the portal. I have a guide waiting for you. He will deliver you to the First Paladin."

"What about you? Why are you staying?" she asked and clutched her rifle tighter.

Sorrow jerked upright to his full twelve-foot height. "Our enemy is upon us. It is a foe you cannot fight. Hurry, else this has all been for naught and your kind will suffer the same fate as mine."

"We can help," Elisa insisted.

"Farisi, please!"

Sorrow knelt again, leveling his face with hers for the first time. "Elisa, you must trust me. I admire your courage, but against what comes, it will falter and fade. There are some nightmares in this universe that humans are incapable of understanding. These monsters that stalk us will devour your souls as they flense your bodies alive. I will not have that weight on my conscience. Please, go and stop my brother from destroying the universe.

"I have come to enjoy your kind, though for reasons vastly different than you might imagine. It has been a pleasure coming to know you," Sorrow explained.

Doubting his sincerity but knowing when there was a fight beyond her, Elisa relented. "Very well. I will get the *Grimfurvor* and deliver it to Tannus. Will we meet again?"

"Our fates are twined. We shall meet, if only for a time. Look for me at the final battle."

"Farisi, we must hurry. I see shapes in the distance," Ah'muf's voice quaked with fear.

She strained against his urgent tugging. The need for conviction arose, threatening to choke her into immobility. The Bloody Man was a part of her life almost as long as she remembered and the prospect of losing him now, without answers or closure, frightened her.

"Sorrow," she called.

"Go, child. It was a cruel twist of fate that threw you in my path, and for that I apologize."

Voice quaking, Ah'muf pointed to the wall of nightmares approaching. "Look!"

Elisa's gaze slid past the Bloody Man and she bore witness to creatures that were never meant to exist. Hulking monstrosities dwarfing Sorrow, they oozed and slid through the darkness. A shapeless blob with seven mouths, each filled with thousands of razor-sharp teeth growled hungrily, as it surged forward. Taller, wider monsters marched beside it. A collection of every child's twisted visions of what hid under the bed. Acid and puss bled from a million lesions. Smoke rose from each footprint. She knew this would be the end of the only constant she ever knew.

"Go! Now, else all is lost," Sorrow shouted above the cacophony of demonic wails.

His right hand flicked out and a giant sword of burning flames appeared. Wreathed in blue fire, the blade was ancient. Wicked. Sorrow charged into the monsters without regard, each desperate act buying time for Elisa to reach the portal and escape. A creature with desiccated flesh slapped the others aside and roared in challenge. Her last glimpse was one of corpses draped over the creature. Each face twisted in endless pain as they screamed without voice. She grabbed Ah'muf and ran.

Battle sounds haunted their footsteps. Unimaginable sounds threatened to burst their eardrums. Raw vitriol pulsed off the monsters in waves, robbing Elisa and Ah'muf of what little strength remained. Sorrow bellowed in response, his power blazing hotly through the unnatural light. A litany of forgotten curses rolled off his tongue with each blow, given and received. Wincing at the sound of flesh tearing, Elisa knew the Bloody Man was not going to survive.

They rounded the corner, where she paused to pay tribute. Bodies melted together. The blazing sword was soon smothered, as Sorrow was buried beneath an unstoppable tide of filth and anguish. Her heart cried out, though she did not know why. Then he was gone. Lost to sight. She raised her rifle and took aim. Doubtful her ammunition capable of stopping monsters Sorrow could not, she owed it to him to at least try.

"Farisi, the portal is close. We must not delay," Ah'muf urged. His voice conveyed the immediacy of their situation. Death stalking them, he longed for a return to his beloved deserts and an end to this cyclical nightmare. "I don't wish to die here. To those … things."

She knew he was right. Death was assured should she stand her ground. Nothing in her meager arsenal was strong enough to quench the original hatred. Elisa lowered her rifle. Her body tensed at the unbridled howl of glee. She snapped around and saw a monster pointing at them. From under its shadows, a pack of creatures burst forth. They ran on six legs and reminded her of an unnatural combination of horse and dog. Fire fell from their backs as they ran.

Elisa and Ah'muf ran as fast as their weary legs could stand. Each step carried them closer to the perceived safety of the portal. Jagged stones of obsidian jutted up at random, so many broken teeth to block their way. Slowed, the pair wound through the maze, ever drawing nearer the portal. Wet sucking sounds tracked their steps. Elisa looked down, for the ground was dry. She found pools of blood trailing behind them. The Forsaken Path was aptly named.

She reached the portal first and readied to fight. The scrabble of claws and venom striking stones neared. Death was but moments away. "Get in there, Ah'muf. I'm right behind you."

"In there? Are you mad?" he shouted over the rising screams echoing off the canyon walls. "Where does it lead?"

Now, you want to question? Sorry, my friend. This isn't the time. "Who cares. We die if we stay here."

Showing an uncharacteristic determination, the desert dweller stood his ground. "I will not go without you."

The first of the dog creatures emerged. Ten eyes in twin rows of five ran diagonally up each cheek. Serpentine tongues flickered, tasting them on the air. Elisa knew true fear for the first time. Eyes wide in dread, she barreled into Ah'muf and knocked them into the column of light. She swore she felt the grasp of claws reaching for her back as the portal claimed them. Lightning clashed and she knew no more.

They ran. Tireless. Impatient. The seven were all that remained of their tribe. Chosen warriors meant to deliver the promise of salvation during the bleakest moments. Spears rattled in their grasps with each footstep. Small pelts circled their waists. Trophies from youth long forgotten. Their quest dominated all, leaving the past unremembered. Withered faces locked on the horizon. Somewhere in both distance and future, awaited the end of their journey. A time of great trial with one outcome.

Sauwgon Hil led. His pace strong. His strength limitless. Born from a primitive tribe at the dawning of time, he rose to become the eldest shaman and a being of hidden power. With the sacrifice of the previous elder, it fell to him to finish their sole purpose for being. Generations failed, doomed to obscurity. Their names were never mentioned. Their stories left untold. Only the prize offered immortality. And only one of them would live to see it.

He knew this. They all did. Immortality was meant to be cherished. Revered among those chosen few who passed the trials. Sauwgon Hil chose his warriors after much deliberation. Tribal elders whispered his lack of strength, a testing of mettle sure to shatter at the first trial. He defied them and now seven remained. His seven. Men vowed to stand by his side until the fire bled from his eyes and crows came to feast upon his flesh. Did they know their deaths were inevitable? He wondered.

"There. Ahead are the caverns."

Sauwgon Hil gestured and his brothers slowed their pace to admire the first trial. Each studied the legends. A map of impossible features drawing them deeper into realms lacking understanding. His heart thundered with anticipation.

"Come. We must hurry."

They ran without words. What was there to say? Each was sworn to the eventual outcome. They were promised a long future of limitless possibility. A rising from the ashes of their old villages and endless days of hunting for their next meals. Sauwgon Hil knew their truth, however, and it was grim. They fled home for the promise of escaping their sins. A thousand dead lay in their wake. Each the victim of deeds best left unsaid.

The seven gained the lower foothills and fanned out in search of an entrance into the mountain heart. Sauwgon Hil was the first to discover the golden path leading deep into the earth. Statues of forgotten warriors in pristine armor, bearing unknown weapons, lined the way. Each was carved from limestone. Sauwgon Hil felt insignificant under their judgmental stares. Summoning the wealth of his courage, he led the seven deeper underground.

Torches flickered to life, blazing a trail ever a handful of paces ahead of them. Cobwebs coated the corners, running along the ceiling. Sauwgon Hil spied small skeletons among the webs, victims to the power of hunger. Ignoring them, he led his chosen on. How deep they went was unknown. How long they walked, the same. Their moccasins scuffed along the clay floor, the only betrayal of their passing.

The torches flickered and extinguished, leaving the chosen mired in darkness. Sauwgon Hil recognized it for the beginning and the end. A sensation they all must face. All but one. He stepped into the cavern and awaited judgment. When the last of his seven joined him, a violent blue light awakened. Blinded, they shielded their eyes and readied spears. Hairs on their arms and necks rose. Instincts screamed of ambush.

Sauwgon Hil knew better. The first trial had begun. Refracted light echoed off seven giant shapes circling the cavern. The shaman stared in amazement as the massive shapes took form. Crystalline, each was a host of endless prisms. Squinting, he witnessed the dark figures contained within each. Seven creatures for seven questers. He did not believe in coincidence, accepting the figures for what they were.

The ground trembled. Stone and crystal broke from the ceiling to strike the cavern floor. Sulfuric fumes wafted from freshly created holes. They had entered the heart of a volcano. Sauwgon Hil's gaze remained locked on the nearest creature. Ignoring the disaster unfolding around him, he sought any discerning feature. Something to provide knowledge of what they faced.

The first crystal cracked, spilling viscous fluids. The figure within stirred. His chosen wailed their fears, embarrassing Sauwgon Hil. The shaman leveled his spear and slowly stepped back. Cracks grew and shattered the tomb. Instead of dropping, the creature spread alabaster wings and hovered a meter off the ground. Grinning, Sauwgon Hil accepted the omen.

"I will fight this terror."

He did not glance at Ferri Juy. The youngest of his chosen, Ferri had the most to prove, despite being loyal to a fault. Sauwgon Hil stepped aside and let the youth attack. There was little else to do. Failure was inevitable, for no man in their history had defeated a dragon. His tail curled around his calf and he watched.

Ferri let out a fearsome roar and attacked. The clumps of hair on his back bounced wildly with each step. The remaining six stayed in place, spears lowered. Ferri took three strides and leapt. The dragon opened its eyes and fixed on him. Rows of jagged teeth lined its mouth, open in anticipation of a meal. Ferri cast his spear, the weapon hummed through the air and struck the dragon below the jaw. Blood fountained. The chosen roared.

Ferri reached for the curved bone sword at his hip and continued to attack. He slipped past claws and struck again and again. Scales chipped away but he could not penetrate the dragon's hide. Ferri attacked until strength betrayed him. His muscles ached, arms sagging under the weight of the bone.

Having had enough, the dragon hatchling ripped the spear from its throat and lifted to the cavern ceiling. Ferri stood below, eager to continue his path of glory. Unimpressed, the dragon tucked its wings and dove. The tiny man met the challenge fearlessly and was swallowed whole for it. Angered at being disturbed, the dragon wheeled about and studied those remaining. The one harboring the most power needed to die first.

Sauwgon Hil expected this and dropped into a crouch. He set his spear down and drew a twisted athame of metal that fell from the skies. Imbued with magics he failed to understand, it filled him with pulsing energy. The shaman held his ground as the dragon neared. Whispering incantations now forgotten, Sauwgon Hil unleashed his full power.

The dragon imploded, collapsing into a brilliant flash of ruby lights. The chosen were thrown from their feet, all but Sauwgon Hil. He alone withstood the eldritch energies unleashed in the cavern and was rewarded for it. A jewel the size of his palm rested at his feet. Marveled, the shaman reached for it. The jewel was cool despite the fumes wafting off it.

"Shaman, have we succeeded?"

Sauwgon Hil's grin exposed his tusks. "Our first task is complete. Ferri Juy paid for it with his life. His name shall now be forgotten."

The others bowed obediently. Task complete, Ferri no longer existed. The past was mired in darkness from which there was no return. His essence was returned to the fabric of the universe. Satisfied the first test was complete, Sauwgon Hil gestured them on with the wave of his spear. The hunt was just begun.

Pain exploded behind her eyes. Gasping, Elisa jerked up and blindly reached for a weapon. The air in her lungs. Blood trickled from her nose. The pounding in her head promised to rip her skull apart. Nausea bubbled up and she emptied her stomach on the ash covered ground. Blinking away the tears, Elisa searched for the monsters. Cold silence met her determination. She was alone.

"A… Ah'muf?" she croaked. The words, despite being spoken softly, hammered deep within her mind. Each syllable a minor anguish.

A breeze pushed through, covering her in a light coat of bright gray ash. Sputtering to clear her mouth, Elisa pushed herself to her feet. Weak knees wobbled, threatening to cast her back to the ground. Using her rifle as a walking stick, Elisa planted the butt on the ground for stability and surveyed her surroundings. The immediate area was slightly less bleak, though far from offering a promise of improvement. Rolling hills stretched beyond her line of sight. Deadened trees peppered the landscape, some stretching hundreds of feet into the sky. She thought she spied the vague light of a second portal far in the distance.

"Farisi!"

Elisa snapped at the sound of Ah'muf's voice. Frantic moments passed before she spotted his outstretched hand nearby. The desert dweller was partially buried beneath a mound of ash and sludge, pinning him to the ground. Hobbling to him, she knelt and pulled. He came free with a disgusting sucking sound on the third attempt. Both travelers collapsed.

"I do not care for this place, farisi," Ah'muf complained after using half his canteen to rinse the foulness from his mouth.

"Bastard could have warned us," she growled. "I think I saw our next destination."

Ah'muf sat up and got his first look at their situation. Hope plummeted and his heart grew heavy. "We are alone."

Realization crawled into her consciousness. Sorrow guided her from reality through the opening stages of the Forsaken Path, only to fall beneath the furor of unimaginable creatures. The possibility of him being gone, forever, awakened stark premonitions for the future. Despair threatened, edging closer to subsuming them both.

"He died defending us, giving us the time to complete our task and right old wrongs," she said after a moment. "We must not let that sacrifice go to waste."

"How are we supposed to contend with this?" he gestured wildly to the landscape. "This is a fell realm we intrude upon. It wants us dead. The Bloody Man was a god. We are mere mortals."

"Faith, Ah'muf. We must have faith," she replied. Her words mirrored Sorrow's sentiment before their parting. "Goti Tai awaits and with it, the First Paladin and his super weapon. We must trust to each other to see us through." *I only hope it will be enough.*

She debated scolding him for his persistent recycling of the same point of view. The repetition of his complaining started wearing on her already frayed nerves. Trying times demanded patience, and she was running out. Elisa collected her gear and took a long pull from her canteen. The tepid water felt good running down the back of her throat, reminding her how dehydrated she was from their flight. A rumbling stomach agreed.

"We need to keep moving," she said. Unwilling to risk being caught by the nightmares that killed Sorrow, Elisa recapped her canteen and readied to march.

"Not a place to wander alone, not even for you, Paladin."

She whirled at the sound of a new voice, rifle slipping off her shoulder and into her hands in a rehearsed maneuver. The tip of her index finger touched the trigger. The cool feel of steel reassuring as she aimed. Ah'muf shuffled behind her, suddenly insignificant without a weapon with distance stopping power. She ignored him and focused on her target.

Emerging from a cloud of haze, the figure halted several meters away. Elisa could not make out any distinguishing features and her hackles rose.

"Come no closer," she warned.

"Is that any way to treat an old friend?"

Confused, she asked, "Show yourself. I don't know you."

"Ah, but you do. What history we shared, Elisa. Through captivity and battles witnessed by titans not meant to live in our times."

"Show yourself, last warning," she said.

The figure blurred faster until stabilizing. Facial features smoothed into definition and Elisa was stunned. Haggard, swathed in crimson robes verging on ruin, the old man stared back with a wry grin. Heavy lines echoed around his eyes, casting darkness on his face. Dark spots covered his exposed flesh. Yet, when she looked closer, Elisa thought she could see through him.

"You … you're dead," she uttered.

He nodded. "Dead, but still needed, it seems. Hello, Elisa."

"Farisi, who is this man?" Ah'muf squeaked from over her shoulder.

"Mollock Bolle. The Prophet."

"Death is but a door to a new reality," the old man confirmed. "We are all meant to continue serving. Those of us chosen, that is. A fell casting of fate, is it not?"

Snorting, Elisa clicked the safety and slung her rifle. Whatever else he may be, Mollock Bolle was no threat to either of them. "Don't get me started. I've been intertwined with the Bloody Man since childhood. It is a foul game I feel might have run its course."

"What do you mean?" Mollock asked.

"I watched him fall under the assault of … monsters before we passed through the portal," Elisa explained. The memory was still too raw, too real to accept. "We have become stranded amidst a grave quest."

"Goti Tai," Mollock said.

"How did you know that?" she snapped; instincts whispered caution. *How do I know it is truly you, Mollock? The last I heard was you died on An'kuruku. Is your shade a trick by my foes to lead me astray?*

Studying him for signs of betrayal, Elisa struggled to remember as much of the man as she could. Half cracked when they met in the Ugri prison cave, he was already to the point of raving about the great secret of the gods. One with the potential of destroying the foundations of the universe. She knew he stumbled upon something no mortal was meant to find. *No wonder the bastard went mad before the end. Some truths are too hard to accept.*

Mollock remained still. His patience acquiescence to her. Lifeless eyes stared back, urging her to quest deeper, into what remained of the wells of his soul. Folding his hands within the frayed ends of his robes, the Prophet waited for her to finish her deliberations before answering.

"I am dead," he said in a failed attempt at levity. "The Bloody Man sent me to guide you through the Forsaken Path. I have been waiting a long time."

"But you only died less than a year ago," she reasoned.

His shrug did little to reassure her. "Time has different meaning in the realm of the dead. For you, it was days. For me? It has been an eon. But none of that matters now. You are here. We must continue."

She paused to look at Ah'muf, silently guessing where his desires sat, before answering. "How far is it to this city?"

"By portals? Some days, perhaps months. As I said, time moves differently here. We cannot expect normalcy on our trek," Mollock replied.

Elisa frowned at the shade. "Even in death you lack the means to be comforting."

"This is not a pleasant time, and mine is limited. I must perform this final task before being admitted to the next realm. Penance must be delivered."

His words bore finality that robbed her of strength. The possibility of enduring a lifetime of struggle, only to find another, equally grueling chore awaiting the moment she closed her eyes for the last time, threatened to steal her resolve. *Ah'muf had the right of it. This is a fell realm humans aren't meant to understand.*

"Can those monsters that attacked Sorrow follow us here?" she asked.

Mollock's hooded gaze twisted back to where the portal lights had been. "I do not know, nor do I suggest waiting to discover. We must move."

"Lead on," she said with slight head gesture.

Bounty hunter robbed of a normal life, desert dweller far from the aridity of his home, and the shade of a man consigned to the grave long ago, the unlikely trio hurried on toward the next menhir and the portal beyond.

High orbit of planet Wexanos.

"Admiral, we have finishing taking on supplies. The fleet is readying to deploy," Captain Samuel said as he halted beside his long-time commanding officer and friend.

Rear Admiral Falchi continued staring off into space. War awaited among the stars, one he was ill prepared to fight. A ragtag fleet of once proud ships of the line drifted behind his line of sight, a sore reminder of how much Nye's civil war had already cost. Hundreds of crew no longer answered muster. Their lives lost to a cause half the population failed to believe in. he often wondered if he was on the right side of the galactic conflict, and even after years of fighting, had yet to discover the answer.

Lines tugged the corners of his mouth down. Bags surrounded his eyes. Fresh patches of gray hair sprouted over his head, bleeding into the moustache he recently started growing. Shoulders sagged from exhaustion. Even in the friendly ports above Wexanos, he failed to find calm. Peace, he decided, was the universal lie.

"Very well, Captain. Have all personnel departed planet side?" he asked. An endless stream of numbers clogged his mind. Guards, ammunition, fuel, rations. Cutoff from the resources of Vau Prime and Prekhauten Command, Falchi was fighting more than just his former colleagues.

"The last flights of Marines are lifting off now, sir," Samuel reported. A half step behind Falchi, he could not conceal the pain he felt from seeing his friend beaten down.

"What of Matthias's platoon?"

Samuel checked his datapad. "First to board."

Were they now? Interesting. If anyone has earned the right to sit this one out, it should be them. "Is Sergeant Asom ready?"

"The ship's Marine contingent is formed up in the main hangar bay, as are the regular Guard units we are shuttling to Mannus Prime, sir. Colors have been presented," Samuel said.

Falchi stiffened, an old pride resurfacing. He adjusted the bottom of his jacket and checked his ribbons through the viewport reflection. "A shame to keep him waiting. Let's go officially promote him before the Marines decide they have better things to do."

Admiral and Captain started the long journey through the belly of their metal beast to recognize a man overdue, though he was quietly promoted several months prior without official ceremony. It was one of the few bright spots of their day capable of stealing their attention from the approaching storm.

EIGHT

3215 A.G. (After gods), the Great Library, planet Wexanos.

"Are you certain this is the correct course of action?" Fistel asked.

Tannus admired the Chief Librarian for his willingness to question. Too few of the followers he acquired over time showed such temerity in the face of what most considered a god. The thought sparked lament, forcing Tannus to abandon his nightly vigil. He turned to regard his closest confidant and voice of reason in an otherwise maddening time. Towering over the yellow robed man, his presence was one of power. Strength. Failure.

Too long, Tannus allowed his brother to subvert the humanity's minds. Time and again, the trio of brothers edged the universe closer to annihilation. An unbeliever of destiny, fate, or any other mortal construct intended to explain their origins, Tannus paused often to wonder if he was wrong. Perhaps there was some cosmic force bent on destroying all life. His people once suffered from similar pains, resulting in genocide. Several lifetimes of effort to prevent humanity from achieving a similar demise stemmed the tide but did little to extinguish the threat.

"I've made a great many decisions that turned out to be anything but," Tannus replied with a grim smile. "Life seldom goes the way we plan, Fistel. Right or wrong, this is the only course offering the remotest chance of victory."

Fistel shook his head. "But to deploy so much of the military assets assembled, we risk being exposed to your brother, or worse."

"Wexanos is a hidden world, my friend. I went to great pains to ensure there was no record in the human archives," he explained. "This is perhaps the most secure location in the entire universe."

"That was before the Inquisitor General started his civil war," the librarian added.

"True, but his vision is limited. With my brother pulling his strings and a hundred wars breaking out across the stars, there is little chance for him to turn his attentions here. Especially with our offensive about to take place on Mannus Prime." His hands slipped behind his back in a rehearsed move, as he started to walk to the landing pads.

"What bothers me more is Tolde Breed leaving with the Blood Witches," Tannus admitted. "Dark forces are at play. We risk losing the war should he fall."

"My lord, he has already fallen once," Fistel reminded.

Not even the favored son of the king of the gods fully understood the magic behind Tolde's resurrection and transference to a new body. Ruma Zzein played her hand close to the chest in this matter, leaving him shunned. Their longstanding relationship held secrets he seldom pried into. Were it not for the warnings voiced by Fistel and the alarm growing in his heart, Tannus might have been willing to overlook this matter as well. His faith in the oracle was unprecedented. In most cases.

"I do not profess to understand what happened, Fistel, only that it was necessary. Finding the weapon capable of stopping Amongeratix is critical, but I truly believe Tolde is the man to wield it when the time comes. His is the most precious of all souls at the moment."

"Why, then, the doubt?" Fistel asked, hurrying his stride to maintain pace.

"It is not Tolde I doubt, nor is it the oracle. It is the secret kept deep within the comet that troubles me," his voice dropped low.

"There is no more secure location in the universe than in their abbey," Fistel wasn't sure who he was reassuring. "Will the Order continue assisting our efforts to find the artifact?"

"I believe so. Agents are deploying to known locations where we have allies," Tannus said. "Not that one of their witches can blend in."

"They do tend to present a signature appearance," Fistel chuckled. "Reports have come in from Crimeat that the Lady Von has gone to ground on her homeworld. Captain August is deploying teams to the surface to root her out and bring her here."

"I sense a 'but'," Tannus said.

"Pinning her down has proven problematic since the disaster at Kharsis. Should she reach your brother or *Behemoth*…"

Tannus paused and held up a hand. "I know, we will be looking at a disaster of unmitigated proportions. I know this, Fistel. We must trust that Captain August and her pirate co-conspirator are up to the challenge in time to prevent Amongeratix from reaching *Behemoth*.

Thinking of it, there is not much to have hope for at the moment, is there?"

"We have been through worse, my lord," Fistel replied.

"Perhaps," Tannus answered, his mind drifting back to battles long past. "But those were different times. This war is going to be the end of everything we know, Fistel. All of it. Even should we manage to pull out victory, the universe will be reshaped into a new entity."

"All our pieces are in motion. What else is there for us to do?" Fistel asked.

Tannus wished there were easy answers. Experience taught otherwise. No matter how many times they clashed, using various means, neither brother discovered the secret to defeating the other. Total victory seemed unobtainable. *Why then does this feel final? Have we at last reached the expiration of conflict? If so, what awaits the final stroke? Shall I know peace after countless centuries or is darkness my ultimate reward*?

"I honestly don't know," he said.

The finality of his tone chilled the librarian. "My lord, I have had the privilege of serving you for far longer than I deserve and I have never heard you speak so. That troubles me more than you know."

"It troubles us both, old friend." Tannus replaced his hands behind his back. "I must consult with my mother. Perhaps she will provide the guidance we seek."

Fistel stayed in place, watching his master stride down a darkening hall as the sun dipped behind the far hills. He found the scene ominous. An ill omen beckoning them to ruin's edge. Fistel whispered a prayer and went about his duties. Every asset they had was in play, requiring his total concentration. A lesser man might have balked, but Fistel had trained for this his entire life. One hundred and seventeen years of service to Tannus taught him one lesson: no matter how prepared the battle plans, they always devolved into raw chaos the moment the first shot was fired.

He had work to do.

Tannus wound down twisting staircases of marble and granite bereft of decoration or grandeur. The heart of Wexanos was buried over a kilometer beneath the surface. A private shrine

Tannus kept hidden from all but his closest confidants. Torches lit the path, forcing darkness back as the lord of Wexanos hastened his step. The weight of eternity bore him down, threatening to break his will when the universe needed him most. It was with troubled heart he reached the bottom floor and opened the massive double doors of oak and birch.

Automatons awakened from their slumber. Two rows of ten foot tall machines crafted in human form and armed with several weapon systems powerful enough to kill a god hummed to life. The red glow of their optic sensors screamed danger as the automatons locked on Tannus. A gift from his brother before madness made him flense his flesh, they defended what Tannus considered the most precious gift in the universe.

"Theta seven-seven," he ordered.

The machines stood down, returning to their docking ports. Tannus admired their design. Each was the equivalent of an entire platoon of human infantry without the mundane needs of rest, food, or water. He once sought to have Sorrow create a small army, if for no other reason than to alleviate the need to involve humans in his endless war with Amongeratix. Those were different times.

Banks of computer screens blinked to life. One wall of the cavern-like chamber was covered in screens streaming data. Tannus scanned them, searching for irregularities more than actual information. Satisfied nothing was amiss, he turned his attention to the giant stasis pod dominating the center of the chamber. Easily long enough for three humans to fit comfortably, the pod buzzed and hummed with lifesaving technologies no other pod contained.

He, Sorrow, and Paradise Tear worked tirelessly on their creation, desperate to save as many of their people as they could before the Armageddon at Occanum. Hundreds of his kind were resting, sleeping for the last three thousand years beneath the very noses of the men and women proclaiming adoration in their names. Tannus snorted. The fools. Mankind had ever been weak in their need for belief in higher powers. They were never satisfied with accepting what they were, and there was no external source of power or wisdom floating among the cosmos. Not one to downplay the Conclave's rigid belief structure, he knew better.

Tannus halted before the frosted viewport and peered within. His mother's face was calm, more serene than it had been in life. She was the only one with the strength capable of keeping the brothers from tearing each other apart. Even when Tannus dared question his father before the entire court, resulting in the banishment of all three, did she turn her love and affection from him. She was his strength. A rock mooring the wayward design of his soul.

His father was gone, turned to dust at the final battle. His uncle was a prisoner of the Blood Witches, destined to travel the stars without voice or intent. Only she remained. The one constant he needed. If only he had not been forced to place her in stasis with the others. Another curse Amongeratix laid among their family. Had he not tried to assassinate her, their conflict might have ended long ago. Peace could reign unopposed, save for the wicked desires lurking in the darkest hearts of men. He sighed, for it was naught but a dream.

"Hello, mother," he said, his voice soft, yet laden with concern. "I wish you were awake to give voice to wisdom. These have become trying times far worse than any our people endured during the madness."

He stared at the smooth lines of her face, angled to perfection no sculptor achieved. No lines choked the corners of her eyes. No age spots decorated her face or the hands clasped over her stomach. She gave the appearance of death. Tannus wondered if she dreamed. If any of them did. They sacrificed their lives for survival's sake, trading laughter and talking within the frozen confines of nothingness. Though he was one of the architects, he bore no desire to share a similar fate. Better he be killed on some forgotten world, than endure eternity like this.

"Can you read my thoughts? Does my voice soothe you? Provide comfort to your dreams? I was never given a choice, and for that I shall never forgive myself. I failed you. Failed you all," he forced the air from his lungs, exasperated by the confession. "Would that I hadn't confronted father that way."

The burden of knowing the war was his fault, the direct result of questions never meant to be asked, often threatened to rob him of strength. Tannus was pragmatic, evaluating each situation uniquely, except for this one. His chastisement carried down through the generations until the scalding in his mind drove him to insanity's brink.

"I am sorry for everything." Tears crept into his voice. "But that changes nothing. My brother is advancing his campaign to achieve humanity's final extinction. I am countering with all I have, yet I feel he has the upper hand this time. There is a finality to this war, mother. I fear none of us will come out unscathed."

He explained the rise of *Behemoth*, the human campaigns, and his quest to find the artifact capable of destroying planets. Tannus omitted Sorrow's efforts, for he knew little of his reclusive brother. That Elisa and Ah'muf were gone, seemingly lost to the universe, was a good sign, though the chances of success were diminished with the death of the Paladin.

The confession felt good, relieving him of immense pressure. Though she had never responded, Tannus chose to believe his mother heard every word. It was the one luxury he kept private. Finished, he placed a loving hand on the viewport, wincing at the cold seeping into his flesh.

"I shall return soon, mother. After I stop Amongeratix from reaching his accursed ship. Perhaps then I can corner him into a position to broker for peace," Tannus hoped. "Do not think less of me, should I fail this time. It is a terrible weight I bear and I seldom feel I am up to the task. War does not become me, nor should it ever. Goodbye mother."

A burst of renewed confidence coursing through him, Tannus began the long climb to the surface. And the war raging on a hundred worlds. Once again it was time to command armies and hopefully, end the silent war that had raged for millennia. Hope was all he had, and he clung to it for dear life.

The *Sayther*, exiting orbit of the Wexanos System.

Uncomfortable was an understatement. The trader ship was far from efficient. Systems leaked fluids, vented precious oxygen, and inspired cold dread as it pulled away from Wexanos's gravity fields. Dim corridors smelled of oils and grease. More than once, he struck his forehead on low running pipes and cables. Hatch doors offered a battered appearance, forcing the passenger to debate how Ishis Gul had come into possession of it. The main drives groaned as power was flushed through them and Matthias swore the ship was going to tear itself apart.

It was a far cry from the pristine condition Prekhauten ships of the line were maintained in, though Matthias found it disconcertingly practical for how it was used. The *Sayther* roared into space, reaching the jump point much slower than the former Guard would have liked. Moments later, it blasted through space, a blur lost amidst a wink.

"Are you sure this boat is going to hold together?" Matthias asked once Wexanos was far behind them.

Ishis Gul laughed, a disturbing nasal sound inspired by his hawk nose. "She may not be attractive, but she has yet to fail me, Matthias."

He balked at the intonation of yet. "Uh huh. How long before we reach our destination?"

After checking the instrument panel above him, Ishis replied, "Many more hours, I am afraid. Do not worry, Matthias. We should make it in one piece. We must. I have lost the escape pods long ago!"

"You know you're mad," Matthias accused.

"Aren't we all?"

Casting an accusatory side glance, Matthias settled back into the torn fabric of his chair and watched the infinity of space slip by. No matter how many times he sat in the cockpit, space continued to amaze him. Decades of service, many spent shipboard, showed him that no two views were ever the same. Space was infinite. A glory too few witnessed, in his opinion. Colorful nebulas, gas clouds, dying stars, and more created a visionary expanse powerful enough to make a man feel insignificant. Out here, he decided, a man might get lost forever.

Like many, he once dreamed of ending his time in uniform and using his savings to travel the stars. Seven hundred occupied worlds offered unlimited possibilities. Also, like many, the realities of life complicated matters to the point his dreams were rendered inconsequential. This was as close as he was going to get. Leastwise until the war ended and some semblance of normalcy returned.

Matthias was tired of war. Tired of seeing comrades fall on worlds he had never heard of before deploying. The mental strain subsumed the human aspect of his nature. He grew cold, detached from his emotions. Matthias often laughed at situations or comments those unassociated with military life found horrifying. He rationed it was his way of coping. Of keeping the darkness from creeping in to steal his soul.

Every combat veteran underwent something similar. Exposed to atrocities and the very worst man could do to each other, it was small wonder more veterans didn't snap. Pushing those memories away and ignoring them was the best a modern soldier could do to maintain sanity in an otherwise insane universe. Matthias suspected it had always been so. How else could society evolve beyond the rough edges? He secretly envied those who had never faced the hell of combat.

"We are entering the Ganid System. Prepare for deceleration," Ishis announced.

Stirred, Matthias looked at the overhead chrono. "What happened?"

"Happened? Nothing. You fell asleep, which I must say made for a boring flight," the smuggler replied.

Asleep? Damn, I didn't realize I was tired. Matthias rechecked his safety straps and clutched the worn, almost abused, arms of his chair. The *Sayther* bucked and rattled, enough he was certain they were about to break up in the atmosphere, before flames spread across the hull as the cold vacuum of space gave way to oxygen rich air. Sweat beaded across Matthias's brow. He had imagined death in countless ways during his time in uniform, but never once did he think this was how he was going to go. Not until today. Ishis Gul was either a certified madman or a genius in disguise.

Ganid II was a small moon sized world with a limited population. Mostly water, the entire world had but one continent. A quick scan showed it was heavily forested. Numerous cities were built over the vast oceans. An aquatic civilization whose primary export was seafood, Ganid II should have gone unnoticed by all but the Conclave's agricultural division. What Matthias found was shocked him.

The *Sayther* drifted over the smoldering ruins of an entire city. Several supports were destroyed, forcing the city into the oceans at a cant. Debris and bodies floated around it, surrounding the city like a halo of regret. Matthias sighed. War had poached the universe of sanity in such a short period of time. He wondered if there was any going back after the dust settled.

They touched down at a small village nestled atop the eastern cliffs of the great continent. The moment the ramp touched down and they deboarded, the surrounding forest came alive. Men and women in dirty gray uniforms emerged with weapons raised. Small tanks and armored vehicles roared from the village and settled within firing range. Matthias held his breath, anticipating a quick, violent demise.

A gruff man with burn scars covering the right side of his face marched up to them. His rifle was perched over a shoulder. The small cigar stub clenched in the corner of his mouth trickled smoke. Deep eyes almost as gray as his uniform stared first at Matthias and then Ishis. His free hand snatched the cigar away.

"I thought I told you not to bring him?" he snarled.

Ishis held up his hands. "Desperate times, Bootleg. Besides, he could use your firepower. There's a big campaign in the Mannus System and his side lacks the bodies to turn the tide."

"Not my problem. We have our own contract here to finish up."

Ishis cast a sidelong glance at Matthias in apology. "We flew over your contract. Looks like the battle is about wrapped up."

"We lost that one," Bootleg replied deadpan. "The gang and I were about to regroup and set matters right."

"There is no time," Ishis insisted. "Our need is dire, Bootleg. You and your company can turn the tide and win the war there."

The mercenary commander slapped his cigar back in his mouth before making a show of turning to his gathered forces. Several laughed. Others broke into wide grins. The rest remained stone faced, as if on cue. Bootleg returned his attention to his visitors. "How much?"

"More than you will ever need," Matthias spoke.

Bootleg spat a wad of brown saliva. "Who said anything about need? This is a matter of want, soldier boy."

"I'm not in the Guard," Matthias's instincts screamed in warning. "You have the wrong man."

"Uh huh. You don't remember me, do you, Matthias?"

Ishis stepped between them, eager to prevent rising hostilities from boiling over. "This is not necessary. Matthias is not part of the Guard. You have my word."

"It must have been eight, nine years ago," Bootleg ignored the smuggler. "My platoon was pinned down. I begged for support but you never sent any. Only a handful survived and when I brought it before you, I was court martialed for failing to follow orders and getting my people killed. Drummed out of the Guard because you fucked me over."

Mind reeling, Matthias staggered back a step. Bootleg, undoubtedly not his real name, clearly remembered him. Pieces fell into place and Matthias began recalling a disastrous campaign on the jungle world Hkarktang. Outnumbered and ill-prepared, the meager Guard forces deployed to stamp out a heretical uprising was forced to retreat, but only after suffering grave casualties rendering his company combat ineffective.

"Bootleg, please," Ishis tried to maintain the peace.

"We were cut off. Your platoon was stranded. I received your requests and tried to deploy air assets, move the artillery forward. Anything I could to buy your people enough time for the evac bird to exfil you. I was shut down. Command decided they couldn't divert any assets," he explained, more to satisfy his recollection.

"You were command, Matthias."

"You and I both know how officers react in the field," Matthias replied. His tone shifted, reverting back to his time as a sergeant major. That old gruff exterior slide over him. He stood taller, meaner. "Blame me, if you wish. I could have done more. I should have done more. None of that matters now. All we once fought and stood for has crumbled. The Guard, like the rest of the universe, is locked in civil war and I need every able body with a rifle I can find.

"You said it wasn't a matter of need. How much do you want?" he asked.

Bootleg's eyes narrowed. The urge to pull the trigger and exercise his ghosts strengthened. It shined through his gaze. Nearly a decade of manifested hatred finally had a target. A viable solution to purging the pain of losing countless friends and comrades. All he had to do was pull the trigger and revenge would be satisfied.

Or would it? Bootleg considered the implications of removing his harshest demon versus the cost to his soul. Killing Matthias was not going to bring any of his men back, nor would it assuage the guilt consuming him. A few moments of satisfaction meant little when compared to the pain Matthias must now live with after confronting an unpleasant episode from the past. Bootleg made his decision.

"How much can you offer?"

"Enough to buy your own gods damned army."

Wary, Bootleg saw an endless stream of credits rolling in, provided they survived long enough to spend them. The campaign Matthias proposed would test their mettle, no doubt pushing them beyond the break point. Risk high, he balanced that by placing faith in his people and their ability to annihilate enemies through rapid aggression.

He tossed the cigar butt on the ground and walked within a step of Matthias. "Go on. I'm listening."

Abbey of the Order of Blood Witches, Acumensiis Comet.

Luma Kai thought her amazement level peaked during her stay on Wexanos. The library world was a hidden gem few among the universe were gifted access to. Sprawling corridors of books and fortunes paled in comparison to the mysteries of the Blood Witches' inner sanctum. Shimmering gossamer halls wound through the massive temple built into the heart of the giant comet. Growing up in a small seaside community far from the bustle of Vau Prime, Luma's greatest joy stemmed from experiencing so many different cultures and societies. None of them compared to the Blood Witches.

"How could they have built all this?" she asked.

Tolde, similarly amazed and confused, had no answer. His experiences with the Order were limited, though increasing with disturbing frequency. Two of the three witches assigned to his missions died on duty, prompting him to wonder how much of a curse he was. Only Sister Alessandra survived her initial task and was rewarded by semi-permanent assignment at his side. She hovered a few steps behind them, allowing their senses time to adjust before burdening them with more.

"It doesn't seem possible, but after all we have been through since the war began, I don't think there is too much that can't be accomplished once our minds are put to it," he answered. "Humanity is a curious breed capable of changing the laws of the universe. If only we didn't get in our own way."

"Humanity is weak, Tolde Breed. We have transcended mortality and the constraints placed upon us through genetic restrictions," Sister Alessandra commented.

She drifted beside them; face concealed beneath the gossamer hood. Static electricity excited her robes, adding a billowing appearance reminiscent of a natural defense mechanism. Born into the Order, she was more detached from the reality of the universe than those who had been brought to the abbey in their youth.

"Your single defining moment is fast approaching. How you act now will determine the end result," she stated.

"I thought you were human," Luma said.

Alessandra turned, her movements ghostly. "Luma Kai, I do not have time to lecture you on the governing of our sisterhood. There was a time when my ancestors were human, but I was born here, among the stars. Some among us remain human, however, and through them the Order discovers more of the universal truth."

"Which is?" Luma asked. Wonder turned to mistrust. The former Inquisitor of the Office of Heretical Persecution readied for betrayal.

"That humanity is flawed. Only through constant evolution can we rise to the standards the so called gods have decreed. Then, and only then, will we finally be able to put war, greed, hatred, and jealousy behind us."

Tolde sensed confrontation and eased between them as they continued walking. "Those are lofty ideals. How can any group rise to such levels without compromising all they stand for?"

He questioned how much the average Blood Witch was told. If Alessandra knew the gods were a lie, would she not just admit it? Why play games for his accord? Tolde thought back to when Tannus showed them the truth, that the gods were little more than an early race who dominated the universe with violence and savagery. Surely the entirety of the Order must know the truth. He suddenly felt trapped in constricting circles of numerous games.

"What if the sole purpose of our Order is to achieve perfection?" she countered. "Enough of this. The Grand Mistress expects you in the cleansing chamber."

"Explain this ritual, please," Luma demanded. "We were told nothing of rituals."

"The Grand Mistress will explain, though I am at liberty to tell you the ritual will cleanse your spirits and enlighten you to be able to stay alive on the comet."

Tolde cocked his head. "Is there danger here?"

"None your weapons can solve. Living in space under constant external pressures has an ill desired effect on mortals. The ritual will provide you the stamina to survive long enough for us to reach our goal. The others will be waiting by now. You are the last."

He had almost forgotten about Paradise Tear and Ragan Sandinsol. Both were assigned to the expedition to stop Amongeratix from reaching *Behemoth*. It was a desperate ploy but one the council deemed necessary, if there was any chance of winning the war. With Matthias off searching for a mercenary army and Fies and his people heading to Mannus Prime, they were the logical choices to send. Tannus insisted there was important work yet to be done on Wexanos and the bulk of their combined strength would be utilized dealing with the smaller fires spreading across the stars. It was risky, but necessary. The enemy continued consolidating power at unprecedented rates, leaving the growing band of allies almost too far behind to catch up.

Tolde understood why Ragan was sent. The youth, stolen from his home and all he knew, was alone. Cast adrift in a universe he failed to understand. Tolde empathized with the boy, knowing how difficult it was to adjust to an entirely foreign environment. It was Paradise that concerned him. Tannus' younger cousin was pleasant enough, having bonded with Luma at some point in their ordeal, but there was an odd aura surrounding her.

They entered a small chamber in the comet's heart. Eyes adjusting to fluctuating brightness, Tolde nodded to Paradise and returned Ragan's nervous smile. Opposite them hovered Ruma Zzein. The Grand Mistress of Blood Witches was impressive in her silence. A dominating figure, older than the comet she called home. She commanded the chamber.

"Tolde Breed and Luma Kai. It does my heart good to see you both again so soon," Ruma began. Her voice boomed. "You have been invited to journey with us in the hopes of stopping Amongeratix once and for all. While there is no promise of success, it is my intent to deny the murderer from gaining his ship and bringing ruin to the universe. To do this, you must be cleansed of mind and spirit. Are you prepared?"

Prepared? This seems an odd time to throw a sudden ritual on us. "As much as we can be. Will it hurt?"

"The supernatural holds many mysteries. Only a handful have ever gone through this process. For some it is ecstasy. Others, a crisis of faith inspiring their darkest nightmares. All are expunged of ghosts, the demons riding their souls, by the end," Ruma explained.

"Will we survive?" Luma asked.

"If strength confides in you."

"That isn't reassuring."

The Grand Mistress remained immobile. "The alternative is far worse. Have you ever witnessed a human body implode from the obscene pressures of space?"

Tolde had heard enough. "Let's get on with this. Amongeratix draws closer to his prize while we debate astrophysics."

A column of golden light sprang from the center of the floor. Sparks resembling winged insects danced around it. Floral scents induced serenity among those present. The Blood Witch raised her arms and whispered ancient incantations learned a thousand lifetimes ago. Ribbons of green and blue swirled, catching the bottoms of her robes.

"So, it begins. Who shall be first to step within the cleansing light?" she asked.

Paradise Tear stepped forward. Her golden hair blended with the light, wreathing her in angelic halos. Hands folded in front of her, she entered the light. Her head cast back. Mouth opened in silent scream as eldritch powers transformed the innermost workings of her body. Paradise closed her eyes. Pulses of energy speared into her. She convulsed with each blow before stepping clear on shaky knees.

Dropping to the floor, smoke billowed off her. Paradise coughed, her lungs filled with renewed vigor. She had undergone this once before, though it was millennia ago and her time in the stasis pod reduced much of her mundane memories. When she managed to stand, her eyes were brighter than Tolde or Luma remembered.

"That was … invigorating," Paradise said. Her words blew out in an icy cloud.

Ruma Zzein nodded and turned to the others. "Who is next?"

The Acumensiis Comet blazed across the universe as it had done for many thousands of years. A haven for refugees and those who did not belong, it was the solemn grounds for what life should have been. Close to five hundred women called the abbey home. They came from across the stars. Unwanted. Unloved. Upon discovery, they experienced life in ways so few were allowed. A peeling back of the curtain.

And it was all falling to ruin.

Two Sisters stood in the shadows of an empty mess hall. The cooks had gone to bed. Tomorrow's meals were prepared, the kitchens cleaned. No one would notice the clandestine meeting. The light pulsing softly off their robes was the only thing marking their presence.

"She goes too far. The Order was not made to accept those who do not belong."

The second agreed. "But what can we do? She is the Grand Mistress. This entire structure was built around her. I fear that if she is deposed, the Order will collapse."

"There is another we could turn to. One infinitely more powerful who will grant us autonomy in the new universe," the first said.

Her tone was that of a snake. Venomous and rancid. Hatred flowed through her words, giving the second pause.

"What power? We already have Paradise Tear aboard."

"As well as a handful of outsiders who should not be here. Ruma Zzein plays a dangerous game with us, and our future."

Confused, the second said, "What other reason than for stopping Amongeratix and preventing Forever Night is there? I do not think she is willing to cast us into the abyss without cause. The others are necessary."

"Bah! Necessary for what? We should expel them at the first opportunity. Vent their bodies into the void and be done with the entire sorry mess," scolded the first.

"You speak of treason."

"I speak of truth," the first retorted. "You and I both have read the signs. We are on a collision course with doom and she brings us nearer with each action. Action must be taken."

"By whom? We are two and your words convince me I should not have sided with you," the second was quick to reply. "This course of action will lead to civil war, or worse."

"Death is the only alternative. Unless we side with him."

"Give up all this Order has stood for over countless generations and become slaves to a foul master with little regard for the creatures he deems beneath him? You overestimate your popularity among the others."

The first swelled beneath her robes with frustration. "I will not stand by and let her tear us apart for vain cause. We were created to be the light across the darkness. Not pawns in a cosmic game without opportunity to win."

"We are entering a critical stage of the war. Beware your next words, Algiss. Should they get back to the Grand Mistress…"

She let the thought fade, hopeful her fellow Sister was keen enough to heed the message. Both women stared in silence for the moment. Each forming complex thoughts to protect themselves from possible betrayal. The Order's most difficult time was fast approaching. Lines needed to be drawn.

"The hour of choice draws nigh, Sister. Be careful which side you fall on."

Wreathed in her robes, Algiss Her slipped away with the unthinkable on her mind. No Blood Witch had ever killed another. It would be a shame for it to happen now.

NINE

3215 A.G. (After gods), Krenz, planet Vau Prime.

He ran. Dogs barked, announcing his trail to their masters. Sunlight bleached the city streets of shadows, but he had no choice. Time was up and the one slim hope for escape was ever a step ahead of him. Cursing his luck, the former crime lord Zoraq Darc was without lifelines. Those he once trusted turned their backs. His mighty empire collapsed, every single associate he once counted on, protected, and employed refused to acknowledge him. Now the end closed on him, eager to cut the threads of his life and render him into the obscurity of oblivion's kiss. Zoraq ran.

His lungs burned. His clothes were torn and filthy. Zoraq was a shadow of his former self. A sad caricature of all he once was. Blisters covered his soles. Every muscle screamed in protest of being misused. It had been three weeks since slipping away from Strannan's headquarters without a word. Three days since the enemy learned of his defection and began their hunt. Three hours since they picked up his trail and tightened the noose. Countless police units ranged across Krenz, beating him out of the bush like an ancient hunt for sport. Unarmed save for a small snub-nosed pistol with just enough charge to ensure he did not spend the rest of his life on a Conclave prison colony, the crime lord struggled to stay ahead of his pursuers.

Mobus Kale's hounds had been on his trail for days, often arriving at his former hideouts well in advance and cordoning off entire blocks and severing many of his avenues of escape. Fear chasing each footstep, Zoraq was running out of options. A flare burst overhead. Artificial red light and smoke drifting down presented tenement faces in a hellish glow. Imagination whispered the sounds of capture marching in unison down the street. He glanced over his shoulder, surprised to find no armed guards in sight.

Zoraq cut down the nearest alley and limped halfway through it before finding a door jarred open a fraction of an inch.

Inspired, he tried to push the door open but it failed to move. Summoning his strength, he slammed a shoulder into the door and was rewarded with a collapsing cloud of dust and squeal of rust and metal as the door opened enough for him to slip through. Debris fell on his head as he entered the darkness.

Zoraq set his back to the door and managed to push it shut with some effort. Alone, trapped in a foreign room, and blinded by near total darkness, he leaned forward and placed his hands on his knees as he tried catching his breath. Muscles trembled from constant strain. Spots danced when he closed his eyes and it was all he could do to not swoon. Battered and broken, Zoraq was a defeated man. At least he was still free and still alive. For the time being.

Risking exposure, Zoraq turned the small light he carried out of necessity on to low power and examined his surroundings. Once sterile metal tables and counters stretched off into the darkness. Racks filled with pots, pans, and other cooking utensils sat collecting dust. He caught the faint odor of rotted vegetables. A bank of cold ovens lined one wall. An open refrigeration unit sat opposite. No doubt the restaurant suffered under the recent martial law imposition, forced to shutter its doors until normalcy returned. He doubted anything would be normal ever again. Fear and anxiety had taken root too deeply.

Zoraq contemplated jamming the back door shut and outwaiting his pursuers. Time was as much his enemy as the local police and their Prekhauten overseers. His one hope of escape lay in just a single bolt hole being undiscovered. Unable to count on his network for support, he had established a series of failsafe options only a select handful knew of. All but one had been eliminated over time, ensuring each position was off the grid.

Cowering in the abandoned restaurant not an option, Zoraq began searching for anything he might use as a weapon. His blaster was less than a quarter charged. Barely enough to put a round in his head should it come to that. He needed more. Zoraq perused a pile of butcher knives before selecting a sleek blade long enough for stabbing. It was the best he was going to find. Determined to avoid capture, the once prominent crime lord headed for the front door.

He slammed his shin on a table leg. Pain lanced through the muscle and he cursed softly. Ignoring the immediate swelling, Zoraq stumbled to the front and the bank of windows showing him the street. Wary, he slid against the nearest wall to lower his profile and poked his head around the window edge.

The street was empty as far as he could tell. A stray dog stalked down the opposite sidewalk. Wind blew trash around. This sector of Krenz was hit hardest with restrictions. He could see where the impact of armored vehicles compacted the road, tearing furrows as they spread their tyranny to each quadrant and city block. Broken illums lay heaped along the way. Instead of providing overhead light, they were shot down and discarded. Zoraq questioned Nye's tactics of destroying the economic infrastructure. Only a fool ignored the will and needs of the people he sought to conquer. The fastest way to insurrection was already spreading across the capitol city.

He peered up into dark windows in search of snipers, spies, or worse. Nothing moved. No one crowded what was one a thriving social destination. The travesty of martial law was laid bare before him. Zoraq studied it for the first time. Any opportunity to bring lasting peace and restore order was gone, abandoned like so many dreams. Krenz was changed.

Satisfied there was no immediate danger he could spot, Zoraq drew a deep breath and placed the palm of his hand on the door. Knowing his stunt was only going to last momentarily, he exhaled and pushed. The door groaned open. The movement slight, yet sounding like thunder to his ear. He slid through the gap, blaster raised. A dog barked in the distance and he jumped. Heart in his throat, Zoraq scurried up the street, hoping it was the right direction. He reached the end of the block and then his carefully constructed world collapsed around him.

A commotion was raised. Armed men and women in dark black uniforms poured from the side streets and alleys. Red and green tracer lines tracked his face and heart. Zoraq froze, locked in fear. The knife clattered to the ground. He tried to raise his blaster to his head but a sniper round took him in the forearm. Blood sputtered. The blaster fell. Defeated, Zoraq fell to his knees and wept.

Boots marched closer. The circle tightened. He caught the crisp polish of Inquisition boots halting before him.

"Zoraq Darc, you are under arrest for treason against the Conclave. Take him away."

Rough hands grabbed him under the arms, jerking him to his feet before locking his hands in cuffs. He was shoved, punched, and prodded into the back of a waiting police carrier.

His last sight was filled with Guards, police, and a handful of Inquisitors staring smugly at what he had become. The once fearsome crime lord of Krenz was no more. All that remained was a humbled shell of a man incapable of forming coherent thoughts. He knew this was the last time he was going to be allowed to smell the open air. Freedom was gone. Zoraq Darc was now a prisoner of the state. Worse, he was a prisoner of Alain Nye and the Inquisition.

The doors slammed shut, swathing him in darkness. The carrier lifted off the ground and sped away to his final destination.

Half a city away, the handful of men and women surrounding Aliz and Captain Julian fanned out across from the old police station. Local law enforcement was being redistributed throughout Krenz, leaving their target building largely abandoned. Intelligence suggested a small detachment remained. More than enough to sound the alarm throughout channels and bring the fury of Mobus Kale's bloodhounds down on the insurrectionists.

"Are you sure you're ready for this?" Julian whispered.

Aliz, thankful for the cover of darkness, scowled at the younger man. She wanted to snap back, remind him of her efforts during the raid on Tatarast Island. There was a steady undertone of her not belonging among the Guards, even today, that burned her. Once the confidante and lover of the most respected woman in the universe, Aliz was reduced to a face among the crowd. Indiscreet and underfoot. The lack of respect depressed her, if she allowed it to manifest.

"Captain Julian, I am very capable of handling myself. As you well know," she hissed, angrier than she intended.

Julian flinched in rebuke. "My apologies, my lady. Still, I would have you stay behind me until the building is secure."

"Of course," Aliz said.

She tightened her grip on her rifle and refocused on the building ahead. She had heard enough, though she made a mental note to confront Julian once the fighting was complete. The young captain could stand to do with a little scolding by his elders.

"Move out," Julian whispered to the squad leaders clustered behind him.

They fanned out in rehearsed movements. Stripped down of all armor and heavy equipment to reduce noise, the Guards and dedicated volunteers who flocked to Strannan's banner after the war began, hurried across the street. Their fire teams hurried behind. Silencers capped their rifles. Julian's mission depended on stealth and speed. Their faces and hands were blackened to prevent detection until they were upon their targets. By then, it would be too late.

The first rifle went off. Then a second. Guards swarmed the entrances. Aliz watched the front doors blow open, followed quickly by two soundless flashes and billowing gray smoke pouring outside. Men and women filed in. Flashes continued, moving up to the second and then third stories.

"Come on," Julian told both Aliz and his command team.

They filed across and lodged against the wall to the right of the door where a pair of Guards remained to secure the exit in case it was a trap. Tense moments passed. Aliz wanted to do more. To help. To be more than an old lady given special treatment. Two Guards stumbled from the smoke. One had an entire leg covered in dark blood. His face was drained of color, reminding Aliz of so many brave Guards who fell on Tatarast and a dozen other engagements since she became part of Strannan's insurrection. The instinctive urge to help inspired her. Aliz grabbed the wounded man by his free arm and eased him to the ground. She snatched a field dressing from his kit and applied a soft tourniquet above the wound. It would have to do until they had time to get him checked out by the medics.

Julian watched her work and knew he was wrong with the way he treated her. Aliz was more than a simple woman given to his charge. She had been hardened by war and tempered by the care only maturity allowed. There was time to rethink his position later, however. The mission needed to be completed first.

"Report," he said to the uninjured Guard.

She saluted, puffing to catch her breath. "Sir, the first two floors are secured. Minimal resistance. We found stores of food, water, and ammo."

"I want this building stripped," he ordered. "Everything that can be used. Destroy the commo equipment we can't transport on foot and start the propaganda. Evacuate the building and reconvene at the safehouse."

"Are you certain this is going to work?" Aliz asked after the Guard hurried back inside.

"Nothing about this mess is certain," he replied. "All I can do is hope, and that is the single most dangerous thing a soldier can cling to. Once we hit enough targets, the enemy should start believing a new faction is moving in to resist them. It's not the best plan, but it's what I have for now."

She thought back over the intricate details of their campaign. The only way to make it work, to divert Inquisition resources from hunting Strannan, was by making Nye and Kale believe new splinter cells were rising and causing havoc throughout Krenz. Similar cells were deployed the same night she and Julian left Strannan that final night. The flames of insurrection were spreading. It was Julian's hope the people would join in and cast off their new master's yoke. Aliz fretted over that detail, for it meant the unnecessary deaths of far too many civilians. Her argument fell on deaf ears. Both military men concluded that a measure of collateral damage was acceptable to achieve their desired results. She fumed and raged but was forced to accept it as a sad facet of a multi-front war.

"You did well taking care of that wound," Julian told her after noticing the distant look in her eyes.

"It was a reaction. I don't know if I saved his life or not," she shook her head. Staring down at her hands, Aliz spied the crimson stain on her cuff.

"You did enough to give our medics a chance," Julian affirmed. "I … I was wrong about you, Aliz. For that I apologize. You have endured far more than I give you credit for. More than anything I have gone through since this war began. Will you accept my apology?"

She pursed her lips, torn between conflicting emotions. "Julian, there are a great many things we are each guilty of. If I were to list them all and continue holding a grudge, our alliance would end in flames. There is no need for an apology. Just don't do it again."

Grinning, Julian said, "We need to move. Sergeant Kolhn, get the wounded on the road and exfil. We don't have much time before reinforcements arrive."

"Sir!"

Aliz watched the dark skinned Kohln hurry into the building. Smoke was seeping through structural cracks. It reminded her of a housefire on her home world from when she was a child, only this time no one came screaming outside. Guards soon began streaming out. Each laden with a heavy pack, hands filled with confiscated weapons. She resisted the urge to go inside and grab her share. Age and seniority had their benefits, though she worried the others might look down on her for not pitching in. She had volunteered for the assignment after all.

"Aliz, we're done here," Julian disturbed her.

"Very well," she said without taking her eyes off the activity. No matter how many times she witnessed the Prekhauten Guard in action, she remained amazed by their diligence and professionalism, even in the face of betrayal by a system they swore to uphold. Her last sights of the raid were a pair of Guards helping a wounded man limp outside.

Safely back in their command center, the Guards filtered through the weapons and intel. Ammunition was distributed to individual fire teams with the majority going into reserve and placed in various hideaways scattered through the area of operations. Each cache held weapons, ammunition, food and water for sustained field operations, should the main command become compromised. Julian worked with what he had and was thankful for the early successes he and his people achieved.

He spent much of the night pouring over maps and aligning future raids to coincide with citywide deployments. Julian's eyes burned from the strain before he realized most of his people were already asleep. Groaning as he stretched, the tired captain tossed his grease pencil on the map before him and decided it was time for sleep. Two more raids were planned for tomorrow, simultaneously in opposite parts of his sector. They were nothing complicated, but enough to throw enemy forces into chaos.

Julian found Aliz sitting on an old bench in front of a grime smeared bay window overlooking a quiet side street. "You should be asleep."

She turned, watching him approach with red streaked eyes. "You're one to talk. This whole operation falls apart without you. I'm just here."

"No, you're more than that, Aliz," Julian sat beside her and followed her gaze down the long quiet road. "You've become one of the hearts of this movement. A symbol the others rally around. I wish I had that level of support."

"What are you talking about? I'm just an old lady past her prime. Your people act more like nursemaids than idolizing warriors," she replied.

The slight hint of crimson flushed his cheeks. Years in service taught him respect was earned, regardless of rank or position. Those men and women fighting for him now made

Julian earn their trust. Suggesting anything less was a disservice to their professionalism. He sensed there was no point in forcing the conversation, so he decided to change the subject.

He hung his head, fighting back a yawn. "Do you miss her?"

Aliz opened and closed her mouth. A tide of emotions threatened to rush her. She remembered quiet nights alone with Lorenu. The way they laughed and shared stories from their youths. Life had been wonderful before Cardinal Phos was elected Cardinal Seniorus. Politics and an endless demand of both time and attention weighed her down after. Their relationship strained, forced to the edge but they refused to part. She and Lorenu adapted, made the most out of what time they managed to find.

Smiling fondly, Aliz said, "She was the best thing that ever happened to me. Soft yet strong. Wise and caring. I wish I could turn back time and convince her not to accept the nomination. Perhaps we would still be together on a distant world, far from the concerns of Vau Prime and this damned war."

"We seldom get to choose our fates," Julian said after some time passed. While he failed to understand her unique situation, he sympathized with her being torn from her life and the driving desire for revenge.

Aliz turned on him, suddenly uncomfortable with the direction the conversation turned. "Did you always want to be a soldier?"

"No. Not at first. I had thoughts of becoming a chef when I was still a child," he admitted. After hearing her chuckle, he added, "Don't laugh. I got to be quite good in the kitchen."

"So, what happened?"

"We didn't have the funds to send me to school. My family has always been, well, not exactly poor but we certainly lacked the credits for nice things. Don't get me wrong. My parents were hard workers who did everything for my sister and me. It bothered me at first, but I got over it. Then a Guard recruiter showed up and I figured it was a good way to start earning right off the jump. I guess this became a career somewhere along the way."

Julian fell silent, becoming lost in memories, both pleasant and not. Aliz studied him, noticing for the first time the heavy lines and dark bags on his face. Much younger than she, he had aged years since the war began. *Haven't we all? Nye seems intent on bringing society to its knees, without any regard for who it hurts. Or how.*

"Can you still cook?" she asked after allowing him space to reflect.

He broke into a wide grin. "Put me in a kitchen and I guarantee you'll forget all out what's happening out here."

She gave his forearm a motherly pat. "I'll hold you to that the first chance we have. Goodnight, Julian."

"Goodnight, Aliz."

The low continent was, from what Davith Strannan gauged, a burned husk of what once was. Mobus Kale and his elite division razed it to the ground with unrepentant fury no citizen under Conclave rule deserved. Entire cities were reduced to rubble. Blackened skeletons lay where they had fallen, a mocking tribute to all life once was. It was by sheer will alone he did not empty his stomach on his boots.

The combination of time and winds swept away much of the stench, though the burn residue lingered long after the embers died. Strannan reflected on the perverseness of it. Orbital imaging showed every settlement, town, and city was gone. Mobus Kale had performed his duties with, in Strannan's mind, misdirected enthusiasm. For what? What did Kale hope to gain from committing such atrocities?

"How could any man do this to his own people?" Strannan muttered.

A pair of young lieutenants shuffled nervously at his side. The latest aides, now that he ordered his forces to disperse into smaller, guerilla units, they represented the best of what he had left. Neither were veterans of more than a few raids during the limited time after the Tatarast Island operation. Baby faced, in his opinion. He longed for someone as capable at reading his moods and interpreting his long bouts of silence like Julian. That man had wit and a mind for tactics. Strannan shifted his gaze from one to the other. *These two are barely away from sucking at their mother's tit. Damnation. Another time, I might have been able to shape them, but now?* He doubted either would live to see the end of the year.

"You can speak," he reminded them in a fatherly tone. "I'm not promoting you to stand there looking confused."

"S...sorry, Sir," they said in unison.

Brass balls. The best I have to work with. "Uh huh. You know, I don't even remember your names. Perhaps you could remind me."

Taller, blond and lithe, the first saluted. "Sir, I am Lieutenant Jash Abernath."

His female counterpart was the polar opposite. Brawny with shifting eyes daring anyone to comment. "Lieutenant Bryn Mal. Sir."

Oh, I like this one. Looks like she has been in a few fights. He glanced at the callouses on her knuckles. "What is your assessment of our current situation, Ms. Mal."

She opened her mouth but closed it faster.

"The truth, please."

Bolstered by his apparent confidence, Mal said, "Sir, this is a total shit show. General Kale's campaign left nothing. We have limited resources, only the supplies we have brought with us, and no hope of concealing our efforts, should they return in force. In short, this is an untenable situation. Sir."

Strannan caught Abernath's horrified expression out of the corner of his eye and nodded. "An accurate assessment, I would say. Why do you think we are here, other than to give our foes a headache trying to determine where we disappeared to?"

"Sir, I … to provide our forces with much needed refit time and to organize plans for retaking Krenz," Mal answered with less confidence.

In truth, Strannan doubted they would ever be able to force Nye to capitulate. Not with the forces he had available to him. The insurrection was on shaky ground. Each action required draining resources and an increased level of complexity that was sure to run out. He felt trapped between the jaws of the mighty sand dragons from the deep deserts of An'kuruku. One moment of weakness and he would be crushed, swallowed, and lost under the weight of impossible odds. *And yet, I have forced all my closest confidants away. Perhaps it would have been better if Kale succeeded in killing me that day.*

"Close enough. Mal, continue voicing your opinions when called for. I want people who can think for themselves, not ones who wait for me to make a move," Strannan ordered. "Abernath, tighten up that uniform. You are an officer in the Prekhauten Guard, not some colonial militia on a backwater world."

They snapped to attention as he waved them off and walked away. The audible smush of Mal's fist striking Abernath in the shoulder was loud enough to make Strannan wince. They might work out after all.

He slipped into his tent, nestled under a cliff overhang and tossed his duty cap on the cot. Instead, it landed in a Guard's lap. Strannan paused, hand reaching for his blaster.

"What are you doing in my quarters, trooper?" he demanded. Squinting in the dusky light, he decided it was not a trooper after all.

The face melted, molding away to one more familiar. One he had thought dead or worse.

"Gedrick Silk. You've returned."

Silk bowed. "General, I would have arrived sooner but was not informed of your … departure from Krenz until recently."

"Your mission to kill Nye didn't succeed." It was more statement than question. If Nye was dead, the entire universe would have heard by now.

"There are new details that have come to light precluding me from the assassination. I barely escaped from Inquisition Headquarters. By the way, I'm never returning to that dreadful place, so don't ask," Silk repressed bad memories.

Frustrated and more than a little aggravated from lack of sleep, Strannan almost collapsed in the chair set beside his field table. "What details?"

"I have learned a terrible truth regarding the true benefactor of this war. Alain Nye has been in league with Amongeratix, possibly for some period of time."

The deposed commanding officer of the Prekhauten Guard felt gut punched. Amongeratix. The scourge of generations. Endless questions arose. The dark son of the Three had been a thorn in the Conclave's side for years. Strannan spent countless hours dealing with allocating forces to recapture the tyrant and was successful only once.

"Impossible," he deflected. "Nye might be a villain, but he would never stoop to unifying with Amongeratix. The man practically led the fight to recapture him after the escape from Crimeat."

Yet, even as he said it, Strannan knew it was far from the truth. The war had its earliest roots around the same timeframe as Amongeratix's escape from the Conclave prison on Prophet Isle. Too many events lined up with that seminal moment. Too many coincidences to be happenstance. Pieces clicked into place and Strannan saw the truth in Silk's report. The implications were staggering. Backed by one of the Three, there was little way Nye could lose his war. The universe would plunge into chaos and all be led to ruin.

"How can we fight the son of a god?" he said, breathless.

Silk wrung his hands together in frustration. It was the same question he'd asked endless times since overhearing the conversation. "There is more."

"Of course, there is," Strannan replied. He made a curt hand gesture. "Well, out with it. You know I detest dramatic pause."

"Amongeratix is loose and in search of some kind of weapon capable of crushing all resistance, destroying humanity," Silk explained. "Or so I gathered."

"You're full of good news. If he comes to Vau Prime, there is no way we can hope to defeat him," Strannan theorized. "I need to get a message to Matthias."

"What are you thinking?"

Rubbing the bone white stubble on his chin, Strannan said, "I'm thinking that we don't have the firepower to fight one of the Three, much less defeat him and if Matthias and his people can't find a way, we are going to have to abandon Vau Prime."

"If we leave now, there will never be another opportunity to reclaim this world. You know that."

He glared at Silk. "You suggest we stick it out and go head to head with the worst killer in human history?"

Gedrick shook his head. "I am suggesting you remember who you are. What if Amongeratix has no desire to rule humanity? It is plausible he only wants to kill his brothers and assert dominance through Nye. If that is true, Nye is the opportunity."

"You had your chance and didn't take the shot," Strannan reminded.

"No. Killing him does little to advance our efforts," Silk said. "But we can turn the population on him. Broadcast it across the stars that he is in league with a true villain."

The option, while having occurred to him earlier, felt shaky at best. Now, with this new information, Strannan felt closer to removing Nye's base of power. The cost would be high. Countless civilians would die, if they turned on Nye and his forces. An unending civil war threatening to return humanity to the dark times before Conclave rule.

"What more do you know of this weapon Amongeratix seeks?" Strannan asked, knowing the monster already had a weapon capable of killing an entire planet. His day continued devolving into the worst-case scenario.

The world suddenly felt smaller. *How much longer before those jaws snap shut and swallow me forever?*

The ice world of Antil IV.

Amongeratix stormed down the frigid corridors of his fortress, ignoring the hushed menials scurrying to get out of his way lest his size and wrath smear them against the wall like so many before them. The lord of Antil was not known for his compassion. Servants came and went with alarming frequency, forcing their overseers to remove eyes, tongues, and hobble them upon arrival. The tundra tribes were cowered remnants of a once proud race. Armed guards lined the corridors at intervals, snapping to attention as their lord marched past.

Amongeratix ignored them all. His mind focused on a singular point of being half the universe away, each footstep was measured, executed hundreds of millions of times over the course of his extended exile. Anger over his brother's decision to openly question their father in front of the entire court festered thirty-five hundred years later. It kept him warm when all else chilled around him.

Hover illum lights flickered as he passed. The very walls of the ancient fortress seemed alive at his command. Amongeratix burst into the main command room. His black cape the color of darkest midnight flowing behind him, he took his well-worn throne. A handful of heads turned his way, acknowledging their subservience. Those who had undergone genetic mutilation remained at their stations, unfazed by their lord's arrival.

"Where is it?" he growled.

Swathed in dark robes, the lead acolyte bowed again. "Master, telemetry reports place the *Behemoth* somewhere in the Orgut System. As far as we can tell, the ship remains undetected by your brothers."

"Show me."

Transparent screens pulled up the ship's location and basic schematics. Amongeratix studied the charts, eyes squinting as he narrowed in on aspects of most interest. With all but basic functioning systems offline, he focused on damage reports. Minor wounds gouged by passing asteroids and other space debris pockmarked the hull. Several chambers in the lower holds were breeched but the ship appeared serviceable. Ready for war.

"Pinpoint exact location."

Computers hummed and buzzed. Sightless menials translated data schemes, processing them to the chief acolyte. The man verified the data before presenting it. "Master, 117.586.992. time to *Behemoth* is less than one standard human month."

One month before he could fully prosecute his war on the universe and reclaim the broken throne for good. Mere days to fulfill the hate filled promise he made Tannus after the disaster of Occanum slaughtered ninety-five percent of their race. Mind racing, Amongeratix turned his attention to additional matters. He still needed an army and the weapon. The skulldaerth were already located and heading to the *Behemoth* through automated computer programs built into place centuries ago. Their awakening was unexpected but timely, affording him the opportunity to apply pressure on Alain Nye.

The universe was already witness to the raw power of his weapon. Redundant systems were no doubt being emplaced throughout the seven hundred worlds to prevent another Kharsis. It mattered not. Once he gained the artifact, there was no stopping him. Finding his wayward agent was another matter.

"Where is the Lady Presha Von?" he asked.

Cocking his head, the acolyte closed his eyes as he interpreted data streams. "Latest reports show she fled Hawker's Gate with a pair of warships in pursuit. We can track her route based on her engine signature, but it will take time. Do you wish us to proceed?"

Hands curling in rage, his fingernails dug into the blanched stone. "I would not have asked if my answer was no. Or should I prepare another acolyte to serve me better?"

"No, Master. Your will shall be done."

Amongeratix scowled yet refrained from destroying the creature. Instead, he channeled his thoughts to the last item preventing him from acting. "Has my army boarded the *Behemoth* yet?"

"The skulldaerth have departed Braewynd as planned. Transports will dock within the next five standard days."

He nodded. All was proceeding. The only factor standing in his way was the disappearance of Presha Von. Amongeratix concluded she was an expendable asset, as were all his human pawns. Until she presented the artifact, he needed her alive. Toying with the idea of deploying additional resources to Crimeat, that most detested world, he continued staring at the monitors.

"Ready my shuttle. Full compliment. I want to be on the command deck of my ship as soon as possible," he ordered.

The words were slow, deliberate, and filled with venom. Menials and acolytes hurried to obey his will. The fortress came alive as soldiers, supplies, and weapons were loaded and stored. The promised war was at last upon them. Amongeratix, lord of Antil IV, remained seated, staring off into the vast whiteness of the snow fields as his mind raced with dreams of wicked temptation.

Tannus and Sorrow had no idea what was in store. Woe be unto them. Laughing, Amongeratix went to board his shuttle.

TEN

3215 A.G. (After gods), PGNV *Indomitable*, en route to Mannus Prime.

Newly promoted Gunnery Sergeant Asom wound through the belly of the *Indomitable*. He knew every inch of the ship, much the same as their former Captain turned Admiral. Serving in the Prekhauten Marines was a great source of pride. He walked with his back straight, shoulders back. The chevrons on his collar gleamed under the bright lights. He still was not sure why he was promoted. In his mind, he was merely doing his job when the ship was boarded. Natural tenacity and honed combat skills took over. Asom advocated for awards of valor for several of his Marines, all without noticing Falchi and Samuel deciding to promote him.

Chagrined, Asom reached the troop decks. The main hangar was filled with an endless line of heavy battle tanks, light armored vehicles, and artillery pieces. Infantry and support troops milled about. Some checked gear. Others played cards. Most were asleep on hammocks strung between the vehicles. Asom never ceased being amazed at the sheer volume of new equipment the regular Guard units received compared to the shipborne Marines. *If I only had a tenth of this level of support.*

He weaved through platoons and companies until finding the squad he was looking for. His first impression was less than stellar. They appeared like every other combat line unit. Bedraggled. Uniforms worn and stained from an endless stream of action. Asom overheard muted conversations and realized they were no different from any unit he served with. Complaining. Joking. Dour and serious. These were men and women who had been on the tip of the spear from the beginning. Legends already. He suddenly felt unworthy of being in their presence.

"You look lost."

Jarred from his thoughts, Asom looked to the speaker and was surprised to find an aggressive looking woman with twin lightning bolts on her bald head standing in front of him. One hand was on a hip. The other rested on her blaster.

"I'm sorry?" he managed.

"It's the tattoos, isn't it? Usually spooks people away," she said. "Who are you looking for, Marine?"

Asom didn't know whether to laugh or be afraid. "Lieutenant Fies. Do you know where he is?"

Her eyes narrowed slightly. "Fies, huh? Yeah, bastard's probably sleeping. I don't know why they promoted him to an officer." She gestured Asom to follow. "Hells, every time he gets promoted, he insists they do the same with me! Tell me how that's fair. Name's Annalilly by the way."

He chose to ignore her. Asom had been in uniform long enough to know banter when he came across it. What bothered him was her intensity. She was enough to give a grown man nightmares. He guessed she was hell on a battlefield, too. For all its tradition and lineage, the Guard was still filled with malcontents and others who did not fit in well with society. They stopped before a sleeping man, whom she kicked with the flat of her boot.

Grunting, Fies snapped, "What in the fu..."

"Got a guest here for you, *Lieutenant*," she said.

Blinking away the precious little sleep he managed since departing Wexanos, Fies cleared his throat and sat up. "Marines, huh? You might have more sense than most of us. Floating around in space must be easier than getting your boots muddy."

"Sir, Gunnery Sergeant Asom of the *Indomitable's* compliment. Captain Samuel ordered me to introduce myself," he reported.

"I didn't know this was a pleasure cruise," Fies replied. "To what do I owe the pleasure, Gunny?"

"My platoon has been attached directly to you for the upcoming campaign," Asom said.

Annalilly folded her arms. "Your boys are rated for ground warfare?"

"It's been a while since I last got my feet in the mud with you grunts, but yes."

Her glare faded to a feral grin. "I like him, Fies. Can we keep him?"

Ignoring her, Fies offered his hand. "Welcome to the club, Asom. I'll let you NCOs work out the details. All I ask is you be ready to deploy when the light turns green."

Asom shook his hand. Their deal concluded, Fies laid back down and placed his service cap over his face.

"Come on new guy," Annalilly told him. "I guess we're not good enough for his high and mighty ass."

Fies growled. "Get out of my AO, Annalilly. I need to sleep."

Asom waited until they were out of earshot before asking, "Is he always like this?"

"Nah. You caught him on a good day," she laughed.

He left the troop bay wondering if Captain Samuel had made a mistake. These couldn't be the heroes he'd heard so much about. If so, the universe was in for a bad time.

"What do you suppose that was all about?" Haggle asked, as they watched Annalilly and the marine walk away.

Jers stared after them, feeling guilty for being more interested in his personal dilemma than the squad's. He glanced at Haggle's cherub face and wondered how the man still had hope. "Dunno, but it can't be good. Maybe we're pairing up with the marines for ship-to-ship action?"

Haggle shook his head. "No way. As interesting as that sounds, I'm not ready to die in space. One of the reasons I joined the army."

"How's that?" Jers asked.

"I figure if I joined the navy, there was a good chance of being blown into space. Which, by the way, is a horrible way to die. I could have joined the air corps but who wants to plummet thousands of feet to their death? No. By joining the army, all I have to do is fall about six feet after getting shot. It seemed the most appealing to me, at the time."

"How does your brain work?" Jers asked.

Haggle was the closest thing he had to a friend, which was saying a lot all things considered. The war robbed him of friends and family. So much so, he often forgot about the days prior to his deployment to Crimeat. Grief combined with guilt plagued him for the longest time after Kastor was killed by Guards he thought were allies. Now, the man's face was barely remembered. Jers felt lost. Dissatisfied with being in uniform, fighting a war he did not understand.

Adding insult to injury was his promotion to sergeant. Fies knew what he was doing. Rapid promotion at the precise moment Jers wanted to leave the Guard forced him to reevaluate his position to the others. They had become his true family. Veterans of several campaigns and brush fights, each was dedicated to the others. It was that sense of selflessness that drew him to the Guard in the first place. He fit in for the first time in his life. Now?

He looked around at the rest of the squad. Beve, the heavy weapons specialist, lounged across the hood of the assault vehicle, his boots dangling over the edge. Hollis was a relatively new addition who joined them just before the Kharsis disaster. Their sniper, Jolent, kept to himself for the most part, content with his thoughts, while the others joked or shared war stories that had already been told a hundred times. Others came and went during his time. Most were lost to memory and the dim reminder that theirs was a fatal occupation.

Haggle caught the glossy look and elbowed his friend and sergeant. "What do you suppose is waiting for us on Mannus?"

"Nothing good," was all he could answer.

A quiet voice in the back of his mind whispered this was it. After the coming campaign, he was done. The only question remaining was how to convince Annalilly and Fies, both of whom supported him when he doubted himself.

Vaade, planet Crimeat.

Trees of a hundred shades of green stretched down the lazy avenues of Vaade. Fountains were filled with children splashing and playing. Couples walked beneath the canopy, stopping to gaze through shop windows and eateries. The soft red and orange glow of light bugs flitting between the leaves presented tranquility among an otherwise clear evening sky. All in all, a pleasant evening far removed from the realities of war.

The novelty was lost on Presha Von as she sat in the small apartment they secured after landing. Trapped on the second floor, she realized she had not been outside in days. Whatever status she once held among the ruling council, evaporated the instant she declared for Amongeratix and plunged her world into war. The fighting on Crimeat might be over, but the scars remained. She was denounced as a traitor with an immediate execution order in place. Coming home was never an option. At least not until it was forced upon her.

Lamenting how far she had fallen, she closed her eyes and thought of happier times. Once considered upper echelon among the nobility, Presha became entranced by the lure of secrecy the dark council offered. Names and faces were concealed, enough that few, if any, of the members knew who the others were. Together they shaped the course of political events across Lethendweil. It was not until the rogue Inquisitor Ursal Prowl introduced the heresy of Amongeratix and the cult of Rengu to the planet, that her life plummeted from its lofty heights.

At first, the lure of ultimate power enticed her. Presha was seduced by converging forces and she lost herself in the addictive pleasures of her oils. Lust drove her actions. Desire fueled her nights. Wicked memories of carnal delights teased her. But it was already far too late to take comfort in past glories. The lure of the oils was lost somewhere during the last few years as she fled Crimeat, became the driving force behind the fall of Hawker's Gate, and now a refugee from the murder of Kharsis. Her life, she decided, was fraught with ruin.

The door groaned open as Geres Auk entered. A giant by human standards, the former strong man for Baron Scura was the most intense person Presha had ever met. There was no sense of humor, no obligation for small talk, and no opportunity to delve into his past. She enjoyed the enigma, but it made for a foul traveling companion. His dour gaze settled on her and she felt tremors crawl up her spine. *The man is a born killer. Capable of snapping my neck with ease.*

"What is it, Geres? Can't you see I am enjoying the sunset?" she mocked.

He grunted but otherwise ignored her banter. "I've made contact with runners for the dark council."

Presha perked up. "How? Where?"

"Through some of the baron's old colleagues. They were hard to find but have agreed to take us to the council," he replied. Geres left out the fact he was forced to snap a few arms to get the answers he wanted.

"I know how to get there. We don't need their help," she insisted.

He shook his head. "We do now. The war forced them to displace, go deeper into hiding. From what I gathered, only a handful remain. The others were either killed outright or cleansed after the baron fell and the war shifted to the stars."

Presha frowned. The council should have been impervious to discovery. Painstaking efforts were made to prevent the ruling council of the lords of Lethendweil from discovering their true identities. How far had times fallen in the aftermath of Amongeratix's escape and Baron Scura's war. She doubted seeking the dark council was prudent.

"Perhaps we do not need their support after all," she surmised.

Geres folded his arms, fixing her with a stern glare. "We risked much to come back here. There are death warrants on both our heads, Lady Von. I don't mind dying, but it will be by my choosing, not these petty nobles from broken houses."

A touch of the poetic in you, eh Geres? I wonder what other secrets you keep deep down inside. "Where has the council moved to?"

"You're not going to like it," he delayed.

The look she gave him suggested she already knew that. "Geres."

"They have occupied certain levels of the abandoned Inquisition prison on Prophet Isle."

She felt her stomach churn. Prophet Isle was the source of the entire war consuming the universe. She heard rumors of a monstrous battle between Amongeratix and his brother Tannus following the prison escape. Hints that another was involved teased her imagination though there was no official word in any report or document. The Inquisition remained tightlipped despite their schism.

Situated north, Lethendweil, Prophet Isle was dedicated to the prison. What sort of villains were contained there no longer mattered as the Conclave ordered the facility shut down after the failed revolution. The red robed cardinals were taking no chances with releasing more than they could control. Presha considered her next move. She had no desire to visit the prison but deemed there was little real choice. Geres's insistence that the dark council was still of service, placed her in a tricky situation.

Ever do I try to regain control of my life and ever it continues spiraling further beyond my grasp. I am doomed to a life of blind servitude, when I should have been a queen.

"You're kidding," she drawled.

The face he gave her, the same one she'd spent the last two years cringing from, stared back blankly.

Pursing her lips, Presha asked, "How do they expect us to reach the island undetected? Security is tighter than ever and we are wanted fugitives. Even if we can get back to our shuttle, there is no way of evading authorities long enough to disappear again."

"There are underground channels available to us," Geres said. "The Baron was adamant about creating alternate escape routes should the war turn against him."

She winced. Not only did the war turn on him, it left him dead on his plateau fortress. Presha briefly considered reaching out to Scura's daughter, Ilsara, but there was no love lost between them. It was a different time, yet old enmities were hard to forgive. The mountain city of Reven was now closed to visitors, partially by the ruling council resolution and enforced by Conclave security. Trust was impossible with the lower provinces, leaving the continent balancing on a dangerous edge.

"I doubt we will be welcomed in Reven, Geres," Presha said. "You, most of all. The young Baroness intoned your penalty shortly after her father died."

"I do not need reminding of this," he growled.

The promise of being drawn and quartered, while the people cheered, soured his mood.

Got you, you bastard. Finally, something to get under your skin. "Come now, Geres. We're not going to let them remove your pretty head. How long will it take for you to get in contact with Scura's network? If they still exist."

"Hopefully, not long," he replied.

She waved him away. "Go, then. The sooner we are safely away from our enemies, the better. This city depresses me."

Fuming, Geres Auk stormed off. Alone again, much as her life continued to devolve into, Presha resumed her watch on the crowded city streets. Vaade once held infinite promise. Dreams of overthrowing the basic power structure and assuming total authority once dominated her thoughts. Now she was fortunate enough to still draw breath. Administering was harder than she imagined. Long months spent running Hawker's Gate after the Conclave was beaten away left their scars. Enough to force her to reassess her thought processes and decide she worked better in the shadows.

A rare moment of weakness overcame her and Presha struggled to control her sobs. Greed and dreams got the better of her, prompting her down easy paths with devious intent. Now, it was all in ruin. Her life became a hollow mimicry of what should have been. Her lands and properties confiscated and redistributed to less deserving individuals who were former rivals. Presha Von had nothing but the clothes on her back and a single, battered ship.

Her thoughts turned to the artifact from Kharsis. The destroyer of worlds. Each night she relived the horror of an entire world dying in a matter of days. Tormented and haunted, Presha struggled with the weight of such a burden. Never in human history was any single individual responsible for such countless murders. The authority bestowed by such an artifact devoured her soul.

No. Not an artifact. This is a weapon. Plain and simple.

Her communicator chimed, bleeping incessantly until she reached for it. Presha's finger hovered over the answer button, already dreading the voice on the other end. She closed her eyes, knowing the promise of pain about to fall.

"Where are you?"

"My lord Amongeratix," she began, her voice catching in her throat. "Unforeseen circumstances forced me to abandon my post at Hawker's Gate. I ..."

"Answer the question, human," Amongeratix demanded.

A tremor of pure terror rippled under her skin. "Crimeat."

The pause from his end sparked thoughts of running and disappearing among the stars. Even a dominant being like Amongeratix would be hard pressed to find her.

"You have returned home. Interesting. Have you been discovered?"

A weight shifted, giving her breathing space. "No, but we were tracked through the shipping lanes by loyalists to the old regime. Geres Auk is currently seeking any still in league with our old alliances."

Amongeratix's voice hardened, if such was possible. "Where is the artifact?"

She froze, trapped in internal debate. Providing him with the location eliminated his need to keep her alive, a state she very much wanted to maintain. However, if she lied or kept the location private, his hounds would be loosed upon her. Having seen his agents in action, Presha knew she was in an inescapable position.

"I have it, my lord," she admitted.

"Do not let it fall into my enemy's hands. I will send agents to retrieve it, and you," he commanded.

"But my lord, what of the loyalist forces?" she asked.

"All that matters is keeping the artifact secure," he answered, the tone noncommittal, vague. "Alert me to your final location for pickup. You have less than one standard week. Do not fail me again."

The line went dead. His last words resonated in her skull. Presha worked herself into a corner, providing her master with impossible truths.

She lowered her face to her hands. "Fuck."

The door burst open. Heavy footsteps prompted her to raise her head. Surprised Geres had returned so fast, she opened her mouth. And fell silent as two massive men, decidedly not Geres Auk, swept through the room. Dim memories suggested she had run into them once before, but where? Weaponless, she had no move.

"Found you, scum," the dark-skinned man covered with tribal tattoos snarled.

His shorter companion slapped a fist into a meaty palm. "We've been looking for you, murderer. All we had to do was wait for your goon to leave. Give us the weapon and we'll let you live. Local authorities might not, but that's hardly our problem, is it?"

"Weapon?" she struggled to find poise.

"Maybe she don't have it?"

The shorter man backhanded his friend. "Course she does. She's just playing stupid. We might need to break a few bones."

"Gentlemen, I have no idea who you are or what you are referring to," she said in defiance.

"Name's Krimpen Mass. This here is Time. You know precisely what we mean. After all, it was you who killed our homeworld. Or did you forget that little disaster, too?"

Time drew a slender dagger. "She's worth just as much dead as she is alive."

"Take a finger, or an ear. She has plenty. Just try not to make it too messy," Krimpen suggested.

"No promises. The bitch killed my family," Time snapped and lunged.

Presha threw her hands up, unwilling to watch her mutilation. The blade never fell. What happened next appeared in slow motion as she watched between splayed fingers. Geres burst into the room and threw a fist to the back of Time's head. The knife slipped loose, plunging to stick in the hardwood floor. Pitching forward, Time threw his hands out to arrest his fall. Krimpen Mass spun, raising his own fists to confront the unexpected threat. Geres was faster. The brute kicked, his boot catching Krimpen in the stomach and dropping him.

Time was back on his feet and whirled to charge his assailant. Geres threw a second fist, narrowly missing Time's chin before they collided in a mass of flesh and fury. Driven back, they crashed through the thin wall separating the apartment's two bedrooms. Dust and wood rained down over them. Time had Geres in a tight grip, crushing the air from his lungs. Geres responded by dropping elbows on him. Blood trickled from several spots on both men as the titans fought to the death. A rib snapped. A nose broke. Two teeth flew across the floor. It took all of Geres's strength to roll them over so he was on top.

"Geres, behind you!" Presha shouted.

He turned his head in time to catch a blow to his temple. Krimpen barreled into him, knocking him off Time. Smaller and outclassed, he struggled to disentangle. Furious, Geres grabbed Krimpen by the back of his head and slammed it into an antique dresser. Wood splintered as the furniture collapsed. He left Krimpen unconscious and went for the wounded Time.

On his knees gasping for air, Time was exposed. Geres wasted no time and kicked the man in the side of his head with the flat of his boot. Time dropped and did not move. Checking each to ensure they were not getting up, Geres doubled over and placed his hands on his knees. His chest heaved as it struggled to fill with oxygen.

"Are you all right?" Presha asked, moving to his side after her initial fear subsided.

He glared at her through the blood dripping into his eyes. "We need to move."

"What about them?" she gestured.

"Fuck them. They won't mess with us again," he said.

She believed him. Presha hurried to her room to gather her meager belongings before they fled into the night. There was no choice but to go to Prophet Isle now. All other options were eliminated. As they boarded the aircab, she thought back on what her assailants accused her of. They sped away with her mind reeling from the revelation that they had nothing to do with the Prekhautens or Amongeratix. *How many others will come forth seeking their revenge for my accused crimes?* She shuddered at the answer.

"Krimpen!"

Stunned, spots forcing him to reclose his eyes, he replied, "Make the room stop spinning."

After great effort, he rolled onto his back and let his hands fall across his chest. Everything hurt, worse when he tried to move. Krimpen felt broken bones stabbing into his flesh. His stomach hurt so deeply, he knew he was going to pass blood the next time he urinated. Surprisingly, it was his mouth that hurt the most. He poked tentative fingers around, groaning upon discovering the hole where two molars had been.

"What happened?" Time asked from across the room.

"We lost." *Bastard took us by surprise and beat the hells out of us. That's what we get for underestimating him. Won't happen again. Next time, big boy. Next time we do it on my terms.*

It took every ounce of strength and no small measure of gritting his teeth to sit up. Lacking strength, he scooted back into the ruined dresser and leaned back to allow it to support his weight. His clothes were ripped. Flesh bruised and bloodied. Krimpen still could not see well, and his head felt like it was being pounded on by a pack of alley brats, but he made out his friend's body.

"You still alive?" he asked.

Time wasn't sure. He remembered watching the boot coming, knowing it easily could have collapsed the side of his head. Combined with the heavy blow to the back of his head when the fight started, it was a wonder he still drew breath. Time lacked medical skills but was wise enough to know he was concussed. "I think so. My head hurts."

Krimpen started to laugh before the pain forced him to stop. "You get a good look at who he was?"

"Yeah. Same man that was with her on Kharsis. Don't seem like we got any luck," Time replied.

"Story of our lives. You need to see a healer?"

Time coughed, spitting a wad of phlegm and blood on the floor. "Need or want?"

"What are you two idiots doing here?" a familiar voice scolded.

Krimpen opened his eyes to slits. Two figures stood in the doorway, blurred and distorted. They gradually came into focus and he groaned as an all too familiar face took shape through the haze. "If it isn't the gods damned pirate boy."

Prekhauten sailors administered to their wounds, much to their protest. Krimpen and Time were insipidly proud men who refused help, even when it was needed. It took the threat of confinement for them to agree to let the medics treat them, and even that proved almost more trouble than it was worth. Pain meds blocked the worst of it, yet left them coherent enough to explain their version of events.

"By rights, you should be dead," Captain August told Time after she inspected the visible damage to his head.

Time broke into a toothy, blood smeared grin. "What can I say? My momma always knew I wasn't smart enough for my own good."

"Lovely," she replied with disdain. "Vicente, who are these two exactly?"

Blackheart groaned, suddenly unwilling to explain how they wound up in his employ and the subsequent sad relationship they shared. By the time he finished, August was almost as confused as she had been upon finding the duo unconscious in Presha Von's room.

"Value of services lacking, what were you doing here?" she demanded.

Hand pressed against the pounding in his head, Krimpen resisted the urge to excoriate her with his customary wit. "We've been bouncing around since Kharsis, landed here, and happened to stumble upon that bitch about a week ago."

"That bitch," Time echoed from the divan across the room.

August glared at him, feeling sorry for the thorough beating they took. "Your plan was what? Make a citizens' arrest and deliver her to the local garrison for the reward?"

Krimpen shrugged and winced as fresh jets of pain rocketed through his skull. "It seemed like a good idea at the time. We even waited for that big bastard she hangs around with to leave."

"Not long enough apparently," Blackheart added.

"I don't like you," Krimpen replied, jabbing his finger.

"You may have acted in your best interests, indeed it would be a benefit to the universe to get a criminal of this order off the streets, but you have made our job infinitely more difficult," August scolded. "Do you have any idea where they went?"

"Lady, we wasn't even awake when they left. How are we supposed to know where they took off to?" Time snarled.

"Save the attitude for those you might impress," August replied. "I'm not one of them, by the way. What you have accomplished is sending Presha Von deeper into hiding."

"So what?" Krimpen asked. "The less the world sees of her, the better."

"Idiot, what if she does to this world as she did to Kharsis? How do you feel about being responsible for the more innocent lives lost?" Blackheart threw back. "We came here to stop her and get the damned weapon back, so it can't be used again."

Time shifted focus from the pirate lord to his best friend. The possibility of her using the weapon again never occurred to them, and now that it had, he refused to be conducive to allowing its use again. Krimpen groaned, rolling his eyes before giving the slightest nod.

"We will atone for our mistake," Time announced. "We will accompany you until she is caught and brought to justice."

"Besides, I want another crack at the big man," Krimpen added.

"Lovely. This day just keeps getting worse," Blackheart said and left the room.

Secret Conclave Prison Facility P-579.

Mobus Kale ignored the masked prison guards bearing alien weapons as he was escorted through the space station. They reminded him of insects with their almost chitinous armor. Who, or what, the Conclave utilized as staff and security for P-579, was a mystery to all but the senior most cardinals, as was the facility they occupied. Built in the center of the Saladiad Nebula, P-579 was referred to as the end of the line by the Inquisition. Housing the worst criminals and heretics in the universe, death was the only means of leaving.

Camera feeds covered every inch of the interior and exterior, tracking movement with heat sensitive guns concealed in the ceilings. The deeper into the station he went, the more heightened security became. Trip sensors dissected the floor at random intervals. Guards increased. Entire corridors were rigged to compress the moment a prisoner escaped from his cell. Vents burrowed deep inside the infrastructure deposited other escapees into space. The end of the line had never been breached. Never had a successful escape attempt. Even if an inmate made it past the initial defenses, there was nowhere to go.

Guards in flowing capes of green obsidian marched in stride with him. He did not protest, knowing visitors were equally susceptible to the station's defense grid. Not a word was spoken between them, though he caught bits and pieces of insect-like chatter. *Aliens. They should have been eliminated long ago, like all the others. A plague on the universe.* Mobus scowled. His dislike for most living beings inspired his ferocity on the battlefield, but it was pure hatred for alien races that defined his character.

They halted before a wall of transparent steel. Locked on the other side was a single man in spartan conditions. Mobus stared at Utan Husk. The butcher of Rofe Kas was clamped to the floor by his ankles. An unbreakable shock collar wrapped around his neck. The filth-stained smock went down to his knees and was his only piece of clothing. Ragged, unkempt hair drifted past his shoulders. His nails were cracked and filthy. Mobus knew the man screamed of uncleanliness.

"Why is he treated like this?" he asked. His tone was laced with anger. "This man was a solider in the Prekhauten Guard."

"Prisoner 74223-A has been sentenced for crimes against humanity. He is no longer classified human," a sterile voice replied over the station intercom. "This encounter is unorthodox, despite being approved by the office of the Inquisitor General. Please conduct your business."

"Open a channel to him," Mobus demanded.

A panel appeared to his right. One of the guards placed the back of his hand on it and a green light blinked on. He nodded to Mobus and stepped back into position.

"Utan Husk, can you hear me?"

Husk's head remained lowered, hair concealing his face.

"Answer me, Husk."

"I know that voice. A ghost from the past," Utan cackled but did not move. "That you, Mobus?"

"It is. I have come to get you out of here," Mobus responded.

Utan laughed. The maniacal sound grated in Mobus's ears. It was the sound of madness. "No one leaves the end of the line. You should know that."

"The Inquisitor General sanctioned your release," Mobus said. "Under special condition."

Utan's head rose. Hair fell away, giving Mobus his first look at what remained of the soldier he once knew. Red streaked eyes glared through years of grime. A grizzled beard and moustache covered most of his face, lending a wild appearance.

"He's the one who put me in here," Utan glowered.

Mobus was thrown off guard. He had not known what to expect. This was not it. The end of the line had pushed Utan Husk to his breaking point. There was a time such punishment might have been considered appropriate. The man was singularly responsible for the largest massacre of civilians by any Prekhauten in the order's storied past. A villain by every measurable standard, he represented the physical manifestation of evil.

"Times have changed. The universe is at war and I am authorized to employ any in my personal service for the duration."

"Who are we at war with?" Utan asked.

Mobus poked his tongue into one cheek. "Ourselves. Guards, release this man and have him cleaned up. I shall await him on my shuttle."

Mobus Kale began the long walk back to his ship. His escort fell in step and marched him away. The wheel was now in motion. Soon, his dreams of seeing Davith Strannan's head on a spike in front of Prekhauten headquarters would become reality.

ELEVEN

3215 A.G. (After gods), Front lines, Mannus Prime.

Torgast tossed the latest stack of casualty reports onto an overcrowded desk and rubbed his eyes. The sun set hours ago, yet his work continued. His commando raid on the enemy command structure resulted in little more than a handful of enemy casualties and the elimination of his entire team. Without a way to break the stalemate in the trenches, he was forced to watch as his army bled itself dry, day by day.

Then there was news from Cardinal Virom from Eger City. His efforts to placate the Inquisition met with failure. Word reached him at dusk they were arriving in the morning to arrest him. The war drained him on numerous levels, leaving a shell of the man. Torgast needed the help Virom promised badly. Stray cannons fired in the distance. They were the least of his worries.

Torgast remembered a time when the sound made him flinch. Hells, the first time he took incoming fire, he jumped in the nearest hole, while those around him stopped and laughed at his expense. War was funny that way. Only soldiers could take the worst aspects of life and treat them with humor. He supposed it was easier that way. Life and death meant so little on the front lines. If he stopped to consider every tally in every report, he might lose his mind. Reducing them to numbers did little to assuage his guilt for ordering them to their deaths, but it did allow him to sleep at night.

"Sergeant Quint! Get in here," he barked.

Jelin Quint, looking unhappy with the chevrons on his sleeves, sidled into the tent. Torgast admitted to a degree of satisfaction with seeing the man thoroughly displeased with his current position. Perhaps not for the same reasons Quint was. The man was pushed to his breaking point and developing a bad drinking problem when the provosts threw him in the brig. Lesser soldiers would have committed suicide by now. He had seen it a hundred times since the campaign on Mannus began. Distraught by the loss of so many friends, Quint teetered on the edge.

"Sir?" Quint asked.

"Tomorrow is going to be a task for you," Torgast began. "I have received word that a pair of rogue Inquisitors are coming to arrest me. This cannot happen. Should my command be removed, the entire army will be surrendered into enemy custody. Officers and senior sergeants will most likely be executed for treason. The rest will either be forced into service or sent to internment camps until the war is over. Where do you think you'll fit in to this new order?"

"Permission to speak plainly?" Quint asked after frowning in thought.

Torgast nodded.

"Sir, seems to me, I would have been fine until you made me a target by promoting me," Quint replied. "That being said, I'm starting to take a shine to being able to tell people what to do. I'd just as soon keep my head on my shoulders."

"I don't disagree with you. In fact, I share the same instincts. We are at a dangerous time in this campaign. Word has it, reinforcements are on the way. In theory, we should be able to break the lines and secure this world."

The news left Quint reeling. Regrets from his unit being slaughtered only a few days ago threatened to push him back into the bottom of a bottle. Listening to his commanding officer explain it might have been for naught, almost casually, riled him. Thousands of good men and women died over the course of the war. For what, went well above his pay grade.

"My question for you, Sergeant Quint, is where do your loyalties lie?" Torgast asked.

Quint rocked back, stunned at being doubted. "Sir, I have always been loyal to the Guard."

Torgast gave a clipped nod. "I need you to execute a specific task, Quint. Once I explain it to you, you can accept the assignment or turn in your stripes and be sent back to the line. No shame. No disciplinary action."

"What sort of assignment, sir?" Quint was hesitant. His instincts screamed this was the sort of thing men got killed for. "I didn't survive this last turn on the line just to die now."

"Death seldom pauses us to consider how we feel, Quint. I have a list of enemy sympathizers within our ranks. They range in rank, but all are detrimental to our coming out of this alive," Torgast explained. "I am detailing you command of a commando squad to round up and arrest everyone on the list. I expect this to be executed quietly, with discretion. Should even one of these traitors sniff word of your coming, the entire network will collapse and we will never get another chance."

He let that sink in, keeping how the coming Inquisitors would no doubt use those same individuals to reinstate order once the command staff was removed. *We just need to hold out for Admiral Falchi to get here.*

Rubbing his chin in thought, Quint asked, "What condition do you want these prisoners in?"

"Alive will be sufficient, though I am quite positive many of them will have different opinions," Torgast said. He collected a datapad off the table and extended it to Quint.

Quint accepted the information. "By dawn?"

"By dawn."

Snapping to attention, Jelin Quint saluted and exited the tent. The promised commando squad was already formed up and waiting. He paused in the doorway as Torgast offered one final word and headed off to his mission.

Discretely. *How in the fuck am I supposed to do that?*

"Are you sure this information is accurate?" Torgast asked.

Cardinal Virom's voice was distorted by jamming. "Enough. You are running out of time, my friend."

He reread the list of names in disgust. "I need some of these people, Cardinal. It doesn't matter who the Admiral sends me, the troops look up and respect half the names you provided. Loyalty goes a long way in maintaining morale. How am I supposed to secure momentum after I am seen arresting senior officers and sergeants?"

"The Inquisition has given you little choice. I tried to dissuade them, but Bela Cass has become most adamant about adhering to the Inquisitor General's demands. I believe her hostility is born from being deployed to Mannus Prime and not a world she deems important enough to allocate Inquisition resources."

"Meaning we are wasting her time," Torgast snorted. He had disliked the rough Inquisitor from their first meeting.

Aggression had its uses, but not among those requiring a more thoughtful demeanor. "What do the gods say regarding this?"

"Remarkably little. Much of what was written decrees man has the right to act according to conscience. Thought laws govern us; it is the passion of our emotions that guide us down the paths to righteousness."

"That is not reassuring, Cardinal."

"No, it really isn't. Let me ask you this, do you feel you are doing the right thing?" Virom chuckled in response.

"Sometimes," Torgast said after a pause. "What fuels your faith? How do you know you are doing the gods' work?"

"Listen to your heart, Torgast. That is the best advice I can give," Virom said. "Best of luck tomorrow."

The line dropped, leaving Torgast conflicted between heart and duty.

"That will be all, corporal," Brigadier Alfan Terroza said, as he sipped his already cooling tea.

He ran a hand through his thinning gray hair and watched as the younger soldier departed. Alone for the first time today, Terroza found it difficult to calm his nerves or focus on anything other than the coming event. Promising to have far reaching repercussions, the return of the Inquisitors from Eger City was the catalyst he needed to recharge his career and get back on the winning side.

Time and a string of setbacks in what he viewed a ridiculous form of warfare, disillusioned him from what Torgast deemed the honest path. *All lies used to slaughter so many. What a fool I was to assume any of us had the authority to struggle for righteousness. No matter. Tomorrow brings a new dawn and an end to this pointless war.*

He heard the tent door brush open, too quietly for any of his staff. "I said that will be all. Or are my order no longer heeded in this army?"

There was no answer. Only the ghostly sound of light footsteps leading to his chair. The cold barrel of a rifle pressed against the back of his head before he could turn. Terroza's blood chilled.

"Brigadier Alfan Terroza, you are hereby placed under arrest for acts of treason," an unfamiliar voice growled. "Please get up and come quietly. This doesn't have to get messy."

Choking back his emotions, the brigadier gently set his cup on the small table to his right. "I don't suppose I have the opportunity to defend myself?"

"No."

Terroza exhaled, knowing it was his final act of freedom. How or why Torgast discovered the mounting insurrection meant little. His career was finished. Guaranteed to spend the duration of the war in a prison camp. His eyes flit to the sidearm casually laying on his cot. Just out of reach. *How much time would it take to reach the gun and end my life? Enough to avoid being shot in the back of the head? Or worse?* The bravado of false theatrics faded as he blanched at the prospect of being shot, whether by his captors or his own hand. Terroza was nowhere near as brave as his battlefield persona. He lifted his hands in resignation and rose.

"Very well. I ask only that my men are given the truth behind my removal," he demanded.

Iron cuffs were clamped around his wrists. Jelin Quint stepped into view. "Brigadier, that is the least of your worries. Get him to the holding pens."

Brigadier Alfan Terroza was dragged away into the night, a victim of his own design. Quint crossed his name off the list and readied to strike the next.

The dice game was well into its fifth hour. Pushing close to midnight, soldiers hooted over winnings and groaned over losses. Pay meant little to the frontline units, though it served as a reminder they were more than mere cannon fodder. Each entrance covered in adherence to light discipline orders, the gathered group was drenched with sweat.

Private Enslo Waq grabbed the fistful of winnings from his last run and stuffed them down his blouse front. He was jeered by his friends when he decided he needed fresh air to properly appreciate his winnings. Waving them off with choice words, Waq slipped outside and breathed. He could not believe his luck. This was the first time he won in over three months, and judging from the stack of bills, was more than that worth of pay. Victory never tasted so good.

He looked up at the sound of a boot scuffing loose gravel and smiled. "Pickings are good tonight, friend! You can take my place. I've won enough."

The newcomer moved swiftly, closing the distance between them. "Private Waq, you're coming with me."

"I don't think so. How do you know my name?" Waq stammered.

Hands shot forward, snatching him by his collar and dragging his face perilously close to the other's mouth. Spittle struck him when the man spoke.

"Make a sound and I'll snap your fucking neck, traitor."

Waq felt his knees give out. "I have money. Take it. Just leave me alone!"

He reached for his blouse and was rewarded with a blow to the head. The world went dark before he was lifted and carried away. Jelin Quint wiped his hands, inspecting the torn flesh of a knuckle. So far, so good.

Inquisitors Bela Cass and Dowan Munn stormed through the Prekhauten camp with perceived impunity. Guards knew their place in the grand order and shied away from the cold black uniforms detailed with a single blue-tinged red rose. The Inquisition was more trouble than it was worth in most eyes. Using this to their advantage, Cass projected authority. The squad of internal soldiers marching in formation behind her added weight as they headed for Commander Torgast's command tents.

To her surprise, she found him waiting. Her eyes narrowed, sensing a trap. Only a handful of usual guards and runners were present, however. Bela projected her voice for all to hear. "Torgast, you are hereby relieved of command and reprimanded to Inquisition custody. Surrender your sidearm. Now."

Torgast pretended to look surprised. "On what authority?"

"The Inquisitor General accuses you of heresy, subject to punishment as we see fit," Bela explained. Her blood was up. These were the moments she lived for. A chance to redeem herself in the Order's eyes and assumed a position befitting her stature.

"You see, that's going to be a problem," Torgast replied. "I have enough Guards who say otherwise."

Dowan sidestepped Bela. "Torgast, listen to reason. There is no need to make this more difficult than it needs to be. You are being accused of the gravest crime. Let us do our job and there will be no bloodshed."

Torgast swept his gaze over the assembled soldiers in obsidian uniforms. Armored with facemasks, they presented a formidable appearance. If only they fought as well as they looked. The Inquisition Guard was largely ceremonial, lacking combat experience. Men and women choosing to hide their faces behind a mirrored sheen, garnered no respect from their Prekhauten counterparts. Torgast pursed his lips. Bela Cass had to have known this, suggesting she was overly confident. It was all he could do to keep the smirk from his face.

"I don't believe I'm going to let you arrest me today," he told her, loud enough his voice swept through the rows of neatly arranged tents.

Bela's face darkened. "Don't be a fool, Torgast. I'll strike you down right here. It makes no difference to me if you come alive or dead."

He gestured to the guard escort with his head. "Going to use your little toys to do it or do you have the stones to pull the trigger yourself?"

"Don't tempt me," she growled.

She shrugged off Dowan Munn's warning hand on her arm.

"What's all this noise?" a voice boomed. "Look lads, the Inquisitor brought her pretty little toys. I wonder if they can fight as well as they look?"

Helmeted heads twisted left and right as throngs of armed Guards emerged to fill the gaps between the tents and the open space leading up to the command tent. Grizzled veterans raised their rifles in expectation. The hum of charging rifles cackled.

"What is the meaning of this?" Bela demanded. "I am under the authority of the Inquisitor General! Stand down and return to your units."

Jelin Quint stepped ahead of the rest of his soldiers. "Sorry lady, we don't take orders from you."

"Torgast, your people will be slaughtered," Bela warned. "I'll have every man and woman above the rank of corporal executed for treason."

Torgast leaned against the tent pole to the right of his door and waved. "Feel free. Though I expect you might meet with some resistance. You see, Inquisitor, this is my army. These are my people. I haven't spent the last two years fighting with them, to abandon them to madness at the behest of a third rate Inquisitor."

Face flushed with rising anger; Bela drew her handgun. "Fool! I have a host of personnel in place to ensure the transition of command to my authority."

"Begging your pardon, but you don't," Quint interrupted. "You can join them in the brig. Well, most of them anyway. Everyone but Colonel Ghez came quietly."

The menace in his voice gave her pause. Confused, Bela Cass realized she was outnumbered. Her bid for power failed and there was little she could do. She raised her blaster and took aim at Torgast. He flinched, twisting away before the fatal shot. A hiss echoed across those gathered. Blood and brain matter splattered. Bela Cass fell dead before she squeezed the trigger. Dowan Munn watched as Quint, smoke trickling from his barrel, stepped forward and kicked her blaster away before turning on the armored squad.

"Drop those guns. Now," he ordered. Quint swung his weapon at the last Inquisitor, when the escorts remained steadfast. "Now, or I'll blow his fucking brains across the area."

"I suggest you do what he says," Dowan stared down the barrel. "I have little doubt his people will do the same to you as he did to Inquisitor Cass. Stand down."

The first weapon lowered. Others followed. Quint jerked his barrel and Guards swarmed the Inquisition to relieve them of their weapons. Fists and elbows were thrown. Rifle butts slammed against helmets. One by one, the Inquisition Guard were subdued and arrested. Dowan Munn watched impassively, hands raised to offer no resistance.

He craned his head toward Torgast. "Perhaps we can discuss the future in your quarters, commander?"

"Sergeant Quint, lock this scum with the others and get them all on the next secured transport to the local prison in Eger City," Torgast ordered.

Quint's glare settled on the Inquisitor. "What about him?"

"That remains to be seen."

Warning bells went off in Quint's mind. Like most Guard, he had little to no trust for any wearing the blue tinged rose. Leaving his commanding officer alone with a man recently arrived to arrest and execute him went against every instinct Quint possessed. This was war. There was little room for error. Especially now.

"Sir, I think I should stay here," he suggested with iron in his tone.

Torgast grinned in appreciation. "Thank you, Sergeant, but I believe the matter is well under control. Report to me once the task is complete."

Salute hesitant, Quint narrowed his eyes and started barking orders to the group of volunteers herding the prisoners. His last sight was Torgast's tent flap closing as the two men went inside.

"This is the moment of your lives that matters the most. A time of confluence, where you can truly cast off the shackles of this mundane existence, abandon the laws enforced upon you by the religious zealots of the Conclave and their Inquisition murderers. This day. This hour. Free yourselves to enjoy the pleasures of a vast universe whose secrets we have only begun to explore. Will you stand with me? Take my hand and elevate yourselves to the image of perfection?"

Kaline stood in the center of a ring of villagers. Most were haggard, exhibiting the signs of a hard life. She empathized with them, appealing to their inert sense of righteousness and values so often ignored by the planet's rulers. Her words incited hidden anger, fueling their sudden and growing need to be free.

Her words were songs on the wind. A melody beckoning potential faithful to the flock. Kaline knew it was a lie. She spoke as she always had but it lacked the emotion Mollock Bolle delivered to the people of An'kuruku in what felt like a lifetime ago. The passion simmered within, despite her inability to summon the same level of compulsion so many thousands obeyed in the brief desert war. She wished she had a fraction of his oratory skills.

"Why should we go to war for you?" a man barely into his twenties, shouted from the crowd. "The government doesn't even know we exist. Why bring them here now?"

Others cheered or grunted their consent. A few tried to shout her down, angered at what they felt threatened their way of life. Most remained silent, cautiously pondering her words. They were a people used to going unnoticed. Ignored by the universe. Kaline's unexpected intrusion not only threatened to end their way of life, it offered to bring them into a world gone mad with the ravages of war.

"No one is asking you to go to war," Kaline insisted. "We are offering the chance to remove those shackles keeping you mired in this village, while the rest of the universe continues to grow, advance, and soar across the stars like kings."

"We have lived this way for generations," an older woman told her.

Kaline twirled, her crimson robes spinning around her legs. "And you have been forgotten. Passed by as other tribes, other races, continue to grow and develop in ways your elders could never dream. Are you willing to let your children and their children remain obsolete? Ignorant of the greater universe in which they belong?"

The elder remained firm. Weathered skin coppered her face and hands. Lines burrowed deep across her flesh. "This is where our youth belong. We are a simple people, immune to the pressures of the greater universe. You come to us unbidden with golden words weaved upon your tongue and speak of war and freedom. Yet when last we looked, it was the outsiders who are caught in a circle of violence."

"This is not freedom. Each day the war rages, on this very planet, your freedom is constricted. What will happen to this village when the battle is brought to you? You lack the weapons, the knowledge of fighting to contend with galactic armies bent on conquest. For that matter, there is no guarantee which side will find you first."

Her voice rose with each damning statement. This was the moment Kaline had awaited. A trigger point capable of pushing the young and dissatisfied over the edge, while breaking the backs of the steadfast elders too blind to understand their place in the universe. Emboldened, she pressed her assault.

"Right now, and only now, you are being given the opportunity to break free. To defend your homes and loved ones from the wicked wrath consuming half the planet," she said. "I do not bring promises of salvation or atonement in the eyes of the gods. No, I'm afraid no mortal has the authority to barter that power. What I am offering you is the power of a god himself."

Whispers and murmurs rippled through the villagers and Kaline concealed her delight.

"My friends, allow me to give you the teachings of Rengu. Take up the cause in his name and your lives will never be the same again. No man or woman will ever have the authority to claim their dominance over you. This is the gift I bring to you."

Bowing, Kaline stepped from the circle and hurried back to the security of her armed escort. Their eyes met, briefly, before she followed him to the small hut they were allowed by the elder council. Paltry accommodations meant nothing to Kaline, for she was here with purpose none could dissuade.

"How was I?" she asked once they were alone.

The Captain sat on a three-legged stool facing the door, rifle over his knees. "Terrifying. I would hate to stand against you for public office."

"What we are doing goes far beyond the constraints of politics, Captain," she replied, refusing to use his true name. His recent revelation inspired fear deep within her heart, a chilling sensation she had not been able to shake since he uttered his name. Unsure whether it was out of respect for his past deeds or that same fear, Kaline vowed to never repeat his name.

His face twisted with disapproval. "This is a dangerous game. I've been to a hundred villages just like this one. Any wrong move, thought, or provocation will result in immediate expulsion or worse. We've already lost one man on this expedition. I don't want to be next."

"You are worried over nothing. I, too, have experience working over these villages. A dozen worlds have been liberated to the will of Rengu through my efforts," she insisted. *Though none as successfully as An'kuruku. Mollock Bolle was a gifted orator. I lack that strength.*

"That may be, but I can't fight off a hundred angry villagers, even if they lack modern weaponry."

She placed a hand on his knee. Subtle. Tender. "Relax. Let the process work. You'll see. Soon we will have willing converts to fuel the cause."

He remained skeptical but placed his faith in her. The natural authority of her demeanor imposed restrictions on his former training. Kaline was beautiful and deadly in equal measure. Accepting her truth, the Captain settled into his watch.

Hours passed. Bright skies gradually turned to darkness. Fires were lit throughout the village. A pair of youths arrived with wood and tinder and an invitation for the offworlders to dine with the elders. Kaline politely refused, much to the Captain's disagreement, with a smile and a promise to take them up on the offer in the morning. They left and time continued passing. It was some time in the middle of the night when the next visitor arrived. A hesitant knock on the hut door roused the Captain from his light slumber. His finger slipped into the trigger well, dancing lightly over the slender piece of metal requiring a mere five pounds of pressure to go off.

Kaline watched his reaction, confirming her fears. "Easy, my friend. I have been expecting this."

She bade their guest enter, patting down her robes to offer a balanced, well-kept appearance, despite the knots twisting her stomach. Kaline was surprised to see the first speaker from their council slip inside. He stood awkwardly, hands clasped before him as he struggled to figure out where to begin.

"Are you sure this is a good idea?"

Samuel looked at his former commanding officer with a raised eyebrow. He may be the current captain of the *Indomitable*, but this was still Falchi's crew and it was all his plan.

"Sir," Samuel began. "It may not be the best idea but it is the only viable one on the table."

Falchi grunted, adjusting his uniform for the fifth time. He wondered how they had devolved to working with mercenaries and worse, inviting them aboard his command ship. Never before, at least not to his knowledge, had a Prekhauten Guard ship of the line stooped so low. *Then again, we have never been forced into a civil war either. Damn Nye.*

"This war will make beggars of us all before the end, Samuel," he said.

Samuel grinned. "Speak for yourself, Admiral. I plan on retiring to a nice quiet resort world in one of the outer sectors as far from Vau Prime as possible."

"Fruity drinks and having your toes nibbled by gueff fish, eh? I never took you for the relaxing type."

Samuel shrugged. "After this? I owe it to myself."

"Don't we all," Falchi agreed. "All right, sergeant, let's welcome our guests."

The sergeant of the guard saluted and blew the ivory whistle to announce the formal welcome of Matthias and the Shadow Hammer command staff. The hard-bitten former sergeant major stepped with an uneasy gait alongside three mercenaries and the smuggler, Ishis Gul. Baleful glares passed between them, with Gul looking decidedly uncomfortable. Falchi dared not guess what passed between them to raise tensions so high.

"Matthias, welcome back," Falchi said after clearing his throat.

"Admiral. It's been an interesting voyage. You already know Ishis Gul. This is Bootleg, commanding officer of the Shadow Hammer mercenary company."

On cue, the mercenary rubbed his palm on his trousers and extended it. Falchi tried not to wince as he accepted it. "Admiral, mighty fine ship you got here. Never been on one this big before."

Falchi looked to Matthias.

"Most of his people are former Guard," the sergeant major explained. The newer models were deployed after their terms of service expired."

"Expired hells! Most of us either deserted or decided the bureaucratic bullshit wasn't for us. We're proper soldiers, you see. Born for the fight and damned good at it, too," Bootleg contradicted. "I hear you got a little problem you need help with?"

Disgusted, Falchi said, "I assume you have been briefed on the situation on Mannus Prime?"

A nod.

"Our mission is simple. Relieve the loyal forces bogged down on the planet and incorporate both them and the manufactories to our war effort," Falchi said. "We need the manpower and the munitions to keep fighting, if there is any hope of retaking Vau Prime from the traitors."

Bootleg rubbed his jaw, the stubble producing a scratching sound. "Not my problem. We'll fight for you. We'll fight with you, but it's going to cost you."

"Those are negotiations for another time," Samuel cut in. "We are currently eight standard hours from dropping into the Mannus Sector. Are your people ready to deploy?"

Bootleg eyed him up and down, passing silent judgment. "Ready enough. Just point us in the right direction and tell us who to kill. We only have one request."

The Guard officers exchanged a wary glance. Having mercenaries onboard was one thing, acquiescing to petty demands, another. Falchi placed his hands behind his back, hoping to portray a sense of calm he did not feel. The sound of infantry companies preparing for the upcoming ground assault grew louder.

"That being?" he asked.

Bootleg jerked his head toward Matthias. "We want him to be your liaison. Me and the sergeant major here have unfinished business."

"Something I need to know about, Matthias?" Falchi turned to his old friend.

Matthias shook his head. Stray locks of graying black hair tickled across his forehead. "Nothing terribly important."

"We go way back," Bootleg added with a bloodthirsty drawl.

Falchi suppressed a groan. The gift of having a five thousand strong compliment of fighters at his command was complicated by rivalries from years past. Too many variables threatened to undo his plans. One push in the wrong direction, or with too much force, and the alliance broke apart, rendering his chances of relieving the siege all but impossible.

"Matthias, are you fine with this?" he asked.

Samuel balked.

"No, but it is the only viable option for now," Matthias replied. "We're at the tip of the spear. One good offensive and the planet is ours, along with the hundred and thirty thousand ground troops. I'll be fine."

Falchi stiffened. "Very well. Bootleg, is it? You have the sergeant major. Additionally, I am detaching a combined army and marine contingent to ensure our two forces act in unison as the campaign advances. This is not negotiable."

It was the mercenary's turn to hesitate. Glancing at each of his staff to gauge their reactions, Bootleg shouted over his shoulder, "Asher, get up here."

The young former Guard sauntered up behind him. Her crimson hair was tied back, lending her a severe look. "Yeah?"

"You're on babysitting duty with the Guards," Bootleg ordered. He returned focus to Falchi, "Good enough for you?"

"For now. Might as well get down to business. Where are we fighting and who do we need to kill?"

Samuel escorted them to a small debriefing room attached to the main hangar. Waiting for them to pass, Falchi grabbed Bootleg by the upper arm and leaned close. "If Matthias dies by anything other than enemy action, I will ensure every last one of your company is killed on that planet. Am I clear?"

A feral grin showed missing teeth. "For now."

He left Admiral Falchi alone, already thinking of how he was going to have to remove the mercenary leader from the equation.

TWELVE

3215 A.G. (After gods), the Forsaken Path.

Spitting out the mouthful of ash, Ah'muf resisted the temptation to pour water over his face. The Forsaken Path was just that. Endless kilometers of ash, dust, and despair. Each day was a struggle to continue. He began to lose hope of seeing the clear skies of his precious desert again. Of finding the happiness he once thought he deserved. Life became an illusion, despite having the woman who held his heart at his side.

Ah'muf caught her watching him. "What?"

She shrugged, a playful gleam in her eye. "Nothing. It just surprises me to watch a grown man bent over lamenting his situation. That and I was checking out your ass."

His face flushed, conscious of his awkward position. "That is not ladylike, farisi."

"What can I say? I'm a woman of the times," she replied and gestured to the corner of her mouth. "You missed a spot."

Frustrated, Ah'muf gave in and emptied his canteen on his face. "What are we doing here? This is not a place for good people. And don't tell me it is to save the universe. At this point, I don't care about anything more than getting home."

She lacked the heart to tell him she doubted they were ever going to see home again. So much had changed over the last few years Elisa no longer recognized herself. She wished she had never met Ah'muf, never left Crimeat, and never agreed to become the Paladin.

"You are mired in doubts."

The mirth faded from her. Elisa turned to the ghost of an old companion. "How can I not be? Nothing in my life makes sense. Here I am, far from home, in a place that should not exist, and speaking with a ghost. If that is what you are, Mollock."

The shade of Mollock Bolle remained silent, as if trapped in thought. In life they had never been friends. Each was captured by the Ugri and escaped. It was a mutual decision to travel together. One he regretted, though in retrospect they were always meant to find each other. A pair of lost souls twisted by fate and forced into impossible situations.

"You would think being dead is liberating," he said. "Instead, I find myself trapped. Locked in an eternal prison from which there is no release. How long have I been dead?"

Elisa stared at him. "Mollock, you were killed on An'kuruku two years ago."

"Two years. Yes. The desert planet. I remember being abducted by a red-haired woman. She … she used me to preach. Prophet," his face dropped. "All lies. Have we ever served ourselves, Elisa?"

"No."

The single word answer sent chills down Ah'muf's spine. He knew bits of their past. Quiet memories she whispered in the dark. The gods were cruel to use mortal lives in their designs. He saw it firsthand in the Deeves.

"We must be moving. Sorrow bought us time but the foe lurking in this realm seeks to devour all. Goti Tai is still far," Mollock advised.

A heavy weight fell upon Elisa's shoulders. It was a familiar burden. One she was forced to bear for as far back as memory served. Elisa came to terms with her relationship with Sorrow and the Three after being forced to flee Crimeat at the onset of the war. Accepting was a far cry from enthusiasm, however. The sole truth she was unwilling to admit was a dream of what life might have looked like if the Bloody Man had not arrived in her village that chill morning.

"What chance have we against those … things if Sorrow could not stand?" she asked.

Her voice was tight, filled with stress and ready to crack.

Mollock attempted to smile. Broken teeth poked through his lips. "My dear, this was never meant for any of the Three to endure. Sorrow did as he was meant to, just as you must. There are many wonders in this realm. Secrets humanity was never meant to know, much less experience as you are about to."

She snorted. Mollock knew secrets. It was the reason for his exile. Elisa looked to Ah'muf to gauge his reaction but the desert dweller sat with his head hung, strands of dark, greasy hair covering his face.

"None of that matters to me, Mollock. You should know that. I have been given a task to complete," she explained. "Finding this weapon and getting it back to Tannus, so he can finally kill his brother, will set us both free. The sooner I return to Wex… home, the sooner I can put this piece of my life behind me and look to the future.”

“We have no future, Paladin. This is our lot. The specificity of our lives. The sooner you accept this is all we are, the easier your task will become,” Mollock replied.

“Easy for you to say.”

“Farisi,” Ah’muf cautioned. His people were superstitious by nature and the thought of provoking a spirit sat ill with him.

Elisa waved him off. “I know. Very well, Mollock Bolle. Lead us to the next menhir so we can reach Goti Tai. This place is doing murder to my skin.”

Ah’muf’s groan carried across the ash fields.

Rain slashed upon them halfway through the day, though Elisa had trouble guessing time on the Forsaken Path. Day and night blended together and were locked in the nascent world of permanent twilight. A far cry from the desert heat or the jungle humidity she grew up with, this was a place of impossibilities. Petrified bushes and long dead trees stuck up from the ash without providing any cover for the travelers. The only thing preventing her head from being soaked was the wide brimmed hat she had worn since her days as a bounty hunter, but even that was little defense against the deluge.

Her faded duster, time worn and weatherproof, swished against her legs, rubbing the tops of her boots to a familiar song she found comforting. Elisa hummed an old tune she picked up during her travels. The melody soothed her, though she did not know the words. She wished there was an opportunity to share it with Ah’muf, for her companion was on the brink of exhaustion and worse. *Just get to this damned village, recover the weapon, and get the fuck out of here. That’s all he needs to get back to his old self.* It was the same lie she’d perpetuated since being transported here.

“Farisi! Look, the lights!” Ah’muf shouted over the din.

Following his finger, Elisa was rewarded with seeing the second portal billowing into the eternal darkness. The column of red and purple lights transformed the landscape into a foul scene, forcing her to look away. Shadows and misconceptions crept into Elisa’s thoughts. The rain lightened enough for them to halt and regain a small measure of composure.

"Mollock, what dangers lurk ahead?" she demanded, flashes of Sorrow's battle with nightmares fresh in her mind.

"I do not know." His flat reply raised the hair on her arms.

She stormed forward to confront the ghost. "How can you not know? You have been here for nearly two years!"

Mollock raised his hands, the tattered robes falling to his elbows. "Elisa, I have been dead for two years. That does not mean I have wandered this realm for that long. Death is complicated and I make no claims to understanding it. One moment I was fleeing for my life on An'kuruku. The next, I was summoned to escort you down the Forsaken Path."

His explanation quelled her growing ire. Elisa hadn't considered Mollock's plight. They never became fast friends during their ordeals, but she formed a begrudging respect for the uncanny recluse. She once wondered how she would have reacted, if their roles were reversed and she stumbled upon the sleeping god and became hunted for the rest of her life.

"I … I'm sorry, Mollock." The admission humbled her.

"Pay it no mind, Elisa. You have concerns of your own and should not fret over a dead man," he replied. "It is safe to assume more adverse creatures lurk where we least expect, though of what sort and how powerful, remains unknown."

"No guarantees," she nodded. Elisa slid her rifle from her shoulder and pulled the bolt to ensure a round was chambered. "No point in delaying either. Ah'muf, are you ready?"

"No," came his answer.

"Let us get one step closer to our goal. I tire of this realm," Elisa said.

The unlikely trio marched closer to their fate.

Ah'muf doubled over and emptied his stomach on the ash and stone. Elisa reeled, slamming into a column of pitted bone hard enough to knock the wind from her. Folding his hands in the sleeves of his robes, the ghost of Mollock Bolle watched as the humans struggled with the portal transition. They were an odd pair. Neither made sense. He felt there was a time when mortal emotions bonded him with Elisa, but memory was elusive in the afterlife. Mollock was far from complicated. It was only after he discovered the truth of the gods that his life devolved. Watching

Elisa and her desert friend together filled him with inspiration, and dread.

"Time is of the essence. If you are recovered enough, we must move on," he said.

Wiping bile drooling from her bottom lip, Elisa shot him a wicked glare. "Easy for you to say. You don't feel pain like us."

"No. I don't feel anything. No pain, no love, no emotion worthy of the name." His eyes filled with sorrow. "It is the great curse of immortality."

Elisa paused before replying. She bore the weight of many sins and admitted often lacking sympathy for those around her. Guilt gnawed upon her soul, threatening to rip it from her flesh. She was lost. Seeing the sadness Mollock bore helped her realize a strategic truth she ignored for too long. Guilt of surviving. Guilt of living. Guilt of continuing, when so many others failed.

"I'm sorry, Mollock," she whispered.

Head cocked, he asked, "For what?"

She began to tremble. "Everything. I should have been there for you. I … I didn't want to believe I was any sort of chosen one. All I wanted was to run and hide for my own selfish reasons. Leaving you on An'kuruku was a mistake."

"You did as your heart called," he replied. "There was no right or wrong answer to your deeds, Elisa. My fate was written the same time as yours. We had different paths."

"But you died," she protested. *Because I wasn't there for you. I left you to die, so I could wallow in my own grief. It isn't fair.*

"As must we all. The power of life and death is not in your hands, Elisa. Death stalks us at will. What we do with our time is what matters, not how the end comes," Mollock explained. "I have no regrets, my friend."

Would that I could say the same. Elisa snorted a laugh and looked around for the first time. Bones the size of buildings stuck up from the ground, poking into the sky at random. An endless field of skulls, rib cages, and more stretched away. Carrion eaters circled high in the twilight. Others perched upon the corpses of the past, waiting. A feeling of evil crawled through her, despite the lack of malice.

"What is this place?" she asked.

"The past. The future. Does it matter?" Mollock replied. "This is where all things return when their time has expired. Fitting, all things considered."

"How so? All I see are the bones of what might have been."

He nodded. "And what was. You have learned a single truth during your trials, Elisa. There are no gods, leastwise none humanity believes to be true, but the path you are upon is the gateway to a great many more you are ill prepared to accept."

Elisa frowned. Until now she had given the end of her quest little thought. Retrieve the weapon and return it to Tannus. Then what? Was her task complete? She doubted it. The Three were fickle and Elisa had a suspicion she was entwined with them to the bitter end.

A strand of crimson hair fell over half her face. Brushing it aside, Elisa asked, "What manner of creatures could have been so large?"

"There are rumors of leviathans in the deep deserts of my home world," Ah'muf said. He moved to stand beside her, his skin pale from the transition. "Great serpents larger than a village, though I have never seen one."

"Echoes of the past," Mollock said. "Guardians of a time best forgotten, yet too close to our futures."

Confused, Elisa gave the graveyard a final look. She had seen enough. The warning was clear. Her future was threatened with a similar fate, should she stray. The bounty hunter hefted her pack, so it rode higher on her shoulders. "It is not yet time to join them, Mollock. How far to the next menhir?"

"Not far, but we must cross a sea of sand laden with danger," the ghost replied.

Great. We go from bad to worse. "Lead the way. We're done here."

Walking under the judgmental stares of the birds clustered atop the bones, the weary band began the march to their next goal.

A great chasm halted their progress. What was once eight, now reduced to six, stood on shaky legs. They leaned on their spears, ragged breaths blowing plumes on the chill air. Emaciated, the survivors were ready to quit and return to the remains of their village. Sauwgon Hil stared at his brothers from beneath ice encrusted eyelids. Their spiritual leader, he viewed their quest in terms of failure.

Limited power became his when Ferri Juy gave his life in the caves. A willing sacrifice born of necessity. Would the others follow suit, if the moment arose? Sauwgon read their futures before the ritual slaying of the former elder and was rewarded with nothing. No insight. No gleam of tomorrow promising the bright dawn they sought. Locked in hesitation, Sauwgon Hil worried he was leading his people to their doom.

"We cannot cross this."

Sauwgon glared at the speaker. A freshly earned male named Fum Haloo. Born of a lower caste, Fum spent his years training to become an acolyte. A disciple of the cult Sauwgon followed, preached, and dedicated their lives to. He should have known better than to question the elder.

"Words of despair serve no purpose to our quest, Fum Haloo," Sauwgon scolded. "Have the others sacrificed their spirits for naught?"

Reprimanded, Fum lowered his head in submission. "No, elder. I spoke from emotion. It will not happen again."

Satisfied the lesson was learned, Sauwgon stepped to the edge and stared down. Red stained cliff walls leered back, beckoning him to step once more and join countless others in the murky bottom. Sauwgon Hil was no fool. The fetishes on his spear whistled from the wind blowing up from the chasm. Death would come in due time and he was not afraid. Death came to all and was not to be feared.

Squinting to peer through the murk far below, the shaman spied the faintest glimpse of movement. They were not alone. The ground began shaking. A flock of scaled birds burst from treetops on the opposite side of the chasm, squawking and hissing a combination of anger and fright. Insects crawled from burrows, streaming in lines between the six. Sauwgon watched the world transform and knew they had come upon their next challenge. A time of trying. A time of sacrifice.

The very ground roared. A hideous sound threatening to burst their eardrums. Sauwgon's weakened legs buckled, nearly pitching him to his death. *Not yet.* Great chunks of cliffside broke free, cascading away. Scree and dust choked the air. The shaman's vigilance was rewarded by the first glimpse of enormous red eyes peering back through the fog. His spear glowed with eldritch power, bolstered from the dragon encounter and infused with Ferri Juy's life essence. Stepped back, Sauwgon Hil was satisfied with seeing his disciples ready for battle.

It was one they would not win. Not with their limited understanding and fledgling power. No. This task was beyond them. Unless he performed magic unseen in a hundred generations. Sauwgon steadied his breathing and waited for their foe to arrive. It was not long.

A monster of stone and wood rose from the chasm. One hundred feet tall and meshed together by clay and detritus, the monster was beyond imagination.

The stench of old earth permeated the air, sickening the warriors even as they attempted to understand what confronted them. Sauwgon gawked after witnessing the confusion and hunger warring deep within the creature's eyes. Such wonders this realm held! He almost admired the impossibility of it all. A longing awakened deep within. The shaman felt desire take shape. A dream unrealized as he longed for the time when such might was his.

Moving to the sound of thunder, the giant placed a palm upon the chasm edge and readied to pull itself free of the prison that had held it for a thousand years. Freedom as a universal constant every creature, great and small, wished. Sauwgon felt a momentary spark of regret. This being, this colossal of old times, should never have awoken. There was no salvation to be had. Only pain and the steady regurgitation into the earth. Life was seldom fair.

Summoning his power, Sauwgon pointed his spear at the creature and whispered ancient words unheard upon the winds for generations. Blue and vermillion light spit from the spear tip, funneling into the creature's chest. Rock and clay burst free, cascading away. Sauwgon unleashed a second and third blast before the others joined him. Enhanced by the late Ferri Juy's essence, Sauwgon felt raw energy coursing through him. Muscles popped and flexed. Old flesh burned away to reveal bronze and alabaster. His hair singed. He felt nothing but unfettered power opening his mind.

Wounded, the creature lashed out. Bone and rock slapped Sauwgon from his feet. He sailed through the air and crashed into a boulder in a cloud of red dust. The others attacked in retaliation. Flames, energy, and raw power assaulted the creature. A rotted tree broke loose and slammed into the ground in front of them. Dust and debris choked the air. Three men were felled. The others redoubled their efforts, taking heart that their assault was having an effect.

Sauwgon choked on the dust, spitting mouthfuls as he rolled to his knees. He watched through tear-streaked eyes as his brave handful attempted the impossible. They had one chance to defeat the creature. One opportunity to win free and continue their quest. Sauwgon crawled over to his staff, grasped the sweat slick handle, and whispered two words into the crystal tip.

Fum Haloo.

A burst of invisible power struck the young disciple between his shoulders, imbuing him with the temporary gift. Bolstered, the youth roared and ran toward the creature. Spear held high above in both hands, Fum leapt the gap between the ground and the creature. He landed high upon the clay chest. Fum grasped a handhold of exposed roots and stabbed his spear with every ounce of energy in his body.

Blinding light escaped the creature as his death cries made the heavens weep. Ancient and irreplaceable, it reeled, staggering on weak legs. Recognition flashed across its face as it locked eyes on Sauwgon Hil. Defeat. A gnarled hand rose, slapping the dazed Fum Haloo to its chest. The snap of bones and squish of flesh bursting was audible above the cacophony. The subsequent explosion, as conflicting energies collided, spread a shockwave of devastation for leagues, burrowing deep into the earth where every living creature turned to ash and was forgotten.

Sauwgon Hil was the first to rise. He used his spear to limp to the sight of the final battle. Of Fum, there was no sign, nor was there any evidence of the creature they'd faced. Naught but a single golden gem lay before him. Instinctively, the shaman collected it and touched it to his spear, where it was enfolded with the spirit of Ferri Juy. His aches and pains diminished. He felt whole again. Without bothering to check on the others, they would be all right or they wouldn't, Sauwgon stepped to the chasm edge and shouted an incantation to the winds. A bridge of golden light spread from his feet, spanning the chasm.

Satisfied this was the way, the shaman turned to his companions four. "Come, brothers. This is how we cross. Destiny awaits!"

He stepped upon the golden bridge without wait, confident in the power his faith resonated.

Planet Inselcor.

Ash filled clouds choked much of the lower atmosphere. Inselcor was far from the main shipping and transit lanes. A forgotten world by all but the chart masters of the Prekhauten Guard on Vau Prime. Seas of lava bubbled, connected by great rivers of molten death. The toxicity of the air prevented terraforming. Few native species called Inselcor home, making it a prime candidate to develop military bases. It was a faulty plan. Casualties were high among the first engineer units deployed. Subsequent colonization efforts proved fatal early on and the Conclave abandoned settling the volcanic world. Countless years later, there was but one settlement on the entire planet.

Sorrow stalked down the well-worn path, ignoring the thorns of the only hearty lifeform on the planet scrapping his flesh and the heat emanating off the lava stream to his left. He was locked in thought, and doubt. It was an old game. One he dwelled on far too often. Events were proceeding at rapid pace. Despite having millennia to prepare, Sorrow inexplicably felt rushed. His brothers remained locked in a conflict far different from any previous. The end was approaching. They all felt it. Only the outcome remained in question.

Sorrow was no hero. He never wanted to be. Some claimed his life was a tragedy, born of desperation and cast into an eerie shadow from which he could never escape. Were they right? His face twisted at the thought. Of every sentient being he encountered, only his mother offered the love he required. His father was harsh, a constant upon the throne with little time for his three sons until Tannus dared question him in front of the court. Punishment was swift. Banishment faster. That decision led to war, and ultimately, annihilation.

Unable to abandon his people, Sorrow was there at the final battle of Occanum where the split factions of his people clashed for a final time. Occanum. Once the sparkling gem of the universe. Generations of history were lost in those dark days. The combined wealth of his species burned to nothing. The travesty unmatched by any before or after.

Oh, he tried. Tried to stop the war from escalating and restore a simulacrum of decency. No one listened. Hatred was too powerful. His only opportunity for redemption came when Tannus approached him with his plan to save as many of their people as he could. The inherent fallacy of it galled Sorrow, for how could either of them decide who lived or died? It was not their place and voiced his concerns. Tannus brushed them aside, claiming that all was lost, if they did not act. Perhaps, Sorrow now believed, it would have been best if they died out.

Instead, humanity spread from the ashes of their civilization and forgot they weren't gods. Forgot the years of slavery dedicated to Sorrow's people. Instead of wiping their names from history forever, humanity committed their gravest crime. They idolized their former masters, confirming an unwanted apotheosis whose repercussions continued to reverberate across the stars. It was far from coincidence they now stood upon that very same precipice. Amused by the realization, Sorrow turned and began the long walk back to his lair.

Automatons guarded the front gates. Each stood ten feet tall and was resplendent in crimson armor that was more ceremonial than effective. Sorrow did not design them for combat purposes. These were decorations intended to prevent prying eyes wandering too close. There was little reason to believe either of his brothers or their advocates would ever discover Inselcor. That didn't prevent Sorrow from establishing security protocols with his creations. Similar to his gifts to Tannus, they warded his lands and ensured all systems operated without fail. His great secret, a private joke between brothers, was Tannus' automatons were created to fight. In retrospect, Sorrow doubted they would last long against Amongeratix, should the villain discover Wexanos.

Sorrow swept by his creations without a glance. Silent watchers, their mechanic gazes remained locked on the ash strewn terrain. Doors hissed open, their pale gray in sick contrast to the bright crimson covering his body. Torches lined the short corridor, unnecessary with their heat. Sorrow spent little on his private defense. His time in seclusion was meant for introspection, not preparation for violence.

Empty rooms stretched deep underground. All were empty save one. Sorrow proceeded at a casual pace to the heart of his citadel. He pressed a hand on the gene lock before slipping inside. A crone sat huddled in a chamber sparse of furniture or mortal trappings. Head bowed, she stared at the ground with blinded eyes.

"Welcome home, Sorrow," she cackled at the sound of his footfalls. "It has been far too long since you last came to entertain me."

"Old Mother, it is no casual encounter I seek. Much has happened of late and I find myself pressed to act, lest all we have striven to achieve falls to ruin," he replied. There was a shameful tone in his voice.

"Do not lower your head on my account. We all must play our parts in this cosmic travesty. What depresses your spirits this day?"

He exhaled a breath he hadn't realized he was holding. "Amongeratix is loose at last. He goes to reclaim his armies and the

Behemoth. I fear we will not be able to stop him this time. Not unless something drastic forces change."

"Change is the one constant we all suffer, Sorrow. Do not forget your lessons," the crone chided. "You have untested strength within your soul. Tannus will not fall, and even if he should, you will discover your true purpose."

Confused, Sorrow said, "One planet has already fallen prey to Amongeratix. Billions of lives lost in the blink of an eye. Evil is at work and our allies thin with each new trial."

"Go to your brother. He will have need of your counsel," she explained.

Sorrow jerked back. "Old Mother, Tannus does not wish to see me. Our last meeting was a poor attempt at maintaining civility."

"He will listen because he has no choice," she insisted. "Go to Wexanos. The time has come at last. We have reached the crucible upon which the future of the universe hinges. Go, my son. Go and save us before it is too late."

Bolstered by the push of confidence, Sorrow bowed to the Old Mother and ordered his shuttle readied.

PGNV *Indomitable*, hours from Mannus Prime.

"No. I won't do it."

"You say that like you have a choice."

"I do. Keep them. I don't need any new bodies. No faces of soon to die cannon fodder haunting my dreams."

Lieutenant Fies sighed and halted midstride. He and Sergeant Annalilly were alone in what should have been a crowded corridor linking the chow halls to the troop compartments. Their argument began after the last bite of what amounted to a final meal before making planetfall. What started as mild conversation, devolved to verbal hostility and then shouting. It was a contest of wills in lieu of the standard "yes, sir" Guard discipline demanded. Compounding matters was the unauthorized relationship they shared. Fraternization was frowned upon under normal circumstances, despite Fies and Annalilly growing close during their time among the rank and file.

"Damn it, Annalilly, we are still Guard. This is part of the job," Fies growled.

Her bald head flushed, highlighting her lightning bolt tattoos. "Fies, I'm tired of watching people die. Especially ones who work for me. Keep your replacements."

He shook his head, sorry for pushing her into a position he once held. "Not how this works. The admiral gave the word. Out of special deference for all we've done, we are being given first picks. You get five."

"Do they come with body bags?" she snorted.

"No. You supply those yourself," Fies snapped. Tired of their game, the platoon leader stalked off. "Get your ass to hangar three. Repos are lined up waiting for a home."

Annalilly glowered at his back.

She burst into the hangar like a storm. Fury bled from her eyes, cowing ship personnel. The senior noncom in charge of replacements stood with a datapad in one hand. His haggard look suggested too many years in service, accented by his pure white hair and grizzled beard. He watched Annalilly coming and sighed.

"What can I do for you, Sergeant?" he asked, already knowing the answer.

She paused, taken off guard by his willingness to confront her. "Lieutenant Fies told me to pick five repos." A glance over her shoulder at the line of Guards left her uninspired. "Where do I sign?"

"They're not cargo pods," he replied and handed her the datapad.

Annalilly scribbled her signature. Forcing her anger, she stepped to the front rank and began her inspections. The first man was too young. The second out of shape, prompting her to wonder how low recruiting standards had fallen. The third wore the gaze of a veteran. His thousand-yard stare bore holes in her and she stepped to the next. She had enough ghosts.

"Name?" she barked at the sixth man.

He snapped to attention. "Sergeant, Private Desril."

Unimpressed, Annalilly asked, "Specialty?"

"Munitions and sapper, Sergeant."

Her squad, now platoon, lacked certain specialties, prompting her to reluctantly say, "Step out of ranks and wait by the hatch."

Saluting, Desril grabbed his bag off the deck and hurried away. Annalilly continued her inspection. Two women and one man joined

Desril by the time she reached the fifth rank. Tired of scanning faces who most likely would not survive the coming campaign, she stopped in front a mountain of a man whose face and hands were covered with scars.

"Where in the gods' deep Hells did they find you?" she asked.

She swore bones ground together when he craned his neck to look down on her. "Costoid Mining Colony, Sarge."

She knew a few miners over the years. Most were as bright as their hammers but were unstoppable when angered. His size alone was enough to give anyone pause. "Uh huh. Name?"

"Palco."

"Let me guess, infantry."

"Trained in it, but can do anything I need to," Palco answered.

Her smirk made him frown. *Big bastard might give Beve a run.* "Welcome to the team. Get your shit and move out."

Palco broke into a grin.

Satisfied, Annalilly marched back to the front of the formation. "The rest of you just aren't good enough for me. Better luck with your next sergeant."

A mix of dejected looks and resentment echoed back at her. Annalilly prided herself on being of few words and had little desire to give the recruits the tongue lashing they deserved. She looked at each of their faces as she collected her thoughts. They blended into men and women, old comrades no longer with her, who played critical roles in her development. Friends. Each was little more than memory. Kastor. Kedrick. The list continued until she felt despair creep into her psyche. War was the worst man could do to each other. Too often, the scars manifested until they drove the bearer mad. Annalilly's greatest fear was letting those ghosts in. She wanted a life after the Guard and knew they were part of the price of survival.

"Listen up and listen good because I'm only going to say this once," she grated. "My name is Sergeant Annalilly. You now belong to me. Make no mistake, each of you is a repo for better people. Don't try to prove yourself to me because I don't care. I expect you all to do your jobs and perform them to the best of your abilities. Anything less and I will dispose of you personally. Provided the enemy doesn't get you first."

Surprisingly, Palco was the only one to flinch. "How many of you have been in combat?"

One raised a hand. Annalilly focused on the lithe female. Corporal Yeves had a haunted look she failed to conceal. Despite that, she stood with shoulders squared and chin out with pride.

"Where did you serve?" Annalilly asked.

Yeves swallowed and said, "Crimeat. I was part of the reinforcement wave after the initial battle."

Annalilly made a note to speak with the corporal later. "Yeves here will fill you in on the horrible details of your job." She lowered her voice. "I don't expect all of you to make it through this one. That's all right. We have a job to do and we're going to do it, regardless of what happens. War is a terrible act and you are about to experience it at the height of terror, violence, and devastation. I don't envy you.

"Does everyone have all their gear? Good, follow me."

Following in single file, Annalilly led her new recruits deeper into the ship, past corridors of crewers preparing for battle. The *Indomitable* was alive with activity. A cloud hung over every person she encountered. The same pall ground soldiers felt in those dwindling hours before an operation began. Electric, intense, terrifying. The kaleidoscope of emotions was both intoxicating and crippling. She decided it was good for her repos to get a taste now before the order to drop.

"Empty bunks are on the right. Grab one, though you won't need it for long. We're scheduled to drop in the first wave. Just under six hours," she said. "Sergeant Jers!"

Jers sauntered over. His uniform was wrinkled, boots dull. The first inklings of stubble spread across his lower jaw and he needed a haircut. "Sergeant?"

"I brought you presents. Get them prepped and ready to deploy. The only one with any combat time is Yeves here. Turns out she fought on Crimeat with us," Annalilly explained.

Unimpressed, Jers fought to keep the depression choking him from his tone. "Welcome home, repos. I'm your squad sergeant. She's your platoon sergeant. Corporal huh? Haggle will like that. Go ahead and drop your gear on an empty rack. Meet me here in five, so I can introduce you to the team."

Standing apart, Annalilly watched Jers closely. She knew he wanted out, to be done with the Guard and disappear. Not that she blamed him. The war was reaping a terrible toll on them all. Events during those final moments on Kharsis haunted her dreams as well, but instead of cowering her, it only intensified her desire for revenge. Jers was at the breaking point. A shell of a man with but one hope; survive. The beep of her chrono announced it was time to go to the final combat prep briefing. Her last look at the squad before leaving to find Fies left her wondering how many of the repos were going to be here after the coming campaign.

THIRTEEN

3215 A.G. (After gods), abbey of the order of Blood Witches, Acumensiis Comet.

Sister Alessandra flowed down the last hall before reaching the Grand Mistress's audience chamber. Though she had been born in the abbey, Alessandra could count the number of times she was given private counsel with Ruma Zzein on two fingers. The prospect of being confronted by the head of the order, potentially reprimanded or worse, sent tremors through her otherwise stern resolve.

She'd taken risks on Rastarok. Each was calculated but all were against her mission parameters. Accepting of any potential reprimand, Alessandra smoothed over her gossamer robes and mentally prepared. Waiting in the antechamber, she realized a human emotion had crawled into her subconscious. She felt the need for companionship. True friends willing to share and endure their trials no matter how disheartening. The bonds formed by Tobas, revealed as the fallen Inquisitor Tolde Breed, and his cohorts on their journey to Braewynd inspired her. A new way of life was exposed to her for the first time, leaving her yearning for the sensation of normalcy unfound among her sisters.

The Grand Mistress's door hissed open. Pale light flooded the chamber in rainbow patterns. Alessandra decided waiting served little purpose and entered unbidden. She found Ruma Zzein hovering cross legged in the center of the floor, head craned skyward to the unending expanse of stars. Alessandra followed her gaze, admiring the limitless potential among their beauty.

"Fascinating," Ruma began. "There is promise among the stars. Lost to so many generations because of greed and hubris. It is a shame. Once, long ago, I was privileged to tour the universe in the hopes of discovering truth."

"What happened?" Alessandra asked after an uncomfortable silence fell between them.

"I found the future instead. In a past life, I was considered an oracle. A reader of futures. It was my predictions that damned the gods and saw humanity rise from the ashes. A curse I have never been able to shake, for it has forever entwined me with the Three." Ruma tore her gaze away from space and settled on the young Blood Witch.

"You were born here, were you not?"

Alessandra bowed. The power in Ruma's eyes was unquestionable. "I was, Grand Mistress. This is the only home I have ever known."

"Many among your generation bear that scar, I'm afraid." Ruma shook her head. "It is perhaps our greatest failing. Several among the Order believed, wrongly, that purity was only accomplished by those born among us. That the others were tainted with latent ills and failings all too common among humanity. I was swayed by their arguments, for a time. That is one of the reasons I deploy you on your missions, so that you may experience life on a different level."

"I saw enough life on Rastarok, Grand Mistress," Alessandra took control of her fate by pushing matters forward. "It is ... incomparable to what we endure in the abbey."

"Did you find what you were seeking?"

Thrown off guard, Alessandra asked, "Grand Mistress?"

"I chose you for a reason. It was a most perilous quest. One not even I was sure of, but it had to be undertaken. Only by allowing Tolde Breed his journey of rediscovery was a chance of victory assured," Ruma explained. "Stopping Amongeratix is paramount to everything this Order has striven to achieve."

"I understand that, Grand Mistress, but why me? What quality do I possess warranting my first mission to be of such lofty importance?"

A thin smile creased her lips. "A worthy question. Alessandra, you have a flame in your spirit that makes you brighter, helps you stand out. I saw your hidden truth and knew it was the only one of our Order capable of ensuring victory."

"But I disobeyed your orders! I let emotions get the best of me and became involved at the end," Alessandra fumed.

That she had been used dawned and left her reeling. Had the Grand Mistress known all along she would disregard her orders and interfere? Tiny branches of possibility opened, forcing Alessandra to rethink her position.

"As I suspected you would," Ruma confirmed. "There are few certainties we can count on in this life, Alessandra. I needed someone capable of thinking for herself in those dire moments where the fulcrum shifted. You are the only one of your rank with the wild spark needed to sift through confusion and balance her sense of duty with raw emotion. Call it using you, if you wish. I did what was necessary for all life."

"Grand Mistress, why are you telling me this?"

Ruma Zzein appraised her younger Sister. The rashness of youth collided with the trappings of the mind to create a powerful witch. *One who might sit upon my dais and lead our Order deep into the future.* "You wish to know why Tolde Breed is so important. Why you risked everything to keep a lone man alive, while others fell and war consumed a continent? The skein of his life is interwoven with Amongeratix. They have clashed several times already and neither has been the clear victor. An interesting confliction. One human male has stymied the greatest menace the universe has seen in ten thousand years."

"I don't understand." Alessandra grew frustrated with the lack of direct answers. "I was told he was important on numerous occasions. What can one mortal hope to accomplish against the eternal evil?"

"It is the power of his spirit that endures, even after his original form is slain and dissolved to dust," Ruma said. "Tolde Breed is the catalyst needed to unite our allies and bring this long war to conclusion."

Before Alessandra could ask another question, Ruma unfolded her legs and rose. "Which is why I am assigning you to him until the end. You each have a part to play in this tragedy."

"Thank you for explaining matters, Grand Mistress," was all that came to her mind.

"Do not be so fast to thank a veiled serpent, child. I have told you much, but I have not yet told you everything." Ruma waited for the witch to settle her mind before continuing, knowing the next piece of information was both vital and damning. "When Forever Night at last arrives, and all players are assembled in the last location, Tolde Breed must die. It is his sacrifice that will ensure victory. You must not stop it, Alessandra, lest all is led to ruin. Do you understand?"

Unsure if she did, Alessandra nodded.

Ruma swept forward to cup her chin, raising her head with motherly care. "It is the way of things. We must all serve as decreed. I have faith in you, Sister. Faith in your passion, your sense of righteousness, and in your conscience. Keep him alive until the final battle. That is your sole charge from this moment. The path will not be easy, for I sense many forces gathering in the dusk of dreams. They will attempt to sway you. Alter your perceptions to their perverted thinking. Stay strong and remember the cost should you stray. Go now. The Inquisitor and his companions are no doubt wondering why they have agreed to accompany the Order of Blood Witches on their quest to stop Amongeratix from reaching *Behemoth*."

Tears filled her eyes as Alessandra walked away.

The die is cast. A final piece placed upon the board. You bear the fate of us all, young Alessandra. I pray you do not fail.

"How much longer do you think they are going to keep us prisoner?" Ragan asked.

Tolde's smile was flat yet filled with understanding. "We are not prisoners, Ragan. There is simply nowhere to go. We are on a comet hurtling through space."

"Sounds like prison to me," Luma Kai echoed from the chair she had sunk into the moment she first sat down. Hours later and she had yet to get up. "At least they are feeding us well and no one's come to bother us."

"Not every prison has bars," Ragan said. "I've spent my time locked away. Most times the guards would come and beat us for no reason. Food was contaminated with spit, or worse. Say what you will, but a prison is a prison."

Tolde wondered what made the young man's life so bitter while acknowledging some events were so draining, they remained in the subconscious long after memory faded. Tolde made a mental note to question the boy later, when opportunity presented.

"I have not spent time behind bars, but I have seen numerous others to their forgotten cells on distant prison colonies," Tolde admitted for uncertain reasons. "All were bad people, though none so much as Amongeratix. You might say he is the reason I am here today."

Luma perked up. Until now, she had heard rumors and slivers of the story of Tolde's first encounter with the wicked Three. She suspected the tale spun through academy barracks and teaching dorms was farfetched, while centered around a kernel of truth. The best legends often turned up disappointing when their truths were revealed.

"How so?" Ragan asked. He knew next to nothing of Tolde and continued struggling with accepting otherwise outlandish claims of identity missing during their long journey across northern Rastarok.

Tolde placed his hands behind his back and started pacing the room. Luxurious by any standard, the Blood Witches left them in a suite adorned with more furniture than was necessary and beds in private rooms. Food and drink were brought to them and a private latrine was made available. Tolde suspected there were few rooms in the abbey as comforting or welcoming.

"I was still a junior Inquisitor when I was assigned to discover how Amongeratix escaped his prison cell on Keltoo. A career Guard named Matthias and his squad was detailed to assist my efforts. We were met by a Blood Witch before setting out on what I have now determined to be the seminal moment of my life. We hunted Amongeratix across space until cornering and capturing him at great cost. So many died that day.

"The villain was imprisoned again. This time on the planet Crimeat. I had hoped my first encounter would be my last, for Amongeratix is the definition of evil."

Luma exhaled sharply, her breath exiting in a shrill whistle as the events on An'kuruku returned.

"I believe he was set free on both occasions, and if not, he certainly had assistance in his escapes," Tolde concluded. "It was his army we fought on your world, Ragan."

"Those skull creatures?" Ragan asked. Eyes wide and filled with fright at the memory of the aberrations responsible for almost wiping out the knights of the Shroud.

"Indeed, and we go now to stop him from regaining command. Several score of pods were launched from Braewynd that day. They have either already docked with *Behemoth* or Amongeratix has secured them in a different vessel. Either way, we are forced into a dire position. Always behind his schemes, like we have been from the beginning."

"What makes you say he was set free, Tolde?" Luma asked, curious to see if her conspiracies aligned with his.

"How else could he have? He was imprisoned for hundreds of years before Keltoo," Tolde theorized. "There is one key factor linking Amongeratix to this current war. The Inquisitor General was an aide, for I met him when I was first summoned to receive my mission briefing. Decades later, he is at the pinnacle of leadership and uses his authority to instigate civil war at precisely the time Amongeratix is freed again. I find those odds too high to be mere coincidence."

"There is no evidence linking the events," Luma frowned. Part of her clung to the old faith, that the Inquisition operated for the betterment of humanity, not the vile deeds of one man bent on conquest and destruction. It was all she had during those foul nights after Tolde died. "Our people on Vau Prime have intercepted no transmissions between the two. We would know if Nye was in league with Amongeratix."

Tolde applauded her commitment, though lacked any such hampering. He saw the universe for what it was. Death changed much about him. "Perhaps, but that is not our mission. Here, today, our sole purpose is to find and destroy Behemoth before the greatest evil the universe has ever know can reclaim his prize. The judgment of Alain Nye will wait."

A conflict emerged within Luma. Her initial idolization of Tolde after his transfer to the Office of Heretical Persecution was diminished by the travesty of reality and his dying. She had yet to face any of her fellow Inquisitors and the idea of being betrayed by the ultimate authority rattled her already fragile psyche. Luma required guidance she was not going to find among the reincarnated Tolde and the host of Blood Witches. That admission shocked her more than any.

"You are saying we must face the Inquisitor General? Accuse him of heresy?" she asked. Eyes narrowed, Luma awaited the secondary blows sure to follow.

Tolde paused, admiring the younger woman for her sense of duty. "I do not know, Luma. What I do know is this war will not end until we defeat Amongeratix. If we can."

"But you just told us he is immortal," Ragan added.

The door hissed open and Paradise Tear swept in. "Haven't you heard, young Ragan? Even gods can be killed."

Tolde and Luma exchanged a private look of concern. Ragan, being the newest of their growing group, had yet to be read in on the great truth and Tolde was reluctant to tell him. Ruining innocence, however convoluted it might be, left the Inquisitor trapped between opposing forces he struggled to understand. Compounding his building misery, Tolde struggled with accepting Paradise. His limited interactions with her left him too deep in the gray. The only solid information he had was she was a weapon who never should have been awakened.

"How can anyone kill a god?" Ragan shook his head in disbelief. "They are beyond us. All powerful and wise."

"If only that were so," Paradise replied. Her voice dipped low, expressing quiet sorrow of thousands of years. "Ragan, there are a great many truths we are kept from. I do not profess to understand them myself but being an integral player in the cosmic game, I can empathize with you. Gods do die. I have seen it firsthand."

She watched his face twist in confusion and her heart fell. "Think nothing more of this, Ragan. We are surrounded by wonders. The Blood Witches have existed for generations, building a remarkable society in defiance of odds. I have been given liberty to take you all on a tour throughout their abbey and into the heart of the comet itself. Should you choose."

"We're being given our freedom back?" Luma asked. Her skepticism echoed in undertones, prompting Tolde to stiffen.

"Of a sort," Paradise replied. "Of course, there is nowhere for us to go! Come, let me show you wonders few of your race have ever experienced. Perhaps it will take your mind off the confusion and immensity of our ordeal."

Ragan leapt at the opportunity. Traveling with the Knights of the Shroud awakened a desire he didn't know he had. To travel, explore a world and now universe previously kept from him. Thrilled with the opportunity, Ragan followed Paradise out the door without further word.

"I don't like this," Luma whispered to Tolde as they followed.

Tolde pressed his palms down his tunic. "There is little harm in it. The Blood Witches will not give access to their secrets and Ragan has no concept of what he has gotten himself into. I should have never taken him off Rastarok."

"Why did you?" she countered.

"A feeling," was his only answer.

High atop one of the meditation towers, concealed from prying eyes and unwanted onlookers, six women sat in a circle. Their hoods cast shadows over their faces, yet all knew the others. It was a clandestine affair, meant to further a cause none fully realized. Dissatisfaction roiled among them for the time of choosing was arrived. Reckoning must be established, if the Order of Blood Witches was to survive to coming darkness.

"Sisters, the time to act is now. Ruma Zzein has committed our Order to a path of destruction that can only lead to our annihilation. All we have lived for will be smote upon the greed of human corruption," Algiss Her snarled.

"We are but six, Mistress. What can we few hope to accomplish against the rest of our sisters?"

Algiss's hood shifted to face the speaker. Contempt filled her voice. "We confront the Grand Mistress and force her to see reason. Six we may be, but that is enough to spark the avalanche required for true change. A passing of the guard to ensure our survival against the Three and the political manipulations consuming humanity."

A third Sister asked, "What happens if the Grand Mistress refuses to listen to our demands? The severity of the costs might not be worth it."

"We make her listen. Survival is the only thing that matters now. Each day we are dragged deeper into human affairs, casting away an entire history of autonomy. Everything this Order once stood for has been abandoned for some vainglorious cause none of us know! The only way to preserve tomorrow is to make Ruma see the truth she has long lost sight of. If she can't, then she needs to be removed. By force, if necessary."

Heads bobbed in agreement. It was a moment they both dreaded and anticipated. A new dawn awaited the Order of Blood Witches. One filled with promise, buoyed by the dreams of those who deemed their role in history to be greater than any mortal construct sabotaged by greed, corruption, and desire. Algiss Her watched her veiled co-conspirators, sensing their growing commitment to her cause.

The first Sister said, "You propose war. Many of the Order will not side with us."

"Once we cut out the cancer holding us back, the others will fall in line," Algiss insisted. "There are few leaders among our ranks. Any transfer of power will be difficult in the beginning, but the masses will fall in line quickly. Order will be restored, and we can continue our path to destiny."

She paused. "There is no other way. Not if we expect to survive the foolishness contaminating our Order."

"When do we strike?"

Finally. "Soon, Sister. Very soon."

The Low Continent, planet Vau Prime.

Residue from Mobus Kale's firebombing choked the air weeks after the event. Those few survivors who escaped the Prekhauten wrath developed respiratory problems starting with a persistent cough. Davith Strannan noticed the same starting among his own people but was handcuffed from preventing it from spreading. His only viable option was to enforce his troops to wear chemical masks and protective suits around the clock.

The former commanding officer of the Prekhauten Guard felt pinned. A lifetime of service resulted in the loss of all he held dear. His career ended the day he was betrayed and blindsided by men and women once sworn to his command. Hundreds, if not thousands, of former comrades were dead; casualties of a war none anticipated. All were slain by those wearing the same uniform, despite having different allegiances. The travesty of it left him hollowed out as he stared down into the cavern being used as his new headquarters.

Lights and power generators removed most traces of darkness, showing him the few hundreds of Guards and old regime loyalists comprising his ranks. Thousands more remained in Krenz to disrupt and undermine Alain Nye's growing reign. Strannan's gaze settled on a handful of red-robed Conclave functionaries who were unable to commit their faith and support to the schism. More problem than help, the religious leaders were the universe's largest problem in his opinion. Complacent in allowing Nye's insurrection, they lacked the moral fiber necessary to take the fight back to reclaim order.

Video feeds from a bank of monitors against a near wall showed him the suppressed coverage of riots erupting across the capital city. The citizens standing up to tyranny were brave, but ultimately incapable of fighting a fully trained and armed Guard unit. It took little imagination to envision streets filled with corpses. Strannan knew his battle strategy was partly responsible, for his insurgent cells fueled that dissatisfaction with martial law and Nye's crackdown on freedoms once taken for granted. Casualties were part of war and there was no time for regrets or to turn back.

"General, there is someone here claiming to work for you."

Stirred from his thoughts of the noose circling his neck, Strannan turned. "I'm expecting no one. Who is it?"

"Claims his name is Gedrick Silk," a bald female sergeant replied. Her dark skin glistened with a sheen of sweat they found constant since arriving on the low continent.

"Send him in. Sergeant, I want him watched from a distance. This is not the time to let our guard down."

"Yes, sir," she said and slipped away to retrieve the shapeshifter.

Terse moments spanned the time before Strannan watched his old friend and agent pass through the curtain hung between stacks of weapon and supply crates comprising the walls of his private quarters. Expectations were low, else the newvids would have spread across the universe by now.

"General," Gedrick said with a genuine smile.

"Silk, what else have you come to report?" he admitted. "Please, sit."

His eyes narrowed, Gedrick took the field chair closest and ran a hand through his voluminous head of dark green hair. "Matters have changed, Davith. I realize I failed to kill Nye but returning with this new information was paramount to mission success. In my opinion."

Strannan paced, hands slipping behind his back. "This is a pivotal moment that will either damn us all or provide the hope the universe needs that there will be a righting of our course. That all is not devolving into chaos and order can be restored. Peace, Gedrick. Peace is the one hope all peoples can cling to. Without it ..."

"There is a window of opportunity, but it closes quickly. I will not murder anyone, not even for you, but I will be here by your side until the end," Gedrick affirmed.

He wanted to run. To flee back to Wexanos under the protective blanket Tannus and the others provided. That was the true fight. The core of the resistance. On the same token, the rebellion on Vau Prime was a hope worth fighting for. Conflicted, he debated the merits of each decision path. A period of humanity was ending. What happened next would determine future generations. He wished he lived in simpler times. The last of his species, Gedrick Silk struggled with his place in history and among his human colleagues.

Seeing the conflict in his eyes, Strannan placed a fatherly hand on his shoulder. "Thank you, Gedrick. Thank you for all you have done to this point. We would not be where we are without your efforts."

They shared a chuckle at their surroundings. "General, I have never once thought I would find myself living in a cave with one of the highest authorities in the universe. Hopefully, the cuisine is appropriate."

"It tastes like ash, which is not entirely a disappointment, given the lack of quality in Guard combat rations," Strannan laughed. "Come, let's find you a spot to sleep and see to a good meal."

"But you just …"

"I know, son. I know. Best you don't think too much about," Strannan cut him off.

Reunited, he felt a measure of his old strength return. The spark of confidence flowed once more and he could envision the future. It was a good place to end the day.

Krenz, planet Vau Prime.

Inquisitor General Nye pulled the trigger and watched the assassin's body collapse beside the other three. All wore Prekhauten uniforms. Eyes narrowed, Alain Nye strode through the bodies and tossed his weapon at the three guards standing in the doorway. Faces hidden behind masks, they tensed.

"What is the point of having security, if you cannot do your fucking jobs?" Nye snapped. "I want this entire building scoured for further infiltrators. Lock it down. No one leaves until they are verified to be who they claim. Bring me any you find alive. Now!"

Saluting, the trio hurried away as a pair of Inquisition officers arrived.

"Well?" Nye demanded.

"Sir, this level is secure. No unauthorized foot traffic has been reported. A company of Guards is en route."

"Where did these people come from?" Nye asked, turning his back in disgust.

The Inquisitor General stopped in front of the wall of windows in his state office and glared down upon the capital city. Hundreds of thousands of citizens, visitors, dignitaries, and insurrectionists lurked within the winding streets and labyrinthine corridors stretching across half the continent. The orange glow of fires raged in the distance, suggesting another night of violence in the name of Davith Strannan. He snorted, fully expecting the assassins' identification to return with connections to the exiled soldier.

The shorter Inquisitor cleared his throat before answering. "Sir, we have teams scouring the compound now. Given the timing of the attack, we believe they were a kill team sent by General Strannan."

"There are only three bodies. If this was a kill team, where is the fourth?"

"We have just started the investigation," the first said. "Inquisition headquarters is a vast complex. Finding one person might prove impossible."

Nye half turned. His face a sheen of hostility. "If you fail to find him, I'll have your execution broadcast to the entire universe. Am I clear?"

"Yes, sir," they answered in unison.

Satisfied with their fear, he made a show of striding across his office with unquestioned authority and sat at the antique desk that had overseen one hundred and thirty-seven Inquisitor Generals. Carved from extinct trees on a dead and forgotten moon, the desk dominated the office. Alain Nye sat behind it a statue. Imposing and unstoppable.

"Has General Kale returned?" he asked.

"No, sir. His shuttle is not expected to return for another four days."

Four days. A lifetime. Nye frowned, considering the implications of the timing. His thoughts drifted toward the Conclave and their host of red-robed fools preening over their loss of power and prestige among the population. He had few allies among their ranks, despite the assurances of too many during his usurpation of authority. The Cardinal Seniorus was reduced to a figurehead stymied by politics and infighting. While Tinnus Har proved a useful puppet, he was ultimately replaceable. The wolves flocked to his shadows, eager for their opportunity to strike and proclaim themselves alpha.

"We must proceed cautiously," Nye theorized aloud. "I believe the time has come for the Conclave to understand their true place in this new universe. How many Inquisitors and subsequent forces are currently stationed on Vau Prime?"

"Several thousand, sir," the shorter man replied as he pulled out a datapad. "If you give me a moment, I can provide you the exact numbers."

Nye waved him off. "That won't be necessary. I want two battalions of shock troops alerted and mobilized, ready to deploy on my orders."

A nervous glance passed between them. "Sir, is that wise? We cannot make war on the Conclave. Think what it will mean to the citizenship. If they see the Inquisition assume total authority now ..."

"Then they will come to learn the truth. The war continues to spread. Rebellion foments on a hundred planets and the Conclave cowers behind their version of the gods. Faith has become corrupted by the desire for power. The universe has evolved and they fail to realize it."

Nye steepled his hands, tapping his chin gently with a forefinger. "Amongeratix is gathering his personal forces and preparing to come *here*. Should he arrive to a scene of raw chaos and dissent, the consequences will be catastrophic. I have not worked so hard for all these decades to fail now. The rebellion must be quashed. Decisively. Immediately."

"Sir, we are fighting the rebels nightly. Guard units conduct raids the moment actionable intelligence is received."

"It's not enough! Every night new raids, new attacks are being implemented across the city. General Kale has failed me. Davith Strannan and his renegade army remains at large with no cessation of hostility. There is no time for inaction, gentlemen. Hesitation will be the death of us all, if Strannan is not removed."

Spittle flew from his mouth. His teeth ground when he closed his mouth. "We are at war. I don't care how many innocents you need to bring in for questioning, how many prisoners are tortured to death. Get me the locations of every terrorist cell operating in this city. The Prekhautens tried. Now it is our turn. I want Inquisitors flooding the streets in force. Our enemies remain successful only so long as the public supports them. Change that and we alter the course of this war. Am I clear?"

He left before either presented an answer. Amongeratix was coming and the planet was locked in raw chaos. Time was running short.

"The warehouse is a front for Guard weapon caches. We hit it and we reduce the enemy's combat effectiveness. Hit enough and they will be forced to pull back, reassess their strategy and redeploy the bulk of their forces in this sector," Julian explained to the handful of junior officers and sergeants gathered around the map table.

Movement in the shadows, announced by the clip of well-worn boots, drew his attention. Julian's face fell when he recognized the woman approaching. Her face was covered in smoke residue and grime. Her shoulders sagged. Jagged tears covered her trousers, suggesting mission failure. Julian excused himself with orders for the command team to continue developing their next course of action.

"What happened, Sel?" he asked once the pair were out of earshot.

Forcing an exaggerated sigh, Sel slipped the rifle from her shoulders and leaned it against a stack of ration crates. "We never got close. Inquisitors and their private shock troops are everywhere. There was no way of reaching the target to plant the charges. I don't know what happened, but the city is being pinched."

Meaning we might have to displace and abandon all we've worked for these last few weeks. "Tell me", he said.

Sel explained the entirety of the mission, from the moment they departed the base to every action leading up to infiltration. Details severe enough to give Julian pause. Destroying the central supply depot funneling food and water to the vast complex of Inquisition, Guard, and Conclave headquarters, which was a city unto itself, was meant to throw the entire sector into disarray, enabling Julian's insurgents the rare opportunity to cause permanent damage, while turning hefty chunks of the local population to their cause.

"Thank you, Sel. Get some food, clean up and get some rest."

She saluted and snatched her weapon and disappeared into the maze their command headquarters became. Julian ran a hand down his face, hoping to ease the mental anguish of her report. Failure to accomplish her mission meant there was no way he could launch the next assault without suffering irreparable casualties. Any good will established among the people stood on the brink of evaporating if Sel's report was accurate.

"Trouble, Captain?" Aliz asked from behind him.

He winced. She was the last person he wanted to see right now. Taking a moment to calm his face, Julian turned. "More than you can possibly imagine. We might be in trouble."

She stiffened, the movement barely noticeable. "It has to do with Sel?"

"She says the city is being swamped with Inquisition forces and I don't know why," he answered.

Aliz folded her arms and said, "I still have contacts in the Conclave. I can try to find out, but I do know there are only two reasons for Nye to do so. Either he is finally tired of our insurrection or there has been another attempt on his life. Either presents harsh challenges. What are you going to do?"

The question stunned him. Until recently, he operated as a surrogate for General Strannan. With the General's forced evacuation to the low continent, Julian was in command of a fair portion of the Guard fighting in this part of Krenz. The burden of leadership had never felt so crippling.

"I honestly don't know, but I don't think we have much time to figure it out, either," he said after some thought. "Can you get through to your people without being discovered?"

Her tight smile surprised him. "Captain Julian, you say that like there's a choice. I'll make the call. With any luck, Nye is already dead and this is a reaction."

Luck, Julian decided, was seldom on his side and that worried him more than he was willing to admit.

FOURTEEN

3215 A.G. (After Gods), PGNV *Indomitable*, entering Mannus Star System.

"All hands prepare for action. Battle stations. All troops report to your drop ships and prepare for immediate deployment."

Jers rubbed the heels of his palms into his eyes to combat the sinking feeling growing in his stomach. Far from his first time in combat, the veteran was trapped in a cycle of thought doing his people disservice. With his focus on going home, Jers was no good to the men and women in his squad. Some had been with him since the start of the war, though the number continued to whittle down as the years dragged on.

Groaning, he pulled his hands away and stared at the new faces. He couldn't help but wonder how many were going to die on Mannus Prime. How many more families had to feel the sting of being torn apart as notifications of their loved ones arrived during the aftermath. It was a cycle of violence he had long gotten sick of. Only Annalilly's insistence of his worth in uniform kept him going, that and the violent promise of reprimand, should he fail any of them in the field. Trapped, he did what every good squad leader does. He lied.

"Make sure you don't leave anything behind. Police up extra ammo and socks. Rations will be dropped along with water and resupply once we establish a perimeter. Remember, everyone you see on the surface will be the enemy. Those of you who have not yet had the pleasure of fighting fellow Guards, are in for a treat. They know everything you do and react the same way. This is the most harrowing situation in which you will find yourselves," he barked to be heard over the din of thousands of soldiers preparing to deploy.

Watching from her position by the drop ship ramp, Annalilly frowned. Jers was being too nice. Unwilling to admit the sad truth. Not everyone was going to survive. Based on reports and intelligence collected since the campaign was first conceptualized, she expected heavy casualties in the first wave. More faces relegated to memory. Forcing the negativity away, she continued listening.

"New people, pay attention to your NCOs and officers. Veterans, keep an eye on the repos," Jers said. His right hand trembled as the pressure of leading his first combat drop intensified. "I want everyone coming home. We fight. We win and we secure this world for the cause. Questions?"

Only two of the replacements met his sweeping gaze, their eyes wide with fear. He didn't blame them. Going into battle was far from natural, despite the art having been executed since the dawn of time.

"Relax already. Me and sarge here have done this a hundred times," Haggle added in support after catching Jers freeze.

"No one gets left behind," Jers managed.

Having seen enough, Annalilly spat her displeasure and barked, "If you are done making love to your people, get them aboard the drop ship, Sergeant. We've got a planet to conquer."

"You heard the sergeant! Load up!" Beve bellowed in his deep voice.

Guards filed by and found their seats. Prekhauten drop ships were notoriously sturdy but handled the turbulence of atmosphere entry poorly. Runnels were dug into the floorboards for vomit. Annalilly watched her people strap in. The banter started not long after the first ranks were in place. Easy ribbing among friends and strangers to relieve the tension. It was always this way. A timeless game played out in every ship before every battle. The closer they burned toward the surface, the quieter it would get, until only the sound of the ship threatening to rattle apart moments before touching down, was heard. Panic and fear settled in as each Guard struggled with thoughts of their own mortality.

Annalilly wished there was another way but war did not care for individual whim. The cold machine of the Prekhauten Guard operated as it always had, with the iron authority born from a position of power. The last man boarded, fittingly Jers, and she was about to follow when a squad of Marines started filing up the ramp.

Gunnery Sergeant Asom halted beside his Guard counterpart. "Sergeant Annalilly, I hope we're not too late for the show."

"How many drops have you conducted, Asom?" She ignored his rank and pale complexion, eyeing him with criticism.

"A few simulated. This is my first combat drop," he admitted quieter than she expected. "Marines don't generally train for ground assaults."

"You're not in the Marines anymore. Welcome to the infantry," she replied. "Until we get on the ground, I want your squad to follow my lead. Most of my people have done this too many times and I just don't have the time to train you up. This is a learn as you go scenario."

His eyebrow rose. "And after?"

"That's when the fun begins. Fighting is fighting, whether you're in space or on the ground," Annalilly answered. "Are your people up for it?"

"After all we've been through? Count on it," Asom affirmed.

She nodded. "All I need to know. Lieutenant Fies is up front with the pilots. Once we breach the lower atmosphere, I'll give the word to unbuckle and make final preparations. There are twin steel cables running the roof. Have your people clamp on until we hit the deck. We're not expecting immediate contact but this is war, so who knows. My team goes first, secure the landing zone and push out for the second and third waves. Take my lead, got it?"

"Fair enough. What happens if the enemy is waiting for us?" Asom asked.

Her grin terrified him. "Kill as many as we can and hope they break." She slapped his armored pauldron. "Relax, this is going to be fun."

Asom never thought of combat as fun and was left wondering who he should be more worried about, the enemy or his counterpart. The ramp closed behind them.

"All ships are reporting ready, Captain."

Samuel glanced at the tactical display. Forty-two vessels comprised their task force. Formidable under most circumstances, though remarkably even against another Guard fleet. Everything from missile frigates to a pair of outdated battleships, the mismatched ships maneuvered into formation around the *Indomitable*. Though he commanded the ship, the coming operation belonged to the military minds of Falchi and Khe-Zhehan.

Samuel turned, hands slipping behind his back in a move he'd witnessed Falchi make a thousand times. He associated true leadership with it and subconsciously adopted it as his own. "Admiral, all ships are moving into position now."

Rear Admiral Falchi stood beside the command chair. Though he once commanded this ship and the Guardsmen aboard, he felt out of place. In other circumstances, he would have been given a state of the art command carrier for a flagship. "Very good, Captain. Open a channel."

A nod from the communications officer and he began his address. "Officers and sailors of the fleet, this is Admiral Falchi. As you know, we are embarking on a campaign to liberate the manufactory world of Mannus Prime. Our brothers and sisters wage war against those who sided with the usurper Alain Nye. Make no mistake, the men and women we go to fight are every bit as qualified to wear the uniform as you and I. We all know someone on the other side. Chances are, we are friends with many of them. Do not let that dissuade you from doing your duty, for they will surely try just as hard to kill us as we will them.

"Captains, you have been given your assignments once we arrive in system. I want all ships rigged for silent running the moment we arrive. No communications until the battle is well under way, or something goes terribly wrong," he paused. Something always went wrong. "I do not feel the need to tell you that this battle will be a turning point in the war. Until now, we have been content to lead small missions with limited risk and reward. That ends today. Once we have declared ourselves a major threat, our foe will pursue us relentlessly—unless we break them here and now. I expect each of you to do your jobs. We will carry the day. Mannus Prime will be ours and with its fall, we can at last begin the planned operation to retake Vau Prime and restore order to the universe. The seven hundred worlds deserve no less. Gods speed and good hunting. Falchi out."

"Well said, sir," Samuel admitted. His heart stirred.

"Are you sure it wasn't a tad dramatic?" Falchi asked. "I believe that was my first official speech to a fleet, Samuel. Nothing like a bit of rousing banter to inspire the troops."

"They should be sufficiently roused, sir." He lowered his voice. "Do you really think we can pull this off?"

"What I think doesn't matter. We have no choice. Our cause needs this world," Falchi replied. "To think, even after three years of war, I am still unused to fighting our own people. What a twisted time we live in."

Samuel agreed. "None of us asked for this war, Admiral. We are all victims of an abuse of power that should have been spotted long before the first shot was fired."

How were we so blind to Nye's ambition? Surely there were signs along the way. Subtle hints of insurrection rising. This failure is just as much mine, as it is the former Cardinal Seniorus and General Strannan's. I pray the cost of our ignorance is not the soul of the universe. "Start the clock, my friend."

Samuel turned to his bridge crew. "Start the clock. All hands brace for battle."

The crew of the *Indomitable* rushed to their stations, a well-oiled machine hungry for their opportunity to right old wrongs. Countless hours of training honed the crew into a modern wonder. There were no repos among them. Each was a veteran hardened by years of civil war. To them, this was just another combat operation.

"Sir, all hands secured. Ship is prepared to drop."

A bead of sweat formed on his temple. "Drop."

The mechanics of space travel made it impossible to physically feel the transition to real space but Samuel swore it threatened to tear his guts out each time. Gripping his chair, he watched as star lines collapsed to bright points. Mannus Prime loomed in the distance. Tactical displays alerted the *Indomitable* of incoming ships, as well as the array of enemy vessels orbiting the planet. He counted and was surprised to find so few. No more than a task force occupied the world.

What they lacked in size, the enemy more than made up for in the pair of orbital firing platforms. Each had the firepower of a pair of dreadnaughts and was capable of weaving an interlocking field of fire to prevent enemy ships from organizing an assault on the surface, while giving time for support ships to shift into position and neutralize any threat. Samuel studied their positions, noticing their proximity to the scheduled drops zones and ability to cover both space and surface threats.

"Helm, what is our position?" he asked.

"One hundred and seventy thousand kilometers and closing."

He glanced at Falchi, who nodded. "Reduce speed to quarter and bring us in to one hundred thousand even. Launch fighters and have the drop ships launch the moment we strike distance."

"Aye, sir," the helmsman responded and began relaying orders.

"Admiral, missile frigates are moving into position. All ships made the translation and are preparing to engage. Would you like the con?"

"Not yet. You may continue deploying the fleet as planned." Falchi knew there was little he could accomplish until the first shot was fired. His strategy relied on the skill of his captains until then. Any ship-to-ship communications effectively removed the silent running and exposed them to enemy monitoring far too early.

He wished Khe-Zhehan was with him. Their combined might of just under fifty ships would break the enemy hold on Mannus in short order, but the Admiral was needed elsewhere. *My first engagement in command of such a force. Am I prepared? Did I learn enough to see a path to victory*? He was about to find out.

"One hundred thousand kilometers," the helmsman shouted.

Samuel barked. "Full stop. Launch fighter screen and get those grunts on the deck!"

He watched as a string of blips emerged on the tacscreen. So, the missile frigates have fired. *Let's hope this gambit pays off.*

"Prepare to engage the nearest platform," he ordered.

If all went accordingly plan, the missiles would disrupt the enemy shields enough to allow the following fighters to sweep in and strike heavy weapons placements. Only then would the full might of the fleet be brought to bear. His one solace stemmed from knowing that whatever punishment the Indomitable faced, the ground forces were going to be cast into a meatgrinder. Tens of thousands of enemy soldiers awaited. Victory was far from assured.

"Commander Torgast, incoming ships confirmed friendly. Drops ships are proceeding to preplanned coordinates."

Torgast whistled, still disbelieving it. When Cardinal Virom first addressed the situation, he thought it far-fetched and implausible. His army was stranded on a world forgotten by friend and foe. There was no way a sizeable force capable of breaking the enemy could arrive undetected. Yet here they were, deploying to help him break the siege lines and put an end to a battle that had already lasted over a year and a half.

"Let's give them some cover. All batteries, lay down a continuous barrage for the next hour," he ordered. The more damage he inflicted from his end, meant the less his counterpart had to throw at the incoming drop ships. He hoped. His junior officers saluted and hurried out the tent. Torgast finished the last bites of his breakfast. "Sergeant Quint, a word."

Jelin Quint, his new rank still uncomfortable on his sleeve, stepped forward. His time in service told him one thing when a commanding officer requested a word. "Sir?"

Torgast tossed his fork on the empty plate and wiped his mouth. "You did well in handling the traitors and our rogue Inquisitors. I have another assignment for you."

"Well sir, I figure you got me out of the brig," he replied. *And off the front lines.*

"The incoming fleet is going to remove enemy air cover and drop a few thousand reinforcements down behind the lines. They're going to need someone to link up and point them in the right direction."

Quint's eyes widened. "Me, sir?"

"You have the skillset, natural tenacity, and dedication we need," Torgast confirmed. "As much as I like having you nearby, there is no one else I can think of worth their salt to execute this mission."

His expression darkened. Being dependable sometimes came back. Trapped between duty and honor, Quint knew there was no legitimate way he might refuse.

"It won't be easy and I don't promise you returning alive," he paused, licking his bottom lip. "I need you to get this done, Jelin. We pull this off and this damned battle will finally end. Every man and woman in the trenches is counting on."

No pressure, right? Chest tight, Quint snapped to attention and saluted. He was surprised when Torgast ignored it and extended his hand instead.

"Sometimes we need to forget military protocol," he said. "I know you won't fail me, fail us. Get over there and get it done. End this fight and get your ass back over here."

"I'll do my best, sir," Quint shook his hand despite the violence rampaging through his stomach.

"Go to supply and get what you need. There's a gunship waiting in your name. Oh, and swing by the S-2 shop and get your orders. They'll hand you contact information and drop zone locations." Torgast withdrew his hand. "Sergeant Quint, it should go without saying that I don't want you taking any unnecessary risks on this one. Get there and lead them in. No one is expecting you to jump into the attack. You're my personal liaison. Remind them, should they forget."

"Understood, sir," Quint said.

His mind remained clouded as he stomped through the endless mud comprising every inch of open terrain in camp. Soldiers called his name, acknowledging his contributions to easing Inquisition pressures and helping Torgast refocus their efforts on the front. Quint ignored them. He'd learned long ago that most bodies in uniform were little more than cannon fodder, passing faces that might or might not be around the next day. Like his friends, some of which had yet to be recovered from their ill-fated attempt at storming the enemy trenches.

Burdened by their ghosts, Quint made his way through the various stations Torgast proscribed and heading to the shuttle pads. The roar of artillery fire bellowed across the battlefield. Over a hundred guns reaped their toll on enemy positions far from sight. He almost felt sorry for the Guards. Almost. Forcing their inevitable fates from his mind, Quint showed his orders to the pilots and boarded. He was surprised to find he was not alone.

"You must be the infamous Jelin Quint."

Quint froze halfway up the ramp. The red robes of office appeared obscene amidst the military drab surroundings. He bowed, acknowledging Cardinal Virom's rank. "Cardinal, to what do I owe the privilege?"

"I wanted to see the man on which so much of our hopes now rest," Virom said as he rose, taking a moment to smooth the front of his robes. "There are dangerous moments in which we live. Torgast is a good man, but he has a blind spot for those in his command. That soft-heartedness tends to place him in danger at the most inopportune times."

"I don't understand what you're getting at," Quint's hand drifted close to the blaster at his hip.

"There is no need for that with me. I was the one who warned our beloved commander about the Inquisitor threat," Virom said. "The Conclave is very interested in your mission, and his success."

"This feels wrong," Quint warned. "I should have you arrested."

"Very well. I am here for one specific purpose." He held up a datapad. "I need you to give this to the ground forces commander. Do not ask what's on it, that is well beyond your clearance level."

He accepted it with a questioning look. "How do I know you're not setting me up? The way I see it, the Conclave is up to its neck in traitors, too."

Virom chuckled. "Meaning I betrayed my Inquisition counterparts to perpetrate some elaborate hoax on Torgast and send your entire army into ruin? He did well in choosing you. If you must know, I am trying to find a way to convince the enemy to surrender before they are annihilated. Making contact with Admiral Falchi's division ahead of the battle not only provides moral support many of the soldiers have lacked but gives them a sense of righteousness as they go to war against their own kind. I have no ulterior motives, Sergeant. Not this time."

"What's to keep me from accessing the documents?" he asked and slid the datapad into his trouser cargo pocket.

Virom shuffled down the ramp. "Absolutely nothing, dear boy. Absolutely nothing."

Quint hit the button to close the hatch. He had a haunting feeling of being set up. The engines flared to life and he had to grab the overhead troop cable to keep from falling over. Too late now, he settled into his seat and debated how long he could wait before skimming through the datapad.

"Phase one complete, Admiral. Both platforms are disabled. Our fleet is engaging the enemy task force as we speak."

Falchi studied the tacscreen. Enemy signatures continued to wink out of existence as their corresponding ships were destroyed. He anticipated full system control within the hour. "Captain, have their communications been jammed?"

"Aye, sir. The moment we announced ourselves. We caught them off guard," Samuel confirmed. He failed to keep the excitement from his voice. "Every drop ship is reporting in. planetfall in moments."

"The Shadow Hammers included?"

"Surprisingly, their ships are pulling ahead of ours," Samuel said with a frown.

"Relax, Samuel. They do it for greed. The promise of a healthy bonus drives them. Let's hope our smuggler friend was right in contacting them."

His previous experiences with mercenaries left him less than enthused about the prospect of relying on them to anchor an entire flank in the most critical operation of the war. Falchi considered himself a practical man under normal circumstances. Though far from ideal, he felt optimistically confident in their chances.

"Captain! New contact translating to real space."

Samuel snapped around. "Where and what class?"

The blood drained from his face as he recognized the signature. *We don't have the firepower to handle this.*

"Its … it's a battleship, sir," the First Mate answered.

"Admiral?" Samuel said.

"I see it, but I don't believe it. Those ships weren't supposed to be commissioned for another few years," Falchi said.

The newest Prekhauten Navy ship of the line was not only ahead of schedule, but it was an apex predator with more guns than Falchi's entire fleet. Bristling with cannons, lasers, and missiles, the battleship hulked over the debris field.

"Weapons spinning up," the helmsman shouted. "Firing!"

Falchi watched as the battleship destroyed two smaller corvettes and one of its own frigates. "All ships full retreat. Samuel, pull up a tactical readout of that ship. Find me a weakness before she kills us all."

He suspected the ship was a prototype. One of the first commissioned after the schism. Resources being depleted on both sides, there was no logical way for Nye or Mobus Kale to push up the production schedules. *But if you're wrong, old man, there's going to be the hells to pay for it.*

"Admiral, why doesn't she have an escort screen?" Samuel asked. The captain of the *Indomitable* was hunched over the computer console, desperately searching for a way to neutralize the threat.

"I can only assume it expected everything to be normal upon arrival. Meaning we have a slight advantage." An idea sparked. "Order all fighters to conduct harassing maneuvers. Hopefully, they'll get lucky and knock out a few of her teeth. Swing the missile frigates around and have them empty their loads into the engines."

"You mean to cripple her?" Samuel confirmed.

"And tear her apart bit by bit, until she's drifting with the rest of the debris," Falchi said.

The last enemy ship blinked off the tacscreen, leaving Falchi's fleet of now forty and the giant battleship burning toward them.

"If I didn't know better, I'd say the captain of that ship is overconfident. That suggests he's new to the position or rank and lacks experience. Open a channel to our new friend," Falchi said.

Samuel nodded to his comms officer. "Aye, sir."

"Enemy battleship, this is Rear Admiral Falchi of the Prekhauten Navy. I order you to stand down and surrender your vessel at once."

Samuel's eyes widened.

"Falchi … you are a traitor and scheduled for execution upon capture. Allow me to provide you the dignity of blasting you into oblivion to prevent the humiliation."

"I guess he's not willing to play nice," Falchi told the bridge crew. "That sounds like a splendid idea, except for the lives of my crew. I trust you will spare them if I surrender?"

The pause suggested he had taken his opponent off guard.

"Perhaps, if every ship stands down immediately. They can spend the duration of the war in a prisoner camp."

"I'm afraid that won't do. Unless you have something useful to say, I believe these negotiations are finished," Falchi said.

Samuel's mouth dropped open, much to the Admiral's amusement.

"I'm going to take delight in killing you my …"

A quick hand gesture and the line was cut. Falchi moved to join Samuel.

"He sounds furious," Samuel said.

"Good. Any captain worth his salt wouldn't have risen to the bait. Our new friend is off his game. Anger drives him, clouds his judgment," Falchi said.

"Giving us a chance," Samuel concluded. "Helm, how far out are those frigates?"

"Seven minutes, sir."

Too long. Samuel asked Falchi, "Can we keep him distracted long enough?"

"Battleship is firing again!"

"Brace for impact!" Samuel shouted.

"Sir, we're not the target."

His eyes flitted across the tacscreen, desperately searching for the target. His heart hammered as he processed the next words.

"They're targeting the drop ships."

Furious, Falchi barked, "All ships reverse course and unleash everything on that gods damned battleship! Fire!"

The *Indomitable* rocked as she spent her fury.

"What the fuck was that?" Fies shouted through his helmet intercom, as a blinding flash splashed across their screens.

The co-pilot craned his head forward for a better view of above. "One of the drop ships … gods damn! There's a battleship up there."

"We don't stand a chance against that kind of firepower," Fies lamented. "Get us on the ground now!"

"Tell your people to hang on. They're about to lose their breakfast," the pilot told him and dropped the angle of the bow.

The drop ship plummeted into the upper atmosphere at top speed. Fies crashed into a metal wall separating the cabin from the hull. His armor dented, taking the brunt of the blow. Tactical warnings flashed as his suit processed new data. Intense pressure crushed his body, despite the armored protections he and the others wore. Cursing, Fies cranked his helmet around to view how the rest of his Guards were.

Three were pressed back in their seats, heads cocked sideways, suggesting they were unconscious. Fies counted them the lucky ones. The others were scrambling to grip anything bolted to the drop ship to keep them from flying throughout the hull. One of the Marines was prone on the deck, unable to move as the ship screamed through the upper tier of clouds. Flames curled around the ship, cradling it with unparalleled violence. The pilots were frantic, hitting buttons and adjusting their ship to compensate for atmosphere entry and desperate not to get hit by the battleship's fury. Debris from stricken vessels burned around them. Casual reminders of the cost of failure.

"Hold on! We're entering the atmosphere!" the pilot shouted over the intercom.

Fies heard a strangled cry in response, followed by every foul word he had ever heard. Grinning at the ridiculousness of it, the lieutenant broke into laughter. Wild and maniac, it spread through the others until the pilots were forced to consider aborting their mission. And like that, it was over.

They broke through the lower cloud layer and angled toward their landing zone, while slowing their descent to manageable speeds. Able to breath freely again, Fies unclamped his boots from the deck and went to check on his people.

"Doc Little! I want biometric scans ASAP. Anyone too injured to fight stays on the dropship," he ordered.

"One minute to touch down," the co-pilot called.

Annalilly clamped her helmet on and barked, "You heard him! On your feet. Power up and prepare to engage."

The landing zone was supposed to be uncontested but she was leaving nothing to chance. The better prepared her people were, the better their chances of survival. She stormed to the rear ramp, weapon in hand. Asom was beside her an instant later. Both were rattled from the unexpected battleship but professional enough to shake it off and do their jobs with maximum effectiveness. One by one, the others followed suit, until only one remained seated.

"Thirty seconds!"

Annalilly issued further orders, wondering who the one was. "No one fires unless fired upon. There's supposed to be friendlies waiting for us. Fan out and form a 180 perimeter ten meters out from the ramp. Move fast and move safe. This is a combat situation, people. Mistakes mean death."

"Ten seconds."

The ramp lowered with the drop ship still in the air. Blinding light flooded the hull. Helmets compensated, darkening the view to prevent the incoming forces from losing vision temporarily. Annalilly's fingers flexed around her trigger guard, index finger staying clear of the trigger well. Sensors activated the instant they registered native lifeforms.

The drop ship rocked as it hit ground. Marines and Guards stormed out in as close to precision as possible, given their lack of training. Annalilly and her Marine counterpart knelt in the center, directing bodies to their correct positions. Men and women rushed past and took prone firing positions in a semi-circle just far enough away from the drop ship's engine wash, as it was already lifting off. Their full complement deposited to Mannus Prime, the ship rocketed back toward space and the nightmare battle raging among the stars.

"Sergeant, report," Fies called.

"Negative contact. One person did not make the drop. Doc said he had internal bleeding from the shock of whatever the hells the pilots did to keep us from getting killed," she answered.

"Push out to one hundred meters. Keep your weapons hot. I don't want any chances taken," Fies ordered.

Turning to Asom, she asked, "Are your people up for this?"

"We're about to find out," he confirmed. "Marines, move out!"

They rose as one. Shipboard fighters used to operating in confined spaces, where any wrong move meant damage or worse. She watched for a moment, impressed by the smoothness in their movements and noting their spacing. *I need to talk to Jers about this later*. The perimeter widened as the combined force moved in search of their contact. The objective was to prepare for unexpected contact and react accordingly. Somewhere in the lightly forested rolling hills was the man capable of leading them to their objective.

She glanced up to watch several heavier ships touch down. Armored vehicles rumbled free and took up support positions. Light artillery pieces came next, their crews establishing temporary fighting positions to provide full circle support, depending on which direction contact happened. Guards marshalled in holding areas at predesignated rally points. Annalilly and her combined force were responsible for taking point, all the way to the enemy trench lines if possible. Right where she wanted to be.

"We got movement ahead. One lifeform."

Accessing the coordinates relayed by Haggle, Annalilly directed her team in that direction. The lone man emerged from a rock outcropping, hands in the air. His rifle was slung over his back and a pair of blasters hugged his hips. The bag at his feet was stuffed with what she assumed to be munitions. She decided to take a chance and remove her helmet.

"Everyone, stand fast. Sergeant Asom, with me," she ordered.

Guards and Marines dropped to a knee and maintained overwatch.

Annalilly halted a few paces away from the man, taking him in with an unimpressed expression. He wore a distant stare to match the scruff on his chin.

"Mind if I put my hands down now? I'm getting tired," he said.

"You're him?" she asked.

He shrugged. "Him enough. Sergeant Quint, personal security for Commander Torgast. Your people have a lot of nice toys. Can they fight?"

She couldn't keep the grin from spreading. "Just point us in the right direction."

He gestured over his shoulder.

"Lieutenant Fies, we have established contact."

His reply cackled through her helmet speakers. "Roger that. Relaying to command. Have your people hold in place and escort him in. We're on the clock."

The sky filled with drop ships, some still smoking and others showing signs of battle damage from the drop. Thousands of infantry, armor, and artillery units pieced together from volunteers, veterans, and deserters flowed to the planet surface. They were complemented by a field force of five thousand mercenaries eager to earn their pay. She continued to watch, knowing this was a sight she would remember for the rest of her life. However long that was.

FIFTEEN

3215 A.G. (After gods), north kingdoms, planet Crimeat.

The air car powered north, beyond the civilization of Vaade and the other major cities of the central kingdoms of Lethendweil. Paved roads and endless rows of homes and businesses gradually gave way to open plains with purple tipped mountains looming in the distance. Grass half as tall as a man waved in the gentle breeze, the subtle reminder that there was a greater life outside of the war, outside of the frantic pace demanded by two sides determined to extinguish the other.

Krimpen Mass stared out the side window, not to admire the scenery but to ignore his companions. Partially recovered from the beating he'd taken at the hands of Geres Auk, the wanderer was a changed man. At least he wanted to believe he was. The truth was, his anger simmered, threatening to erupt into flame the closer he got to discovering Auk's whereabouts and the opportunity for payback.

A low chuckle drew his attention. His viper gaze fell on his companion and longtime partner in crime. "What?"

Time gestured to his face. "You look like you're trying to swallow a mung fruit."

Grimacing, Krimpen resisted, barely, touching the swelling on his face. Bruised and discolored, he was fortunate not to have lost any teeth from the blow. That encouraging thought aside, half his face had swollen and refused to go down, threatening to reduce vision in one eye, while leaving him in a constant surly mood.

"Funny. I don't remember you taking a boot to the face," he chided. "Oh, that's right. You were knocked out by that point."

"I'm just making an observation," the bigger Time shrugged.

"Keep your observations to yourself next time," Krimpen snapped. "How much longer until we reach the port to this damned island?"

"Several hours yet," Captain August answered. "I suggest you relax and recover your strength."

"Recover my … I'll be ready to fight whenever you need me," he sputtered to Time's chagrin. "Recover my strength."

"Tried to tell you," Time said, innocently enough to provoke a scowl.

"He has a point, you know," Vicente Blackheart said to August. "We are against the clock on this one. Presha Von is escaping, and with that damned weapon she used on Kharsis. If she gets off world without us stopping her …"

"I know, Captain, but there is little more I can do. This vehicle is overloaded and we are at maximum speed already," she replied.

August lacked the desire to continue her explanation. The pirate lord knew there was a communications blackout directed at Prophet Isle and the nearest cities, preventing outgoing transmissions from escaping the surface. The noose continued to tighten around their quarry, but Presha Von proved elusive under the best circumstances. The fallen noblewoman of Crimeat should have been in custody several times over since announcing herself a major player in the war. So many others failed where she was attempting to succeed. Odds were not in her favor.

Pressed to deliver results before Von delivered the weapon to Amongeratix, August and her ragtag team of less than desirables were the only viable option in this sector, leaving her struggling to reconcile her mission with her emotions. She was a career officer who had been on track for a ranking position in the fleets. The outbreak of civil war derailed that, but she found a new home with Admirals Khe-Zhehan and Falchi. She felt like she belonged more to them than the previous Prekhauten Naval command. Unquestioned loyalty defined her, yet this assignment pushed her to the limits of all she found acceptable. Pirate and now minor villains, August spent as much time watching her back as looking for her target.

"My crew is ready to land the instant we get confirmation she is here," Blackheart pushed. "We have enough skimmers to keep any aircraft from launching."

"The *Solstice* is more than capable of incapacitating any vessel this planet has. Thank you, Captain. I shall keep your recommendation in mind, should we fail to apprehend Lady Von," August used her most convincing diplomatic tone.

Blackheart flashed her a nasty side glare before his face smoothed back into place. "As you say, however, I would be a fool not to remind you how many times she has slipped our grasp.

Do not continue to underestimate this woman, Captain August. She is as cunning as she is wicked."

"Desperation drives us all to extremes. We shall discover Von's whereabouts, eliminate her hideout and apprehend all of her compatriots," August affirmed, though her words rang hollow.

"Not before I get a crack at the big bastard that busted my face," Krimpen growled.

"Almost busted your face," Time corrected.

Their banter, barbed and insipid, reminded Blackheart why he regretted hiring them on Kharsis to begin with. There was only so much he could take and the pair pushed him closer to drawing his blaster and ending their discussion permanently. Frustrations continued mounting in the former pirate lord. His universe was shattered, a hollow remnant of what had once been a lucrative crime syndicate spanning hundreds of systems. Now, he was reduced to a single, battered ship with a thinning crew and was shackled to the Prekhauten Guard. It was enough to make him wish he had stayed home and learned the family business. Almost.

Vicente Blackheart liked to think of himself as evolved. The events of the past few years challenged that narrow point of view. He came to understand he was much smaller and more insignificant than he thought. The pirate network was all but destroyed and he was now inextricably associated with his former rivals. The irony did not amuse him. Forced to bide his time, and bite his tongue, the pirate sank into himself and began developing his escape route. All he needed to do was find Presha Von, kill her bodyguard, and take the weapon for himself. Wealth beyond imagination awaited, if he happened upon the right bidder.

"How do you know these two?" August asked him.

Rolling his eyes, Blackheart said, "Old acquaintances I wish I'd never hired. They've caused more trouble than they are worth and apparently aren't that good in a fight."

"Pull this car over and I'll show how good I can fight," Time growled.

Krimpen added, "Our lives were perfectly fine until you came along. Now look at us! Orphaned and recovering, and for what?"

"This ain't our war," Time nodded.

"No, it ain't."

August decelerated and the vehicle ground to a jarring halt, hovering inches off the ground. "Listen to me, I am only going to say this once. The two of you have officially been conscripted by the

Prekhauten Guard. You are going to assist us in apprehending the criminals on Prophet Isle. Failure to do so will result in your summary execution. Am I clear?"

The sell swords exchanged a private glance, though she caught hints of fear in their eyes. Rubbing his jaw, Krimpen sighed. "How long until we get there?"

"Not much longer." Satisfied, August resumed the winding journey north.

They arrived at the port town of Dretl just before dusk. August parked their confiscated vehicle at the nearest prefect station, for the Guard never made it this far north during the occupation two years ago, and they went in search of a transport willing to fly them across the Ghel Sea to the former Inquisition prison on Prophet Isle. The jagged teeth of the Bothwel Mountains loomed ominous in the growing gloom to the east. She prayed it was not an omen.

"Who are we supposed to meet? This town doesn't look like it's seen any authority for generations," Blackheart asked. "My kind of town."

"No one in particular. The only thing that matters is contacting a pilot willing to cross the sea at night," August explained.

Thunder rumbled in the far north and a chill wind blew in. A storm was approaching, threatening to ruin their plans and leave them further behind Presha Von. The deeper their hunt stretched into the Lethendweil wilderness, the more their quarry slipped away. August prayed there was a pilot daring enough to assist them.

She gave Blackheart an appraising look. "Captain Blackheart, I believe this is a task best suited for your particular talents. Find me a pilot and ship."

"I thought you'd never ask," he broke into a grin. Blackheart started walking, waving over his shoulder, "This way, gentlemen. The ocean is brisk and there's a tavern filled with tired sailors."

"Good, I can use a drink," Time replied and followed.

Krimpen, still holding his face, told August, "Those two are going to get us all killed."

"I've been saying that for a long time now," she said and followed the others.

They walked side by side, Krimpen hurrying to catch up. Fresh waves of pain jarred his face with every step, increasing his desire to avenge his embarrassment. His mind raced through the possibilities awaiting them at the end of the journey and one thought continued sticking out. He cast a sidelong look to the female Guard captain, quietly appraising her. She seemed intelligent enough, dedicated to her duty, and was in general disapproval of the pirate lord. All hallmarks establishing her as a prominent figure he could come to admire.

"I have a question," he started, finishing the thought only when she slowed. "What are you after in all this? I know about the weapon, and that woman is nothing but trouble, but don't you Prekhautens have more important issues to solve?"

"How do you mean?" she tried to deflect.

"The civil war is spreading and nothing either side is doing can keep it hidden from the universe. Your side is coming out on the losing end. What purpose does stopping Von have to you bringing the traitors to heel and restoring order?"

The sound of her tongue clicking the roof of her mouth was surprisingly loud. "Just because we are at war, with ourselves, does not negate the obligation we hold to preserving the status quo and ensuring life—all life—continues to hold meaning. We are fighting to continue a way of life that has existed since humanity rose from the ashes of the gods."

"That's not what I asked. I want to know what you are getting out of this," he countered. "And what makes you certain life should continue on the same path, if all it has done is lead us to the nightmare we're trapped in now?"

August knew he made a valid point, though she was reluctant to openly admit it. Duty and honor were important parts of her life for so long, she often failed to consider thinking for herself. Professional officers placed themselves last, as any good leader should and the ruling members of the Conclave and Inquisition had forgotten. His unexpected line of questioning helped open a sore she was unaware of.

"Governing seven hundred worlds is no easy task. There are a score of pop up wars on any given day, interplanetary disputes consuming precious hours, and the threat of heresy developing where we least expect it," she tried to rationalize. "What we have may not be perfect, but it gives the population a fighting chance at equality and the opportunities everyone else has."

"Captain August, I thought you were a smart woman," Krimpen chided. "You're a fool, if you think there is universal equality. Prejudices run deep, no matter how high or lowborn a person is. I think the Conclave turns its back on matters that does not directly affect it."

"Such as?" she asked.

"Take Time. He was born to a low-class family and sold into indentured servitude when he was young, just so they could afford to put food on their table. Where was the Conclave? Like it or not, the fools on Vau Prime sit in their opulence, ignoring the plight of billions, while taking in the perks and benefits the luxury of wealth maintains. There has to be a better way."

"You imply a systemic issue."

Lightning crashed over the sea.

"I do. How many other races have been driven to extinction because of the Conclave's indifference? Are they any less important than humanity?" he pressed, sensing her growing disquiet. He knew he struck a nerve by the way she stiffened uncomfortably.

"No one race or being is more important than another. I was raised to treat everyone based on their actions, not their species or sex. Alas, I cannot speak for the rest of humanity," she replied after some thought.

"No," his voice fell. "You can't. Just keep one thing in mind as we go forward."

August, already reeling from the unintentional assault on all she thought she knew and understood, waited patiently.

"Don't make the mistake of trusting everyone in charge of you, just because they are in charge. One thing I've learned from this mess is that we are devolving into factions with private motives. This war will damn us all before the end," Krimpen finished and replaced his hand to his jaw.

Rain fell. Tiny drops at first, before developing into fatter, heavier bombs striking them. Villagers hurried to get out of the weather, knowing the worst was yet to come. August and the others followed suit, ducking into a portside tavern where Blackheart was already halfway through a mug of ale and a round of questioning. He caught them entering, water dripping from them in fouled puddles, and gestured toward an empty table.

The room was mostly empty, though filling up the harder the storm drove in. August followed his lead and sat with her back to the wall. A lifetime of service left her ultra-aware of her surroundings, heightening her level of situational awareness. She took nothing for granted, especially the fact she was the only person in Dredl wearing a Prekhauten military uniform. Feeling out of place, she kept a hand under the table, close to her blaster.

Blackheart arrived a moment later with his conversation partner in tow and in time with the barmaid. Krimpen and Time showed no hesitation when ordering, forcing August to follow suit, so as not to arouse suspicion more than it already was.

"This is Captain Edsen. He's willing to take us north," Blackheart told them.

"For the right price," Edsen added. He wore his shoulder length hair tied back in a tail. The stark white of it at odds with his forest green tunic. Tiny scars peppered his hands and arms. Rugged, he had every look of a fisherman. "That island ain't what it used to be, not since the monster was freed from his prison."

"That was years ago," August made the mistake of answering first.

Edsen's eyes narrowed. "Your people might be welcome down south in the bigger cities, but we don't have much use for you up here. Prophet Isle is a cursed place now. There're rumors of strangers coming and going, people gone missing and worse."

"What could be worse?" Time asked.

"You don't want to know, friend," Edsen shook his head. "But I can take you there. Can't promise a ride back."

"That has already been arranged," August affirmed.

Blackheart's frown was a brief flash. Tracking Presha Von on the ground made sense, until now. He failed to understand why August hadn't recalled their shuttle or requested additional support from the *Solstice*. They had more resources at their disposal than any planet side and she was concerned about aesthetics.

"Then what do you need me for?" Edsen asked. He drained the rest of his mug and slammed it on the stained wooden table.

"We are trying to maintain a low profile, Captain Edsen. Get us to the island safely and you will be rewarded handsomely for your efforts." Her voice strengthened, imbued by the rank and stature commanding a starship afforded.

The fisherman balked. "Fine. I was just asking. No harm done. When do you want to leave?"

"Now."

The finality of her single word prompted both Krimpen and Time to look up from their cups in surprise. Until now, she had been a figurehead with no real authority, almost hesitant in her ministrations with them. There was no mistaking her demeanor or the confidence associated with stepping back into a role she'd held for most of her adult life.

Blackheart slapped Edsen on the back with a wide grin. "See, that wasn't so hard at all!"

Her first glimpse of the old Conclave prison evoked despair. Even after two years, there were still signs of an epic battle in the surrounding area. Blast marks scored the building of onyx. Vegetation crept in to reclaim what was once natural. A haunting atmosphere settled over the land. A pall threatening to reduce her will before stepping foot into the prison proper. She glanced up at the abandoned guard crenellations, mouth dropping at the size of the gaping hole in the side wall facing her.

"This is a fell place," Geres Auk said from her side. His rifle was in hand, anticipating foul play.

Presha Von had never felt more insignificant than in this moment. Any pretense of power or the illusion of being in charge abandoned her the closer she got to reconvening with the dark council. Once a prominent member of the group where no one knew who the others were, Presha was reduced to a refugee on her own planet. She prayed for a measure of respect to remain among some of the survivors, but without knowing who was dead and who the replacements were, all she had was hope for the opportunity to prove herself.

"There is residue magic here. Dark powers were unleashed, even worse than those comprising the bindings to keep Amongeratix locked within," she replied. "I have no desire to go further."

"You must," Geres said. "The council expects you. I have no doubt they already watch us. We must be careful. I do not trust them."

"Nor I," she agreed. A breeze tossed her greying hair softly over her shoulders. She sank deeper into her crimson robes. "But they are our only hope of escaping the Prekhautens and reaching Amongeratix."

Geres looked down on her, silently questioning her misplaced dedication to a monster responsible for the deaths of millions. Loyalties clashed with common sense. He bore no love for the Three or their schemes but was sworn to defend Lady Von. Perhaps it was his failure to keep Baron Scura alive that drove him to greater fervor. He knew there was but one fate awaiting. Geres Auk was going to die before the war ended. Of that, he was certain, for his choice of allegiances provided the catalyst of his own demise. Ironic, all things considered.

"Give me the word and I will kill them all," he whispered.

Presha reached out to pat his forearm for reassurance. "I know. Come, there is no point in delaying the inevitable. Let us see what our hosts have in store. At the very least, this stage of our journey is ending."

She warmed herself with thoughts of delivering the weapon to Amongeratix and concluding her part in the war. It was a singular task she never wanted and was still unsure how it fell into her hands. *Foolish woman, you know full well how this happened. All you wanted was power, a controlling hand in Lethendweil's council of lords. You couldn't wait to jump as soon as that damned rogue Inquisitor came to you with whispers of greatness. Look what your desires have wrought! A broken woman on a desperate gambit to save her neck before the hangman comes.*

He allowed her to take the first step forward, knowing the simple act allowed her to feel in charge once again, restoring some semblance of authority when she needed it most. He cared nothing for such trappings. It was his life to serve whoever desired his services the most. Life in Reven was far from kind. The Plateau was covered in snow and ice for most of the year. Since joining Presha Von, he was harried across the stars with dogged foes eager for their blood. He failed to recall the last time he chose a job where luxury was the standard.

They left the artifact stashed in a secret compartment aboard their ship. The dark council might be the silent backers of the council of lords, but they did not need to know her true purpose. So far as they were concerned, Presha Von was returned to make amends. Geres spied movement in one of the upper story windows. A flash of shadow gone just as quick. His lip curled up with anticipation. The game was on.

They were within meters of the entrance when several figures emerged from the prison, barring the way in an open display of mistrust and borderline hostility. Geres judged them to be hired guards. He used his size and domineering presence to project confidence. One guard shifted under his predatory glare. Message delivered.

"Put your weapons down and step back, so we can search you," the apparent leader ordered. His voice flickered with sudden uncertainty.

"That's not going to happen," Geres said before Presha opened her mouth. The need to establish control of the situation compelled him to override any placating attitude she was prone to showing.

"The council orders it. None may pass with weapons," the guard reaffirmed. "These are difficult times. Comply or turn back."

Presha placed her palm on Geres's abdomen. "We shall comply with the council's wishes. My associate was exercising caution. As you say, these are difficult times and knowing who to trust is not an easy task."

Satisfied with her complacency, the guards shuffled forward and relieved them of weapons, patting them down for any concealed. They collected Geres's arsenal and surrounded the pair before leading them into the bowels of what had been a state-of-the-art prison facility. Skeletal remains lined the halls. The tattered remnants of Conclave and Inquisition wardens. Presha ignored them, for their purpose had been served.

The guards led them down three levels to an abandoned command center, where they were told to wait until summoned. Geres paced, his patience worn thin. Presha watched him, wondering what great hate kept him so intense years after his life was all but shattered by Baron Scura's failed bid at seizing control. A spark ignited in her mind and she finally understood it was the rebellion combined with Amongeratix being freed that sparked the entire civil war consuming the universe. *Was Scura part of that plan? Or had he been a useful dupe camouflaging the truth as enemy factions crawled into position?*

Her security depended on his mental balance and she feared he was close to breaking. There was but so much a person could handle before their mind snapped. She and Geres had already been through so much. The odds of finding peace at the end were slim. Presha bore the mental scars of victory and defeat. Guilt for her actions on Kharsis threatened to crush her, defeating any notion of value or worth she might have held. She was, in all regards, the most violent murderer in the history of humanity. Such a title wore down her resolve. More than once, she considered suicide, for the alternative of living with her decisions was much worse.

Once they were alone, Presha turned on Geres. Anger flashed in her eyes. The pent-up rage of marginalization and impotence. "You had no right to speak for me! I am a Lady of this land and not to be treated like cattle. My station still commands respect, Geres Auk."

The deeply tanned flesh of his arms rippled as he flexed. Geres's voice was calm, despite his outward hostility. "I did what was necessary to keep them from killing us. We are not welcome here, *Lady* Von. You would know that, if you paid attention. Whoever these council members are, they are not the ones you remember. Much has changed on Crimeat since we left. You have walked us into a pit of vipers hungry to lash out at whoever they believe wronged them."

Fuming, she clenched her tiny fists and trembled. "That does not give you the right to …"

"Say thank you and move on," he interrupted. "Your status is withdrawn. No one here cares for who you were or what you pretend to be. I suggest you use your new reputation when we are summoned. They will respect you out of fear, not your past."

That would mean accepting what I am! Her mind screamed back at her. The fragility of her situation left her bereft of her emotional shell. She felt the tug of temptation, luring her to succumb to reality and become the monster others considered her. All she had to do was reach out and let the fall do the rest. Presha Von. Murderer of worlds.

A door in the back of the room opened and the guard captain entered. He paused in midstride after seeing the conflict change in her face. Reassessing which prisoners offered the most danger, he thumbed off his rifle's safety. "The council will see you now, but only you. Your bodyguard is to remain here."

Presha straightened her back, eyes dancing with the subtle hints of madness. She was close, so very close to accepting her truth and ascending. Yet for each temptation, there was resistance. A measure of her old self attempting to reassert itself. She felt her mind straining and it frightened her.

"Geres Auk is free to go where he will," she snapped and stormed past the bewildered guard.

"Best follow her before she does something rash," Geres waved the man off with a feral grin.

Swallowing his confusion and rising concern, he hurried to catch up. It was already too late. Presha Von stood in the center of a room that once contained a massive oval table where senior leaders convened their private meetings with their overseers on Vau Prime and beyond. Darkened computer screens filled one wall, empty caricatures leering down upon those assembled. Seven figures in black robes were arrayed before her, each concealed within the shadows of their hoods. Presha scoffed, recalling how she sweat for no reason in the cause of righteous anonymity. Fools. The faces beneath the masks might have changed but their narrow dogmatic views of the world remained stagnant.

"Why am I am summoned like a dog when I come openly for assistance?" she demanded. "Is not the purpose of this council to influence events and the course of our futures? Why do you cower in an abandoned prison wreathed in eldritch magic, when there is a planet waiting to be conquered?"

"You are in no position to ask questions of us, Lady Von. We have summoned you to atone for your sins."

"It was your manipulation which caused our downfall. You must atone."

She swept her gaze across them, straining to catch a familiar inflection or speech pattern. Was it possible all members were new? If so, this was not the meek council she once pretended to influence.

"Atone? Where was this council when Scura fell? When the Conclave deployed thousands of Guards to control Crimeat? Where was the council when deciding which side this planet would support in the war?" her voice rose, echoing. "You claim the moral high ground without understanding your pathetic influences have been rendered irrelevant. All I see standing before me are relics of a forgotten past. Betrayers of history and lacking the fundamental cause we once stood for."

"ENOUGH!" bellowed the man in the center. He stepped forward, his movements predatory. "I have long listened to the impotence of your rage, *murderer*. Oh, yes. We know what you have become and it does not impress us. After you left, you abandoned us, we were forced to reconstitute and adapt into a body none were prepared to accept. It was your betrayal that made us this way. Forced us to come here, among the twisted labyrinth of dark powers and forgotten hostility. Do not come before us claiming the moral high ground. You are not our better. You are our damnation."

Confused, her mind reeled under the strain of misreading the situation, again. Presha squinted, trying to break through the darkness beneath the hood. She discerned the slightest hint of recognition in her accuser. A voice from her distant past. But who?

"Who are you?" she asked, the strength fleeing her tone.

He took another step closer, dominating her view, and slowly lowered his hood. Presha gasped. "Have you forgotten me already?"

"You, you're supposed to be dead!" Denial rang true, for she stared into the face of a ghost. A man she hoped to never see again. One who tortured her endlessly, making her life a living hell. Her father.

The ship loomed over the first transport pod. Monstrous, it was both sleek and antiquated with obscene angles and thickened hull reminiscent of early human innovations. Black as space, the ship was a modified cargo hauler fitted with enough weaponry to deter pirates and present a formidable appearance to any who would challenge. Guns tracked the pods, searching for signs of betrayal. The vibrating hum of engines slowing rattled the ship. Nameless, it was a predator.

"My lord, we have reached the last transport and are preparing to secure it now."

The vessel captain remained focused on his readout screen, unwilling to meet the sour gaze of his master. Scores of blind menials more machine than man comprised the bridge crew. Madness stole their vision as well as their humanity. Servitude to the foulest of the Three made them … something else. Only the captain remained intact. It was more punishment than blessing.

Amongeratix lounged on the command throne, with a leg draped over one arm, indifferent to their ministrations. Little more than useful tools, every human in his employ stretching across centuries died in abject misery, despite their proclaimed loyalty to him and his reclamation campaign. They were insects and he treated them as such. Through these long years, he often longed for the camaraderie of his own kind. Of a brother to commiserate with and share stories. Ever filled with vengeance, Amongeratix lacked the companionship his species was based on.

That emptiness left him hollow, giving him renewed purpose in his quest to reestablish dominance in the universe. Humanity confused his kind for gods, failing to understand the truth before it was too late. How or why this evolution occurred was irrelevant now. Amongeratix harnessed their ignorance and twisted it to serve his purpose. For those under his thumb, it was a willing sacrifice. The symbiosis of ideologies instilled since he first arrived on Antil IV and claimed it for his throne world. Generations of servitude were bred into the population until it was expected and honorable.

"Master of the Ship, finalize boarding operations. I want the last of my army on board in quick order," Amongeratix ordered. "I am going down to view my prize."

"Yes, Master. All hands, execute reclamation operations. I want weapons and tactical on full alert while the ship is exposed," the captain barked. The ruthlessness in his tone conveyed his station, for his was a once noble family continued to serve in graduated positions of power.

Leaving the bridge, Amongeratix made the long stroll down to the cargo holds. Lost in ancient memories of the creation of his private army, the giant ignored the horde of menials working beneath him. Those who failed to get out of his way in time, were crushed or smashed into the bulkhead. Doors hissed open, revealing the sprawling cavern that was the main cargo hold. Hundreds of workers toiled to dock and secure the first transport. Their black uniforms reminded him of the depths of space, while reducing each to a roiling mass of flesh and blood without distinction. The cargo master tucked a datapad beneath his arm and hurried to intercept his lord before Amongeratix reached the boarding ramps.

"We have secured the transport and are maneuvering it into the back of the hold to facilitate room for the others," he said, hurrying to catch up as Amongeratix continued to stride past. "My lord, it is not yet safe to enter. We don't know what contaminations are within."

"I made these creatures. There is no danger to me," Amongeratix snarled. "Get this pod opened. I wish to inspect my prize."

Acceding his wishes, the cargo master bowed and held back as the giant stormed up the space damaged ramp, where a trio of menials busied clearing debris from the access panels. Amongeratix struggled to contain his excitement. It had been centuries since his army was interred within the temple of Braewynd. His initial plans to conquer the planet and use it as a forward operating base in his war against humanity were derailed by the unexpected interference of both his brothers. The battle was furious, but Amongeratix was forced to abandon his temple and his army. Yet for reasons he failed to understand, his brothers were content with sealing away the army of skulldaerth after deactivating them and emplacing wards to prevent him from returning.

The fools. Every general knows to destroy his opponent's weapons and capabilities and his brothers, in all their glorious ignorance, thought the threat was extinguished. Amongeratix intended to make them pay. With recovery operations underway, he no longer needed the stronghold of Braewynd or the influence it presented to that sector of space. All that mattered now was to board his army and claim *Behemoth*, which he guessed was already being hunted. Tannus may be a fool, and Sorrow off kilter, but they were just as wily as he.

"Open the hatch," he commanded.

The menials hurried to obey, eager to avoid the displeasure of their lord, lest he cast them into the void. His impatience barely contained, Amongeratix was rewarded by airlocks hissing open. The others were not so fortunate. One menial was blasted with enough force to melt his flesh. He fell screaming and went still after hitting the deck. Noxious gases seeped free but had no effect on Amongeratix. Perhaps it was his twelve foot stature preventing him from catching the brunt of the fumes. Perhaps it was advanced genetics. He cared not. The only thing that mattered was laying his gaze upon the army he meant to conquer the universe with.

Lumens awakened as he brushed past the remaining servants and entered the pod. Rank after rank of dormant skulldaerth awaited. They remained in stasis, unable to move or age. His eyes drifted over their inert forms and knew happiness for a shining moment. At least until he discovered fully half the pod was empty. His warriors were missing. Eager to get to the bottom of the mystery, Amongeratix needed to get in contact with Zhagurim, his lone agent deployed to secure the temple. For any of his prized possessions to be gone suggested matters went poorly. It was with restrained fury he stormed out of the pod and headed back to the bridge.

"Get the rest of these transport pods on board now! We have a war to wage and I am tired of delay!" he bellowed and was gone.

The cargo master's knees trembled long after his master disappeared. The smell of warm urine surrounded the man. Embarrassed, he turned his wrath upon the surviving crew. Any displeasure exhibited by Amongeratix was to be meted out upon those less fortunate at every convenience. It was their way of life. Operations continued.

SIXTEEN

3215 A.G. (After gods), the Forsaken Path.

"Ah'muf, run!" Elisa shouted and leveled her rifle at the nearest attacker. Sighting quickly, she slipped her finger in the trigger well and exhaled before squeezing.

The round sped the gap between her and the monster threatening Ah'muf. The terrified desert dweller wailed as he felt the hot breath of a creature that made no sense on his nape. Running on goat-like legs, the head and torso reminded him of a deep desert worm. A mouth filled with teeth and three tongues lashed and gnashed as it attempted to succeed where so many others already failed. A string of corpses stretched back to the portal.

The bullet struck between where eyes should have been. A fountain of dark, almost black blood spurted across Ah'muf's back as the beast died. Unwilling to turn for fear of the others emerging from the ground, he ran harder. His lungs burned. Muscles ached. Sweat and dust caked his face, threatening to drip into his eyes. Forced to climb, Ah'muf reached for handholds to gain Elisa's elevated position. She fired, and again. Flecks of loose stone, sharp and stinging, cut him. He collapsed beside as she busied reloading.

"Are you injured?" she asked without looking.

Gasping for air, he laid on his back and closed his eyes. "I can't keep doing this. There must be a better way."

The ghost of Mollock Bolle materialized. There was sadness in his eyes. "Another way? No. This is the only path to Goti Tai. Any deviation will result in you being lost for eternity."

"Easy for a ghost to say," he snorted in reply.

"You think I wish to be this incorporeal form? My life was never easy, but I much prefer it to this substance-less existence in which I am trapped," Mollock said. His voice lacked emotion. "All life wishes to continue, often past its time. When death does come, it is meant as respite. A means of escaping the endless years of toil and trial. Becoming whatever I am was never meant to be. I long for the time of darkness. Of oblivion."

"Hey, philosopher, there'll be time to lament once we are clear of these damned creatures," Elisa snarled. She settled back behind her sight.

A dozen creatures stalked them. Though slowed, they followed the trail of corpses, suggesting either an uncanny sense of smell or unwavering sonic tracking abilities. Regardless, they died easily enough. Elisa and Ah'muf first encountered a knot of them feasting on the corpse of an unknown creature too close to the menhir. The battle was short and fierce, leaving both sides awash in gore. It was only Mollock's warning that forced his friends to move.

Hours passed, though it might have been moments, as time was distorted on the Forsaken Path. Elisa found herself wishing for Sorrow. His size and fury would make quick work of the creatures. Like most of her life, she was left without those she needed most. The tragedy continued the older she became. Now, she was the protector, responsible for herself and Ah'muf. *Paladin. I can barely keep myself alive and I'm supposed to do it for two? We're not going to make it out of here alive.*

She fired and was rewarded by another creature pitching sideways. "Mollock, what are these things and how can we beat them? I don't have an endless supply of ammo."

"An unfortunate occurrence. I do not know their name, only that they are alien to this realm. What little I know suggests they became lost here several millennia ago and subsist on the flesh of their own. You are a delicacy for them. The opportunity to feast on something different," Mollock answered after some thought. "There is a nest in the vicinity, but it is buried far underground. Your best chance is to keep moving. I can show you the way."

"He seeks to kill us," Ah'muf hissed with rasping breath.

"To what purpose? I am your guide to Goti Tai. Follow me, quickly. They are almost upon you," the ghost replied.

Elisa's rifle cracked again. "Time's up. We need to move."

Mollock disappeared and reappeared several meters away. "This way. There is an old village nearby. Perhaps we can lose the creatures within. Hurry."

Elisa pushed off and slung her rifle. "Let's move, Ah'muf. I'm not going to lose you here. Not after all we've been through."

"Farisi, I cannot go on. The path has taken too much from me already," he panted.

"Move or I'll shoot you myself," Elisa snapped. As much as she cared for the desert dweller, she was in no mood to be a nursemaid. "Mollock, is there anything you can do to slow those things down?"

The ghost cocked his head, sands and debris blowing through his shade. "Perhaps. Keep on this course. I will rejoin you shortly."

He faded again, leaving the foreigners to carry on as fast as their battered bodies could manage. Elisa heard the screams of their pursuers rage upon the wind as the ghost attempted to draw them off. Knowing the ruse would not last long, she ran faster and was rewarded by catching a glimpse of several two-story ruins looming ahead. Every footstep drew them closer. The odd pair hurried for their lives, unsure whether the false protection offered by the ruins was enough to keep them alive long enough to reach the next menhir and the portal beyond. She decided to trust to hope, despite a lifetime of disappointment.

Instinct guided her. That primordial sense of survival all creatures are born with. Elisa felt her past rush by with each stride as death closed. Fleeting images of standing among the corpses of her village, the Bloody Man looming over her. Watching Mollock Bolle die on An'kuruku. Meeting Tannus before being whisked away to the Forsaken Path and cast into a role she was neither ready for, nor willing to accept.

Ah'muf ran at her side, falling into stride and blissfully unaware of the struggle occupying her mind. Tears filled her eyes, but she would not let one fall. The culmination of her experiences formed the core of who she was, and who she will be. To ignore that meant hesitation, a surefire call to a dismal demise. Elisa took each fractured moment and forged them into a thing of strength she used as her struggles continued to lengthen.

"There! I can see the ruins," she shouted between strides.

They ran until their legs threatened to give out. Dust kicked up with each footfall. Hot wind swarmed over them. Bodies glistening with sweat, she longed for the early days of being locked in a world of ash and shadow. Here, in this juncture, there was light and torment. An ill combination, without the inherent peril. Elisa squinted in the brightness, nearly tripping over what was once a perimeter wall. Being so close to potential salvation filled her heart with renewed vigor. She ran faster.

They dashed by the first remnants of houses. Calcified ruins of unfamiliar stone. Whatever cataclysm occurred here was lost to time. Victims of the unstoppable force of nature, or something worse. She dared not consider the alternatives, for they wore upon her soul like grinding teeth. The ruins welcomed them. Shadows of the past leered from empty window frames and behind blasted walls. Elisa caught movement out of the corner of her eye and ignored them. Time enough for the past once they were safe.

She slowed after judging they'd reached the village center. Spinning to face the nightmare creatures, Elisa slipped her rifle into her hands in a well-rehearsed move. She knelt as her vision blurred and darkened around the edges, her head swooning as she threatened to lose consciousness. Placing her firing hand on the ground to steady herself, she scanned the roads for signs. Empty. No sound or trace of their pursuers. She almost felt relief that Mollock had succeeded.

"Farisi, where are we?" Ah'muf asked with strained voice.

He was tired, pushed to the edge and teetering on the brink of giving up. The only positive he clung to, was how alike this realm was to his desert home. Dry heat assaulted him, aging his skin and leaving his mouth parched. He welcomed the change, for it was a small relief. More than anything, he wished to leave, to return to a realm that made sense and lacked impossible monsters intent on his destruction. Such choices were beyond his ability to control, alas. He was trapped, with a woman his heart belonged to, without the possibility or means to escape until Elisa completed her task. *Damn the gods. Damn every last one of them.*

"I don't know," she replied. Her finger slipped off the trigger. "Mollock said to make for the ruins. Here we are."

"I don't see the ghost," he muttered, distrust rising as his mind refocused.

"I don't see our pursuit," Elisa countered. She had felt the growing animosity Ah'muf exhibited toward the ghost of Mollock Bolle and wondered what it was based in. Surely not jealousy. Even when he was alive, Mollock was little more than a traveling companion, forced into a joint situation. She found his ways eccentric, almost manic. "We should get to high ground just in case."

"Can these creatures not use stairs?" he asked.

"I'm not willing to find out. Come on."

They paused to drink from their canteens. The faintest grumbles of empty stomachs echoed from each. Time enough for food after they secured a defensible position. She led them through the far end of the ruins, amazed at how petrified every exposed surface was. Elisa walked close to one building, tugged off her glove and ran a hand over the time-smoothed surface.

"Like glass!" she was amazed. "What could have done this to an entire village?"

"I have no desire to find out, though there is a strange sense of serenity here," he replied. "Almost peaceful."

A tremor deep in the ground rocked the area. Elisa staggered, using her hand to prevent from toppling over. However serene the ruins might be, there was latent danger constructed into the fabric of this realm. It was a casual reminder that nowhere was safe.

"Ah'muf, in this realm, peace is the great lie," she warned and replaced her glove.

She led them to the nearest structure with a serviceable stairwell. Neither spoke, for both devolved into their private torments—inspired by the culmination of their journey. Despair lurked nearby, whispering supple illusions of things yet to come. Elisa dropped her back against a partial wall and rested her rifle on what had been a windowsill. For the first time since entering this realm, she allowed a deep breath while staring out over the high ground. The pillar of lights marking the last portal, were clear in the distance. Dark clouds roiled around the edges of her sightline, threatening but never nearing. She failed to understand anything and it left a hollow chill in the corners of her mind.

"You should eat. Who knows how long it will be until our next meal," she suggested. Her tone was harsher than intended and she regretted it.

He rummaged through his pack before producing a pair of military field rations. "How can the space soldiers maintain such strength and health eating food such as this? It has been but days and my stomach rebels at the thought!"

She snorted her amusement, wondering if she should go on to detail some of the worst of what she had eaten during her time as a bounty hunter. In the wild, one never knew when or where their next meal was coming from, if at all. A hungry woman will eat anything she can, given the right circumstance. Elisa decided to allow him his personal misery, if only to keep him from expressing feigned shock at her unscrupulous past.

"Get some rest. We stay here until Mollock returns," she said. "I'll take first watch."

"Ah, farisi. How did we land in this awful predicament?" he asked through a yawn.

"I wish I knew."

She resumed her gaze on the area leading into the ruins, but there was no sign of Mollock Bolle.

Ah'muf awoke much later. Any feeling of rest was dashed by the sound of Elisa's rifle. Scrambling, he slipped his pack on and followed her line of fire. They were found! The ground teemed with masses of creatures bubbling up from the ground. Whatever the ghost had done, he only managed to stir the entire horde. Three were down but were already being trampled over and devoured by their bloodthirsty kin.

"Farisi, we must flee!" he shouted over the roar emanating from the masses.

She'd already judged their predicament and came to the unfortunate conclusion they were trapped. Escape was all but impossible at this point. The best she hoped for was to take as many of the nightmare creatures out before they got her, that included doing Ah'muf the favor of ending him before he was torn to shreds. Sickened, she kept close watch on her ammunition count.

The ghost of Mollock Bolle reappeared behind them. His transparent face fallen with despair, as the realization that all he once fought for and was commissioned by higher forces to defend, was come to ruin. His ruse failed. They were going to die in a forgotten village on the outskirts of insanity. He caught Ah'muf's eye but remained silent. Seeing fate played out in his ghostly eyes, the desert dweller closed his and prayed. The beasts were within fifty meters.

To his dying day Ah'muf would never know if what happened next was in answer to his prayers or an act of fate. The ground trembled and broke, cracking in massive gaps, stretching deep into the bowels of the world. Noxious fumes spilled free, choking the creatures in waves before a series of tendrils touched the light of day for the first time in centuries. Globs of melted flesh dripped from each, splashing the ground with an acidic hiss. Fetid and diseased, a mass of greyish body roiled below, unwilling to break into the light after a history of darkness.

Ah'muf emptied his stomach at the sight and stench choking the village. He watched through watered eyes as each tendril opened at the end and a score of smaller grasping tentacles whipped out to begin snatching the creatures in midstride. Elisa stopped firing and even Mollock watched the unexpected involvement with awe. Hundreds of the creatures were pulled into the depths. Their screams echoed deep into the maw.

"Run," Elisa said and hurried down the stairs without waiting to see if the others followed.

They escaped the nightmare ruins, accompanied by the cries of dying monsters and unholy creatures never meant to enter the waking world. Elisa's heart hammered. Through the thunder of each beat, she picked out the slap of Ah'muf's moccasins close behind. Buildings collapsed into dust and all that once was disappeared into the memories of an extinct race in an impossible realm, where possibility and reason collided for control.

The horizon blazed with the green-purple glow of the next portal. She took Mollock at his word and hoped this was the beginning of the end. Goti Tai awaited and she lacked faith in reaching it unharmed. The Forsaken Path reaped a wicked toll on mind and soul. They kept running until the sounds of slaughter were lost on the wind.

Sauwgon Hil stared at the desiccated remains of two of his faithful. They died much the same at those before them. Little more than chewed upon bones, their names were all that remained. The shaman frowned, failing to comprehend what eldritch powers had been unleashed in the phase of their hunt. Could the sky dragon be so powerful as to command the nature of this world through whim? Those few disciples remaining lost their confidence and faith. Broken, they teetered on the brink of failure. He felt their desire to run, to flee back to the ruins of their society and pretend none of this happened, and he did not fault them for it. Human emotions were unlike anything he'd ever encountered. Those who remained had yet to master their minds and it was up to him to force them through that barrier, so they may become elevated. If they survived the quest.

"Our brothers did not die in vain," Sauwgon addressed them. "They join the others. Sacrifices of mind and spirit, so that our people might continue to live. Our journey draws to an end. Salvation approaches and now is the hour in which you must find the resolve to continue on. To bear the brunt of horrors unimagined. Only through strength and perseverance can we exist in this new world. Do you stand with me, brothers? Here, at the precipice of evolution, I beckon you to fulfill your oaths and become what we were always meant to be. Are you ready?"

A sandal scrapped the sand. A cough insulted his intellect. Only one met his eyes with grim determination and even then, he saw defeat lingering in the shadows. Sauwgon Hil raised his spear to the sky and whispered an incantation. The others would fall. Of that he was certain. Their lack of conviction sickened him. Their sacrifices evolved into something more than he expected when they set upon this journey.

Who he was and what he thought to become were separate entities incapable of surviving in the same body. With each death, he gained immeasurable power and mental acuity. Each life essence gifted him, imbuing his weathered flesh and fragile bones with renewed vigor, as well as the certainty that he was the only one meant to survive the quest. By right of dominance, Sauwgon Hil was meant to evolve. To become more than any of them were capable of conjuring. Who or what remained concealed in the haze of tomorrow. Armed with that vision, the shaman spoke the words binding his two fallen comrades.

Dark clouds swirled overhead, forming from his imagination. Lighting slashed through the gloom, brightening the purple sky. The hairs on his flesh stood on end. A dribble of urine leaked down his leg. Raw power was unleashed. A reckoning upon which the fate of an entire civilization rested. Sauwgon threw his head back and howled. The primal scream was lost within the cacophony. The others crouched, throwing their spears down to cover their bleeding ears before madness claimed them.

A bolt of lightning split the ground between them, casting them away like a handful of pebbles. Insignificant. Meaningless. Kinetic energy blasted through Sauwgon's protective magic and struck him in the chest. His tunic and chest hair burned. His eyes smoked as the energy sought escape, the taste of freedom that was unavailable. Trapped, it smoldered in his lungs even as his body warped and transformed to contain it, to make it his.

An idea struck. One he was at once ashamed of and surprised it had not struck sooner. The shaman looked to his fallen kin, still dazed from the energy burst. Three remained. Neither the strongest nor the brightest. Time slowed as his steps echoed the debate raging in his mind. One of the disciples stirred, rolling onto his stomach. Sauwgon thrilled with exhilaration as he leveled his weapon. Moral constraints flickered, threatening to halt his designs before he exhaled a pensive breath and committed the unthinkable.

Green flame of raw energy pulsed out to strike the disciple in the chest as he tried rising to one knee. Blood and flesh evaporated into pink steam, until nothing remained. The dead man's power flowed into Sauwgon. Muscles bulged. Energy unparalleled surged through his veins as he turned on the second man. Moments later but one remained and he was spared for reasons neither understood, or anticipated. On his knees, the disciple placed his empty palms outward, daring the shaman to end his life.

"You do not fear death?" Sauwgon questioned, spear pointed at the man's heart.

"What is to fear? We are the last of our kind. Death is assured. If this is to be my end, at least my sacrifice will provide you the strength to continue," he replied. "Kill me if you must, Sauwgon Hil. I fear nothing."

The madness flickered before dissolving. Sauwgon straightened and extended a hand to help his final disciple to his feet. They were alone in a world they did not understand, confronted by demons and monsters of the foulest imaginations. Where their journey took them remained elusive, but the shaman knew they were close to finding the dragon and unlocking his full potential. Eager to claim his reward, Sauwgon led them deeper into the realm of madness.

Secret Inquisition Prison Facility, planet Vau Prime.

Screams were drowned out, dampened by the soundproof walls in the cell half a kilometer underground. Gaunt faced guards stood outside, flanking the windowless door. Dim lights cast the corridor in shadow. A fitting gift for foul deeds. Blinding slivers of light flashed beneath the door, seeping through the inch gap to illuminate the high gloss shine of the guard's boots.

The Inquisitor General stormed down the corridor in his resplendent white uniform. The bluc tinged rose petals were the only color, bright and inviting. It was the symbol of unmitigated power recognized throughout the universe. Nye's desires flowed through him, naked for all to see. Knowing the time for pretense was long past, he wore his treason openly. Armed guards marched at his back. A squad of the loyalist and feared Inquisitors in uniform. Reflective masks concealed their faces.

"Open the door," Nye commanded, as the pair of guards snapped to attention with his arrival.

"Sir, Inquisitor Deahs requested not to be disturbed until he successfully retrieved the information you desire," the younger of the two guards said with shaky voice.

Nye's eyebrow rose in disgust upon noticing the man's knees trembling. "How long have you served the Inquisition?"

"Less than a year, sir."

The second guard subtly moved away in anticipation of violence to come.

Nye stepped closer, until his breath fogged the young Inquisitor's rank epaulettes. "Do you know who I am?"

"Y… yes, sir."

Leaning close to whisper, Nye growled, "Then I suggest you get out of my fucking way before I have you torn limb from limb and flensed alive. Am I clear?"

Barely managing a nod, the Inquisitor moved aside, while his counterpart keyed the access code. Nye strode in before the door was fully open. His escort remained outside, weapons trained on the guards. Alain Nye gave the room a brief inspection. Aside from a small chair for his master torturer, there was naught but a second chair with the prisoner hooded and strapped at forehead, chest, wrists, thighs, and ankles. Pools of drying blood spread across the dark floor. Flecks dripped wetly down the walls.

"Inquisitor General, I did not expect you so swiftly," Master Torturer Deahs bowed after taking a thin blade out of the prisoner's right lung.

"How is our guest?" Nye asked. His stomach churned at the pile of toe and fingernails at his feet.

"I believe he is willing to speak to you, though he proved most resistant at first," Deahs replied. "I was almost impressed. Alas, men lack the strength they once held."

The body trembled in that familiar way all men had, when they at last understood the end was upon them. That all their dreams were cast to the vagaries of fate as the walls closed in upon them. Were the circumstances not so dire, Nye might have found amusement in the moment.

Forcing down his nausea, the Inquisitor General grew apprehensive, almost giddy at the prospect of finally being able to end the rebellion and secure Vau Prime well ahead of Amongeratix's arrival. "Remove his hood. I want him to look me in the eyes."

The Master Torturer hurried to obey. His slender frame was bent, twisted both inside and out. Whatever rot compelled him to perform acts of depravity, poured out through his deadened eyes. Streaks of white assaulted his retreating hairline, further developing his sinister appearance. Deahs undid the strap around the prisoner's forehead and jerked the hood free in an effort of showmanship going unappreciated by his victim and superior.

"Zoraq Darc, scum of Krenz and former crime lord. It is a pleasure to finally make your acquaintance," Nye studied the broken man. Lips were cracked. His nose jerked to one side. Both eyes were swollen almost completely shut and his eyebrows appeared burned off. Disgusted, Nye continued, "How long we remain this close to one another remains to be seen. I understand you have information for me."

Zoraq tried blinking but his right eye remained shut. When he opened his mouth to speak, a dry croak issued forth. A gesture from Nye prompted Deahs to give the man a sip of water. The crime lord's tongue poked free, eager to lap every precious drop.

"Speak," Nye commanded.

"I know where General Strannan is and how many forces he left behind in Krenz," he struggled to say.

"And? I already know Strannan has fled the capital. You leave me unimpressed. Perhaps Master Deahs has not broken you as much as he believes," Nye suggested.

Menace laced his words, an undercurrent of wickedness impaling Zoraq with the promise of a bleak tomorrow.

"Pl... please, I know more. The rebellion is spread across the city in cells. They are led by junior officers and the former Cardinal Seniorus' lover," he hurried to say.

Aliz? She yet lives. Interesting. It appears my scouring of leadership was not as thorough as I was led to believe. "She is naught but an old woman. Her influence in galactic affairs has long waned. You'll have to do better than that. Where is Davith Strannan?"

His chest collapsed as the breath fled him. Zoraq lowered his head, the words he knew must be said, now hesitant. Loyalty, for what it was worth, accounted for the slightest measure of his soul and it manifested when he least needed it. Ultimately, there was little choice. Death was the only option and Zoraq Darc had never been accused of bravery.

"The low continent. He took his command team and now coordinates the rebellion from there," Zoraq whispered in shame. "Where I do not know. He did not keep me in his confidence after learning of my intent to depart."

Nye straightened and adjusted his uniform blouse. "There, Deahs, you see, he can be reasonable. Thank you, Zoraq Darc. Your intelligence will break our enemy's spine for good and it will be by your tongue I can at last secure this world and focus on the rest of the universe. You have done the Inquisition a great service and for that you shall be rewarded everything you deserve."

Gesturing for the torturer to join him in the corridor, Nye bore a glint of true happiness, for the game had turned in his favor. "I want every known rebel cell, names, families, every actionable piece of intelligence you can glean from that scum. Once you are satisfied he has no further value, you are free to dispose of him however you see fit. Either way, I want him dead by nightfall and make sure there is no evidence. As far as the universe is concerned, Zoraq Darc is just another casualty of war."

"It shall be as you command," Deahs' grim demeanor brightened at the prospect of being given free rein to utterly destroy the man in his cell.

Eager to be away from this place of pain, Alain Nye whirled about and headed back to his offices. Mobus Kale needed to be given a direction to point his newest weapon.

The low continent, planet Vau Prime.

The drop shuttle barreled through the atmosphere in a halo of red-gold flames. One passenger was strapped within. A man filled with venom and the aroused desire to fulfill his mission and regain favor among the command. Betrayed by those he once served loyally, Utan Husk longed for redemption. Promised a lifetime of confinement, he was surprised to have one of the senior Guard commanders, a general no less, come to retrieve him with a pardon and the opportunity to continue a mission the gods assigned him. Gripping the security straps locking him in place, Utan grinned.

He closed his eyes and hummed a tune his mother once sang him. The lullaby brought comfort when life spiraled out of control, offering hope that he was on the correct path and his efforts would be rewarded when his last breath escaped him. Utan needed to believe. Worship of the gods was driven into his core from childhood and he continued to exemplify that praise in all he did. Knowing he did his mother proud, Utan focused on the task at hand.

Mobus Kale was adamant about eliminating the target while keeping his reasons private. Not that the one-armed general lacked transparency. Utan saw through him. Saw the machinations of one mired in his inability to accomplish the mission himself. Knowing he was being called in to finish such a priority task buoyed Utan's spirits. Old strength invigorated his resolve. Years of being kept on limited rations, with little exercise, robbed him of his former glory. Transit time from his prison to Vau Prime, the jewel of the civilized universe, afforded the opportunity to eat and drink to his content.

His body screamed in protest as Utan pushed unused muscles to the edge of their endurance. Hunting the former Guard commanding officer was his highest profile mission yet. One certain to garner infamy as his legend spread across the stars. Utan Husk relished at the thought of adding Strannan to his tally. Not that he bore the General any ill will. Their paths never crossed and he doubted Strannan knew his name, much less his reputation. A board of commandants presided over his general court martial, leaving the upper command echelon clear to persecute military actions across the seven hundred worlds.

"General Davith Strannan," Utan mused once the roar of entry lessened. "I am coming for you. Are you prepared? Have you made peace with the gods?"

The drop shuttle hurried to the scorched planet surface, where destiny awaited. A confluence of fates that would shake the foundations of the world. Utan Husk sang louder.

"The asset is deployed," Mobus confirmed.

His irritation at being called upon, rang in his voice. The heir to the Prekhauten Guard, Kale found little need to clear his affairs with either the Inquisition or the Conclave. Neither body provided the prestige they once held. One devolved into utter uselessness, while the other was filling its ranks with the depraved. Madness was tearing Vau Prime apart and he played his part in it. Razing the low continent to eliminate the rising cult of Rengu was harsh but justified in his opinion. Anything less than a show of dominance allowed for resurgence. Alain Nye failed to see matters the same and the split began.

Nye's voice betrayed little emotion. Mobus noted the Inquisitor General was growing more confident in his schemes. It was an arrogance ill served in the Guard, and if Mobus played it correctly, might prove Nye's undoing.

"You took your time. Matters are progressing behind schedule, General Kale. Vau Prime was to be pacified a year ago. Your vendetta against Strannan has cost us," Nye scolded.

Mobus was thankful the transmission lacked imaging, else Nye would have seen his glare of disdain. "Eliminating Strannan was the only option to advance our cause. I did not anticipate the cult uprising on the low continent, else the totality of my efforts would have focused on the renegade. Do not mistake my redirection for lack of focus. I have done all you requested. The Guard has matters of its own that need seeing to."

"I am well aware of your internal power struggles, General Kale. Just as you must be reminded who put you in your current position," Nye threatened. "Generals are easy to come by. If you cannot finish the mission of securing this planet, I may have to find another venue for your particular talents."

Mobus lashed out, smashing a computer console with his metallic hand. Sparks danced across his fist, scorching the cuff of his uniform. Squeezing his eyes shut, he replied in a slow, measured delivery, "Do not threaten me, Nye. I have returned to Vau Prime with a weapon capable of ending Strannan while I weed out and destroy the rebellion plaguing *your* city."

His heart beat faster as the pause lengthened. Paranoia, ever lingering on the edges of his fragile sanity, whispered conspiracies. Suggestions of betrayal and worse. Mobus wished he still believed in the gods, but their childish lore offered little for a military man to cling to. He believed in what he could see, not what his conscience dictated must be, because a man in a red robe proclaimed it so.

"I am transmitting data gleaned from a prisoner. See that you use it wisely. I expect the rebellion crushed in one fell swoop," Nye ordered. "This war has lasted long enough. It is time we took it to the stars and reminded the universe who is in control. Do not fail me in this, Mobus. Our future depends on it."

The transmission squelched and was silent, leaving Mobus Kale brooding. Control. Ever the dream of weak men seeking validity in a world indifferent to their whines. Alain Nye suffered from inadequacies prompting his lust for power. Only, Mobus knew his secret. Knew that the true strength behind the schism was the greatest monster the universe produced. Amongeratix, volatile son of the king of the gods, was awake and in play. Mobus suspected his two brothers were desperate to stop him, for they were ever seeking ways to remain apart from the detritus of humanity. Where did that leave the Conclave? He knew Amongeratix was collecting ancient armies and moving on Vau Prime. Would he retain Nye and the Cardinal Seniorus and allow them to reign over the human empire or would he fulfill his millennia old quest to reign once again?

The unknown thrilled him, while providing the spark of inspiration Mobus finally understood he lacked for too long. Seven hundred known worlds was a vast opportunity. Filled with dreams of empire, Mobus Kale accessed the files.

SEVENTEEN

Abbey of the Order of Blood Witches, Acumensiis Comet, en route to intercept *Behemoth*.

"Lord Tannus has already admitted the truth of his people. You are but a handful of mortals in the entire universe with this knowledge, which is why I have decided to trust you further."

Tolde and his companions stood arrayed before the Grand Mistress of the Order of Blood Witches in a half circle. His hands were clasped before him, patiently working through the riddles deliberately unveiled. Placing his trust in Tannus left him uneasy, for though they were allied, those alliances were easily shifted. Being brought back from the dead proved enlightening for the former Inquisitor. *Why was I resurrected? What grand design am I part of and why is no one willing to tell me?*

Ruma Zzein continued. "It goes without saying that all you see within this chamber is sensitive. Not even the wealth of my Order has seen what lies beyond these doors."

They were deep within the bowels of the comet, beneath the bottom floors of the abbey. Blue, yellow, and green lichen glowed, brightened by the power wafting from each of the three Blood Witches in attendance. Ages worth of dust coated the path. The walls were roughhewn, stone filled, with a thousand jagged edges. Magic permeated the air despite evidence of men with picks and tools having carved the passage. Wide enough for two abreast, the ceiling was uneven, forcing them to stoop, and in Paradise Tear's case, crawl to reach the small chamber they now stood in.

"I must hold each of you to a vow of secrecy. No mention of what you see within shall ever be uttered," Ruma stared each in the eye, searching their souls for signs of treachery or betrayal.

One by one they nodded or replied aye. The risk associated with opening her vault of secrets to so many was measured and weighed against the coming Forever Night. Disturbances in the flow of space and time left her questioning her path. Destiny was ever a stranger. Ruma knew she should have been dead and forgotten a thousand times over. For reasons beyond her ability to interpret, her life continued. Missing the truth of why haunted her private moments. Since fleeing captivity, with Tannus' help, she continued evolving in ways alien to all.

"Very well. Follow me and do not touch anything. Eldritch magic wards this chamber." She locked eyes with Tolde.

The Inquisitor swallowed, unable to shake the feeling she was speaking directly for his benefit. "What lies beyond?"

Ignoring him, Ruma opened the door and flowed inside. A strange metallic hum vibrated up from the floor, filling their mouths with an iron taste. Dark, save for a handful of soft orange lights surrounding a capsule, unceremoniously placed in the center. Cables and a host of wires connected the capsule to a bank of computers built into the far wall. All lights and diodes were dim, save one that glowed a haunting green. Tolde's eyes widened. He had seen this before.

"Who is it?" Paradise asked before he opened his mouth. The edge in her tone brought him on edge.

Ruma hovered beside the capsule, hands folded within her robes. Her head lowered. "The scourge of the universe, Paradise Tear. This is Rengu."

"The god of death?" Ragan chimed. Sweat beaded his brow, dripping from the tips of his tangled hair to run down the sides of his face.

"He should have been killed at Occanum. You had no right to preserve his life," Paradise growled.

"This decision was not made lightly. Much thought and effort went into securing his body, though why, I have often wondered," Ruma made no defense. What was done was done. "Rengu is the source of all evil plaguing humanity today. Cults in his name have spread like fires, a precursor to Amongeratix's assault. Tannus and I believe Rengu still has a part to play. A final gasp before his time expires, though what, I do not know."

"My uncle cannot be trusted, nor should he be allowed to draw another breath. I was there, Ruma, when the final battle all but wiped my people out. It was Rengu who slew Tannus' father and now I find this monster alive and in your care."

Ruma anticipated her hostility, for it was a demon she also struggled with. "Decisions needed to be made, Paradise. Tannus believed, as do I, that the preservation of life was more important than rivalries and differences. Keeping Rengu alive was a calculated risk."

"I must speak with my cousin," she planted her feet and crossed her arms. Paradise stood over ten feet tall, dwarfing the others. "He has much to answer for."

Ruma remained stoic, unimpressed with the outburst. She knew truths Paradise Tear failed to comprehend, including why Rengu was still alive and how much he was able to tell them before going into stasis. An event occurring years after her own entombment.

"I understand your frustration, even your anger, but there is much you have not been told," she decided to peel the edge back a little to see how the giant might react. "Do you know why it was deemed important to place you in stasis and keep you hidden for so long?"

Confused, some of the hostility drained from her glare.

"You are the only one capable of either awakening or destroying your kind. Tannus foresaw continued trouble with Amongeratix and created the stasis pods, with Sorrow's help, to operate through a single genetic code. Yours. Paradise, you are the only living soul in the universe with the power to save or damn your people for eternity."

"I thought you were gods?" Ragan whispered louder than intended.

The echo of his words rattled throughout the chamber to strike Paradise between the eyes. Her heart strained with new grief, as old wounds were reopened. Tannus kept that secret from her, and to hear one of humanity's youngest awaken with raw skepticism, threatening to undo all his life had been built around, the combination left her rattled. She knelt before Ragan.

"Gods? We were never gods, though many of our kind found the notion of apotheosis quaint enough to perpetuate the lie," she explained. "My kind were no different from you, Ragan Sandinsol, save for a penchant for violence. I … I wish it were not so."

Reeling as his mind struggled to accept the impossible, Ragan desperately wished to return to his home world and the comfort the ignorance his former life provided. Like so much else, he discovered the desire lacked follow through. The young thief was trapped in a world he did not understand, with beings who should not exist. His sense of adventure was dying each day and he damned Tolde for accepting him.

"Why keep him alive?" Luma Kai asked. "His name is responsible for thousands of deaths."

"Would his demise prevent the spread of ill in his name?" Ruma countered. "Rengu will atone for his crimes when the proper moment presents itself. Until then, he remains a quiet secret among the stars. One not even Amongeratix can guess."

Another Blood Witch hurried into the chamber. Her chest rose with ragged breath. "Grand Mistress, you must come quick. There is an urgent matter you need to attend!"

Ruma Zzein spun on the young sister. "I left instructions not to be disturbed. What is the meaning of this?"

The folds of her hood shifted as the witch glanced at the Grand Mistress's guests. She paused with unease. "I … it is for your ears alone, Grand Mistress."

"Speak plainly. I have nothing to hide from anyone here," she hissed.

Rebuked, the young witch bowed. "It is Mistress Her. She is leading a delegation to your quarters to demand your resignation. She says she will take the Order by force, if you choose to ignore her."

Insurrection. So, it appears Amongeratix has reached those beneath me after all. "How many sisters have answered her call?"

"I do not know, Grand Mistress, but the hall was filled with supporters as she marched. Mistress Mlth dispatched me as soon as she received word."

Vipers at every turn. Even with an unknown number at her call, Algiss Her was not powerful enough to claim leadership over the entirety of the Order. *What game do you play, Algiss?* "Return to Mistress Mlth and inform her that I will handle the matter personally. She is not to interfere unless called upon. My friends, perhaps it will be best if you return to your quarters for the time being. There is a reckoning approaching and I would not burden you with our internal affairs."

Tolde stepped forward, curiously unwilling to allow the one responsible for his resurrection to fall against a tide of unexpected malfeasance. Where the burden of loyalty sprang from was beyond him, though it felt right. "We shall stand beside you, if it is all right with you. There is already too much betrayal spread across the universe."

"Tolde, are you sure?" Luma questioned. "They control powers we don't comprehend, much less have a counter to."

"My mind is clear on this, Luma. The Grand Mistress requires our assistance, even if it is to merely observe," he replied.

"Fucking hells."

Paradise rose. "My faith in you is rattled, Witch, but I shall stand beside you as well. You and I must have a reckoning when this war ends."

"I don't want to die," Ragan squeaked.

"No one is asking you to, kid," Tolde said.

Luma cocked an eyebrow. "We kind of are."

Tolde placed a fatherly hand on Ragan's shoulder. "Stay behind me. We will protect you."

He followed Ruma from the chamber.

Alone in the gloom, Luma watched them go. "Who's going to protect us?"

"Ruma Zzein! Come forth and atone for your sins!"

Algiss Her dominated the corridor. Her width presented bulk, accented by the followers coerced to her point of view. Many lacked faith in the Order's present course of action, being too young to understand the principles of foundation. Idealists, they suffered from the warped teachings of one already soured on outdated beliefs.

The Grand Mistress emerged from a side corridor. The door opened without sound, providing her the opportunity to come upon her betrayer's flank unawares. "What is the meaning of this? How dare you question our actions?"

Algiss Her whirled, her robes twirling around her frame as she struggled to keep surprise from her voice. "Ruma Zzein, you have led this Order astray. Our mandate, from your very own lips, has always been to avoid human entanglement. We were meant to be warders, watchers from across the stars, without bias or prejudice. Your decision to ally us with Tannus circumvents all we have sought to achieve, reducing us to mere slaves in a never-ending war."

Smoothing her robes, Ruma reached up and lowered her hood, allowing all to see her face. Ragan gasped for he expected a wizened crone, not the image of a woman frozen in time. Were it not for the combination of fear and reverence, he might have found her beautiful after a fashion. Old scars lined the right side of her face. Cruel reminders of the torment suffered during her time as Oracle. Magic could conceal them, but they had become boon companions as she strove to create a utopian society humanity might one day admire.

"Forever Night approaches. I acted befitting that knowledge. The rest of you return to your quarters. I will treat with Mistress Her alone." The strength of her authority echoed down the hallway. Whatever folly Algiss inspired among them, there was no denying the raw power Ruma Zzein held. She prayed it was enough to prevent the inevitable.

"They are committed, Ruma. Do not ignore them. New leadership is needed. You must stand down," Algiss restated.

"A threat, Algiss? Do you forget who it was that found you? Orphaned on that speck of an island your people called home? Abandoned by family and friends. I took you in when no one wanted you. I treated you like a daughter. An heir to the wisdom of the universe and you squander it on dreams of pious grandeur," Ruma snapped. "Where is your honor? Or has Amongeratix bought you entire?"

Static lines of power surrounded the Mistress of Novices. "How dare you accuse *me* of treason? I have stood by your side for centuries. This Order is nothing without my work! I should be Grand Mistress by now but you continue to affront my devotion. Step aside, old woman, and I will let you live. You have my word."

"The word of a traitor means little, even during the best of times," Ruma clenched her fists, collecting power while subtly positioning herself between Algiss and the others. "You have become twisted, Algiss Her. I give no further warning. Stand down."

"Or what?" Algiss dared and threw her fists out.

Bolts of power lashed through the air. Lights flickered and burst. A novice screamed, fleeing. Sparks and flames danced between the two most powerful women in the abbey. The explosion of two lethal powers colliding threw several to the floor. Robes caught fire, the witches within screeching. Ragan dropped to his knees, hands covering the trickle of blood leaking from his ears. The Inquisitors reached for weapons they did not have, leaving the giant Paradise Tear the only viable defense.

Infuriated, Algiss Her doubled her assault, funneling every ounce of raw energy into her second attack. Wall panels cracked and splintered. Ancient marble crumbled under the extreme pressures. A younger witch burst apart in a spray of red mist, violent enough to break the once stolid will the group arrived with. Blood Witches fled for their lives, leaving the two most powerful of their order vying for control. Seizing the advantage, Paradise took off after them, accompanied by a slew of cursing and oaths suggesting an unpleasant demise.

"Back into the stairwell!" Tolde shouted above the roar of battle. He shoved Ragan out of the battle zone, confident Luma was on his heels.

Once secure from stray blasts of energy, the trio watched as the titanic struggle evolved into an indescribable nightmare. Buffeted by repeated impacts, they struggled to avoid being struck. Tolde watched in abject horror as Ruma was driven back. He sensed a shift and wished Paradise remained at his side.

"Your time is ending, Grand Mistress! I have the power now," Algiss bellowed. "You should have abdicated when you had the chance. Now I will end you. The universe will forget your sad legacy, as a new order will rise from the ashes of your failure."

Shadow and illusion grew her presence, so she loomed over the weakened Grand Mistress. Algiss raised her hands, curled into claws sparking with electricity. Madness filled her eyes, born of promises and false hopes. The Mistress of Novices allowed a single thought to dominate her mind, casting aside all rationale and companionship.

Back against the wall, the soft sound of Ruma's slippers touching the floor for the first time was remarkably loud. Smoke billowed from her robes, their gossamer fabric losing luster. Scored in a dozen places where fragments of energy broke through her defenses, Ruma had never been tested this much before.

"I have failed you, Algiss. You, of all my students, should have been treated with greater caution, for ever have you lacked the internal fortitude to do what must be done," Ruma taunted. "That inability has brought you to ruin."

"Feeble words from a defeated relic," Algiss shouted. "I am going to take great pleasure in watching you die. My only regret is you will not be alive to witness Lord Amongeratix assume control of the Order and this comet."

"That … is your final mistake."

Ruma's voice was barely a whisper. Suppressed hostility flashed in her eyes as her face clouded over with rage she had forgotten dwelled deep within. The Grand Mistress of Blood Witches rose to her full height, dwarfing the larger Algiss. Tremors rippled through the corridor. Fists clenched, she hovered closer to her prey.

Algiss threw up a protective ward a split second before Ruma's attacked shredded the ward and burned through her fingers. Little more than blackened stubs, Algiss was robbed of her ability to defend herself. The assault continued. Lash after lash permeated the younger witch's mind and spirit, threatening to break her into incoherent ruin. Flesh and robe dissolved to ash. Hair burned away, leaving a twisted mess.

"I have dedicated my life to stopping the predations of Amongeratix and you willingly turn to him for guidance! Oaths were sworn. Fealty expected. The lord of despair is a wicked creation who should never have been born and you would deliver the keys to this abbey to him on bended knee! Algiss Her, I strip you of your title, your powers, and your standing within the Order. Outcast I name you! Heretic!"

Her voice rose with each syllable. One of Algiss's eyes burst under pressure and she slumped to the floor as a final bolt of power struck her between the eyes. All magical abilities, stripped, the broken shell of a woman wept as she attempted crawling away. Ruma stalked behind, suddenly unsure whether to kill her or consign her to a fate far worse than eternal darkness.

Luma's gasp dissolved the tension, forcing the moment past. Blood mingled with an unknown yellow tincture to trail Algiss down the hall. Never had the Inquisitor witnessed such vulgar displays of power, not even during the battles on An'kuruku, when an entire army was turned to glass. Magic, she decided, was a wicked creation best relegated to the past.

Kneeling beside her former friend, Ruma passed judgment. "I will not kill you, Algiss Her. Consider this my last act of respect to you. Crippled, bereft of the ability to heal, and shorn from all that you have known for hundreds of years, you will live out your life until that final miserable moment when your heart stops and you realize there is nothing beyond the veil.

"Go, go to your new master and tell him you have failed. You are now a thing of the past. Another failure in a growing list," Ruma gestured the two witches who accompanied her to Rengu's crypt. "See she is placed on a shuttle. I want every Sister who aided her, bought into her lies, or plotted insurrection removed from my abbey. Do not perpetrate violence unless necessary. Some may merely be deluded by soft whispers of power. Traitors they may be, but I hold no ill toward them. Go."

Gathering what remained of the Mistress of Novices, they hurried to obey. Ruma turned to her companions, those faithful chosen upon whom the fate of the universe rested, while replacing her hood. "It is unfortunate you witnessed our private matters. Are any of you injured?"

All they managed were cold stares in reply.

Jungle village, planet Mannus Prime.

Kaline stared off into the fading sunset. The sky, serene as any she encountered on the numerous worlds she had visited, was awash in darkening pinks and reds. These were the simple moments she took pleasure in, freed of the burdens placed upon her. The Captain was off to their shuttle on a supply run. His protestations of leaving her alone in a potentially hostile village were ignored and, judging by the serenity she felt staring into the growing night, warranted.

Alone, she closed her eyes and thought of a different time. A time where the course of her life changed forever. It was unexpected, and not entirely welcomed. Never considered a people person, Kaline preferred the solitude attributed to her former lifestyle. The less contact with others, the simpler her life remained. At least until that fateful day several years ago …

She greeted the dawn much the same each day. A hot cup of caf in her tiny hands and a hunger to appreciate life's simple bounty. Dawn was her favorite time, when the world yet slept and but a handful were awake to enjoy the majesty of a swift sunrise. Working the night shift at the planetary observatory helped. She stifled a yawn, wincing at the familiar burn of her tired eyes.

Her only companion was an android with limited vocal function. More machine than man, XC-99 maintained the electronics and ensured all telescopes were tracking the moon's satellite defenses. Not that Kaline minded. She preferred the silent company. Unable to stop a second yawn, she decided it was time to finish her logs and go home. A spark plunging down through the thin atmosphere caught her eye. Gone as quick as she spied it. Kaline attributed it decreased mental function after a long, droll night. She turned away, thinking nothing more of it.

It was her greatest mistake. Kaline arrived home to find an alien shuttle sitting in front of her living quarters. Her rank afforded her the liberty of an independent home, much to the jealousy of her peers and neighbors. She seldom considered their woes. Life was an individual effort. How could any expect to become something, if they sat around and waited for a handout?

The man waiting on her doorstep was small, hidden beneath robes of onyx and crimson. His close-cropped hair was streaked through with thin grey lines. Hard eyes filled with determination stared at her beneath a weathered face. Though he presented little threat, Kaline found his presence unsettling.

"Who are you?" she demanded with shaky voice.

"Are you Kaline Quo'les?" he ignored her.

She stiffened. A host of words, empty threats, played out in her mind, yet she stood silent. Paralyzed with fear. Her legs betrayed the slightest tremble.

"I a... yes," she was unable to take her eyes away.

"Good. I do so hate wasting time," the stranger replied. "I have come a long way to find you, Kaline."

"How do you know my name?" A measure of strength awakened when confronted by the promise of danger. "I am no one. What use could I possibly have for you?"

"That is a tale long in the telling. It is written among the stars that yours is a destiny of greatness," he rambled. "How long have you gazed into the heavens, wondering what future awaits you? There is majesty among the stars, kept from every man by those twisted powers who have consumed the universe for three thousand years."

Heart hammering in her chest, Kaline leaned closer, eager to hear more. His tone dripped honey, luring her mind to places she seldom imagined. Questions arose. The Conclave protected the universe from heresy, from subversion under the promise of preventing life from devolving as it had for the gods before.

"What if I told you the foundations of human existence were built upon a lie?" His voice was soothing, whispering confidence.

He followed her gaze to the skies, a grin revealing impossibly white teeth. "You have suspected this? Thinking you were meant for more. A future of greatness. Do not deny the desire in your heart. I see through you, Kaline. I sense the moment of your time approaching. All you need do is take my hand and all shall be revealed. All shall rest at your fingertips. You, Kaline Quo'les will be a name remembered throughout the course of the human future."

A wizened hand stretched out. Kaline's mind filled with conflicting thoughts. His speech awakened latent emotions deep within. She was tired of being ignored. Tired of going unnoticed as her peers enjoyed their lives. A forgotten woman, bereft of a true life, Kaline admitted the hard truth of wanting more. Her hand reached back.

"What must I do?" she asked in a breathy whisper.

"The first step has already been taken. Yours is a future that will burn brighter than a thousand suns. Oh, what sights I have to show you. Come, there is much work to do."

She followed him blindly to his shuttle, leaving the hollow shell of her past behind.

Kaline opened her eyes to the warmth of the first rays of sunlight kissing her face. Memories of her journey to whims of Rengu were at once pleasant and tormenting. Liberating the minds of the downtrodden and forgotten proved a far easier task than she imagined, even after years of performance. How many converted to her subtle promise was unknown, though she suspected in the thousands. Fewer remained alive. It was the sad cost of devotion and she would have traded none of it. Accepting that hand was the single greatest moment of her life.

Hesitant footsteps clomped up the slope behind her. Kaline frowned. Like all pleasant moments in her life, this one ended. "What is it?"

"Ah, Mistress Kaline, I have gathered those willing to hear your words."

Back to the villager, she broke into a grin. *So, it begins.* "Very good, young Bao. I knew you would not fail me. Are they prepared to open their hearts and minds to the glory that is Rengu's wisdom?"

"I do not know, but more are willing to listen," Bao replied. He was bowed. Mind already clear of doubt. The first convert.

"Listening is the beginning. The most important part," Kaline smiled.

The warmth of her gaze fell upon him and Bao blushed.

"When my Captain returns, have him wait outside. I would not want your friends feeling disassociated by his armed presence," she cooed.

Bao nodded and accompanied her to the gathering.

Krenz, planet Vau Prime.

"This doesn't feel right," Aliz whispered. "Where are the authorities?"

Crouched at her side, Julian swept his binoculars across the building façade. "I don't know. The place should be filled with people."

Reports suggested the local precinct was ignorant of the threat, going so far as to conduct business as usual, despite rumors of losses in the surrounding neighborhoods. Julian found the idea of attacking a precinct full of loyal prefects doing their best to keep their citizens safe and their streets clean distasteful, but orders were orders. He suspected most of the men and women he was responsible for killing or displacing were only trying to do their jobs, neither inherently good nor evil. The sad truth of war was innocence suffered first.

"We need to get closer before I commit to the assault," he continued. Risking lives for no gain served no purpose. The enemy was already closing in, and until now, he remained a step ahead. *But for how long? This game won't last forever. My people are strained, pushed to their limits with no sign of relief. I fear this campaign will be the end of us all.*

Unconvinced, Aliz shook her head. "It could be a trap."

"There are no guarantees in war, Aliz, and we need this station to secure the sector," Julian countered.

"Fine, but must you go? Our people need you alive more than your conscience needs to be salved."

He frowned. Aliz was ever the mother and it showed in the level of care she exhibited toward the rebellion. Under her withering concern, Julian relented. "Very well. A commander's place is to command, not lead the assault. Tage, take three with you and recon the block. Don't get caught."

Aliz watched four figures slip from the shadows. Silent professionals, they obeyed without question. She admired their fervor, if not their eagerness to spill blood. All remained citizens of the Conclave, regardless of which ideology they served. How man killed his fellows with so little compunction was lost on her. She longed for the days of decency, but in retrospect, decided they were far behind them now. Lost before the war began.

Slipping a look at Julian, she wondered what was going through his mind. No stranger to battle, she often imagined the steel it took to lead soldiers, knowing some would not return. Such weight would drown an average person. The one battle she fought in left her mind reeling with questions and doubts. Her one way of reconciling the harsh truths was by comparing it to decisions Lorenu Phos was often criticized as being ruthless. *Did her orders result in death? Was I purposefully left in the dark about the vile necessities of leadership*? Aliz shuddered. Layered secrets burdened her, threatening to subsume her mindfulness when she needed it most.

What happens when we spring the trap?

"Aliz, you need to be ready to move, if this goes sideways," Julian watched as his scouts disappeared, slipping into the prefect building.

She forced out the heavy breath in her heart. "Just like we rehearsed."

"Just like that," he echoed.

"Captain, movement on the second story. Third window from the right."

Julian shifted but found nothing. "I don't see anything."

"It was there, sir. I swear."

He tried to think who the speaker was, while looking harder. The voice was unfamiliar and decidedly young. Too young to play at war when he should have been in school. "I still don't see anything. Are you sure it wasn't one of ours?"

Gunfire erupted from within the building. The window he had been watching blew out with a puff of flame and black smoke. A charred body fell to the ground. Julian caught the sound of military vehicles moving in, their telltale engine whine sparking dread. Even with the weapons and equipment confiscated during the raid on Tatarast Island, only went so far against armor. Options thinning, Julian knew retreat was the only viable solution.

"We're about to get pinched," he told Aliz before directing the rest of his raiding party. "Hit those windows. I want Tage at least the chance of getting out alive."

Small arms fire lashed across the darkness, striking the prefect headquarters with unrepentant fury. A trio of men squirted out a side door. They wore prefect uniforms and were cut down for their patriotism. Julian jerked at the unexpected sound of gunfire to his right. Smoke trickled from Aliz's barrel.

"I knew teaching you how to shoot was going to come in handy," he said after seeing the ill-hidden look of horror in her eyes. Julian recognized her strength the moment she wound up in his care, though now he wondered who was watching after who.

"We must all make sacrifices, Captain," she replied. "What are we going to do about those?"

Aliz gestured with his chin to the first armored personnel carrier emerging from the night. Tracking, Julian relaxed enough to think straight. Light armor, prefect issue. Kale's forces had yet to react. *Or they are waiting for us to break and run before slaughtering us. I need a new lifestyle.*

"Get your head down, Aliz," he warned, reaching for the cylinder weapon at his side.

She burrowed as deep into the coarse rooftop as she could, keeping her head raised just enough to witness what came next. Julian slid the weapon onto a shoulder, flicked on the small targeting computer and aimed. Aliz had seen these before, on Tatarast. Their lethality provided an immediate impact on the battlefield. One she prayed was enough to demoralize the prefects from engaging further. War was such a terrible waste of life.

"Fire in the hole!" he shouted.

Those nearest ducked. Julian fired. Plasma burned out the back of the tube as the thermal projectile rocketed toward the carrier. The prefect in the passenger seat dove out the door an instant before the blast struck and penetrated the industrial grade armor. Men and metal melted into slag. She felt the heat on her face. Emotions welled. Aliz sympathized with the brave prefects within. No one deserved such a fate.

"That did the trick, but I fear we've overstayed our welcome," Julian said. "All teams, displace and retreat. Rendezvous at point alpha. Move!"

Aliz gripped his forearm. "Captain, what of the men in the building?"

Battle sounds were all but finished. Only the cackling of flames sang across the night. He shouldered the rocket. "We can do nothing for them, Aliz."

"But you don't know that!" she protested. Heart heavy with the loss of so many, she railed at the thought of abandoning men to their doom. She had to know if any yet lived. Needed to know. If only to calm the ache in her heart.

His shoulders slumped. Defeated. "Aliz, we have been through this before. If any live, they will exfil and regroup. I can't risk more lives on a whim."

She knew. Of course, she did. Knowing did little to reduce the burden of guilt weighing down her heart. The dam broke. Tears spilled free. Years of pent-up frustrations colliding in the aftermath of yet another engagement. Nodding, she allowed him to pull her up and hurried to their escape vehicle before worse than prefects arrived to secure the scene.

"I am tired of losing people, Julian," she whispered after settling in her seat. "So very tired of it all."

He gunned the engine and sped away after ensuring no one else remained behind. Julian kept his gaze on the road. "I know, Aliz. I know."

They soared over the empty roads, each lost in that strange land between private thought and lament. He was thankful for the droning engines, for they prevented him from hearing her weeping. Life would have been better, if he'd stayed home and took up the family bakery. So much better.

EIGHTEEN

3215 A.G. (After gods), Western approaches, planet Mannus Prime.

"Medic!"

Annalilly heard the telltale double thump before diving on the wounded man. The grenades went off, blowing their force up instead of out and saving her life in the process. Dirt and debris rained down upon them. Ears ringing, she pushed off her comrade to give Doc Little room to work. His uniform was drenched in drying blood. His aid pack was already half depleted. Despite her orders, he remained without a helmet. The hollowness in his eyes was one she expected to find up and down the lines, in those fortunate enough to survive.

"How is he?" she asked.

Lines of tracer fire filled the sky overhead. Little stuck an index finger in the wound, feeling for the foreign object. "Should be fine. It's a minor flesh wound."

Annalilly left him to his patient and sought out her heavy weapons team. Another round of explosions threw her to the ground. Stone and shrapnel pelted her armor. The battle stretched for half a kilometer to her flanks. Their movement to contact was successful, drawing enemy rearguard action before she was ready to retaliate.

"Gods fucking damn it," she snarled. "Somebody put suppressing fire on that fucking position, now! Beve!"

"Sergeant."

"You got a bead on that bastard shooting grenades?" Annalilly crawled behind a small boulder and poked her head out just far enough to scout the engagement area. Trees and uneven terrain prevented her from seeing too much. Grumbling, she switched her helmet to thermals.

Beve's rumbling voice responded a moment later. "Yeah, I got em."

"Do you need an invitation?"

Grinning behind his visor, the heavy weapons specialist slipped his fingertip into the trigger well. "Nope."

"Then put a hole in his gods damned chest."

He fired three times in rapid succession as he trained his rifle on each target hunkered down in what appeared to be a log bunker. The third man was hit before the first was dead. "Targets eliminated, Sergeant."

About time. Annalilly lifted her head a little higher. The immediate threat removed, she began counting targets. Too many, prompting her to wonder just how caught by surprise the enemy was. "Yeves, Palco, I want that line peppered with grenades and thermal rockets. Burn them out. The rest of you stand by to assault. No one stops until we clear their position, understood?"

"Heads down!" Yeve's baritone rang across the intercom.

Hell unleashed before she received confirmation. Annalilly watched with mute fascination as trees exploded. Body parts sailed into the air. It took little to imagine what they were enduring, for she had been on the receiving end one too many times. Sympathy, however, was in short supply. Without waiting for the detonations to end, she pushed to her feet and charged.

"Now!"

Soldiers crawled from their positions, reluctantly following her lead. Sporadic small arms fire dropped one or two. Annalilly opened fire. Odds of hitting a target were slim. She sought only to keep their heads down long enough to cross the distance. Then the fun began. Raw nerves reaped an emotional toll. Her adrenalin surged through her veins. Thirty meters. Palco's second barrage landed and broke the defender's will. Enemy Guards picked up and ran only to be shot in the back. Others threw their hands up, unwilling to endure more brutality. A select few continued the fight. These true believers drew Annalilly's vengeance.

Rifle tucked in the shoulder pocket, she swept across the battlefield with immaculate precision. Enemy soldiers pitched back, their lives cut short by her fury. Haggle slid beside her and emptied his belt fed grenade launcher. The sonic whumps of detonating forty-millimeter phosphorus rounds vibrated up through their boots, as white-purple flames engulfed more traitors. Annalilly broke into a wild grin, savage and mirthless. She discovered she enjoyed this. The ruthless slaughter of armed men and women intent on seeing her dead. It was the ultimate game.

One of her Guards fell forward and was still. Arms and legs crumpled beneath him, head twisted sideways. The visor prevented her from instant recognition, as well as any accusatory glare. Tactical readouts scrolled across her screen, detailing the fallen. One of the repos. Losing a soldier was never pleasant but she thanks the gods it was not one of her friends. Obscurity made the loss less unacceptable. There'd be time enough to mourn him after the smoke cleared.

She shouted her frustrations and pushed forward. Annalilly leapt over fallen trees, pausing but once to reload the power charge in her rifle before leading the assault into the enemy trench. Sporadic fighting continued as opposing forces clashed in a battle of wills. Knives were drawn. Rifles turned to blunt instruments. She dampened her helmet's speakers to keep the cries and screams from the wounded out of her head.

A blade slashed toward her head. Annalilly ducked back and brought her knee into the man's stomach. She was surprised to find most of the enemy lacked proper Guard armor, suggesting they were fighting rear echelon or reserve troopers. Following her knee strike, Annalilly allowed her momentum to drive her body weight into the stricken man and to the ground where she snapped his neck. A second foe popped up from the nearest fighting position, grenade cocked back to throw. She drew her sidearm and shot the woman in the face. Body and grenade dropped into the hole. The resulting explosion ensured the threat was eliminated.

Hollis and Jolent rushed past her, firing steady streams into a squad of retreating soldiers. An inspection up and down the lines showed most resistance was crushed. Defeated Guards threw down their weapons, raised their hands and were escorted away from the fight. Others fought to the bitter end, trying to take as many foes with them before they went back to the dirt. Suddenly claustrophobic, Annalilly ripped off her helmet and breathed deep.

The acrid stench of battle filled her nostrils. The iron tang of blood. The despair of loss. Dirt, sweat, and emotion invigorated her. Medics rushed to the next fallen Guard. Litter bearers carried the wounded back to the line of departure, where a robust aide station was set up. Several Guards slumped down, backs against trees as they struggled to understand what just happened. The crackle of an incoming transmission forced her to replace her helmet.

"This had better be good," she snarled.

"Situation report, sergeant," Fies voice cut through her latent hostility.

I liked you better when you were just a squad leader. "First emplacements are clear. Enemy in full rout. Casualties are minimal. Requesting position to follow and continue engaging."

"Negative. Call back coordinates and prepare for artillery support," his voice was mechanical, bereft of emotion.

Translation, we can't afford to waste lives. "Roger. Coordinates as follows."

Asom's heart thundered as he closed the gap between forces. The Marine was used to close quarter battle, confined by inanimate corridors. Engaging the enemy in an open area covering kilometers was unlike any experience in his time in uniform. He insisted on keeping his Marines together during the assault, though there was never a real sense of resistance. Army and Marines tended to mind their affairs, while developing an unsteady alliance. Annalilly had no problem with it and he was able to concentrate on keeping his people alive.

They moved with awkward precision, each struggling to come to terms with the unwritten laws of surface warfare. The disassociation did little to negate their lethality. Asom and his squad assaulted with the ruthlessness that had become a Marine standard. His first few rounds struck a man in the upper chest and head, vaporizing him as he fell. The Marine beside Asom grunted as his chest plates stopped a stream of incoming rounds. Three grenades followed, exploding at the stricken man's feet.

Rock and dirt splattered Asom. His ears rang from the detonations. Force of impact drove him to a knee. He caught the strained gurgle of his fellow Marine dying. Pushing off the ground with his free hand, Asom redoubled his resolve. *Close the gap. Eliminate the threat.* Killing the enemy meant a great deal less than keeping his people alive. A task ripe with failure. Explosions rippled up and down the line. Men and women fell. Bushes and trees shredded. He kept running.

Squads of soldiers burst from the haze. A desperate last stand. They came screaming, wielding bayonets and combat knives. This Asom understood. Aiming at who he assumed to be the ranking officer, he squeezed the trigger. The woman dropped, clutching the spreading redness over her stomach. Her death stalled the advance, allowing the Marines to crash into their disorganized ranks. Asom struck first, plunging his blade into the exposed neck of the nearest soldier. Twisting, he ripped the blade free and launched into the next target.

A blow to the back of his helmet staggered him. Asom turned, firing without looking. Two rounds caught his opponent in the throat, nearly severing his head. Asom grunted when a massive weight barreled him to the ground and started pummeling him with a rifle butt. Marine armor was different from regular Guard. Made of composite material to withstand all but the strongest weapon impacts, his armor was built to take a beating.

The soldier landed on Asom's chest, pinning his legs. His blows trailed up from the sternum to helmet. Each thrust wild, momentum nearly succeeded in breaking through. Asom brought his arm up, blocking the next blow and opening the opportunity to punch his attacker's elbow with his other hand. The exposed limb cracked. He looked up to see bewildered pain twisting the soldier's face and a shower of blood washed down with bits of skull and brain matter. Groaning, Asom pushed the corpse off and snatched his rifle. He doubted he would ever learn who saved his life and it didn't matter. Dead was dead.

"Keep moving, Marines! We're not letting these Guard troopers win the day."

He once spent a few moments wondering what others thought of him before the notion became foolish. Almost as foolish as he felt barking encouragement to his people. Asom rose through the ranks listening to leaders do the same, figuring it was good enough to inspire their Marines, so it should be good enough for his. The thought brought a chuckle that spread to his squad. Chuckle turned to uncontrollable laughter, as what remained of the enemy was overwhelmed and rendered combat ineffective.

"Corpsman up!"

Blood raised, Asom advanced on the enemy defensive position to give his medics room to operate unhindered. Explosions and small arms fire became sporadic, trickling from the intense barrage, announcing the beginning of the firefight. Bodies became visible the closer he got. It was a sickening sight. Splashes of crimson painted what foliage remained. Craters pockmarked the area, punctuated by burnt trees. Deciding he preferred the intimacy of fighting in space, Asom followed Annalilly by removing his helmet and stalking through the rubble to her.

"Hell of a fight, eh?" she smirked.

Pulling a swig from his canteen, Asom wiped his mouth with the back of his hand. "If you say so. Is it always this bad?"

Annalilly rounded on him. "This bad? This was nothing. A minor skirmish. The real fight won't come for a few days, not til we close in with their main army. That's where the fun begins."

"We live different lives," he muttered.

She nodded. "That we do. You mean to tell me you've never been in the shit this bad before?"

"Wasn't much need until this war started," he replied. "Our duties revolved around escorting dignitaries, ranking officers. I was never in a real scrap until about a year ago. Got a medal and a promotion out of it."

There was no hint of bragging in his voice, more sadness for serving during a period of civil unrest. Life seldom cared for the whims of its participants.

"Stick with my people. You'll get plenty of fancy medals to put on your chest before this is done," she lamented. *If you live that long. War isn't for everyone.*

The first artillery shells rocketed overhead. Soldiers raised their weapons to cheer. Every round meant the potential of having one less enemy to face when the push came.

"Come on, let's get some grub. I'm famished."

He stared at the red specks coloring her lightning bolt tattoos and wondered how much violence this woman had seen to make her harder than a mountain. Asom followed. The first hints of hunger awakening.

Jelin Quint scratched at the stubble growing on his chin. Never one to grow facial hair, his face was in a constant state of itching or feeling weighted. The one time he tried to grow a beard lasted a handful of days, until the itching phase. Unable to bear the irritation, he shaved it off and never considered it again. Time in the field, on campaign, left him little options.

His right hand fiddled with the datapad Cardinal Virom slipped him before departing. He'd read it once, en route to the rendezvous and it left him rattled. Never trust the clergy to look out for you. Filled with enemy troop strengths and dispositions—how Virom came by this intel was questionable at best—there was enough information for the reinforcing division to crack the enemy siege lines and end the campaign. All good facts, until he scrolled through a dossier of the enemy chain of command and discovered his brother, whom he thought long dead, commanded.

Wouldn't mother Quint be shocked to learn her elder son yet drew breath. Rumored to have been killed during a trade dispute on the backwater world of Ninean, Banno Quint was the meanest dog in the neighborhood. His reputation and quickness to action resulted in being promoted faster than his peers and assigned to increasingly difficult units. Ninean was meant to be a peaceful negotiation, until someone fired on the compound housing half the delegates. Talks ended and the Conclave ordered the heresy stamped out. Jelin decided his brother was responsible. *Bloodthirsty bastard probably set the fire himself.*

Knowing the information would spread as soon as he handed the datapad over, Jelin suspected narrowed eyes would seek him out, silently questioning whether he was equally treasonous. *Why couldn't I have bought it with the rest of my unit? None of this would be happening and I could have died lacking this terrible knowledge.* Fighting his brother was no issue. They never got along. Jelin feared he wouldn't be able to overcome the stigma once Torgast and the others found out. *But doesn't the Old Man already know? He must have figured it out by now. Not like Quint's a popular name. Just how screwed am I?*

"Sergeant Quint, do you have anything to add?"

Caught off guard, Jelin dropped his hand and fought off a grimace as the itching spread across his lower jaw. "Excuse me, sir?"

The junior lieutenant staring at him had every character trait of a hard man. Rumored to have risen through the ranks, he commanded an entire brigade, prompting Jelin to surmise the allied forces lacked leadership. Regardless of his position or experience, the men and women surrounding him displayed unquestionable loyalty. He was one of theirs.

"Sir, I was given this right before heading your way." He handed the datapad over. "Contains all the intel you should need to begin sustained operations."

Fies glanced at Annalilly. "Looks like the Admiral was right. Our friends in the Conclave came through after all."

She snorted. "Remains to be seen."

Where Quint found Fies to be quietly inspiring, he was terrified of the tattooed platoon sergeant. Madness smoldered in her eyes. He'd seen it before, right before the hard parts of the battle erupted. Some were consumed by that fire. Others rose above it to reap a wicked toll. Banno was such a man. *What kind of outfit have I fallen in with?*

"All right. I want a firm line established along this route here," he pointed at the terrain map covering the table they surrounded. "Double pickets. We might have bested our enemy today, but we are outnumbered and outgunned. Get your people fed and bedded down. Make sure they change their socks. Nothing stops a soldier faster than bad feet. Triple guard rotation throughout the night. This is a combat op, no slacking. Questions?"

"Sir, what time are we kicking off the advance?" a haggard sergeant with a timid demeanor asked.

"Orbital bombardment should commence at dawn, Jers. I want the line moving one hour before. We hit their supply lines, artillery parks, and anything else they have lurking behind the front. Do not, I repeat, do not become bogged down. Keep moving at all costs. If we need to pull back, we do it across the line. One unit displaces and we lose everything. Understood?"

Heads bobbed.

"Good, dismissed."

Squad leaders and platoon sergeants broke away in groups or alone. Junior officers huddled nearby discussing tactics and theoreticals of what might happen. Nothing was left to chance. They were too small a force for that. Every trigger puller was necessary. Jelin had been in quality units before, but there was something about this one. Desperate to be sure, they operated like a machine, even with the compliment of Marines in their midst. *This is what I've been missing. That sense of belonging. Of knowing the other man has my back. Lucky bastards.*

He knew what had to be done. Sucking in a deep breath to steady his nerves, Jelin waited for the crowd around Fies to clear. "El-tee, I need to talk to you."

Failing to keep the yawn from stretching his face, Fies said, "Quint, I wanted to thank you for providing the intel for us. You were a great help today."

He didn't see it that way. In fact, Jelin did nothing more than watch the battle. Pleasant as that was, he felt wrong for it. "Wasn't nothing, sir. I wish I could have done more."

"Don't we all. What can I do for you?" Fies responded.

Red lines streaked his eyes. For all his preaching of letting the soldiers get sleep, he hadn't been able to close his eyes since the terror of not knowing if the enemy battleship was going to target his ship next. Chunks of debris from the massive ship continued to burn up in the atmosphere as they were caught in the gravity well and sucked to the surface.

This is it. No turning back now. One confession and I'm back in irons awaiting my court martial. "Well, this isn't going to be pleasant, but I need to say it. It's about the enemy commander, sir."

A sucking feeling in the pit of Fies's stomach robbed him of strength. "Go on."

Jelin ensured they were out of ear shot from everyone else. "He's my brother."

Fuck.

Bootleg depressed the firing pedal and watched the enemy armored aircar evaporate in a puff of flames. Grinning, he swept the turret of his Aggravator class tank for more targets. Columns of black smoke billowed from a dozen fires. The enemy rear-guard fortress wasn't expecting an armored assault and paid for that error. Vehicles burned. No building was left standing. The mercenary had no idea what strength he faced, nor did he care. The threat was eliminated, opening the way for his Shadow Hammers to plunge into the enemy's guts once they were given the green light. Not bad for a day's work.

"All elements, stand down. Infantry sweep forward and secure the position," he barked to his company. Mischief gleaming in his eyes, he looked over to the opposite side of the cupola. "Hey, Matthias, you reckon we should take prisoners or just run 'em through now and save the hassle?"

Matthias rolled his eyes but showed no other reaction. Men like Bootleg were a pox on ordered battle units. He failed to recall the man's true name or his infractions, making the mercenary's vendetta all the more curious. Figuring there would be time enough to make right when the smoke cleared, Matthias remained focused.

"You know Guard policy. Prisoners have the same rights as everyone."

"Too bad I'm not in the Guard anymore. You've gotten soft, Sergeant Major. There was a time I'd watch you punch a few rounds through someone's face if he pissed you off," Bootleg teased. As much as he wanted to goad his former commander into brash action, he remembered Admiral Falchi's threat. The Shadow Hammers might be good on the ground, but nothing in their arsenal could stop an orbital bombardment. Best to play nice until the campaign ended and he got paid.

"Order your people to escort the prisoners back to the command area."

Bootleg spit a mouthful of dark fluid mixed with flecks of leaves. "No fun. That's a lot of mouths to feed, but I wouldn't want you to disappoint your boss. Be a shame if you got a blemish on your record. Albus, see to it none of our guests are injured. Have Doc patch 'em up, if needed. Once you drop them off with them Guard boys behind the lines double time it back here. We got a battle to plan."

"Right, Chief."

Matthias watched a hatch open on one of the aircars and Albus slid out, waving his weapon and shouting. Nerves often ran high right after a battle, and though this was but the overture to what Matthias envisioned as a long campaign, the Shadow Hammers got their appetites whet. Satisfied, Matthias resumed his attention on the decimation before them.

There was no finesse in the mercenary assault. The combined armor and infantry attack struck the enemy lines with blunt force, overwhelming resistance in mere hours. Any professional aspect the mercenaries had was lost amid their savage brutality. Matthias wondered how many of the dead he once knew. The sad cost of war was not in governments or entities, it was the loss of friends and familiar faces. An occasional loss was expected, the odd empty place at the table, but the wholesale slaughter of so many, that entire units ceased to exist, left him appalled. His loss of appetite for battle grew the older he became. War, he decided, was a young man's game.

"You done admiring the scenery?" Bootleg snorted.

Constant chiding starting to wear on him, Matthias did his best to ignore it. "We need to keep pushing forward and link up with the rest of the strike force. Time is against us."

Eyes narrowing, Bootleg replied, "I know my job, Matthias. Unless you're in a hurry to get what's coming?"

"Just do your job," Matthias snapped. "You'll get your chance when the smoke clears."

"Chief, I got the numbers," a distorted voice broke the immediate tension.

"Send it," Bootleg resumed his attention on his unit.

"Seventeen dead, thirty-eight wounded, zero missing. We have eighty-one prisoners. Some aren't going to make it."

Seventeen dead. For what? This miserable rock isn't worth a drop of our blood, yet here we are. Just like our Guard days. "Police up the bodies for grave detail and get everyone loaded up. It's time to get back in the war. Refit and resupply immediately. We've got people counting on us."

He turned to Matthias, "Not one damned word."

Eger City, planet Mannus Prime.

Cardinal Virom rubbed his hands together as his nerves threatened to get the best of him. His mind raced with dark thoughts. Falchi's armada arrived and made their ground forces drop but the unexpected arrival of the Prekhauten battleship threatened to undo all. He felt trapped in his offices, while good men and women died above him. Sworn to uphold humanity and ensure the continued faith and stability of society, Virom was at odds with his position. The Conclave stood on the brink of irreversible change. At war with itself, the priests and cardinals who once called themselves allies, were now turned on one another under the justifications of righteous proclamations. *But who is right?*

The sun was rising. The first hints of light cracking the curtain of darkness. There was a time he enjoyed the hour. A time gone as the dread of each new day promised to bring them all closer to unwelcome demise. Virom questioned whether his time as a member of the Conclave was at an end. The desire to wear his robes faded, despite his acknowledgement of conscience that all sentient beings deserved the opportunity to enhance their lives through divine worship. His qualifications clashed with the current downtrend in ministry affairs dictated by the Forum tucked away on Vau Prime.

Feeling trapped, Virom attempted to rub away the growing ache in his temples. The how and why of the war meant little at this stage. One side was going to win and the universe would be forever changed. Which side remained to be seen, though the longer the fighting went on, the more he suspected Alain Nye would reign supreme. Until then, Virom vowed to minister to the people of Mannus Prime, when allowed, and provide comfort to Torgast's forces. There was little else the Cardinal could do.

"This is Admiral Falchi calling for Cardinal Virom."

Chills rolled up his arms. Virom turned, eyes wide. He gestured for the young priest monitoring the communications station to open the line.

"Admiral, this is Virom," he almost shouted.

"Good to hear your voice again, Cardinal," Falchi admitted.

Heart pounding, Virom settled into his high back chair. "We thought you were lost in the engagement with the battleship."

"It was a tough enough fight but we had the weight to win through, though at great cost. The skies over Mannus Prime are now in our control."

Head dipping, Virom failed to imagine the mixed sensations of fighting against a superior foe in the coldness of space. Violence was never his vocation, choosing wisely to leave it to braver men and women. "Was your deployment successful, Admiral?"

"Enough. We lost a few drop shuttles with all hands, but the bulk of our ground forces are deployed and engaging the enemy west of the lines. Can you contact your ground forces commander and have him establish communications with my fleet?"

Meaning he expects to have company before this is finished. Virom made up from his lack of battle knowledge with guile. He conspired with Torgast to block outgoing transmissions from the orbital firing platforms, cutting lines with forces on the ground and Prekhauten staging bases in the sector. It proved just enough for Falchi to swoop in undetected.

"Relay your message and I will ensure he receives it," Virom confirmed. "I already have a liaison to your ground command. He should be arriving shortly, if he has not already. Admiral, there is another problem. I have one of the planetary Inquisitors in custody. Would it be possible to shuttle him to your fleet so he is no longer a burden or threat to the local population?"

Virom winced as he spoke. The Inquisition presented his greatest threat. With Bela Cass dead, authority went to the treacherous Dowan Munn. The thin Inquisitor had tried to coerce Torgast into working together after the execution. After listening to all Dowan had to offer, Torgast gave the man a chance to subvert enemy units to his cause. He was escorted to a neutral position, watched under heavy surveillance. Light infantry units attacked simultaneously, revealing the attempted rescue effort. The enemy was beaten back and Torgast had Dowan confined. The cost in life was great, with several hundred dead on both sides. Virom doubted any one man was worth such a toll.

"As long as you don't mind if I jettison him into the void the instant he tries anything," Falchi stated. Always the no nonsense sort, Falchi grew harder the longer the war extended.

While Virom did not know the man personally, Falchi's tone suggested his seriousness. "Understood. Thank you, Admiral."

"I'll have a shuttle dispatched to you upon receiving your coordinates. Falchi out."

The line went dead, leaving Virom confused as he failed to understand the significance of the enormity of so many moving pieces. Were he a less cynical man, he might have dared to hope.

Massed artillery fire blew holes in the heart of the enemy camp. Impossible damage continued under the punishing rain of plasma and high explosives. Clouds of black smoke hovered over the battlefield. Bits of entrenchments, bodies, and more rained down. A hellish storm, the barrage continued for the better part of an hour. If he listened closely, Torgast swore he heard the mindless screams of those Guards enduring the assault. While he did not envy them, he knew each casualty was one less fighter to defend against the next phase of his campaign.

Up and down his main lines, Guards watched their counterparts suffer. There were no cheers. No elation for victory. Months of fighting in the trenches robbed their spirit. Those still motivated to fight, looked on with regret, knowing they had endured the hell of an artillery barrage too many times. Unimaginable suffering spread on the other side of the front. Friends lost. Morale shaken. Hollow stares for the rest of their lives. Going unreported by either side, was the rising number of suicides. Brave men and women who performed every task asked of them but were unable to live with the consequences. That pain gnawed away all resolve, until the soldier believed death provided the only relief. It was the greatest travesty of the war.

Torgast watched from a command bunker built into the front trench. Junior officers and sergeants came and went with orders. There was an excitement in them he had not felt for months. One of Torgast's biggest complaints was in not having armor to force the advantage. A duel of elite infantry divisions devolved into a static nightmare.

Thousands of lives were lost to the grueling atmosphere of trench warfare. His men needed a boost.

The artillery expended ammunition at a great rate, sparking the rumor mill. Torgast told very few of the incoming forces landing on the opposite side of the engagement area. Once the landings were confirmed and Falchi's forces engaged with the enemy would he have the word spread. It was his intent to force his opponent to divide his attention, thus weakening his response to whichever assault he felt was primary. Torgast did not envy his counterpart.

"Commander, we have an incoming message."

Torgast lowered his binoculars. "From whom?"

"Sergeant Quint, Sir."

He concealed his pleasure. Quint was providing more than his worth since being taken off the line and assigned to his personal protection detail. Men like Jelin Quint were hard to find in a lengthy campaign.

"What does our good sergeant have to say?" he asked.

"Contact has been established with arriving forces. All units are pushing forward. Sergeant Quint reports enemy rear pickets have been engaged and eliminated. He expects to be within range of the rearmost supply depots by morning and requests your orders."

Far better than expected. Torgast flexed the fingers of his left hand. "Tell him to advance and destroy all enemy units in their path. Secure the supply depots, if practical. Destroy them if not. Regardless, hold position after. We will draw the enemy's attention with an assault on their lines."

He hoped to draw the focus back on him, allowing the newly arrived armor elements to punch up through the enemy's center, breaking their camp and scattering any organized defenses remaining. Not foolish enough to expect immediate victory, Torgast ran through alternative plans. Victory or defeat remained subject to whim and willpower. He refused to consider the worst-case scenario until it happened.

"Relay orders to Generals Desril and Hamma. I want their divisions prepared to advance by dawn," he added. "Lift the artillery barrage. Our friends across No Man's Land know we have help by now. No point in wasting ammo."

Men and women saluted and raced to convey the orders. He felt an electricity spreading for the first time since the Mannus campaign devolved into this nightmare. It was a dangerous moment capable of robbing his focus when it was most needed. Torgast exhaled, forcing his nerves to calm and resumed watching the final salvos rocketing overhead.

Later in the day, tired and unable to pay attention, he stumbled into the officers' mess for the chance to relax his troubled mind. A handful of subordinates occupied some of the tables. They nodded or murmured greetings. Torgast feigned enthusiasm before dropping into an empty seat. One of the cooks presented him a tray of blanched vegetables, an unidentified meat that was almost too stringy to eat, and a slice of bread. The bread was the only appetizing part of the meal. There was no point in chiding the mess staff. They cooked what little supplies were available. Still, not bad for having spent eighteen months on the line.

He was surprised to see the red robes of Cardinal Virom sweep into the mess after swallowing his last mouthful. They weren't expected to meet for another few days, suggesting too many possibilities Torgast was not prepared to accept. He gestured with an open hand and Virom sat.

"You look tired," Virom said, after waving away the mess sergeant.

"It's been a day," Torgast nodded.

"One might argue it has been momentous," Virom tested. "I assume you have heard from your man on the other side?"

"I have. Everything is moving according to schedule."

Virom accepted a mug of caf with a thin smile and inhaled the heavy aroma. "I needed this. What would your army do without fresh caf?"

Torgast snorted. "Rebel. The food may not be the best, but this is better than a year's backpay."

"I sense worry in you, Torgast. This is the hour where the tide shifts. As you said, all is proceeding according to plan."

Torgast admired the Cardinal's enthusiasm without reciprocating. "Nothing goes right in war, Virom. I'm trying to stay ahead of this by building a counterstrategy, should our friends on the other line get their act together. Why are you here?"

"Because of our friends on the other line, as you say," Virom did not hesitate. Time was of the essence at this late stage and he wanted

Torgast fully armed to make his decisions. "Sending Jelin Quint was an interesting move on your part, and I will not disagree with it. However, you should be aware that he is the brother of your counterpart."

Face falling, Torgast leaned conspiratorially close. "What are you telling me, Virom? Did I just provide my enemy with an invaluable asset?"

"That remains to be seen, though I have every confidence in Jelin's loyalty to your banner," Virom said. "Belief is far from solid, however."

Feeling foolish for not having added the names until now, Torgast struggled to keep his poise. Jelin Quint was worth his weight in credits and his brother was equally vicious on the opposing front. He could only hope the brothers did not see eye to eye. Otherwise, the entire campaign was in jeopardy.

NINETEEN

3215 A.G. (After gods), Northern Ocean, planet Crimeat.

Krimpen Mass emptied his stomach again, prompting him to wonder how much remained before the organ itself flowed out. Bile dribbling from his bottom lip, he closed his eyes and whispered prayers for it to end. The soft chuckle from across the cabin infuriated him, just as it had the last three times. He was in no condition to retort, however. Each time he made to speak, the now familiar rumble in his belly echoed. Weak and aching, he cocked his head with a gleam and pointed a finger. It was the best he had.

"Stubborn, isn't he?" Blackheart said.

August and Time watched their companion, careful to move their boots away from the vomit covering the deck. The storm continued, hammering the small craft and forcing it closer to the ocean surface. What was little more than a standard hour's trip had gone on for three, with no trace of land in sight. Long enough, the Guard Captain suspected foul play.

"How much longer before we reach port?" August shouted over the roar of crashing waves slapping the hull. She longed for her command chair in the cold comforts of space.

"Can't tell! Haven't seen a storm this bad in a long time," was the reply.

Frowning, she crossed her arms and nestled into the webbed seating.

"I don't think Krimpen is going to make it much longer," Time lamented. "He's a dry land sort."

Scowling, Krimpen opened his mouth before clamping it shut. His face bore a green sheen and was covered with sweat.

August peered over the pilot's shoulder to the raging storm outside. "I don't think we're going to make it, if this pilot doesn't point us back in the right direction."

"How do you mean?" Time asked in a whisper.

August leaned close and lowered her voice. "Check the compass. We should have been heading north. This ship is moving east."

"Why would he do that?" Time asked. He sat straighter, moving his head to either side, slow enough to avoid detection.

"I don't know, but I need to find out," August replied. She unbuttoned the strap securing her blaster to her thigh.

Blackheart caught the move out of the corner of his eye and followed suit. She waved off his questioning look.

"Edsen, are you sure we are heading in the right direction?" she asked.

Silence dominated the cabin. August had her answer. Rising in one swift movement, she had her blaster nudged against the back of his head. His shoulders slumped.

"I asked you a question," her voice was stern, commanding.

"Please, I'm just doing what I was told," he whined. "They said they'll kill my family if I don't cooperate."

She pressed harder. "Who said?"

He jerked the controls, pitching the small craft off kilter. August crashed into the hull, blaster skittering away. Krimpen vomited again, a mournful dirge filling the cabin. Time pushed his friend over with a heavy boot and lunged for the ship captain. The shuttle dipped toward the ocean. Waves crashed over the prow, as lightning struck nearby. Through the gloom of night, Time caught the distinct outlines of rock formations looming.

Grasping the pilot by the hair, Time jerked him back out of the seat and slammed a fist into his exposed face. The man fell limp to the deck, even as Blackheart slid into the empty seat and attempted to right the craft before they drowned. Twin engines groaned under the strain, already filling with saltwater. The tiny band, minus Krimpen, collected to stare over Blackheart's shoulders, as their world narrowed to a watery view. Muscles straining, the pirate pulled the craft out of its pitch and leveled off.

"Let's not do that again," he said, teeth still ground together.

August gave a reassuring pat on his shoulder. "Point us west and get us on the ground."

The tiny ship altered course. August turned to address Time when a bolt of lightning struck the upper hull. She hit the bulkhead and dropped, blood spreading from her temple. Sparks showered around her. Lights and power flickered and the craft dropped.

"Gun!" Time's heavy voice filled the cabin.

Captain Edsen drew a concealed blaster from his boot and took aim at Blackheart's back. Black smoke filled the cabin. Finger slipping into the trigger well, the pilot's eyes narrowed with anger. He never saw the boot lash out and catch him in the side of the face. Darkness swirled and he dropped. The blaster skittered away. August picked herself up, pressing a hand to her wound. She stared at the unconscious pilot and then to Krimpen Mass. Disbelief filled her.

Krimpen grinned, pieces of food and filth clinging to his teeth. "Told you I felt fine."

His eyes rolled to the back of his head and he collapsed.

Time nudged both men with a boot. Neither moved. He looked down on his friend without sympathy. "Idiot."

"Tie this bastard up," August said quietly. Every sound a hurricane in her head. "Gag him too. We can't afford any more surprises."

"On it," Time confirmed and removed the pilot's belt.

Satisfied, she turned her attentions to the beleaguered Blackheart. His forearms strained, veins popping. Sweat rolled down his face. She caught his dire reflection in the windscreen. Their options were limited. Her naval experience suggested the craft was running out of power, and with land unseen, they risked the potential of a watery demise.

"How much longer?" she asked.

Blackheart shook his head. "Better strap in. This isn't going to be nice."

"Keep us in the air as long as you can," she told him. "I'm going to make a call."

"You risk letting Von escape. There's no way her people won't intercept the communications," Blackheart warned.

"We don't have a choice."

Water splashed over the windscreen. They were moments away from plunging beneath the waves. August stumbled to the rear compartment and prayed.

The glow of a single fire lit the chamber. Built deep within the earth, the remnants of the dark council were determined not to be discovered by the ruling council of lords, at least not until their strength was marshaled and they stood a chance of finally completing their goal of overthrowing the planetary government. A trickle of wind sifted through cracks in the foundation, suggesting a network of tunnels and natural caverns existing long before the Inquisition prison.

Presha Von cared for none of that. All that mattered was delivering the artifact to Amongeratix and escaping the devolving situation her life had become. Her eyes burned from lack of sleep. The rumble of her stomach reminded her she hadn't eaten in too long, and there was a hollowness to thought process she struggled with since learning her father was alive.

Frustration expressed as tears, leaving her rattled. Presha's confidence was shaken. All she had striven for these long years was broken. Cast asunder by a wicked tide, unfeeling and uncaring of her personal whims. Separated from Geres Auk, Presha was trapped with conflicting thoughts. The sound of the door behind her opening brought her back to the present. She used the heels of her hands to wipe her eyes before sitting straighter, in an attempt at regaining what dignity she had remaining.

"Decades of your life wasted, and for what?" her father's stern voice resonated throughout the chamber. "Your mother and I trained you from birth. You were meant to be the one to secure our place in the planetary order. Yet, instead of success, I find only failure. Presha, you have disgraced our name and brought a curse upon this world."

Her hands balled into fists. "I did all that I could, father. If I was so damned important, why weren't you there for me? Why did you disappear and allow me to fail?"

He sidled around to the opposite side of the table and curled his hands around the back of the empty chair. "You think my leaving is excuse enough for you? The dark council was hand selected, by myself and one other, to influence and direct political energies on Crimeat. You were chosen to become my successor and rule this world. I left when your strength was ascendant. What you did with that power is your fault. Your misunderstanding. Your failing. Do not seek to cast blame upon those who moved mountains for you. Even if you are too ignorant to understand it."

Olex Von leaned closer and she noticed how grey his hair had become. Lines creased his sun weathered face. There was a faded gleam in his eyes. Presha shook her head. "The council was primed. We were changing the world. Half of the ruling council was eliminated in one night. All was proceeding according to plan until *he* escaped."

"Escaped? Or released?" Olex asked. He refused to say Amongeratix's name, lest the monster suddenly appear.

Presha looked her father in the eyes. "What do you mean?"

"You have no idea what powers you have aligned yourself with," he muttered.

Her voice dropped. "You abandoned me. Where else was I supposed to turn? Baron Scura? His family is weak. The name is now a pox on this world."

The scrap of his chair being pulled back crawled down her spine. He sat, exhaling a lifetime's pressure. "Why did you join forces with him? How?"

The anger left her. Defeat resumed its customary place. "I had nothing, father. No one until the Inquisitor arrived one afternoon."

"Ursal Prowl," he snarled. "The man was a snake, unworthy of his station."

She nodded. Curled locks fell over half her face. "He whispered promises of power too tempting to ignore. I was meant to be the proctor of Crimeat once Amongeratix began his reign and the Conclave was deposed. It … it was a dream."

"Prowl was never meant to be more than a minor player," Olex affirmed. "His death is no great loss. What promises did Amongeratix offer I could not?"

"He charged me with greatness. My path took me across the stars to a place called Hawker's Gate. I was important, for a time, unlike any experience I have had on this planet. I mattered. What can you offer me in his stead?"

"Mind your tongue, child. I have done more than you will ever know," Olex growled. "There are many powers at work in the universe. Do not make the mistake of believing your precious Amongeratix is the only one. His facet of hatred is but a glimpse into a darker world."

Presha erupted in fury, unable to maintain poise. "Damn you! You question my past, while ignoring my questions. Where were you, father? Why did you abandon me, when you knew I would need you most?"

"There are matters you must not be made aware of, lest your mind be influenced before you are ready," he said after some thought.

She jerked back. "Influenced? By whom? Father, you speak in riddles, while accusing me of treason and cowardice."

"Crimeat has been forgotten by the powers that be. The vacuum needs to be filled. What if I told you there was another power rising? One capable of righting all wrongs through the delivery of ancient truths humankind is too fragile to accept," Olex drawled, teasing her. "I was forced to abandon the dark council after Amongeratix was set free. His malevolence cannot be contended with. There is no strength in the hearts of men capable of defeating him and I would not see you or any I love spiral under his control."

She slapped a palm on the granite table. "Yet, here I sit, minion to the great monster of the universe. Have you any idea what I have done? The sins I have committed?"

The color drained from his face. "I have heard whispers. Rumors of atrocities on a distant world. I did not want to believe them."

"Nor did I, yet I alone am responsible for the deaths of millions," she said in a haunting whisper. "I do not deserve to continue, to live as a monster. My name is cursed across the stars. Should this war go badly, and the Inquisitor General's forces find defeat, I will be hunted down and executed in front of all seven hundred worlds."

"And you will deserve such fate," her father cautioned. "Do not mistake my tone, daughter. You performed a vile act and must atone for such crimes when your time is served. That is between you and your maker."

She rose to leave. There was nothing more to say, for a father's love meant everything and she was no bereft of his. The chasm between them widened, perhaps irreconcilably. Whatever she imagined their reunion would produce, dissolved into mist between them. Presha was lost now more than ever before.

"Sit down," Olex bade. "I don't know where you think to escape to. We are on an island surrounded by men and women sworn to defend the new council. Not even that ape of a protector of yours is strong enough to defeat us. Wasn't he in Scura's employ?"

"He found his way to my side." *And is the only one I can truly trust.* "Father, where did you go?"

He clasped his hands together and leaned forward. "That is not a story fit for this conversation. We are here to discuss your future, in so long as I have any power to help it."

Sensing the upper hand, Presha grinned inwardly. "I must reach Amongeratix and deliver the weapon to him."

His eyes widened. "You have brought the object of destruction here? To your home? Are you mad? There is nothing to stop it from being used."

"It is in my possession and I have a determined bodyguard, unless your zealots have killed him," she quested.

Olex waved her concern off. "Your man is fine. He is confined and under guard until you and I reach an accord, or he attempts to escape. What is your purpose for returning to Crimeat after these long years?"

She calculated, a measure of her old self resurfacing. Regardless of who the dark council members were, she held an elevated position capable of saving or damning them in equal measure. The choice remained hers, for the moment. "I will speak my plight to the entirety of the council alone. I do not appreciate having to repeat myself."

"Mind your tongue, girl. I am still your father," Olex scowled.

Am I though? You have grown weak in your old age, father. A faded glory of better days. What did you find, searching in the dark corners of the universe? "I am who you raised me to be. All the lies, manipulation, and subterfuge are heaped upon your legacy, father. Place me before the council and I will deliver my proposal."

"You try me."

"I have spoken my mind," she folded her arms and fixed him with a stern gaze that had frozen lesser men. "Get me before the council."

"Very well. You shall have your audience, though I make no promises of the outcome. Guards will be along to escort you back to your temporary quarters."

He rose so sharply, Presha took a step backwards, breath catching in her throat. Olex stormed off without another word, leaving her wondering what she had gotten herself into and whether her ticket off world awaited or if she was damned to spend the rest of her days in the abandoned prison, forgotten by any and all.

The Great Library, planet Wexanos.

Tannus buttoned his tunic without worrying over the wrinkles covering his chest. At his side, Fistel fretted. He finished collecting what little belongings his lord and master requested, and having already overseen a covert security detail mobilizing, remained plussed upon seeing the casual distress Tannus showed of his appearance.

"You dote like an old mother," Tannus chided. "I am going to meet with my brother, Fistel, not the king of the universe."

"One must have standards, regardless of the situation," the chief librarian snapped back. "Banak and his team are already aboard your ship."

"He's not going to stab anyone, is he?" Tannus asked with raised eyebrow.

Fistel brushed him off. "Only if needs be. You tend to run in foul circles, my lord."

"Such has been my burden for thousands of years, Fistel. You don't know Sorrow means to betray me."

The seriousness in his tone left an odd flavor on Fistel's tongue. "I have met your brother but once, and the experience was less than pleasurable."

Memories of fresh blood dripping off the giant upset his stomach. Much as he enjoyed his service to Tannus, Fistel found the other brothers wicked and unworthy. Too many issues arose whenever Tannus dealt with his brothers, leaving the chief librarian laden with decades of frustration. Compounding his misery was the possibility of Wexanos being discovered by either Amongeratix or the Conclave.

"Are you certain this is a wise idea, my lord?" he insisted.

Tannus grinned. "Dealing with my brother is seldom considered wise, Fistel. Still, it must be done if there is any way to avoid plunging the entirety of the universe into war."

The librarian froze, fixing a queer look at the giant. "Aren't we already at war?"

"Unfortunately, but not every world. There is still time to preserve humanity. I cannot accept a fate similar to my people," Tannus lamented. "Someone needs to survive, if only to pave the way for the next species."

"Thousands of years old and you continue pining for days gone by," Fistel shook his head. "This is a dangerous game. We cannot change the past, no matter how promising you view the future."

Tannus sagged, the wind stolen from him. He sat and tried to remember a time where he did not fret over the continuation of his species. "I should have tried harder to prevent humanity from worshipping my people as gods. This is the greatest lie perpetrated upon a people, Fistel. Another lament, as you say. Now my best bet is to prevent this knowledge from spreading. I will not be responsible for the fall of mankind."

"You may not have a choice, my lord," Fistel countered. "Your brother is intent on either destroying the universe or crushing it under his heel."

"I wish I knew what game he played, but he proves elusive. Regardless of my personal preference, I feel the climax to our long struggle barreling toward us and I am ill-prepared to defeat him." Tannus fell silent, eyes downcast.

Worry filled Fistel. "Forcing you to listen to Sorrow's madness."

"Unless you can think of a better way."

Fistel remained quiet.

Inquisition Headquarters, planet Vau Prime.

Alain Nye stared out over Redemption Boulevard. His stern gaze viewed the city, his city, with contempt. Millions of citizens called Krenz home. No doubt tens of thousands wished to see his head on a post outside of his citadel. Several times that number brokered no opinions and these were the sheep he considered far beneath his concern. Too many people were content with being told what to do, how to live, when to die. They were minor cogs in the great machine, yet necessary to his ascension. His sneer reflected the inner workings of his mind. He judged much of the universe's population unnecessary.

The Inquisitor General often thought of burning the universe down and starting over, molding society in his image. It was a worthy dream, though one doomed to failure. His pledge to Amongeratix rendered all notions of individual reign void. Rendered down, he was little more than a puppet to a much greater being. Fortunately, Amongeratix was still far from Vau Prime and intent on private affairs. Alain Nye had a small window to enact his plans, thus ensuring his necessity under the next regime.

"Perhaps Mobus had it right," he muttered to his reflection. "Best to burn it all down."

He clasped his hands behind his back and turned. Time was now of the essence. A lifetime spent striving toward one goal was reaching its conclusion. Ever since he was first exposed to the secrets of the Inquisition, Nye felt the pull of something greater than himself. He wanted it all. The power. The prestige. It was intoxicating.

Nye remembered languishing beneath previous Inquisitors General. Farius Graeme was a decent enough man, but his vision was limited. He was content with allowing the Conclave to dictate through their aloof visions of an outdated model. The fools failed to realize they rendered themselves obsolete. Mankind no longer needed faith to exist. In fact, Nye believed the faith in the old gods prevented man from achieving his full potential. *Of course, the gods aren't gods at all. Won't that destroy the Conclave*!

Nye's desire to expose the Conclave as frauds, fueled his hatred for the red-robed cardinals. Their failed assassination attempt caught him off guard, for he did not think them capable of doing the hard right. More the fools them. Alain Nye vowed to not make the same mistakes. Though confronted by setbacks and minor defeats, his plans continued on schedule. That schedule was ready for its next evolution.

A pair of faceless guests stood behind him. Swathed in dark robes, the Vaumagian Assassins had become familiar assets. The Inquisitor General had mixed emotions concerning them. The Order had already failed him once, leaving a foul taste in his mouth for many months after. He made his displeasure well known to the chapter masters and was assured those responsible were dealt with accordingly.

"Do you understand what it is I demand?" he asked.

They nodded as one.

"I need to hear you say it. Too much is on the line," Nye insisted.

"We are to claim the life of the Cardinal Seniorus and as many of the inner Forum as possible before termination," the assassin on the right said.

Her voice was metallic. Mechanical. Nye's skin crawled, unnerved with the way they spoke without a face.

"Do not fail me again," Nye warned. He left the rest unsaid, silently wondering if he had the military strength to defeat the entire Vaumagian order.

"It will be done."

"Go. I expect a full report from your masters upon the conclusion," Nye dismissed them.

The clip of his polished boots as he strode to his sleeping quarters, ended the conversation.

Prophet Ilse, planet Crimeat.

August stood on dry land and thanked the gods for her good fortune. Their craft plunged beneath the ocean surface, hurrying to the bottom moments after her transmission to the *Solstice* was cut off. Each person made their peace with whatever god they worshipped. Final prayers were oathed once Blackheart announced they lacked power to resurface. Death was a foregone conclusion and a fate she never imagined. Only the pilot was spared the worry as he remained unconscious.

The craft jerked, but it wasn't from striking bottom. All eyes turned to the roof as the tiny craft was pulled upward. Water streamed in through several cracks, adding urgency to their fears. Time shouted with glee as they broke the surface. August slumped, the adrenaline fading with understanding. A rescue shuttle from the *Solstice* found them and secured the craft with magnetic clamps. They were safe, if for the moment only.

Reflecting on their plight, August refused to look at the ruined craft again. The pilot was secured and placed in Prekhauten custody for the attempted murder of a capital ship officer. She was satisfied with where that left her and the others. The storm was breaking far to the east, sparing the coastline much of its fury. Waterlogged, wounded, and furious with the betrayal, August wasted little time issuing orders. The time for subterfuge was over. If Presha Von hadn't known she was being hunted, she did now. It was time to put the entirety of the power under her command on full display.

Surprisingly, it was Vicente Blackheart voicing concern. "Are you certain this is a good idea? We have no idea what sort of defenses await us, nor do we know more about tricks she may yet have. We could be walking into a trap."

"Of course, we are, Vicente. The difference is we are prepared for it. We have two ships in orbit capable of reducing any barrier or obstacle she might have emplaced. I want Lady Von to tremble with fear as we approach," August vowed.

Blackheart stared at his counterpart, confused by the sudden change of attitude. Still shellshocked from events on Kharsis, the former pirate lord longed to be free of his predicament. Long months of plotting revenge on Presha Von were culminating in an unexpected scenario. He feared the Guard captain teetered on sanity's brink, when level heads were needed most.

"Captain August, this woman has a weapon capable of killing worlds. Our ships offer little challenge against such power," he cautioned.

She rounded on him, drawn up in full military posture. "What then, do you suggest? Hmm? We abandon our mission now that we are so close to completing it? Or perhaps we should go to speak with her under the white flag of parley? I thought you were made of sterner material."

"Were circumstances different, I would put you to the sword for your mockery, but we must focus on the quarry. Presha Von must not be allowed to murder this world," Blackheart growled. "Hells, we don't even know where she is. The bitch could have already fled the planet."

"All outgoing craft have been logged and accounted for, Captain Blackheart. No vehicles have departed from this island in the past three days," the shuttle pilot informed him. Her golden hair blended with the sand over her shoulder, lending her an otherworldly appearance.

"We were hours behind her," August said after catching his eyes narrow in calculation. "I am landing a detachment of Marines. You may deploy whatever forces you wish. Together, we will find Von, crush any resistance, and reclaim the weapon before it can be used again."

Blackheart struggled with his sudden crisis of conscience. There was a time he would not have hesitated and obliterated Von's position from space and picked the ruins for bones. Damning the Prekhauten Guard for softening him, he considered the implications of ending the hunt prematurely. There was risk of many unnecessary deaths, and despite the prize awaiting success, the scars promised to haunt him long after the war ended.

He thought of his depleted crew. Of the thousands of lives lost in the wreckage of Drespai. Of the cosmic death cry of Kharsis. *How many more must die before the god of death is satisfied? I fear my mind cannot stand much more.* A vision of Sedge filled his mind's eye. The scarred old veteran was the closest thing he had to a friend since abandoning his life of luxury and striking forth to make a name for himself in the pirate world. Blackheart knew Sedge's secret. That the old man was a former retainer of his father's sent to keep a watchful on the wayward son. Family. Until now the word meant little.

"Are you certain we can finish this?" he asked.

Her eyes lit with intensity. "We can and we shall. For the greater good, Vicente. It is time the villains were brought to justice."

"Justice is of little concern to me, August. I am more accustomed to revenge," he countered.

"Are you two finished? I'm soaked through, starving, and haven't used the head in far too long," Krimpen Mass interrupted.

His soured expression prompted the captains to burst into laughter. Time joined them soon after, doubling over as he was unable to stop.

"I hate you all," Krimpen cursed.

Two platoons of Prekhauten Marines landed in their position with light armored vehicles and array of weapons capable of leveling the strongest fortification. Seasoned veterans, each was determined to avenge old wrongs and complete the task assigned to them by Admiral Falchi. They'd caught snippets of intel from the ship's crew, whispers of battles being fought across the universe as the small force tried to reclaim lost ground. Many had friends in units deployed to Mannus Prime, Barrumtel, and other worlds. While hunting down Presha Von was their charge, it was the one thing standing in their way of returning to the fight and doing their part.

Though small, the force was strong enough to execute limited strikes on solitary targets. August did not doubt their capacity, nor lethality. Pinning down Presha Von and securing the weapon were her immediate concerns. She watched the deployment proceed with pride. Each Marine knew his and her jobs and performed as only she knew they could. The three men behind her inspired her only source of doubt. They continuously proved thorns in her side, amusing as their banter might be at times.

A sidelong glance showed them arguing, always arguing, over how best to proceed, as if Krimpen Mass and Time were equal partners in command. What they said was irrelevant. Since finding the odd pair beaten and sore in an abandoned room in Vaade, they proved little more than a distraction. August suspected they were fighters given their bravado and misplaced sense of righteousness, combined with viciousness. Perhaps, given opportunity, they might become useful to her mission. Otherwise … Time threw his hands in the air and stormed off, leaving Krimpen and Blackheart locked in heated debate.

"This job is going to kill me," she muttered and resumed overseeing the deployment.

"That's not what I said at all. Did your concussion rattle your brain?" Blackheart fumed.

Grinding his teeth, Krimpen folded his arms. "Careful, pirate. It's been a while since I lost control."

To his credit, Blackheart did not back down. "Does it look like I care? What I said was you and your partner are free to do whatever you want with Geres Auk. He's not my concern. I want the woman and the weapon."

"What about her? Don't suppose the Prekhautens are in a hurry to turn a blind eye to you absconding with the one weapon capable of murdering entire worlds," Krimpen taunted. "I wonder if Captain August has approved your plan?"

"Careful now, Krimpen. This isn't a game. I've got a score to settle as well," Blackheart tensed, mind working through the different angles being presented.

"We all do. I was there, same as you."

Vicente Blackheart visibly relaxed, if just. Hiring Krimpen and Time continued proving to be his second biggest mistake. The first was aligning with the Inquisitor General to secure the weapon. *At least these fools haven't sold me out yet. Scores. I'll take Nye's head quicker than Von's, if it comes to that.* Plots formed as he drowned out Krimpen's veiled protests. Intricate circles with overlapping outcomes. The how of accomplishing all he wished remained elusive and left him locked in debate. Too many problems continued presenting themselves, leaving him forever behind. Blackheart needed that one move, the important key, to defeat his enemies and re-secure his rightful place in the universe's hierarchy.

Somewhere along the way, Krimpen fell silent. The bigger man stared hard at the pirate, marveling at the way his eyes were glazed and locked in private struggle. Never considered among the brightest of men, Krimpen Mass frowned. The argument was lost, or pointless. The result was yet to be determined. Muttering in frustration, he left Blackheart mired in whatever quagmire his mind created.

"Did he agree?" Time asked.

His hawk-like gaze remained on the deploying force of Marines and pirates. The motley assortment was impressive in its own way but did little to fill him with hope of an easy victory. Past experience told him the coming fight was going to prove more than any were willing to accept.

"If by agree you mean he didn't say no, sure."

Time grinned. "You worry too much. How's your face?"

"My face? What does that have to do with anything?" Krimpen fumed.

Time gestured. "It gives you an unpleasant appearance. Almost as if you are trapped between crying and anger."

"You do remember Kharsis? Our home?" Krimpen almost shouted. "I don't want that to happen again. Not here. Not ever. We have to stop her, Time. For our people."

Laying a meaty palm on his shoulder, Time's voice lowered. "We will, Krimpen. For all of them."

TWENTY

3215 A.G. (After gods), the Forsaken Path.

Winds swept through the ruins. Elisa and Ah'muf pulled their overcoats tighter in a desperate attempt to save their exposed flesh from the stinging bites of sand being whipped at them. Adding insult, the ghostly form of Mollock Bolle drifted across the wasteland with rare impunity. He fell silent after the second hour, sparing them the torment of running commentary on the world they endured and what awaited. Here, caught in perpetual twilight, the beleaguered group slogged closer to the end of their quest.

"Mollock, we must get off the road! We cannot continue through this storm!" Elisa shouted about the mournful wail slashing through the ruins.

"There is a place ahead, large enough to shelter you until the storm passes," Mollock assured her. "It is not far."

He drifted ahead, leaving the pair locked arm in arm, suffering the abuses of a realm that did not want them. Elisa watched the ghost through slit eyes until he disappeared. Her mind wandered. Her life was one misadventure after another, yet as much as she wanted to attribute her current predicament to the deceased Mollock Bolle, it was another who deserved the honor. Meeting Mollock as prisoners of the Ugri sparked a three-year running dilemma, but it was Sorrow's unannounced arrival in her village that determined the course of her life. The one positive was meeting Ah'muf on An'kuruku. He had been a constant presence in her life since. She squeezed his arm tighter, prompting a timid yelp.

Elisa was a strong, determined woman who felt out of place among the Three. She found it difficult to no longer think of them as gods. Tannus' revelations on Wexanos inspired fear, where none once resided. Humanity worshipped the gods for thousands of years, without ever knowing it was a lie. The greatest con in history and she was part of a small, but growing, number who knew the truth. That alone marked her for death by the Inquisition. How does one go from worshipping a god to accepting them as just another species? She lacked answers but knew if such knowledge became commonplace it would tear society apart.

The weight of responsibility pressed down, threatening to break her before completing her task. Elisa forced the issue of gods and morality from her thoughts. Hefty decisions belonged to those more powerful than she. The bounty hunter turned her focus inward, to the twisted path culminating with her appointment as Paladin. She often wondered why she was chosen. How? Sorrow never spoke plainly, leaving her confused and more than a little frightened. It was during those dark moments Elisa tried to remember her family.

The more she thought of her mother the less she remembered. Faces blurred, until naught but smeared images lingered on the edges of her inner sight. Once she clung to hope that the Blood Witches might provide a way to circumvent her failing memory. The longer the war stretched, the less she worried. Enigmatic and far from personal, the witches were aloof to the needs of the universe. Perhaps Sorrow would grant her one boon by allowing her to return home and find the clarity she desired.

Ah'muf squeezed her arm, gesturing wildly at an overhang just ahead. The ghost of Mollock flickered in the shadows. They were safe. Elisa felt no elation. No great joy from finding succor as the heart of the storm passed. The longer she marched upon the Forsaken Path and her path to destiny, the more she lamented bringing others into her plight. Spiraling thoughts surrounded her heart. No matter how far they traveled together, she felt only growing remorse for bringing the desert dweller into her life. His professed love provided a measure of hope, but little else, the more death reared to oppose them. She resisted the urge to apologize, again, and led them toward Mollock and safety.

She collapsed in an exhausted heap the instant she escaped the biting sands. Ah'muf slumped beside her, glaring up at the ghost. Mistrust blazed in his eyes, for though he lacked much of the experience Elisa had, he knew wrong. Elisa watched them from the corner of her eye, curious to see if Ah'muf dared risking the ire of the dead. It was a pointless thought, for Mollock displayed indifference in all he said and did. Even tempered, he brought an odd balance to the chaos of her life.

"Mollock, do you know where we are?" she asked, once it became evident no confrontation approached.

He stared off into the wall of sand howling just outside. "This is Goti Tai. We have at last reached our destination."

Elation sparked. Elisa felt the haunting limits of false energy surge. "We made it?"

"Against all odds," Ah'muf muttered. "Thank the gods."

Mollock fixed him with a curious look, forcing Elisa to pray for silence. "There is yet much to endure before we find the First Paladin and recover *Grimfurvor*. Dangers lurk."

"What worse can this realm throw at us?" Elisa asked, disbelief mocking her tone. "We have already bested every challenge. I am ready to end this chore and return to reality."

"Is this not a mirror of reality?" Mollock asked. "We exist in a place forgotten. Wedged between life and death. Uncomfortable, yes, but a situation I have grown accustomed to."

"I do not wish to remain here long enough to follow suit," Ah'muf interrupted.

Elisa nodded. "Nor do I. Mollock, how much further before we find the First Paladin?"

"A day. Perhaps two. The Forsaken Path is never constant. Distance matters little, for this is a place that does not make sense," Mollock answered. If he was bothered by the desert dweller, he made no show of it. "The First Paladin is ensconced deep within the city center. Beware though! Every challenge you have faced thus far, pales in comparison to what is yet to come."

"You continue speaking in riddles, Mollock," Elisa warned. "Speak plain, so that we may prepare for tomorrow."

He squared on them. "Very well. To reach the First Paladin and retrieve *Grimfurvor,* you must confront the one creature that haunts each of our thoughts. You must confront yourselves."

"That doesn't sound so hard," Ah'muf said.

Elisa stayed quiet. She knew too well how hard the task was Mollock presented.

"Rest," the ghost of Mollock Bolle said. "Many dangers yet await. You shall have need of all your wits and strength before then. I shall stand watch."

"Are you certain?" Elisa asked out of reflex.

"I do not need rest or sustenance," he ignored her concern. "I am, much to my despair, eternal."

"You cannot fade? Become one with the universe?" she asked.

"I do not know, though I long for the moment when I at last dissipate and exist no more. This form vexes me to great ends. I am tired of being trapped without a body."

She caught the hint of sadness in his voice and wished she might be the one who delivered his final reward. He deserved that much. Elisa decided to weep over him when neither of her companions watched. Lesser men deserved better.

"Farisi, my eyes burn. My muscles ache. I must rest, lest I not be able to accompany you to the end," Ah'muf pleaded.

Her soft grin warmed him. "Sleep, Ah'muf. We will depart once the storm finishes. I have a feeling there is no hurry."

"No hurry?" he questioned. "How can that be?"

"Mollock said as much. Time matters little in this realm. We could have been gone from the others for years or naught but a day," Elisa theorized. "The only way to discover the truth, is by returning home."

Unsettled by the thought of escaping reality for years, potentially decades, Ah'muf frowned. "What if we have missed the war and our foes now reign?"

"I don't believe that is so, my friend. Sorrow would not have sent us upon this quest if the possibility of being obsolete existed," she said. "When we retrieve this *Grimfurvor* and return home, it will be precisely when we are needed the most. Rest now. There is still long to go."

Her gaze lingered on his face until he stretched out on the dirt floor and closed his eyes. He was asleep moments later, leaving her alone with a ghost and the fragments of thoughts threatening to rend her mind apart. *Am I ready to confront myself?*

The prospect terrified her more than it should have. A lifetime of misunderstandings, piled upon the foundations of bitter resentment, warred within her mind. Her strength stemmed from years of forged destiny. Elisa was a hard woman with a buried softness. She often wondered how different life might have been if the Bloody Man never visited her village. Where once dreams filled her tender heart now naught but bitterness remained. Confronting the demons of her past was dangerous under the best of circumstances. Unable to sleep, she scooted next to Mollock.

The ghost kept his gaze on the storm. "It is a dark night, Elisa. You should rest. Tomorrow will prove more taxing than you imagine."

"I don't know if I am ready to face my past," she whispered.

Small chunks of aged stone whisked past, striking time-pitted walls in passing. "Such things are not for us to decide. The only way to secure the weapon and exit this realm is by doing the very thing you are reluctant to do. A new age must dawn, Elisa, if the universe is to continue. We all have parts to play. The how and why do not matter, though I once believed they did."

"Aren't you concerned of fading?" she asked, uncomfortable with the directness of his answer.

He fixed her with an unreadable gaze. "I am already dead. What more use am I to the powers that be? Elisa, you will collect allies along your journey. Some will fall aside. Others will abandon you when you need them most. Many, including your desert man, will stand by your side to the bitter end, even though it means their demise. Life is cold, unfeeling. If you are not capable of confronting yourself, who is?"

"I know what I must do but the worry in my heart gives me pause," she admitted. "How will I know if I succeed?"

"That much should be obvious," he replied. "Rest. The trial ahead will not be easy. Clear mind is necessary to overcome the demons of your past."

"Easier said than done," she snorted.

His stance softened, betraying the last remaining hint of mortality. "My life was never fulfilling. I moved from job to job. Village to village. Never belonging to any tribe, nor feeling comfortable with family. I believed there was greater destiny ahead, always on the edge of the horizon. How wrong I was! I lament that dark times swallowed my future the day I stumbled upon the great secret."

"The gods," she concluded.

He nodded. "I was prospecting, eager to stake claim and reap the rewards before others swarmed the area. I think now I was never a confident man. Boisterous perhaps, but never one to fully believe in myself. Finding that tunnel should have been the beginning of a new day. One I was destined to emerge from, a new man. How deep into the earth I delved, I do not know, but my journey ended in a small cavern forgotten by time and man alike.

"It was there I first saw her. Pristine. Innocent almost. She was both beautiful and horrid to behold. Man should never come face to face with those he worships. I knew immediately what I gazed upon, for such radiance pulsed off her sleeping form. The gods were real. Forgotten by most.”

“Mollock, they were never gods,” Elisa said. Sadness filled her eyes. “It was all a lie.”

“Yes. The gravest injustice to an entire species,” he agreed. “How many others knew what I did? Did they go mad? Or was an unexpected softness awakened when confronted with our own mortality?”

“What did you do?” she asked.

A sigh escaped him. “I ran. For all I was worth, I ran. Foul creatures, the likes of which I will not speak of, hounded my steps. Wherever I went I brought death and despair. For a time, when cast upon wits end, I hid. The monsters faded, replaced with nightmares and worse in the quiet hours of the night. Broke and frightened, I stumbled into Ugri lands, and well, you know the rest.

“I was never a bad man, Elisa. I stand firm behind that, but I was weak and greedy. The price of that greed was death,” Mollock fell silent.

She pitied him, though was loath to admit so. They were of the same world but with vastly different lifestyles. Both were trapped between what might have been and what must be. Elisa longed for a simpler time. An age without the burdens heaped upon her. Such was not her fate. All that remained was discovering how she met her demise, for surely there was no hope for survival, once she delivered the weapon to Tannus.

“We have both been robbed of our future, Mollock,” she said with a frown. “Troubled by meddling beyond our comprehension.”

“Get some rest, Elisa. Your mind must be sharp, if you are to face your truth.”

She left him, alone save for the howl of the wind.

The Low Continent, planet Vau Prime.

The scrape of steel over flesh echoed throughout the small canyon. Over and over. Carrion birds and rock lizards scampered off. The aroma of a small fire filled the air, reminding them of a fouler time, when survival was not guaranteed. The skinned corpse of stone hyrax roasted on a spit. None of it was necessary, but the lone man occupying the camp was compelled to reconnect with a world that had all but forgotten his name. There were times when the old ways were more important than simple comforts.

He was the last of his people. The others were naught but charred remains ground beneath armored vehicles and thousands of boots. Fools all. Shaved, he rinsed off his face before patting it dry with the remains of a towel. The growl in his stomach reminded him it was time to eat. He knelt and whispered a prayer in thanks for the small bounty cooking and the scraps of his life.

Boot steps drew his attention. Almost too faint to pick up over the cackling fire. His eyes flashed open. His hand dropping to the antique blaster at his side. The man spied the source of his distraction easy enough. Another person strolled through the canyon slot into his camp without fear or regard. Curious, he kept his blaster in the holster. It had been so long since he last spoke with another human, much less saw one alive.

Still, caution was prudent. "That's far enough, friend. I'm not a violent man but I ain't no fool neither."

A thin smile flashed the dull yellow of neglected teeth. "Fair enough. I'm just passing through and smelled your fire. Been a while since I last ate."

He viewed the newcomer, taking in the faded stitch of his clothes and the stubble on his face. Nothing felt out of place, until his gaze tracked down to the newness of the boots. "Might be willing to spare a bite or two. There's few enough of us left down here."

"Times are tough all over," the stranger said. He gestured to the opposite side of the fire. "Mind if I sit? Been on my feet for a while now."

"Seems to be the story for those of us still alive," was the reply. "What village you coming from?"

"Does it matter? Ain't none left." He shook his head. "Damned Guard swooped in without warning and killed everything in sight. Naught but a wise man turned and run."

The camper bobbed his head. "True words, friend. You part of that cult got everyone riled up?"

Firelight reflected in the stranger's eyes. "Naw. Never saw the point in putting blind faith in one god. I been all over this universe. Seen too much to put stock in it."

"We all need the gods, friend. Only way to stay sane when the world goes mad. Where'd you say you come from again?"

"Didn't. The past is the past. Best leave it there. That meat done?"

Alarms went off in his mind. The stranger's tone became harder. Meaner. "Done enough. Reckon you best get your fill and head on. Ain't room enough for us both here and I ain't trying to draw Guard attention."

"They still operating down here?" the stranger asked with genuine interest.

"Here and there. I heard rumors of a group not far down south way. Hiding in the rocks like me and you."

"Down south, you say? I might just need to take a stroll down there and see," the stranger said. "Got a score or two to settle."

"Bad business tangling with them, even if they ain't the ones who torched the continent," the camper replied. "What's your name, friend?"

Utan Husk dropped any pretense of being a survivor. His body stiffened. "That's the one question you shouldn't have asked, *friend*."

"I ain't trying to start trouble. Man's got to be careful these days," he defended. The snap of his holster being undone echoed.

"It's far too late for that." Utan was on his feet closing the gap before the camper reacted.

Letting out a loud burp, Utan tossed aside the leg bone and leaned back against the rust-colored rock wall. Disappointed in not gleaning more useful information from the holdout, the former Guard bore a perpetual scowl since slipping his blade over the man's throat. Utan already knew Strannan and his people were deeper south. But where? The answer eluded him, leaving a foul taste in his mouth.

He cast his gaze around the campsite, wondering how desperate the final hours of Mobus Kale's purge were for the people of the low continent. Utan longed for the sensation. The palpable fear overwhelming the senses during that last moment. Killing his first man since being freed, offered little relief to the pressure mounting in his mind. He needed more. The rush of knowing he was responsible for removing a lifeform's existence inspired his depravity, giving him reason to continue. Reason Kale reawakened.

Utan studied the corpse at his feet. Deciding he needed to blend in more with what locals remained, he took to shaving his head and face. He scuffed the tops and side of his boots to reflect as much struggle in surviving the aftermath of the purge as possible. Once done, Utan rummaged through the campsite for any useful items. He'd been issued transport, weapons, and enough gear to see his mission through but there was no way he could blend in. He needed another way.

The second option was to present himself as a volunteer. Intelligence reports suggested Strannan's force was dispersed and weakened, making it ripe for reinforcements from every sector. Utan was trained in infiltration but lacked the patience for subterfuge. Years spent in prison, abused and debased of humanity, left him unwilling to surround himself with others for extended periods.

There was no real choice. Utan decided to spend the rest of the night in the safety of the canyon and head south in the morning. At some point, he planned to ditch his military gear and adopt a peasant attitude and pray the good General Davith Strannan was forgiving.

"Of course, if he recognizes me, the whole plan goes to shit," he chuckled to the fire.

Utan laced his fingers behind his head, stretched his legs, and closed his eyes. One problem at a time.

Warehouse district, Krenz, planet Vau Prime.

Down to a handful of soldiers, Julian felt the end of the campaign approaching. None of it was his fault. He'd done all he could within Strannan's mandate before Mobus Kale returned to reinvigorate his campaign to secure the core world. How many friends and soldiers under his command who were either captured, killed, or missing astounded Julian. Ever the professional, he took each loss personally.

What began as an effective guerilla campaign, was reduced to escape and evasion as Kale unleashed fresh divisions of shock troops into Krenz. The city was flooded with armed men and women. Traffic slowed. People were ordered to remain in their homes under penalty of heresy accusations. Inquisitors under Alain Nye's thumb ranged the shadows. It wasn't uncommon to learn of vague disappearances in the darkest hours of the night. Foul times had fallen, with no dawn in sight.

His fire team slipped through abandoned alleys, avoiding the integrated camera security system. It took ten days for public sentiment to turn against them. Mobus Kale's purge turned families against each other. Friends into foe. Mistrust was rampant and the only way Julian's people escaped was by shutting down all external communications and going deep underground.

The lower levels were foul places, long given over to the seedy criminal element. Prefects and Inquisition enforcers refused to police them. Too many casualties in the past stayed their hands, though both organizations monitored all that went on beneath their thumbs. Men like Zoraq Darc elevated themselves to stations far above their birth lots. It was here Julian hoped to evade capture and rebuild his insurgency. Getting there was his first obstacle.

Weapon at the ready, he was back in his element. It had been years since the young captain last led an infantry patrol but some training was ingrained so deep, you never forgot. Julian glanced over his shoulder to his soldiers. Veterans all, they appeared little more than dark shapes in the night. He'd long stopped wondering if they felt the same fears gnawing upon him. Worrying about death was the worst mistake a field soldier could commit. The idea drove some mad, while others completed a self-fulfilled prophecy. Julian knew his understanding of warfare was limited. He concluded long ago that it was best left for others to ponder. All he needed to do was keep himself and his people alive, for as long as possible. Better said than done these days.

The street market was empty. Its customers and hawkers having gone home before sundown. Curfew was strictly enforced in the civilian districts. It took several arrests and unexplained disappearances before the population realized General Kale was serious. Since then the Prekhauten Guard ruled with utter surety. Julian counted on that fact this night. He reckoned areas like this the best access point to enter the underworld of Krenz. If he was right, there was little chance of discovery by armed patrols. Prefects were no different from soldiers. Once routine was established, the inevitable slackening of awareness began.

He took a final look left and right before jerking his head and headed into the street. The others followed single file at three meter intervals. Heart pounding, Julian expected the report of a sniper's shot. Only when he reached the relative safety of the market did he exhale. One by one his soldiers joined him, dispersing into the market to avoid presenting a large target. A quick head count and they were on their way.

Julian followed the heads-up display on his wrist guard. The holographic imaging was the latest Guard tech, confiscated during their raid on Tatarast Island. He figured it was the best piece of equipment in his kit. Grinning, he felt like a child with a new toy. They moved at his speed. Muzzles swung across intersecting fields of fire. What they lacked in heavy weapons, the tiny squad more than made up for with tactical and special operations experience.

They reached the far side of the market and paused, taking defensive positions, while he rechecked the map and gave the others opportunity to catch their breath. Julian's element abandoned their former position hours ago, after receiving intelligence of an impending raid too large to be coincidence. Fortunately, there were contingency plans in place. Julian split his task force into small, twenty-man units with orders to rendezvous at alternate positions throughout his sector of the city. Other elements continued to operate, forcing Julian to ensure their actions remained separate, lest the entire campaign unfolded.

The soft huffing at his side broke his train of thought. Julian gave Aliz a false look of confidence. "So far, so good."

"How much further?" she asked, choosing to ignore him.

"There's supposed to be an egress point just beyond this stall. After that, a stairwell down and we should be good to go," he replied. "Aliz, I can't vouch for what happens next."

She laid a hand on his forearm. The sleeve was damp with sweat. "Julian, no one is asking you to. I have been through this before. The underworld is no place for decent folk, but these are not decent times. If this is the only way we can survive, so be it."

He winced. "I don't know …"

"Captain, you've led us this far. I have every confidence you will get us where we need to be. The others look to you for strength and guidance." She leaned close and whispered, "Don't let them down now. Not after we've come so far."

An eerie calm settled over him, reducing his apprehensions. Still far from safety, he felt the first stirring of hope echo in the corners of his soul. Perhaps there was a chance. Just one moment of luck required to see them ensconced in a seedy part of society he knew little about.

"Very well. We need to keep moving," his voice rose enough for the others to hear. "Close ranks. I don't want anyone getting separated. Not now. Sergeant Gies, you have the rear. Anyone comes close, put a hole in them."

"Roger that, sir," the scar-faced redhead snarled and slunk into position.

"It's now or never," Julian told Aliz.

He pushed open the concealed door with a nod from her. Darkness swept out to meet them, curling long tendrils around the captain. Julian clicked the thermal imaging scope attached to his rifle with the tip of his pinky and cleared the immediate area. His hands sweat in their gloves, an uncommon sensation for the veteran. Taking a deep breath, he led his people down. Winding stairs sucked them deeper underground. Every footstep echoed like thunder down the winding corridors of Krenz. Certain the element of concealment was lost, Julian decided to pick up the pace.

A dull thunk told him Gies was on the staircase, moving down after securing their entry point. Satisfied, Julian cleared the third landing and paused. A head jerk sent two others barreling down before him. The rest of the squad followed. All but Gies and Aliz. Doubts collided with concerns, twisting his face in the shadows.

"What is it?" Aliz asked after noticing his consternation.

"Are you sure this is a good idea?" he asked.

She sighed, having struggled with the suggestion for days. "No, but it is the best one. All we need to do is make contact with his people. They have no love for the Inquisition."

Julian's shoulders shook with a snort. "After what happened to Zoraq, they'll be hard pressed not to execute us on the spot. I'm taking an awful risk here, Aliz."

She thought back to the first time she made this journey. Broken, defeated. Aliz reeled from the murder of her lover and best friend. She watched Lorenu die a thousand times each night for months, until finding the courage to reclaim their honor and seek a measure of revenge. She found it with the criminal underworld and their enigmatic leader, Zoraq Darc. Now he was dead, after spending over a year fighting alongside loyal Guards, the integrity of his former position was in question.

"This entire war has been one risk after another. Momentum has shifted back to our enemies. Our list of allies thins daily. We need them, Julian. If only to stop the bleeding long enough to restart our offensive," she replied.

He paused in thought before breaking into a grin.

"What?" she asked.

"You're doing it again. That motherly tone of authority," he answered.

Aliz rolled her eyes and hurried after the squad. Chuckling, Julian followed a step behind.

Time slowed the deeper they went. Along the way, Aliz slipped to the head of the tiny column, figuring it best when they encountered Zoraq's former associates. Her assumption was correct. They reached the seventh subbasement before scores of men and women emerged from hiding to surround them. Weapons pointed at each, freezing them in place. She felt Julian nestle beside her protectively and lowered her rifle. Most of the shadows were human shaped, though she thought she spied the hulking figure of a Bagath in the background.

"Who's in charge here?" she demanded. Her voice boomed in the unnatural darkness.

"Don't seem like you're in much of a position to be giving orders, grandmother," the reply came from the center of the group.

She felt Julian stir and reached over to keep his rifle pointed down. "My name is Aliz and if I were your grandmother I should have scolded you once again over."

Murmurs ran through them. The scuffing of boots shifting in uncertainty. A man stepped forward, the chewed remains of a cigar in the corner of his mouth. His hair was greasy with an uneven beard clogging his chin. Wiry by any standard, he hoisted his rifle over one shoulder. It was the darkness in his eyes that drew her attention though.

"Aliz, huh? I'm surprised you came back, but now you're here, how about you tell us what happened to Zoraq?"

She gripped Julian's rifle tighter until her hand bled white.

Low Continent, planet Vau Prime.

"Just hold still!"

Jash Abernath eyed his counterpart with mistrust. Boots spread shoulder width apart, he stood six feet away from the larger Bryn Mal. A fingernail sized token rested between his feet.

"Are you sure about this, Bryn? We never went through knife fighting," he almost whimpered.

Bryn's face hardened. She pointed her dagger at him. "Look, Jash, we're both professionals here. Besides, the General needs us both in top fighting condition and I haven't missed yet."

"That doesn't mean you won't this time," he cringed as she took aim.

"I'm hurt," she replied, without meeting his gaze.

Bryn cast the dagger, watching with glee as it burrowed into the token with a satisfying thump. Jash closed his eyes, thankful the experience was over.

"Your turn," Bryn announced after clapping her hands with raw delight. Knifework was never her strength. She preferred pummeling others into submission.

"Both of you, in here now!" Strannan's baritone barked from within the command cave.

Jash hurried to obey, leaving Bryn to collect her dagger before entering the general's private quarters. She brushed past the stacks of supplies and ammunition crates forming the walls to his sanctum. It was a far cry from the luxuries of office in Krenz, but these were desperate times. The rebellion teetered on the edge of collapse, and if the snippets of intelligence she'd overheard were half accurate, their position was becoming more dire daily.

Bryn joined her counterpart at the position of attention and saluted. Davith Strannan waved off the formality. A far cry from Krenz indeed. "What was that commotion a moment ago?"

Jash blushed, leaving Bryn to answer. "Sir, we were practicing with the bayonet."

A bushy eyebrow rose. "Trying to stay sharp, is that it?"

"Yes, sir," they said in unison.

"Uh huh. Stand at ease," he ordered.

They clasped their hands behind their backs, curious to the summoning. Strannan, ever the professional, didn't waste time.

"Plans for our continued campaign continue evolving. Word has reach me from Krenz, that several cells have been eliminated or gone radio dark. One can only suppose Mobus Kale ran them to ground, either capturing and killing them or forcing them to abandon their assignments. The latest cell to go dark is Captain Julian's. I have it on good authority he continues to fight, though our foes draw their noose tighter.

"What does that mean for us? I can see the question in your eyes. The answer is simple. We must prepare for a renewed offensive here. If just one of our people talks, and they will, for Nye's interrogators are ruthless beyond imagination, it will spell our doom." He paused to run a hand through his thinning hair. "Word has already gone out to any allied elements in space. We must be prepared to evacuate the home world.

You two will ensure all elements are packed and ready to move on short notice. There can be no mistakes. Make it happen and report back to me upon completion. I'm sure I'll have another assignment for you by then."

They snapped to attention and saluted before being waved away. Strannan leaned back in his chair and watched them leave, reminded of the impetuousness of youth.

"Those two will keep you on your toes," Gedrick Silk, said as he slipped by them. "Ordering the retreat?"

Strannan shook his head. "Just getting prepared. What have you got for me?"

Checking to ensure no one was within earshot, Gedrick took the empty seat across from Strannan. "I went to the spot of the disturbance like you asked. It was a ship. A small shuttle touched down. There were signs everywhere. Whoever piloted it was gone, along with the ship. It's a good bet we're not alone anymore."

"Damnation. I was hoping for more time," Strannan cursed.

"It doesn't look like we have it," Gedrick said.

Their position on the low continent was always precarious. Both men understood that the moment the decision to abandon Krenz was made. Logic suggested Strannan fled to less obvious places. Once it was evident off world transportation was unavailable, Mobus Kale would turn his steel gaze south. His obsession with finding and killing Strannan overrode any tactical sense. It made him dangerous, almost as much as it made him foolish. Strannan needed to capitalize on that before it was too late.

"Ramp up the defenses but do it quietly. I don't want to play our hand too soon," Strannan ordered. "Are you going to stick around?"

Gedrick rubbed the stubble on his chin. "I didn't risk everything sneaking back onto Vau Prime to leave you in your most dire moment, Davith. I'll stay long enough to discover who our spy is."

"After that?"

His expression remained neutral. "We'll see."

TWENTY-ONE

3215 A.G. (After gods), Abbey of the Order of Blood Witches, Acumensiis Comet.

Traces of the rebellious assault were largely removed. Magic cleansed the stains, driving the memories of Algiss Her and the others into obscurity, as their legacies were stripped from official records. The Grand Mistress decreed all traitors excommunicated, to be destroyed on sight. Instead of retreating to her sanctum, Ruma Zzein prowled the corridors. She offered reassurances to those in need, encouragement to others, and oaths of vengeance to a special few. Morale began to rebuild, despite the miasma of distrust echoing through the abbey.

Menials and lower ranked Sisters bowed and stepped aside as she passed, for she had become a hurricane within their walls. Raw power danced upon her robes, and for the first time in generations, Ruma strode without the comforts of her hood concealing her face. Now was not the time for secrecy or subterfuge. Deciding to bare her anguish for all to see, the Grand Mistress forced herself back into the spotlight. She was the vision of strength, to be feared and awed in the same breath.

Ruma glided down repaired corridors, the marble gleaming to perfection once again. She found her guests in one of the dining halls, their restrictions lifted after knowledge of their deeds during the insurrection circulated through the Order. Sister Alessandra sat among them, picking through a half-finished plate. She rose when Ruma entered.

"Please, remain seated," Ruma bade. "I cannot express gratitude enough for all you have done for my … this Order. The Blood Witches are in your debt, such as it is."

Tolde swallowed a partially chewed mouthful before replying, "We did what was right, Grand Mistress. I do not profess to understand you or your ways, though our shared experiences have taught me the value of what you do for the universe. What will you do with the traitors?"

A mischievous gleam entered her eyes. "This is the reason I come to you now. It appears our paths continue to align. We have discovered Algiss Her and the others have docked with the object of our pursuit."

"*Behemoth*?" Luma gasped.

Ruma nodded. "Indeed. I have been blind."

She went on to explain how Amongeratix breached her psychic defenses a year ago, surmising he seduced some of the Sisters to his side. Shame rang throughout her speech. It was no easy thing to admit failure on such monumental level. The others listened without interruption. Being guests, their input was reserved.

"We have successfully tracked *Behemoth* to a nearby star system. It is unknown whether Amongeratix has rendezvoused yet or not, though I suspect he is still in transit," she concluded.

"Meaning we have the opportunity to get aboard and scuttle the damned thing," Tolde theorized.

"We don't know what horrors await us," Paradise Tear interjected. She knew her cousin more than any of them and her fear showed in her tone.

"It is a chance we must take," Ruma softened her words. "Paradise Tear, you have been a staunch ally for centuries. Our friends will have need of your intimate knowledge, if there is any hope of success. Amongeratix must not be allowed to dock with his ship."

"What if he does?"

Ragan's question stunned the room into silence. Heads turned, regarding him with cold disappointment. Unused to the greater universe, the youth's innocence proved refreshing—if untimely.

The Grand Mistress faced the youth, admiring his audacity, despite the ignorance presented. "Ragan, Amongeratix is the greatest threat humanity has ever faced. Should he regain command of his warship, entire worlds will burn."

Gulping, Ragan shrank under her tone.

Sister Alessandra drifted closer to him for support. "Ragan, you must understand, we are at a dire time. Everything this group has done for the past three years has been to liberate your kind from the depredations of the gods. *Behemoth* is the most powerful vessel in existence. It has more guns, cannons, and weapons than an entire fleet. We do not expect you to understand, for the universe is a far vaster construct than any you encountered on Rastarok."

"There is no shame in asking questions, young Ragan," Ruma added after catching the shift in conversation. "It is through acquiring knowledge, our futures become enhanced." She cast her gaze upon the others, freezing their blood. "Know this, we stand upon the crossroads. Our one chance of achieving success was in keeping *him* from reaching *Behemoth*. Those odds shrink by the moment."

"Meaning we must strike now," Tolde affirmed. "Can you get us to the ship before he docks?"

"There are ways," Ruma nodded. She said nothing further.

Paradise Tear folded her arms, face crossed in consternation. "Our task is made more difficult by the defection of Blood Witches. We cannot fight whatever horrors await within the dark halls of that ship and a cadre of magic users."

"You may have a detachment of Sisters to assist you. This raid is of the utmost importance and cannot be left to fate. The time has at long last arrived when the Order of Blood Witches will return to the center of the universe. Our time of anonymity is expired."

Surprised with the admission, Tolde thought back to his experiences with the Order. Until Rastarok, the witches assigned to him met grisly fates. Their deaths weighed upon him. For the Grand Mistress to willingly deploy a squad or more at his disposal, suggested the importance of what must come next.

"How soon can we depart?" he asked.

"Soon," was her reply.

Grand Mistress Ruma Zzein slipped from the dining hall, allowing them to continue eating in silence.

Sister Alessandra was summoned a short time later. She found the Grand Mistress locked in reflective thought high above the abbey. The chamber was small by comparison to her offices. Cushions piled in the center were the only decoration. Slate colored walls shielded her from space. Bereft of light, Ruma found it essential for calming the voices in the corners of her mind. Life often overcame her, forcing her away from the balance once achieved during her exile.

Alessandra bowed and waited in silence.

"Alessandra, I find myself taking you into confidence more than I expected," Ruma pulled her hood up.

"It is an honor, Grand Mistress," Alessandra replied with honesty.

A snort, so soft she almost missed it, suggested otherwise. "You question my actions. Perhaps doubting whether Tolde Breed is capable of defeating our foe."

Stunned, Alessandra remained silent.

"It is all right. In other circumstances I would question myself," Ruma added. "Such odd times we live in. I know stopping Behemoth is Tannus' priority but I have another mission for you. Algiss Her must be stopped. Amongeratix cannot be allowed to harness the power of our Order. Destroy our former friends."

"It will be done, Grand Mistress," Alessandra said.

"Do not make the mistake of believing this an easy task. Algiss is more powerful than you imagine. The spells I placed upon her restricting her magic will not last long once she realizes what happened. There was a time I groomed her to take over the Order. A worthy successor to my life's work." She shook her head. "Killing her will be my greatest failure and your highest achievement to date. Should Amongeratix gain access to our kind, the future is lost."

"Is it possible?"

"There was a time I thought otherwise but I have been blind for too long. Too many mistakes are being made," she admitted. "I would be lying if I said my confidence was not rattled."

Alessandra listened with muted shock. To suggest the most powerful woman in the Order, a guiding light so many looked to throughout the centuries, was fallible, threatened to undo confidence when it was needed most. She opened her mouth but a brittle hand stayed her protests.

"No, do not pander to me, Alessandra. I am mature enough to recognize truth when struck by it. I place a terrible burden on your shoulders and expect much from you," Ruma said. "I wish our roles reversed. There is a reckoning coming. Alas, I am required to rebuild the damages done to our halls and help the younger Sisters rediscover their strength and … faith."

"What of Lord Tannus?" Alessandra asked. "Does he not have capacity to deal with his brother?"

Ruma flinched. "Tannus has another task before him. One he cannot afford to ignore. Think no more of it. We have all the tools we are going to get. Can you do this?"

"Yes, or I shall die in the attempt."

Ruma stared out from beneath her hood. Sadness filled her eyes, for she had listened to far too many friends' oaths similar throughout the years. Her past was a graveyard of memories. She prayed Alessandra and the others were not about to join them. Experience suggested otherwise. The moment she worked so hard to deliver was fast approaching and Ruma struggled with base human emotions she once thought she had managed to shed. She watched Alessandra head off and wondered if being human was such a bad thing after all.

Tolde slid the charging handle of his rifle back and forth several times to ensure smooth operation. No soldier, the former Inquisitor had been forced into too many combat scenarios. He longed for the security Fies and his Prekhauten element provided during earlier missions of the war. They were the hammer needed to break his foes. Closing his eyes, he recalled his first meeting with Matthias during their hunt for the escaped Amongeratix. Like most Guards, Matthias was rough around the edges and eager to get into a fight. Age and experience tempered that flare some. Now he was alone, save for a handful of friends. They would have to do.

"Do I get a gun?" Ragan asked.

Tolde met his innocent eyes, trying to imagine the youth confronting Amongeratix. Young enough to be his son, Tolde regretted taking Ragan from his home world. No one deserved to suffer through what must come, especially not one so young.

"You won't need one," he replied. "Because you're not coming."

Luma Kai lifted her head, shock written on her face.

Ragan's shoulders slumped. "What's the point of me being here? I stood by your side all the way through Braewynd. I'm not afraid."

"No, you are a brave young man, but we are about to face an evil beyond your comprehension." Tolde walked over and placed a hand on the youth's shoulder. "You saw what these witches are capable of. Even that is child's play to Amongeratix."

"The others are going with you," Ragan fumed.

"They have all proven themselves in battle," Tolde reiterated. "I cannot focus on the task at hand, while looking over my shoulder to you."

"It's not your decision!" Ragan was on the verge of losing control. He'd been taken from everything he knew and cast in the midst of a universe he never knew existed. The shock of loss roiled in his mind, leaving him confused and more than a little scared. "I left Rastarok because of you. I was promised a future where I can become what I want. You brought me here for a reason."

"Your future dims with each passing moment. Rushing to meet the monster is a track toward death, availing you nothing," Paradise Tear said from across the room. Her face darkened as she noticed the brazen defiance only youth produced. As much as she wanted to reprimand him, a soft spot opened in her heart. The universe needed more like him. "I will watch over your. Your heart is strong, though I fear it may not be enough. Stay by my side, no matter what! If it is your destiny to survive, you will."

"What if it's not?" his voice lowered.

The question went unanswered as Sister Alessandra and half a dozen Blood Witches swept into the room. Faces concealed beneath hoods, the Sisters hovered with hands folded in their robes. Alessandra blazed with power. Conviction flared in her eyes.

"We have been given leave to depart. The traitors must be stopped. Is your team prepared?" she announced.

"As much as can be. Do you think we have the firepower to stop the others?" Tolde asked.

Alessandra stiffened. The colors of her robes swirled in angry patterns. "Leave them to us. Your primary task will be disable *Behemoth*. Destroy it if possible."

"We're wasting time," Tolde avoided the obvious. His mind raced to the complex task of crippling a monstrous warship that had endured millennia drifting through deep space. *From one impossible task to another. Is this all my life has become? An endless string of frustrations, determined to see my demise?*

Alessandra turned to her companions, "Collect the extra equipment. We must depart immediately."

Tolde and Luma exchanged wary looks as they followed the Blood Witch cadre down the battle-scarred corridors. Nothing in their careers prepared them for what was to come. Both wondered if they were the right tools for the job or if they were heading to a slaughter.

Planet Mannus Prime.

The night was alive with the sounds of insects and creatures. A cacophony of noise enough to drive the unsuspecting mad. Kaline sat with her eyes closed. She was soothed by their symphony. Reminded of a simpler time. Her breathing was shallow. Strands of crimson hair lay across her face, tickling her soft flesh. The crunch of a twig snapping echoed from behind.

"What is it, Captain?" she asked without opening her eyes.

He settled beside her, weapon in hand. "Rumors, Mistress. A mob is forming. They want your head. We should retreat to the shuttle."

"There are always rumors. How we deal with them, determines our course," she replied.

She felt the heat of his breath on her neck. Anger. Frustration.

"I don't have the firepower to stop them all," he snapped.

Kaline blinked rapidly as her eyes adjusted to the quasi-darkness. "We are not without allies. The word of Rengu spreads. Have faith, my friend."

"Faith doesn't stop fanatics, Mistress. We are in real danger and must displace," he insisted.

Craning her head toward the village, Kaline spied the flickering tips of rising flames.

"See, it already begins," she said.

I see it, all right. That's our doom coming for us. "Kaline, what do you suppose will happen when a mob of angry villagers storms our position? We are exposed, outnumbered, and in an untenable position. No matter how many villagers have been swayed to your quest, it will not be enough. I have seen the violence men perpetrate on one another when riled. This cannot end the way you envision."

"Rengu is with us, Captain," she insisted.

Shadows began moving in the night. Detaching from trees and boulders, they slipped through the darkness, ever drawing closer to Kaline's position. Rising, the former Prekhauten brought his rifle to the ready position and expertly thumbed the safety off. Adrenalin surging, he fell back on old training.

Kaline rose beside him, a staying hand on his rifle. "Welcome, friends. Welcome to the embrace of Rengu."

"Ain't no time for friends," growled a thick voice. "We've come to see you gone."

Fucking told you. "Get behind me," the Captain whispered through clenched teeth.

Nonplussed, Kaline pressed, "Come now. We are not adversaries. Have I not brought gifts with promises of liberation?"

She picked out distinct figures. Tribal elders and the older generation. Those unwilling to allow their outdated way of thinking to be subsumed. Kaline knew their kind, for they were the bane of her quest.

"Your lies will see us on our knees in chains," a woman scowled. "Time has come. You aren't welcome here. Time for you to go."

The Captain slipped in front of her before she could protest. "Anyone comes closer and they don't see the dawn."

A green laser emanated from beneath his barrel, lining up on the chest of the nearest villager. They paused, unsure if he was bluffing.

"He can't kill us all!"

Snarling, he replied, "Doesn't mean I won't try."

Others approached, bearing torches. Cursing, the Captain knew he was about to lose the night advantage. Without knowing if they were armed, he risked being either gunned down or overrun and captured. These backwater villages seldom requested prefect support, choosing instead to handle matters by themselves. Visions of being hung or tied to the stake taunted him. His fingertip touched the trigger.

"Please," Kaline begged. "Will you not listen to reason?"

She doubted a day would come where she understood what happened next. A rock sped from the night to strike a nearby tree. The crack of her defender's rifle split the air. A body fell. Men and women broke into a roar and charged. Several more shots erupted before she was grabbed by the arm and thrust back. The Captain tossed a small object into the onrushing crowd and ran as fast as he could. Mind struggling to comprehend, Kaline hurried to keep pace.

The explosion was condensed, destroying everything in a three-meter radius. Cries of pain joined those of rage. Kaline winced, desperate to drown out the horrid sound. Her visions of a golden future for Mannus Prime evaporated in the flames of dissatisfaction. Yet rather than succumbing to rising despair, she felt something snap deep within. She was infuriated. Her master entrusted her with turning worlds to his whim. She had never failed … until now.

"Keep running!"

His voice bellowed in her ear. Threats reverberated throughout the night. The hungry pace of boots and moccasins slapping the vegetation. Her heart pounded so loudly she thought her head would split. Kaline knew terror only once before. Here, now, threatened with death, she rediscovered it.

A second group of people emerged just ahead. They charged. Kaline saw death for the first time and it was a human face. Shaking herself free from the Captain's grip, she was determined to meet her fate on her own terms. Scores of villagers swept by them. Their raw stench overpowering her senses. Confused, Kaline caught the eye of the first man who came to her seeking the wisdom of Rengu. Hope sparked.

The villagers crashed into each other. Two ideological groups eager to defeat the other by any means. Former friends and family members punched, kicked, gouged, and tore at each other in the name of a cause too few understood. Kaline marveled at the sight before once again being dragged away.

"We can help them," she protested.

He grunted. "There's no helping this madness. The shuttle isn't far. There's still time to escape before it's too late."

"But the …"

"This planet is lost!" he shouted. "Now, if you don't get your little ass moving, I will knock you out and carry you. Move!"

She ran. What choice was there? The forest stretched forever. A moving threat she feared. Letting go of her, the Captain slowed enough to key a series of commands to the small computer attached to his vambrace. Lights blazed just ahead. The shuttle. They were almost to safety, and he hoped, their way off a world gone mad. One that clearly did not want them.

They burst from the tree line and spied the dull grey metal of their salvation. Kaline felt her heart soar. They were safe. She allowed herself to slow and then walk. Sounds of the battle were far behind, posing no legitimate threat.

"Wait," the Captain warned.

She followed his pointing finger to the back ramp. A lowered ramp. The pilots were on their knees beside the shuttle, hands on their heads and a trio of armed villagers behind them. Dark splotches covered their faces.

"We don't want trouble. Give us our pilots back and we're off this world," the Captain didn't allow Kaline to negotiate again. "All you have to do is back away. Leave us be and we'll do the same. Enough blood has been shed this night."

"Way we see it, there wouldna been any blood at all if it weren't for you," the biggest man growled. "We was fine before your woman started weaving lies."

"Now our people are dying," the one to his right said.

"Because of you," said the third.

Tired of pointless rhetoric, the Captain raised his rifle and fired three successive shots. Each struck a villager in the forehead. They pitched backward, trailed by thin ropes of blood. He stalked off before the last man hit the ground, securing the landing area.

"Are there more?" he asked the pilot after the visibly shaken man rose and strayed over.

"No. The rest took off into the forest at the first sounds of fighting."

He looked the flight crew over for any injuries preventing them from performing their duty. The Captain jerked his head. "Get this thing cranked up. I want us airborne as soon as possible."

Pilot and copilot hurried aboard, leaving the Captain and Kaline. She refused to look him in the eye, though why was her private reason. The mouth of Rengu felt defeated, embarrassed, and humbled. She placed a sore foot on the ramp.

"It was for the best," he said softly. "Mannus Prime is one world. There are others. This is not the end, just a setback."

Ignoring him, Kaline boarded the shuttle and reflected upon her humiliation.

Behemoth, Deep space.

The small craft blazed through space, eager to escape the punishment earned by those aboard. Over a score of Blood Witches outcast from the Order fled. It was a worthy sacrifice, for the alternative was obliteration. They had placed their faith in Algiss Her. In her honeyed tongue. In her promises of a new tomorrow. The dawn broke and it ended disastrously. Deciding their lives were more important than their principles, the former Sisters abandoned their oaths in search of the one being willing to offer succor.

Amongeratix.

The thought of aligning with a power strong enough to enforce their will, thrilled the more naïve, while the older, experienced Sisters secretly worried they were all damned. They huddled together, consoling the loss of unity. A separation from the entity that was the Order. Algiss Her listened to their murmurs without interest. Humbled by her failed power grab, the former Mistress of Arms wallowed in agony. Her face was scarred. She felt the ache deep in her bones, a constant reminder of her poor judgment. If the others around her were concerned over her plight, they failed to show it.

Quiet conversations circled the cabin. Thoughts of what awaited conflicted with what was left behind. Their unique position left them strangers in their own bodies. More than one fallen Sister suspected her powers would fade or abandon her now that they were separated from the Order. Algiss listened to their petty concerns, struggling with her desire to see Ruma Zzein and the entire abbey obliterated. Hatred flourished with every breath, until it consumed her. The cold dark of space permeated all and allowed her to turn her focus inward. To besting her former friend and mentor, so that she might finally assume her rightful place in the universe.

Algiss glanced out the viewport. Stars passed. She ignored her broken reflection, choosing instead to see the fabric of existence. Those pricks of distant light turned to glaring demons. The first inspirations of madness awakened and Algiss Her realized she liked it. For too long she lived under the stringent rules of another. Forced to endure policies inspiring more questions than moments of calm. The Order of Blood Witches was steeped in tradition and mystery, but Algiss allowed herself to admit those walls were more of a prison for her than salvation. She wanted more, needed more.

Freedom was at last within her grasp, though she no longer clutched at the dream of ruling the Order. Removed from her shackles, Algiss was able to see her true self for the first time in decades. She was no longer a puppet. No longer a minion, slaving away under the rule of another's vision. At last, she was in control of her destiny. She vowed to make the universe burn.

"Mistress?"

Algiss snapped around, fixing the younger Sister with a baleful glare. Flickers of flame licked from her eye, forcing the woman back in shock. "What?"

Her voice seethed.

Swallowing hard, the Sister said, "We are approaching the *Behemoth*. What are your orders?"

Orders? They still see me as the authority figure. A woman of stature. What are my orders? She stared at the thirty women huddled before her. Scared, confused, ripe with terror. They were the lesser Sisters of better women. But they were hers. Algiss stiffened, drawing to what height she could manage through the agony consuming her.

"We will pledge our services to Amongeratix but not our lives. His is the true power in the universe and destined to win this war, but we shall never serve another again. Ours is the right of rule and we shall take our place in the center of humanity. All shall bend their knee or pay with their lives," her voice rose with fervor. "Never again will we be bowed or broken! I say this unto you now, today is the beginning of a new era. A time of glory for the new Sisterhood!"

She fixed them with a wicked gleam. "Which of you will step forward and join me? The universe is ours. All that remains is to take it."

They huddled in the semi gloom, curious and unsure. A Sister gasped. Another pointed. Algiss Her frowned at their childishness. Doubts crept in. Had she chosen poorly? Were these Sisters lacking? Then she spied the source of their dismay. Algiss held up an arm and stared in wonder as her gossamer robes solidified into a sheen of deep crimson. Raw energy warmed her, flushing her body with a heady combination of elixirs and toxins. Strength poured into her muscles, relieving aches and healing wounds. Her breath exited in plumes of ragged steam. When the transformation ended, she was a different woman. A dangerous one.

"You see! I have been granted the strength of our master! Come, embrace me and become one with his power," she demanded.

The first Sister rose and tattered her embrace. Compelled by the majesty in her voice, the others soon followed.

Sauwgon Hil marveled at the scene laid out before them. Moss covered stones rose high into the sky. A skeleton of immense proportions sat before each, their flesh long since removed by the ravages of time and wind. Each bore a dull crown. Sauwgon knew them for what they were. Great kings of men reduced to abandoned memories. They were the refuse. The forgotten paths less taken. Failures. Heart hammering as he strode through the first giant shadow, Sauwgon clutched his staff.

The soft kiss of wind teased his hair. A groan drew his attention, deep and grating. The shaman turned to see the first skeleton's skull twist down at him, judging him with empty eyes. The sword in his hand, crusted over with rust and age, shifted ever so slightly. Sauwgon understood the peril they were in. He recognized the test and did not envision surviving. More than twenty skeletons littered the area he and his lone apprentice were to travel. Trapped, the shaman knew they could not back out and go around. The defenders of the glade would slaughter them both should he attempt it. There was but one option. Sauwgon glanced to his last disciple.

"It is time," he said.

The pain of his words etched across his face. Sauwgon asked for sacrifice from the only other member of his tribe left. Once he was gone, the shaman alone would remain, should he escape the field of skeletons. It was no easy statement to order the death of one so close, but they were doomed from the start. With no females in their number, it was but a matter of time before the end arrived. His endgame held more significance than the continuity of species, however.

Rather than succumb to eventual demise, Sauwgon refused to back down. He was close to the end. He felt it. The lure of unimagined power just out of reach. The buzz of a thousand insects filled the glade, trembling the ground with an awful roar. His last disciple gripped his spear tighter and boldly strode to the center of the glade. Skulls turned on him, balefires burning deep within their empty eye sockets.

The first rose, a towering figure of diminished greatness, raining moss, dirt, and debris. Swallowing his fear, the last disciple roared and charged his foe. Sauwgon watched with fascination as stone clashed with steel. Flakes of rust showered the combatants. Knowing the significance of the sacrifice, the shaman felt he must witness, but time was drawing short. It was with heavy heart Sauwgon turned his back on the last disciple and hurried away. Not every death was meant to be witnessed.

Bandy legs carried him away from the scene. More skeletal guardians awoke, eager to join the conflict. Sauwgon grimaced at the sound of aged bones grinding together. Imbued with the strength of the fallen, the shaman hurried along. Destiny awaited. He crashed through debris littered cobwebs of giant spiders. Raw power blazed from his spear, melting web and insect alike. A blood curdling scream echoed through the stones, announcing the death of his last disciple. Unlike the others, there would be no collection of power. His lifeforce spent, the disciple would fade to dust and bitter memory. A worthy sacrifice for Sauwgon to achieve his final evolution.

The shaman watched the surrounding world shimmer out of focus. Brilliant lines of color stretched before him. The ground pitched and yawed. Chasms opened in the sky, great rents showing him glimpses of another reality, filled with gaping mouths filled with teeth and disproportioned heads with a million eyes. He watched the birth of stars and their violent demise. The secrets of the universe were laid bare for his pleasure. A heady sensation warmed his body. His muscles vibrated as tentacles of light coiled around his arms and legs and dragged him forward. He obeyed. What else was there?

Reality folded around him. Sauwgon Hil gasped as his flesh dissolved, dissipating in the light. This was his gift. His final reward for a lifetime of searching. Memories assailed him. The moment he first decided there was more to life, to existence. His quest for knowledge as he delved deep into the mysteries of the unknown. Quiet secrets whispered in his ears when he was alone, beckoning him to seek the truth and become more than the sum of all his people combined. Their toxic promises inspired him to learn more. To seek the fortune of the ages. Here at last, he stood upon the precipice. Tilting his head back in exultation, he closed his eyes and left the last vestiges of mortality behind. Oblivion greeted him with open arms.

TWENTY-TWO

3215 A.G. (After gods), Western front, planet Mannus Prime.

"Grenades first. Then we storm the line," Annalilly whispered to the group of squad leaders crouched around her.

Darkness prevented her from seeing their faces, their silhouettes little more than indistinct shapes in the night. She knew them by the shapes of their heads. Funny what details leaders associated with their troops. Jers was to her immediate right. His lack of enthusiasm worried her. Having already expressed his desire to end his time in service, the veteran's dire approach to each engagement was starting to wear on his soldiers. Annalilly knew she needed to stop it. But how? She considered going to Fies and requesting Jers be relieved, but they were in the middle of a campaign with limited supplies and fewer reinforcements.

"We go in five. I want intervals and blue force trackers on. Once your squads have secured their targets you hold in place," she continued even as she decided attaching her command staff to Jers's squad was in everyone's best interest. "Understood?"

Heads bobbed.

"Take your places. No quarter," Annalilly finished. She snatched Jers's vambrace when he rose. "Jers, I'm sticking with your squad tonight. You still have the immediate command."

"Yes, Sergeant," he replied, voice bereft of emotion.

She caught the hesitation in his stance. The way his shoulders stooped. Perhaps it was her imagination. Weapons, armor, and equipment weighed and it was no small task to bear Guard kit through an increasing string of firefights. Throw in lack of sleep and limited rations and Jers was pushing the end of his rope. They all were. Annalilly refused to accept any weakness. The only thing mattering was completing their mission and securing the enemy trench line. She decided to confront him afterward. If they both lived.

Exhaling the breath choking her lungs, Annalilly stood. Her knees ached. *Damn, I hate getting old.* The sad truth was she had far more days being sore. Fresh aches and pains teased her with approaching retirement. Only, there didn't seem any chance of retiring, not with the universe locked in civil war. Choosing to focus on the approaching mission, Annalilly decided to let the future stay where it belonged. She had enough problems maintaining the odd combined force under her thumb. The responsibility of so many lives rattled her. Every life lost was a reflection of inadequate leadership, or so she had been led to believe.

Shaking the cobwebs from her mind, Annalilly checked the chrono on her helmet's heads up display. The numbers fled, counting down to zero. Her pulse quickened with the anticipation of what came next. Thermal sensors picked up scores of small objects launching through the air, those responsible were on their feet and creeping forward a moment later. *Time to go.* Detonations erupted up and down the enemy trenches, spitting gouts of flame amid a shower of dirt and debris.

Annalilly roared over the helmet's intercom. A blood curdling sound, both inspiring and terrifying. Caution escaped her as she gave herself to the awesome thrill of close combat. Gone were the doubts and fears, replaced by the unflinching desire to stay alive another engagement. She followed Jers's squad with her command staff, a group she never thought to control, a few meters behind, intent to remain out of the way. The assaulting elements hit the trenches before the enemy recovered from the grenade strike. Heavy rumbles echoed in the background, prompting a tight grin. The artillery brought by Sergeant Major Matthias was clearing its throat. *Good. Kill all these bastards.*

Sporadic rifle fire pierced the darkness up and down the line. Her orders were specific: spare the rifle when necessary and give the foe the blade. Bodies leapt into the trench. Annalilly scanned the immediate battlespace and noticing several cooling bodies leading up to the trench. Medics were already squirreling through the night, climbing over bodies to get to the wounded and passing up the dead. She didn't envy their jobs. Better to make the mess than have to clean it up. She hit the sandbag-lined lip of the trench and halted her tteam, while the grunts cleared room.

Damage from the grenade assault was severe. Limbs and burned pieces of equipment littered the area. Men and women screamed. Others were run through with bayonets. She was ordered not to collect unnecessary prisoners. The definition of which lay within her scope to execute. There were other units engaged in the firefight. Let them worry about prisoners. She had scores to settle.

"Sergeant! We've secured this section. There's a command bunker twenty meters down the line," the report cackled in her helmet.

Annalilly nodded, an old habit ingrained into her by previous platoon sergeants. Cursing, she opened the channel. "Roger that. All squads, sweep and clear the trench and prepare for counter assault. We regroup and move when called. Squad leaders, I want an accurate headcount, living, dead, and wounded. Green reports are due in ten."

Movement coming out of the trench caught her eye and she slid her weapon left. It took a split second for her HUD to identify. Ignoring her orders, she fired one ion round between the startled woman's eyes. No prisoners. A heavy machine gun erupted from down the line, belching blue-white flame into the impure night and announcing an end to the element of surprise. The real battle was just beginning.

Asom longed for the tight corridors of his ship. Open space fighting was terrifying and he wanted his marines to exfil the moment the campaign ended. They didn't belong in the mud with the rest of the grunts. He reluctantly admitted ship to ship action was no prize fight. The intimate space opened slender avenues of approach but the risk was greater. Recent event splayed over in his mind, confusing years of experience. The only constant lay with Annalilly and her platoon. Each and every one of them was crazy.

Leaning his forehead on the nearest sandbag, Asom thanked the gods his marines made it through the assault unscathed. Annalilly's follow up orders came through, stealing his moment of peace. Regardless of where he fought, Asom was a professional. He hefted his rifle and started moving through his platoon barking orders.

"Marines, listen up! I want head and ammo count asap. Doc, see if any of the connecting platoons need your services," his voice was strong. Confident. "Everyone else prepare to move. We're going to clear out that tree line next and you can bet these sons of bitches aren't going to give it up as easy as this lovely trench."

Laughter echoed back. That was good. Levity meant they were alive. Twisted as frontline troop humor tended to be, it was the telltale sign morale remained high and they were focused on the next mission. Heads in the game, his old gunnery sergeant used to say. Nothing to do but wait for the reports to flow in, Asom activated his armor's hydration system and took a long drink of lukewarm water. The taste was almost fetid but would have to do until they were cleared to remove helmets and drink from their canteens.

A check of his chrono said the assault lasted less than ten standard minutes. Dozens of bodies filled the trench and the immediate area ahead of him. Guardsmen cut down trying to escape the frenzied attack of former comrades eager to kill. Most didn't get far. Those few who had were no doubt relaying stories of overwhelming forces surging through the night. Nothing inspired fear like a successful firefight in the middle of the night, when the sane were supposed to be asleep. He snorted his amusement. Then the bark of machine gun fire sent a sheet of death into his area.

Marines caught in the open were gunned down. A head popped from the shoulders. An arm was sliced off. Bodies scurried back into the safety of the trench, while others dragged the wounded down behind them. He grimaced at the thought of leaving marines in harm's way, but the wounded were always secondary concerns. Light thumps sounded in the night. Mortars. He cursed as the heavy whump of impacts ranged up and down the line. Most missed, though one or two found their targets. With nowhere for the kinetic energy to go, the results were devasting.

"Heavy weapons! Get me a bead on those fucking machine guns," he shouted over the mounting chaos. "Do it now or we're all dead!"

Marines planted their heavy weapons on the bank and zeroed in on the nearest grove of trees. Asom let them work. He had other matters to attend to. Keying an external channel, he said, "Cold Steel Seven, this is Marine One. Fire mission. Danger close. Grid coordinates relaying to you now. Request ten rounds of H.E. Fire when ready, over."

"Copy, Marine One. Keep your people's heads down. This is going to get nasty," came the reply.

"Roger, Marine One standing by for confirmation."

He counted, slowly. The rounds were already screaming overhead by the time he heard them.

"Rounds out," the artillery center confirmed.

The night erupted in a nightmare of flame and liquid death. Asom's visual dampeners protected his night vision and allowed him the opportunity to watch the mayhem consume the trees. Successive rounds destroyed everything over man height.

The force of impact sped into the trench with unabated fury. Debris struck several marines. Others were buffeted by the blow. The ground trembled, threatening to tear asunder beneath their boots. Asom decided it was more dangerous than the threat of being vented into space.

It took less than two heartbeats for the barrage. Two heartbeats in which he felt the rawest terror of his life. He knew what was coming next. Anticipation filled him. Asom gripped his rifle tighter and propped a foot halfway up the trench wall.

"All elements, advance and destroy enemy units to the front."

He was the first out of the trench. "Kill them all, marines!"

Their roars were matched by the belch of twin machines covering their assault.

Jers ran for his life. Every footstep was potentially his last. Each breath among the final few in his short life. At the sharp end for three years, he didn't understand how the others weren't cracking as well. The squad leader killed two enemy Guards while securing the trench, and despite his best intentions, readied for the second phase of the assault. Falchi and the others wanted this to be the push. The last action to secure Mannus Prime, defeat a massive enemy army, and get the war moving in their favor at last. Jers saw it as the end of days. The niggling feeling in the back of his mind whispered he wasn't going to leave here alive.

"All elements, advance and destroy enemy units to the front."

"You heard her, move out!" he shouted, releasing the breath he hadn't realized he was holding.

The words sound foreign, almost alien, though he knew he issued the suborder. Despite the growing sensation of wanting to escape, Jers remained professional. He was trained to obey, adapt, and perform at higher levels than ordinary civilians. The Prekhauten Guard prided themselves on being the most disciplined and combat ready unit in the universe. Jers was part of that tradition.

He wondered if that was the reason Annalilly put him in charge. The crunch of his boots on broken terrain amused him for some reason. He ran in line with the others. A solid wave of armored ferocity. Jers idly mused what those forces he had attacked over the years felt like, seeing the unstoppable tide of grey and silver rush toward them. He felt it at Hawker's Gate and again on Kharsis. The urge to flee so strong, it prevented him from moving. He imagined the stench of hot urine running down legs, as death approached. Intimidating. Petrifying. Only, these weren't ragtag militia or planetary defense forces. These were veteran Guardsmen. The contest was even.

Jers hit the ruined trees and whistled at the raw devastation greeting them. Broken and twisted trees jutted from the ground, bloody spears in the night. There were so many body parts, he doubted anyone would get an accurate count of dead and missing. The artillery may be far away and frowned upon by most frontline grunts, but they were gods in wait for the Guard in trouble. He failed to understand why they weren't used more often. Surely the mercenaries Matthias brought back had enough firepower to level most, if not all, of the enemy fortifications all the way to the heart of their lines. It was his experience there was nothing so demoralizing as surviving an artillery barrage. He almost pitied the bastards on the receiving end.

Almost.

The ruination stretched for hundreds of meters in every direction. Jers found it comforting, knowing there was no way anyone could survive this and remain combat effective. It was a tender mercy, saving him from the worry of immediate harm. He didn't know who was in overall command, but experience taught him they were not going to stop and consolidate their position again. Not until reaching their final objective. The battle was joined and it was all or nothing to the very end. One army was going to break. He prayed it wasn't them.

Matthias listened to the cry for artillery support. His heart quickened. A lifetime of fighting among the ranks urged him to abandon the Shadow Hammers and get back in the fight with the men and women he trusted. Bootleg and his five thousand strong force were nothing but mercenaries, in it for the money and the glory. Whatever honor they once held as Guardsmen, was long used up. They were the ultimate battlefield predators and he despised being among them.

Cannons barked their replies up and down the armored lines. Matthias wished Falchi would authorize continued orbital strikes, eliminating the enemy force and the need for more Guards to die in what he deemed a pointless civil war. Ask ten Guards what they were fighting for and nine wouldn't have an answer. He supposed it was the great tragedy of it all. The greed of a handful skewed the entire seven hundred colonized worlds into unending war that continued escalating on unprecedented scales. It was enough to make him weep.

The only way to end the war and restore order, as well as humanity's faith in their ruling bodies, was to cut the head off their enemy. That head belonged to Amongeratix. The Inquisitor General and others may be executing the war from a human level, but it all originated from the millennia old hatreds of one being who failed to realize there was no place for him in the new order.

"All vehicles, let's roll. Grunts have cleared the way. Now's our turn," Bootleg barked.

Matthias felt his vehicle lurch as the armored task force rumbled into action. Though he failed to understand why the grunts were forced to move first, he was thankful for the heavy fist such a large armored force deployed. With most of the enemy's combat forces dedicated to the opposite side of the battlefield, the Shadow Hammers were the wrecking ball the army needed.

Two full divisions stretching on a front of fifteen kilometers, stepped off the line of departure after a brief artillery barrage and a handful of infiltration raids designed to soften the enemy's outer defenses. Matthias longed to be back with his people, the men and women he trained with, bled with, and spent countless nights under a foreign sky with. They deserved his loyalty, not the ragtag mercenaries who either fled military service or were forced to depart under less than honorable conditions. Any reconciliation would come long after the last round was fired.

He and Bootleg were on a collision course, where only one would walk away. The former sergeant major cast a wary glance at the hardened mercenary across the turret. Matthias struggled with trying to remember working with the man. Decades worth of military service stretched into a hazy past, leaving Matthias at a loss. He encountered thousands of Guards. Why was this one man so difficult to recall? Bootleg's grievances were severe, worthy of a court martial under the best of circumstances, and he was adamant about making Matthias pay. But for what exactly? Missing a key component, Matthias felt trapped in an endless maze. Perhaps there was no way out.

The bark of the main gun firing shredded his thoughts. Fire slashed the night up and down the Shadow Hammer lines. Whatever they lacked in military discipline, was made up with their ferocity in combat. Unencumbered by standard Guard rules of engagement, the mercenaries were free to reap whatever toil sated their thirsts. From what Matthias had already witnessed, that thirst was unquenchable. He prayed none of the targets being mowed down were friendlies.

"Are you going to open up with that gun or do I shoot you now and dump the body?" Bootleg's angry growl slashed into his headset.

Matthias swallowed his pride, as he was forced to every time he spoke with the man. "There are no immediate targets. Firing now is a waste of ammunition."

"Course, it is," Bootleg sneered. "We got the ammo and we got the enemy. Who knows, soldier boy, you might get lucky and reduce the odds a little before we get into the shit. Now open fire or I will."

Turning the light machine gun on Bootleg and eliminating the threat was a viable solution, though it left Matthias at the mercy of the rest of the company. He decided it was best to keep playing by the rules, twisted as they were. Their time of reckoning was coming. Fast. He flipped the safety off and depressed the firing pedals. Blue-white streams of superheated death zipped into the night.

The light assault vehicle kicked into gear and hurried across the rubble strewn terrain. Originally meant to carry soldiers into battle during lightning assaults, the vehicle was large enough to fit ten fully equipped fighters in the back. Armed with twin 9.88 mm machine guns capable of shredding a human body and protected by three-inch-thick composite armor, the vehicle earned the nickname of dragon.

Jelin Quint stood behind the sights of one of the machine guns. He preferred riding shotgun on the dragon to slogging it across the battlefield on foot and was thankful no one forced him to spearhead the assault with Annalilly and her people. He knew a suicide mission when he heard it. Survival rates were destined to be low. He glanced back at the huddled men and women cowed in the back of the open cargo space. One fell round and they were done for, but that was a price to pay for speed and lethality.

Mired in shadow, Quint's imagination took root. Each face was a soldier he served with. A fallen warrior during the ill-fated assault responsible for all but wiping out his company. They leered back at him, questioning why he deserved to live, while the others fell. Tears welled as emotions threatened to subsume him. *I'm not strong enough for this. I should have died with you.* Yet here he remained, a pivotal figure at the spearhead advance of the final push to secure the planet.

Quint failed to understand what Torgast saw in him. He was a broken man, haunted by personal demons. The prefects were right to lock him away where he couldn't do anyone harm, most of all himself. A breeze kissed his face, slapping his nostrils with the stench of fresh death. Time enough to lament later. First, he needed to survive the night. After that, perhaps he might atone for the cardinal sin of abandoning his comrades.

Shaking the cobwebs away, Quint focused on the pressing issue placing him in the initial assault wave. His brother. The sergeant was consumed with guilt after learning it was his own flesh and blood commanding the enemy. Though they were never close, and rarely communicated, Quint felt conflicted at the duality of his loyalties. Blood was everything on the planet he grew up on. How would his family react to learn brother fought brother? *Damned disappointed is how they'll feel, you daft bastard. Pa might be turning in his grave right now.*

Quint snorted. It served the old man right. Banno was always the favorite son, leaving Jelin begging for the scraps of attention he seldom received. After Banno joined the Guard, Jelin followed, but with the intent of taking an entirely different career path where he could make his own name and reputation. Never in his wildest schemes did he imagine they might square off against each other with the fate of entire armies in play. He supposed it was a cruel irony the universe was so fond of playing.

The thin voice crackling over the intercom was harrowing. Quint gripped his weapon tight. "Keep your heads down. Incoming orbital bombardment commencing in three … two … one."

The night erupted in a blinding flash.

Torgast ducked as the bone numbing sound of orbital strikes thundered across the skies. Thankful for the seclusion of his tent, the Guard commander was far too seasoned to allow his men such an unseemly sight. His mind shifted to the men and women deep within the enemy fortifications. Regardless of which side they fell on in this schism, they were all once loyal Guardsmen. Torgast was wise enough to know no one believed they were the bad guys. Not even the people he was determined to kill. Strapping on the last of his armor, he snatched his helmet and headed out. The front awaited and, he prayed, so might the last battle of this impossible campaign.

Guards nodded in greeting, strictly enforcing the no salute order as it suited their internal sense of defiance. Torgast didn't mind. Being sniper bait was not on his agenda. He had witnessed far too many junior officers fresh out of training demanding their due respect, only to have their brains paint the nearest sandbag wall moments later. Fools. Why weren't they taught respect is earned, not given?

He gained the forward command post in time to watch bright columns of red light spear down from space. Admiral Falchi's orbital bombardment was in full operation. The tactical lasers were powerful enough to melt bone, without destroying the environment. Torgast lamented the loss of life. Some part of him wanted the opportunity to speak with prisoners and convert them back to the side of the righteous. Perhaps it was a dream, a fanciful illusion every field commander has before the final dawn. He owed it to his conscience to try. What sort of man would he be, if he didn't?

A sea of unfamiliar faces greeted his arrival. Secure within the blackout confines of the bunker, each paused to acknowledge the field commander. Torgast waved them off and sought out the senior Guard. There was work to be done this dark night and no time for pleasantries. It struck him as the heavy flaps were drawn over the door behind him that he missed having Sergeant Quint at his side. The man was borderline broken and battling as many ghosts as enemy soldiers, but he was loyal to a fault and quick witted. He wondered if he had done the right thing by sending Quint with the liaison force.

None of that mattered when he laid eyes on Cardinal Virom among the huddled senior officers and sergeants surrounding the battlefield map. Seeing Torgast approach, the elder Cardinal slipped free of the intense conversation debating tactics and timing. He clasped Torgast's forearm with familiarity.

"Cardinal, I had not expected you to attend the front for this," Torgast began.

Virom's smile was thin. The message was clear. You should not be here. "Come now, my son, what use does the Conclave serve, if not to calm the fears of its constituents during their darkest moments of crisis? How are you, Torgast?"

He ran a hand through his thinning hair. "I'm about to send ten thousand of my best over that berm, into a hail of fire that has kept us locked in position for the better part of a year and pray Sergeant Quint and the other faction have synced their assault perfectly. How do you think I feel?"

"These are trying times," Virom bobbed his head. "I received word from Krenz earlier today. They want you to surrender your command and stand down all forces."

"Of course, they do," he snorted. "I suppose I'll be taken in for some sort of re-education?"

A dark pall fell over Virom's face. "Point in fact, you and all of your senior leaders are to be executed on spot. Your units will be folded into existing battalions and redeployed across the universe to continue Nye's insurrection."

"Comforting. At least he's doing me the favor of not having to witness my people fall to corruption," Torgast waved the concern off. "Cardinal, by the time this battle is finished, those fops on Vau Prime are going to have more problems than taking my head. What of our guests?"

"The Inquisitors are behaved enough in their cells. My personal guard has them locked away under the royal palace. I don't suspect either will see the sun for quite some time."

"The Inquisition is fiercely protective of their own, Cardinal. Be careful," Torgast warned. He expected a rescue attempt, but from whom or where, was beyond his purview. Military intelligence continued monitoring the situation for any actionable chatter, allowing the field commander to earn his paycheck.

Another round of orbital strikes hit the enemy center. Torgast forced himself not to flinch. "My apologies for being late. Where do we stand on the assault?"

Those surrounding the table saluted. Torgast waved them off. There was no time for military formalities. Not with the battle already underway. A dark-skinned colonel cleared her throat. Her light brown eyes shined in the artificial light, contrasting the grime on her uniform.

"Sir, we have all assault elements staged on the line of departure and are awaiting the end of orbital bombardment to commence our attack." Her voice was crisp, authoritative and betraying none of the latent concerns gnawing at her.

Torgast studied the maps. Two full divisions, nearly ten thousand Guards, massed along the trenches. It would be the largest assault since the campaign began, and if the gods willed it, a crippling blow to their enemies. He tried to ignore the numbers as individual beings. Men and women of flesh and blood about to step into the breach. How many would not return? And of those who did, how many more would never be the same again? The laments of a soldier nestled in his mind, Torgast brushed his fingers over the terrain features.

"This is a bold maneuver, Colonel. We risk everything on the whims of people who have not been on this planet. Not been in our fight," he reminded them.

The injection of a new fighting force inspired them. He saw it in their eyes. Bereft of support for so long, his army was on the verge of demoralization, and worse, collapse. Admiral Falchi's unexpected arrival with not only a functional battle group but thousands of infantry support was the boost his people needed. They saw the end in sight. Torgast felt the renewed energy among the ranks as he passed through to the command tent. They wanted the fight. Wanted to end this war and move on to the next. No one knew why they were fighting. Hells, he still hadn't figured it out. All that mattered now was the men and women to their left and right. The rest would sort itself out after the dust settled.

Stiffening, the colonel replied, "Sir, our people are ready. This is the moment we have waited for since being deployed here. The end of the war is in sight."

"Making this our most dangerous hour," Torgast agreed. "Make no mistake, our enemy will do everything they can to prevent our victory. We must continue adhering to the same discipline, the same standards and levels of situational awareness that have seen us this far. Anything less will result in disaster." He paused. "Which is why I will be joining the second wave."

Gasps rippled through them. Virom stepped forward.

"Torgast!" he exclaimed.

Staying their concerns with an open hand, the commander offered a thin smile. "I have sat behind a desk or in a bunker for far too long, while our people bled. I ordered Sergeant's Quint's company to attack and he alone survived. What sort of battlefield commander would I be to hide behind a sandbag wall, staring through binoculars as the final push played out? No, my friends, I will not be swayed. A commander's place is in the field."

If for no other reason than to assuage the guilt riding my conscience.

"Once our navy friends stop clearing their throats, I want that first wave out of the trench and moving. We cannot afford delay or give the enemy time to recover. Use artillery and mortars to cover our approach," he ordered.

"What about prisoners?" a portly captain asked.

Torgast grimaced. "They are of secondary concern. Anticipate any frontline troops to be diehard believers in their cause. The first wave does not stop. Keep pushing. Break the lines and we end this today. I want their battle standards in my fist by nightfall. Second and third waves will secure prisoners. Assaulting elements keep pushing. This is the only chance we are going to get. End this war today. Am I clear?"

Nods and murmurs of *yes sir* echoed around the table. He felt their motivation combined with a natural hesitancy he shared. Months of prolonged engagement corroded their fighting spirit, making them pause when they ordinarily would have pressed. Everything rested in their hands now. These brave men and women willing to stand up to tyranny and do the right thing in the face of overwhelming odds. Victory or defeat, Torgast was proud of every last one. He snapped to attention, presented his best salute, and spun about. The time for talk was finished. Now, it was time for war.

He didn't exhale until exiting the tent. Frustration and apprehension flushed his body. Torgast almost wished he smoked. Anything to ease the tension and make him feel human again. The tent flap rustled behind as Cardinal Virom joined him.

"This is not a wise move on your part," the older man cautioned.

Lances of supercharged energy funneled down from space to strike the center of the enemy camp. "Cardinal, when have I ever been considered wise? Give me today and you can remind me tomorrow just how much of a fool I was."

Another blast rocked the ground. *Kill those bastards. Kill them all.*

High orbit, planet Mannus Prime.

"Missile launch detected."

Warning sirens screamed across the bridge as the *Indomitable* crew surged into action. Falchi stood, hands clasped behind his back in a gesture of complete calm he did not feel. Chunks of the destroyed battleship continued breaking up and drifting into the planet's gravity well. He was surprised by his opponents' renewed ferocity. What should have been a resounding defeat only served to inspire greater attacks. Falchi didn't understand their tactics. They were outnumbered, outgunned, and fighting a losing battle to his ragtag fleet. What did they hope to gain?

"Launch countermeasures and prepare for impact," Captain Samuel announced from his command chair. "Target firing solutions on the perpetrator and blow them from my battlespace."

Falchi's eyebrow rose. Through years of service together, he had never heard Samuel speak so. It was refreshing to hear his protégé filled with passion, yet similarly distressing. The longer the war drew on, the more it forced unpleasant changes on the participants. He feared Samuel was but the latest in a growing list of casualties. Impressed as he was, the admiral longed for the return to normalcy. Civility. *War makes monsters of us all.*

"Enemy frigates moving into sector seven."

Samuel glared at the tactical display. Common sense said to cut and run. Unable to fathom what games the enemy played at, he took a deep breath before issuing new orders.

"Bring up a squadron of corvettes to neutralize movement and send in all available fighter wings. Break them now."

He swiveled his chair to face his mentor and friend. "Sir, what are they up to? We have them outgunned and outmanned. There is no logical reason to continue this engagement."

"I have been wondering that myself, Samuel. Losing that battleship should have been the nail in their coffin."

"Whoever commands their battle group is either a madman or has another trick up his sleeve," Samuel grunted.

The *Indomitable* rocked as counterbattery fire slashed across the distance to the incoming missiles. One by one, they detonated far enough away from the hull to prevent major damage. Flights of fighters chased each other across the debris field. Capital ships burned from a hundred fires, fueled by enormous supplies of oxygen. The nightmare landscape stretched across the event horizon as the two fleets battled for supremacy over Mannus Prime.

"Captain! New signal entering the system," the helmsman shouted above the din of the command staff.

Heads snapped toward the screen. Falchi caught himself leaning forward to get a closer look at the metal monstrosity pulling closer to the battle. Dull gunmetal grey, the ship was a barge of sorts, though not one he had ever seen. Any markings or characteristics were scrubbed, leaving the ship akin to a floating derelict. To his trained mind, there was no purpose for this vessel to be entering the airspace.

Samuel was a step ahead of the admiral. "First Officer, bring up specs on that barge. I want to know weapons' capabilities and how much of a threat she is."

"Aye, Captain," the golden-haired officer replied. Her fingers danced across the keys. Frowning, she turned to Samuel, "Sir, there are no weapon signatures aboard. She is running on low propulsion, almost adrift."

"It's no accident she's here," Falchi cautioned, lest any of the crew lower their guard. His right hand gripped the back of the captain's chair.

That was all Samuel needed to confirm his suspicions. "Weapons, blast that thing out of my A.O. and plot firing solutions on the largest enemy capital ship. This engagement has gone on long enough."

As if on cue, the barge's engines kicked in and she began picking up speed. Falchi's face drained of color when he recognized the tactic. "Order all ships in that thing's path to evade at once! Shields to full. All other craft are to concentrate their fire on the engines. Stop that barge!"

"Sir, what's going on?" Samuel asked, his eyes glued to the screen.

The enemy barge plowed into the front picket line without incident, as friendly cruisers and light attack craft peeled away in a last-minute attempt at following orders. Torpedoes fired from a dozen ships converged on the barge, detonating deep within the iron bowels. Still it kept coming. Falchi felt dread crawl up his spine. What game was the enemy playing?

"Admiral, barge drive signatures are spooling up to critical mass!"

"Detonation in thirty seconds!"

Falchi punched the back of the command chair. "All vessels pull away. Clear the blast radius. Now!"

The rest of the allied fleet broke away, but it was not enough. The enemy barge, packed with enough explosives to destroy a small moon, exploded seconds later. Several ships were incinerated in the blast. Their tattered hulks burning into the planet's atmosphere. A strike cruiser too slow to escape began imploding from the engines forward. Falchi watched in horror as flames raced ahead of the destruction. Hundreds of lives lost. Other capital ships sustained major damage to shielding and hull integrity. Then the wave hit *Indomitable*.

The ship rolled. Tiny explosions consumed the interior. Ceiling panels sparked and fell. Crewmembers were pitched to the deck and into bulky equipment panels. Smoke began filling the bridge as warning sirens blared. Knocked to his knees, Falchi pulled himself up and assessed the damage. Blood trickled down the left side of his face. Screens flickered, went black, and lit up with real time data from the explosion.

A new set of icons flashed on the screen and his heart sank.

"Enemy battlegroup translating to real space in sector three."

Face tightened in a grimace, he glared at the tactical officer and growled, "Order all ships to engage."

TWENTY-THREE

3215 A.G. (After Gods), Prophet Isle, planet Crimeat.

Presha Von paced in her cell. Her father would insist it was a chamber, but there was no coating the fact she was all but a prisoner to the new dark council of Crimeat. Scenarios formed and played out in her mind, each focused on besting the issue and keeping her head where it belonged. So much had changed on her homeworld since Amongeratix and the Inquisitor General began their long-prepared war on the universe. A pallor of fear lingered everywhere she went, culminating with the paranoia wafting from the council members. Survival might be harder than she assumed.

Tired of pointless movement that did little to assuage her concerns, Presha sat on the cold metal bed. Her feet dangled; hands clasped upon her lap. Low energy lights built into the ceiling pushed back the darkness just enough to remind her of the ridiculousness of the situation. Half the universe was hunting her and here she was, trapped in an Inquisition prison that hadn't seen use in almost three years. She might have found it entertaining, if not for the promise of what was yet to come.

Reflection had never been her strong suit. She preferred the cold statistical reaction to a situation, whether it was assuming command of Hawker's Gate or fleeing across the stars to bear witness to the murder of Kharsis. Presha longed for a return to normalcy, though she secretly knew it would never happen. Meeting Amongeratix was the worst thing that could have ever happened to her. Before him, she had a promising political career and was in the process of securing her destiny under the guise of the dark council. Greed interfered as gold-laced words dripped from the tyrant's tongue. Presha fell for it without hesitation. She snorted. Ironic, considering she was sitting in a Conclave prison cell not far from where he was once kept.

The thump of bootsteps echoed down the abandoned corridor. Presha doubted there were other prisoners being held here. Wishing for a weapon, she slowed her breathing as the repetitious sound halted before her door. Archaic keys, a symbol of the purported purity the Conclave wished to impose upon the universe, fumbled and clicked in the lock.

She was amazed by the simplicity of it. Days ago, she was soaring across the stars on a vessel capable of traveling faster than the speed of light and today she sat in a cell warded by keys and guards. The indignity of it chafed her.

The door creaked as it swung open. Her initial thought was to leap at the guard and render him unconscious. It was only the bulky shadow creeping across the floor to bathe her in darkness that stalled her aggression. Presha glanced up at her father, eyes widening to the point the lines crowding the corners of her eyes appeared as great rents in her flesh.

"You are the last person I expected to see," she sniped and folded her arms.

Olex Von's scowl pressed his thin lips together. "Do not push me, daughter. This is not the planet you abandoned those few years ago. The council is debating over your fate. My hands are tied."

"Why father, I had no idea you cared so much," Presha's voice was a low growl caught in her throat. She hopped down from her seat. "Am I to be executed now? Is that why you have come?"

"Hush your tone, girl. There are forces at play you have no concept of," Olex warned. He loomed over her. A hint of breeze scrapped the bottom of his dark robes across the floor. "I still have pull within the council, but my time is limited. There is someone you must see. He is both wise and powerful."

"Geres Auk has all the power I need," she replied. The edge was gone, replaced by the well-practiced tone she once used on Hawker's Gate. "Where is this mystery man?"

"We must go deep into the earth," Olex explained. "He has not seen the light of day for many years, nor do I believe he wishes to. The Equerry is quite mad but bestowed with the gift of foresight. If there is a way out of this situation, he will find it."

Doubtful, Presha knew this was her only chance of escaping the inevitable death being decided by the dark council. She tipped her head, the slightest incline, and gestured her father to lead.

He stepped to the door before warning, "Presha, keep your hood up and do not look the Equerry in the eye. It is an … unpleasant sight for even the most hardy."

Her stomach twisted. Dark images swirled in the caverns of her mind. She had witnessed so much during her service to Amongeratix, it took little imagination to conjure fresh nightmares.

"Quickly. Follow me," Olex whispered.

They hurried to the far end of the hall, stepping over debris to reach a slender stairwell. Presha was surprised to find the steps carved from the finest marble. They were also coated with a layer of dust. She bore daggers into her father's back. *Is he leading me to my end at last? Father dearest, a servant of powers he fails to comprehend.* Longing for a weapon, Presha focused on her surroundings.

How far underground they went, she didn't know. The winding staircase bottomed out, guarded by a pair of intricately carved pillars. Images of snakes and mythic creatures swirled around in rising patterns, all under the watchful gaze of giant beings. Fires raged behind each, though the presentation was lost on Presha. She searched for anything she could use to combat her father should he prove treacherous, but the chamber was immaculate.

The walls were hewn from the rockface, polished or worn down with time and diligence, suggesting this was older than modern civilization on Crimeat. Presha admired the sterile atmosphere, for this was the most impressive structure she had ever entered. A low ceiling provided a claustrophobic feeling. Suppressing the growing desire to flee, she continued after her father. Each footfall was the sound of delicate thunder rippling into the distance.

Torches sprang to life. The archaic flames a reminder of darker times. Presha struggled to recall the last time she needed flames to light her path. Eventually the chamber narrowed. She spied an ancient wooden table filling the center. The luster was gone, chipped away by time and decay. A raw stench overpowered the air. Bile tickled the bottom of her throat. Blinking through tears, Presha at last noticed the fragile man hunched over a book at least a foot thick.

His black robes carried the same dust coating. Ichor ran down his lower face, and the cowl over his head concealed his eyes. Presha's instincts flared. This man chwas dangerous, though in ways she failed to understand. Without glancing up, the man flipped through the dust eaten pages until finding the one he sought. A skeletal finger traced over lines. Its nail was chipped and impossibly long. Dark mists spewed from his mouth as he coughed.

"The day of conquering shall at last arrive. One shall stand forth from our ranks to claim his rightful place among the stars. The savior. The slayer of humanity."

Presha recoiled. The equerry's voice sounded as a death rattle. The cold mockery of living death. Tiny fingers of fear slithered into her subconscious. She had traveled half the universe since fleeing Crimeat after the failed insurrection attempt and encountered a host of mysteries and creatures beyond imagination. What she saw in the shriveled husk of a man before her turned her stomach. Few things screamed danger as much as the equerry. *Father, what dark powers have you sold your soul to?*

"You speak of Amongeratix," she suggested.

The equerry ignored her. "It is a prophecy from old times. An age when humanity struggled from the reigns of slavery. The gods may be forgotten by many, but they have long memories. He is coming. Balance will be restored."

Presha cracked her knuckles and scowled. "Speak plainly. Amongeratix has returned and wages his campaign across the stars. The Conclave is locked in civil war, threatening to tear all we have built apart. How much more can we accept before the Three dominate again?"

His hooded head turned, fixing Presha with a baleful glare. "Prophecies are often misread. I have consulted the powers lurking in the night. They all agree. It is not a *he* we await for the revival."

Her mouth went dry. "What do you mean?"

"You, Presha Von, are the destroyer of worlds, come to bring ruin to us all."

High above, locked in his cell, Geres Auk caught the first whispers of madness howling in the quiet corner of his mind. He broke into a grin and began pounding a fist on the cold iron wall. The warrior turned protector at last understood his role in the universe. A reckoning approached. He pounded harder as the howling increased.

"Daughter, I … I am sorry," Olex admitted as he paced the room.

His hands were clasped behind his back. His jaw set in consternation. Forgotten fatherly instincts resurfaced and it was all he could do not to whisk his only child away from the torment and horror of the future.

Presha regarded him coldly. They seldom crossed paths after her mother died. Unsuited to be a parent, she viewed Olex as an errant guardian, ineffective and pointless. She struggled with finding a spark of love in her heart, but time produced thick callouses.

"I have always known I was destined for a life greater than any on this planet," she said after much thought. "Amongeratix and I have crossed paths numerous times since the dark council helped free him from these very walls. He is a cancer upon which our species rots. If what this equerry says is to be believed, he is no longer the preeminent threat to our survival. It is me."

"The creature speaks in riddles and misdirection," Olex scoffed. "Believe not when he claims you are the harbinger of doom. You are my daughter and heir to my house. Nothing more."

"Father, how can you be so sure?" she replied. A gentle hand swept through the creases of her dress. "You did little to raise me. Indeed, you had no idea I was part of the council. Ever since I was a child, I dreamed of power. Of controlling men and women to achieve my goals. Is it so far-fetched to imagine the universe at my fingertips?"

He stopped midstride. "You speak madness. This place is cursed. A haunting laid down by eldritch magic. It is clear what I must do. Give me a little time and I will get you out of here. You should not have come back."

Her laughter pierced the gloom. "Where else can I run? Agents of the true Inquisition hound my moves. They know what it is I bear in my possession and will stop at nothing to secure it. I am the threat they have long feared. Nowhere in the universe is safe for me."

Olex considered her, struggling to accept his daughter with what she had become over the past few years. Grown to a fine woman, she bore striking resemblance to his wife. But the similarities ended there. Presha was headstrong and determined, like him. Ruthless at times, her cunning nearly resulted in the complete usurpation of the ruling body of nobles. It was by a throw of chance she became the most wanted woman in the universe.

"Is it true?" he asked, unwilling to finish the thought.

Presha opened and closed her mouth in second thought. How much did he know? In truth, how much did anyone know of her deeds on Kharsis? She blew out a steady breath before her confession. "Yes, though perhaps not as you were led to believe. It was by chance alone I activated the artifact and killed the god on Kharsis. His death unleashed a defense mechanism that killed all life, rendering the planet a dead rock."

He gasped. Horror etched in the lines of his face.

"How was I to know what would happen? I do not believe I am evil, for no one truly does. That does not excuse the wickedness of my actions, for millions are now dead by my hand. These are difficult times. I did what was asked of me. No more. Do you judge me harshly, father?"

She withheld the full truth. That she was too eager to obey Amongeratix's command and prove her worth. It was an act of aggression born from the desire to be needed and to exact a measure of revenge against the Conclave forces that pushed her out of her roost on Hawker's Gate. Guilt riddled her mind since. Flickering images of dying plant life and citizens crumbling into ruin teased her at night. She was a shell of the woman she once was. A gift from the cruel gods and a whisper of what awaited all humanity.

Ignoring the question, he instead asked, "Where is this artifact now?"

"It is safe, and far from here," she answered. "You need not worry of Crimeat suffering a similar fate."

Any notion of rescuing his daughter faded with the contempt in her tone. "Why did you come back, Presha?"

"I had nowhere else to go."

The storm abated sometime during the night. Blackheart removed his hat and squeezed the water from it. Prekhauten weather gear proved notoriously poor quality. Their small command tent leaked relentlessly, drenching them all to the bone. It was a small price to pay for the knowledge they were closing in on their prey. He paused after catching huddled figures staring.

"You look like a drowned rat," Krimpen Mass snorted.

Ever at his side, Time chuckled through his pain.

Blackheart scowled but held his tongue. There was no arguing with either man.

"He's not wrong," August seconded. Her eyes never left the scroll of data on the small pad before her.

Fuming with impotent rage, Blackheart waggled a finger at them all. "Just wait until I get back on the deck of my ship and away from this madness! I never should have agreed to ally myself with brigands and worse. Do you have any idea where I come from?"

"Oh, we know," Krimpen nodded. "Me and Time here, we done our research. You are the spoiled brat of a wealthy family."

"Famous one, too," Time added.

"S'right. Why do you think we're sticking around? Figure the reward keeps getting higher, the more we do," Krimpen said.

"There's no reward, you idiots. This is life or death. We're not here to play your simple games," Blackheart scolded. He threw his hands up.

Krimpen pointed back at him. "Careful, friend. We ain't the ones to fool with. Me and Time got a score to settle with that big bastard. You give us his head and we're square."

"Quiet down, all of you," August warned. Her hand flew to her earpiece. A thin smile crept across his face a moment later. "Reinforcements are on the way. If you three can keep from killing each other, I am going out to meet them."

The sound of Blackheart grinding his teeth followed her outside. August shook off their negative effects and breathed the damp night air. Despite inhuman magics and the god-rot surrounding the old prison from when Amongeratix escaped, she was reminded of warm summer nights during childhood, when she and her sister would go down to the water's edge to catch the multicolored glowing insects of her home world. Fond as the memory was, August expected it would forever be marred by what must be done here.

Footsteps drew her attention. Without her helmet, August was forced to rely on natural senses. Shadowy figures emerged from the night. They spread out and took up positions forward of the tent without a word spoken. Their leader halted before her and saluted.

"Captain, I have two platoons of Marines with me. Where do you want us?"

Relief washed over her face. August knew they were coming but it had felt like an impossibility until setting eyes on her Marines. "Sergeant Talore, good to see you. Did you encounter any resistance?"

"No, ma'am. The locals stayed inside for the most part. Guess they've had enough of the Guard poking its nose around," Talore replied. His voice was thin and ill-suited to a man of his size. "Pirate giving you trouble?"

She made a show of rolling her eyes. "No more than usual. Have your people take up a static line defense until we figure out our best avenues of approach."

August left out how much was at stake. The casual reminder was enough for less than spectacular moments, but the fate of the universe hung on her decisions. Some things didn't need to be said. She led him back into the tent and allowed him time to remove his helmet before starting.

"We have determined there is one main access point. Here," she pointed to the small holographic map from her activated datapad. "Amongeratix's escape produced a number of smaller, less accessible rents in the perimeter. Each is large enough to allow squirters out without being noticed."

"I can have snipers emplaced for that," Talore confirmed. "Any idea how many targets are within?"

She shook her head. "The Conclave went to great lengths to ensure this was one of the most secure facilities in the universe. Every attempt at digital or thermal imaging has failed. Residue from the former shielding permeates the atmosphere. Our scanners have been haywire since we arrived. Worse comes to worst, I will call in an airstrike from *Solstice*. Have your people been briefed on their primary targets?"

"Yes, ma'am. Most of us had friends at the Gate," Talore said. "We've been itching for some payback ever since."

"Sergeant, this is not a revenge mission. We are to capture alive at all costs. Presha Von may hold the key to stopping this war," August said. Her tone was less than convincing.

Talore stiffened but did not comment. His eyes swept over the graphics. "What sort of diversion do you want to draw them out?"

"I think a few well-placed plasma rounds should be sufficient," she replied.

Krimpen's eyes widened. Until now, it was a matter of hunting down their quarry and exacting a measure of revenge for the wounds they suffered in Lethendweil. Heavy weapons never figured into his thinking, nor the damage they were capable of inflicting. He cleared his throat with a not-so-subtle cough.

"Is everyone forgetting the important part?" he demanded. "There's a crazy lady in there with a planet killing weapon. You get her mad enough and this is another Kharsis."

"Lots more people here than back home," Time added.

"Relax, gentlemen. I have no intention of repeating the past," August told them. "Sergeant, should it come down to that, I want no trace of Lady Von's head remaining on her shoulders. Understood?"

"Clear, ma'am."

"Good. Deploy your people, Sergeant. I want this ended tonight," August ground through clenched teeth.

Marines moved off into the night, leaving her alone with a pair of addle-brained misfits and a pirate lord she still wasn't convinced she could trust.

Planet Occanum.

Tannus took his first steps upon his ancient home world and felt the crushing weight of eternity pressing down on him. Memories flitted past. Some good. Others not. The same niggling doubt he carried for thousands of years resurfaced, prompting him to question if he truly was the catalyst for everything that had occurred over the span of the Conclave's reign. It was a pointless exercise. What was done was done and there was no returning to any semblance of what had been. Alone in a foreign universe, Tannus found carrying on more tiresome as the years fled past.

Dust kicked up in billowing clouds with each footstep. An ugly landscape of dust stretched before him, accented by the forever darkness of space. Home. He snorted. Naught remained but ash and bitter scars savaging the planet. Once, majestic cities dominated lush forests and rivers. Occanum teemed with life. It was the fitting center of the universe from which his kind ruled with utter surety. Once, but no longer.

All that ended the day he questioned his father in front of the court. The subsequent banishment led to an irreparable schism and then war. Tannus cringed at the memory of that final battle that all but eliminated his race. Desperate months hiding a paltry remnant of his people, with the aid of his cousin, Paradise Tear, as the warring factions tore each other apart. Together, Tannus and Paradise hid over seven hundred of their kin across the universe, one to each occupied planet. It was a last-ditch gambit doomed to fail if Amongeratix ever discovered the truth, for his brother ever suffered from the pains of jealousy.

They were placed in statis one by one and left to sleep until the time arose when they would be needed again. He sealed them in and used Paradise's genetic coding to activate the pods. She was the key to their survival. Tannus placed her in stasis with great reluctance, for he knew he would need others to speak with as time wore on. How she was discovered on the shores of the Bo a few years prior remained a mystery to them both and placed them all in renewed danger. Amongeratix was quick to learn of her retrieval and made it his purpose to find her and unlock the codes of his sleeping people.

"You drift into the past, brother."

Tannus jerked back to reality. It had been long since he last confronted his brother. "Sorrow, what is the meaning of this? Ever you seek to dissuade me with your games."

The Bloody Man emerged from the darkness. His blood covered body a stark contrast to the bleak grey of their surroundings. "Tannus, you must learn patience. We are entering the final stages of the long game. Now is not the time to rush forward blindly."

"I am a busy man, brother," Tannus growled. His patience was sorely beset. "Why did you summon me to this place?"

Sorrow extended his arms in a sweeping gesture. "This was our home. I know you remember, even if you are too jaded to find the brightness of it."

"Father ended any love I once held for *home* when he cast us out," Tannus replied. "I never wanted any of this, Sorrow. The war. The destruction. The … responsibility."

"None of us did, though you were set to continue his reign," Sorrow added. Genuine regret reflected in his gaze.

Tannus turned, avoided his brother's stare.

"Amongeratix is getting closer to enacting his final plan," Sorrow continued after a moment. "We are not ready to stop him."

"This delay further puts us back."

"Brother, he is ready to launch his assault on Vau Prime," Sorrow pressed. "Should he usurp the Conclave, he will have access to the largest military force in the universe. We will not be able to stop him with our meager forces."

Tannus' eyebrow rose at the term *our* but he held his tongue. "I have elements in play as we speak. Should they succeed, we will have more than enough military backing to continue the war. However, sacking Vau Prime is concerning."

"And seemingly, inevitable, if we cannot disable *Behemoth* and leave his army stranded in deep space," Sorrow concluded.

Sly bastard. How much else do you know, I wonder. What spies have you in my midst? "What of the Paladin?"

Sorrow jerked back, not expecting the question. "She is … on the Forsaken Path."

"Learning the truth of our origins," Tannus frowned. "Has the Prophet reconnected?"

"You know he was killed on An'kuruku during the battle to rescue Paradise Tear," Sorrow used his own play to throw Tannus off guard. "I have no doubt his shade has found her, however. She will return with the totem and we will at last be able to force our brother to see reasoning through his storms of madness."

"Amongeratix will not relent after so many millennia. You know what must be done," Tannus said.

Sorrow held up his hands. A drop of blood spilled to the ash and was swallowed. "I will not kill my own brother. No matter how dire our position becomes."

"That choice may not be up to us, brother," Tannus said. "The future is in motion. I will go to the Grand Mistress of the Blood Witches for guidance. She has never failed me."

"You know what she will caution."

Tannus turned to leave.

"I know."

His words were whispered on the still atmosphere. Tannus closed his eyes, wrestling with ancient demons. He knew what must be done, and despite three thousand years of coming to accept it, was loath to.

Sorrow watched him go. Tears flowed down his cheeks.

Capital District, Krenz, planet Vau Prime.

They stole through the shadows. Golden faced killers with murderous intent. Three Vaumagian assassins stalked the night in search of their prey. None spoke. There was no need to. Each was enhanced with telepathic biometrics capable of sending and receiving messages from their kin. Science evolved them into the perfect killing machine, and though they often met with failure, they were the most feared weapon in the known universe.

The faceless killers glided down alleys and disappeared from the human eye as they crossed near empty streets. With the curfew in full effect and a host of firefights breaking out nightly across the city, there was little concern of being discovered. Armed patrols in light anti-armor vehicles prowled the main avenues. Huddled bands of pedestrians scurried away, eager to return home without being stopped, or worse. Krenz was a nightmare landscape of military oversight. Whatever hold the Conclave once held here, was gone.

Stolen from their parents at birth, the assassins were raised to despise humanity. Each underwent an augmentation process making them more machine than human. They were wholly subservient to their masters by the time training and indoctrination ended, making them the ultimate weapon in an increasingly dark universe. Single file, they slipped into the shadows and disappeared down a string of forgotten sewage tunnels running the length of the central district.

Abandoned for centuries, the tunnels were a brittle piece of history few bothered with. Improvisations in waste management negated the need for antiquated technology. Some were permanently encapsulated and shut down to prevent security breaches into the government complex. Others, like the one they followed, remained delicious secrets to those who wished their business to be conducted without oversight.

They were under the exterior wall and heading closer to the Conclave headquarters in moments. Broken down maintenance robots filled entire sections. The assassins sped by, assured no alarms would be tripped in their passing. Their employer was specific in his instructions. Reaching an intersection with five branches, the leader flowed into the second from the right and picked up his pace. They were close. Hurrying to meet their deadline, they ran as fast as they could. Onyx capes trailed after. The only sound of their passing was the occasional drip of water splashing from the ceiling.

The assassins gained the end of the tunnel. An access door blocked their way. Halting, the leader produced a digital key and pressed it against the control panel. The red locking light blinked green and the door slid open. The assassins drew daggers as they entered the Conclave subbasements. Dim lights illuminated these floors. Used for maintenance and storage, few of the clergy ventured this deep. It was a fallacy that would be fatal beyond repair tonight.

None of the assassins expected to survive. It didn't matter. They were tools to be used and discarded as their masters saw fit. So long as the mission was successful and the employer pleased with the results, each killer considered his purpose fulfilled. That narrow mindset was instilled in them from the first moment of conscious thought. They climbed a string of stairs, for the lowest levels were constructed long before the modern conveniences of technology. Limestone crumbled beneath their boots but up they went.

A second door blocked their way, and the leader again bypassed the security systems. Their employer spared no expense, or tool. His desire for this foul deed to be completed before the night ended was relayed to the masters. The urgency of their assignment did little to deter from their professionalism. Vaumagians were machines of singular purpose.

Brighter lights now lined the halls. The floors transformed from dust laden dirt to immaculate tile. Skeleton crews comprised the night shifts, and they were few and far between. The oppressive black of the assassins' uniforms stood out against the soft tan walls. Rather than fret over their obviousness, they moved faster. They were under strict orders to avoid all contact, to the point of aborting their mission, should they be discovered. Footsteps echoed in the tunnel behind them, followed by the sound of two men laughing and talking. The leader glanced at the chrono counting down on his faceplate. They were meters away from the access shaft. Discovery now meant mission failure.

A warning light flashed on their faceplates. The trio slipped into a slight alcove to avoid detection. The leader pressed his gloved thumb against the genetic entry of the access shaft and was rewarded with the camouflaged passage hissing open. They were within and the door sealed before the workers ambled closer. The leader discarded the glove and the stolen genetics embedded in the microfibers in a flash receptacle as the tiny compartment rocketed up through the spine of the Conclave's inner sanctum.

They slowed and stopped soon after. Each assassin crouched, expecting contact as the door slid open. Quasi-darkness greeted them. Helmets converted to night vision. Thermal sensors drilled into their optic fibers provided immaculate sight through the gloom. The leader stepped forward into the apartment level of the highest members of the Conclave. There were no guards. No roaming sentries to ensure their wards were protected. A critical failing in the wake of the murder of the previous Cardinal Seniorus. The assassins crept now, earning their name as they began to stalk their unsuspecting prey. Down the hall they went, until they arrived at the final door.

A quick glance to the others confirmed all were prepared. The leader used his last keycard and accessed the private quarters of the Cardinal Seniorus. The rooms were pitch black. A rustle in the far room suggested their target was sleeping, stirring in restless slumber as his universe steadily burned around him. Each step the assassins took was deliberate. The others cleared the rooms, ensuring they were alone, as the leader inched closer to his target.

The assassins converged on the last door. The last obstacle preventing them from completing their task and returning to the anonymity of obscurity. Cocking his head, the leader considered an infinite number of possibilities. His concern over the final door being unlocked, and them not being provided an access code wore on his shoulders. Was the mission too easy? Did the Conclave suspect treachery? It was not his place to question, or reason plausible scenarios. He gripped his dagger tighter and wedged the door open with the toe of his boot.

No alarm sounded. No armed guard met them with blasters firing. Only the quiet of night and the steady rise and fall of their target's chest beneath the sheets remained. The third assassin turned to watch their egress point. The second hurried back to the apartment's main doors. The leader stalked within and raised his dagger with each passing step. A foot from the bed and the occupant shifted. The leader froze. Advanced technology in his robes allowed him to blend with the darkness. He counted to five, and once assured the target was still asleep, completed his journey.

The dagger plunged down.

Inquisitor General Alain Nye sat in his favorite chair staring off into the artificial lights of Redemption Boulevard. He tapped the arm nervously with his left hand and gripped a glass with the last sip of the evening's liquor in his right. The golden fluid sloshed to the lip before settling. Nye discovered an alarming truth over the course of the last few months. He learned his anxiety levels rose with each new challenge. Being one of the most powerful men in the universe was not supposed to be like this.

Disappointed with the current trajectory, Nye decided the time was right for a total overhaul. He willingly allowed the bloodthirsty Mobus Kale his campaign of subjugation and torment. Anything to remove the insidious Davith Strannan and his band of insurgents from Vau Prime. They were the one obstacle impeding his success. Remove them and the planet was secure. Then he could look to the stars and begin retaking precious systems who proclaimed their independence as the Conclave and Insurrection tore themselves apart in civil war.

Compounding his miseries was an accelerated timeline. Amongeratix was in increased contact with his headquarters. The vengeful son aimed to claim the center of humanity as his first prize and transform it into a brutal seat of power. Nye was under no illusions as to what would occur. The histories were filled with instances where Amongeratix won. Entire populations were slaughtered at whim, ruining planets for generations. Every moment Nye delayed securing Vau Prime set up the inevitable conclusion to the grand human experiment.

Frustration furrowing his brows, Nye downed the last of his drink. He hadn't spent decades scheming to lose everything to a tyrant. A savage whip of the wrist sent the glass crashing into the wall. Bits of shattered glass spilled across the immaculate floor. *Time. I need more time!* It was the one item there was none left to him.

His private channel activated from his desk. Nye glowered at it, expecting more dismal news. Failures piled around him these days. "What?"

"It is done."

The line went dead.

Alain Nye sank back into his chair. The wind stolen from him. A thin smile crawled across his face. One less obstacle remained.

TWENTY-FOUR

3215 A.G. (After Gods), the Forsaken Path.

"Are you certain?"

The ghost of Mollock Bolle cocked his head. Not even death unlocked the mysteries of mortal communication skills to him. His limited time with Elisa on Crimeat failed to inspire any deep lasting notions of camaraderie or friendship. She had been a fellow captive, trapped in a struggle neither understood. She, on the other hand, rose above the constrictions of her station to become a powerful force rival to the Three. He wished he was born with the inner strength, but he'd always been a coward. Mollock thought his plight ended as he drew his final breaths. It was a fool's wish. Fate had more in store for him. The crimson of his robes was faded now. The lines beneath his eyes deeper. He saw his reflection in a grime smeared mirror upon their entrance to the forgotten city of Goti Tai. Mollock longed for the peace of death as he stared at a face he failed to recognize. His soul was tired. Perhaps, just perhaps, helping Elisa was his key to eternal rest.

"I have seldom been certain, Elisa," he replied. "This realm is unlike anything either of us have experienced. The mortal laws do not abide here."

She glowered at him. "That is not reassuring."

"All I know is, that I am to guide you to the First Paladin," Mollock said. "He is here."

Elisa hung her head, greasy red locks dangling over her face. "I never asked for this."

"None of us have."

She raised her head and looked him in the eyes. "Why us? What was so special about the two of us, that sent us far from all we knew and loved, to this miserable pit of a realm?"

It was a pointless question. Mollock knew neither were loved by any. Her old life was robbed during an encounter with the Bloody Man. His vanished the night he discovered the truth of the gods. Prophet and Paladin. Their fates were forever intertwined. At least so far as the Three had use for them.

He shifted closer to her in a vain attempt at comfort. "We are doing this for the greater good of seven hundred worlds and the continuity of our species. Amongeratix is a relic from the distant past. He should have vanished with the rest of his kind."

"But he did not. Instead, he rises every other generation to plague us, kill us, and devolve us back to the slave state our ancestors languished under," Elisa growled. "I have studied much of the histories during my time with Tannus. They detail what the Conclave has kept secret for three thousand years. We were little more than chattel.

"Forgive me, Mollock. I latched upon a moment of weakness and took it out on you unfairly. I may have no desire to serve as the Paladin but it appears I have no choice," her shoulders slumped as she exhaled. "Our lives were ruined the moment we made contact with the gods. I would not have the whole of the universe suffer, if my actions can stop Amongeratix and end the threat of the gods' return for good."

A thin smile creased his weathered face. "I knew you would find reason through the madness. Come, the First Paladin is at the ancient heart of Goti Tai. Let us end this stage of the quest as heroes."

Heroes. The notion sent shivers down her spine. Never in the entirety of her existence did she imagine herself a hero. She followed the shade, hoping against hope he was right. Her body was sore. Her heart pained at having brought the man she loved to this godsforsaken realm. A quick glance showed her Ah'muf marching alongside without comment. *He's a good man. Far better than I deserve.*

"Courage, Ah'muf. Our quest nears the end. Soon we will see our friends again," she whispered.

He bobbed his head. "It is not that I worry with, *farisi*."

She empathized with his arguments. None of them wished to be here yet wishes were the last consideration. Elisa learned to accept who she was meant to become, rather than remaining in the dismal past. It did little to assuage her guilt for having dragged him along, even though she knew she had nothing to do with it. Ah'muf followed his heart. And that was ever a dangerous proposition. *Does he know he is the iron I lean on? Can I tell him without insulting that foolish desert pride?*

He reached out to gingerly touch her forearm before hefting his pack higher and striding ahead.

Bastard.

The endless maze of Goti Tai might once have been majestic. Wind worn building jutted from the sand and dirt, suggesting stunning architecture, unlike any they had ever seen. Once Elisa might have scoffed at the notion, but that was long ago. She had fled the cold comforts of her home world and spanned the breadth of the universe in search of purpose and meaning. She found it here, of all places, at the broken end of the bottle with time running out. A dozen worlds filled her memories, each more incredulous than the last. Whatever Goti Tai was today, she had no doubt it was once the jewel of this realm.

Brief images of Crimeat becoming a wasteland teased her mind's eye. Elisa held no love for her home, but neither could she willing accept its demise. There were good people on Crimeat, freed from the influences of the Three. They deserved better than to fade into a forgotten past, naught but dust and ruin.

"We are nearing the end," Mollock announced over a swirling wind whipping through the ruins. "The First Paladin is not far now."

"What of our hunters? Could it be true we have lost them at last?" Elisa hoped.

She was tired of fighting impossible creatures ripped from the depths of her darkest nightmares. The sheer impossibility of all they'd seen and survived mocked her sense of realism.

Mollock kept moving. "I have no answer for that, Elisa. We must move swiftly. I feel my soul being stretched. As if my time here is finite."

They rounded a corner and were confronted with a lone avenue forward. The path of no more than two hundred meters rolled up a gradual slope to an unsuspecting home. It had one door and no windows. What remained of the roof was filled with holes. Nothing about it suggested value. Twin rows of statues lined the path. Each portrayed a squat reptilian-being with a natural shell on its back and a wicked spear in its right hand. Clearly warriors, each glared straight ahead. Hundreds of immaculately carved teeth lined their mouths. Guardians.

Elisa surmised it was once the place a worthy being would spend his days. The answer to all her questions, problems, and dreams lay just ahead. She took her first step on the final stretch and faltered. Now that she was here, the bounty hunter found her steps heavy. Her legs refused to obey. Random thoughts swirled through her mind. She lost the will to continue.

"Mollock! I can't move," she tried to shout.

Her voice came out a strangled warble.

The shade turned, unaffected. "The guardians do not want us here."

Tears spilled down her cheeks. "Stop them. We must find a way."

Ah'muf cried out and fell to the ground. Pain lanced his veins, forcing him to curl into a tiny ball of bruised flesh. A great horn blared across the sky. As one, the guardians stepped onto the path and turned toward the intruders. Spears leveled. Hissed breath beat hard on the wind.

All this way, only to be killed by a fucking turtle! Elisa wanted to laugh. She wanted to shout her outrage to the skies, but no words came. Her throat constricted. Time was almost up. Every step the guardians took brought her inevitable demise. Where the strength arose from, she would never learn. It was that inner wellspring where hope so often clashes with despair that gave her the strength to resist. To combat the magic freezing them in place. Inch by precious inch. Elisa's fingers curled around her blaster. She drew. The guardians moved closer.

Her veins felt afire as she curled her fingers around the comforting grip. Every inch gained was won through maximum effort. Sweat poured down her face. Elisa squinted and pulled with all her might. The blaster tugged free, rising through great exertion. Every moment a struggle, she slipped her index finger into the trigger well, relishing the cool feel of metal on flesh. Inch by inch, she brought her blaster higher until she was confident she would at least strike one of their attackers before being sliced to ribbons. But which one?

There were no discernable differences in them. Each was the exact replica of the one standing beside it. A menacing figure dredged from the depths of ancient despair to protect Goti Tai and keep its secrets. Her eyes the only unfrozen part of her, Elisa scanned the gathering crowd for any sign of weakness. It proved a pointless endeavor. Not a one had a distinguished feature marking leadership or command. Frustrated, she made peace with firing until she no longer could. The trigger clicked with each subtle move.

A crimson glimmer caught her eye. Could it be? Elisa narrowed her focus on the object. There, transfixed at the base of the throat of the center defender was a fist sized crimson jewel. It was worth a try. Hope threatened to rise, and Elisa fought to keep it contained, lest the disappointment of failure proved too much. She took aim. The enemy ground forward one agonizing step at a time. Dust clouds kicked up with their approach. She felt fear surge through her veins with each step the enemy took. They were close enough to spy the serrated edges on their spear tips. Death promised to be painful. She squeezed the trigger with all possible strength.

The superheated energy round struck the defender to the right of the target, tearing great chunks of petrified flesh away in a spark of ash and fury. Panicked, Elisa took a calming breath and fired again. And again. The second evaporated the defender's lower jaw. The third struck true. As one, the defenders froze in place. Elisa found she could move again. She fired another round just in case. None moved. It was then she noticed how close the spears were to her. Another few steps and she would have been skewered.

A groan behind her suggested Ah'muf was recovering. She risked a glance over her shoulder and was relieved to see the desert dweller picking himself up from the dust. The shade of Mollock Bolle wasted no time and shifted through the impossible ranks to the base of the steps leading into the temple. After seeing he was neither assailed nor confronted, Elisa decided it was time to move. Magic, she learned over the past few years, had a way of shifting without warning.

"Ah'muf, we must hurry. This is our only chance," she urged.

He shook his head, dust and debris falling from his greasy hair. "Chance to run into another trap. This place has a fell undercurrent."

She grunted in agreement. "Like it or not, this is where we are meant to be. The Bloody Man would not have sent us here for no reason."

Together they hurried through the massed ranks of armed defenders until they stood beside Mollock. Her heart pounded as she wove through the frozen statues. Visions of being trapped in their midst toyed with her. It was, she decided, a most devious way of eliminating potential desecraters or looters. Gaining the steps, Elisa let out a long breath she hadn't realized she'd been holding.

Every step of her journey had been fraught with peril, from being the sole survivor of her village to fighting her way across the stars as she slowly accepted her role as Paladin. It was a thankless task. She wondered how her former companions were faring in their unique journeys. Tannus was convinced this was the final push to rid the universe of his kind and his brother's threat. Elisa had doubts. She spun at the massive grinding sound behind her, rifle sliding from her shoulder and charging in a well-rehearsed move.

To her amazement, the defenders marched back to their original positions. Their task complete. *Looks like we passed the test. Now, to see what this First Paladin has in store for us.* The unlikely trio climbed the temple steps. Each was conflicted with warring emotions none were prone to discuss. Elisa studied her friends. Certain this was the end for Mollock, the shade of the Prophet expected to be released back into the ether once his task was complete. He strode confidently ahead, a weary look etched upon his brow. The promise of freedom beckoned and his longing to at last depart the realms of life surged. Ah'muf was a different story. Determined to stick by her side out of love, the desert dweller had dreams of returning to An'kuruku and forgetting all that had happened since first encountering her in that café, what felt like a lifetime ago. His bravery was a fragile shell ready to break.

Elisa ignored her personal feelings. They did little to influence her actions. She had become a machine in the service of a greater power. It was a life forfeit of desire. Want and need reduced with call to higher purpose. The bounty hunter turned savior ached to be done with her task. To put the Bloody Man behind her, and at last, discover if she could survive with a life rebuilt around who she wanted to be. That dream was stolen from her youth. Robbed of any potential life, Elisa knew nothing else. The scars left to her psyche were permanent. Victory or failure, she was trapped with who she was.

They entered the gaping darkness of the temple. Eyes struggling to adjust to the gloom, she halted just inside the threshold. Echoes of their footsteps reverberated deep into the dark. She lost sense of dimension. Another test? Perhaps one final cast of the die to ensure she was worthy of receiving the Grimfurvor. Growling her frustration, Elisa was tired of playing games.

"Show yourself!" she demanded of the dark. The trill of her voice repeated. "I am Elisa of Crimeat, appointed Paladin and champion of light. We have come far and will not be denied now!"

Champion of light? Where did that come from?

A pale light beamed down from what she judged the center of the chamber. A hundred meters away, Elisa stared at the frozen column.

Then she saw it. A lone figure swathed in dark robes sitting beneath the light. The First Paladin. An endless search across seas of monsters and increasing challenges at last drawn to a close. Her heart froze. What if she had journeyed this far only to be rejected as unworthy?

"At last, you have come. I have waited long for one such as you."

The voice bounced in her mind. Clear and concise. She risked a look to the others and knew they had heard it as well.

"Come closer, Elisa of Crimeat. I am Vishon Risa, the First Paladin."

She lifted her leg to move forward, halting with her boot inches from the ground. Cursing her self-doubt, Elisa forced her foot down and strode ahead with false confidence. The doors slammed shut behind.

Sauwgon Hul closed his eyes in a pointless attempt at calming his rising nerves. He had come so far since that fateful day he and his disciples set forth to discover the hidden truths leading his people to ruination. Now, he was the last. Their extinction a foregone conclusion, the shaman bristled with unimaginable power. He vowed the others did not die in vain, for the prize at the end of the journey went beyond mortal comprehension. Unable to focus, Sauwgon pushed himself to his feet and stretched.

His muscles were sore from the increasing challenge demanded of him. How far he journeyed, he did not know, only that every footstep brought him closer to the end. Mind ablaze with myriad possibilities, Sauwgon clutched his staff and was instantly recharged as the power from his disciples flowed into him once more. Their collective conscience whispered in the deepest corners of his mind, threatening to drive him mad with their impulses and combined hatred.

You betrayed us, shaman.

Lies! It was all lies!

A curse upon your bones. You will suffer once you join us.

"Be silent, all of you," Sauwgon chided. "All proceeds accordingly. This is how it must play out."

Murderer! You led us to our doom.

"I offered the chance for immortality," Sauwgon countered.

By entrapping us in the prison of your psyche. What glory can be found?

"It is not glory I seek, but survival."

No, Sauwgon. It is a path of lies you boldly march down. All for naught. Soon you shall be dust and with it, the end of our people. A curse upon your name.

"This is why I am the last. You are all fools! None of you have the vision I do. You were all found wanting," he fumed. "Be gone from me now. Your usefulness is ended."

Be careful what you wish for, shaman. It may not turn the way you expect. The white dragon is cunning.

The voices fell silent, their steady accusations ringing in his ears. When at last Sauwgon opened his eyes, he discovered he was in a new realm unlike any of the others he had traveled through to this point. Amethyst crystals the size of houses peppered the landscape as far as he could see. Dark clouds, tinged red, crowded the land. His neck tightened at the thought of being choked by their menace. Sauwgon Hil had witnessed many things during his life. None appeared so dire as the nightmare he now experienced. The ground trembled beneath his feet. Rivulets of lava burned between onyx sand and stone. It was, he deemed, a fitting place to end it all. With heavy heart, he took his first step forward.

The ground lurched as his moccasin struck. Sauwgon struggled to remain standing. Winds whipped sand and dirt at him, slashing into his flesh with vehemence. He laughed at his rising audacity. Challenging the will of the gods themselves, the shaman marched ahead more determined than before to gain answers. The feathers on his staff fell flat as the winds died. Sauwgon ignored the change. He knew the land feared him. Feared what he represented. Nonplussed, he picked up the pace.

Jagged mountains loomed ahead. Wreathed by lightning, he knew this was where he needed to be. Sauwgon channeled the strength of his disciples and was rewarded by their energy funneling through his veins. Each strength combined within him. His muscles grew. His stamina soared. Golden fire flickered from his eyes. He felt the change and it buoyed his spirits. The gods had much to answer for, if indeed there were gods. Above all else, Sauwgon wished to learn the secrets of the white dragon and why it chose his people to visit demise upon.

The shaman passed between two massive amethysts and was frozen mid-stride. He strained and surged against the invisible energy containing him but it was to no avail. Trapped, Sauwgon realized this was his final test. One last challenge to prove worthy. He gritted his teeth and prepared for the worst. It was not a long wait.

Funnels of rock and dirt burst from the ground in massive pillars. More than he easily counted. Through the perpetual darkness in each funnel sparked the slightest hint of light. Flames caught the air and grew. Twenty-five feet high, each broke free of its constrictions and formed the shape of men and women. All were blanketed by hungry flames licking the tepid atmosphere like newborns. Sauwgon blanched at the sight. Not even with the power of his disciples could he hope to defeat such massive beings. They, he decided, were to be the bearers of his destruction that would forever wipe the stain of his memory from existence.

Brandishing odd weapons the likes of which he had never seen, the flame giants turned on him. Their faces shocked him, for each was blank. Empty holes of darkness for eyes and mouths, the flame giants lacked mortal definition. Sauwgon struggled to comprehend what they were. Crowns of flames circled their brows. He felt the regal hatred pulsing off them, as if he were an affront to all they held dear.

Sauwgon Hil closed his eyes and began chanting words of power. They hummed in his chest, vibrating deep within the well of his soul until the ground beneath him trembled. The power web constricting him faltered. His strength grew. Sauwgon felt invisible as one hand broke free. He slammed his staff on the ground with as much strength as possible. Arcs of raw power flashed.

"I shall not be denied," he whispered.

Sauwgon brought his staff down again. Bolts of white-yellow energy speared forth, one for each of the flame giants confronting him. They rocked back, if slightly.

"I shall not be denied," his voice gained intensity.

Another blast of power flowed from him. The webs of power snapped. He was free. The trap dissolved, echoes of its strength drifting across his frame. Sauwgon opened his eyes. The flames burned brighter. He felt the land feeding him. Power, after all, recognized power. The flame giants hesitated, not expecting him to pass their test. Those nearest Sauwgon hefted their weapons.

"I shall not be denied!" he bellowed above the howl of the wind.

The shaman glared at the approaching giants. Their weapons perplexed him, for they were constructed of fire, an extension of their owners. Each was shaped like a spear but had several appendages. Sauwgon took the offensive and jabbed his staff to the giant on his right as he mouthed a spell. Water bubbled from the ground at the giants' feet. Steam hissed as it touched their flesh. Doubling his efforts, Sauwgon was rewarded by a wall of water gushing up to challenge the giants. Their weapons flickered before extinguishing. A minor victory, for more than a score more awaited their turn.

"Who's next?" Sauwgon challenged as the first two fell back.

They surged forward as one, quickly encircling him and lowering their weapons until the points of each was but inches from his face. Sauwgon Hil braced himself for the fight of his life. He slashed with his staff, inviting the last battle. Weapons clashed in a shower of sparks.

Behemoth, deep space.

Algiss Her, newly crowned Queen of the Red Sisterhood, gazed into the emptiness of space. She was unsettled by it and had been for years. The cold confines of the Abbey of Blood Witches left her with an unhealthy attitude toward space travel, and more importantly, the rising possibility of being devoured by the great blackness stretching into forever. Hands clasped together within the sleeves of her robes, Algiss knew any serenity she enjoyed could not last. The time of Forever Night was fast approaching, barreling at her with unprecedented fury. It was a conflagration the universe could not survive. She prayed she had been in time to save herself and a small portion of sisters who joined her cause.

Old hatreds stewed upon her brow. She was ever stymied under Ruma Zzein's outdated doctrine. Ever desirous of power, Algiss made her peace with abandoning all she swore to uphold and align herself with the growing power of Amongeratix. He was all too willing to accept her fealty and promise to bring war to the universe. Standing upon the bridge of his command ship, Algiss knew his was a strength that could never be undone.

Menials crewed the ship. The spoiled combination of failed genetics and mutations rendering each a pale mockery of humanity. Algiss viewed them with disgust. In her mind, there was no place in the future for such creatures. Two other sisters monitored the menials. Their crimson robes brought unholy light to the otherwise gloom of space.

Silent watchers, they represented the only strength active aboard *Behemoth*.

A quiet squawk disturbed the silence. Algiss snapped her head about to determine the source. Menials gibbered to one another in agitation. Her chest tightened. Old fears rising to taunt her mind. Scarred horribly from her failed coup attempt, Algiss Her knew she had been discovered. Red robes fluttered as a Sister drifted to investigate.

"We are registering a pair of power sources approaching the ship," one of her Sisters said, after studying the computer terminal.

Her tongue caught in her mouth before Algiss forced out, "Is it *them*?"

"Unknown signatures," the Sister replied.

Algiss clenched her fists. "How far out are they?"

"The first is still well over three hundred thousand kilometers. The second twice that."

"I want all weapon platforms operational and ready to engage before either ship gets closer. Activate any defenses onboard and prepare for battle. We must not let this ship fall into our enemy's hands."

"But Sister Her, we do not have positive identification. It could very well be Lord Amongeratix come to claim his flagship."

"And it might very well be Ruma Zzein and her Inquisitor reborn come for our heads," Algiss snapped. "I will not return to that den of villainy again."

Rebuked, the Sister bowed her hooded head. "We stand ready to serve."

As it should be. "Deploy our Sisters throughout the ship. I want one stationed at every potential boarding point. Let the fools come. We shall show them a welcome they will come to regret.

"It will be as you command," the Sister bowed again and began barking orders to the menial crew.

Algiss Her knew it was but a matter of time before her treason caught up to her. The Order of Blood Witches was ruthless in their pursuit of perceived wrongs. Time was running out. Her one chance of survival now rested in an antiquated battleship drifting through space and a subhuman crew with no concept of mortality. The odds of winning, depending on who was aboard the approaching craft, plummeted with each passing moment. She was determined to go down fighting, however, and was more than prepared to dole out what vengeance remained in her heart.

Behemoth continued on. Its course was set millennia ago. A time of great confluence approached, and with it, the fate of all life in the universe.

The Low Continent, planet Vau Prime.

Heavy winds reduced visibility to little more than a few meters. Ash and dust clouds swept across the low continent in a storm of unparalleled fury. Utan Husk marched across the wastelands, determined to reach his goal and complete the one task that had provided purpose during his incarceration. Hate fueling him, the former Guardsman was buffeted by the wind. Each step required strength. It was a struggle to remain upright, while the storm raged. Sand lashed the little exposed flesh. Lacerations crisscrossed his face. Tiny blood spots spread. Utan ignored them. Funneled down to a creature of singular purpose, he trudged closer to revenge and General Davith Strannan.

Violent memories mocked his approach. Pummeled under their torment, Utan rewatched each death by his hands over and over. He'd done what his commanders demanded. Subservient to the cause and the lofty moral decay of the Conclave, Utan Husk executed each mission with unparalleled lust. He didn't remember when the killing became a passion. The transformation was gradual until he thrived on the adrenalin rush the act of taking life produced. Prekhauten command took notice of his deranged attitude and made efforts to remove him from the field. What followed remained redacted until Mobus Kale went looking for expendable assets.

Utan had no qualms with his lot. He'd done terrible things and knew there was a reckoning coming, in this world or the next. All that mattered was finishing the task he had dreamed of for so many years. After that, nothing else mattered. Clamping his lips tighter to prevent the ash from slipping through, he kept moving. Step after step. Meter by meter. Rigid discipline pushed one foot in front of the other. Though infantry, Utan never cared much for walking. Advancing technologies should have nullified the need for basic foot soldiers. The Guard failed to adapt, leaving countless veterans disgruntled, and in his estimation, easy to manipulate.

He walked for three days after killing the lone survivor in his camp. Utan felt no pity over the man, for he was an obstacle and a liability. The risk of being discovered, knowing Strannan would have a network of lookouts and scouts peppering the area for kilometers in every direction, was too high to allow anyone to see his face. Even a lonely soul begging for some good to come from the burning. Conscience unburdened, Utan moved on.

His supplies were running low. Finding anything to eat or drink in this desperate land proved all but impossible, forcing him to tighten his rationing. Hunger pains cramped his torso. His tongue was almost too big for his mouth. His lips were cracked from the constant exposure to harsh conditions and his throat was perpetually dry. It was the worst he could remember, and there was no end in sight. All he had to guide him was a compass he knew wasn't working correctly and the looming shadow of a mountain range directly ahead. Reckoning Strannan was hiding here was a calculated risk.

Nothing in the intelligence brief he received from General Kale and his staff indicated they had the slightest clue to the rogue general's whereabouts. Utan figured it mattered little at this point. The human body was conditioned to last no more than seventy-two hours without water. He was nearing the end of the clock. If Strannan wasn't in the mountains, the most Utan could hope for was finding a stagnant pool or underground lake. Otherwise …

Day fled to night. The winds slackened, if barely, allowing him to move faster. The mountains were growing larger. He could feel victory. If nothing else, it would be a reprieve from the merciless sun. Utan was exhausted by the time he crept into the first gentle foothills. The dark black rock faces jutted from the ground like broken teeth, a visual reminder of the damage Mobus Kale and his campaign committed not only to the people of the low continent but the land.

Cool wind kissed his cheeks, marking the first pleasantness he'd had in days. Come the dawn, there would be enough opportunity to hide from the sun, and perhaps, avoid being pelted by the wind and ash. Utan removed the cloth from around his head and wiped the sweat. Freed from the fabric, his head instantly became cold. Repressing a shudder, he leaned back against the nearest rockface and closed his eyes. The back of his head thumped against the stone, a casual reminder tougher times were still ahead. He was exhausted. Utan considered himself a tough man, but everyone had limits. He was fast approaching his.

"Keep your hands where we can see them," a thin voice commanded.

Utan opened his eyes to narrow slits, scanning the shadows. "I didn't come looking for trouble."

"You shouldn't have come at all," a second voice replied from the opposite side.

At least two. Armed. They are either bandits or Guard.

"Don't seem to have anywhere else to go, thanks to those damned Guards," he lied. "I been on the move for months now. Don't suppose you folks got enough space for me just for the night? I, I don't think I can go on without a good rest and some hot food."

A third voice, perched higher up, said, "We don't take in strangers, not unless they came with a specific purpose in mind."

"What purpose would that be?" Utan asked.

Boots crunched the gravel. "You tell us. No one walks these mountains without a reason."

Guards. Looks like I found you, Strannan. "Fair enough. I'm tired of being mistreated by them who is supposed to protect me. Rumor has it, there's some real nasty folks hiding out in these parts. Collecting an army to strike back, if it's to be believed."

"You a soldier?" the second voice asked.

"Who's asking?" Utan snapped back.

The third man grunted. "You got that right. He's got the killer gleam in his eyes. Either that or he's a bandit."

"Ain't much to bandit around here, not since those fuckers from Krenz came down a'killin'," Utan played up the accent.

The first man emerged from the shadows. His uniform was battered, clearly worn through numerous engagements. Scoring on his chest plate suggested he was a lucky man. He walked with a limp on his right leg.

"Seems to me you're looking for some payback," he suggested.

Utan shrugged. "Depends how you mean."

Eyes shifting to the movement, he tracked the female stepping closer. Her rifle remained trained on his head. *Interesting.* She wasn't ready to take unnecessary chances. Utan almost approved of her demeanor, knowing far too few Guards were willing to go beyond their standard rules of engagement.

"He's got that cold killer gleam in his eyes," she said. "Give him some food and water and send him on his way."

"We need the manpower, Lieutenant," the first man said.

Bryn Mal scowled. "We also don't need the trouble. Man like this is bad news."

"Hold on now," Utan protested. "I ain't done nothing to you. Want answers? Aye, I can fight. Did my time in the Gameli Sector."

The Guards exchanged a glance. Bryn Mal edged closer. "Nasty business. I lost some good friends there. You get hit?"

"A few times," Utan answered truthfully.

She nodded. "How do I know you're here for the right reasons?"

"Because I don't have a reason. You say you need fighters. I can fight. Feed me, give me a few power packs, and point me at the enemy," he said.

"Works for me. Follow me," Mal ordered.

Utan fell in line beside her. The pair of rifles pointed at his back did not go unnoticed.

They wormed deeper into the mountains through a maze of jagged stone until Utan had little idea which direction they came from. He felt numerous gun emplacements in overwatch during the trek. Strannan may be disgraced, but the man had not lost any of his bite. Martial prowess was a developed skill, making Strannan the most lethal man on the low continent. Doubting his escape chances, Utan followed the Guards through a series of security positions and carefully camouflaged checkpoints. His dedication was rewarded by at last entering the hidden lair.

The noise within suggested hundreds of Guards, rebels, and willing insurgents were cramped into the cavern. His nostrils flared the deeper he went. The scents of latrines, unwashed uniforms, and body odor roiled his stomach. Utan was treated better in his cell.

"All right, *friend*. This is where we part ways. Quartermaster will see to your kit and find you a place to bunk after admin assigns you to a squad," Mal explained. "This isn't going to be pleasant, but you'll soon get all the fight you could ever want. Good luck to you."

He made an effort of a half-hearted salute and watched her depart. So far, so good.

TWENTY-FIVE

3215 A.G. (After Gods), Forward battle positions, planet Mannus Prime.

Jers pulled his combat blade from the neck of the woman he just killed and wiped the blood on the mud at his knee. The body, already limp and cooling, lay beside him. He regretted the manner in which he committed the act, but secrecy was demanded for this mission. Command whispered they were nearing the final push to break the enemy and claim Mannus Prime. He didn't care. All Jers wanted was to survive and escape the deepening madness inspired by the war. Sliding his blade back into place, he brought his rifle up and scanned for enemy soldiers.

Heat signatures detected by his helmet confirmed those nearest to him were friendlies. Prekhauten command went to great lengths to ensure a minimization of friendly fire incidents. They never counted on an open civil war. Jers took little comfort in having his closest companions at his side, however, for they all held the potential of turning traitor. In his estimation, it was a muddled affair, producing too much angst and trauma. He needed an escape.

"All squads, prepare to move out."

Lieutenant Fies's disembodied voice crawled over the intercom. One by one the Guards clicked acknowledgement. Jers tapped the button on the side of his helmet, changing the blinking icon on his visor to solid green. He drew a deep breath and climbed to his feet. The outer trench was secure. Additional forces already on Mannus Prime were pushing on the far side of the battlefield, giving the invaders from Falchi's task force an open door into the enemy camp. None of that concerned him more than a passing fancy their fight might be over sooner, and with fewer casualties than initially anticipated. Jers let the thought pass and focused on surviving.

"Move forward."

They stepped off in line. Jers trained his weapon on the nearest trench line and verified his squad was moving with him. Nine blips registered in his computer. He considered them fortunate to last this long relatively unscathed, but war had a nasty habit of leveling the field. He clutched his rifle tighter and picked up the pace.

"All elements, stay online," he said on their private channel. "I don't want anyone getting there before me."

"Copy."

"Roger."

Only one failed to respond. "Beve, you hear me?"

The deep rumbling of the squad's heavy weapon specialist hurt his ears. "I got you, Jers."

Bereft of vegetation, the land between trenches was a mud packed nightmare to cross. Each boot squished or splashed. Darkness prevented the Guards from seeing the ground clearly, but at least there were no branches or sticks to step on and snap. Thus far, surprise had been achieved. Jers expected the enemy waiting in their trench for the command to open fire and cut down the attacking force. How could they not know?

His helmet picked up the first enemy heat signatures. Jers clicked his safety off. His squad knew their orders. Close to a minimal distance and engage at will. The time for secrecy was over. This was their great push to snap the enemy rear and bring in the heavy armor provided by the Shadow Hammer mercenary brigade. He envied the men and women riding in their metal monsters. They didn't need to worry about mines or tripwires. Only the turret gunners were concerned with snipers. The rest were securely ensconced within inches of armor.

His rangefinder dropped to ten meters. Jers brought his rifle up and sighted on the first target. He squeezed the trigger with the cool precision of years of training. Until the war started on Crimeat, he had never fired his weapon in anger. Now, he couldn't stop. He was rewarded by watching the thermal imaging of his target's head evaporating in patterns of red and blue. As if on cue, the rest of the squad engaged their hated foes.

Jers almost felt sorry for the men and women in the trench. He doubted they were bad people. Most were like his squad, just doing their jobs. It was a shitty way to die. Focusing on a small command bunker to his right, Jers hurried. His calves burned as he sprinted across the uneven terrain and grasping mud. Jers gained the trench and tossed a grenade into the bunker entry. The explosion blew out bits of debris and flesh, almost knocking him down. Grunting, he jumped into the trench and sprayed his rifle inside the ruined bunker before entering. A handful of bodies, two wearing officer pins, were within.

The rest of his squad slipped into the trench. Biometric readings on his visor said all were still alive. He viewed it as a good sign, but the battle was just beginning. One way or another, the battle for Mannus Prime was coming to an end. Jers leaned against the ruined guidepost and exhaled a deep breath.

"You're not taking the night off on, are you, sergeant?"

He reluctantly opened his eyes and was rewarded with the menacing figure of Annalilly standing before him. "No, sergeant. Just catching my breath."

"Good. We've still got a lot to do." She pulled off her helmet and wiped the sweat from her scalp. Jers still found it odd to see her bald. "See to your squad. Water and ammo. We're not stopping here. Soon as the armor arrives we make the push."

"Roger that," he replied.

Annalilly tugged her helmet back on and broadcast to the command net. "Trench line secure. Bring those big bastards in."

The rumble of heavy engines echoed across the battlefield.

"All armor elements begin your assault."

Matthias felt a surge of adrenalin at the call. A far cry from his experiences on An'kuruku against the subverted forces of Amongeratix, this was a test of wills. Both armies were of similar training and weaponry. Evenly matched in terms of firepower, it was a war he never wished to see and one he couldn't escape. *I should have stayed retired. Damn Strannan.*

On the opposite side of the turret, Bootleg gave the order to attack. The Shadow Hammers, despite their fervent desire to kill Matthias at campaign's end, were highly skilled and ready to unleash a second round of misery upon their targets with the ruthless abandon of men and women fighting for money.

"What do you say, Matthias? Ready to kill some more traitors?" Bootleg chided.

Matthias ignored him. There would be a time of reckoning soon enough. No need to fuel the fire. The tank lurched forward and was soon speeding toward the first trench. Artillery shells roared overhead as the ground batteries softened up previously untouched defenses. His people were out there, fighting and dying in the night. Matthias longed to be with them but needs must. Service with the mercenary company was the price for securing their contract. It sat ill with him. Too many friends and former comrades already lay dead or wounded in filling hospital tents. He tried telling himself it was necessary to reforge the universe and save them all from the depredations of the Three. The lie had sustained him until now.

Blinking infrared marking lights lined the paths cleared of mines. Matthias looked back to see the armored column funnel into wedges. Once within the enemy perimeter, they would fan out in a broad line of destructive energy. The goal was to push to the camp's center and cut the head from the beast using the honed tactic of speed and ferocity. While Matthias bore no animosity for the Guards on the opposing side, he understood the need to eliminate as many of them as possible. Not only did they heavily outnumber his forces, they had proven a devout will to adhere to the commands of a corrupt regime. For such a crime, there was but one recourse.

Guards lined the path, waving the tanks and armored personnel carriers forward with raw enthusiasm. Matthias grinned. Nothing bolstered morale like seeing the giant armored beasts claiming dominance on the battlefield. Several Guards raised their rifles to the sky in cheer. He waved to them, simultaneously scolding their command structure for allowing this temporary lapse of focus. His heart surged when he felt the main gun powering up beneath his feet. Meters fled by as they approached the kill zone. This, Matthias decided, was what war was always meant to be.

"Passing second trench. All vehicles resume positions and fire at will."

Matthias gripped the firing handles on the crew served weapon moments before the tank lurched as it fired its first round.

Gunnery Sergeant Asom felt his mouth drop open as the raw destructive power of an entire brigade of armor opened fire. Nothing in his experiences in space combat were comparable to the awesomeness of the scene. Flames belched from barrels, followed by streaking lines of tracer fire as gunners targeted and picked off enemy soldiers with alarming speed and efficiency. It was a game of death far beyond his ability to comprehend. Not for the first time, Asom longed to return to the spartan comforts of the *Indomitable*.

"Stay calm, Marines. This one isn't our fight," he chimed over the intercom as a company of support vehicles pushed through.

The Marines had done their job, securing their section of both trenches and ensuring safe passage for the armor. He imagined their looks matched his. Ground warfare was not their specialty, and for that, he was thankful. Asom gathered his wits as the tanks fired again. Subsequent explosions shredded the night sky, bathing all in an unnatural inferno. The artillery fire lightened the deeper the advancing elements penetrated, affording Asom the opportunity to collect his thoughts and focus on the next stage of the assault. They, like the Prekhauten infantry to their left and right, still needed to push forward and clean out the rot infesting Mannus Prime.

He switched channels. "Sergeant Annalilly, this is Asom. My people are ready to advance."

"Copy, Asom. Standby for orders."

Cold. Methodical. She was an enigma he failed to understand. A consummate warrior, Annalilly was perpetually caught between a professional soldier and bloodthirsty tyrant. The dichotomy confused him. He preferred leaders with a direct mentality, eliminating confusion and striking at the heart of the matter right off the bat. The ground rumbled at the flow of armor continued into the enemy camp, robbing Asom's attention. Abandoning thoughts on the worrisome Guard detachment, he focused on the raw power of the brigade they were tasked to support.

Asom rechecked his squad vitals. Only one dead and a few wounded, nothing serious. He considered them fortunate. Were this shipboard action, his Marines would have suffered far worse. A green icon flashed and turned red. Asom spun, bringing his rifle up in the same motion. The shout went over the intercom before he could blink.

"Sniper!"

"Who got hit?"

Cursing. Bodies shuffled for cover. Asom watched their medic hurry to the body. "Busck, talk to me. Who bought it?"

"It's Starkweather. He's still breathing, but barely," the medic confirmed. Her voice threatened to break with anger.

"Get him under cover ASAP," Asom ordered. To the rest of the squad he barked, "Find me that fucking sniper and take him out!"

Marines fanned out, shifting their direction of approach to meet the threat. Asom made for the wounded man. A second round slashed across his night vision. Blood fountained from Starkweather's neck between his helmet and chest armor. The Marines opened fire. Ion rounds tore the nearest trees apart. Branches and heavy leaves fell in torrents. A heavy machine gun ripped streams of superheated death into the night.

Asom tore his gaze from the carnage in time to see Busck pitch backward. Her arms flew into the air as she fell. Dead before she hit the ground. He spied the hole in the center of her helmet visor and realized wounding Starkweather was a ploy to draw in more valuable squad members. It was a vicious style of warfare, one the Prekhauten command officially outlawed. Medics were supposed to be immune to slaughter on the battlefield. Hatred welled in Asom. The enemy had changed the rules. For that, they would die.

"Ivan, get that grenade launcher in play," Asom roared over the escalating din of battle. "Somebody kill the fucker! Now!"

The thump-thump-thump of the grenade launcher dominated the area. Acrid smoke drifted across Asom's vision, blotting out the target area in the split-second before grenades detonated. Marines rushed forward as the last round pelted them with rock and debris. Asom gave a last look to Busck and Starkweather, now both dead, and hurried into the fray. He was rewarded by one of his men gesturing with his rifle to the small blood trail leading away from the fight.

"We wounded him at least," Asom growled. "Isen, Grath, with me. Find me the body. Everyone else fall back and prepare to advance with the rest of the infantry."

He watched his people stalk back to their line of departure. The armor was plunging deep into the rear lines of the enemy camp. Nothing seemed capable of stopping them. Asom began the hunt. The trio formed a wedge and moved out. The blood trail grew larger and Asom knew death was only a matter of time. He spotted a discarded rifle smeared with blood. A few meters later, there was a broken helmet. They were close.

Asom passed between two massive trees and saw the boots first. Tracking right, he followed them up the legs, waist, and torso to find the sniper leaning back against a tree. Blood bubbled on his lips. What remained of the body was a pulped mess from the grenades. One eye was swollen shut. The right arm cauterized below the elbow. Asom felt no remorse. No pity for this killer. Prekhautens were meant to have honor, not fight like this.

Lowering his rifle, Asom drew his blaster and leveled it at the sniper's head. Asom pulled the trigger.

Doc Little pressed the bandage to Desril's thigh. "Hold this down while I tie it off."

"Of all the fucking places to get hit," the squad sapper growled. He punched the ground.

"Quiet already," Little snapped. "It's tough enough doing this without being shot at."

"Where's the rest of the squad?" Desril asked.

"Why?"

"Why? You don't expect me to sit this one out, do you? I got a job to do," Desril fumed.

Little jabbed a stubby finger at him. "I don't care what you do, but you can't fight with your leg like this. Understand?"

Snatching his rifle, Desril pushed up and took an unsteady step. Pain lanced up and down his leg, angering him further. He took another step, forcing through the discomfort, until he was confident enough to keep going. Hobbling after the rest of his squad, Desril didn't give the medic another look.

Little scowled but packed up his gear rather than put up a fight. Others were going to need him soon enough. Zipping up his field kit, Doc Little placed his hands on his knees and exhaled. A meaty hand reached down to help him up.

"You need a vacation," Haggle told him.

Small arms fire picked up. Little paused to drink some water from his canteen. "Doesn't look like it's going to happen tonight. Is anyone else wounded?"

"Not yet, but the night's still young."

"I always wondered what it would be like to fight against our own people, but this … this is a nightmare," Little admitted.

Haggle removed his helmet and wiped the sweat from his brow. Clumps of hair were matted to his forehead. Dark circles clung to his eyes. They'd been fighting on Mannus Prime for over a week now. A full week of continuous combat operations. drawing them toward the final confrontation with the bulk of enemy forces. The assault promised high casualties, even with the more than one hundred thousand additional forces on the other side of the battlefield.

"Have you spoken with Jers lately?" Haggled asked.

"No, why?"

Unsure how to express his emotions, Haggle worried over his best friend. Their time in uniform was filled with escalating consequences, culminating with the invasion to retake this planet. Everything had been fine until their deployment to Kharsis. Neither man was the same after. Haggle struggled with nightmares from the dead planet. He was hurting but lacked the outlet to vent his pain. Jers, he knew, suffered worse.

"Never mind. Just keep an eye on him. We're making the final push and I don't want anything happening to him."

Little's eyebrow rose in silent question. Soldiers were cryptic at times, proving frustrating when diagnosing issues. Even after years together, the medic found the tight bonds of infantrymen difficult to decipher. He nodded and shoved his canteen back into place. They were a family; the only family each other had in dark times.

"Will do, but I've got plenty of wounded to keep me busy," Little reminded.

Haggle peered down at the dark pool at Little's feet. Desril's blood. He hadn't seen action this fierce since the attempt to retake Hawker's Gate. Even that failed attempt paled in comparison. Rifle and machinegun fire roared through the night. Crimson lines of tracers arced to and from enemy lines. With the outer trenches smashed, it was a matter of time before the enemy folded. The fighting, once infantry units engaged with their counterparts, promised a bloodbath of unprecedented proportions. *Maybe Jers has the right of it.*

The ball of flame and black smoke curling into the sky was immediately followed by a shockwave throwing Haggle and Jers to the ground.

Matthias spat a mouthful of blood and wiped the grime and soot from his eyes. Vision swimming, he opened his mouth to stop the ringing in his ears. He gripped what remained of the machine gun mount in the hopes of stabilizing his balance. Stunned, Matthias crawled from his hatch. Fires burned across the top of the tank. Thick funnels of black smoke curled around him, a dedicated reminder that death was coming to claim its due. Fresh waves of pain arced throughout his body. A veteran of a hundred wars, Matthias finally understood the fragility of his profession.

Managing to drag his legs free, the Guardsman spotted Bootleg. The mercenary was half out of his hatch, face down on the tank's turret. He wasn't moving. Matthias crawled, still unsure if his legs worked properly, across the blazing tank. There was no love lost between them, but he was trained to never leave a man behind. His uniform sizzled as he crawled across the metal alloy. Vaguely aware of shouting somewhere in the armored belly, Matthias gripped Bootleg's utility belt suspenders and pulled with all his might. Slowly, the mercenary came free.

Unconscious, Bootleg was little more than dead weight. Matthias strained as he pulled and dragged them both to the tank's edge. The vehicle was slanted at an angle. Half the right side was blown away, pieces of track and armor scattered for meters. A building roar prompted him to move faster. It reminded Matthias of the heavy shipping vehicles used on populated worlds. He grasped the edge of the turret and looked down. It was a fifteen-foot drop with no handholds or places to climb down. Grunting, Matthias rolled Asher over the side, and waiting to see where the man landed, followed.

The ground was soft, abused from the passing of so many heavy armored vehicles and a thousand pairs of boots. Matthias landed with a fleshy thud and rolled clear of the destroyed tank, as a blast of flame erupted from every hatch. The soldiers within were incinerated, ending their cries. It was a small mercy, Matthias concluded as the stench of fuel and roasted flesh choked him. Beside him, Bootleg stirred. His nose was broken, and his left cheek was swollen bad. Soot stained his face, and his hands were blistered and raw. Beaten up, but alive.

"Wake up, damn it," Matthias shouted over the din. "Wake up before the whole damned thing goes up!"

He slapped Bootleg, hoping the fresh pain would induce his consciousness. The mercenary blinked rapidly before emitting a low groan. Matthias rose to his knees, helping the dazed Bootleg to the same. They leaned on each other for stability before Matthias dared to rise. Tears welled as he forced through the pain. Nausea roiled within and he vomited what little was in his stomach onto his boots.

"Not what I wanted to wake up to," Bootleg groaned through clenched teeth.

"Get up. This tank is going to blow," Matthias ignored him.

The broken pair limped and hobbled back toward friendly lines. Or so they hoped.

Corporal Yeves thought she had been through hell on Crimeat during the initial campaign against rebel Guards. That minor action paled in comparison to the nightmare unfolding around her. The push into the enemy perimeter was in full swing, but as usual, intelligence proved faulty. Whatever rearguard the enemy was supposed to have had was suddenly bolstered by frontline combat troops of equal caliber as the attackers. It was the type of fight she both longed for and loathed.

Slapping in a fresh power pack, Yeves aimed at the trio of enemy soldiers advancing on her right flank. The middleman carried a squad sized light machine gun capable of shredding Yeves's squad. Squeezing the trigger, her first three shots went wide right. The enemy realized they were under fire and dove to the ground, making it all but impossible to eliminate. Frustrated at her lack of aim, Yeves had one other option.

"Palco, do you see that machinegun team fifty meters out on your one o'clock?" she chimed into her helmet's open channel.

A thick spitting sound. "Yeah."

"Take them out. I got no shot."

Lines of blue-white blazed from his position, shredding the small mound separating the enemy soldiers from Yeves's line of sight. Grass and dirt burst apart under the fury of the machinegun. Palco kept firing until all three heat signatures started turning blue in his scope.

"Done."

Yeves blew out the breath she hadn't realized she was holding and bumped her forehead against her rifle's carrying handle. One threat removed. Gods knew how many more awaited in the burning darkness.

Jolent glared at Hollis. He felt useless and decided to take it out on his spotter. The squad sniper was too far behind the action and falling further back by the moment as the armored spear thrust deep into the enemy's exposed belly. Once the last line was broken, there would be an all-out push to capture the enemy command and end the war. And he was about to miss it.

Normally, Jolent enjoyed the luxury of being in a secluded position and doing what he did best. War was easier from a distance.

Others scorned him for not being up close and personal with the foe, but they failed to consider how he stared into the eyes of most of the soldiers he killed. Their faces haunted him every time he closed his eyes. It was the lingering effects of violence that forced him to remove the humane portion of who he was, leaving in its place a man as cold and emotionless as the rifle in his hands.

"It's not my fault!" Hollis protested. Her armored shoulders rose as she shrugged in frustration. "We're infantry. There's no way to keep up with those tanks."

Growling under his breath, Jolent took a final look through his scope. Nothing but a handful of prisoners being escorted back to the line of departure. He was out of the fight and furious.

"We need a ride," he said.

Thankful for the night, Hollis gave him an incredulous stare. *Where in the hells am I supposed to get a vehicle? He's lost his mind.*

"Did you hear me?"

"Huh? Yeah, I heard you. Where am I getting this mysterious ride? The war is already up there," she said.

He gestured to the nearest line of prisoners. "Let's ask one of them."

A prisoner? "You're going to get us court martialed."

"Not if you get us ahead of the advance, so I can use this damned thing," he shook his rifle. "Let's go."

Cursing under her breath, Hollis hurried after the squad sniper. Her life continued getting more complicated. And she hadn't even been promoted yet.

"Jolent, Hollis, where in the hells are you? We've got a fight up here," Annalilly's voice snarled over the open channel.

Saved by the boss. "Moving, Sergeant. Transmit your coordinates, so we can find you."

Jolent stopped in midstride and adjusted his direction. The search for a vehicle would have to wait.

Commander Torgast watched the updates scroll across the massive screen in the forward command bunker. A steady flow of information detailed every bit of action happening across the entire battle sphere. Too much for any one person to accurately track. A full squad of analysts and data pushers filled the bunker, tracking and breaking down every report from the front. Torgast often wondered how they managed. Battles were much easier when directing them from the front, this was an exercise in madness. A handful of low-ranking officers surrounded him, waiting for new orders as the battle unfolded.

Once the orbital bombardment halted, it had been raw chaos as his finest assault divisions surged out of their trenches and across the divide to engage the dazed enemy. Losses were high, for even though the enemies were the victims of a dazzling assault from space, they remained trained professionals. Torgast's forces closed to within fifty meters before they were met with withering defensive fire. Scores died in those first few moments. Each one a loss deeply felt by comrades and commanders.

Torgast squinted at the real time board tracking progress. Friendly forces were marked by blue dots. Enemy red. Soon they would converge in one mass of purple. A section of enemy line broke, a deep bulge of blue pushing into the mass of forces. Torgast's heart quickened. The prospect of breaking the lines and collapsing the defense a distant tickle in his mind. He wanted the battle to end. Needed it over to salvage his command, reconsolidate his assets and claim Mannus Prime for those still loyal to the Conclave. They were close. Oh, so close.

Incoming artillery fire slammed into the ground up and down the first trench, knocking Torgast and a few of his officers to the ground under a hail of dirt and pebbles streaming from the bunker's ceiling.

Picking himself up, Torgast said, "I thought we knocked out their howitzers. Where the hell is that fire coming from?"

"Sir, it appears there is an active firing battery orbital bombardment missed," one of the analysts reported.

"No shit," Torgast growled. "Where? Get me the coordinates and relay to our artillery. We can't protect our assault, if the enemy has indirect fire capability."

Not to mention direct fire, once my people get within range. Torgast recalled the one time he witnessed the destructive force of a full battery unleash direct fire. The destruction was catastrophic and left him haunted for many weeks following. He had no desire to repeat that.

"We have them, sir."

He stalked to the computer terminal. "Pull it up on screen. I want drones in the air to strike whatever the artillery doesn't kill."

"Bastard Battery, fire mission …"

He caught the command through the clamor of incoming and outgoing communications. It sent a thrill through him. A second salvo struck the trenches, killing and wounding dozens of second wave forces. Torgast caught the familiar whump of outgoing rounds and narrowed his gaze on the main battle screen taking up half the bunker wall of the tactical operations center. The enemy firing battery was well concealed beneath a fortress of sandbags and natural fortifications. Torgast was a professional infantry officer, but his experiences gave him enough knowledge of combined arms doctrine to appreciate the artillerymen's efforts. Hunter killer drones hovered on the edge of the scene, eager for the strike.

Rounds slammed into the battery. Torgast watched a cannon tube explode from a direct hit. Soldiers ran, only to be cut down by shrapnel from the point detonating bunker busting rounds his people wisely used. White-grey smoke occluded the scene as a second salvo struck. Then a third. The travesty of human slaughter sickened him, despite its necessity.

Red tracer lines stretched from the drones to targets hidden in the haze. Low density armor piercing rounds slashed from the sky to strike down those enemy soldiers the artillery failed to kill. It was a slaughter. One Torgast would rather not watch, but though the casualties were enemies, could do no less. Every Prekhauten Guard deserved a warrior's demise. Satisfied the threat was eliminated, the commander breathed a sigh of relief. One threat down.

His thoughts soon turned to the men and women engaged on both fronts. Faceless strangers sworn to uphold oaths to a failed government system, who had no idea there was a war of attrition consuming Mannus Prime. The worries of the Conclave were beyond his control, however. The politics of Vau Prime were half the universe away. Torgast knew the situation would settle itself. Until then, he would continue doing his duty. To the last man. While most of the thousands of Guards streaming into the enemy lines were faceless, there was one he kept in his thoughts.

Torgast prayed he hadn't sent him to his doom.

Jelin Quint bordered on the edge of giving in to the madness growing within. Each moment of battle threatened to unleash his captured fury. Revenge for his company who was so ruthlessly slaughtered in an ill-conceived assault. Vengeance for those who would never be able to go home. Retribution for the families torn apart by the loss of their loved ones. The burden of guilt fell upon him, demanding he pay homage to the ghosts of the dead, and if the gods were willing, take his rightful place beside them. It was a game he was ill suited to play.

So much of his life had been wasted in the pursuit of vainglorious endeavors. Jelin Quint was never a practical man, though he prided himself on unparalleled professionalism and the constant drive to be the best soldier he could be. He thought that lost after his drunken arrest and assignment to the ground commander's personal detail. Torgast offered him a second chance to prove his worth, here at the end of the line. Jelin resigned himself to death upon being attached to the incoming ground forces. He welcomed the advancing demise and eternal slumber, only possible through putting his rifle down for the last time. The gods had other plans.

His focus shifted when Cardinal Virom stalked into the belly of the transport to deliver the last piece of news Jelin expected. His brother was alive and well and commanding the enemy forces. *Seven hundred known worlds in the universe and that bastard was within arm's reach.* Jelin never got along with his siblings. They were a vicious bunch, more interested in furthering their individual careers, than building any type of family legacy. Banno was presumed dead, lost in action on planet Ninean several years ago. The loss drove their father to the bottom of a bottle and saw their mother wither away to an early grave. For that crime, Jelin could never forgive his older brother. Learning he was still alive inspired new anger and the lusting desire for revenge.

The firefight raged around him, slowly developing into a battle for the soul of the planet. Medics rushed forward to secure the wounded as the armored spearhead plunged deep into the exposed underbelly of the supply trains. Jelin was no strategist but knew enough that no army could survive long without food and ammunition. Perhaps once the breakthrough turned to rout, he would be able to confront his brother one final time.

"The Shadow Hammers just lost a tank."

Jelin pulled his gaze from the rising conflagration several hundred meters ahead of the mobile command center. Assigned to light infantry units throughout his career, Jelin had no love for the lumbering armored hulks. While they provided protection and a steel fist capable of ending battles early, they reduced his ability to move and react to contact. Six in one hand …

"Sounds like they need some help," he said.

Lieutenant Fies ignored him. His focus fixed on the men and women of his platoon, as they ground deeper into the maelstrom. He should be there, with them. Promotion reduced his need for frontline action, relegating him to a distant leadership. Or perhaps it was his association with Tolde Breed transforming him from a simple line officer to a command level authority.

"Let me take a squad forward," Jelin pressed. He bristled at having to remain behind the attack, but Torgast's orders were clear. Coordinate and liaison with the reinforcements. For a man who never wanted to fight again, Jelin Quint ached with the need to get in the fight. "There's bound to be wounded."

"Not if they were trapped within the hull," Fies replied with strained words. Still, he couldn't afford to divert combat power for the effort. "Fine, secure the wreck and pull any mercs out of there. Do not engage unless fired upon. I'm not getting my ass handed to me by your boss because you were reckless."

Jelin grinned and hurried off.

Doc Little finished wrapping Matthias's wounded shoulder. Ruined bits of armor were stacked nearby. Refusing to be administered to until the worse wounded Bootleg, Matthias swallowed his pain as a squad secured the site. Being behind the assault was by no means an assurance of safety, especially in a fluid battle. With thousands of moving pieces, Matthias found it curious a pair of faces he recognized came to his aid.

"Sergeant Major," Jelin acknowledged, as he dropped to a kneeling firing position.

"Just Matthias," he winced. "Little, is he going to be all right?"

"I need to get him back to the field hospital," the medic said. "Might lose a leg if we don't make it fast."

Matthias stared at the sedated mercenary. Whatever hatreds the man vowed in making his deal with Falchi, seemed petty in light of recent events. Worse than losing a tank, the mercenary company was down a commander.

"Where do we stand with the assault?" Matthias asked.

Jelin gestured forward with his chin. "Last I heard, we were engaging the rear defense troops. My brother is no doubt sending some of his fighters to slow us."

Brother? Why is it always a sibling rivalry? I should have stayed retired.

"Your brother is …"

"Banno Quint, commanding officer of the enemy forces on Mannus Prime."

Of course, he is.

TWENTY-SIX

3215 A.G. (After Gods), Prophet Isle, planet Crimeat.

Marines sprinted through the darkness to reach the main entrance of the former Conclave prison before snipers eliminated the pair of men guarding the doors. Talore was the first to reach the relative safety of the building. Breathing hard from the run across broken terrain, the Marine sergeant made a quick head count before ordering the breaching team into action. Shape charges were slapped onto the frame. He watched as the detonator was placed in the center.

"Fire in the hole!" Talore shouted.

The Marines ducked aside and took cover before the blast tore the doors from the structure in a blast of directed kinetic energy. Helmets switching to infrared, Talore led his people inside. Smoke occluded much of the immediate area. They took positions on either side of the entry, front ranks kneeling to provide the second rank a clear shot.

"This isn't right," Talore muttered. "Where is the resistance?"

He ordered a pair of scouts to range to the end of the short hallway, while the others finished securing the offices and general workstations. There'd been no intelligence of who the Conclave kept prisoner here or how so much devastation was brought down upon the structure and surrounding areas. Talore was glad he wasn't here when it happened. Neither had Captain August or their pirate companion been able to confirm how many enemy combatants were within. It was a no-win situation from his point of view. That meant casualties.

"Status."

Talore frowned. "Captain, we have the initial area secure. No sign of the enemy. Proceeding now."

Whether you like it or not.

"Copy. Command element is approaching your position. Remember the mission, sergeant."

"Yes, ma'am." *How could I forget?* The murdering Presha Von had much to atone for. Talore lost family on Kharsis, distant cousins to be sure, but blood nonetheless.

What remained of the room to his right was once a security guard station. Reinforced windows and an empty weapons rack behind the elongated central desk confirmed as much. A bank of dead computer screens lined the far wall. Talore figured the prison lost power after the last prisoner either escaped or was transferred. A thin film of dust covered the floor. Cobwebs and other nasties filled the corners and ran across the ceiling. He was starting to think their information was wrong, that Presha Von was not within, when a warning light blinked on his visor.

"Sergeant, we got movement."

"Hold your fire and identify," Talore ordered. "The last thing we need is to kill an unarmed friendly."

"Roger."

Gripping his rifle tighter, Talore aimed down the hall at numerous shadows detached from the walls. Wraith-like, they stalked toward the Marines like hunters. Flesh prickled, he slipped his finger in the trigger well and clicked the safety off.

"Captain, are you seeing this?" he asked. "We're about to have company."

"Have you identified?"

"Negative. I suggest you hold in place. This might get hairy," Talore said. He already knew the answer. Ever since they fell into orbit, his captain was itching for a fight and the opportunity to shut down this aspect of their mission. Not that he blamed her. Working hand in hand with a pirate crew went against everything he was taught to believe. Wars, Talore decided, were tricky that way.

"Just hold on, Sergeant. We are almost there," August replied.

Biting his tongue, Talore was reminded how glad he was he never got commissioned. There were situations when being an officer was unbearable.

August slipped into the abandoned Conclave prison a step ahead of Vicente Blackheart, much to the pirate's glowering frustrations. She knew he wanted revenge for all Presha Von had done to him and countless others since the war began, but she had her orders. None of them involved killing the target. August was forced to remind him a final time that she was to be taken alive. It was an ill sitting command with the pirates on the ground, for they were men unaccustomed to civility and the rule of law.

Though, I can't blame them. With the Conclave disintegrating before our eyes, I fear lawlessness is about to sweep across the stars until it consumes every planet. We are stranded in desperate times, with no clear endgame. She shook off the bleak vision of the approaching future and hustled to Talore's side.

"What do you see?" she asked.

He kept his gaze funneled through his scope. "Captain, there are a handful of figures moving at the far end of the hall. Each time we advance, they fall back. Their biometric signatures are unlike anything I have encountered. Almost as if …"

"They are ghosts," Blackheart concluded.

August cast a withering glare. "Don't be ridiculous. This was a Conclave installation. Ghosts are figments of imagination and literary fancy."

Blackheart shook his head. "Do you know who was kept here? There was but one prisoner and he is the worst of the worst."

She racked her memory, desperate to find any trace of who he was referring to, but alas, until arriving on Crimeat, she had no idea the Conclave had secret facilities here. Secrets within secrets. "If you have useful information, it would behoove you to tell me now."

Blackheart swallowed. "I'm not surprised you don't know. The Inquisition likes to keep its doings private, even from the cardinals."

An Inquisition prison? "Vicente, who was kept here?"

"Amongeratix."

Helmets shifted his way. August felt her skin prickle. The golden hairs standing on end. The nastiest of the Three. While Amongeratix was halfway across the universe, according to last reports, his presence lingered in the walls, choking the very air they breathed. Knowledge was a terrible weapon.

"What do you suppose behoove means?" Krimpen Mass whispered through clenched teeth. His jaw ached worse than before, the pain meds having worn off.

Time shrugged. "Something to do with cows, I guess."

Krimpen slapped him in the back of the head for good measure. "Idiot. Does it look like there's any farm animals here? This was a prison. 'Sides, you heard the Marine. Ghosts and such. We've entered a curse."

"I don't believe in curses, Krimpen. C'mon. We can handle this," Time growled and joined August. "Cap'ns. Mind if we take a crack at this?"

"We don't know what we're facing," August said.

"Be our guests," Blackheart almost spoke over her.

"I got first shot on that big bastard," Krimpen snarled, as the pair stalked after the roiling shadows.

"What?" Blackheart asked. "I don't want to die here and they don't seem to have a problem with it."

"This is not how we do business, Ca …"

Time suppressed a laugh. "They really don't get along, do they?"

"Not our problem," Krimpen Mass said. "What if these things really are ghosts?"

"Guess we'll find out."

They waded into the mass of darkness choking the end of the hall. The light surrounding them faded, threatening to choke them into obscurity. Time stepped in front of his companion and drew his blaster. They'd been itching for a fight since the debacle in Vaade. Embarrassment aside, Krimpen recognized the threat to every soul on Crimeat, should they fail in their attempt at capturing the universe's most hated criminal. Refraining from giving in to raw emotion, he didn't recall any restrictions regarding Geres Auk. Some men, Krimpen Mass decided, were meant to be mauled.

Shadows fled at their approach. An inexplicable survival instinct forcing them into hiding as the manifestation of fury entered their midst. If Krimpen or Time understood the ramifications of their actions, it remained a silent revelation. Both men halted and moved back-to-back. The hallway was calm for another heartbeat before shadows launched from the walls in attack. Static energy cackled across the space between them. Stabbing bolts of invisible force bounced off flesh. Repulsed, the shadows renewed their assault with what fury remained.

Bracing for the inevitable, the intruders coiled, seeking a target for their fury. Shadows swarmed them. Krimpen and Time punched and slashed with their fists but struck nothing. Frustration combined with fear, as they slowly began to realize they might have marched to their doom. Krimpen drew his blaster and fired. The round spliced the nearest shadow, who parted in swirls of eldritch sorcery before reforming and attacking.

Krimpen ducked under a sweeping blow meant to decapitate him and laughed when naught but the rush of wind tickled his scalp. No blow fell upon them. Confidence grew. Whatever powers guarded the prison were but haunting memories of what once was. They had no power over the realm of the living. A façade best left to ignominy. The shadows ceased their attack, content to surround the intruders until a new plan was formed.

"What is going on?" he demanded. "We should be dead already."

Time held out a hand, allowing the nearest shadow to pass through. "Nothing. I felt nothing. What are these creatures, Krimpen?"

"How should I know?" he snarled. "What I do know is we can't kill them and they don't have any ability to harm us. I feel like this is a sick joke."

"Joke or not, our prize lies beyond," Time pointed to the stairwell at the edge of sight. "Do we wait for the others to catch up?"

"Where's the fun in that? Come on. We've got a bad guy to hunt," Krimpen grinned. Gaps where his missing teeth were mocked the false darkness.

Disappointed from the anti-climactic results, Time swatted the nearest shadow with the back of a hand and was rewarded with watching it evaporate, only to coalesce once more when he was past. Ghosts.

"Lord Von, intruders have entered the prison."

Olex Von knew it was an inevitability. Once his wayward daughter returned to Crimeat and his life, the father knew bad times approached. Her coming was the harbinger of doom. The feral mentality of the new dark council prevented him from establishing a sense of security in the aftermath of the initial events at the dawn of the war. Though he moved swiftly to claim what he viewed as his rightful place, Olex's plans ground to a halt with Presha's return. It was an inconvenience he did not want or need.

"Who?" he demanded.

Presha paled. Her smaller figure shriveling under his baleful glare. "The Prekhauten Guard. They have hunted me since Kharsis."

"Nonsense. With the civil war growing, the Guard has no resources to devote to a peaceful world. You are inflating your importance, daughter," he scolded.

She remembered her spine just then. Presha Von was once among the most powerful figures in Amongeratix's rising insurrection. A swath of destruction followed her since her initial departure from the cruel restrictions of her home world. She wished she had never given in to base impulses. Declined command of Hawker's Gate and never set eyes on the planet killing artifact that continued ruining her life. Hope of escaping her pursuers and finding a quiet life dwindled each day. Trapped within the prison, Presha Von felt the noose tighten.

"This is no time for your delusions, father. My enemies have tracked me down. Whatever ideations you hold for the future are now in jeopardy," Presha insisted. "This is a most dangerous game neither of us can afford to play."

"Speak plainly. You may have carved a bloody path across the stars but you are still my daughter," Olex said. "We have defenses."

"Not against them, you don't," she almost sobbed. "They will stop at nothing to garner revenge against my crimes. I ..."

He squared on her. "What?"

Unable to withstand the scrutiny of his gaze, Presha discovered a moment of weakness and hid her face in her hands. Her shoulders trembled. Strands of unkempt hair dangled over her face, concealing the private torments threatening to break loose. Olex, uncharacteristically placed a fatherly hand on her shoulder.

"Tell me, daughter," he whispered.

Sniffing to clear her nose, she wiped a forearm over her eyes. "Perhaps I should answer for my crimes and let them take me. Father, I have done terrible deeds, worthy of my neck in the noose."

"Your life, or death, is not theirs to decide," he cautioned. "I am in command here and if they want you so badly, they must come through me. We are not defenseless, Presha. I told you this. We will be fine."

She shook her head, torn between the weakness of a daughter trapped in a world beyond her reckoning and the knowledge of crimes against humanity deserving execution. It was an unending misery driving her to the fringes of insanity's grasp. Presha once thought she was strong. Invincible. Her attempt to gain power in the Council of Lords, under the tempered hands of Amongeratix, exposed the faults in her thinking.

Doubt arose for the first time. Crippling and threatening. This game she played outclassed her at every turn.

"Very well. What must we do?" she asked.

Warning alarms sang out. Her eyes went wide. It was too late.

Geres Auk lifted his head to the sound of the alarms. A dweller of solitary madness, he sat in his cell with quiet reflection. Now that the paths of the universe were opened to him, he felt liberated for the first time in his young life. A natural brute, he had bounced from one employer to the next, ever seeking to enhance his reputation and rise above his lowly station in life. Born into poverty, Geres resorted to his fists when education failed him. Soon he was in the fighting pits close to Ugri lands where the law was often confused and ineffective. Nothing he did compared to the freedoms of attaching himself to Presha Von, not even the head of security job he secured with the former Baron Scura.

Geres never knew what he wanted from life or where it would lead him. The sudden clarity he reached in this prison cell, awaiting judgment by the dark council, enlightened him to a universe filled with endless possibilities. Reborn through the crucible of fervor, Geres Auk was a new man with a clear definition of tomorrow. First, he must find Presha, and a way off Crimeat to rendezvous with their worthy master.

The voices were a constant whisper. Reminiscences of all that had permeated the walls of the prison complex during Amongeratix's incarceration. They soothed him, coaxing the giant with temptations undreamt. He didn't care why he was chosen, only that he was. The deliverer of vengeance upon the mortal realm. Imbued with the courage of conviction, Geres Auk felt unstoppable.

The alarms continued; adrenalin surging through him. Time was almost up. The voices whispered urgency. Find the woman. Find *Behemoth*. Never had his purpose been clearer. Geres jerked to his feet and was at the door a step later. He pressed his face against the small glass to look for any signs of his captors, though they refused to acknowledge such. The halls were empty save but for the flickering ceiling lights. Frowning, Geres attempted to slide the door open. Metal groaned but did not budge. Anger surged in him and he began pounding his fists upon the fragile metals.

Whatever Blood Witch spells once used to imprison Amongeratix were gone, their influence used up. Vibrations rang from his fists to his boots. A dent formed. First one, then another. Twin depressions growing with each blow. A vertical crack began, running down the center of the abused door. Geres grew motivated and renewed his assault. When the door could take no more punishment, he stepped back and planted the flat of his boot on the damaged section. The door tore free and clanged to the hallway floor. He was freed. The beast loosed from its cage.

Weaponless, he stalked off in search of Presha Von and the promise of salvation.

The Marines hurried after Krimpen Mass and Time. Talore had difficulty reconciling with whom they were and what the odd pair represented. Neither mercenary nor soldier, he drew the inescapable conclusion that they were a pair of miscreants in search of violence. What other answer could there be? In a way, he envied them. Focusing on the task at hand, he glanced back to ensure Captain August and the pirate were close by. Losing either threatened an unduly demise to his otherwise stellar career.

The sound of blaster fire echoing a level below grabbed his attention. Battle was joined, but with who? What? A figure in a midnight cloak detached from the wall and ran toward him, knife in hand. Confident it was no illusion, Talore swung his rifle and fired without aiming. The figure doubled over and pitched forward, knife tumbling from his grasp. Talore put another round in him to ensure he was dead before moving on.

"Sergeant, we must be wary," August warned. "This man did not show up on my thermal sensors."

"Sorcery," Blackheart muttered.

"Enough of your superstition, Vicente," August warned. "Sergeant Talore, are you getting any readings on our targets?"

"Hard to distinguish with the interference we're getting from this blasted building. I don't know who made this, but it wasn't meant to be spied on," he replied.

That eerie sensation crawling over her seconded his opinion. There was nothing by the book about this facility. They ran a database check on it before the assault and she failed to find any record of the

Prophet Isle prison. *Whoever made this, indeed. Secrets layered upon secrets. No wonder the Inquisition is at our throats.*

"Keep pushing. We can't afford to let Krimpen and Time disappear," she ordered.

"You heard her, Marines. Weapons up. Identify your targets and shoot to kill," he relayed to his people.

Crowded behind Blackheart, the pirates he'd brought along were a mixture of aching to be set loose and desperate to return to their ship. Men and women who participated in the fiercest action on Kharsis and lived through the torments of that fateful moment. It was a delicate balance Vicente Blackheart struggled with, as he questioned the strength of his spine in these dark times.

August, as if sensing his indecision, turned her helmeted head to him. "What say you, Captain? Are your people ready to claim their due?"

All depends on the final toll. "We'll do our part. Don't you worry about that, Prekhauten. We've been through worse. You just give us a clear shot at Von and we'll call it square."

"We need to find her first," she reminded. "Move out."

Following the Marines, August hurried down the stairs to join the fight.

Several more assailants broke from the walls, each armed with curved blades that were ultimately ineffective against Prekhauten armor. They died under withering vengeance, only a space marine was capable of. August ordered one of the corpses stripped of its cloak, intending to investigate the strange material at their first convenience. Too many mysteries consumed the prison and every answer discovered might help her cause as the war progressed.

Krimpen Mass and Time cared nothing for the worries of the Marines. Their ire risen, they charged without regard for personal safety into the throngs of defenders filling the hallway. Convinced they were closing on the target, Krimpen broke into a sprint and started firing into the masses of black cloaked warriors. Several dropped. A handful turned to flee, but the majority banded together and met the crazed intruder's charge. Chaos ripped a hole in the fabric of reality. Bodies clashed. Curses uttered.

A blade slashed across Krimpen's forearm. The red line spread when he crushed the attacker's face with a devastating blow. *Why aren't they using blasters*? Then it dawned on him. The shadows. The whispers of ghosts from Blackheart and his people. None of the defenders expected an intrusion. They were confident in their concealment. That meant there were no reinforcements coming. No frantic calls for outside assistance. However many people remained within the prison was all they were going to get. He broke into a savage grin.

Time had already pushed a hole in the center of the defenders. His size and strength overpowered the smaller men and women swathed in black cloaks. They fought with the recklessness of never having been trained, making them easy targets for Time's experience. Sidestepping a dagger throw, Time snatched two men at the same time and smashed their heads together. The satisfying thunk of bone and flesh cracking before they dropped unconscious, was a delicate symphony he longed to immerse himself in. There was no remorse. No mercy given. No quarter asked. In Time's mind, each person coming after him was associated with Presha Von and became vilified to him. Guilt by association was a terrible price.

Ion rounds speared through the knot of bodies. Several dropped. Time felt the burn and sizzle of a round as it sped past his cheek. The rate of fire intensified as more Marines got online and initiated their assault, catching Krimpen Mass and Time in the middle. How neither man was hit was a blessing. Krimpen closed his eyes and froze in place, praying to whatever god would grace him, that he made it through unscathed. Remarkably, Time began laughing. A deep bellow reflecting the madness every combatant experienced.

Then it stopped.

The hall consumed in smoky haze, bodies littered the ground. Some writhed in agony. Most were still. Marines rushed forward, Talore in the lead. He looked the bigger men up and down for injuries, silently grateful for his team's aim. After watching them fight, Talore had no desire to fight either. Movement from the far corner drew his attention before he could speak. Two figures, hoods down, blocked their way. He failed to recognize the older man on the right, but the woman sent alarms ringing through his helmet's identification system. Presha Von.

"Stand easy, Marines. No one fires unless I give the word," Talore warned.

"Presha Von, you are under arrest for crimes against the Conclave, the Inquisition, and most of all, humanity itself. Surrender and make this easy," August's voice rang with authority as she slipped between Time and Talore.

She removed her helmet, daring to show her face without regard for personal safety. Reckless, it was the sort of move any soldier would respect.

"You cannot have her," the man at Presha's side said. "Depart this place at once. You are in violation of a private land agreement."

"This … facility belongs to the Inquisition," August ground out slowly. "Do not tempt me with foolishness. I have orders to bring her in. You are not on my list."

August drew her blaster. "We can do this the easy way or the hard. It matters not. One way or the other, you will be in custody and the universe shall rejoice."

Presha shrank at her father's side. The hatred broiling in him presented an unwanted struggle. Here was a man who raised her with cold disdain, or so she envisioned, standing up to the greatest military authority in the universe. Unarmed. Olex was many things in her eyes. Hero was not among them. She watched with rapt attention as the Prekhauten refused to listen to him. He had to know there was no escape. The secret protections of Prophet Isle remained unspoken. His followers were shattered. The new dark council, already a fragile mockery of what once was, broken. One, she knew, had already committed suicide. Others attempted to flee, no doubt being round up by additional Marines waiting in the night. A few lay dead with what she termed cultists. It was a small price to pay, yet each body represented a growing number of souls forever trapped in her legacy.

Presha knew she had one final move. A last ploy to end the string of violence and restore order to her influences on the universe. It was a horror she once delighted with as a child, but time and temperance showed her how wrong many of her ideations had been. Drawing the slender blade tucked into her belt, Presha sidestepped closer to her father.

"Father, I'm sorry."

His head turned as the blade slid between his ribs and into his heart. Olex Von blinked once in confusion and sagged to his knees. Unwilling to allow him to suffer on her behalf, Presha decided taking his life was the kindest mercy she could show. She plunged the blade deeper and twisted. He gasped in pain and his once handsome brown eyes rolled back in his head. He was dead before he hit the cold floor.

"Drop the weapon!"

"Hands over your head!"

Commands were shouted, but she failed to hear them through the sound of her sobs. She was responsible for murdering a planet, yet this one death was her greatest crime. Boots slapped over the broken tiles. Rushing to apprehend her. No doubt rounds of torture awaited, for she was a notorious criminal, with inside information on the great enemy scouring the universe. Keeping her alive was in everyone's best interest. Resigned to her fate, Presha dropped the knife and obeyed. Her part in this sad tale at last complete.

Eyes closed, she felt more than saw the hulking figure of Geres Auk burst past her. Unarmed, he dashed toward the stunned Marines. Murder burned in his eyes as the whispers spurred him on. Presha was amazed by the boldness of his actions. For her. It was all for her. That knowledge reduced what she had just done to foolish pride, hollowing her out to the core. She flinched as Geres bellowed and attacked. In the short span of minutes, her life had devolved to a living hell.

Time slapped his friend on the chest and pointed at the charging bull of a man. Wild, unkempt hair flowed behind him. His clothes were torn and worn through in places. His boots echoed the insanity of the situation with each thundering step. Time started to draw his blaster when he recognized the face. Crazed or not, it was the same bastard who'd thoroughly beaten them in Vaade. Retribution was at hand.

"Not weapons, Time. We do this the right way," Krimpen snarled from his right.

Time's hand slipped from the blaster and he cracked his knuckles. They charged. It was a battle of titans, threatening utter annihilation. He ducked to avoid the blow aimed at his face, catching Krimpen's fist smack into Geres' exposed ribs on the other side. Blows rained between the three. Bones snapped. Blood flew. A nose was broken. A tooth knocked loose. They fought as animals, each hungering to end the nightmare with the trophy kill.

Time wrapped his arms around Geres' waist and tackled him to the floor. A well-placed boot cracked against the top of Geres' skull, enraging him further. None of them felt the rumble deep within the prison bowels. A groaning as the earth tore, as if from the fury of the combatants. The walls trembled, cascading sheets of dust around them.

Geres got his foot clear and punched a kick into Krimpen's stomach. He then snatched Time by the elbow and twisted as Krimpen doubled over with a whuff. The screams of pain reverberated up and down the hall. Using momentum, he smashed Time's face into the wall and flipped over to his feet. Geres spied Presha Von, weak and alone, out of the corner of his eye and remembered why he was here. Forgetting his opponents and ignoring the soldiers, he dashed back to Presha, snatched her up by the waist, and fled down the darkness of the hallway.

The Marines stepped back as one, weapons trained on the madman attacking their allies. Talore was impressed with the ferocity exhibited between them. It was a fight that could only end with slaughter. Then the impossible. Geres Auk seized advantage, beat the two men off and escaped … with their target.

"After her!" August shouted.

Talore, disturbed by what he'd witnessed, order his men to open fire. Killing Von served no purpose, but it was a risk he was willing to take. The thought of tangling with that madman soured his stomach. "Move out! Capture Von. Kill the other."

Sprinting, they were no match for Geres Auk's long stride. Weighed down by armor and uncertainty, the Marines quickly fell behind.

August swore, the first break in professional decorum. She slammed her helmet against the wall repeatedly until her anger was slaked.

"That didn't go well," Blackheart said, somehow relieved his people did not have to face the madman Geres Auk had become. Some fires burned too hotly to extinguish.

August rounded on him, jabbing her blaster at his chest. Pirates recoiled, prepared to exact revenge, should she kill him. "Von is escaping, but the artifact is here somewhere. Send your people to search every room. I want it found. We can still salvage the day."

Mad. We've all gone mad.

They discovered the world killing artifact in an old administratum office. Excited Marines raced back with the news and a request for assistance. Much larger than a normal human could carry, the ancient metal took six Marines to haul to the surface, grunting and groaning the entire way, as the power flickered in and out. The tremors begun during the firefight, continued with worrying acceleration. August urged her people to work faster. They scoured any computer system still operational and filtered through every office for any actionable intelligence. Satisfied there was nothing left, the contingent headed to the surface.

A fresh storm rolled in, blanketing Prophet Isle with heavy wind and rains. Blackheart was convinced the island was angry. His words fell on deaf ears until lightning began blasting the prison. A wretched scream came from deep within the earth. Several men and women were knocked down. A rent grew in the ground, running through the prison's center. The ground cracked and broke until a chasm opened to swallow the prison like a hungry demon released from the bowels of the underworld.

August stared in mute horror as the prison disappeared, dragging all down with it. Several pirates fell to their knees in prayer as old superstitions came alive. Armageddon had come to Crimeat and swift wings of vengeance. When at last it finished, naught remained put a gaping maw stretching deep into the center of the planet.

Blackheart wiped the tears from his eyes and moved beside August. "It appears our mission is finished."

"We don't know if Von survived."

"Does it matter? The artifact is in our hands. Nothing remains of the prison, or those strange bastards in dark robes," he said. "I've had my fill of this hellhole."

She considered the situation. A tactical victory, but an incomplete one. Presha Von was the prize, but the artifact meant one less enemy weapon in their vast arsenal. August needed time to assess all that had transpired since being assigned this mission. The only aspect working in her favor lay in securing the artifact aboard the *Solstice* before Blackheart made a play for it. Their alliance was forced, tepid under the best circumstance and intolerable under the worst. Trust never evolved between them, prompting August to establish backup plans. The game stretched long into the night, and for now, gave her the upper hand.

"Agreed. There is little else we can accomplish on the ground," August said. Keying her comms, she ordered, "*Solstice*, this is August.

Deploy retrieval shuttles for all forces and prepare to depart. We've done what we came here to do."

"Roger, Captain."

She faced Blackheart. "I imagine this means our alliance is ended."

"So, it appears," he nodded.

"What will you do now?"

He tugged the corner of his moustache. "As you said, Presha Von is presumably still out there. Hunting her down with satisfy my crew, those who were at Kharsis. Unless you care to hand over the artifact and we go our separate ways?"

He lacked the heart to tell her how he originally became involved in this sordid tale. How the Inquisitor General hired him to retrieve the artifact and then betrayed him. The deepest wounds always begin with a small cut. For all his bravado, Vicente Blackheart was tired of the chase. Of constantly looking over his shoulder for the assassin's blade. The once respectable merchant thought about heading home and putting it all behind. But what adventures could be had hiding behind a desk?

August's expressionless face told him enough. "I don't know what to do, but I know one thing, Sharlyn August. The universe is a vast place. Perhaps our paths will cross again."

"Perhaps, Vicente Blackheart." She extended her hand. "Perhaps."

TWENTY-SEVEN

3215 A.G. (After Gods), Deep space, *Behemoth.*

The Blood Witch shuttle rocked out of the hull, bound for the antiquated battleship favored by Amongeratix. Imbued with magic to deaden the larger vessel's ability to detect them, the small compliment of soldiers, witches, and remnants tensed in anticipation of what came next. The assault had been rehearsed since leaving the Acumensiis Comet. Every nuance and chance thought for and addressed. That this was a suicide mission went unsaid, for each bore the burden in their own fashion.

Tolde Breed, resurrected and placed within a new body, gripped his rifle while grappling with doubts. Dying served little purpose, but he had performed his task. By rights, he should have been forgotten and gone, not awakening in a different body on a distant planet. The travesty of his life became his greatest challenge to overcome, for his mind struggled with every waking moment. Worse, he saw that same doubt in the eyes of his companions. All but the youthful Ragan Sandinsol. Theirs was an odd relationship he had yet to figure out.

No time for that now. We are entering the monster's mouth. Death becomes our boon companion, for he is ever hungry. Exhaling, Tolde struggled to remember the last time his nerves got the best of him before an operation. A knee bounced. His mouth was dry. A veteran of a dozen campaigns and harrowing adventures, Tolde felt no better than a raw recruit thrust into the frontlines. *Surely this is how Ragan feels. Or is it?* The youth survived the quest to find Braewynd. Now he was thrust into yet another impossibility, with no idea what was about to happen. Ever the young are forced to suffer. Tolde lamented his inability to convince Ragan to stay aboard the comet where it was safe. No matter what followed, their fates seemed intertwined. The former Inquisitor resigned to watch after the youth, all while knowing there were no guarantees in battle. He closed his eyes and sighed.

Luma Kai stared at Tolde through slitted eyes. Her trust was building, but he had yet to prove himself to the point where she would stand by his side in the direst circumstance. They had only worked together for the better part of a year before his untimely demise, and much of that separated out of necessity. She'd never been a believer of the afterlife, making his return a haunting reminder of how small she was in the scope of the universe.

He had earned a measure of that trust during the failed insurrection on the comet. His actions saved many lives, including her own and showed Luma just how important some bonds were, regardless of distance or … events. The balance required to continue walking this same path intensified with each new task. Ultimately, Luma Kai recognized that only by setting aside her prejudices and focusing on the mission, would they find a measure of success. Even then …

Their eyes met and she looked away quickly. How could he not know there was unease among them? The impossibility of it frightened Luma, for Tolde was a man she aspired to be; confident, professional, never thinking of himself until all other possibilities were satisfied. He was, she concluded, the perfect Inquisitor. Now they were within moments of docking with *Behemoth* and about to enter the lair of nightmares.

"Ten seconds to outer shield breach," the pilot announced.

Hands gripped braces. The passengers sank deeper into their seats in the hopes of remaining stable as they passed through the ship generated atmospherics and electrical field. None but the contingent of Blood Witches were used to such maneuvers at velocity. Harrowing enough under pristine conditions, a false move meant them smashing against the hull.

"Once we get inside, we stay together," Paradise shouted over the whine of engines as they sped up. "We only have one chance at disabling the engines. Does everyone remember their roles?"

Heads bobbed up and down, except for the Blood Witches. They stood still, unaffected by the distortion gripping the shuttle. *Behemoth* was ancient and protected by countless evils, beyond mortal imagination. Amongeratix was ever the cunning one of his brothers. An unstoppable force determined to enact his will. It already played out over a dozen worlds. The universe burned as he grew in strength, gathering his power for the return of the gods.

"Brace for touchdown!"

Paradise grabbed the handle dangling from the ceiling and spread her legs. She wore her old armor. Tannus had kept his stored all these centuries as she slept. The mystery of who discovered her and how she was expunged from stasis to land on planet An'kuruku, was a subtle mystery none had the opportunity to explore, though she feared the answer had much to do with the outcome of the war. Darkness filled the cabin the same moment the shuttle lurched and landed on the deck. The sound of her heartbeat thundered between her eyes. The slightest hint of doubt awakened to clash with the fear of being on her cousin's ship again. Then the side hatches slid open and the occupants dispelled into the docking bay.

Paradise led the charge, ignoring her insecurities. Never the warrior, necessity forced her hand. Long rifle charged and a pair of blasters at her hips, she outdistanced her companions as she burst across the empty docking bay floor. lights flickered, casting the already drab interior in waves of distorted light and darkness. No alarms greeted them. No angry crewers determined to halt them. She found the emptiness disturbing. She made it halfway to the pressurized doors leading to the central corridor before the first signs of trouble reared.

The round missed them all, burning a deep gouge in the decking. Metal and alloy melted as the acidic mixture spread at their feet. Ragan Sandinsol thought he had endured nightmares, but this was unlike anything he had seen during the quest for Braewynd. Skeletal warriors and wizardry showed him a realm of impossibilities. His first few moments on *Behemoth* elevated those lessons with dire effects. Liquid capable of melting metal! If his friends back home could hear him now. The former street thief tucked close to Tolde and ran for his life as a second unseen weapon fired another spray from the opposite angle.

Ahead, Paradise Tear was firing her rifle at the nearest weapon. Energy rounds scored holes in the interior bulwarks, but the lethal spray continued. Ragan caught a pair of witches, beings of immense power he failed to understand, raised their arms in unison and cast a crimson net of raw energy at the second weapon. Everything it touched dissolved. Ragan ran faster, though the uncertainty of another such weapon roaring to life in front of him terrified him. The shockwave from an explosion pitched him face first into the decking and his world went dark.

Tolde crawled to his knees and reached for the unconscious Ragan. "Get up, damn it! Ragan. Ragan, can you hear me?"

The younger man moaned, blinking rapidly to clear the webs from his stunned mind. Bells rang in his ears and his body ached from head to toe. Tolde's rough hands jerked him upright and they stumbled for cover.

"What's happening?" Ragan asked, after slamming into the nearest concealed bulkhead.

"Our enemy has allowed us to land," Tolde explained. A second explosion too close to the shuttle, covered the front of the craft in flames.

Ragan shook his head, still unaware of his surroundings. "We should leave!"

"Can't. The mission comes first, boy," Tolde said. "Are you injured?"

"I … I don't think so."

"Good. We need to keep pushing forward. Sister Alessandra will handle the threat here."

Uncertain, but also unwilling to die, he followed Tolde's lead as they sprinted across the short open space separating them from Paradise Tear and Luma Kai. Both women were firing at the nearest acid thrower and were rewarded by a jet of smoke and the weapon dropping down toward the deck. Luma continued firing until the weapon tore free from the ceiling and crashed down in a shower of sparks.

Consolidating their forces in a small perimeter, Tolde was surprised to see the Blood Witches joining them so quickly. Thin tendrils of smoke lifted from their robes. A pair of sealed doors forced the group to an untimely halt. Confident all immediate threats were negated, they paused to catch their breath.

"The main engine room is down the corridor on the other side of these doors. I anticipate more obstacles, not to mention the traitor Sisters," Paradise said.

"We should leave a rear guard for the shuttle," Alessandra suggested.

Loath to reduce their combat power, Tolde disagreed. "Doing so serves no purpose, if we don't have the strength to destroy the engines. We're going to need everyone we can get."

Paradise wiped the sweat off her nose. "Agreed, Sister. The engine room is our top priority. Disable the engines and escape."

Dissatisfied with the answer, Alessandra agreed to the plan. That she secretly desired to exact a measure of vengeance on Algiss Her influenced her decisions. Never had there been a rebellion among the Blood Witch ranks. That any Sisters continued breathing, was an affront to all the Order stood for. Sister Alessandra was known for her patience and thus resigned to stalking down her prey, opposed to charging blindly forth.

"Stay behind me and keep moving. Time is our enemy," Paradise ordered and hit the activation panel. The doors hissed open, revealing a long, darkened corridor stretching into the abyss. "Move."

Algiss Her watched the battle transpire from the bridge, unimpressed with the intruder's audacity. A tickle of fear motivated her, for the prospect of losing *Behemoth* before Amongeratix could reclaim it, was akin to a death sentence. The newly anointed Crimson Mistress felt her future slipping away.

"Are any of those skeleton warriors awake?" she demanded.

"No, Mistress. It appears only a moderate defense system guards this ship's interior."

Angered, Algiss said, "Send a pair of Sisters to stop them. We cannot let this ship fall into enemy hands!"

A young novice cleared her throat. "But Mistress Her, we do not know their intended targets. This ship is vast and we are few."

Algiss lashed out with raw energy, throwing the young woman against the computer terminal behind her. The screen went dark as the novice rolled onto her stomach and planted her hands beneath her. Others present stiffened, failing to meet Her's stern gaze. Darkness coalesced around the Crimson Mistress in waves. Unspoken powers awakened from the blackness of space and time stretched forth to taint her soul.

"Do not question me again, child," she ground through clenched teeth. "Deploy as many forces necessary to stop them immediately. Lord Amongeratix is about to dock. See this is ended before he does and bring me the heads of the those involved."

Crimson Sisters hurried to obey.

Tolde Breed stood upon the precipice, staring down into infinity. The how and why of it didn't matter. All he knew was what his eyes told him. The deck was gone. Replaced by infinite darkness. A single, foot wide space remained. Enough to walk across but with no room for error. Worse was the rising agony he felt twisting his insides. As if decades of abandoned pain reached out in search of a new home. Tears streamed down his face. The brittle reminders of unchecked agony. He knew the others would be in similar condition, should he look behind him. Only Paradise Tear stood unaffected by the magic of *Behemoth*.

The giant woman wasted no time in crossing the bridge. Her strides were confident, betraying no hint of mortal emotion. Tolde admired her for that. Summoning what courage remained, he took his first hesitant step onto the bridge. An updraft blew his hair in the silent promise of an eternal plummet, should he step wrongly. Closing his eyes to refocus, Tolde wobbled. He threw out his arms to rebalance, lest he drop over the edge. A gasp from behind was enough to inspire caution. Yet, he knew by delaying he raised the chances of failure. Tolde Breed took another step. Then another. Soon he was being grabbed by the shoulder and pulled to safety by Paradise.

"It is an illusion," she told him. "A clever one playing on our unique fears."

He offered a dubious look but remained silent. Ragan and Luma Kai followed. Watching them was worse than doing it himself. Tolde's knuckles bled white until they reached safety. The Blood Witches followed, either unaware of the threat or unconcerned, as they drifted over the deck to reach the others. The moment the last Sister finished, lights blinked on and the floor became whole. An illusion indeed.

"I don't want to do that again," Luma announced.

Tolde gave her an appraising look and asked Paradise, "How much further?"

"Not much. Our journey is almost complete," she confirmed.

Why then, am I anxious? The automated defenses in the docking bay should have permeated the entire ship, yet the tiny group traveled un-accosted for what felt like miles. They'd run through a gauntlet of minor traps along the path. A hall filled with flames without heat. Floating blocks of ice slamming into each other. A massive serpent with two mouths that spit blood. None of it was real, and despite Paradise's reassurances, Tolde discovered new fears with each trial. Was this ship naught but a means to bend reality and warp the human mind? He didn't want the answer, knowing what damage it might bring.

"Keep moving," Paradise said and struck out again.

They made it to the engine compartment doors before the first sign of true trouble reared.

Blasts of malformed magic lashed out from the shadows. It was only through quick thinking Alessandra cast a protection ward, dissolving the energy mere feet from the others. A second blast struck but she was better prepared and flung it back on her attackers. Flames burst in the darkness as an enemy witch staggered out of her concealment. Luma Kai shot the burning woman several times until she dropped dead to the deck. The second witch redoubled her efforts to destroy them.

The Blood Witch beside Alessandra was caught in the chest with a blast of funneled energy, slicing through the wards with ease to pierce her heart. She died with a gasp a moment before Paradise Tear leapt across the space between forces and snatched her foe by the throat. Colored sparks of magic surrounded them as the renegade witch struggled to survive. Paradise ignored the magic as it scored her flesh and squeezed harder. She did not stop until she heard the distinctive pop of bones breaking. Head tilting back, the corpse collapsed in a mass of crimson robes.

"We must hurry," Alessandra said. She knelt beside her fallen sister, closing the woman's eyes in a final gesture of humanity. "Algiss Her will pay for this."

"Mission first, Alessandra," Paradise reminded.

Tolde was unwilling to delay and hurried to get the doors open. He and Luma took the advance, sweeping their weapons and scanners across the massive chamber in search of signs of life. Once he confirmed they were alone, Tolde took in the sheer impossibility of what faced them. Power cylinders twenty meters across stretched up to the ceiling conduits, linking together in a mass of cables and tubes. He stopped counting at twelve. With little knowledge of what made a ship work, Tolde could only wonder what his primary target should be. Getting to the engine room was one thing. Knowing what to do, another.

Luma unstrapped the pack from her back, the loss of weight a blissful relief to her strained shoulders. "Look for computer terminals and any active banks of machinery. The witches will handle the bigger stuff."

"What about those?" he pointed at the nearest column.

Luma shook her head. "We blow that and the whole ship goes up."

How does she know that? Tolde took off his pack and withdrew the first shape charge. "Ragan, follow Luma and place them where she tells you. Hurry. We are running out of time."

The street thief grabbed the charge and ran to the nearest terminal.

Charges planted and minor equipment disabled or destroyed, the small band fled back toward the docking bay. It was a frantic pace, unheeding the hidden dangers lurking ever out of sight. Tolde struggled to keep pace with the lengthy strides of Paradise Tear. It was the first time he felt invigorated, hungry for success and that measure of retribution that had eluded him since his untimely demise on Kharsis.

A myriad of thoughts collided in the confines of his mind. Endless days of suffering promised closure with the destruction of *Behemoth*. The plan was to regain their shuttle and escape to space before blowing the charges. There could be no chances taken, for the bulk of the ancient ship demanded respect. He imagined fleets of such craft soaring across the stars in pursuit of expanding their empire. No doubt they secured the seven hundred known worlds, but how many others no longer existed thanks to their long war? How many human populations were obliterated on the whims of madmen intent on total domination? What little Tolde learned of the gods, he now scoffed at the name, suggested they were nothing more than technologically advanced savages, who ruled without wisdom or benevolence. That humanity found the mechanisms to escape and thrive in their absence, was a brutal reminder that the universe did not take sides.

A nagging sensation accompanied him ever since docking and it had grown each harrowing moment aboard Amongeratix's ship. Old memories returned to haunt him. From his first escape from Inquisition custody to the nightmare aboard the derelict ship where most of Sergeant Matthias's men were killed. It was the Blood Witch who helped secure Amongeratix but she paid for it with her life. Ever since, Tolde had been weighted by the guilt of survival.

The second escape on Crimeat confirmed his worst fears. That a person of power was assisting Amongeratix in his quest for domination. Many ills plagued the universe, setting one of history's worst villains loose to reap havoc devolved an already unstable political and social situation. Tolde Breed paid for his involvement with his life. A fitting tribute to a lifetime of service against heresy. Being brought back to life remained beyond his ken, forcing deeper introspection into what life meant and what purpose he had to fulfill. That he was inexorably attached to Amongeratix, hounded his steps through time.

Lost in reflection, he failed to notice they had traversed the length of the main corridor and were approaching the yawning mouth of the docking bay—to find it blocked by a half a dozen women in crimson robes. Tolde skidded to a halt and checked the charge on his rifle.

"Behind us!" Ragan shouted.

Looking back, Tolde saw another six renegade Blood Witches blocking the corridor. They were trapped.

Central Trade Routes, en route to the Core Planets.

Kaline refused to speak. Their defeat on Mannus Prime left her in an odd place. Unaccustomed to being thwarted, she thought back on the string of successes leading her to this point. Many worlds had fallen in Rengu's name, and should Amongeratix and Nye fail in their insurrection, it would take the Conclave generations to reclaim them. Mannus Prime should have been no different. It was a planet ripe for conquest. One she had seen a hundred times before. It was then she lamented her greatest asset. The one man capable of oratory brilliance, that played on human emotions and reached deep into the psyche to produce results. She missed Mollock Bolle. His untimely demise on An'kuruku threw her quest into disarray and she now began to accept that she had never recovered.

Her list of allies thinned to non-existence, Kaline struggled with finding the strength to move on.

"Mistress Kaline, we are cleared from Mannus Prime and ready to receive new orders. Where shall we go?"

She looked up into the Captain's expectant face. He showed no emotion. Betrayed no hints of doubt. Years of military experience honed him to a well-oiled machine. To him, she remained the expedition's leader. His sworn allegiance remained, to the bitter end.

Her voice caught, forcing Kaline to clear her throat. "I don't know, Captain. My heart tells me there is still a chance to subvert Mannus Prime."

"Intelligence suggests the rebels are close to securing the world. If it falls, the lanes will be filled with retreating craft. Slipping back to the surface shouldn't prove difficult in the confusion," he replied.

"Is it the right thing to do?" she asked.

"That is not my call to make. You lead, I follow, though I am fearful for your safety. Our relations with the locals is not productive."

"Thank you for your candor," she said. "Would that others had your strict adherence to duty, we would not be in this position. Very well. Take us back to Mannus Prime. I would give those villagers a final opportunity to enlightenment."

Leaving her alone to relay orders to the flight crew, the Captain felt content for the first time in years.

Kaline felt the ship slow before turning. She was going back to the scene of failure and panicked retreat. To her humiliation at the hands of savages. Knowing there was schism already in play, Kaline felt her chances of success rise. Conversion was, after all, the bittersweet endgame for all she strove to achieve. She intended on unleashing the manifestation of Rengu upon the villagers. The population of Mannus Prime would pay for its ignorance. Pay for her humiliation. She could think of no better end than the chaos of slaughter about to be delivered.

Krenz Underworld, planet Vau Prime.

"Where have you taken him?"

The masked man ignored her as he continued laying out an array of rusted and wicked tools. The lone light, shining directly over them, offered little illumination in the small chamber. Sounds of life tickled her ears, promising hope and salvation, while simultaneously whisking it away as if on whim. Frustrations turned to fear at the prospect of what was to come.

"Answer me, damn it. Where is Captain Julian?"

"Captain, now, is he?" a male voice said from behind her.

Restrained, she could not turn to see who addressed her. Regret sank her, for she had given away too much.

"You're not going to get anything else from me," she said defiantly.

"We both know that isn't true, Aliz. When last we met, you were in the company of our boss. Now he is dead and I want to know why."

Aliz balked. "Dead? By whose hand?"

"As his companion, I was hoping you could tell us."

The man settled into the chair opposite her. He was tall, thin, and had rich dark hair hanging past his shoulders. A three-day beard occupied his lower jaw, lending a sinister look. It was the eyes, predatory and merciless, that fixed her attention. Aliz was already far too old to wander among the underworld, much less the criminal side of it. A woman who should have been broken a thousand times over, she remained defiant in the face of the fragments of Zoraq Darc's network.

News of his death, while not surprising, was difficult to swallow. Never an ally, Zoraq helped her through difficult times following the assassination of her lover, Lorenu Phos. His resourcefulness working outside of legal constraints made him valuable in a time where she needed it most. Convincing him to join with Strannan and the rebellion took effort but proved beneficial for all parties. That is until the assault on Tatarast Island. It was there the criminal mastermind learned the true horrors of war and saw his future if he failed to alter course. Aliz was disappointed when he left the rebellion, but not distraught. Men like Zoraq Darc followed their own destinies. Even if meant going to their doom.

"He was alive and well the last time we spoke," she said. "Zoraq decided it was time to part company. I tried to dissuade him from going but he would have none of it. He slipped away into the night. I never saw him again."

Metal scrapping metal. A torturer's tool being sharpened.

"He was beaten, broken, and ruined. All while still alive. Or so they tell me," he elaborated, narrowing his gaze on her. "As one of the last people to see him alive, I wonder if you felt betrayed and had your revenge upon him. Things to ponder, don't you agree, Aliz?"

"We were never friends and yes, I tried to convince him to stay with us. Regardless of what was said, we did not part as enemies."

He leaned forward, elbows on the table. "I wonder if your soldier friend would say the same?"

"What has he to do with any of this? Captain Julian has done nothing but fight against the tyranny unleashed by Alain Nye since the coup began. He is a noble man, determined to save what remains of the Conclave, before it is too late."

He snorted. "It's already too late. Those bells tolled long ago, Aliz. Everywhere I go, Prekhauten patrols stop me, searching me, and asking for registration papers. They choke the population, forcing us into our homes and preventing any form of public gatherings. My people are hunted to extremes, tortured in the streets and slaughtered as examples. Do you have any idea how many friends, how many family members I've lost to *your* war?"

Aliz strained against the bonds pinning her wrists to the table. "My war? This only became my war after Nye murdered my ..."

His eyes lit up. "Go on. Your what? Who did they kill, Aliz?"

"My lover," she said in a whisper. Her shoulders slumped. The fire went out of her voice. In place of the strong rebellion leader, was a broken and fragile old woman well past her prime and cast adrift in a world she did not understand. "They killed my lover."

He sat back in the small metal chair, folding his arms across his chest. A gesture with his head and the torturer began packing his tools. "We are done here. My name is Edam Boone. Call me Zoraq's successor in these matters."

Edam rose and made for the door.

"Wait," Aliz called. "What happens next?"

A glance over his shoulder stared deep into her heart. "Next? I decide whether you are lying or not."

The door slammed shut behind him. Aliz lowered her head and fought against the wave of tears threatening to burst free.

"Let her sit for a while," Edam told the handful gathered around him.

"Do you think she is telling the truth?"

He snorted. "About being Phos' lover? Yes. There was no lie in her voice, though I question all that has happened since the murder."

"What of Zoraq's death?" the torturer asked. His beady eyes were crossed, lending him a perpetually confused look. "I am not convinced she didn't betray him."

"Perhaps, Thopos, but we must be wary of conspiracy theories. Aliz told me all she needed to, whether she knows it or not. Let her get the pain out of her system. We will have need of her in the coming days," Edam said.

Thopos cocked his head, the thoughtfulness uncharacteristic of Edam. "How so? She is old and broken. Whoever she once was, is gone, Edam. This war claims a heavy toll on all of us."

"Think on it! She was Lorenu Phos' lover, perhaps more. She can serve as the rallying cry for everyone being subjugated by the tyranny consuming Vau Prime. I may not hold to lofty ideals but I do know the universe is suffering under this oppression. Imagine if the untold trillions had a face to support. To look up to during their darkest hours. It could be the beginning of a new day for all of us."

Thopos frowned. He knew the value in people, a skill honed through years of dealing with the scum and villainy of the Vau Prime underworld. Each person reaches a point of diminishing returns and he saw that in Aliz. She was defeated, ready to break. What value was there in such a fragile state? "You play a dangerous game."

"I want to be free again, Thopos," Edam said. "Curfews and martial law are just the beginning. Those who do not conform to the Inquisitor General's new regime will be weeded out and eliminated. We've already seen it. I am tired of living in fear. The old ways were great for us but the Conclave often turned a blind eye to our endeavors. Hells, they sent Aliz down here to liaison with us how many times? All I'm asking for is a little time and trust. We can turn this around. We can."

"You put all our lives at risk, Edam," Thopos scolded. "I don't like it. We should either kill them or dump them halfway across the city. Let the Inquisition find them. Perhaps that will remove the heat from our necks for a change."

The hopeful expression on Edam's face fell.

"But," Thopos held up a finger. "I'm willing to give it a shot. As you say, we have nothing left to lose."

Edam broke into a grin and hugged the smaller man in an awkward exchange. Their network was devastated, shrinking with each action. He was desperate to find any advantage before the noose drew too tight.

"You won't regret this," he said, unable to contain his joy.

Thopos grunted. He already did.

Julian was herded into the small room blindfolded. The Guardsman was at the end. His life forfeit to whatever disturbed powers now ruled the universe. Focusing on the past string of failures leading to this point, Julian lamented being unable to do more for Strannan and for Aliz. Thoughts of escape did little for him. He was seasoned enough to understand his predicament, and without a working knowledge of where he was, Julian reluctantly accepted his time was ending. The travesty of it rocked his core.

Pain lanced his eyes as the hood was ripped away and light struck him. Blood flowed unrestricted through his wrists again after his bonds were cut. Julian cast a hand to shield his eyes, hearing the door slam behind him. Honed defenses kicked in. He stepped back, blinking away the spots occluding his vision, until he felt the cold press of the wall. His legs tensed, anticipating the launch of sudden attack, but none came. Confused, he counted heartbeats until his vision cleared. What he saw left him confused. There, seated at a small table with drink and food, was Aliz. She struggled to control her laughter.

"What's going on?" he demanded. Stiff pride harshened his words, and he instantly regretted his tone. She wasn't the target of his ire, merely the recipient. "Why aren't we dead yet?"

"It appears Edam Boone is a thinking man," she said between giggles. "You look foolish like this, Julian. We are no longer in danger, I think."

"That isn't reassuring," he replied. Julian took the empty seat opposite her. "Are you sure the food isn't poisoned?"

"Would it matter, if it was?" she replied. "We are trapped in their world, at their mercy. As I was saying, Edam Boone is unlike his predecessor. Zoraq Darc was a man after his own needs. That selfishness led to his downfall. They found his body a few days ago."

"The Inquisition?" he asked.

She nodded. A hint of sadness remained in the corners of her eyes, stretched thin by the lines gathered around them. "He wasn't a bad man, Julian, regardless of what we may believe. I like to think of him as misguided."

"Self-serving is closer to the truth," he grunted and poured a mug of water from the pitcher between them. "What's our next move?"

"We did come looking for them," she suggested. "The insurrection is on its knees. We are losing now, far more than winning. Numbers and supplies dwindle, while our enemies increase their grip. What choice have we but to stay with these people and find a way to survive?"

"We can continue the fight," he said. Darkness smoldered in his gaze. "Everything we've done, Aliz, cannot be thrown away on a whim. Yes, we are being beaten back, but the resolve never wavers. This is the only opportunity we are going to get before Nye assumes total control. I say we fight. The network is still there. By combining our two forces, we can break the enemy. Bleed them enough and they will turn away."

"A war of attrition?" her mouth dropped open.

"Is there any other kind?"

For all her admiration, she found the Guardsman frustrating on multiple levels. Obstinate and infuriating, he often let his military side shine through in the face of reason. That dominating trait forced issues where none existed, setting them on opposite sides. In another lifetime, he might have been a son to her, but the universe was filled with the broken dreams of other lifetimes. Aliz accepted their positions for what they were, soldier and statesman. Only, she was never a politician. She was the quiet, unrecognized voice lending strength when the Cardinal Seniorus needed it most. Even then, it wasn't enough. She reached a tiny hand across the table to grasp the back of his.

"We will get through this," she said in a motherly tone. "I know we will."

The door jerked open, allowing Edam Boone to sweep in unannounced. "How remains to be seen. Please, don't get up. We have much to discuss and little time to do so in."

Aliz exchanged looks with Julian, neither comprehending. She opened her mouth to speak but Edam cut her off with a wave.

"You wish to live. We wish to live. There is only one way to achieve this," he told them. "I have a plan."

TWENTY-EIGHT

3215 A.G. (After Gods), The Low Continent, planet Vau Prime.

Nestled deep in a cave system far from any civilized remains, the men and women still loyal to General Strannan and the Conclave planned their return to Krenz. It was a desperate moment, for word had reached them of the splintering of insurgent cells in the capital city. A stranglehold on the major population centers was increasing and Strannan was helpless to halt it. Those still alive were desperate for aid. By all accounts, numbers dwindled daily as Mobus Kale's enforcers hunted them down.

Strannan sat with his only friend and advisor, the shapeshifter Gedrick Silk. They discussed matters long into the night, for Gedrick was deep into his quest to discover who was spying for the Inquisitor General. A handful of leads failed to pan out, however, forcing the men to rethink their operation.

"I wish Julian was here," Strannan ran a hand over his scalp. "This is a damned wretched mess and only getting worse. How can our spy be so well concealed? I handpicked every soldier who followed me down to this cursed land."

"These are desperate times, Davith," Gedrick cautioned. "It is easier to accuse than to investigate thoughtfully. What I witnessed in the Inquisition headquarters was frightening on many levels, not the least of which was Nye's following and their growing fervor."

"Making what we need to accomplish more important than before. Damnation!" Strannan smacked a fist into his open palm. "Lieutenant Abernath!"

The young Guardsman hurried in and saluted. His uniform was shoddy, disheveled and frayed in too many places. His face bore a gaunt look, as if hollowed from a bright future. "General."

Strannan appraised his young aide and worried the man was a reflection of the entire command. "Where do we stand with the task I appointed you?"

"A handful of recruits trickle in daily, but with so few, it remains fairly simple to do a quick background check. The issue Lieutenant Mal and I are facing is our growing inability to access databanks. Sir, I fear the enemy is closing in."

Gedrick quickly added, "It was but a matter of time."

Grunting, Strannan said, "No doubt Kale is salivating at the prospect of bringing his personal vendetta to a close. We need a win. Has anyone been in contact with Captain Julian or Aliz in the last week?"

"Not that I am aware of, sir," Abernath replied. His tone implied his desire to be done with conversation and sent back to his task.

Realizing the dead end, Strannan shifted the conversation. "Have any of the new recruits come with combat experience?"

"A handful, though there was one man who bore a lethal demeanor. Vicious looking man, if I remember correctly, sir," Abernath said after some thought. "He has the look of a killer burned in his eyes."

Strannan exchanged looks with Gedrick but neither spoke. "Very well, I can only pray others will arrive with that same intensity. I don't suppose you got his name?"

"No, sir, but I can get it shortly."

The general waved him off. "Never mind. Keep trying to raise Julian. I need to know what is happening up there, if we stand any chance of reclaiming the city from Nye."

Gedrick cleared his throat the moment Abernath departed. "Are you really interested in having trained killers in your midst? We might as well court the Vaumagians."

"I need fighters. We have a solid base here but lack the experience necessary to win," Strannan explained. "Find this man, Gedrick. See what he offers. If there is even the slightest potential, bring him to me."

"Be careful what you wish for. Desperate times often reduce our capacity to think clearly. I will do as you wish, but I fear for you, old friend."

The shapeshifter departed with his head lowered. A cold sensation ran down Strannan's spine. Yes, he was desperate, but the only way to succeed was to throw everything he had at the problem. Even if it meant doing the unthinkable. Trapped in an endless cycle of regret and indecision, the former commanding general of the Prekhauten Guard struggled with the sensation of a hand grasping for him from behind.

Utan Husk sat with closed eyes and meditated. His mind was heavy with what lay ahead. Years of agony and the rising desire for revenge were so close to finale, he struggled with biding his time. The great enemy was near. Oh, so near. Davith Strannan had been the one thought that kept him sane during his imprisonment, and while the briefest hints of madness flickered in and out, Utan felt strength grow the closer he became to his target.

Night had fallen, leaving much of the motley assortment of soldiers and want-to-be's fast asleep. Utan snorted at their lack of professionalism. No unit he served in was as complacent as the group assembled in the caves around him. It was testament to Strannan's ineffectiveness to lead, and by association, a death sentence for any foolish enough to get in his way. This night was for knife work. Crawling from his cot, Utan snatched up the pair of daggers under his pillow and stalked off in search of his prey.

No one stopped or questioned him. The negligence, while appreciated, appalled him. Quiet urges surged through him. Kill them all. End all Strannan stands for and be free at last. Whispered promises of a golden future where Utan Husk could stride among the stars with unparalleled liberty, enacting his brand of justice on those deserving souls, fueled his steps as he crept closer to Strannan's private enclosure. Emboldened by the lack of interior security, Utan found himself at the wall of supply crates designating Strannan's area before he knew it.

There was no hesitation. No second thoughts to muddle the course of the future. Blades clenched tightly, Utan drew a calming breath and rounded toward the entrance. He was almost surprised to find it guarded. A burly female Guard officer stood in silence beside a junior sergeant. His eyes fluttered, struggling with the eternal war with sleep. Utan struck at the officer first. His blade punched down, deflected at the last moment as she spied him from the corner of her eye and threw up a blocking arm.

Blade hit bone. Utan, infuriated, swept his second blade through, slicing across the top of her unprotected chest. The lieutenant shouted a warning and collapsed. Blood pumping, Utan leapt over her and plunged his first blade down the sergeant's throat and into his chest cavity. Confusion spreading across the man's face, Utan twisted the blade before ripping it free. The sergeant was dead before he hit the ground.

Utan Husk pressed against the stack, anticipating a flurry of activity after the alarm was raised. Silence dominated the immediate sections of the cavern. He had been stealthy enough to carve open the path to his ultimate prize without raising alarms. Trusting his skills, Utan stepped over the bodies, and after curling his fingers around the curtain edge, peeled it back and slipped inside. Deadly intent in his every move, he struggled to contain the raw energy threatening to consume him. His right arm trembled as he fought with himself for control.

The soft snoring coming from the cot just ahead encouraged him. Utan Husk raised one arm as he stalked the final few meters to his long-awaited prey. The ease of it all raised the hairs on his neck and arms. How could the most powerful man on the low continent sleep in total confidence? No matter, Utan decided, his death was an inevitability at this point. He crossed the final steps and leered down on Davith Strannan.

Scarred, beaten and abused, the general was not the demon who haunted him during those long years in confinement. Instead of an all-powerful being wielding the fates of subordinates with impunity, Utan found an old man past his prime. Wrinkles and spots aged the general beyond his years. What hair remained was sparse and stark white. Utan almost felt sorry for him. A moment of regret threatened to unravel all. The weakness of the human spirit breaking through the crust of madness consuming him. Disgusted with himself, he slipped a finger over the blade's edge and drew blood.

Rediscovering his resolve, Utan crouched over Strannan, pressing a palm on the man's chest and the dagger to his throat. "Davith Strannan."

Eyes opening slowly, Strannan focused on the apparition pinning him down.

"Shhh, this doesn't need to be loud," Utan whispered.

Strannan stared back in silent defiance, but there was something missing. Utan growled at the insult, as he realized Strannan had no clue who he was.

"You don't remember me, do you?" he snapped. "My name is Utan Husk, General. Utan Husk. You sentenced me to life in prison for doing what *you* ordered. I killed countless people in your name. For the Conclave. For the future. What was my reward? To rot away in an obscure cell, forgotten by civilization."

"Utan Husk?" Strannan asked.

Utan whipped his dagger across Strannan's throat and stabbed him in the chest repeatedly. Anger took control, as ropes of blood flew, painting the walls and his face in unabated fury. Utan stabbed again and again, until strength abandoned him. It wasn't until he roared his frustrations to the universe that he realized he wasn't alone. Another figure slipped in behind him. Utan caught the clip of many pairs of boots swarming the entranceway. Eyes bleeding hate, he pushed off the corpse.

The shot echoed after Utan felt the burning pain punch through his spine and through a lung, before bursting free from his chest. Coughing a mouthful of frothing blood, he spasmed as a second, then third round, took his life. Utan Husk slipped off Strannan's body and hit the floor with a fleshy thud. Life fleeing him, he stared into the accusatory eyes of the man he just killed. *At least my name was the last thing that bastard said.* Darkness swarmed the corners of his vision. Calm beckoned. A final mockery of all that was his life. The irony of it insulted him. Utan closed his eyes. He felt his heartbeat slow. Thump-thump. Thump-thump. Thu—

Gedrick Silk lowered his blaster, smoke steaming from the barrel. The murderer was dead but it was too late to save his friend. Ignoring the body on the floor, Gedrick knelt beside Strannan and closed his eyes. There was no point in feeling for a pulse. No rise and fall of the chest. The universe had lost a great man. Gedrick Silk lost a better friend.

"Goodbye, Davith Strannan," he whispered. "You deserved a better fate. Perhaps now you can find peace as your long struggle ends."

Jas Abernath halted a pace behind him, staring down at the impossible scene. "What do we do now?"

Gedrick cocked his head, placing a comforting hand on Strannan's chest. "How is Lieutenant Mal?"

"Medic says she'll make it. Sergeant Dree did not fare as well," Abernath replied. He couldn't pull his gaze from the body.

Gedrick nodded. At least some good was salvageable. "Find out who this man is. I want to know if this is just the beginning or a one-time event."

"You never answered my question."

Exhaling the ache from his soul, Gedrick rose. "No. I didn't."

Forum Meeting Chamber, Krenz, planet Vau Prime.

One by one, the crimson robes flowed into the hundred seat Forum. Murmurs spread through the Cardinals as they tried to discern the purpose of the unscheduled meeting. Close to one hundred of the top clergy in the universe were gathered—ostensibly to discuss matters of state and the wellbeing of the member planets. An endless cycle of decision and argument worthy of those precious few acting as the hands of god.

A squad of armed Prekhautens marched in after the last Cardinal arrived. Weapons charged and in hand, they formed ranks in front of the Cardinal Seniorus dais and blocked the exits. Dissent broke out among the Cardinals. This was not the first time they were arbitrarily summoned on whim. With no clear leadership, whispers of Tinus Har's assassination, the Conclave was adrift in chaos. Several sided with Alain Nye, acknowledging him as the rising power. Those still loyal to the old ways, were forced to hold their tongues and bide their time until a day of reasoning returned to Vau Prime.

"What is the meaning of this?" Cardinal Porii Daam shouted to quiet the crowd. "We are not cattle to be toyed with."

Inquisitor General Alain Nye stepped out of the shadows, hands clasped behind his back. The war had aged him but he had never been more determined. His time of ascension was fast approaching. Soon, the time of the Inquisition would spread among the stars, burning all foolish enough to oppose it, until naught by compliance remained. It was inevitable. His strength was already flowing off-world. The earlier decision to disband the Forum and reeducate those members of the clergy who failed to see his point of view, proved an initial failure, prompting Nye to recall the Forum members—those still living and unimprisoned.

He stared up at them now, unimpressed with their false piety. *How many know the truth of the gods? How many are complicit in the great lie?* The travesty of their nature offended him. Generations prior once agreed to withhold the secret from humanity, knowing that should it get out, the universe would devolve into chaos. Already enclaves were burning under the subversion of the cult of Rengu. Vau Prime might have been cleansed but far too many worlds were awakening to the distant call to rebellion through Rengu. His own allegiance to Amongeratix, hesitant as it may be, presented a different dynamic. The web spun out of control, each new thread crossing the last with increasing intricacy, until he almost lost track of his goal. The dance was both enticing and haunting.

"Calm yourself, Cardinal Daam. This is not the first time we have done this," he said. The microphone attached to his uniform at the top of the buttons amplified his voice with unquestionable authority. "Cardinals of the Forum, the last time I stood before you, I demanded complete loyalty. Some of you gave your oaths that day. Others were … removed for their defiance. Though I disbanded this body, it became clear I yet have need of you.

"Why then do you persist on hampering my efforts to rebuild unity among our factions? How much more blood must be shed in tomorrow's name for you to be satisfied I am serious? By your defiance, you place entire populations in jeopardy. The newly restructured Prekhauten Guard is prepared to assume control of every planet under Conclave rule, imposing martial law without mercy," he drew a breath.

"However, I am not here to admonish you. Each of you knows the cost of rebellion, and for those still mired under the illusion of ignorance, some of you will fall to the Inquisition. Today, my friends, I come to offer condolences for your loss."

"What is this game, Nye?" Cardinal Thent demanded. "What loss?"

Feigning shock, Nye stepped back. A ripple went through the Guards. The rattle of weapons shifting stilled the gathering. "Why, Cardinal Seniorus Tinus Har is no longer with us. My offices learned of his passing just this morning."

A middle-aged woman with violet eyes rose. "Impossible. We would have heard of this much sooner than your spies."

"I can assure you, Cardinal Shri, my information is both accurate and unfortunate. With the death of the Cardinal Seniorus, I have decided there shall be no more. The order is hereby relegated to serving the Inquisition in all matters of faith and heresy. You will each be escorted back to your living quarters and held under guard until I can ascertain the levels of your loyalty."

Reclasping his hands behind his back, Alain Nye strode away with utter surety. "Oh, and Cardinals, there will be no further warnings. I suggest you all take this time to decide where your futures lead. Good day."

The doors opened and a full company of Guards with Inquisitor escorts flowed in. Nye walked out with a measure of clarity. No doubt Amongeratix was coming to solidify their union and bring a new order to the universe. The Inquisitor General found himself whistling as he took his time heading back to his office.

"Enter."

Mobus Kale tore his gaze from the holoscreen of data. Artificial light reflected from his bared metal arm. Surgeons initially suggested skin grafts and replicated flesh to lend him the appearance of normalcy. Mobus scoffed at their false concerns. Flesh, he had come to understand, was a mortal weakness holding him back. Let them see his augmentics and cower as word of his approach spread. Such was true years ago when he first lost his arm. Such remained true today.

A grizzled colonel stepped to his desk and rendered a crisp salute. "General, we have received the news you are waiting for."

Clicking the screen off, Mobus leveled his gaze on the man, failing to recall his name. "Is he?"

"Our spies have confirmed Utan Husk killed General Strannan."

At last! Years of rising tension seeped through his pores, no longer any reason to remain pent up within mortal confines. Mobus was caught between emotions. He felt joy at removing an obstacle and the one man capable of ruining his plans. Sorrow for the loss of a one-time mentor, but never friend. Disappointment in failing to execute the man himself.

"Are you certain? There can be no error," Mobus warned.

"Yes, sir. The body was witnessed."

Leaning back in thought, Mobus pondered his next moves. Eliminating Strannan was a major step forward. Once word spread throughout the city, resistance would crumble. What few active insurgent cells remained would either go deeper underground or fade into the general population. In effect, the battle for Krenz was nearing finale.

"What of Husk?" he asked.

The man was a wildcard. A loose end needing to be handled before Mobus could move forward. Dangers surrounding him, there was no room for error.

"Eliminated. One of Strannan's officers killed him before he could escape." There was no remorse in the colonel's voice. Men like Husk were a violent commodity, only to be used when the worst case scenario demanded it. His death was no loss, for the newly reorganized Prekhauten Guard or the chain of command.

"One less problem to deal with," Mobus mused. "Very good, Colonel. Send the order to all elements in the field. I want the insurrection crushed and total control of Krenz in my hands as soon as possible."

"Yes, General." He saluted again and left his commanding officer brooding.

The game had changed.

Exile. The only thought keeping Tinus Har, the deposed Cardinal Seniorus and former puppet of Alain Nye, from ending it all. After the botched assassination attempt, he was trapped between conflicting ideals. Either stay and confront his assailants by proclaiming a new age for the Conclave and its subjects or remain a continued target for the deviance sweeping the capital. Neither appealed to him. Decades of service to waning ideals, working through the hierarchy to reach the ultimate plateau was whisked away by a power move intended to eliminate one of the three ruling factions. Had he not pushed so hard for Lorenu Phos' removal, he might have been surprised.

The shuttle sailed through the darkness of space, oblivious to the trials of the man within. Tinus gathered what possessions he could, securing a small fortune in the process, and slipped away in the middle of the night. If not for the anticipation of Nye's betrayal, he would have been the victim of the assassin's blade. Emotions gripped him, preventing the blissful promise of rest from claiming him. He felt rage at being abandoned by those he worked so hard to cultivate to his ideals. Anger at the knife thrust in the spine Alain Nye delivered. Sorrow at leaving everything behind to carve out what meager living he could for his final years. Worst of all, none of it made any sense to him.

The plan had been to share power. Not consolidate it in one man's hands. Lacking support, Tinus Har was forced to flee without so much as announcement. How could there be one? Broadcasts were already being distributed throughout the seven hundred worlds bemoaning his death. He had become, to all effects, a ghost. Compounding his lament, he had no safe place to travel. His home-world of Mannus Prime was the site of the largest ground battle between Prekhauten factions. He had no allies, nowhere to go to ground.

Yet Tinus remained undeterred. The assassination was a setback. One he intended to counter with a hammer strike of his own. It was but a matter of time. Wheels in motion, he began the long road to redemption. All he needed now was a place to start. That an army of willing sycophants to enact his will. Uncomfortable grin twisting his face, Tinus thought of better days.

The lone shuttle continued on, the universe unaware of the approaching storm.

On his knees, head hung low, Sauwgon Hul's breath was ragged. Fires burned in his lungs. Victim of a thousand cuts, he was depleted. The magic imbued from his chosen disciples was bled out. Every fingertip was scorched to the bone. The stench of cooked flesh tickled his nose. Greasy strands of hair dangled over his face and shoulders. Sweat covered his body, muscles trembling in the absence of flames. Every torture devised by men and gods was burdened within his soul, the madness threatening to tear his already fragile sanity apart.

The giants were gone, defeated by his hands. Now alone, the shaman found he could not rise. His body ached for nourishment. Parched, his tongue filled his mouth. Starved, his stomach clenched in spasms. His fingers trembled, desperate for a drop of water. Lips cracked, nose broken, Sauwgon pitched forward in a boneless heap. Dust rushed into his open mouth, filling it with putrid flavors. He choked and lay still. Of the entire journey, this was where death at last came for him. The end of his people. Last of the precious bloodline begun ages past. Sauwgon Hul would disappear into anonymity, his name never remembered. The insult mocked his final breaths.

A roar filled the soot-stained skies. The ground trembled with thinly disguised rage. Such ancient power awakened him. Sauwgon found the strength to lift his head and gazed with wonder upon the massive creature filling his vision. The white sky dragon emerged from a golden halo wreathed in fire. A rent between time, space, and reality.

Through the curtain of golden light particles raining down upon the wounded land, Sauwgon spied a green land filled with crystal blue rivers. Tears filled his eyes.

"Sauwgon Hul. You have passed the trials. You alone have been found worthy of ascending."

The disembodied voice of the sky dragon penetrated his bones. A trickle of strength electrified him. Sauwgon pushed up from the ash, kneeling once again. Yet instead of being bowed, he raised his head with the defiance that had seen him through these many trials reborn.

"Who are you?" he asked, voice hoarse and breaking.

The sky dragon hovered above him. Angelic wings flapping on a light breeze. The winds cooled Sauwgon's face, providing relief from the heat and dryness.

"I am here to escort you to the golden realm, where you will at last achieve your potential and rise above the constraints of your fading flesh. Will you join me?"

Gaze fixated on the dragon's face, Sauwgon spied qualities akin to his own. Could this be an ancestor returned? The possibility made him giddy. He stretched forth a desiccated arm, grasping to touch the warmth of the dragon's flesh. Particles tickled the ruin of his fingers.

"Can you be true? After so long, am I to be relieved of this form?" he asked.

"There are many wonders in the universe you are not yet aware of, Sauwgon Hul. Take my wing and become more than the line of your people from the beginning ever could. I am future, past, and present in one. The sum of every experience imagined or real. I am … eternal. Accept my strength and join me, brother."

Brother. The word awakened stunning admissions. He was born an only child to a barren mother. The impossibility of his birth was heralded as a miracle among his tribe. He was the chosen one, meant to deliver eternity to his people. Oh, how wrong they had been. Here, at the end of all things, Sauwgon Hul was the lone survivor in a game of attrition.

"Yes. Yes, I shall take your hand. Lead me from this misery. I am ready," he proclaimed.

The dragon bobbed, lowering to within an arm's length of the shaman. "You are not quite ready. There is one final task you must accomplish before the gates can open."

"What? What must I do?" Desperation crept into his tone. He was so close.

"You must leave behind the name Sauwgon Hul and with it your mortal flesh."

Tears flowed freely. The end at last delivered, he bowed in submission. "This I shall gladly do."

"Then rise, brother and be forever known by your true name."

"What is my name, oh mighty sky dragon?"

"You … are Rengu."

Dragon and man touched and the world exploded in a cascade of brilliance.

"Did you feel that?" Ah'muf asked as the world trembled beneath them.

Elisa placed a palm flat on the vibrating dirt. The temple ruins coughed dust. She felt the anticipation coursing through it, yet how could such be possible on a mere building forgotten by time and space? She feared the answers but looked to Vishon Risa regardless.

"So it happens," the First Paladin murmured. His gaze, unfocused, stared up to the semi-darkened oculus in the center of the ceiling. "Do not concern yourselves with this. A moment in history, rebirths in a distant realm forgotten by space and time. Nothing you do can alter it, for it is the convergence of past and future. What has happened before, so shall again. All that matters to you is stepping across the threshold and claiming what is yours by right, Paladin."

The name chilled her. Elisa was first named Paladin by Sorrow on the snow covered north of Crimeat. Then she failed to discern its importance. Time and experience detailed a better picture, humbling her on multiple levels. Base instincts screamed for her to run. Flee this place and find what measure of life she could before the end, for surely the agents of Amongeratix would be ruthless in their persecution of all who opposed him.

Ignoring her mind, Elisa knew the only possible opportunity for survival was by following Risa's words and claiming the Grimfurvor, the weapon rumored to have the power of killing a god. Perhaps it was all foolish legend, inspired by dreams of the impossible and lonely imaginations of lesser people. Perhaps not. Real or not, she was determined not to be the one to pass such opportunity by. If claiming this weapon, as Sorrow explained, was the key to ending the eternal war and restoring peace to the universe, who was she to abandon those depending on her?

"What must I do, Vishon Risa?" she asked.

Ah'muf wailed quietly from behind.

"No tricks. No games. Stretch forth your hand and claim *Grimfurvor*. If you are found worthy, the blade will accept you," his easy smile alarmed her.

"If not?"

He shrugged. "Another will come. Another always comes."

Unexpected doubt awakening within, Elisa wondered how many more Sorrow had set upon this path. Unfortunate souls found wanting and removed from existence. True fear whispered from the corners of her mind. *Run, Elisa. Do not tempt fate. Death hounds your heels, eager for the sniff of flesh.* Pushing those ruinous voices aside, Elisa gained her feet. The universe may be ending but it would not be by her indifference.

Lacking confidence, she stalked across the chamber to the lone item. *Grimfurvor* sat upon an ivory pedestal, swathed in unnatural light. She felt the hum before she heard it. Tiny hairs on her arms standing on end, the closer she got. Shimmering walls of light danced around the weapon. Elisa stared in mute awe as *Grimfurvor* shifted from a blade to a small blaster, then a hand grenade, sword, and axe. Was this the promise of true power? A changling material conforming to its user? Could this kill Amongeratix?

She forgot when, but somewhere during her travels, Elisa was told the truth behind killing a god. She scoffed at the time, thinking the advice incredulous, yet a measure of truth resided in every fabrication. The best way to kill a god was to stop believing. Time would tell if this was true or not. For her part, she wasn't willing to find out. Having seen the destructive nature of the Three, Elisa knew what needed doing, and what was expected of her. They all deserved to be put under the blade for their continued crimes against humanity. Determined to enact her will, Elisa felt the wash of anticipation flow through her. Tiny fingers reached for the impossible weapon.

A thought struck and she stayed her hand inches from the energy field. "Vishon, what does it mean to be a Paladin?"

The wizened man smiled. Warm, fatherly. His weathered skin, the color of deep rust, cracked through the effort. "A worthy question. To be Paladin is to serve as a champion. Unparalleled in virtue, courage, and fortitude. To willingly set aside personal desire for the greater good and to do, unquestioningly, what must be done in the name of life."

Do what must be done. Words meant to become a mantra. Doubt slipped from her as unexpected revelations awakened. Her desire to eliminate the supposed gods served as the driving factor in her life. She was the hammer of fury. A vengeance to be reaped in the name of every innocent soul dragged down to the abyss. Elisa stiffened with the discovery of righteousness. Paladin. Avenger. Deliverer. She stretched forth once more and curled her fingers around ancient *Grimfurvor*.

An electric jolt flashed through her system. Tears burst free. Her heart hammered. Where once defeat dwelt, now fountained a wellspring of strength, energy. Elisa felt more alive in the first few moments of touching the weapon, than in her decades of life. This was the culmination of all she was ever meant to be. The promise of a new dawn, where she might finally be freed from the ghosts of her past. She wept as a string of unfulfilled promises crashed together, breaking upon the shores of her resolve. Elisa pulled and *Grimfurvor* came free, eager to fulfill its task and find a peace long due.

"Good. Very good, Elisa," Vishon Risa crooned. "Long have I waited for the one to come and deliver me into the oblivion I deserve."

Elisa spun. "What do you mean? Are you not the First Paladin?"

He swept his arms out. "The ruler of all you witness before you. Yes, I, Vishon Risa was elected to be the First Paladin. A warden of humanity and guardian of all souls. Long have I stewed in the reek of my failures, for I have been trapped in this place for many lifetimes. No other has survived the trials. Before your arrival, I cannot recall the last time I spoke to another. You are my salvation, and damnation, for my purpose is at last ended. You now claim the title of true Paladin and I shall be resigned to my eternal rest. Thank you, Elisa. Now go. Return to your realm and do what you were created to do. May you find success where so many of us have failed."

She obeyed without question. The finality of his tone removed doubt. Grabbing Ah'muf, Elisa hurried from the temple, even as a wave of darkness settled over them. They were slipping through the cracked doors, when she thought she caught a sigh of elation abruptly cut off. The doors closed behind her.

The shade of Mollock Bolle stood upon the steps, hands clasped in front as he patiently awaited her return. Though his part in the tale of the gods was ended, he found merit in being allowed to witness the opening salvo of humanity's rise. The time of forever shackles was drawing to a close. Elisa caught a hint of serenity unlocked in his eyes and felt her heart clutch.

"Is it done?" he asked.

"You have to go, don't you?" she replied, ignoring him.

He spread his arms, gesturing to the world around them. "Such is the way of things. We were never close, you and I. An alliance born through necessity, I think. That does not mean I grieve any less for our final parting."

"What does he mean, farisi?" Ah'muf asked. The desert dweller was tired of confusion, of being trapped in a realm of clutching impossibilities. His longing for the day when their task at last finished and they might find a life among the stars, grew stronger each day.

"His time is at last finished," she supplied. "Mollock Bolle can finally find peace."

"A long journey," the shade confirmed. "Stop Amongeratix. End the war. You are the one hope our kind has remaining. End the threat while there is still time. I have always known you were special, Elisa. There is a fire within you capable of greatness. Find it. Use it."

Mollock began losing definition. His image flickered as it faded. A final gesture and wave and he was gone. What wisps of shadows remained, blurred into the nothing surrounding them. Elisa felt a tear form, though she was unsure why. They were never close. Never considered one another friend. What little time they spent together, ended in tragedy. Yet he was the Prophet, and his task was complete. A day for closure.

A whirlwind of colors filled the gap in his absence. Elisa stared wide eyed as it spread. Glimpses of a better world filled with greenery and life beckoned. She knew it was their way home. Their one chance at returning to reality and ending a cycle of violence stretching back thousands of years. The weight of generations thrust upon her shoulders, Elisa clutched Ah'muf's hand in hers and stepped into the portal.

TWENTY-NINE

3215 A.G. (After Gods), Front lines, planet Mannus Prime.

"How are you feeling?"

Bootstrap opened his eyes, slow and reluctant. Waves of pain coursed through him, despite the medication the field surgeon gave him upon admittance. His mouth was dry, lips caked together. When he spoke, his voice was a shadow of its former self. "Like I've been beaten up one side and down the other. Where am I?"

"Field hospital. You're out of the fight, mercenary."

Squinting through the brightness of the tent's light, Bootstrap processed the voice. "That you, Matthias? I figured. Just can't kill you like you need."

"That's war," Matthias replied.

Failing to rise, Bootstrap landed back on the cot and closed his eyes. "What happened?"

"Tank took a direct hit from some nasty weapons. Your crew was killed. I barely got you out before the whole thing went up."

Pesin. Ger Fulan. Daldre. All gone on a whim. He struggled remembering the events leading up to his wounding. Bits of random images flashed but nothing steady. Most of the battle was a blur.

"Might as well relax. Doc says you're out of the fight," Matthias continued. "You have a fractured spine. Should heal but it will take time. Asher was sent back and assumed command in your absence."

Asher. Good choice. "Why are you here? Come to gloat?"

"Got a bad leg and severe burns. I get to sit this one out too."

Bootstrap snorted. "Just a pair of old cripples, aren't we?"

"Seems like it."

"Why did you save me? I've been threatening to kill you since we agreed to this fool plan," Bootstrap asked. "A normal man would have left me for dead."

"We don't abandon our own," Matthias said. "You know that. What's done is done. You're going to have to wait to kill me."

"Don't think I'll forget," Bootstrap admitted and dropped it.

He had much to think on and plenty of time for it.

Columns of enemy Guards flowed through the ranks. Weaponless, hands locked overhead. Haggle whistled amazement as he lost count after a thousand. Sounds of battle rang over the field. Somewhere ahead, the two allied forces were converging on the center of the camp where fighting was the fiercest. Those most loyal to the Inquisitor General and his usurpation would stop at nothing to prevent the inevitable. He knew it was a lost cause, for the vast firepower being brought to bear, would soon crush all resistance. It was but a matter of time.

"Did you ever think we'd see this?" he asked.

Jers raised his head. Exhaustion dulled his eyes. "Does it matter? They could have surrendered weeks ago and saved us the hassle."

Resentment laced his words. Jers, already tired of war, saw the end approaching. Serenity filled his soul over his decision. He knew it was the right thing to do. Unable to bear the responsibility for the lives of those beneath him, Jers best served the war effort by stepping away. His one dilemma sat in when and how to tell Annalilly. Under normal circumstances, his resignation was considered desertion and punishable with death by firing squad. The war on Mannus Prime was anything but normal. He watched the endless stream of enemy Guards with the sadness from recognizing a complete and thorough failure of all he held dear.

"But they didn't," Haggle reminded. "Would you respect them if they did?"

A look of disgust twisted his face. "What are you babbling about? They're the enemy."

"That doesn't mean they're still not Guards. Some of these were our friends, Jers. I keep looking at the faces to see anyone I recognize."

"Don't bother. They chose their side, just like us," Jers scolded. "We lose when we start treating the enemy like friends."

"We lose when we don't," Haggle whispered and fell silent.

A series of explosions along the forward line of troops stole their attention.

Jelin Quint ducked before a wave of debris slammed into his turret. Cries from the wounded flooded the open channel in his helmet, carrying with them a host of bad memories. He rewatched his friends fall, cut down by the withering rain of fire pouring up from the trenches. The full travesty of war laid bare by the knowledge he alone had survived. *We are all damned on this rock. It's just a matter of when.* Closing his eyes to escape the past, Jelin was grateful for the slap on the back of his helmet.

"You okay?"

He nodded, still unsure if he was or not. They had broken through to the exposed heart of the enemy fortifications, and in conjunction with the massed infantry divisions pushing from the opposite side of the battle, were squeezing his brother's command. Fighting grew fiercer the deeper they penetrated. Banno Quint's elite units were here, trapped in the heart of the war. He knew many were untested on the trenches, having sat in quiet reserve for months, as the regular line troops bled each other dry in a series of failed assaults. This time was different. The end was in sight. No more tomorrows.

Twisted over the anticipation, Jelin popped back up in his hatch and curled his hands around the firing triggers of the crew-served heavy weapon in front of him. The vehicle lurched and continued its path deep into the enemy's ranks. Clouds of black smoke choked Jelin. He felt the sweat collecting on his scalp, pressed in by his helmet's padding. Wars, he concluded, were meant to be fought by younger men than he.

"All units hold in place."

Jelin shook his head, positive he'd heard the last message incorrectly. "What did she say?" he asked the vehicle commander.

"Repeat. All units hold in place. Enemy command is offering their surrender."

That sneaky bastard. I knew he didn't have the stones to fight. "We should keep going. This is a trick."

No one answered. Why would they? He was the only one who knew his brother commanded the opposition. The only one with knowledge capable of defeating him. The others were tired of fighting, seeing their comrades fall. No good soldier wanted to fight. The men and women who'd come to Torgast's aid accepted the surrender for what it was—the cessation of hostilities and a chance to live another day. How could he blame them?

"All elements, what is Sergeant Quint's location?"

Did she just say my name? Jelin resisted the urge to depress the triggers as confusion and frustration clashed.

"Command, this is Fies. He's with me," the lieutenant replied.

"Roger, El-tee. His presence is requested at the surrender. Transmitting coordinates to you now."

Jelin didn't know the woman on the other end of the communication, but he didn't like her. Unable to contain his professionalism, he blurted, "What do they need me for?"

The delayed response suggested the caller bordered on disciplining his lack of etiquette. He closed his eyes, struggling to imagine why he was being called forth. The conclusion hollowed him. *How does Banno know I'm here?*

"Unknown. Double time it over there, Sergeant. Time is wasting."

He caught the slight click of lines crossing over.

"What's this all about, Quint?" Fies asked.

How do I explain this one? "I'm not sure, but there is something you should know, sir."

Quint and Fies hopped out of the command vehicle and headed for the cluster of officers and senior sergeants in a small clearing between two armies. Stacks of weapons littered the area, many of them thrown into a crater from an orbital impact. It occurred to Fies no one bothered considering what to do at the end of the battle. That tens of thousands of Guards would surrender, wasn't a discussed topic in any of the planning sessions. Repatriation was a possibility for some. Fies refused to believe they were bad people, simply because they fought for the opposite cause. He guessed most were loyal Guards, doing what they were ordered. There was no crime in that.

A grizzled master sergeant walked up to them, eyeing Quint from head to toe. "You Quint?"

"Yes, Sergeant. What's this a ..."

"This way," he jerked his head and turned back to the gathering.

Quint passed Fies a distressed look and followed. What he saw awakened a sense of disappointment he hadn't known he possessed. There, beyond the wall of dirtied and bloodied Guards, stood his brother with arms folded. Defiant in every regard. Banno's haughty look turned to disgust as he spotted Jelin.

"I figured you were lurking in this rabble," Banno called. His booming voice rumbled across the area.

"Banno. You're supposed to be dead," Jelin snorted.

"Surprise."

"Sergeant Quint, your brother requested your presence before offering his formal surrender," a major he didn't recognize explained.

"Uh huh." Jelin ignored the man, eyes fixed on Banno. "Well, I'm here. Sign the document and let's get you hauled off to a Conclave prison world. You've cost me enough already."

"Oh, little brother, I haven't even started," Banno leered. "The only way I'm surrendering is after I kill you."

Exhaling, Jelin rolled his shoulders. He began removing his armor, after handing his rifle to Fies. "I figured as much. Let's get this over with."

On equal terms, brother charged brother. Soldiers roared their approval. Others flinched, preparing to attack. Not a single officer moved to stop the confrontation. Jelin swung first, his first cracking Banno's jaw hard enough to send ropes of spittle flying. His reward was a gut punch that drove the air from him.

"You were always the weakest of us, Jelin," Banno taunted. He rubbed his jaw, giving Jelin time to catch his breath. "Mother's little runt. I've hated you for years, but learning you were attached to that fucker Torgast's command, gave me purpose. I don't mind losing this battle, as long as I get to kill you first."

Jelin rushed, tackling his brother around the waist. They collapsed in a flurry of punches and kicks. A rib snapped. A tooth broke free. Jelin roared in pain as his brother dug a thumb into the corner of an eye. Banno pressed his attack, pressing his forearm against Jelin's throat, with as much strength as he had. Jelin tried rolling, but the weight on him was too much. He brought his knee up, catching Banno in the groin. The older brother slipped off, allowing Jelin to deliver three quick strikes to his ears before scrambling free.

Sputtering as fresh air flowed again, Jelin spat a mouthful of blood. He heard the familiar sound of a blade slipping free. Banno never did fight fair. Eyes watering, he braced. Banno didn't disappoint. He lunged for Jelin's chest. A quick strike to the heart and the end of a lifetime of jealousy and disappointment. He never made it. Jelin stepped into the blow, taking a glancing slash across his arm, while simultaneously punching Banno in the throat and hooking a leg behind

Banno's knee. The larger man fell back, Jelin on top of him. Blow after blow rained down on Banno, transforming his face to a bloodied mess. Somewhere the blade fell free and Jelin snatched it. He had it pressed to his brother's throat, drawing a thin red line before stopping.

"Enough! This ends now," Jelin snarled between labored breaths.

Hatred flared in Banno's eyes. "Do it, you miserable excuse for a brother. Kill me now and go running back to mommy."

"You get to live, brother. Spending the rest of your days in a prison cell, forgotten by the universe. Death is too good for someone like you."

He punched Banno between the eyes, knocking him out. Seeing their commander sounded defeated, stole the energy from his army. Those still in possession of their weapons cast them down. Their fight was gone. Fies came forward to help Jelin off his unconscious brother. The war for Mannus Prime was over.

"Admiral Falchi, we've received an urgent message from the surface. The enemy has surrendered."

Falchi, ever resolute while in uniform, stood straighter as unseen forces slipped from his shoulders. The initial purpose for coming to Mannus Prime was fulfilled. The hard part started next. He knew they needed to move fast to secure the manufactories and begin producing ammunition and equipment. Alain Nye would be furious with the loss, making Mannus a constant target, until it was either destroyed or back in his grasp. Falchi refused to allow that. A convoy of construction vessels were en route to ring Mannus with defense platforms, satellites, and spaceports for the battlefleet Falchi intended on stationing in orbit. If Nye wanted it, he was going to pay a terrible cost.

"Captain Samuel, I believe it is time to see just how loyal our opposition is to the Inquisitor General's ideations for the universe," Falchi said. *And more than time to appoint a field general to our growing army.*

Samuel grinned. "Aye, Admiral. My shuttle is fueled and waiting."

"Very well, Captain. Let's go see what all this fuss was about."

Torgast made his way through the endless kilometers of destruction. What had once been verdant fields, was now little more than mud and broken lives. Entire companies of Guards were confined to quarters, as his leadership cadre assessed their individual loyalty. Those deemed to be innocent to Nye's schemes, were taken away to be blended into other battalions, while those adamant in their cause, were arrested and processed for transport to a prison world. A great many more were done with fighting and released from their oaths of service. Perhaps, if they all laid down their weapons, men like Nye would never come to power.

Two days had passed since the brothers Quint ended the war. Time with which Torgast came to grips with the secret perpetuated by the stalwart Cardinal Virom. Had he known … Red robes, the only stop of brightness in an otherwise drab world, the Cardinal walked alongside Torgast, passing messages of hope and encouragement to those Guards along the way. He reasoned they needed a true Conclave presence, now more than ever. The moral victory bestowed upon the victors soon passed to the vanquished, helping bolster ranks and swing decisions by those still on the fence. Virom knew better than to accept his presence alone as the reasoning behind their conversions. He quietly assumed it was the absence of the Inquisition, lending authority to the Conclave, proving the righteousness of his cause in the process. At this stage, Virom was willing to take any victory.

They found a host of leaders assembled in the former command tents of Banno Quint. Torgast saluted Admiral Falchi and acknowledged the others before settling into an empty field chair. Virom sidled down beside him, eagerness written upon his face as the future was discussed.

"Commander Torgast, it is my pleasure to make your acquaintance at last," Falchi began. "Now that we are all assembled, it falls to us to determine the future of Mannus Prime, as well as our persecution of the war against the usurpers. Before we begin, there is one matter that must be addressed. Torgast, our army has more than tripled in size since this battle. We now have the combat strength to take the fight to our enemies, rather than wait to be assaulted. This unexpected growth presents new challenges, however."

"I don't follow, sir," Torgast said.

Virom kept a secret smile.

"Every army needs a good leader. Someone willing to place the needs of subordinates first and do whatever is necessary to ensure mission success, while always thinking of his people. The job is yours, if you want it."

Mouth agape, Torgast spread his gaze around the room to the sea of faces, some known, others not. Everyone, including Jelin Quint, offered a nod of approval. Torgast rose, hands shaking. He was a career officer, but the unexpected civil war left his future in limbo. Without the proper command hierarchy, there was no room for advancement. To hear Falchi offer him the opportunity to continue to serve the men and women who won this war, was unexpected, and most welcomed.

"Sir, I would gladly accept command of this rabble," he said, throat dry.

Falchi broke into a wide grin. "Very good. Oh, and I'm going to have to promote you. Having a mere commander in charge of an entire army is unheard of. Congratulations, Brevet General Torgast."

The tent broke into cheers.

"He deserved it," Jelin said to Fies once they ceremony concluded and they were alone again. He looked to the odd collection of sergeants and soldiers spread out nearby. Many were cleaning weapons, repacking their gear, or sleeping. Seeing them tugged his heart. He missed the camaraderie. The sense of belonging.

"Lot of good people here," Fies nodded. His gaze flicked to Jers. "Some of that I can control. You provided an invaluable service to the platoon and I'm in need of a new squad leader. Are you up for taking the reins on this band of miscreants?"

Stunned, Jelin was speechless. There was nothing special about this squad. They were much like every other small unit in the Prekhauten Guard, only they weren't. Their bonds were forged through experiences, unlike most others. He heard the laughter of the heavy weapons specialists as they shared a private joke. Saw the young medic roll her eyes in mirth. Three Guards were engrossed in a dice game. They were much more than a squad. They had become family somewhere along the line.

"I think I can handle that, sir," Jelin said.

Annalilly slapped him on the back, eliciting a wince as the sting spread through his shoulder. "Welcome to the team."

Jers listened. He was happy for Jelin Quint. The man had lost everything just a few short weeks ago, pushed to the edge and left for broken. No one deserved to live out their days mired in survivor's guilt. Guards like Quint needed a home. There was no better place than with the men and women in this squad. Only a handful remained from prewar days. A host of faces and names filled the ever-growing roll call of lost comrades. Kastor. Kedric. Boller. The list stretched back, all the way to those frantic first few days on Crimeat when all this was a supposed small defection by rogue Guards.

The battle's end left Jers spent. He had nothing else to give. How his squad pulled through the siege of Mannus Prime unscathed, was nothing short of a miracle, but he knew it couldn't last. New names would join the ghosts of those lost. It was inevitable. He refused to stick around long enough to see any more of his friends fall. The fragility of his soul pleaded for release, lest he become the next tragic casualty.

"On your feet, Jers. We've got a conversation to be had."

He groaned at Annalilly's perpetual growl. *Was the woman ever happy?* Obeying, Jers followed her away from the squad to a quiet area just out of earshot. Once alone, she squared on him. He briefly wondered whether they were about to fight.

"You still intent on quitting?" she demanded.

Shit. "I am. I'll desert, if I have to."

Frowning, Annalilly produced a small datapad from her blouse pocket. She handed it to him. "No need for that. You and I have never been that close, but I respect you, Jers. Hells, I might even love you in that weird way only soldiers who've been through shit and battle can do. Doesn't mean I agree with you, but at least I respect it."

"What's this?" he asked, taking the pad.

"Your papers. Sergeant Jers, you are officially relieved of your rank and all responsibilities associated with service in the Prekhauten Guard. Congratulations, you are officially a civilian."

The pronouncement stunned him. He almost collapsed as his knees gave out. A free man. No more wars. No more death. Only the chance to prove his worth as a contributor to the universe, for good or bad. Months of dreaming and now, in the blink of an eye, it was finished.

"I …"

"Save it. You're a good man, Jers. Better than me," she snorted. "Go and make something of your life. You've earned it. I'll take care of the others. Maybe one day, when all this insanity is finished, we can meet on a distant world and remember the good times. We owe it to ourselves.

Now go, before I get sappy. Say your goodbyes and ensure you do a proper turnover with Sergeant Quint. He's a crazy bastard but good to have in a fight. We'll get you back to Wexanos. I'm sure Tannus can arrange transport to whatever world you want to plant your flag."

"Thank you, Annalilly," he mumbled and did the unthinkable. He hugged her and refused to let go, as tears rolled down his cheeks. Consumed by emotion, Jers never noticed her returning the deed.

The random act of kindness was not lost on the squad, however. Haggle spotted them first and word quickly spread. Leaving their weapons and gear in place, the squad surrounded Jers and Annalilly and joined in the tearful goodbye.

"I'll give it to you ground pounders, you all have a bond most of the rest of us will never know," Asom admitted sometime later, as they sat around a small fire cooking their food.

The Marine never once felt comfortable fighting on the ground. A never-ending cascade of new ways to die presented at every turn, leaving him rocked. What he desired now was the close confines of his ship and the opportunity to direct battles as he saw fit. He'd lost seven Marines on Mannus Prime, each a terrible blow. Their places were already filled from the ranks of prisoners. Wars never lacked the bodies to put in uniforms. Training them would take time and more than a measure of trust, but he was already looking forward to it.

"I never thought about it," Annalilly replied. Her deadpan delivery remained constant, no matter how dire the situation turned. "We just look after each other, same as you space jocks do. This was a hells of a fight, wasn't it?"

He nodded, staring out over the devastation their assault accumulated. Ranks of armored vehicles lined the way back to the rear assembly area. The Shadow Hammers who survived the battle busied refitting their tanks for the next engagement. Rumor had it Matthias and Bootleg had made peace and were now discussing future operations. Asom knew better than to believe everything he heard, but the duo proved a formidable blow when needed. Perhaps it wasn't the craziest thing he heard this day.

"Hard to believe we made it through," Asom agreed.

"Bloodied, but alive," she added. "It's been a pleasure working with you."

"You as well. Never thought I'd have the opportunity to say that to a ground pounder."

"Never thought I'd say it to a space jock."

He laughed. Old rivalries remained despite the changing of all they knew. The civil war showed no signs of slowing down. Other worlds were under siege. Millions of Guards busied fighting each other in forgotten reaches of the universe. Asom didn't suppose their paths would cross again. A fact filled with melancholy. He extended his hand.

"Sergeant Annalilly, it's time to head back to my ship. Next time, let's do this in space, where I can feel comfortable instead," he chided.

Her eyes widened. "You must be mad. Risk being vented into space? No, thank you. Surface warfare might not be ideal but at least if I get shot, I only have to fall a few feet."

She took his hand.

He couldn't argue with her logic. Offering a final nod, Gunnery Sergeant Asom stalked off, barking orders as he went. "Marines! Ruck up! Time to go home."

Time to go home. No truer words were ever spoken. Annalilly watched them walk away for a bit before turning to her own platoon. The fight for Mannus Prime might be finished, but the long war continued.

Homes burned. Chaos descended from the stars to rip the quiet jungle community apart. Brother fought brother, as conflicting ideologies emerged. A new power threatened the old standards long established through generations of meticulous cultivation. That power was Rengu. Hatred burned as brightly in those new adherents to the forgotten god as it did their village. No one was safe. Scores of bodies already littered the village. Lacking modern weapons, they died by sword and spear.

Kaline watched it all through her enhanced night vision goggles. Her wrath consumed her, yet she was unable to move from this spot. Beside her, the Captain cradled his rifle in anticipation of unrealized threats. Their return was far different from how they fled. Angry villagers forced them away, but it was through harnessing that anger and boiling it over into open hostility, Kaline thrived. These people were beneath her. Contempt twisting her features, she watched with glee as they tore each other apart.

"Beautiful, isn't it, Captain?" she cooed.

Face hidden behind his issue helmet, the former Guardsman remained silent. He had seen the power of words too many times on the battlefield. The results were always the same. Bodies. Regret. The pomposity of righteousness spewed to the victors. All of it sickening. How many more needed to die for vanity's sake? It was an ages old question without answer, for the madness of men stretched deep into the soul.

"You knew this was my intent," she added after becoming uncomfortable with his silence. "Did you not?"

"Doesn't make watching it any easier to stomach," he said.

"This needed to be done. We cannot allow lesser beings to dictate where the word of Rengu is spread. His fires will consume this planet from here. Our purpose is fulfilled," Kaline said. "All you gaze upon now belongs to Rengu."

A man of unquestionable loyalty to those under whom he served, the Captain never put stock in blind faith. Man was a thinking creation, capable of overcoming the old fears. Religion was a dying construct, one designed to keep the masses in check, while those in power reaped the benefits. He never once met a clergyman worthy of devotion. The authority in Kaline's tone awakened new questions. Ones he was afraid to explore.

"Would these people best serve Rengu by remaining alive? This is wholesale slaughter, not religious rebellion."

"This is the gods' will."

The finality of her tone ended the conversation. His unease grew as the depravity of the scene below heightened. Dissatisfied with pointless death, he longed for the day when he could at last put down his rifle and walk away. Movement from the corner of his eye drew his attention to the left. Sensors picked up a body of villagers moving in their direction. Elevated heat signatures left their intent without doubt. *Here we go again.*

"Mistress, we need to get you back on the shuttle. Now."

She flinched at the force of his tone and looked where he pointed. Men and women, some speckled in blood, emerged from the undergrowth with murderous intent. Torches blazed in a few hands. Others brandished archaic weapons promising a brutal demise. Kaline stepped back, despite her defiance.

"Brothers and sisters! This is a time to rejoice. To give tribute to Rengu for his many gifts," she began. "We have come so far! Go back to your village and deliver his justice to those unbelievers, so that we may rise again as one."

"Lying bitch!"

"We're done listening to you!"

"Twisted the whole village. Now it's your turn!"

A rock sailed through the crowd and struck her chest. Kaline cried out and staggered back. The mob charged, spanning the distance in a harrowing moment. Battle instincts took over as the Captain's first round took a villager in the stomach. The man pitched forward, others clambering over him to get their prize. A nightmare scenario unfolded. One that should have been predicted, based on their last encounter. Frowning behind the security of his helmet, the Captain fired as fast as he could. It was not enough.

"RUN!" he shouted to Kaline.

The stunned woman gave him a final look, as if understanding his intent, and hurried back to the waiting shuttle. Unbearable weight pressed on her conscience, for his was a willing sacrifice in the name of a cause far greater than himself. Or so she chose to believe. Kaline fled as fast as weary legs carried her. Each step brought her closer to safety and an undeserved escape from this planet. Her heart bemoaned the echoing sounds of gunfire as they abruptly cut off. Alone and friendless, she vowed to lament the Captain's loss.

A stray bolt from his rifle sizzled through the air past her to strike the blackened hull of the shuttle. Ducking, Kaline picked up her pace, lest she be killed by her champion's weapon. A fitting demise to a mission of ego. Confused with how quickly the situation devolved, Kaline admitted the brashness of her decision. They never should have returned. Now her Captain was dead out of vain ignorance. A proud man, with questionable morals, but one who never once waivered from her side. Alas that she never knew his name.

Cheers erupted from the crowd. Kaline risked a glance back and was appalled to see the villagers stripping the former Guardsman of his armor and clothing, before hoisting his lifeless corpse over their heads. Arms and legs dangled, slapping the backs and chests of those villagers. It was the momentary glimpse of his empty eyes staring back at her that ripped Kaline's heart out. She became lost, a victim of her own greed. Doubts flickered to life, awakened by the primal desire to abandon her mad quest and accept the inevitable.

Rocks started pelting her. More struck the soft ground to either side as she ran. Kaline struggled through the bog of doubt and found solace in the knowledge of her Captain willing to die, so that she might escape. A glorious demise for a better man. Refusing to allow his memory to fade into oblivion in a nameless village, Kaline gained the safety of the shuttle ramp. The copilot fired several shots from his blaster, enough to deter the bloodthirsty mob and allow her the time needed to climb aboard. The shuttle was in the air before she gained the top of the boarding ramp. Lurching, Kaline grasped the nearest strap hanging from the ceiling to prevent from dropping back to the already shrinking earth.

Dull thumps pinged the shuttle's undercarriage. A few more rifle shots struck without causing damage and the ramp closed shut. Confident she was safe, Kaline listened to the sounds, now barely distinguishable above the roar of igniting engines. The copilot disappeared after helping her to her seat. An act of humiliation getting the best of her frayed nerves. She closed her eyes and leaned back into the webbed seating.

"None of this was meant to happen," she mumbled. "Now, you're gone. My lust for power and a twisted need for revenge, robbed your life when I needed you most. What is left?"

The darkness mocked her. Kaline stretched forth her senses, desperate for a measure of reassurance, but none was to be found.

"Mistress, the pilot wishes to know our destination."

Cold regard from the copilot disturbed her. Kaline thought to chastise the man for ignoring her loss of companion. Heroes deserved better. Yet how? Reluctant introspection showed a woman alone, bereft of a once robust support network and thriving ministry. Her devotion to Rengu fundamentally transformed all she had once been. That past now occluded by dementia and hollow glories, teased Kaline. Where to go indeed?

Feelings of abandonment crept in. Her psyche flooded with empty emotions. Gone. It was all gone. Kaline felt true fear for the first time, rocking her to the core of her soul. Rengu's influence faded, leaving a broken woman in its place. What little confidence remained in her was fragile, desperate for purchase to be renewed. Kaline lacked even that. Each time she closed her eyes she witnessed the Captain's inglorious demise, mocking all she once stood for.

Returning to An'kuruku to assemble a new army was a distinct possibility, though the desert planet already languished under a wave of poverty and desolation caused by her rebellion, though she suspected it had more to do with Amongeratix's unexpected arrival. No, she needed to find a new world to start anew. One who did not know the tortures of the gods. Kaline vowed, there in the quiet of the shuttle as it rocked through space, to avenge her Captain and remove the stain of Rengu from the universe altogether.

It was the least she could do.

THIRTY

3215 A.G. (After Gods), Deep Space, *Behemoth.*

The wave of magic slammed into the unsuspecting witches. Green flames engulfed the center woman as the others fell back to regroup. Sister Alessandra pressed the attack, desperate to turn the ambush on the renegade witches. Taken off guard by a withering salvo from small arms, the Crimson Sisters protecting the landing bay entrance broke.

"Keep moving! We must get to that shuttle," Alessandra said.

Her voice was strained from her use of power. Sweat poured down her face, dripping into her eyes. A flicker of movement as two others joined her. Timers on the engine bombs were ticking down, narrowing the strike force's chances of escape. Bolts of magic flared from behind, striking bulkheads and splashing against one of the witches. Her scream as her right arm melted from the elbow down, reverberated through the group.

A few Blood Witches threw up a protective barrier, deflecting most of the incoming magic to the walls where ochre flames charred the abused steel with unmitigated fury. Holes opened, revealing cabling and support frames. A trio of witches combined their power and returned fire. Their magic was dispelled with ease. Steam from a burst pipe flooded the separating space, transforming the battleground an eerie shade of color and shadow. Bolts of raw energy collided, as the dual cadres attempted to destroy each other.

Unable to engage on both fronts, Alessandra frowned. The defenders were regathering and throwing magic back, forcing her to stay engaged. Warning klaxons sounded and the pressurized bay doors opened. Alessandra got her first look into space and the looming starship preparing to dock. There was little doubt as to who commanded. She prayed whatever force *he* brought was manageable. Otherwise …

The rear would have to deal with their own problems. She had her own to deal with. Unless Alessandra found a way to break the enemy and open an egress to the escape shuttle they were doomed.

Paradise Tear watched the woman to her right disintegrate, molten drops of flesh and bone dripping to the deck and discovered the depths of her fury. She unleashed a withering blast from her rifle and charged. Undaunted by mortal energies, she stepped into the line of fire and was immediately struck by magic. She winced in expectation, but upon discovering she remained unharmed, broke into laughter. The Crimson Sisters opposing her stepped back, suddenly uncertain of their abilities.

Turning to the others, Paradise shouted, "Secure the landing bay. I'll handle this."

The giant burst forth, firing from the hip as she closed the gap. Paradise Tear was among the enemy in a pair of heartbeats. She fired into the cowl of one witch and was rewarded by a gout of blood pumping forth. A blast of magic struck Paradise's shoulder, forcing her to turn and slam the flat of her rifle into the assailant. The broken weapon clanged as it hit the deck. Enraged, Paradise attacked with a flurry of kicks and punches. The handful of witches confronting her held their ground and died as a reward.

Grunting from exhaustion as the last witch collapsed in a crimson heap, Paradise frowned at her ruined weapon. Confident the threat was eliminated, she rejoined her companions and was dismayed as she recognized the face peering back at her from the docking ship's bridge. Amongeratix. The destroyer of worlds had come to claim his ship. They were too late. Drawing the imbued sword from behind her back, Paradise Tear strode through her friends to meet the new threat. Death's mocking laugh echoed in her mind. She had never held the strength to best her cousin.

"Tolde Breed, take the others, flee back through the ship and evade whatever forces are set upon you. I will lead my cousin from the landing bay and give you time to escape," she said.

The finality in her tone induced an unexpected struggle in the Inquisitor. Her importance to the future of the universe was a subject dear to Tannus, prompting the giant to implore with Tolde to keep her from harm's way. Should Paradise fall here, the fate of every living soul stood in jeopardy.

"We cannot leave you," he replied. "Tannus was adamant in this."

She offered a sad look on him. "Tannus is not here. None of you have the strength to withstand Amongeratix. Only I can delay him. Do this, Tolde. Save the others. You are a special man and have a destiny to fulfill."

Confused, his fingers tightened their grip on his rifle. The boarding ramp extended from the ship, followed by a massive shadow of the one being capable of striking fear in Tolde's heart. A handful of previous encounters did little to diminish the nightmarish majesty of the most hated of the Three. Resolve bled from his weakened knees, yet he remained defiant. Unable to abandon his friend to certain demise, Tolde accepted his fate and moved beside Paradise.

"No, Tolde. I must do this alone." She knelt to stare him in the eye. "This is not my end. Amongeratix is raw power, but he will not kill me. I am the key after all. He needs me alive to enact his plan. Go. Flee while you can and return to Tannus."

His heart hurt, wounded by her words. Many lives depended on him leading them to safety. She was right. There was nothing he could do. "Very well. May we meet again, Paradise Tear. I will not rest until you are among us again. You have my vow."

"One I gladly accept," she said.

Rising, Paradise brandished her sword once again and prepared to give her cousin a proper greeting.

"You heard her, we need to leave. Now," Tolde shouted.

Sister Alessandra gawked at him. Her blood raised, the witch was building her power to throw at Amongeratix. Tolde had seen this before and the results were horribly predictable.

"Alessandra, we must do this," he urged.

Sparks danced from her fingertips then flickered out. "Sisters, follow the Inquisitor."

The strike force gathered and sprinted back into *Behemoth's* interior under Paradise Tear's watchful gaze. They were proof not all was lost. That some good remained in the universe and it had the heart to stand up to tyranny. They rounded the corner and were lost from sight. It was better this way. Some matters were strictly for family.

The first tremors rippled through the ship's core. Her eyes widened. The bombs were detonating.

Ragan pitched forward as he lost balance. Luma's quick reaction to snatch his collar from behind, the only thing preventing him from slamming into the undulating decking. Dazed, the youth failed to comprehend what was happening. No warrior, he insisted on accompanying what he now viewed as a doomed quest. Madness hounded his every step. Nothing made sense. Ragan stalked the corridors of an impossible vessel unlike anything on Rastarok. His early dreams of seeing the stars were a far cry from the twisted reality mocking his youthful innocence. No experience in his young life, including the quest to find Braewynd, compared to the devilish torments of wild magic and fury consuming him since joining Tolde on the Blood Witch comet. Cursing his stubbornness, Ragan ran behind Tolde as the sounds of battle raged.

That they were going the wrong direction, was not lost on him as successive blasts ripped through the engine room. Sirens screamed through the beleaguered vessel. Every groan a death rattle. Imagination got the better of him, as he imagined *Behemoth* tearing apart, leaving them drifting frozen through space for eternity. Ragan regained his stride and kept moving. Away from the witchery being unleashed and the giant killer who had just boarded.

Hurrying down the corridor, Ragan stayed a step behind Tolde. Though the man was no longer Tobas, the Inquisitor continued treating him in a fatherly manner. Endearing, it provided Ragan an outlet he lacked during his youth on Rastarok. He didn't know what initially drew him to Tobas, but their bond strengthened with each passing crisis. Portions of the ship exploding beneath him, Ragan worried this was the end.

"Where are we going?" he gasped between breaths.

"Keep moving!" Tolde shouted.

He did. The alternative meant death. Luma Kai was in front of him, her light footsteps almost gliding over the ancient decking. What little he saw of *Behemoth,* suggested the vessel was older than humanity. A titanic juggernaut wreaking havoc across the stars unrestrained. Ragan gleaned snippets of information about the gods and how their internal strife led to the rise of the Conclave and the near destruction of all in the gods' realm. He shuddered at the thought of an entire fleet of ships this powerful ranging through space and time. How could anything stop them? *Behemoth* buckled again, lurching port as a trio of explosions threatened to tear her hull apart.

Keep running, Ragan. Keep running.

*

Paradise Tear gripped her sword, fingers bleeding white. It had been long since she last sparred with Amongeratix, and if the past were any indication, she would come to rue this decision. Licking her dry lip, she swept her gaze over him and was surprised to see he was unarmed, then she remembered he was coming to claim his command ship. What need would there be for weapons on his own vessel? Amongeratix finished descending the ramp and stood with feet spread shoulder width apart. Challenge issued.

He waited, ever out of reach; a caged predator ready to bring ruin to any opponent. Paradise struggled with the urge to flee, to escape with her friends in the mad hopes of surviving long enough to gain the sanctity of Blood Witch abbey. Their fates were no longer in her hands, however, all she controlled stood before her. Committed to the battle, Paradise stalked forward.

"Cousin, this is not way to begin a family reunion," he taunted. "Would that Tannus were here instead perhaps I might find challenge."

"I'm afraid I will have to do," she replied.

A gleam entered his eyes, giving her pause.

"Oh, yes. I believe you will do nicely. I've been searching for you, dear cousin. Of all in our twisted little family, you are the one I have desired most," he said. "Your defeat will spark the new age I am bringing to the universe."

She halted midstride, nerves failing. "What madness are you talking, Amongeratix?"

Paradise knew the truth. That hers was the genetic code capable of activating the artifact without mortal intervention and slaying what remained of their people. Two beings possessed the knowledge of where the remnants of her people rested. Tannus and Paradise Tear. Her one solace in confronting Amongeratix lay in knowing she was of no use to him dead.

"Ever your words spew poison, cousin. End this charade of righteousness and return to the quiet skulk of your frozen planet," she seethed.

From childhood his inability to accept taunts spurred roiling vengeance in the furnace of his soul. Amongeratix harnessed that fire and used it during the final war that left his people a ragged collection of survivors and withered corpses. His was the way of pain. The only way to cleanse the universe was by eliminating what remained of that once proud race. Humanity already fell upon its knees in supplication. Soon the crown would be his.

Amongeratix beckoned her with an open palm. "Come, cousin. Let us test your martial prowess one final time."

She leapt, her sword slicing through the empty space he just occupied. Laughing, he welcomed the challenge.

Algiss Her watched in awe as Amongeratix made quick work of his cousin, even as the Crimson Mistress stewed over the loss of so many of her disciples. Damage control and fire suppression systems turned the ominous calm *Behemoth* offered upon her arrival to chaos. Those Sisters still alive were ordered to help mitigate the damages in the engine room, lest the ship fail altogether. The surviving intruders disappeared within the ship's bowels. A minor irritation without Paradise Tear, Algiss ignored them and worked to save the ship.

A final glance at the holoscreen showed Paradise on her knees, head bowed. Pieces of her broken sword lay on the deck nearby. The outcome was never in doubt. Algiss snorted and watched as menials crawled from the shadows to bind the giant. She viewed the extent of Paradise's wounds. Her face darkened with bruises, she was thoroughly beaten. Amongeratix had but a single scratch across his lower jaw.

"Mistress Her, we have found the intruders. They are making their way back to the shuttle bay."

Algiss drummed her aged fingertips on the console before her. Killing them meant little in the scheme of things. She achieved her goal of finding *Behemoth* and preparing it for Lord Amongeratix. Pursing her lips, she watched as the image flipped. The ragged handful of survivors stormed down a corridor swathed in shadows. Their energy and haughtiness torn from them.

"Let them flee," she said.

"Mistress?" the witch asked.

"We have what we came for. Let Ruma Zzein discover the truth of failure. She will think hard before sending a second expedition," Algiss explained. "I want those fires out and repairs begun before I return."

"Where are you going?"

Algiss fixed the young witch with a smug glare. "To greet our new master."

Sister Alessandra, fists clenched with gathered power, sidled to the doorway and peered into the massive landing bay. She scanned everything, ready to unleash her fury on whatever target presented itself. One by one, the others fell into a line behind her.

"How many?" Tolde whispered. He stood a step behind, rifle raised.

She gave him a deadpan look. "None. The bay appears empty."

Empty? That should be impossible. They'd only left Paradise to battle Amongeratix a few minutes ago. Tolde expected throngs of enemy soldiers to have converged on the scene, watching as the titans battled. All he heard was the low whistle of oxygen filtering through the ship's systems. Of Paradise Tear, there was no sign.

"We need to move," he said. The words caught in his throat, loath as he was to abandon an instrumental part of their team.

"Agreed," Alessandra said. "I will lead. Shepard the others aboard the shuttle and prepare for takeoff. We must not dally."

Keeping her opinions private, Alessandra swept into the bay. Electricity danced between her knuckles. Violet sparks of energy aching to be unleashed. Tolde hurried the others to their vessel, and after taking a fast headcount, followed Luma Kai into the hold to sweep for enemy. Once clear, the others filed up the ramp. Tolde instructed Luma to fire the engines as he returned to the bay to search for any planted explosives. Alessandra met him at the ramp.

"This is odd. There are signs of battle. Look, here is a piece of Paradise Tear's sword," the Blood Witch explained. "But I can sense no presence anywhere near us. It's almost as if …"

"Feels like a trap to me, Sister," Tolde said. "We must leave now, if we are going. Otherwise, I'm heading out in search of her."

Alessandra laid a comforting hand on her shoulder. "I know. Come, we must report to the Grand Mistress and inform her our quest has failed."

The ramp closed behind them and the shuttle roared back into the eternal emptiness of space once again. The Acumensiis Comet was far away, giving the passengers ample time to lament their losses and fume over all that had transpired. They spied no signs of external damage, as *Behemoth* faded behind them.

Amongeratix stormed onto the bridge of his command ship, taking in the collection of women in crimson robes arrayed before him. Anticipated, he spied Algiss Her a step ahead of the others. The Crimson Mistress bowed in supplication.

"I see you have begun awakening my ship," he barked.

His very words were thunder.

"We have, my lord. *Behemoth* will soon be ready to take to the stars once more," she replied.

A low grunt, casual with its disregard, rumbled from his throat. "What of the explosions I heard? Has our foe left us crippled?"

"Menials have awakened and are combating damages as we speak, but we need more crew."

"Do not concern yourself with such. I have entire ships filled with crew en route as we speak. This has been a day I have long desired." He swept his arms wide, encompassing the bridge with familiarity. "Mistress Her, you have done well, but your task is not yet complete. We are about to take our war to the stars."

"Ever have I desired revenge against those who held me back," she hissed.

His eyebrow arched. "Revenge, yes. We shall all find a measure of redemption during the coming crusade. First, I have a special task for you. Detach a compliment of your witches to ensure our guest is properly secured. We have a long voyage ahead and it would not do to have Paradise Tear left wanting."

Algiss Her bowed again and snapped her fingers. Three witches fell in beside her, eager to begin the imprisonment of Paradise Tear. The first steps toward retribution.

Sorrow's keep, planet Inselcor.

A plume of molten lava erupted, bathing the shores in steam and anger. Sorrow watched the scene play out with disinterest. Any amusement he once found in the ebb and flow of the rivers of lava was faded, lost to growing concerns over his inability to mitigate his brother's hatred. Ever had their struggle raged, until it devoured entire worlds and drove all involved to crippling madness. No good came from his meddling. Of that, he was certain.

Recovering from shadow wounds obtained during his time on the Forsaken Path, Sorrow wished he had stayed with Elisa to the end. The quest to find the First Paladin and secure *Grimfurvor* was paramount to all he had done over the last three thousand years. Amongeratix was a disease needing to be excised, if life had any chance of continuing. Perhaps the hands of mortals could succeed where he failed so many times. It was a cultivated dream evoking twisted emotions, for he knowingly ruined a woman's life to entertain his base desires. Should this scheme result in failure, it would all have been for naught. The price, albeit steep, was one he was willing to pay. Life must be allowed to go on. The great enemy proved too much of a liability. Already his strength grew. Sorrow feared he was too late. Feared Elisa had failed in her quest, or worse, was found unworthy.

He shifted, wincing as ripples of fresh pain crawled across his ribcage. The Prophet was dead, his purpose fulfilled, leaving the Paladin alone to fight the gathering darkness. Sorrow never imagined, those many centuries ago when he established the positions, how the endgame would play out. The vagaries of uncertainty threw obstacles at every opportunity, often stymieing his plans in infancy.

Cursing his inability to extricate himself from complex games, Sorrow was forced to watch the long move play out. Vaguely recalled conversations with Ruma Zzein in her capacity as oracle, now so long ago, dust collected around the edges, the Bloody Man felt the approaching confluence ripple through his veins. She warned him of Forever Night before the schism rendered his kind all but extinct. Scoffing at the idea of the grand cataclysm, Sorrow decided it prudent to take precautions. Elisa was his last, best hope. A fool's gambit cast in the guise of mortal flesh and blood.

He knew she bore hatred for him. How could she not? His arrival in her village those many decades ago was ordained. Choosing Elisa was no mistake. Sorrow knew what he was doing. Unfortunately, for the child, a life altering event was required to set her on the correct path and develop her into the tool he needed. Not a day passed where he failed to lament slaughtering that village. A lifetime of guilt over the necessary murders of all Elisa held dear, as he shaped her mind and spirit into a weapon. Perhaps there would come a time where he might explain his motivations to her. That she was the object of an ancient prophecy foretold millennia before her birth and the one bright spot in a dismal future.

Why he required such measure of acceptance stretched deep into his core, for he was ever the lonely child ignored by his parents. Once the feud began between Tannus and Amongeratix, he felt silenced. Sorrow tried, and failed, for centuries to cement his place in his father's eyes and was left wanting. That abandonment by the one who was meant to love more than any other wounded his soul. A panoply of mixed emotions clashed within his warring mind. Bereaving his lot in life, Sorrow took Ruma Zzein's words for gospel and set about creating a self-fulfilling prophecy. When the dust of the final war settled to ashes, he anticipated basking in eternal praise for his efforts.

Refocusing on the raging current forcing fresh lava down the slope and into the expanding seas beyond, Sorrow prayed for Elisa's return to his brother and perhaps an end to their eternal war. He was tired. They all were. But for the war to end, Sorrow knew one of them must die. Which one? He closed his eyes and dreamed of better times.

Low Continent, planet Vau Prime.

Gedrick Silk stared deep into the flames as they consumed Davith Strannan's remains. The service, brief as it was, ended some time ago, stealing away most of those who'd attended. The shapeshifter's mind was troubled. Strannan was the one human he confided in. A sole beneficiary to what remained of Silk's race. Here, at the end of a legacy, Gedrick couldn't help but feel as though he failed his friend. Hints of betrayal danced the outskirts of the investigation into the murder. Something sinister lurked just out of reach, hiding in plain sight, he suspected.

Gedrick refused to rule out other subversive agents buried in their midst. The remnants of Strannan's command on the low continent was ripe for infiltration. A purge was in consideration, for the insurrection could ill afford to lose more senior leadership. The train of thought led Gedrick down dark roads. Boogeyman leering from the shadows, he knew that should he head down the path in search of spies and traitors, the entire war effort would derail. There must be a better way. But what?

The matter of Utan Husk, whoever that was, perplexed him. At the moment of his death, Husk was convinced his name would go down in infamy, yet none in Strannan's inner circle recalled who he was. A minor contrivance unanticipated by the staff. In the absence of orders, and while those few witnesses reeled in shock, Gedrick ordered Husk's body stripped down and dumped in a nameless chasm deep in the mountains, never to be found, never remembered. The fate of murderers demanded no less.

One matter resolved, Gedrick moved swiftly to ensure their movement did not collapse overnight. A plan formed. One only he was capable of pulling off. Gedrick Silk stood before the flames, until naught but a mound of smoldering ashes remained. He owed Strannan that much, perhaps more. Dawn approached, the first inklings of pink shredding the veil of grey and black stretched across the world. Longing for the kiss of the sun's first warmth, Gedrick tilted his head back and closed his eyes. These quiet moments offered him the promise of a better tomorrow. He did not move until he felt the whisper of sunlight caress his face. Satisfied, Gedrick began the long walk back into the caves and the awaiting confusion.

He was not disappointed.

A score of senior enlisted and officers crowded the briefing table. Quiet, but heated, arguments circled. Angry fists were shaken. Vehement heads shook disagreement. Gedrick felt their alliance fracturing, forcing him to step in and do the unthinkable. Spying the young lieutenant Strannan appointed to his personal staff, on what Gedrick assumed was whim, the shapeshifter took measure of the fell gathering.

"There's been no word from Krenz in days. If any cells exist, they have gone deep underground. Our cause is lost. It is time to look for means off world," a brevet general said.

Gedrick recalled none of their names. He was no soldier, no developed strategist. A man of the universe, Gedrick was the one hope they had to avoid capture and subsequent torture.

A female colonel rolled her eyes. "Abandon the capital? Are you mad? If we leave Vau Prime, there is little chance we can return. The war will be lost."

"This war is already lost! General Strannan is dead. We are leaderless and our foe has discovered the means to infiltrate our forces. What else is there at this point but self-preservation? I will not die under Alain Nye's Inquisition."

"Such news should not be discussed openly. We do not know who is listening," Gedrick said after clearing his throat.

"This is a military matter, Master Silk. I don't recall your presence being requested," the general sneered.

"Perhaps, yet I, alone, possess the ability to keep this campaign going," he replied, "whether it is here on Vau Prime or elsewhere."

Flustered, the general slapped a palm on the table, spilling a canteen. Gedrick watched the liquid flow, spreading through papers and onto datapads.

"What madness is this? I should have you arrested. Perhaps it was your foul influence that led to Strannan's demise."

Gedrick rose, gaze fixed upon the upstart general. His opinion of Prekhauten leadership diminished with each passing comment. They were fragile, pushed to the edge and ready to break. None among them knew his true nature, a fact he worked painstakingly to keep secret. Cracking his neck, Gedrick shimmered and began his transformation. The event lasted but a handful of heartbeats and when it was finished, those assembled stared upon the visage of their late commanding officer.

"Impossible," a sergeant major whispered.

"What devilry is this?" the general asked. His face was drawn, cheeks pale.

"I am a shapeshifter," Gedrick explained. "I am also the sole reason this war will not end today. While you are correct, I am no strategist or soldier, I can keep the memory of Davith Strannan alive. With your support, of course. Tell me what to say and when. Lend me your years of experience during those rare moments when Strannan must be seen in the public eye.

"We cannot afford to allow our enemy to learn of their success. Strannan did not die in this godless place. Wounded, perhaps, but he lives. It is the only opportunity to keep the fires of hope alive," Gedrick said.

He grunted and shimmered back to his original form. "What say you? Will you help me? I cannot do this without you, nor do I think I should. Strannan trusted each of you, vested confidantes in a maddening world. The swirl of chaos taints all we do, yet there is still a chance to prove our worth and bring the Inquisitor General to his knees."

Shaking her head, the major said, "We have been fighting a losing battle for the better part of a year now. Nye holds every advantage."

"Plans were already developed to flee Vau Prime. I say we enact them now and save what we can," the general said. "Regardless of what this … imposter brings. We are alone in the universe. No help is coming."

"That is where you are wrong," Gedrick replied. "What if I told you, a great army was assembling, one filled with dispirited ranks of loyal Guards and crews of valiant sailors? That forces beyond your imagination gather to bring the war to Nye and his allies? My friends, we are not alone. A power is rising and it can sweep aside the detritus of filth humanity has been mired in for so long. We can cut out the rot and rebuild all that was lost. All it takes is a little faith and the iron will of the Prekhauten Guard."

Nodding to Abernath, Gedrick left the room. Some arguments were best had without witness.

Abbey of the Order of Blood Witches, Acumensiis Comet.

The abbey was abuzz with unbridled excitement. Whispers of a grand event permeated the gloom of the recent rebellion. Damages were already repaired. A handful of novices promoted to full Sister to replenish the ranks. It was a time of great change, for the old ways no longer sufficed to keep them safe. Grand Mistress Ruma Zzein ordered sweeping changes to all Algiss Her once commanded. Loyalties were tested, for there could be no repeat of the defections. Arms training intensified. Full blooded witches developed their powers for the coming war. The level of activity engulfing the normally quiet abbey halls proved invigorating.

Ruma Zzein watched the stars through the bay viewing ports circling the navigation chamber. Sogress B'mn sat in her command chair, telepathically directing the comet on its eternal course through the universe. The head navigator was several hundred years old and unparalleled in experience. Her counsel was one of the few Ruma sought during times of distress.

"You do poorly disguising your emotions, Ruma," Sogress chided.

"Only with you, old friend," Ruma smiled.

"You are concerned with the mission to *Behemoth*."

A statement of fact more than question.

"Shouldn't I be? I fear I have sent them all to their doom," Ruma said.

Sogress made a sucking sound. "Nonsense. You did what needed doing. Algiss Her's insurrection is a stain upon our legacy. Should she succeed in joining with Amongeratix, he will at last have many of our secrets at his disposal."

"You're not making a valid case to calm my nerves, Sogress," Ruma frowned. "Ever has he longed to unravel our Order. His hatred for me transcends common sense."

"Yes. One would figure after thousands of years it would be time to move on and find a new target for his ire."

"Amongeratix does not forgive, nor forget. He will not rest until I am destroyed."

The sorrow in her voice tugged Sogress' heart. She loved Ruma as much as she had ever loved anyone. The Grand Mistress provided her the opportunity to develop her skills and rise to the challenge of being more than expectations limited her to on her home world. It was an unrepayable debt.

"We are a long way from Forever Night, Ruma," she reminded. "Forces are in play beyond our control. Enough to provide hope in the gathering darkness. I should not be the one to tell you to maintain your hope."

"You read my mind."

"Being a telepath has its advantages. How long are we going to continue this charade, Ruma? Tell me what ails you true."

Drawing a reluctant breath, Ruma said, "Algiss Her's insurrection. She threatens to unravel all I have worked toward. We are weak, Sogress. The Order inches to the precipice. What can I do to prevent the approaching anarchy?"

The Navigator pretended to think before answering. A centuries old game. "You are stronger than you believe. We have endured many trials through the years. Algiss is not the first to turn her back on you."

"What if I made a mistake?"

"Not even you are capable of predicting every future. Let this play out. All is as it should be. Are these not the words you have spoken to a thousand sisters?"

Ruma winced from the sting of her words. A slight hesitation, enough to arouse suspicion, altered the mood. How could she explain word of the failed mission to destroy Behemoth, already reached her? Worse, the mission lost their most valuable member. Ruma Zzein lamented all that had happened but took small comfort in knowing Paradise Tear was still alive. Amongeratix needed her. There was yet time, though ever ticking down as the impossible game drew to conclusion.

"There is more," Sogress said.

A thin smile creased Ruma's face. "I never have been able to fool you. Yes, the mission failed. Paradise Tear is now prisoner of her cousin. We are behind yet again."

"A familiar position. What of the reborn Inquisitor?"

"Alive."

Sogress nodded. "Then all is not lost."

"Not. It is not, but the way forward will not prove easy, for him most of all," Ruma agreed.

"These matters are beyond our control, Ruma Zzein. Matters must play out as they are intended. The young Inquisitor must fulfill his purpose in this game of destinies. Time for lament once the curtain of dust settles."

"He deserves better."

"Again, this is not for you to decide. Forever Night approaches. The players are in place. All we can do is guide them to their eventual ends," Sogress cautioned. "Tannus' fury will be unmatched."

"Yes, he will need to be talked out of acting. Ever has he fumed at his brother's arrogance. Should they clash now, all will be thrown into jeopardy."

"That is another matter altogether."

Ruma rose, smoothing the front of her gown. A ceremony to promote the new Mistress of Novices was due to begin, ushering in a new age in the Order of Blood Witches.

The Acumensiis comet sailed on, ever in search of its approaching destiny.

EPILOGUE

3215 A.G. (After Gods), Great Library, planet Wexanos.

Tannus sat in quiet rumination. Agony and rage warred for possession of his conscience. Ever trapped in a cycle of second guessing, his regret for allowing Paradise Tear to accompany Tolde Breed to the Blood Witches' comet tormented him with casual grief. No matter what he did, he could not escape the masterful plans of his errant brother. Amongeratix remained a step ahead. Tannus felt his grasp on the situation slipping, devolving as enemy powers gathered and grew stronger. The universe was balanced on the tipping point, plunging down to chaos was but a hushed breath away.

Yet, all was not lost. The crusade to claim Mannus Prime was a resounding success. Tens of thousands of loyal Guardsmen now flooded the ranks, making them a formidable army to stand against the rising tides pulsing from Vau Prime. Munition factories already resumed operations, pumping out weapons and ammunition in volume for the allies. No stranger to war, Tannus knew those brave souls standing beside him were hard pressed for help, yet while Amongeratix held the upper hand, he was rendered immobile.

And now he held the key to destroying the last vestiges of their race. Should Amongeratix crack her genetics, he stood to gain the forbidden knowledge concealed for ages. Once the rest of their kind was gone, there would be none left to prevent him from bringing utter ruination to the universe, reshaping it in his violent image and ruling for eternity. For the first time since being freed from the Conclave prison, Amongeratix stood a real chance of success. Humanity, still in its infancy, would never recover.

Frustrated, Tannus stalked through the Great Library in search of counsel. He found the Chief Librarian tending one of the many rose gardens decorating the exterior. The weathered old man stopped pouring water on a bush of violet flowers, set the can down, and awaited his lord. Tannus never understood the blind allegiance but welcomed it, nonetheless.

"Fistel, how long have you served me?" he asked.

"Many decades now, almost nine," Fistel replied. "Long enough to know when you are reluctant to broach a subject."

Tannus grinned despite himself. His experiences with humanity began long ago and continued heightening with certain individuals. Fistel was his match in many arenas, dueling wits most of all. "Am I doing the right thing?"

The Chief Librarian's eyes widened, and he licked his lower lip. "My lord, you have been at war with your brother for longer than I can understand. Every opportunity to find advantage and at last know peace, must be assumed. The only real question is what must be done."

"Each time we speak, you remind why I entrusted you those many years ago," Tannus said. "Long have I anticipated this final campaign, yet now that we are in its midst, I find myself mired in doubts. It is no easy thing being eternal."

"Even gods die. Nothing remains eternal," Fistel reminded him. His fatherly tone stripped Tannus' hardened shell, exposing the fragile youth who once challenged his father in front of the entire court and began a war. "Amongeratix will do as he must, just as you shall. We have scored a great victory on Mannus Prime, and if my sources are accurate, Crimeat with the retrieval of the artifact. Two out of three isn't bad, my lord."

No. Two out of three is just the beginning.

Tannus left his confidante to his roses and returned to prepare for the arrival of his allies. Victories and defeats were exchanged, but much yet remained before he was ready to take the war to his brother one last time.

Artificial lights groaned to life and Akin Brohl opened his eyes for the first time in over two thousand years. Crusted and caked together from the long sleep, pain danced across the corneas. Unused muscles ached as he tried sitting up. The unnatural sleep preserved his youth, a dangerous ploy by now forgotten powers. Any atrophy or desiccation negated by eldritch magics. Hale and dangerous, the God Slayer remained eternally in the prime of his life. No hair draped from his chin. No luster lost from his piercing gaze. He was, in a word, perfection. The counter to a memory of conspiracy perpetrated by the old gods.

The hammer of justice, Akin Brohl held to no past life, no memories of childhood or the sweet embrace of a doting mother. He was shaped by unremembered creatures desperate to find freedom from the tyranny of the gods. Akin took to his assignment with zeal. He raged across the stars as the god war, threatened to destroy all. Dozens of the elder race fell by his hands. A fitting tribute to his creators. All he knew was death and the stagnant period of waiting. Awake once again, the God Slayer dressed and sought out his weapons.

The time had come once again to carry his crusade to the stars. The blood of gods needed spilling.

THE END

To be continued in A Time For Tyrants

Welcome to Ghendis Ghadanisban. City of god-kings. City in turmoil.

The god-king is dead! Whispers of murder spread through the city known as the Heart Eternal. His death allows an ancient evil Razazel to return and resume its quest to dominate all life. As if that isn't enough, warring factions threaten the jewel of the desert. The only way to prevent this is by a group of reluctant heroes to escort a young boy filled with the dying god's essence to the ancient mountain of Rhorremere so the god-king can be reborn.

It is a quest bound to claim lives, for evil never stops.

Far off in the mountains, a squad of stranded space marines sells their services in the hopes of being rescued. Their search brings them in conflict with too many enemies. Forced to join the quest, it is a decision that may prove their ultimate doom.

Fate and destiny clash as agents of good and evil set forth to stake their claim.

Welcome, friends, to the Heart Eternal.

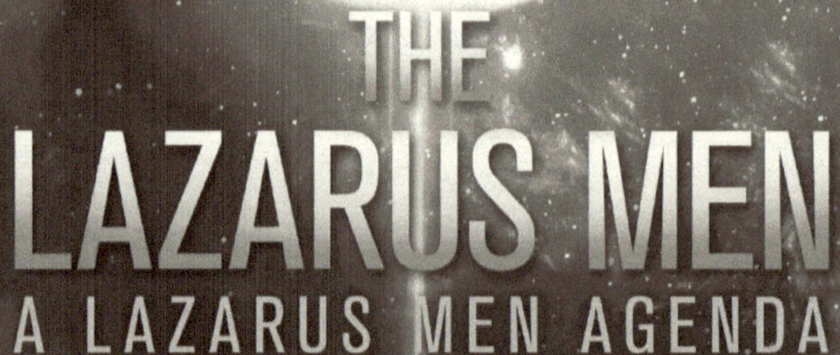

THE
LAZARUS MEN
A LAZARUS MEN AGENDA
CHRISTIAN
WARREN FREED

Welcome to the world of the Lazarus Men.

A thrilling sci-fi noir adventure combining the best mystery of the Maltese Falcon with the adventure of Total Recall and suspense of James Bond.

It is the 23rd century. Humankind has spread across the galaxy. The Earth Alliance rules weakly and is desperate for power. Hidden in the shadows are the Lazarus Men: a secret organization ruled with an iron fist by the enigmatic Mr. Shine. His agents are the worst humanity has to offer and they are everywhere.

Gerald LaPlant's life changes forever the day he accidentally witnesses a murder and discovers an alien artifact in his pocket. Forced to flee, he is chased across the stars by desperate men who want what he has and are willing to stop at nothing to get it. Along the way Gerald meets a host of villains and heroes, each with hidden agendas. If Gerald has any hope of surviving, he must rely on his wits and avoiding the one thing that could get him killed more than the rest: trust.

For he has the key to the galaxy's greatest treasure. Half want him dead. Half need him alive.

It's a race against time to see which wins.

THE CHILDREN OF NEVER

A War Priests of Andrak Saga

CHRISTIAN WARREN FREED

The war priests of Andrak have protected the world from the encroaching darkness for generations. Stewards of the Purifying Flame, the priests stand upon their castle walls each year for 100 days. Along with the best fighters, soldiers, and adventurers from across the lands, they repulse the Omegri invasions.

But their strength wanes and evil spreads.

Lizette awakens to a nightmare, for her daughter has been stolen during the night. When she goes to the Baron to petition aid, she learns that similar incidents are occurring across the duchy. Her daughter was just the beginning. Baron Einos of Fent is left with no choice but to summon the war priests.

Brother Quinlan is a haunted man. Last survivor of Castle Bendris, he now serves Andrak. Despite his flaws, the Lord General recognizes Quinlan as one of the best he has. Sending him to Fent is his best chance for finding the missing children and restoring order. Quinlan begins a quest that will tax his strength and threaten the foundations of his soul.

The Grey Wanderer stalks the lands, and where he goes, bad things follow. The dead rise and the Omegri launch a plan to stop time and overrun the world. The duchy of Fent is just the beginning.

The follow up to the L Ron Hubbard Writers of the Future award winning short: The Purifying Flame, the Children of Never is an all new novel set in a world of raw imagination.

BIO

Christian W. Freed was born in Buffalo, N.Y. more years ago than he would like to remember. After spending more than 20 years in the active duty US Army he has turned his talents to writing. Since retiring, he has gone on to publish more than 20 science fiction and fantasy novels as well as his combat memoirs from his time in Iraq and Afghanistan. His first book, Hammers in the Wind, has been the #1 free book on Kindle 4 times and he holds a fancy certificate from the L Ron Hubbard Writers of the Future Contest.

Passionate about history, he combines his knowledge of the past with modern military tactics to create an engaging, quasi-realistic world for the readers. He graduated from Campbell University with a degree in history and a Masters of Arts degree in Digital Communications from the University of North Carolina at Chapel Hill. He currently lives outside of Raleigh, N.C. and devotes his time to writing, his family, and their two Bernese Mountain Dogs. If you drive by you might just find him on the porch with a cigar in one hand and a pen in the other. You can find out more about his work by clicking on any one of the social media icons listed below. You can find out more about his work by following him on:

Facebook: @https://www.facebook.com/ChristianFreed
Twitter: @ChristianWFreed
Instagram: @ christianwarrenfreed

Like what you read? Let him know with an email or review.

www.ingramcontent.com/pod-product-compliance
Lightning Source LLC
Chambersburg PA
CBHW060939190726
48286CB00005B/1347